MW01505237

A Means to Freedom

A Means to Freedom

The Letters of H. P. Lovecraft and Robert E. Howard: 1930–1932

Edited by S. T. Joshi, David E. Schultz, and Rusty Burke

Hippocampus Press

New York

A Means to Freedom:
The Letters of H. P. Lovecraft and Robert E. Howard: 1930–1932

© 2017 Robert E. Howard Properties Inc and/or Lovecraft Holdings, LLC. Used with permission. ROBERT E. HOWARD and related logos, names and characters likenesses are trademarks or registered trademarks of Robert E. Howard Properties Inc. in the United States and certain other territories. H. P. LOVECRAFT and related logos, names and characters likenesses are trademarks or registered trademarks of Lovecraft Holdings, LLC in the United States and certain other territories. All rights reserved.

Certain referenced stories and related names, logos, characters and distinctive likenesses herein may also be trademarks or registered trademarks of Conan Properties International LLC, Kull Productions Inc, Solomon Kane Inc or Robert E. Howard Properties Inc.

No portion of this book may be reproduced—mechanically, electronically, or by any other means, including photocopying—without written permission of the copyright holders.

H. P. Lovecraft's letters published with the permission of the Estate of H. P. Lovecraft, Robert C. Harrall, Administrator. Robert E. Howard's letters published by permission of Robert E. Howard Properties Inc.

"With a Set of Rattlesnake Rattles": *Leaves*, Summer 1937; reprinted in *The Howard Collector*, vol. 1, no. 1, Summer 1961; reprinted in *The Howard Collector*, Ace Books, 1979

"The Beast from the Abyss": *The Howard Collector*, vol. 3, no. 3, whole no. 15, Autumn 1971; reprinted in *The Howard Collector*, Ace Books, 1979; an abridged version, with illustrations, was published as *The Last Cat Book*, Dodd, Mead & Co., 1984

Cover art by David C. Verba depicting Main Street (circa 1900s), Cross Plains, TX.
Cover design by Barbara Briggs Silbert.
Hippocampus Press logo designed by Anastasia Damianakos.

Hippocampus Press, PO Box 641, New York, NY 10156
www.hippocampuspress.com

Second Softcover Edition, 2017
ISBN 978-1-61498-186-2 (Volume 1)
ISBN 978-1-61498-188-6 (2 Volume Set)

Contents

Introduction

When H. P. Lovecraft (1890–1937) wrote "The Rats in the Walls" in late summer of 1923, he included some sentences in Gaelic—lifted from Fiona Macleod's "The Sin-Eater" (1895)—to indicate his narrator's cataclysmic descent upon the evolutionary scale. Writing to Frank Belknap Long a month or two later, he noted: ". . . the only objection to the phrase is that it's *Gaelic* instead of *Cymric* as the south-of-England locale demands. But as with anthropology—details don't count. Nobody will ever stop to note the difference."[1] But one person *did.*

"The Rats in the Walls" was published in the March 1924 issue of *Weird Tales.* When it was reprinted in the June 1930 issue, the writer Robert E. Howard (1906–1936). observed the s eemingly insignificant linguistic matter and concluded that, by using Gaelic instead of Cymric, Lovecraft was implicitly adhering to an alternate theory about the successive waves of Celtic settlement of England. Lovecraft, in a letter that does not survive, apparently admitted his pilfering of the Gaelic phrase from "The Sin-Eater" and presumably added that his use of it did not have any broader significance. In this odd manner, the correspondence of two of the towering figures of American weird fiction began, to cease only with Howard's suicide six years later.

Howard made no secret of his admiration for Lovecraft's writings. Lovecraft could scarcely have failed to notice the enthusiastic comment that appeared in "The Eyrie" (the letter column of *Weird Tales*) in May 1928, three months after the appearance of "The Call of Cthulhu":

> R. E. Howard writes from Texas: "Mr. Lovecraft's latest story, 'The Call of Cthulhu', is indeed a masterpiece, which I am sure will live as one of the highest achievements of literature. Mr. Lovecraft holds a unique position in the literary world; he has grasped, to all intents, the worlds outside our paltry ken. His scope is unlimited and his range is cosmic. He has the rare gift of making the unreal seem very real and terrible, without lessening the sensation of horror attendant thereto. He touches peaks in his tales which no modern or ancient writer has ever hinted. Sentences and phrases leap suddenly at the reader, as if in utter blackness of solar darkness a door were suddenly flung open, whence flamed the red fire of Purgatory and through which might be momentarily glimpsed monstrous and nightmarish shapes. Herbert Spencer may have been right when he said that it was beyond the human mind to grasp the Unknowable, but Mr. Lovecraft is in a fair way of disproving the theory,

1. HPL to FBL (8 November 1923); *SLL* 1.258.

> I think. I await his next story with eager anticipation, knowing that whatever the subject may be, it will be handled with the skill and incredible vision which he has always shown."[2]

Lovecraft, for his part, does not appear to have made any public statements about Howard's work prior to initiating his correspondence with him, and references even in his letters before 1930 are scant. But, when he first heard from Howard, he wrote to August Derleth: "[Farnsworth] Wright [editor of *Weird Tales*] has just forwarded a scholarly & interesting letter from the W.T. author Robert E. Howard, concerning my 'Rats in the Walls'. I think I shall write Howard shortly, for he seems to be an exceptional chap. I like some of his work very much, though he makes too many concessions to the popular fiction ideal."[3] In a letter written shortly after Howard's death, Lovecraft stated: "I first became conscious of him as a coming leader just a decade ago—when (on a bench in Prospect Park, Brooklyn) I read 'Wolfshead'. I had read his two previous short tales with pleasure, but without especially noting the author. Now—in '26—I saw that *W.T.* had landed a new big-timer of the CAS [Clark Ashton Smith] and EHP [E. Hoffmann Price] calibre. Nor was I ever disappointed in the zestful and vigorous newcomer. He made good—and how!"[4] There may be a bit of exaggeration here, as there are few indications in Lovecraft's surviving correspondence of the time that he took any particular notice of Howard's work, especially since that work was of a very different sort from the intellectualized, cosmic horror that Howard himself rightly recognized as the hallmark of Lovecraft's own fiction. But in any case, it is evident that, when the correspondence was initiated, there was considerable respect on both sides.

This is not the place for a detailed or comprehensive analysis of the Lovecraft-Howard correspondence.[5] What we can do here is to trace, in broad outlines, the significant threads of discussion and what the ebb and flow of the correspondence reveals about the intellects and psychologies of the two writers. At the outset, the discussion is largely academic, focusing on somewhat technical (and, in many particulars, now outmoded) disquisitions

---

2. *WT* 11, No. 5 (May 1928): 711–12; rpt. in *H. P. Lovecraft in "The Eyrie,"* ed. S. T. Joshi and Marc A. Michaud (West Warwick, RI: Necronomicon Press, 1979), pp. 27–28.

3. HPL to AWD (20 June 1930); *Essential Solitude: The Letters of H. P. Lovecraft and August Derleth,* ed. David E. Schultz and S. T. Joshi (New York: Hippocampus Press, 2008), 1.268.

4. HPL to E. Hoffmann Price (5 July 1936); *SLL* 5.277.

5. See Rusty Burke, "The Lovecraft/Howard Correspondence," in *The Fantastic Worls of H. P. Lovecraft,* ed. James Van Hise (Yucca Valley, CA: James Van Hise, 1999), pp. 143–49; S. T. Joshi, "Barbarism vs. Civilization: Robert E. Howard and H. P. Lovecraft in Their Correspondence," *Studies in the Fantastic* No. 1 (Summer 2008): 96–125.

on etymology, the migration of ancient peoples, and related matters. Howard appears intent on proving his intellectual credentials by lengthy quotations from encyclopedias and other scholarly works. It is of some interest that actual rough drafts of some of Howard's letters to Lovecraft survive, suggesting that Howard was particularly keen on presenting his arguments in the most convincing manner possible. Lovecraft's letters, in all likelihood, were his customary handwritten epistles written with considerable haste and not a great deal of forethought, although the substantial book-learning Lovecraft had at his disposal comes through in many passages.

It is, however, not long before the central focus of the correspondence—the relative merits of "civilisation" (as conceived by Lovecraft) and "barbarism" (as envisioned by Howard)—emerges. How this discussion began is not entirely clear. In April 1931 Howard tells Lovecraft that he is working on his first story involving Conan the Cimmerian, "The Phoenix on the Sword." Although, of course, Conan is Howard's prototypical embodiment of barbarism, there was nothing in the correspondence at this time to lead to a dispute. The trigger appears to have come a full year and a half later, when Lovecraft, in response to Howard's passing comment that "I am unable to rouse much interest in any highly civilized race, country or epoch," launches into a vigorous defence of the cultural supremacy of Greece and Rome. This was a subject that Howard was not likely to take lying down, for it was especially the Romans who were the chief foes of the Britons and Celts whom he regarded as his spiritual ancestors.

In the long and tortured course of this debate, as in the other debates in which the two writers engaged, it appears that both Lovecraft and Howard were talking past each other. Howard repeatedly maintained that his taste for barbarism was a mere preference that conveyed no judgment on the relative merits of the two types of life; this stance may have been partly disingenuous, for at times Howard does reveal a distaste for what he regards as the effeteness of civilization—or, at least, some exemplars of it—that go well beyond matters of mere preference. Lovecraft, in turn, while purporting to accept Howard's non-judgmental stance, nonetheless attempted to present a wealth of arguments claiming that civilization was somehow intrinsically superior to barbarism. His ultimate argument was a quasi-scientific one, in which he maintained that civilization involved a greater "amount of pleasurable energy-conversion," whatever that means. Lovecraft simply could not conceive how *anyone*—especially one whose intellectual and creative faculties he admired so much—could prefer barbarism to civilization.

This whole discussion was complicated by two ancillary discussions—the relative merits of physical versus mental functions, and the relative merits of frontier life as opposed to settled life. It should not surprise us that Lovecraft (the prototypical scion of pseudo-aristocrats from a long-settled Eastern city) and Howard (the at times aggressively anti-intellectual offspring of a frontier family in a Texas that had scarcely emerged from frontier life itself) should take opposite sides of these issues. Once again, both authors commit gaffes of various sorts—as when Howard, perhaps unwittingly, seems to equate the achievements of Michelangelo and a heavyweight boxer, and when Lovecraft (perhaps responding to Howard's own overcolored portrayals of life in the Texas of the near and remote past) envisions fisticuffs and shootings at every street-corner in the Southwest.

It must, however, be pointed out that the two writers did agree on one point—that of race. The letters leave little doubt that both Lovecraft and Howard were imbued with prejudice against African Americans, Jews, and other minorities, and certain passages in these letters do not make pleasant reading today. Lovecraft, in relating the history of Rhode Island and of New England, found occasion to note that the "foreign overrunning of America . . . [is] the most tragic event in the continent's history" (4 October 1930), while Howard, although engagingly relating the oral ghost stories he heard from the local Negroes ([c. September 1930]), could not help lamenting, "I'm afraid that in a few generations Texas will be over-run with mongrels." The conventional defense of these views—that Lovecraft and Howard were merely expressing the prejudices of their times—falls to the ground, at least as far as Lovecraft is concerned, given that many of the more advanced thinkers of the period (with whom Lovecraft would surely have wished to align himself) were abandoning such racist presuppositions in the wake of anthropological advances that definitively refuted any notion of the biological "superiority" or "inferiority" of the various races of humanity.

At times the correspondence becomes quite rancorous. In a letter of 27–28 July 1934, Lovecraft wrote:

> I believe that there are *certain real and specific reasons* for considering civilisation as different from barbarism in a direction intrinsically favourable to man's degree of importance, enjoyment, symmetry, and completeness in the cosmic flux; a direction to which we may logically apply the term "upward" (as based on the only scale of progressive organisation in the cosmos), and which we cannot help endorsing if we are friends rather than enemies of mankind.

That last comment sent Howard off the deep end. Clearly taking the remark personally, he bitterly rebuked Lovecraft for calling him an "enemy of mankind," and was not much mollified when Lovecraft asserted (perhaps disingenuously) that the remark was not in fact directed explicitly at Howard. For virtually the rest of the correspondence, one senses a latent resentment against Lovecraft on Howard's part, exemplified by numerous sarcastic references to Lovecraft's own preferences.

It should not, however, be assumed that the correspondence was a hostile one. One of the great virtues of these letters is the transparent manner in which each author unconsciously reveals his own tastes, predilections, heritage, background, and aesthetic principles. Howard's exhaustive chronicles of Southwest history, with its array of gunfighters, posses, and romantic legendry, make it understandable why Lovecraft predicted that Howard would one day "make his mark in serious literature with some folk-epic of his beloved southwest"[6]—a task that, aside from random stories set in Texas, Howard did not live to undertake. Lovecraft, in turn, informs Howard copiously about the 300-year history of his native region, writing powerfully about the lingering psychological effects of the Puritan theocracy and its witch-fears, the beauties of the Rhode Island landscape, and his deep-seated sense of connection with New England, Old England, and the heritage of Greece and Rome.

Political and economic matters come up for discussion in the latter stages of the correspondence—understandably so, given the turmoil of a nation in the throes of the Great Depression. Lovecraft's attraction to what he would elsewhere term "fascistic socialism"—the withholding of political power (specifically, the right to vote) to the few, conjoined with the spread of economic wealth to the many—ran into difficulties when Howard backed him into a corner in defending Mussolini ("Do not judge the sort of fascism I advocate by any form now existing"). Lovecraft delivers some pretty telling blows against the democracy (he would term it ochlocracy) being practiced in the United States ("Democracy—as distinguished from universal opportunity and good treatment—is today a fallacy and impossibility so great that any serious attempt to apply it cannot be considered as other than a mockery and a jest"), but has trouble defending his "fascistic socialism" from Howard's charges that, based on current and past history, the "untrammelled freedom of expression" that Lovecraft claimed as a desideratum would be in pretty short supply if his political system really went into effect. The crux of the issue rested on the two authors' different understandings of what constituted "personal liberty." Howard had lamented in March 1932 that "Personal liberty, it would seem, is to be a thing of the past"—an exaggeration that Lovecraft properly refuted. But it was not to be expected that two individuals from such widely differing backgrounds could see eye-to-eye on this or related issues.

In the end, perhaps the greatest value of this correspondence rests precisely on the stimulating discussion engendered by two quite different personalities. Howard summed up the matter keenly in a letter of December 1935:

---

6. HPL, "In Memoriam: Robert Ervin Howard" (1936), *CE* 5.217.

> My life has been almost antipodal, in its associations, to yours. I've had little acquaintance with scholars, artists and literary people, whereas these types obviously have formed the bulk of your companions. Not being familiar with these types, it's easy for me to misunderstand their ideas and opinions. I'm also but little fitted to deal with abstract ideas which do not, apparently, have any connection with everyday reality as I know it. I've never had much time to devote to theories and philosophies. . . . On the other hand it seems obvious from your own arguments that you've had little if any first-hand contact with the rough sides and the raw edges of existence; if you had, you couldn't possibly have some of the ideas you have, and so many of my views and statements wouldn't seem so inexplicable and outrageous to you. It is inevitable that we should constantly misunderstand each other.

Throughout their six-year discussion, Lovecraft's and Howard's differing perspectives on virtually every feature of life show themselves—and the result is a richly diverse correspondence in which fundamental issues of intellectual, social, and political life are debated with the vigor that we would expect from two such powerful personalities.

—THE EDITORS

A Note on This Edition

This edition of the correspondence of Robert E. Howard and H. P. Lovecraft has been compiled in a somewhat unusual manner, in that the originals of Lovecraft's letters do not survive. They apparently were destroyed inadvertently by Howard's father, Dr. I. M. Howard, in the 1940s. Prior to that event, however, extensive transcripts of the letters had been made under the aegis of August Derleth at Arkham House, for eventual publication in Lovecraft's *Selected Letters* (1965–76). We have had access to the transcripts, but it is clear that certain parts of them have been transcribed in a garbled fashion; also, the transcripts are not complete, as some apparent cuts have been made. Some letters apparently were lost by Howard himself. Originals of some of Lovecraft's postcards to Howard survive and have been consulted for this edition.

Howard's own letters—nearly all of them typescripts—have been made available to the editors. We have sought to print them as faithfully as possible. We have silently corrected what are clearly stenographical errors. In a few cases, we have added an editorial "[*sic*]" to alert the reader to an error that exists in the original text; in other cases where misspellings or other errors occur, it can be assumed that the error is in the original.

To minimize the number of endnotes, we have relegated a considerable amount of information to the bibliography and glossary of names, found at the end of volume 2. All works by Lovecraft, Howard, and others mentioned in the text (with the exception of some stories in *Weird Tales* mentioned in passing) are included in the bibliography, with full bibliographical information on their first appearances and additional information on the editions used by Lovecraft and Howard, the presence of the work in their respective libraries, and other relevant information. Names mentioned frequently in the text are cited in the glossary of names.

Abbreviations

AHT	Arkham House transcripts of Lovecraft's letters
ALS	autograph letter, signed
ANS	autograph note (e.g., postcard), signed
AWD	August W. Derleth
BMM	Howard, *Bran Mak Morn: The Last King*
BO1	*The Best of Robert E. Howard: Volume 1, Crimson Shadows*
BO2	*The Best of Robert E. Howard: Volume 2, Grim Lands*
BSA	Howard, *The Black Stranger and Other American Tales*
CA	Howard, *The Complete Action Stories*
CAS	Clark Ashton Smith
CB	Lovecraft, *Commonplace Book* (numbers refer to entries)
CCC	Howard, *The Coming of Conan the Cimmerian*
CE	Lovecraft, *Collected Essays,* five volumes
CL	*The Collected Letters of Robert E. Howard*
CSC	Howard, *The Conquering Sword of Conan*
D	Lovecraft, *Dagon and Other Macabre Tales*
DAW	Donald A. Wandrei
DH	Lovecraft, *The Dunwich Horror and Others*
EIH	Howard, *Echoes from an Iron Harp*
ET	Howard, *The End of the Trail: Western Stories*
FBL	Frank Belknap Long
FF	*Fantasy Fan*
FW	Farnsworth Wright
HC	*Howard Collector*
HPL	H. P. Lovecraft
HS	*The Horror Stories of Robert E. Howard*
JHL	John Hay Library, Brown University
KEA	Howard, *Kull: Exile of Atlantis*
LL	S. T. Joshi, comp., *Lovecraft's Library: A Catalogue* (numbers refer to entries)

LR	Peter Cannon, *Lovecraft Remembered*
LS	Howard, *Lord of Samarcand and Other Adventure Tales of the Old Orient*
MM	Lovecraft, *At the Mountains of Madness and Other Novels*
MW	Lovecraft, *Miscellaneous Writings*
NAPA	National Amateur Press Association
REH	Robert E. Howard
REHB	Rusty Burke, *Robert E. Howard's Bookshelf.*
RHB	R. H. Barlow
SHSW	State Historical Society of Wisconsin, Madison
SLH	Howard, *Selected Letters,* two volumes
SLL	Lovecraft, *Selected Letters,* five volumes
STSK	Howard, *The Savage Tales of Solomon Kane.*
WF	Howard, *Waterfront Fists and Others*
WT	*Weird Tales*

The editors are grateful to Glenn Lord, Patrice Louinet, Rob Roehm, Paul Herman, Scott Connors, Larry Richter, John Haefele, Alton McCowen, Margaret McNeel, Donnell Clark, Jack Scott, David Hardy, Dennis McHaney, Will Murray, John Locke, Morgan Holmes, Mark Hall, Rob Preston, Alistair Durie, J.-M. Rajala, and Bobby Derie for their assistance.

1930

[1] [nonextant letter by Robert E. Howard]

[c. mid-June 1930]

[2] [nonextant letter by H. P. Lovecraft]

[c. late June 1930]

[3] [TLS]

[July 1, 1930]

Dear Mr. Lovecraft:

I am indeed highly honored to have received a personal letter from one whose works I so highly admire. I have been reading your stories for years, and I say, in all sincerity, that no writer, past or modern, has equalled you in the realm of bizarre fiction. I realize that it is the custom for enthusiastic readers to compare a favorite author with Poe, and their comparison is seldom based on any real estimate, or careful study. But after a close study of Poe's technique, I am forced to give as my personal opinion, that his horror tales have been surpassed by Arthur Machen, and that neither of them ever reached the heights of cosmic horror or opened such new, strange paths of imagination as you have done in "The Rats in the Walls", "The Outsider", "The Horror at Red Hook", "The Call of Cthulu", "The Dunwich Horror"—I could name all the stories of your's I have read and not be far wrong.

Thank you very much for the poetry. I should like very much to see more of it. "The Dweller"[1] especially intrigued me, as I found in it much of the quality of your most powerful prose stories—a sudden Door-like opening on absolutely unguessed conjectures, that sets a sort of inarticulate madness that howls for expression, clawing at the reader's brain.

I am indeed gratified that you have liked my efforts in Weird Tales, and I thank you very much for your kind comments on them.

I am going to impose on your good nature to the extent of discussing my reasons for believing the Cymric peoples were first in the British Isles. My education on the subject is meager but it is one which has always interested me greatly, perhaps because of the dominating percent of Gaelic in my own veins. Such authorities as I have read seem very conflicting in their views and often self-contradictory, so perhaps already research has rendered my ideas absurd and rediculous. However, I shall venture to commit myself.

Admittedly, your theory, as put forth in your letter, is logical, well grounded, and in many cases, unanswerable, by my scanty knowledge, at least. However, it seems to be the general trend of recent researchers to believe that the separation of Gael from Brython occurred before the conquest of Britain, and that the language of the Britons was merely a branch of the Continental Gaulish. There seems to be a difference between Gaelic and Brythonic which runs back into the mists of antiquity and seems to suggest a vastly ancient separation and possibly a development in different parts of the world. As regards present-day Cymric or Cymreag, I attach less significence to it as a Celtic speech than most do. The use of "s" in Gaulish, which did not extend in the same manner to Brythonic, seems to point to a variance after Brythonic separated from Gaulish, either on the Continent or in Britain. You are quite right in saying that Welsh or Cymric departs from the Aryan root stock far more than does present-day Gaelic. I consider that the language—Cymric—has been so mixed with Mediterranean, Latin, Saxon and Scandinavian languages that it retains but little of the pristine Celtic quality. However, I believe this mixing took place at a comparatively modern date and that the language of the ancient Gauls and Britons was as close to the Aryan root as that of the Gaels, with the exception of the "qu" sound which the Gaels retained longer than the Brythons. I take this to mean that the Brythons earlier branched away from the Aryan stock and came into contact with other races sooner than did the Gaels.

The modern trend seems to point to a generally recognized theory that the first Celtic invasion consisted of Goidhelic peoples, who swept over Europe at the end of the Neolithic Age. These, according to many historians, were followed by a wave of Brythonic people who conquered them and drove them into Ireland, Scotland and perhaps Cornwall. Later still—about the first century B. C. another wave of Gaels came into Ireland and later spread into Scotland.[2]

My theory conflicts with this view and I will frankly admit I have no grounds whatever for many of my notions on the subject and will make no attempt to prove them. I have not studied the results of latest researches and there are many flaws that I myself can see in my theories.

My idea is that the Brythonic peoples were the first to branch away from the Aryan stock somewhere on the plains of Asia, and that they and not the Gaels brought the Bronze Age into Europe. My reason for this view, that is, in regard to the bronze, is the fact that Caesar found the Britons still using swords of copper and bronze. If, as some historians maintain, bronze using Gaels preceded and fled before Brythons wielding iron swords, it seems to me that the Britons should have opposed the Romans with weapons of the latter metal. I believe that the Gaels were those Celts who remained in the original homeland of the Aryans after the ancestors of the Brythonic races moved westward. Living among Aryan tribes they retained the original Aryan language longer. I believe that their roaming, which began centuries later, followed a different course from that taken by the Brythons; that they came to the Mediterranean Sea and followed its shores westward, intermingling to some extent with the peoples they found there. This would account for the original trend of scholars to class the Irish as a Mediterranean race, and account also for the numerous words of Hamitic or Semitic affinity in the Gaelic language. Whether the Gaels or Milesians lingered in Egypt as mercenaries and whether they spent some time in Spain before coming into Ireland, as the legends say, I am not prepared to defend, though I believe it to be extremely likely. O'Donovan and O'Reilly's Irish-English dictionary shows clearly the connection of many Gaelic words with Hebrew and Greek words, though the last is natural with any Aryan language, of course. The author in his preface states that the work of the Earl of Ross and General Vallancy show that a large element of Phoenician exists in even modern Gaelic. The question is, however, whether this element was brought in by the Gaels who collected it on their wanderings, or was introduced by traders. I, personally, think it very likely that the Celtiberians of Spain were closely allied to the Gaels, and possibly themselves the ancestors of the Irish and Scotch. As they were allies or tributaries to the Carthaginians, their speech must have been mixed largely with Phoenician.

Bishop O'Brien of Cloyne scoffs at the legends representing the Gaels wandering from Scythia into Egypt and thence to Ireland, but admits that the Celtiberians were doubtless among the early settlers of Ireland.

I quote some extracts on the Celtic subject, some of which seem to bear out parts of my notions and some of which seem to refute them entirely, as I have said before.

"The view that there was on the continent an older group of Celts who preserved the Indo-European sound qu (the so-called qu group) and who were followed by a conquering group, who changed that sound to p (the so-called p group) is now most generally discarded. Though we know but little of the language of the ancient Belgae, it is sufficient to class it with that of the Celts and perhaps to identify the Galates and the Belgae. Anyhow it is clear that **Γαλάται** and **Κελτοί** [are] two distinct words, and that neither of them has anything to do with the modern names Goidhelic and Gael." (The Encyclopedia Americana.)

I quote the same authority which says a division of the Celtic race: "Correct in a purely linguistic sense devides the Celtic languages into a K group (Goidhelic) and a P group (Gaulish and Brythonic). The most notable characteristics which set off the Celtic languages from the other members of the Indo-Celtic family are: (1) The fall of initial and intervocalic; this change which is common to both branches of Celtic, took place before 1000 B. C. and before the Goidhelic Celts separated from the Brythonic Celts and the invasion of Britain, (2) the change already refered to, (viz. of qu to k and p) which took place after the separation, old irish *coic,* Old Welsh *pimp,* five, (3) the change of the Indo-Celtic e (long) to Celtic i (long), Latin *verus,* Old Irish *ifr,* true, (4) the change of vocalic r and l to ri and li.

"Were it not for a common vocabulary the Brythonic group of Celtic would be separated by an unbridgable gulf from the Goidhelic. This cleavage is observable from the earliest monuments and is chiefly due to the following factors: (1) The different treatment of the Indo-Celtic qu, which at a very early period became p in Brythonic but which in Goidhelic was for a long time preserved and then, even in the Oldest Irish, changed to k (written c) Gaulish agrees in making this change with Brythonic of which, to that extent at least, it may be regarded as a prehistoric type. E.G. Gaulish pempe, five, Old Welsh pimp, Breton pemp, Old Irish coic; Old Irish macc, Welsh map, son."

I think the reason for Brethonec or Cornish more nearly resembling Gaelic is as I quote from The History of Ireland, edited by Henry Smith Williams: "Early writers pointed out a Goidhelic element in the topographical nomenclature of West Britain, and concluded that the country was once occupied by the Goedel whence they were driven into Ireland by the advancing Cymri. This was a natural and reasonable conclusion at the time. But our present knowledge compels us to adopt a different view . . . . the numerous traces of Goidhelic names found there are derived from an Irish occupation in historic times."

This appears to me to further point to a much later entrance of the Gael into the British Isles. The more or less simultaneous invasions of Wales and Scotland by the Gaels seem to me more the expansion of a new, vigorous and growing tribe than the reviving growth of an ancient and conquered nation. I quote Bede:

"At first this island had no other inhabitants but the Britons. . . . When they had made themselves masters of the greater part of the island, the Picts from Scythia . . . . accordingly sailed over into Britain. In process of time Britain, after the Britons and Picts, received a third nation, the Scots, who migrating from Ireland under their leader Reuda . . . . seized . . . . settlements amongst the Picts."[3]

I think such Latin authors as mention the above matters agree with this account, in that the Britons precede the Picts and the Picts, the Scots or Gaels. The legends of the various races coincide with it, as do, I think, the narratives of the British historians, Gildas and Nennius.[4] I have not read The Irish Annals[5] nor The Pictish Chronicle[6] but if I am not much mistaken both agree in placing the arrival of the Gaels much later than that of the Picts and Britons. It seems to [me] that if, as most historians maintain, the Gaels had been living in Ireland where they had been driven by the Britons, for so many centuries, they would have come into Scotland at an earlier date, for the main British population seems to have been confined largely to the southern part of the island.

I believe that the Gaels landed first in Ireland. Henry Smith Williams' History of Ireland: "The last of the prehistoric races of Ireland were the Scots or . . . . Milesians. At the earliest period . . . . it was occupied by a sparse population . . . . Tuatha Feda, doubtless of aboriginal Iberic race of western and southern Europe." These were soon conquered by the Celts. "It is not necessary" (quoting from the same history) "to suppose that all the tribes included under this name (Firbolgs) came at the same time. The effect of their immigration now appears that in the north the people were Cruithni or Picts . . . . in the east and center British and Belgae tribes; and in Munster when not distinctly Iberic, of a southern or Gaulish type."

To further establish the identity of these first Celtic invaders I here quote from The Catholic Encyclopedia which contains a very exhaustive study of all Irish subjects. Speaking of the early history of "Ogygia, or the Ancient Island. The Firbolgs . . . were kindred perhaps to those war-like Belgae of Gaul. The Milesians certainly belong to history though the date of their arrival in Ireland is unknown."

I quote again from Williams' History of Ireland: "This struggle (the conquest of Ireland) was brought about by the arrival from abroad of a new tribe or the rise of an old one. The former view seems the more probable, for at that time great displacements of the Celts were taking place subsequent on the conquests of the Romans and some of the displaced tribes may have migrated to Ireland. The victors in the struggle appear afterwards as Scots. (Gaels.)"

I frankly admit that I base my theories as to Celtic occupation of the Isles largely on the Milesian legends. I firmly believe that subsequent research will prove these supposed myths to contain more truth than is generally supposed. Gibbons[7] sought to refute the so-called legend that Ireland was the original home of the Scots, maintaining that the Gaels spread into the smaller island from Scotland, but the converse has since been proven. In like manner I believe that other legends of the Irish will be some day confirmed. Zimmer in his "Kelt-Studien" says: "We believe that Meve, Conor Mac Nessa, Cuchulainn and Finn Mac Cumhail are just as much historical personages as Dietrich of Berne or Etzel."[8] And if the Ossian legends are to be accepted largely, I see no reason for denying the old Dananean myths at least a grain of truth, a base of fact. If British or Belgic tribes were holding the eastern and central part of Ireland before the coming of the Gaelic Milesians, it seems natural to think that like races were already firmly established in Britain, which island being so much nearer the mainland.

I do not subscribe to the theory which makes Partholan[9] and his followers Gaels. I see no reason to suppose that the first Celtic invaders of Ireland were of the same tribe as the last. If, as some historians maintain, Partholan and his men were Gaels, and the later Milesians came from Gaul, how is it that they escaped the wave of Brythonic invasion that is supposed to have occurred during the long gap between the coming of Partholan and the coming of the Milesians?

I believe that Partholan and his men were as represented by Irish legend—Egyptian or Phoenician sea-farers. I believe that the Fomorians were Finnish or Germanic pirates living in Jutland, and that the ensuing waves of Nemedians, Firbolgs and Tuatha De Danann were British invaders, or possibly Belgae. Firbolg or Men With Bags seems to be merely the Gaelic manner of pronouncing Belgae. The Milesians I believe to have been the only true Gaels, Scythic Celts who left the Aryan steppes much later than the Brythonic peoples and who after centuries of wandering, eventually came into Ireland.

Another and possibly more obscure reason for my belief is this: most of the Gauls and the Britons seem to have been of a large blond type, with light eyes and yellow hair, the true Aryan complection. But according to certain traditions, the Milesians were dark of a "Spanish" type, when they invaded Ireland. According to these traditions, the Milesians or Gaels retained the Aryan height and light eyes—generally grey in this case—but were dark of skin and hair. This departure from the original Celtic stock might have taken place in Ireland after the invasion, despite legends to the contrary—might have merely been a result of the conquerors mingling with their Mediterranean subjects. But I think it points to long residence or wandering among Hamitic or Turanian peoples before coming into the British Isles. It seems to me that if any great mixing between Aryan and aboriginal Mediterranean took place in Ireland, it would have been between the earlier peoples. But the Nemedians and Tuatha De Danann are usually represented as being very fair. I believe the typical Gael to have been tall, grey eyed and black haired, and that more recent traditions representing heroes as fair, either meant some man in whose veins Brythonic blood predominated, or else the legends themselves became changed in the same manner that caused Cuchulainn, "a small, dark man" in early legends to become a golden haired giant in the later legends.

But after all, these classifications are more or less unimportant, since Gaelic, Cymreag, Brethonec, Brezonec and Gaulish are all parts of the great Celtic race and language which left its mark in more places than is generally realized and formed the base for so many modern languages, though its influence is largely forgotten in the passing of the ages.

I must crave your pardon for taking up so much of your time. I had not realized that I had strung out such a lengthy discussion in so much detail, and hope I have not bored you too much.

I hope that you will have the time and inclination to write me again when it is convenient for you, for I enjoyed your letter very much, and I strongly hope to read more of your stories in Weird Tales soon.

Cordially,
Robert Eiarbhin Howard

P.S. I took the liberty of writing this letter on the typewriter as indeed, I do all my correspondence; I write such an abominable hand, I can scarcely read it myself.

R. E. H.

Notes

1. It is not known what HPL had sent REH in the way of poetry. "The Dweller" is sonnet XXXI of *Fungi from Yuggoth* (1929–30). Since HPL sent REH the ms. of the (nearly) complete poem not long after (see letter 4), it seems that HPL may have sent

a clipping of the poem from its appearance in the *Providence Journal* (7 May 1930), along with some others.

2. Goidelic languages (including Irish, Manx, and Scottish Gaelic) are one of two groups of modern Celtic languages. They originated in Ireland and are distinguished from the other group of Insular Celtic tongues—the Brythonic—by the retention of the sound *q* (later developing to *k*, spelled *c*), where Brythonic has developed a *p* sound. Both sounds are assumed to be derived from an ancestral form **kw* in the Indo-European parent language (the asterisk identifies a sound as a hypothetical and reconstructed form). Because of the *k* (or *q*) sound, the Goidelic languages are sometimes referred to as Q-Celtic.

3. Bede the Venerable (673–735), *Historia Ecclesiastica Gentis Anglorum* (*Ecclesiastical History of the English People*), Book 1, Chapter 1, "Of the Situation of Britain and of Ireland, and of Their Ancient Inhabitants"; trans. William Hurst, 1814.

4. Gildas Bandonicus, a Celtic monk of the 6th century; author of *De Excidio Britanniae* (*Concerning the Ruin of Britain*) in the 540s. Nennius was an 8th-century historian who is a major source for tales of King Arthur; author of *Historia Brittonum* (*The History of the Britons*).

5. "The Irish Annals" is a collective term referring to a number of historical documents recording the history and legends of Ireland up to about the beginning of the 18th century.

6. The Pictish Chronicle, ms. COLB. BIB. IMP. PARIS, 4126. There are several versions of the Pictish Chronicle. The so-called "A" text is probably the oldest and the fullest. The text seems to date from the reign of Kenneth II (971–995), since he is the last king mentioned and the chronicler does not know the length of his reign. The manuscript itself is, however, a 14th-century copy.

7. Edward Gibbon (1737–1794), *The Decline and Fall of the Roman Empire* (1776–88), ch. 25.

8. This quotation apparently derives from the article "Ireland: Irish Literature," by Douglas Hyde, in *The Catholic Encyclopedia* (1910 ed.), 8.118. The same abbreviation is there used for Zimmer's *Keltische Studien.*

9. Legendary leader of the second "invasion" of Ireland. Various traditions assign him different places of origin, but all are in the Eastern Mediterranean region. He and his followers are said to have defeated the Fomorians (who may have been a race of divine or semi-divine beings), but after a short time in Ireland, all expired of a plague in a single week. The most important source for Partholan is probably the *Lebor Gabála Érenn* (*The Book of Invasions*). HPL mentions Partholan in "The Moon-Bog" (1921).

[4]

10 Barnes St.,
Providence, R.I.,
July 20, 1930

Dear Mr. Howard:—

I was greatly interested in your letter of the 1st, which I found awaiting me upon my return from a week in Boston & vicinity. The high opinion you express regarding my efforts is surely encouraging in the fextreme, & makes me anxious to get the time to produce something new. "The Dweller" is one of a long series of weird metrical attempts in something like the sonnet form—& since you express a wish to see more, I am enclosing a ms. which contains some thirty-three.[1] You don't have to read all these things through, if they tend to get tiresome—& there's no hurry about their return, although I'd like to see the ms. (my only typed copy) eventually. Ten of these will appear in *Weird Tales*; others have been taken by other publications, while a goodly residue are still unplaced.

Since last writing you I have read "The Moon of Skulls", & am fascinated by the suggestion of unholy antiquity brought up by your Atlantean city & its subterraneous crypts. I shall look forward eagerly to future work of yours—or rather future & present, since I have not yet had a chance to read the latest W.T. with your "Hills of the Dead".

Your observations on Celtic philology & pre-history proved immensely fascinating to me, & wholly bely your modest claim of "meagre" knowledge of the subject. In truth, my own vague smattering sinks into total negligibility beside the array of facts & reasonable deductions at your command. As a rank layman, I am really entitled to no opinion at all—but you certainly incline me to adopt the later opinion in the Cymric-Gaelic matter so far as a layman's choice of theories may extend. I can see that the argument from which my random assumptions rose is now an outmoded one, & that contemporary research has delved much deeper for foundations. That Gaelic & Cymric elements were separated far back in the Celtic race's continental experience, & that the Cymric culture was first to be permanently seated on the greater part of the island of Britain, would seem to be the accepted idea nowadays; & I certainly have no grounds for doubting it. All the linguistic facts which you cite tend to prove an early separation & parallel growth of Gaelic & Cymric rather than a divergence of the latter from the former as a late corruption; & it is perfectly reasonable to attribute the Gaelic place-names of South Britain to relatively late Gaelic occupation of the soil. The details of course must still be regarded as open to research; but I fancy the matter of early Gaelic-Cymric separation is pretty clearly demonstrated. I must wholly discard the crude assumptions I had held in this matter.

Turning to your individual theories—here, of course, my ignorance continues to disqualify me as an intelligent arbiter. Since I know nothing of any Celtic language on the one hand, or of any Semitic language on the other hand, I can hardly do much in the matter of testing alleged affinities. I must point out, however, that according to most of the conservative statements I have read, the supposed affinities of Celtic to Eastern speech do not bear the light of profound analysis—this applying both to the widely credited Phoenician element in Cornish (popularly attributed to a semi-prehistoric tin trade) & to the subtler & less commonly maintained resemblances broached in certain works. I have understood the view of sober scholarship to be that the alleged resemblances are purely accidental, or produced by the unconsciously biassed interpretations of scholars who worked with a theory already formulated. One need not point out the vast number of cases in which this matter of spurious linguistic interpretation has occurred in perfectly good faith. The distorting & filtering effect of a preconceived theory on the human powers of observation & correlation are much greater than was realised until recently; & we have as evidence the serious & bona-fide blunders of such men as Prof. Rafn of Denmark, [2] who honestly thought he made a Norse-Punic interpretation of the mixed jumble of lines (now believed to be Indian, Portugese, & English markings superimposed) on the celebrated Dighton Rock* in Massachusetts;[3] Prof. Le Plongeon,[4] who actually believed he had deciphered the wholly undecipherable Mayan hieroglyphics, &—very recently—Dr. Barbosa & Gen. Roudon of Brazil, who only last year imagined they could see a coherent Punic text in markings on the rocks of an Amazon tributary—which turned out to be natural fissures & weatherings. All this makes me disposed to be cautious about statements concerning Celtic-Semitic linkages, since the major body of conservative opinion is—or was the last I knew—so definitely reluctant to consider them genuine. Here, though, I may be behind the times—hence I reserve judgment until I hear how 1930 scholarship stands on the matter. If leading philologists have changed front, I am perfectly ready—as one without first-hand data—to change with them. It is not, I think, the view of the standard ethnologists that the Gaels had much Mediterranean or Oriental experience. Rather do they trace the southern element in existing Irish & Welsh people to another preëxisting stock which was not Gaelic at all. The *existing* Celtic-speaking races of Britain are admittedly an ethnic problem of some complexity; but authorities do not seem to extend this complexity back to the *original* users & importers of the Celtic dialects. It seems to be the idea that all the *originally* Celtic tribes were purely Nordic-Aryan—tall, light, yellow or reddish-haired people whose wanderings had been predominantly northern, and who assimilated comparatively little alien blood & culture. The Celtiberians would seem to be a dark Mediterranean stock, originally non-Aryan in speech and culture, who had suffered a Celtic conquest & had succumbed to the language & folkways of the superior race—of whose actual blood they had relatively little. Since this Mediterranean or Iberian stock originally extended north into the British Isles, it is not remarkable that the case there has analogies with the case of the Spanish peninsula; but there is one major difference in that the Celtic *blood* actually predominated in Britain & Ireland, so that the surviving stock remains largely Celtic-Nordic in physical type, (the most notable mass exception being the Welsh, where the Mediterranean blood predominates) & quite overwhelmingly so in speech & institutions.

---

*this rock is only about 25 miles from Prov. I have seen it myself.

But aside from this matter of Oriental influence, I surely see no insuperable objection to your view that the Gaels first entered the British Isles *after* instead of *before* the Cymri. Evidence still would seem to be highly nebulous and conflicting, so that dogmatism in either direction could not but be a mistake. The matter of bronze swords is perhaps not wholly *conclusive,* since an iron-using race could readily drop back to copper & bronze if deprived of easy access to workable iron deposits by some geographical change; but it is at least an *indication* which ought not to be disregarded.

You are right, too, I think, in believing that early Irish legendry ought to be carefully examined for its historic significance. Legends do not spring out of thin air, & actual direct experience is just as frequent an ingredient as the allegorical mythology, patriotic imagination, unconscious distortion, & transferred experience (i.e., attribution of events occurring in one place or historic stage to another place or historic stage) which form parallel ingredients. It is the business of the historian & anthropologist to sift the existing legendry very closely & analytically—examining the evidence both external & internal, & eliminating whatever would appear (from intrinsic cast, conformity to known myth-patterns, or discrepancy with previous well-correlated data) to be fabulous. The residue may well be tested seriously for historicity; & some of it stands a good chance of eventually being linked with the known stream of facts, and located on the chronological scale.

One of the best check-ups for legendry is *archaeology*—the intelligent examination & correlation of prehistoric artifacts, considered in relation to the artifacts of other known groups, & to the geological & physiographical qualities of their site. In the British Isles, so far as I know, the testimony of the earliest objects & deposits is such as to indicate a so-called *heliolithic* culture both in Britain & Ireland—i.e., a culture of definite nature, known & identified elsewhere, & having certain unique & unmistakable characteristics such as mummification, the rearing of megalithic monuments in circles or otherwise, the worship & association of the sun & serpent, the use of the "swastika" symbol,[5] etc., etc. Nothing discoverable comes before this—until, of course, we get back to ages definitely pre-human in the fullest sense, the age of Challean, Foxhall, & Sub-red-crag artifacts, & of the Piltdown skull. Now the heliolithic culture, which extends all the way from Ireland across Europe & North-Africa to Arabia, India, South China, Melanesia, Polynesia, & even Mexico & Peru, is pretty definitely associated with the small, dark Mediterranean race, & is known to have had nothing whatever to do with any branch of Nordics. It probably arose in the Mediterranean region & spread in all available directions—in many cases overriding previous primitive cultures & influencing other races. But where its artifacts are *the earliest,* as in the British Isles, we may reasonably conclude that it was the first culture of any permanence on the given site, & that its users were of the Mediterranean race that evolved it. I believe, therefore, that it will be difficult to prove that the British Isles (possibly a part of the continent at the time of first settlement) had any civilised, half-civilised, or even advancedly savage inhabitants prior to the coming of the dark neolithic Mediterraneans. The sub-human reliquiae represent stocks which could scarcely have survived the glacial periods, & it is my guess that the incoming Mediterraneans found the terrain fairly well devoid of bipedal fauna. There may have been some of the squat Mongoloids now represented by the Lapps, for it is known that they once reached down extensively into Western Europe; being probably the stock amongst whom the *witch-cult* (a fertility-religion arising in a pastoral & pre-agricultural age) and rite of the *witches' sabbath* took their source.[6] But evidence seems to have been against their having penetrated the British area to any extent. It's true that the Celts share most vigourously the myth-cycle of *fairies, gnomes,* & *little people,* which anthropologists find all over western Europe (in a distinctive form marking it off from the general Aryan personification system which produces fauns, satyrs, dryads, etc.) & attribute to vague memories of contact with the Mongoloids wholly prior to their invasion of Britain. Since these fair Nordic Celts found a smaller, darker race in Britain & Ireland, there is a tendency on the part of some to be misled, & to assume that the "little people" legends allude to contact with *those* dark aborigines. This, however, can clearly be disproved by analysis of the myths; for such myths invariably share with the parallel Continental myths the specific features (or tracks of these features) of having the "little people" essentially *repulsive* & *monstrous,* subterraneous in their habits of dwelling, & given to a queer kind of hissing discourse. Now this kind of thing does not apply to Mediterraneans—who are not abnormal or repulsive from the Nordic standpoint, (being very similar in features) who did not live underground, & whose language (possibly of a lost branch, but conceivably proto-Hamitic, Hamitic, or even Semitic) could scarcely have suggested hissing. The inevitable probability is that all the Nordics met with this old Mongoloid stock at a very early date, when it shared the continent with the northward-spreading Mediterraneans & with the remnants of other paleolithic & neolithic races now lost to history; & that after the ensuing conquest the defeated Mongoloids took to deep woods & caves, & survived for a long time as malignantly vindictive foes of their huge blond conquerors—carrying on a guerilla harassing & sinking so low in the anthropological scale that they became bywords of dread & repulsion. The memory of these beings could not but be very strong among the Nordics, (as well as among such Mediterraneans & Alpines as may have encountered them) so that a fixed body of legend was produced—to be carried about wherever Celtic or Teutonic tribes might wander. But this is rather a digression . . . . . especially since your theory does not deny an early dark race in the British Isles, but merely postulates that, among the Celtic-speaking invaders, the light-haired element was of earlier advent than the tribes who spoke Gaelic. Whether the Gaels were light or dark when arriving in Ireland would still seem to be an open question; & not an altogether vital one, since a very slight contact with a dark race is sufficient to darken the pigmentation of a blond stock. Thus the Gaels might have had their dark hair before reaching Ireland, yet without having undergone any Oriental wanderings. A very superficial wash of Mediterranean or other brunet blood, obtained in Western Europe, could have turned the trick. Of course the race would still produce many blond specimens, just as the blond type still exists in Britain & Ireland despite the dark races which have contributed their blood; but the presence of a substantial dark element would doubtless attract special notice among the still unmarked Celts, (who had perhaps preceded the Gaels or Milesians to Ireland, & had not so far fused with the aborigines to any degree) causing the latter to regard them as a "dark people" & so describe them in legendry. Dark hair, eyes, & skin pigmentation are certainly the more basic type for *homo sapiens,* so that the few specialised types who have assumed other characteristics easily fall back to the old pattern whenever the least predisposition occurs. That is, it is hard to make brunets blonds, but easy to make blonds brunets. A few blonds coming among a brunet people produce no alteration of the physical type, whereas a few brunets coming among a blond people will soon cause that people to produce a very high percentage of brunet descendants. There must have been a vast preponderance of blonds among the total invading stock of Ireland, since so many blond types (even in regions unaffected by the later Teutonic blood) are produced there today. Just how this blond blood was distributed among the several waves of invaders we cannot now say—nor is it likely that we shall ever know. The old legends, admittedly subject to change and interpolation, cannot well be more than a general indication & source of suggestions.

But at the same time I think you are right in attaching importance to the indicative & suggestive value of the legends. They are probably distorted so far as details, proportions, historic emphases, & chronology are concerned, yet there is much reason to think that they bear a real relationship to the successive waves of prehistoric conquest in Ireland—whether those waves be all Gaelic or otherwise. I do not know the legends at first-hand, but as I gather them here and there I do not find Partholan represented as Egyptian or Phoenician, as you assume. My impression is that the tales make Partholan & his men *Greeks*—indeed, my impression was so strong that I wrote a story of Ireland years ago, in which I adopt that assumption myself (for fictional purposes only).[7] But according to legend, Partholan's race all perished in a plague, & left no descendants after about three centuries of occupation. Incidentally—this same fate of extinction is also alleged to have overtaken the second wave of invaders, (the Nemedians) reputedly from "Scythia". In considering these geographic & ethnic attributions, we must remember the relatively limited horizons of the bards who shaped the legends. In the tribal period when the myths took form, "Greece" & "Scythia" might have meant almost anything considerably removed from the coast of western Europe; for these names were very vague rumours in the days of the Lebar Gabhala, much as the names of Cambaluc, El Dorado, Prester John, the Great Cham,

Eipango, & the Isles of Spice were to the western Europeans of the Middle Ages. The Fomorians—sea-raiders—do not seem to have colonised the country much, but to have waged a piratical warfare on the Nemedians. You are probably right in considering them northern pirates. It would also seem probable that, as you say, the Firbolgs & Tuatha De Danam were from Britain—*Cymri,* according to the theory which you hold; though I had previously fancied them Gaels—the date being too early for the differentiation of the Cymric type as I had envisaged it. Of course, they *could* be Gaels, assuming that a wave of this stock had passed over Britain & was being driven out by advancing Cymri. I still think this probable though one cannot be certain at present. It is my impression that a large part of the later Irish people must be descended from the waves of invasion recorded as Firbolg & Tuatha De Danam. The Milesians *undoubtedly* were Gaels, whether or not the *only* Gaels who ever entered Ireland. Personally I cannot think that they were the only ones, since the legends do not indicate any linguistic or cultural difference from the already resident tribes—& Cymric differs so much from Gaelic that the contrast would be very marked if it existed. On the other hand, the Milesians are held to have been *related* to some of the resident tribes, especially those of Ulster & Munster. Candidly, I really think that most of the invaders of Ireland from late neolithic times onward were Gaels of one sort or another, (& various subdivisions are exceedingly probable) whoever the invaders of Britain may have been. The story is assuredly not a simple one, & many wholly unrecorded immigrations probably occurred—accounting for peculiar physiognomical types in western Ireland & northern Scotland found nowhere else in the world today—but it seems to me that the great preponderance of Britanno-Hibernian invasions was by Celts, *relatively* untouched by Oriental blood, language, or culture, & that those entering Ireland were preponderantly Gaelic. It does not seem to me remarkable that the Brythonic Cymri failed to conquer Ireland in the pre-Milesian period—if indeed they did so fail—since the island may well have been defended powerfully enough to deter a race already busy with the subjugation & settlement of Britain. It is very probable that the Cymric conquests ended with Britain; & that Ireland, after receiving Gaelic refugees from that place, (Firbolgs—Tuatha De Danam) became too formidable to encourage Cymric invasion. Of this, however, we cannot speak with certainty. What is more of a puzzle to me, since accepting your assurance that the Gauls of the continent were probably Cymric, is how the certainly Gaelic Milesians got to Ireland, & where they directly & immediately came from, at the late & almost historic date generally assigned for their advent. Probably, I suppose, they came from Eastern Europe, or perhaps from some part of Spain or Southern Gaul where they had held out against other elements for a long period. I have doubts regarding any Oriental theory. Not only does Gaelic fail to show any Oriental influence which *conservative* philologists can recognise, but the late date ascribed to the Milesian invasion brings it far along in the recorded history of the Eastern & Mediterranean world, so that any large & powerful element like the wandering Gaels would have been noted in recorded history if present in these regions. You are doubtless aware that the Milesian invasion is set at a very late date B.C., & by some even in the A.D.'s. No great tribe wandering through the Oriental fringes of the Graeco-Roman world could have so wholly escaped notice. Far more likely is the idea that the Milesian Gaels were dwelling in some part of the Western world still in a primitive & relatively unhistoric state. The Milesians of legend come out of nowhere—& the Eastern & classical worlds of their probable period were far from nowhere! It may have been the Roman advance in Western Europe which sent them roving still farther westward.

But pardon all this rambling. In a layman's way I find the subject of prehistoric anthropology fascinating—hinting as it does of the dramatic and the unknown—since I am only too eager to pour out a flood of suggestions, based on ill-digested smatterings of knowledge, on the slightest provocation. I wonder what you think of the recent theory of Prof. G. Elliot Smith,[8] which has gained surprising ground in the last decade, that

(a) *civilisation* is not a natural & inevitable, but purely accidental step in a race's development; a step which is vastly more likely not to occur than to occur.

(b) that there is only *one* civilisation in the history of the world—that of the Nile valley; *all* others, (even the Chinese, Mexican & Peruvian) being derived from it by migration or transmission, & all notions of independently evolved cultures (beyond a simple neolithic stage, at which races tend to stagnate) being errors & delusions.

(c) that we commonly overestimate the antiquity of neolithic Europe, & that later neolithic races were contemporary with the great Eastern civilisations, picking up many of their inhibitions from these.

Personally, I can't swallow *all* this, though I concede that most of the different cultures around the Mediterranean—& perhaps this Tigris-Euphrates—must have had a common source. I think that civilisation is an inevitable consequence of the long & settled existence of an intelligent race, & that any such race would develop an independent culture if left long enough without having a ready-made culture transmuted to it. I furthermore think that a large part of the civilisations of China, Mexico, & Peru were certainly original & autochthonous, no matter how many details they may have *later* absorbed from the spreading Nile-born world-culture. Young Frank B. Long (a friend of mine whose *Weird Tales* work you have probably noticed) & I argue interminably on this point, he being a Smith-adherent. Recent researches in the matter of Mayan culture, pointing unmistakably toward autochthony, seem to sustain my position of scepticism.

But I will take up no more of your time with this disjointed wandering. Rest assured that I do not think your theories at all extravagant, & that it [does] not involve much of a wrench to make me a convert to most of them. In closing, let me add that my friends Long & Clark Ashton Smith (whose work you must know) have repeatedly praised your tales, Long being especially enthusiastic about "Skull Face". He also likes your verses exceedingly.[9]

Most sincerely yrs
H P Lovecraft

Notes

1. To date HPL had written thirty-five sonnets for *Fungi from Yuggoth,* but his typescript long omitted the two concluding poems in the event that he might yet write others. He did not, but his typescript of the cycle long consisted of only thirty-three poems (CAS had one such copy). When RHB prepared a new typescript for HPL in September 1934, "Evening Star" and "Continuity" (numbered XXXIV and XXXV as when HPL had first composed them) were included. It was not until 1936, when RHB planned an edition of the complete cycle, that it achieved its present form, with "Recapture" (mid-November 1929) inserted as the antepenultimate poem and "Evening Star" and "Continuity" renumbered to accommodate it.
2. Carl Christian Rafn (1795–1864), Danish antiquarian, early advocate of the theory that the Vikings had explored North America centuries before Columbus and Cabot.
3. Dighton Rock, at Berkley, Massachusetts, is an 11-foot-high "glacial erratic" boulder that once rested on the shore of the Taunton River. It is covered with petroglyphs attributed to sources ranging from Portuguese explorers to Native Americans.
4. Augustus Le Plongeon (1826–1908), author of *Vestiges of the Mayas* (1881), *Sacred Mysteries among the Mayas and the Quiches, 11,500 Years Ago* (1886), and other works.
5. A swastika is an equilateral cross with arms bent at right angles, all in the same rotary direction, usually clockwise. It is a symbol of prosperity and good fortune widely distributed throughout the ancient and modern world.
6. HPL derived this theory (now regarded as extremely unlikely) from Margaret A. Murray's *The Witch-Cult in Western Europe* (1921).
7. See letter 3, n. 8.
8. Sir G[rafton] Elliot Smith (1871–1937), author of *The Evolution of Man* (1924) and *The Migrations of Early Culture* (1929). Smith was a vigorous proponent of the theory that Egypt was the source of European civilization. See *The Ancient Egyptians and Their Influence upon the Civilization of Europe* (1911).
9. To date, nearly half of REH's appearances in *WT* had been verse.

[5] [ANS][1]

[No postmark, n.d.; enclosed with letter?][2]

Old Salem with its spectral memories (the prototype of my fictional "Arkham") is only about 60 miles from Providence. I was there last week—also visiting ancient Marblehead. (a coastal village which has scarcely changed in the last 200 years—the original of my "Kingsport.") I love these ancient places where the architecture, memories, & atmosphere of other centuries still linger. Providence is rather an old place itself—redolent of the 18th century,—so I have grown up as something of a natural antiquarian in an unsystematic way.

Notes

1. [Front:] Main Entrance, Old Witch House, Built 1635, Salem Mass. [HPL's note:] more likely circa 1660.

2. HPL had visited Marblehead and Salem shortly before 10 July 1930 and c. early Nov. 1931 with W. Paul Cook.

[6] [TLS]

[August 9, 1930]

Dear Mr. Lovecraft:

Let me first thank you for the opportunity you have given me to read your poetry; I need not tell you that I appreciate your kindness highly. You have, in this sonnet-cycle, accomplished a superb artistic work, to my mind. It is not for me to say which of the poems were best; I read the whole with complete enjoyment. To say that some were superior to the others would be to imply that certain facets of a diamond were superior in luster to the rest. In expressing a preference for some of the poems, I do not by any means seek to imply an inferiority of the others. But I was especially taken with "The Book" "Recognition" "The Lamp" "The Courtyard" "Star-Winds" "The Window" "The Bells" "Mirage" "The Elder Pharos" "Background" and "Alienation."

I am glad that you liked "The Moon of Skulls" and hope my future efforts meet your approval. And I am highly honored to know that Mr. Long and Mr. Clark Ashton Smith have noticed my efforts. Both are writers and poets whose work I very much admire, having carefully preserved all of their poems (as well as all of your's) that have appeared in Weird Tales since I first made my acquaintance with the magazine.

I scarcely need say that your comments on historical and prehistorical matters I found to be highly interesting and instructive. You touched on a number of phases of which I am totally ignorant, and in matters wherein our views differ somewhat, I candidly admit that I am not scholar enough to present any logical argument. Your observations regarding the Mongoloid aborigines and their relation to the fairy-tales of western Europe especially interested me. I had supposed, without inquiring very deeply into the matter, that these legends were based on contact with the earlier Mediterraneans, and indeed, wrote a story on that assumption which appeared some years ago in Weird Tales—"The Lost Race". I readily see the truth of your remarks, that a Mongoloid race must have been responsible for the myths of the Little People, and sincerely thank you for the information. As the present Mongolian is more or less repellant in appearance to the present-day Aryan, how much more must the primitive or retrograded type of Mongoloid repelled the original Aryan, who was probably superior in physical comliness to moderns!

As regards Partholan, legends I have read seem to differ, some ascribing his origin to Greece, others to Egypt. Donn Byrne[1] in his romances speaks of "Partholan of Egypt", and maintains that the present names of MacPartland and MacFarlane are an evolution from Partholan, though the chief's entire band of descendants seems to have been wiped out by the plague. The Firbolgs and the Tuatha De Danaans, as you know, were represented to have been descendants of those Nemedians who escaped the swords of the Fomorians and returned to Greece, whence they had originally come to Ireland. Returning at different times, they were bitter rivals until the coming of the Milesians, from Spain by way of Egypt and Scythia (according to legends.) Firbolg, or Men With Bags is supposed by some to be merely the Gaelic way of pronouncing or indicating Belgae, which, if correct, would seem to point to a Continental or Brythonic affinity.

Regarding Oriental phases in the Celtic language, you are doubtless right in attaching little significance to it. Indeed, the likenesses of Gaelic to Semitic, seem too slight to warrant basing any theory upon them—though the thought is entirely too fascinating from a fictional point of view for me to ever abandon it entirely. I quote here all the evidence I have been able to find that points to a linking of the languages—scanty, I will admit, nor do I indeed put it forth to hold up any theory of mine. I quote from O'Reilly and O'Donovan's Irish-English Dictionary published by Duffy and Co., Dublin, more than thirty years ago. No very modern authority, to be sure.

"The old Irish, began their alphabet with the letter B, and therefore the Irish called it Beith-luis-nion from its first three letters."

(This agrees with certain Eastern races, though it is certainly but a trivial point.)

"However, in imitation of other learned languages, and particularly the Latin . . . . . . the modern Irish thought proper to begin their alphabet with A. This letter . . . . is not unlike the Hebrew Aleph, and the Chaldean and Greek Alpha."

Concerning the word Bel-ain, meaning the circle of Belus or the Sun, it is said: "Ain or ainn in Irish signifies a great circle; and Bel or Beal was the Assyrian, Chaldaean, or Phoenician name of the true God, while the patriarchal religion was generally observed. This name was afterwards attributed to the Sun when those oriental nations generally forgot, or willingly served from the worship of the true God and adored that planet as their chief deity. It is very certain that the primitive Irish observed this idolatrous worship of the Sun under the name of Bel or Beal, whatever part of the world they derived it from, as appears very manifestly by those religious fires they lighted with great solemnity on May day; a fact which is evidently proved by the very name whereby they distinguished that day, which is still called and known by no other name than that of La Beal tinne, i.e. the day of the fire of Bel or Belus . . . . . I shall finish these remarks with observing that the word Ain or Ainn, is the Celtic original upon which the Latin word Anus was formed; it was afterward written Annus . . . . to mean solely and properly the solar circle or annual course of the Sun."

"The name of this consonant (B) in Irish approaches much closer in sound and letters to the Hebrew name of the said letter, than either the Chaldean Betha or the Greek Beta, it being in Irish Beith and in Hebrew Beth. Beth signifies a house in Hebrew, and Both in Irish is a very common name for an open house or tent. It is to be observed that the Irish consonants, b, c, d, g, p, t, by a full point or tittle set over any of them, do thereby lose their simple strong sound, and pronounce after the manner of the Hebrew bh, ch, dh, gh, ph, th, which are simply and genuinely aspirated; on the other hand, it is to be particularly noticed, that the now-mentioned Hebrew consonants, by them called Begad-Kephat, memoria causa, by fixing a dagesch or full point in the middle of any of them, do thereby also lose their simple aspirate sound and pronounce strong like the Irish b, c, d, g, p, t; so that the addition of a full point to the above mentioned Hebrew consonants changes them into their corresponding letters of the Irish. By this kind of reciprocation between the Irish and Hebrew languages, the antiquity of the Irish or Celtic seems to be sufficiently demonstrated; although it must be confessed that the using a full point in either of the languages is of a late invention."

"The Irish D also agrees with Gr. Th or Theta, in like manner with the Hebrew Daleth or Dh, which, by putting a full point over it, becomes a D. The Irish language is industriously censured by some critics for admitting a superfluous D or Dh at the end of several words . . . . . . And we find a near coincidence of that redundancy in the Hebrew language; thus in the Hebrew raah, to see, leah, to toil or labor, etc., the final letter He or h, is not pronounced, but, like the Irish Dh, becomes a mute or quiescent letter.

"It (E) is in Irish called eabha, the aspen-tree; and is not unlike the Heb. heth.

"It (F) is called fearn, the elder tree. It is the same with the Hebrew vau, because the figure and sound of both letters are very nearly the same.

"(G) The very figure of the letter g, in some of our old parchments, is not essentially dissimilar to some of the cuts of the old Abrahamic and Phoenician gimel. The Hebrews call this letter gimel, as we are assured by grammarians, from its crooked figure, bearing some resemblance to a camel, which in Hebrew is called gamel or gamal; and to observe it, by the by, gamal, as well as camal, is the Irish for a camel.

"(M) We think it well worth observing here, that our language bears a perfect resemblance, in the disposition of its pronouns, to the manner of ordering them in the Hebrew; for the latter devide them into classes etc. The prepositive are set before words, and the subjunctive are written in the end of words; both equally determine the person.

"(N) It is called Nuin, the ash tree. In Hebrew it is called Nun, from the sound.

"(O) It is the positive vowel of the diphthong oir, the spindle tree; and we find this diphthong in the Hebrew: as, Heb., Goi, Lat., gens.

"(P) The Greeks, to observe it, by the by, have taken their (word for tower or castle) from the Phoenicians, their first instructors in letters, in whose language it is Borg, which is plainly of the same root with our Irish word brog or brug, a strong or fortified place, also a lord's court or castle; whence the French Bourg, the German Burgh, and English Borough, do in a larger sense signify a town. We find the like affinity in many words between the Greek and Latin and Irish languages: as, Ir. cairg and carga, Easter; Latin, pascha, and Chaldaice, pascha, which is derived from the Hebrew Pasach or Phase; Lat., transitus, the Passover. It hath been observed before that the Lingua Prisca, or the primitive Latin tongue, was chiefly formed upon the Celtic and the truth of this assertion is abundantly confirmed through the whole course of this dictionary. Celtic coib, Lingua Prisca cobiae, Latin copiae."

The remarks regarding Celtic likenesses to Greek and Latin and other Aryan languages are of course, beside the point. Nor is there any particular reason, I admit, in supposing that the Semitic semblances are other than mere coincidents or later additions to the language, borrowed, perhaps, from the Latin. However, I can not but believe that the ancient world was knit more closely together than is generally supposed.

As refers to the worship of Bel, I have read somewhere that the Celtic term Bally, meaning town refers to Baal, the Semitic god, which worship, it is averred by some was introduced into Ireland by Phoenician traders and settlers after the Milesian invasion (setting the date of that invasion further back than is generally accepted) or was brought into Ireland by the Gaels themselves. But attempting to untangle legends and find some phase on which they all agree, would seem to be an endless task—too puzzling for my scant knowledge, even if I could read them in the original. One legend for instance, has the Gaels wandering into Egypt to serve as mercenaries, just at the time the Hebrews are leaving, and another legend has it that the Milesians were already well settled in the Egyptian barracks when the Jews arrived, and that it was malcontents among the Gaels who went into Goshan and stirred up the Hebrews to revolt. Another legend makes a powerful Irish family named Cusac the progenitors of the Cossack race, while of course you are familiar with the many tales of the Lia Fail, the Stone of Destiny which Jeremiah (reputed to be a Jap named Gera mia, Giver of Stones) is supposed to have brought into Ireland with him and on which the present English kings are crowned.[2]

I have read an interesting theory put forth by some historian whose name I cannot now recall, (I can remember faces and events but find it almost impossible to remember names and dates) but as closely as I can remember his idea was something like this: That western Europe was first settled by a nomadic tribe of Celts whose language was the basis of modern Gaelic; that these primitive Gaels were driven into the outer fringes by the more powerful Brythons who became Gauls, Belgae and Cymri. That the legend of Partholan refers to the first settlement of Ireland by these Gaels, and that the plague to which is ascribed their destruction really refers to an invasion by Britons, who disposessed them of the more fertile parts of the island. That the Fomorians, Nemedians, Firbolg and Tuatha De Danaans were various waves of Brythonic peoples from the larger island. That meanwhile a powerful branch of Gaels had taken refuge in the mountains of Spain or southern Gaul, where they resisted the assaults of the Brythonic Gauls, and retained all their tribal characteristics, as a primitive race of mountaineers is likely to do, and that it was these people, who, giving way before the Romans, crossed over into Ireland and became the Milesians of legend. He explains their relationship to various tribes of Ireland by the fact that many of Partholan's Gaelic descendants still maintained a desultory warfare with the conquering Britons.

His theory seems plausible in many ways, though I do not concur in all his suppositions. Of course, I really have no right to quarrel with a historian, but when the historians quarrel among themselves, even such a slightly informed layman as myself is likely to draw his own conclusions. I am ready to accept the above mentioned idea that the Gaels came to Ireland from Spain or southern Gaul; indeed, the legends seem to confirm that, if legends can be said to confirm any historical fact. But I strongly doubt the assertation that the Gaels preceded the Brythons into any part of western Europe, and I hold—with the obstinacy of ignorance no doubt—that the Gaels followed an entirely different route into Europe than that taken by the Brythons. I am probably all wrong, but I believe that the Gauls or Brythons are supposed to have come out of Central Asia, crossing northern Russia, possibly the Scandinavian countries, and coming down into France through Germany.

I have no real reason to uphold my belief, but I believe that the Gaels came the other way—the southern route, so to speak, across Asia Minor and Africa and up into Spain. This trek must have taken place at a very early date, in the first dim dawn of history when the movements of all tribes and nations were very vague and easily lost to the recorders. They probably lived for many centuries in southern Gaul before they went into Ireland.

But as I said, my ideas and sources of information are so nebulous that they are not worth imposing on any one. I wont ramble in this direction any further except to say that in regard to the relationship of the Gaels to tribes already in Ireland, I do not imagine that the Gaelic invasion was a sudden flood of entirely unknown people. I suspect that Gaels had been filtering into Ireland for some time in one way or another, and there were probably a number of settlements in various parts of the island, doubtless near the coasts.

Professor Smith's deductions are interesting, though I cannot say that I agree with all of them. I believe, like you, that civilization is a natural and inevitable consequence, whether good or evil I am not prepared to state. As to the single civilization theory—no doubt the Egyptian culture greatly influenced the rest of the world to a large extent, though I had thought that as early as 6000 B.C. the pre-Semitic Sumerians had a civilization somewhat superior to the contemporary Egyptian one. Perhaps the Grecian culture had a basis of Egyptian, transmitted through the conquered Cretans, though it appears to me that the Hellenic invaders, rather than adopting it as their own, reared a separate civilization on the ruins of the Mycenie civilization. I cannot think that the Nile valley culture affected the people of China, Mexico and South America overly much, though there may have been more intercourse between these early races than we think. Possibly, as he says, later neolithic races were contemporary with the Eastern civilizations; I seem to have read somewhere that the early Cretans were supposed to have been in the tag end of their own particular New Stone Age when they first came into the knowledge of the Egyptians. That seems to me to be a more or less minor point.

And now I come to a point where I must impose on your good nature. I mean by that, I am about to ask a number of questions about subjects wherein my ignorance is exceeded only by my interest. Let me first say, in partial explanation of my lack of information on the subjects about which I am going to inquire, that my failure to inform myself has been less lack of interest than lack of opportunity. Western Texas is no particular seat of culture, and it is almost impossible to obtain books on obscure and esoteric subjects anywhere in the state. The greater part of my life has been spent on ranches, farms and in boom towns, where there were quite often neither book shops nor libraries within a hundred miles, and my studies were mainly in snatches, in spare moments when I was not working at something else. Only the last few years have I been able to devote the greater part of my time to writing and studying, so you can readily see why my education is not all it should be.

But the questions. I have noted in your stories you refer to Cthulu, Yog Sothoth, R'lyeh, Yuggoth etc. Adolph de Castro, I note, mentions these gods, places, or whatever they are, only the spelling is different, as Cthulutl, Yog Sototl.[3] Both you and he, I believe, have used the phrase fhtaghn. A writer in the Eyrie, a Mr. O'Neail,[4] I believe, wondered if I did not use some myth regarding this Cthulhu in "Skull Face". The name Kathulos might suggest that, but in reality, I merely manufactured the name at random, not being aware at the time of any legendary character named Cthulhu—if indeed there is.

Would it be asking too much to ask you to tell me the significance of the above mentioned names or terms? And the Arab Alhazred, and the Necronomicon. The mention of these things in your superb stories have whetted my interest immensely. I would extremely appreciate any information you would give me regarding them.

Hoping to hear from you again, and again thanking you for an opportunity of reading your poems,

Sincerely,
Robert E. Howard

Notes

1. Brian Oswald Patrick Donn-Byrne [Donn Byrne] (1889–1928), Irish historical novelist. REH is known to have read *Hangman's House* (1926), *Crusade* (1928) and *Destiny Bay* (1928).

2. REH appears to confuse Lia Fáil (Irish for Stone of Destiny)—a standing stone at the Inauguration Mound on the Hill of Tara in County Meath in Ireland, which served as the coronation stone for the High Kings of Ireland—with the Stone of Scone, commonly known as the Stone of Destiny or the Coronation Stone kept at the now-ruined abbey in Scone, near Perth, Scotland, and used for centuries in the coronation of the monarchs of Scotland, the monarchs of England and, more recently, British monarchs. (Edward I captured the stone as spoils of war and took it to Westminster Abbey, but the stone has since been returned to Scotland.)

3. Adolphe de Castro's "The Electric Executioner," which HPL had revised, contained some of HPL's own mythological elements but with the names given an Aztec cast.

4. N. J. O'Neail in "The Eyrie" (*WT,* March 1930); see Joshi and Michaud, ed., *H. P. Lovecraft in "The Eyrie,"* p. 31, and McHaney, *Robert E. Howard: World's Greatest Pulpster,* p. 23. See also *SLL* 3.166.

[7]

10 Barnes St.,
Providence, R.I.,
August 14, 1930

Dear Mr. Howard:—

[. . .] Concerning early Europe and the "little people"—I remember the interest with which I read "The Lost Race" in 1926. For fictional purposes it is perfectly proper—perhaps even *best,* on account of the dramatic simplicity of the idea—to attribute the British legends to forgotten races in the British Isles themselves. That is what Arthur Machen has done with such marvelous skill and potency—giving the wild hills of Wales an aura of hidden fear and dark fascination which no reader of "The Red Hand",[1] "The Black Seal", or "The Shining Pyramid" can ever forget. But in sober fact, it seems most probably to lay the myths to the squat Lapp-like or Esquimau-like aborigines of the Continent—especially since they exist in vivid form (as *kobold* legends etc.) amongst northern Continental races who were never in prehistoric contact with Mediterraneans. More about the heritage of these primal Mongoloids can be found in that important anthropological work, "The Witch-Cult in Western Europe", by Margaret A. Murray (1921).

All your remarks on the Irish legends, and the supposed affinities betwixt Gaelic and Semitic tongues, proved largely new and highly interesting to me. I had never before seen a detailed statement of the mooted linguistic resemblances, and am infinitely glad to have the transcript you furnish—which I shall preserve carefully. As you remark, resemblances to other Aryan tongues on the part of Gaelic mean very little in relation to the debated point—and so far as the *alphabet* is concerned, we very well know that Western Europe had no alphabet until the Greek characters slowly filtered north and west. The Greek names of the letters naturally have a Semitic base, since they were taken directly from the Phoenician. Thus in naming E "eabha", the Celts undoubtedly had the Greek *eta* rather than the Hebraeo-Punic "*heth*" in mind. It is the disposition of modern scholars, I gather, to deny the *direct* origin of any western alphabet from the Phoenician or Carthaginian. Even the Punic characters of the Teutons are traced to obscurely transmitted Greek influences. But as you say, it is very likely that separated ancient races had many more individual contacts than history records, so that certain anomalous and outwardly unaccountable borrowings are not to be wondered at so vastly after all. We really know very little of the details of prehistoric tribe movements, so that dogmatism in any direction is rash and presumptuous. Assuredly, the fiction-writer ought not to be tied down to any tentative claim of the moment's anthropological scholarship.

Smith's theory of a single origin for all civilisation is set back somewhat by those scholars who maintain that Mayan mathematics had certain points in advance of Egyptian or any old-world mathematics of the same period. The Sumerian question which you bring up is also another hard nut to crack, although Smith meets this matter with some ingenious arguments, comparisons of artifacts, and criticisms of the generally accepted tables of ancient chronology. You would find his writings highly interesting and thought-provoking. His latest and most inclusive book—"Human History"—arouses young Long to almost lyrical ardours of admiration. I have not read it as yet, but mean to do so as soon as possible. Smith is probably right so far as the nations of the Mediterranean littoral are concerned—that is, Egypt flowered so early that her neighbours couldn't help picking up ideas at a time when their own culture-state was very primitive and receptive. But I think S. is wrong in claiming that none of these neighbours would have been likely to evolve any culture without this accident-born prototype to imitate. Greek culture obviously consisted of a substratum modified out of all resemblance to its ancestry by the institutions of the conquering (Nordic) Achaeans, and incorporating many elements which filtered out of Asia Minor and Egypt. The Achaeans were blond barbarians who brought to Greece practically the same elements which the Celts and Teutons brought to the British Isles and to Gaul. The difference in resulting culture must be traced to the difference of the environing conditions they encountered.

Regarding the solemnly cited myth-cycle of Cthulhu, Yog Sothoth, R'lyeh, Nyarlathotep, Nug, Yeb, Shub-Niggurath, etc., etc.—let me confess that this is all a synthetic concoction of my own, like the populous and varied pantheon of Lord Dunsany's "Pegāna".[2] The reason for its echoes in Dr. de Castro's work is that the latter gentleman is a revision-client of mine—into whose tales I have stuck these glancing references for sheer fun. If any other clients of mine get work placed in W.T., you will perhaps find a still-wider spread of the cult of Azathoth, Cthulhu, and the Great Old Ones! The Necronomicon of the mad Arab Abdul Alhazred is likewise something which must yet be written in order to possess objective reality. Abdul is a favourite dream-character of mine—indeed that is what I used to call myself when I was five years old and a transported devotee of Andrew Lang's version of the Arabian Nights. A few years ago I prepared a mock-erudite synopsis of Abdul's life, and of the posthumous vicissitudes and translations of his hideous and unmentionable work *Al Azif* (called ***Τό Νεκρονόμικον*** by the Byzantine Monk Theodorus Philetas, who translated it into late Greek in A.D. 900!)—a synopsis which I shall follow in future references to the dark and accursed thing.[3] Long has alluded to the Necronomicon in some things of his[4]—in fact, I think it is rather good fun to have this artificial mythology given an air of verisimilitude by wide citation. I ought, though, to write Mr. O'Neail and disabuse him of the idea that there is a large blind spot in his mythological erudition! Clark Ashton Smith is launching another mock mythology revolving around the black, furry toad-god *Tsathoggua,* whose name had variant forms amongst the Atlanteans, Lemurians, and Hyperboreans who worshipped him after he emerged from inner Earth (whither he came from Outer Space, with Saturn as a stepping-stone). I am using Tsathoggua in several tales of my own and of revision-clients—although Wright rejected the Smith tale in which he originally appeared.[5] It would be amusing to identify your Kathulos with my Cthulhu—indeed, I may so adopt him in some future black allusion.[6] Incidentally—Long and I often debate about the real folklore basis of Machen's nightmare witch-cult hints—"Aklo letters", "Voorish domes", "Dols", "Green and Scarlet Ceremonies", etc., etc. I think they are M's own inventions, for I have never heard of them elsewhere; but Long can't get over the idea that they have an actual source in European myth. Can you give us any light on this? We haven't had the temerity to ask Machen himself.[7]

With best wishes—

Yr most obt and hble svt

HPL

Notes

1. The epigraph to HPL's "The Horror at Red Hook" (1925) is from "The Red Hand."

2. The Pegāna stories of Lord Dunsany are found primarily in *The Gods of Pegāna* (1905) and *Time and the Gods* (1906); in *The Complete Pegāna,* ed. S. T. Joshi (Oakland, CA: Chaosium, 1998).

3. "History of the *Necronomicon.*"

4. "The Space-Eaters" (*WT,* July 1928) and "The Hounds of Tindalos" (*WT,* March 1929).

5. CAS introduced Tsathoggua in "The Tale of Satampra Zeiros" (1929; *WT,* November 1931), but HPL's "The Whisperer in Darkness" (1930) contains the first reference to Tsathoggua in print. HPL cited Tsathoggua extensively in "The Mound" (1929–30), ghostwritten for Zealia Bishop, but *WT* rejected the tale and it was not published until 1940.

6. HPL did so, referring to "L'mur-Kathulos" in "The Whisperer in Darkness."

7. The names, so far as is known, were invented by Machen. HPL had obtained Machen's address (and addresses of several other contemporary writers of weird fiction) from AWD for the purpose of having W. Paul Cook mail Machen a copy of the *Recluse* with "Supernatural Horror in Literature." Cook did so, but HPL never wrote to Machen himself; nor did he write to any other of his idols or peers.

[8] [ANS]

[Postmarked Quebec, Canada,
1 September 1930][1]

This place surpasses all my expectations—a veritable dream of archaic city walls, castellated cliffs, silver spires, narrow, zigzag, precipitous streets, & the leisurely civilisation of an elder world!

Regards—

H P Lovecraft

Notes

1. Front: Unknown.

[9] [nonextant letter by H. P. Lovecraft]

[September 1930]

[10] [TLS]

[ca. September 1930]

Dear Mr. Lovecraft:

I envy you your sojourn in Quebec. From what I have read and heard of the city, it is indeed the most archaic city in the New World. I should like very much to go prying around in out-of-the-way places, redolent with the musk and decay of antiquity—but I've never had the time or money.

I am highly obligated to both yourself and Mr. Long for the loan of "A Man from Genoa." I have not gotten the book yet, mail service being rather irregular in this part of the world, but I am looking forward to its perusal with the greatest anticipation.

I was amazed to learn that August W. Derleth is only twenty-one. He must have begun marketing his work at a very early age, for it seems that I have been reading his stories in *Weird Tales* for years. My friends and I have often commented on the excellence of his products and wondered why he did not try his hand at longer stories.

I have noted Mr. Dwyer's letters in the Eyrie, and remember the poem you mention.[1] I cannot at present recall Mr. Talman, though I have undoubtedly read stories by that author. Thank you very much for giving me the addresses of these gentlemen, also Donald Wandrei's. I am usually so busy I dont know when I'll have time to write them, but I mean to do so as soon as possible. Correspondence with such gentlemen, as with yourself, is a rare treat and an honor.

As regarding the Persians, and their relation toward the Aryan race as a whole, about the only difference between them and the Mesopotamian races seems to me to be a more kindly attitude on the part of the Persians toward conquered races. They were cruel, but we do not find the systematic and continual butchery of subjugated peoples as was the case with the Semitic races. To me there is a strange and powerful fascination about this wayward branch on the Aryan tree; it stirs my imagination to contemplate those proud, half-naked blond savages riding down out of their mountain fastnesses to ravage the rich lands of the plains—their whirlwind conquests and appallingly swift moral and physical disintegration. Indeed Croesus might say he conquered his conquerors, for Lydia's looted wealth played havoc with those hardy barbarians. I suppose a strong Turanian strain had filtered into the Persian bloodstream before they came into the plains. We read that their youths were trained to do only three things: ride, speak the truth and bend the bow. If you will notice, the bow is basically a non-Aryan weapon, and one which the Persians must have taken from some Oriental neighbor. The Greeks never esteemed its use, and archery was little thought of in Rome's regular legions, though their auxillaries practised the science effectively. The western races seemed partial to hand-to-hand fighting, a natural preference, considering their superior strength and statu[r]e.

The Celts were not bowmen, nor were the Germans. True, no Eastern nation ever equalled the skill and science of the medieval English archers but I think even this can be traced indirectly to non-Aryan influence. The Normans brought the bow into England and it was arrows that decided the day at Senlac. But the bow came into France with Hrolf and his Norsemen, and the Danes particularly had been using the weapon skillfully for centuries. It is very likely that the Scandinavian peoples learned the effectiveness of the bow while still roaming the steppes of Northern Asia, by contact with some bow-and-arrow Turanian people, and brought that knowledge with them when they overflowed over Greater Sweden, into the Baltic countries and later all over the world. Of course, I do not mean that they really introduced the bow to the other western nations as a hither-to unknown weapon. But I mean that my belief is that archery as an art and science of war, originated with the Mongoloid races, was imparted to the eastern-most ancestors of the Danes and was spread by them over Europe.

For the bow is connected and interwoven with Oriental history from the very dawn of history. We read of the prowess of the Pharaohs, shooting from their war-chariots and slaying lions and Hittites impartially; the Philistines give back from the fury of Saul and shower him with shafts from a distance; the Babylonians and Assyrians war with heavy bows, curved in an exaggerated fashion; the Persians and Scythians exchange heavy flights of whistling shafts before they close in battle. And to come to a more recent date—the Roman legions reel before the cloud of Parthian arrows, the Crusaders fall before the Turkish bows, and the wild riders of Attila, Genghis Khan and Tamerlane wipe out whole armies without coming to sword-points.

As regards the Armenians, I am inclined to the theory that they represent a race whose original type was Semitic, who fell so completely under the dominion of their Aryan conquerors that they forgot their original Semitic language, and retained the later-acquired speech through following centuries of re-Semitizing.

I agree with you that the Tuscans influenced Roman physiognomy and character greatly. And that brings up another question—who were the Tuscans and from where did they come? I would certainly like to see your views on the subject.

I shall watch for the tale, "Medusa's Coil,"[2] you mentioned. Regardless of the author, if you instilled into the tale some of the magic of your own pen, it cannot fail to fascinate the readers.

As regards African-legend sources, I well remember the tales I listened to and shivered at, when a child in the "piney woods" of East Texas, where Red River marks the Arkansaw and Texas boundaries.[3] There were quite a number of old slave darkies still living then. The one to whom I listened most was the cook, old Aunt Mary Bohannon who was nearly white—about one sixteenth negro, I should say. Mistreatment of slaves is, and has been somewhat exaggerated, but old Aunt Mary had had the misfortune, in her youth, to belong to a man whose wife was a fiend from Hell. The young slave women were fine young animals, and barbarically handsome; her mistress was frenziedly jealous. You understand. Aunt Mary told tales of torture and unmistakable sadism that sickens me to this day when I think of them. Thank God the slaves on my ancestors' plantations were never so misused. And Aunt Mary told how one day, when the black people were in the fields, a hot wind swept over them and they knew that "ol' Misses Bohannon" was dead. Returning to the manor house they found that it was so and the slaves danced and shouted with joy. Aunt Mary said that when a good spirit passes, a breath of cool air follows; but when an evil spirit goes by a blast from the open doors of Hell follows it.

She told many tales, one which particularly made my hair rise; it occurred in her youth. A young girl going to the river for water, met, in the dimness of dusk, an old man, long dead, who carried his severed head in one hand. This, said Aunt Mary, occurred on the plantation of her master, and she herself saw the girl come screaming through the dusk, to be whipped for throwing away the water-buckets in her flight.

Another tale she told that I have often met with in negro-lore. The setting, time and circumstances are changed by telling, but the tale remains basically the same. Two or three men—usually negroes—are travelling in a wagon through some isolated district—usually a broad, deserted river-bottom. They come on to the ruins of a once thriving plantation at dusk, and decide to spend the night in the deserted plantation house. This house is always huge, brooding and forbidding, and always, as the men approach the high columned verandah, through the high weeds that surround the house, great numbers of pigeons rise from their roosting places on the railing and fly away. The men sleep in the big front-room with its crumbling fire-place, and in the night they are awakened by a jangling of chains, weird noises and groans from upstairs. Sometimes footsteps descend the stairs with no visible cause. Then a terrible apparition appears to the men who flee in terror. This monster, in all the tales I have heard, is invariably a headless giant, naked or clad in [a] shapeless sort of garment, and is sometimes armed with a broad-axe. This motif appears over and over in negro-lore.[4] I do not know what sort of tales modern darkies tell. For years I have lived in a section where negroes are very rare. Indeed, no colored person is allowed to remain over night in this county.

But through most of the stories I heard in my childhood, the dark, brooding old plantation house loomed as a horrific back-ground and the human or semi-human horror, with its severed head was woven in the fiber of the myths.

But no negro ghost-story ever gave me the horrors as did the tales told by my grandmother. All the gloominess and dark mysticism of the Gaelic nature was her's, and there was no light and mirth at her. Her tales showed what a strange legion of folk-lore grew up in the Scotch-Irish settlements of the Southwest, where transplanted Celtic myths and fairy-tales met and mingled with a sub-stratem of slave legends. My grandmother was but one generation removed from south Ireland and she knew by heart all the tales and superstitions of the folks, black or white, about her.[5]

As a child my hair used to stand straight up when she would tell of the wagon that moved down wilderness roads in the dark of the night, with never a horse drawing it—the wagon that was full of severed heads and dismembered limbs; and the yellow horse, the ghastly dream horse that raced up and down the stairs of the grand old plantation house where a wicked woman lay dying; and the ghost-switches that swished against doors when none dared open those doors lest reason be blasted at what was seen. And in many of her tales, also, appeared the old, deserted plantation mansion, with the weeds growing rank about it and the ghostly pigeons flying up from the rails of the verandah.

There is a legend that was quite popular in its day in the Southwest, which I am unable to place. That is, I cannot decide whether it is one of the usual inconsistencies negro-folk-lore often displays, or a deliberate Irish invention, intended to be a bull.[6] That is the one about the headless woman, who strange to say, was often heard grinding her teeth in the angle of the chimney, and whose long hair flowed down her back!

Negroes are an interesting study. There used to be darkies who vowed they could see the wind, and that it was reddish in color. They said that's why the pigs squealed so when it began to get cold—they too could see the wind and were afraid of it. And there was one Arabella Davis, I remember, whom I used to see, when a child, going placidly about town collecting washing—I mean when I was a kid, not Arabella. She was a black philosopher, if there was ever one. Her little grand-daughter tagged after her, everywhere she went, carrying Arabella's pipe, matches and tobacco with as much pomposity as a courtier ever carried the train of a queen.

Arabella was born in slavery, but her memories were of a later date. She often told of her conversion, when the spirit of the Lord was so strong upon her that she went for ten days and nights without eating or sleeping. She went into a trance, she said, and for days the fiends of Hell pursued her through the black mountains and the red mountains. For four days she hung in the cobwebs on the gates of Hell, and the hounds of Hell bayed at her. Is that not a splendid sweep of imagination? And the strangest part is, it was so true and realistic to her, that she would have been amazed had anyone questioned her veracity.

But here I am rambling on indefinitely. Thank you very much for the kind things you said about the "Bran-cult." I notice the current Weird Tales announces my "Kings of the Night" for next month's issue. I hope you like the story. Bran is one of the "Kings". I intend to take your advice about writing a series of tales dealing with Bran. If you can get Machen's address from Mr. Derleth, I'll see what I can do. If Machen answers my inquire at all, his reply should be very interesting. I have always been fascinated by his work, though I will say, frankly and with no intent to flatter, that I consider him inferior to yourself as a horror story writer.

I hope you will have—or possibly I should say, will have had, when this letter reaches you—an enjoyable visit in Quebec. I repeat I envy you. It has been so long since I have taken a trip of any kind, I feel as if I were taking root. For instance, it has been two years since I have been across the Mexican

Border. I live in a section of the country not particularly stimulating to the imagination, unless the inhabitants' continual struggle against starvation can [be] said to be a stimulant. The drouth hit this country hard, and please do not think I exaggerate when I say that many tenant-farmers and their families are at present subsisting entirely on parched corn. There is no grass; the people eat the corn that belongs by right to the farm horses, and the farm-horses eat mesquite beans. Soon the beans will be gone and the horses will die; the people will die too, unless the government aids them.

But I have rambled long enough; pardon me if much that I have said has been boresome.

Most cordially yours,
Robert E. Howard

P.S. Thank you very much for the picture of Paul Revere's home. I note that it is surrounded by stores and shops of Italians. Its a pity that all the landmarks of American history seem to be in the process of being swamped by the tide of foreign invasion. The same process is going on on the Gulf coast, and in the Rio Grande valley country.

R.E.H.

P.S.S. I have received Mr. Long's book since writing the above; I have not yet had time for a proper study of it, but from my first perusal, I can see that [the] poems come up fully to all expectations.

R.E.H.

Notes

1. Bernard Austin Dwyer, "Ol' Black Sarah" (*WT*, October 1928). In the parody "The Battle That Ended the Century" (1934) by HPL and RHB, the two main characters are "Two-Gun Bob, the Terror of the Plains" [REH] and "Knockout Bernie, the Wild Wolf of West Shokan" [Dwyer].

2. Revised by HPL for Zealia Bishop. *WT* did not publish it until January 1939.

3. The Howards lived in Bagwell, Red River County, c. 1914.

4. REH used this story as the framework for "Pigeons from Hell."

5. Neither of REH's grandmothers was "but one generation removed" from Ireland.

6. An Irish "bull" is a statement that appears to contradict itself, or contains an unconscious absurdity, as when Sir Boyle Roche warned the House of Commons of ruffians who "would cut us to mince meat and throw our bleeding heads on that table, to stare us in the face."

[11] [nonextant letter by H. P. Lovecraft]

[c. September 1930]

[12] [TLS]

[c. September 1930]

Dear Mr. Lovecraft:

I am very glad that you enjoyed your visit to Quebec so much, and your vivid description of the city fills me with an intense desire to see it for myself. It must indeed seem a detached fragment of an older world. Your description of your voyage, and the sunset view of Boston harbor fascinated me as much as your stories have fascinated me. It must indeed be a unique sensation to a landsman to see only billowing waves for horrizons. A sensation I have yet to experience. Outside of a steamboat ride or so on the Mississippi and a few short launch rides on the Gulf, my experiences on the water have amounted to nothing. Thank you for the post card pictures.

I have re-read "A Man from Genoa" many times and each reading has strengthened my first estimate of the author—that he is truly a magnificent poet.

I quite agree with your praise of Mr. H. Warner Munn. I have been reading his work in Weird Tales for many years and consider it of the highest quality. I should like very much to see the history of light weird fiction you say he is preparing, as well as your own survey. I believe you said your article was published in The Recluse. Do you suppose I could obtain a copy containing it?

Your remarks on the Etruscans interested me very much. I am sure you are right in believing them to be of a very composite type of Semite and Aryan. Its a pity no more is known about them; doubtless their full history was a spectacular pageant of wars, intrigues and culture developement. Where did they have their beginning? What unknown tribes went into their making? Was it conquest, friendship or pressure from some common foe which brought together and mingled these alien race-stocks into one people? Was this mingling accomplished in three or four generations or did it require the passing of a thousand years? In what secluded valley did these people slowly and peacefully climb the ladder of evolution or over what waste-lands were they harried by what nameless enemies? Did they spring into being in Italy, or did they come from some far land? And if the latter, what drove them from their original home-land and what chance flung them on the Italian coasts? These are questions whose answers we doubtless shall never know, and after all, may be asked of almost any race.

I was also interested in the theory of type-differences in the Semitic races, of which I had never heard before. It sounds very plausible, for there always seemed to me to be a basic difference between, say the Bedouin Arab and the Jew, even allowing for the long centuries of different environment and ways of living. That is an aspect of history full of dramatic possibilities; a clean cut divergence of type existing back to the very dawns of time. An ancient feud between the ancestors of the desert dweller and the fertile valley dweller, symbolized by Cain and Abel and by Esau and Jacob. The real basis of the Arab's hatred for the Hebrew having its roots in primordial racial feud rather than religious differences of comparatively modern times. I must weave that thought into a story some day.

Your remarks about the early history of Rhode Island were highly educational to me. I am so confoundedly ignorant about the history of my own country. I only knew, vaguely, that in its early days Rhode Island was a wealthy, tolerant and non-Puritan state. Its a pity the Revolution played such havoc with the plantations. I imagine, that, as you say, there has been a great deal of literary tampering with the original folk-lore of the state. You are right too, in remarking that what is close at hand tends, ordinarily, to lack interest.

For instance, I have been repeatedly urged to make an article or tale of a certain murder-ranch which lies several miles west of here, and on which, some thirty years ago, a series of unspeakably ghastly crimes were enacted, and on which skeletons are every now and then found to this day. However, I have not the slightest idea of putting it on paper—more especially as one of the men who committed some of those crimes is still living and at large!

You are quite correct in saying that demonry of one's own race is more real and vivid than that of some other race. That is why, I suppose, that tales of Puritan New England and such Scandinavian sagas as that one dealing with Grettir the Strong and his battle with the vampire, seem more gripping and grisly than stories of Indian magic and negro voo-doo.

What a deformed branch on the tree of progress that witch-craft phase of Puritan New England became! To what basis do you attribute it—religious fanaticism stretched beyond human boundaries and producing abnormalities, or an inherent abnormality in the people that produced the fanaticism? To me the aspect of that age and its people is beyond all comprehension. I frankly cannot begin to fathom the dark mental perversity that brought such grisly Chimerae into being. A fantastic idea presents itself to me persistently, that the littoral had something to do with it; perhaps the cold New England winters that cooped people into houses and turned back the pages of time to the ice-fringed shores and snowy forests these peoples ancestors knew before they came into England. We know that the Scandinavian peoples are prone to dark brooding and paranoidal impulses. Can it not be that the cold, overcast skies, the brooding hills and dark mysterious woods brought forth a latent insanity lurking in these persecuted and creed ridden people? Lingering racial memories and superstitious fears breaking from the long sleep of centuries to take on monstrous shapes.

I have long been sure that there was Celtic blood in your veins and sure, it is great honor is due you as a descendent of the great O'Neills. How many times has my blood tingled to read of the deeds of Shane and Hugh and Eoghain Ruadh!

Teutonic horror-tales, as you say, have a quality all their own, and most grisly, striking a different note than the lore of more southerly races. As regards your own horror-story style I would say that it is basically Gothic, but that it is not handicapped by the too-ponderous, rather unwieldy and rather barren narrative style we are apt to associate with Teutonic literature. The Celtic influence is readily seen, to my mind, in the smoothly flowing style of your tales. Altogether, if I may venture to say so, your horror-work seems to me to lean toward the Gothic in conception and the Celtic in execution. You certainly seem to have as much connection with Celtic tradition as Machen.

As for myself, I can lay scant claim to either school, my tales being more on the action-adventure style than the true horror-story. If I had any particular method, I suppose it should be Celtic, since the great part of my blood is of that race. My branch of the Howards came to America in 1733 and the first of the American line married an Irish girl, an example from which no Howard has since deviated, to my knowledge. Behind my English name are lines of purely Gaelic Eiarbhins, O'Tyrrells, Colquhouns, MacEnrys, and Norman-Irish Martuins, De Colliers, FitzHenrys. Yet there is a Scandinavian strain at me, for one of the MacEnrys of my line married the daughter of an Irish woman and a red-bearded Dane who first opened his eyes on the cold shores of the Skaggerack.

It seems to me that I have heard somewhere before of the "moonack"[1] but I could not swear to it. I wish I had the time and money to go carefully through the Old South and gather negroid traditions systematically. As it is I only remember snatches heard years ago. There are very few negroes in this part of Texas and these are nothing like the "old-timey" ones.

I remember the idea of whippoorwills and psychopomps in your "Dunwich Horror" and how I was struck with the unique grisliness of the notion; did the Puritans bring the belief with them from England or did it spring up in the New World?

The tale of the murdered traveller is, as you say, quite common in all sections and reminds me of one, very old, which was once quite prevalent in the Southwest and which must be a garbled version of some legend brought over from Scotland. It deals with three brothers stopping at a lonely cabin high up in the mountains, kept by an evil old woman and her half-idiot sons. In the night they cut the throats of the older brothers, but the younger escapes. Now enters the really fantastic part of the tale. The younger brother flees across the mountains on his fleet horse and the old woman mounts and pursues, carrying a cane held high in her hand. Again and again the boy eludes her, but each time she holds the cane high and sings a sort of incantation:

"Sky-high, caney,
"Where's Toddywell?
"Way over on the Blue-ridgey mountains!
"Haw back!"

Perhaps in the original tale, the answer is given by the cane. Anyway, the cane points out the way the boy has taken and the pursuit is renewed. Eventually the fugitive gains "a pass in the mountains" and escapes. When a youngster I always shuddered at the mental picture that tale brought up—the lean and evil hag with her lank hair flying in the wind, riding hard across the dark mountains under the star-flecked skies, gripping her gory knife and halting on some high ridge to chant her fantastic incantation. But it is but one of the many bloody tales that once flourished in the Scotch-Irish settlements of the Southwest.

About that ghost-switches tale outside the door—that always struck me as being about the most grisly in its implication of any ghost-tale I ever heard—more so because of its nameless suggestions. The fault I find with so many so-called horror-tales (particularly including my own) is that the object of horror too swiftly becomes too solid and concrete. It takes a master of the pen, such as Machen and yourself, to create a proper SUGGESTION of unseen and unknown horror. The illusive shadows lurking at the back of the brain are so much more monstrous and blood-chilling than the children of the actual mind. I'm not saying this like I'd like to say it. But the rustle of leaves when there is no wind, the sudden falling of a shadow across a door, the furtive trying of a window-catch, the sensation of unseen Eyes upon one, these give rise to speculations more monstrous and terrors more cosmically icy, than any chain-clanking apparition, or conventional ghost, that appears in full glory. When a writer specifically describes the object of his horror, gives it worldly dimensions and solid shape, he robs it of half its terrors. Somewhere, somehow, there must lurk in the dim gulfs of our racial memories, titanic and abysmal horrors beyond the ken of the material mind. For how else are we able to half conceive and fear entities we are not able to describe? Seek to draw their images for the conscious mind and they fade away. We cannot shape them in concrete words. Well, I seem to be repeating myself without saying yet what I'm trying to say. But I'll say this: humanity fears floods and starvation, foes and serpents and wild beasts, but there are fears outside these concrete things. Whence come these fears from the OUTSIDE? Surely in its infancy mankind faced beings that live today only in dim ancestral memories, forgotten entirely by the material mind. Otherwise, why is it we half-visualize in that other, subconscious mind, perhaps, shapes beyond the power of man to describe?

Your mention of the Italian invasion of New England brings up a phase of American life that always fills me with resentment: that of the overflowing of the country with low-class foreigners. I've seen it happen in Texas. The state is slowly being taken over by a South and Central European population. Louisiana is already over-run with Italians; they were brought in to work the corporation-owned plantations and they swarmed into the cities. Conditions in the Latin Quarter of New Orleans are of almost unbelievable filth and depravity.

Almost the same conditions exist in South Texas on the great cotton farms. These farms, owned largely by men in other states, are worked entirely by Mexicans. As each farm consists of from three to eight thousand acres in actual cultivation, it requires the work of many hands. A Mexican thrives on wages that would reduce a white man to starvation. I have seen the huts built for them by their employers and overseers—one roomed affairs, generally painted red, one door, two or three glassless windows. There are no chairs, beds, tables or stoves. The Mexicans sleep on rags thrown carelessly on the floor and cook their scanty meals of frijoles and tortillas on open fires outside. The death rate is enormous, the birth rate even more enormous. They live like rats and breed like flies.

But while I dislike the methods used in bringing huge droves of Mexicans across the river to stuff the ballots on election day, or to compete with white labor, still I look with tolerance on those already here, and prefer the Mexican to the Italian. After all, the Mexican has some claim to priority, for his ancestor greeted Cortez. These in Texas and along the Border are predominantly Indian; the Spanish strain is very slight. In the interior you will find many find old dons of almost pure Castilian strain, living a lazy, old World sort of life on their wide-spread ranchos. But like most of the better class of foreigners, we seldom get any of that sort as immigrants.

There is a great deal of romance about these descendents of Cortez' knights. I recall just now one Ramon Macias, an aristocratic Mexican if there ever was one, son of General Macias, "Calles' Butcher", as the general was called. Ramon was a sort of black sheep. He had pure Latin features but his eyes were grey and his complection lighter than mine, and he was a true descendent of the men that broke the Aztec empire. I saw Ramon fight one Sandi Esquival ten gruelling, bruising rounds one night in San Antonio, when I knew that Ramon had a bullet in his back that prevented the proper use of his right hand. A handsome lad he was then, but a few years later I saw him again and could scarcely suppress a shudder; some bravo's knife had left a grisly scar clear across his face that twisted his lips into a permanent snarl.

But pardon me; I'm prone to wander off the subject and meander around quite aimlessly. I was speaking of the foreign influence in America. There is, for instance, a town not many miles from San Antonio called New Braunfels—a German settlement.[2] The only non-German inhabitants are a small colony of factory workers who are looked on with much resentment by the townsmen. Its merely a bit of transplanted Germany; German architecture, German food, German language—even German laws. Its a beautiful little town, the cleanest as to appearance, of any town in Texas. You'll see portly, bearded gentlemen strolling down the streets sedately puffing at gigantic pipes, just as they must do in Potsdam, Dresden or Dusseldorf. Just a little bit of Germany, that keeps itself apart from the rest of America. They strictly obey their own laws, but they dont—or didnt—like laws enforced on them by American officers and judges. This I well know, for when I was there six years ago, I was mistaken for a Ranger and thought for a bit I was going to be mobbed! And that would have been infernally embarrassing because, with the usual perversity of luck, I wasnt packing a pistol that night; had left it in the hotel.

Still, the best immigrants we get in Texas as a whole, are Germans. They are thrifty, law abiding and hard working; superior in living standards to the Mexicans and Scicilians who swarm to our coasts.

I'm sending you a picture you may find interesting: a snap-shot of the Alamo, in San Antonio. Its just about surrounded with modern buildings but it still retains some of the look of a by-gone age—built in 1728, I believe.[3] I'm not superstitious, but standing in the Alamo I have the same sensations I've had standing under the Dueling Oaks outside New Orleans—as if the place were haunted. San Antonio is a picturesque town, with the narrow river winding in and out all through it, with its broad plazas, old missions and cathedrals, and adobe houses shouldering modern buildings.

Most cordially yours,
Robert E. Howard

Notes

1. *moonack:* the ground-hog or woodchuck. Among the negroes, the name is applied to a mythical animal supposed to have a baneful influence (*Oxford English Dictionary*).
2. See letter 4, n. 15.
3. REH probably refers to the church building at the Alamo, the most commonly recognized of its buildings, which was begun in 1758. The mission itself began as a collection of crude buildings in 1718.

[13]

10 Barnes St.,
Providence, R.I.,
October 4, 1930

Dear Mr. Howard:—

[. . .] I agree with what you say about *suggestion* as the highest form of horror-presentation. The basis of all true cosmic horror is *violation of the order of nature,* and the profoundest violations are always the least concrete and describable. In Machen, the subtlest story—"The White People"—is undoubtedly the greatest, even though it hasn't the tangible, visible terrors of "The Great God Pan" or "The White Powder". But the mob—including Farnsworth Wright—can never be made to see this; hence W.T. will always reject work of the finest and most delicate sort. Of course, there is such a thing as *excessive* indefiniteness, especially among novices who do not really understand how to handle cosmic suggestion. Crude writers use the old trick of calling a hidden horror "too monstrous to describe", merely as an excuse for not forming any clear picture of the alleged horror themselves. But the skilled author who knows what he is doing can often hint a thing much better than it can be told. Drawing the line between concrete description and trans-dimensional suggestion is a very ticklish job. In the greatest horror-tale ever written—Blackwood's "Willows"—absolutely nothing takes open and visible form. I shall be interested in seeing what you think of the course I steer in my newest attempt—"The Whisperer in Darkness"—just sent to Wright. I fear, though, he will refuse it on account of its length and lack of speeded action. By the way—you succeed very often in suggesting a cosmic horror beyond the concrete. You do it in "Red Thunder", in the Valusian tales,[1] and in your descriptions of African ruins. The keynote of such suggestion is the *implication* of fundamental disarrangements of natural law, especially as relates to space and time. Unholy *survivals,* intrusions from other worlds and other dimensions, etc., are the kind of thing having the richest possibilities.

Yes—the Etruscans certainly form a rich field for the speculative imagination. There is room for a novelist's work in the vast blank forming their pre-Roman past, and I wish that you would try handling them some day. They could be connected with fabulous and vanished civilisations in Africa or Atlantis or elsewhere, and represented as the last transmitters of terrible secrets from the Valusian elder world. The dark and mystical character of their religion well lends itself to such exploitation. There is likewise, as you suggest, room for much dramatic reflection in the heterogeneous personnel and history of the Semitic races. My own guess is that the Alpine-Semitic type—the queer-eyed, queer-featured type which we historically regard as *Jewish*—was originally confined to the fertile valleys and plains, and did not include the *early* Jews at all; these latter being that homogeneous with the Arabs, and thus chiefly Mediterranean. The Assyrians, as shewn in their sculptures, are extreme examples of this Alpine type; and the Phoenicians and Carthaginians appear to have belonged to it. When the nomadic Jews conquered the cities of Canaan, they probably found this type prevailing there—the difference being clearly shewn in cultural ways. The two elements were mutually antagonistic, but eventually amalgamation occurred—the established and numerically preponderant Canaanite stock of course engulfing the relatively small but ruling element of Mediterranean Hebrews. Thus the Jew of historic times is probably more of a mongrel Canaanite of Alpine ancestry than a descendant of the original Hebraic group. Moses—if he was indeed an historic character—would probably find Mohammed or Saladin more like himself in blood and features than he would find any of the prophets of the later Jewish line. It is obvious that in *prehistoric* times the Hebrews and Arabs were virtually one. When the Arabic Hyksos or Shepherd Kings conquered Egypt, they brought in myriads of Jews as friendly supporters—these latter becoming a slave-race when the reviving native-Egyptians expelled the Hyksos. It was this period of enslavement, I fancy, which first broke the spirit of the Jew, and gave him that readiness to submit to conquest which has made all his cultural heirs so peculiarly hateful to our unbroken and liberty-worshipping Western race-groups. The Arab of today is a better representative of the prehistoric "Abrahamic" Jew than any type historically known as Jewish. Altogether, there is great stuff in the Semitic peoples—a powerful mentality, and marvellous stamina in limited directions—but somehow they have never been able to coördinate themselves into any solid and enduring fabric comparable with the Aryan world as a whole. In my opinion, the greatest single Semitic civilisation—notwithstanding the opulent glories of Babylon, the well-knit culture of Judaea, and the political-mercantile prowess of the Phoenicians and Carthaginians—is that of the Islamic Caliphs in the Middle Ages. We have seen this consistently underrated because it was the enemy of our own ancestors in the Crusades, but impartial investigation reveals it as indeed one of the greatest and most intelligent cultures which has ever existed on this planet. From the 7th century to the Renaissance the Saracens were virtually the only mentally alive people west of China and India; and when the Renaissance did finally start to regain the lost intellectualism of Greece, it was more through Arabic mediation than directly. Most of the Greek scientific works were known to our mediaeval forefathers in Latin translations *from Arabic translations,* instead of in versions taken directly from the [Greek. We know Ptolemy's] great astronomical work not by its original name of Μεγάλη Σύνταξις, but by its *Arabic* name of "Almagest". When the history of the Dark Ages is re-written by some historian or archaeologist of the millennially remote future, we shall see how naively distorted and erroneous our present common conceptions are. Popularly, we think of the Italo-Gallic area as the prime theatre of significant action, and subordinate everything else in comparison; yet in sober truth, this played-out Latin region amounted to relatively little. We overstress it because it was the last place where the full classic civilisation flourished, and the first place where the newer Renaissance culture gained headway; yet in real truth it held little more than barbarism between 700 and a period varying from 1100 to 1400. The old Western culture was dead for the time being—its remnants going westward rather than staying in the south, and being probably more visible in Ireland than in Italy. Byzantine culture was by all odds the leading Aryan civilisation—though of course it had ceased to be Western in spirit, and was altogether static and uncreative. Overwhelmingly superior to any of these remnants of the West's shattered past was the vital, virile, all-embracing civilisation of the advancing Saracens. While our own Nordic race was on a more primitive plane of expression, and the prostrate Latin cultures were nothing more than senile remnants, the Islamic Arabs were facing the universe with all the passionate intellectual curiosity and aesthetic fervour of a highly-evolved, healthy, and burgeoning young race—reviving and extending the science of the Hellenistic world, and crystallising a set of intelligent, humorous, tolerant, and beauty-loving folkways indescribably superior to our own barbaric folkways of the same chronological period. The Arabian Nights gives us a vivid glimpse of this brilliant, mature, stimulating civilisation—and it is an eternal pity that we were destined to fight against it instead of learn from it. However, it is fortunate that we did not allow it to conquer us. If we must regret the Crusades, we certainly need not regret the earlier victory of Charles Martel. Great as the Saracen culture was, it was essentially the culture of a Southern and Semitic race; and in no way adapted to the instincts of Celts and Teutons. Though we might have profitably *borrowed* much, we could never have been comfortable as integral parts of the full fabric. It was best that we kept free to shape our own ways—kept independent and still plastic, and finally adopted the revived classical culture of our Aryan kindred rather than the fundamentally different importation from the East. Eastern importations don't fit us very well, and I am rather sorry that we had one of them saddled on us (in common with the later classic world) in the form of Christianity. This religion is Semitic in spirit and doctrine, and has probably retarded us more than it has helped us. We have indeed never really accepted it, but have merely hypocritically paraded a somewhat Aryanised form of its externals. It would have been much better for us to have kept some form of our natural and ancestral polytheistic pantheism—a type of emotional outlet infinitely better suited to our instincts than the intruding systems which historic accident foisted on the Western World in Constantine's time. Still—we avoided the complete cultural Semitisation which Saracen conquest would have brought, and ought to be very thankful for that. We were very close to an Arab conquest in the 8th century; and had the battle of Tours turned out differently, there is no telling what the history of Europe might have been. But anyway—in the Dark Ages the high spots of civilisation were not Rome and Paris, but Bagdad, Damascus, Medina, Cairo, Granada, and Cordova. Political instability and disunion made this brilliant culture comparatively short-lived as a dominant world-civilisation; but it burned scintillantly in its heyday, and had so deep a fundamental vitality that it cannot be called wholly dead even now. It is of course decadent in the extreme; yet still survives in Palestine, Arabia, and North Africa, and is not beyond all hope of some sort of renaissance some day. To me it has been a perennially fascinating thing ever since I read the Arabian Nights at the age of five. In those days I used to dress up in a turban, burnt-cork a beard on my face, and call myself by the synthetic name (Allah only knows where I got it!) of *Abdul Alhazred* [2]—which I later revived, in memory of old times, to confer on the hypothetical author of the hypothetical Necronomicon! But I never carried Orientalism as far as our fellow W.T. contributor E. Hoffmann Price, who (so Wright tells me) has travelled in the East and is familiar with the Arabic language.

As for local American history—if my remarks on R.I. were new to you, I am sadly afraid that corresponding remarks on any state west of the Alleghenies would be equally new to me! That is the trouble with a nation of such wide and diversely derived territory. Really, each average American is a citizen of his own section alone in the fullest sense. Of the whole fabric, he knows the political externals and high spots as textbooks and casual reading have sketched them; but his knowledge of intimate details, folkways, sources, backgrounds, and deep cultural trends is generally confined to the vaguely-bounded subdivisional unit in which he grows up—or at least, to that unit and the spatially and chronologically contiguous units which have shared its fortunes in the historic stream. Nor can things naturally be otherwise. The wonder is that so wide and diverse an empire can remain as linked and homogeneous as it does. The Hellenic world couldn't do it; and the Roman world, after doing it for a while, fell apart very quietly and thoroughly when the thin cord snapped. For my part, I can't get any inner subjective sense of the reality of any America outside the colonial area. New England is around me, so I feel that very vividly as a tangible force; and the other colonies of the early days are almost equally real to me because of their visible historic relationships. New York, Pennsylvania, Maryland, Virginia, and the Carolinas—each represents a system of pageanty which registers sharply, familiarly, and correlatedly on my consciousness and memory; together with England, Lower Canada, and the West Indies, whose linkage with our history was of comparable intimacy. But outside this compactly linked historic zone my sense of reality lessens. The diminution of perspective becomes emphatic, and the objects recede. Westerly America takes its place, with me, beside Continental Europe and the rest of the distant world, as something *objective,* to be *read of and learned about* rather than *experienced.* Broader historic study and travel would undoubtedly enlarge my radius, and I mean to have a try at it some day. My present limitations are largely determined by my unusual degree of absorption in the 18th century—a period for which I have a curious and only partly explicable affinity. I never feel quite easy because fashion won't let me wear a powdered periwig and small-clothes!

Rhode Island arose not merely as a *non-Puritan* but as an *anti-Puritan* colony—it being the recognised refuge of such persons and groups as found the gloomy theocracy of the Massachusetts-Bay intolerable. It is amusing to note, in looking up R.I. genealogies, how frequently one's first R.I. ancestors will be recorded as having come from England to Massachusetts, and *then,* in anywhere from a month to a decade, having reëmigrated to R.I. The colony was founded by Roger Williams, a clergyman whose opposition to the Massachusetts doctrines caused his expulsion from that colony in 1636. He had originally been a Church-of-England curate in London, and had hoped to find a more liberal world in New England; but five years of Salem and Boston shewed him that the Puritans were worse than the established order. In June 1636 he and 12 companions landed on the west shore of a steeply plateau'd peninsula called by the Indians Mooshassuck, and situate betwixt the Seekonk river and the head of Narragansett Bay, just outside the boundaries of the Plymouth Colony. They were the first whites there—but they stuck, and the village of Providence which they founded and named on the spot is today the second city in New England. The place where Williams landed, attracted by a spring of fresh water, is only about five blocks straight down a precipitous hill from where I now sit writing; and is at present being made into a small commemorative park. Once this colony was founded, it began to attract liberal-minded people by the thousand. Not only did religious radicals come to the Providence region to live in the town or establish rural domains nearby; but religious and political *conservatives,* weary of Puritan cant and gravitating back toward the Church of England, came in large numbers to the large boot-shaped island of Aquidneck 20 to 30 miles south of Providence off the east shore of the bay. There they founded Portsmouth in 1638, and Newport in 1639; later spreading over to the west shore of the bay and establishing vast mainland domains where they lived in patriarchal fashion with many slaves. Aquidneck, by the way, is the original *Rhode Island.* (probably a corruption of the Dutch *Rood Eylandt,* or Red Island, so named from abundant reddish clay, rather than a comparison to the Isle of Rhodes, as commonly supposed. The Dutch surveyed the region, without colonising, in 1614—it having been first explored in 1524 by Verrazzano, an Italian in the employ of France.) The name reached out to include the rest of the colony at a much later date. By the middle of the 17th century, the R.I. region had developed into two distinct parts, between which considerable rivalry existed—the Providence area around the head of the bay, peopled by restless religious radicals clustering about Mr. Williams and living mostly as small farmers; and the Newport area close to the sea on the lower end of Aquidneck Island, peopled by men of greater substance and conservatism and tending toward stock-raising and larger-scale agriculture. In Providence the Baptist faith gained ascendancy, while in Newport the Church of England came to the fore, with Quakers and Congregationalists as secondary elements. The rivalry between the two sections cropped out repeatedly—especially when they sent representatives to London to arrange for a colonial patent. They wished to act as one colony, in order to present a united front against the hostile and encroaching Puritan groups in Mass. and Connecticut; (who claimed most of our territory for themselves!) but each wished to get a little bit ahead of the other. In 1644 Mr. Williams got a patent from Charles I which put the name of the Providence-Plantations (i.e. the group of towns consisting of Prov. and its neighbours) *before* that of

Rhode Island; (i.e. the Aquidneck group headed by Newport) but in 1663 Newport got ahead when securing a fresh charter from Charles II after the Cromwellian usurpation . . . . her emissary John Clarke succeeding in having the official name fixed as "Rhode Island *and* Providence-Plantations". That remains the *legal name* of our commonwealth *to this day*—although popular usage gradually transferred (circa 1700) the name R.I. to the whole of the colony as a matter of natural abbreviation. The growth of Newport at first wholly eclipsed that of Providence, both materially and culturally. In 1657 the "Narragansett Country" across the bay was exploited by a land corporation, and large estates sold to planters from Newport, as well as to prosperous newcomers from Massachusetts—Church-of-England men, Quakers, and Congregationalists. This was the beginning of that famed and wistfully mourned squirearchical chapter in Rhode Island history, to which the Revolution gave the blow which finally ended it. Meanwhile the quarrels of both Newport and Providence with the Puritans were incessant. Mass. and Conn. tried to start boundary disputes which would have robbed us of half our tiny territory, and Mass. in particular bitterly hated us because we gave harbourage to *Quakers,* whom the Puritans persecuted unmercifully. Our only really good neighbour was the *Plymouth Colony,* founded in 1620 by Pilgrim separatists outside the Puritan fold. The Plymouthites, however, were often bulldozed by the arrogant Boston Puritans into acting unfavourably toward us—and in 1691 (under the new charter which established the royal Province of the Massachusetts-Bay with enlarged boundaries including even Nova Scotia) the Plymouth colony came to an end and became part of our hated enemy Massachusetts. (By this time, though, Mass. was less formidable; being under a Royal Governor instead of the Puritan theocracy) In 1675 came the deadly King Philip's War against the Indians, and here again the Puritans proved an adverse influence. This war was engineered by Wampanoags, a tribe inhabiting the Plymouth Colony, of whom R.I.'s Narragansetts were only loosely-knit allies. Among the Narragansetts, only a few embittered chiefs sided with Philip; and if let alone we could easily have kept the tribe under control and preserved the unbrokenly cordial relations which Mr. Williams had established. Up to 1675 our record with the Indians is as spotless as William Penn's—and it would have remained so had Massachusetts minded its own business. But no! That wouldn't have been like Boston! Late in 1675 the Mass. rulers sent a body of mixed Mass., Plymouth, and Conn. troops into the Narragansett region without our permission and against our wishes, and on one terrible winter's night descended on the tribe's retreat in the swampy woods and massacred every living redskin they could find—men, women, and children alike. This is the "Great Swamp Fight" of history—the Lord's Brethren against the wicked pagan! This was virtually the end of the Narragansett nation. The pitiful remnant amalgamated with the Niantics from across the line in Connecticut, and thereafter went steadily downhill. In our golden age of 1700–1775 they were a weak, decadent element, who tended more and more to amalgamate with our runaway negroes. They were still recognised as wards of the government, with a legal tribe status, till about half a century ago; when they became too few to justify recognition. Today the pitiful survivors—with their negroid taint—hardly number a hundred—yet still exist on their original soil, and hold tribal gatherings twice a year.

About the middle of the 17th century (in Providence not till 1681) began that development of maritime commerce which was to outclass agriculture in bringing prosperity to Rhode Island. Newport began privateering about 1653, during the Dutch war, and after that a trade with the West Indies developed. Newport became a focus of vast wealth and commerce, and finally a genuine seat of culture—it being the place where the Narragansett planters had their town houses and held their cultural diversions. Newport was to the Narrag. country what Charleston was to the Carolina lowlands, or what Williamsburg and Fredericksburg were to old tidewater Virginia. No northern state was more like the South than colonial R.I., and in the course of time very cordial relations with the Southern Colonies sprang up. We also had very close ties with the planters of the West Indies—Barbadoes, Jamaica, etc. When the Edict of Nantes was revoked in 1685, Rhode Island shared in the influx of French Huguenots which gave New Rochelle, N.Y., New Paltz, N.Y., and Charleston S.C. such a valuable element. Of course they could settle nowhere else in New England, but here they were welcome, and gave such hereditary names as Ballou, Tourtellot, Bernon, Ayrault, etc. *I almost but not quite* have Huguenot blood, for my great-great-great-great-grandfather Benjamin Whipple had for his *first* wife the daughter of Gabriel Bernon, founder of King's Church in Providence . . . . but I am descended from his *second* and English wife. Another incoming element which did *not* mix with the English was the rich *Jewish* group in Newport. This group began to appear about 1676, attracted by the growing commerce; and were tremendously influential until the Revolution ruined and dispersed them. They built a great synagogue (still standing) in 1763, and aided all the current civic and cultural movements. They were of Portugese origin, but came by the way of Holland and the Dutch West Indies. By 1815 or so the last one left, and such later Jews as have filtered into Newport (reopening the long-closed old synagogue) bear no relation to them. Trade and privateering were the financial life of Rhode Island in 1700—and it must be admitted that we share the culpability of New York in harbouring and dealing with "privateers" whose separation from downright piracy was more shadowy than actual. Mayes, Bauber, Tew, Bradish, and Kidd (guilty or innocent) were all winked at in our seaports, and Lord Bellomont wrote many a despairing letter to our Governor Samuel Cranston. After 1700 our ships specialised in the "triangular trade"—"rum, niggers, and 'lasses". A vessel would go down to Cuba or Martinique and stock up on cheap molasses, bringing it back to Newport or Providence (and Bristol and

Warren, after a grant of George II gave us a strip of Mass.—formerly Plymouth-Colony territory along the east of the bay) to be distilled into cheap (and often watered) rum. This rum was then taken to the West African coast and traded to the black chiefs for slaves; (one cask would at first buy a prime young buck nigger, though prices went up after competition developed) the resulting cargo being taken to the West Indies and traded for more molasses to make into rum . . . . and so on . . . . . and so on . . . . . . And thus the great fortunes of Rhode Island were founded. Enterprising captains used to like to tap fresh trading areas from time to time—where fewer ships had called, hence where the native chiefs were less shrewd in bargain-driving. Accordingly many Rhode-Islanders went as far up the great African rivers as their vessels could navigate. This, in the days of small, light-draught ships, was sometimes a long way—hence we may imagine some of them in pretty strange and perilous and sinister regions; surrounded by warlike tribes of problematical attitude, and close to the primal secrets of a cryptic and haunted continent. You ought to be able to get an Afro-Atlantean story out of some of those voyages—fancy David Lindsay of Newport, Obadiah Brown of Providence, or Simeon Potter of Bristol stumbling on the Cyclopean ruins of some Valusian outpost with likely slaves for sale! What blacks were not sold in the West Indies were generally brought to Rhode Island for the Narragansett planters and others. There was not much slave trade with the Southern American ports until the late 18th and early 19th century, when Congress gave the industry a time-limit and declared it legal only until 1806. Then, with our Southern planters clamouring for as many blacks as they could get before the prohibition went in force, the Rhode Island skippers had a feverish spell of racing between the Guinea coast and such ports as Charleston, S.C., with as many niggers as they could possibly pack into their vessels' holds—the triangular feature being abandoned, and any cheap trade article being given to the black chiefs. It was only then that the inhuman evils of unsanitary crowding began. Previously it had been to the interest of the captains to deliver the blacks in as good condition as possible. Charleston will never forget how Rhode Island stocked her with niggers a century ago. When I was there last spring an old man told me how well-known the Providence and Newport sailors used to be along the East Bay St. waterfront, and pointed out a building which had once been their favourite tavern. After 1806, though, R.I. vessels dropped the trade, and left the illegal "bootleg" traffic to the Maine skippers who specialised in it. In Charleston the blacks were landed at the foot of Queen St. (present Clyde Line docks) and auctioned off at once in the still-standing buildings (locally called "Vendue Row") lining that street between the wharves and East Bay St. None of these raw African niggers were ever sold in the famous "Old Slave Market" in Chalmers St., which all the guide-books mention. That was reserved for high-grade house-servants.

(According to ships' records, R.I. vessels carried 7958 slaves, in all, to Charleston.)

Meanwhile the Narragansett planters prospered in a more modest way—eventually specialising in dairying and horse-breeding. "Narragansett pacers" and "Narragansett cheeses" were known the world over. Sheep were also kept, the wool export being considerable. Estates ran up to fabulous sizes; 2000 to 12,000 acres in many cases. (Think of this in a colony whose total area is only 1300 sq. mi., including the bay!) My ancestor Robert Hazard (whose wife lived to be just 100, and is the only centenarian in my ancestry) had 1000 acres in all—500 in one place, and the rest scattered. Another forbear of mine, Thomas Stanton, had a plantation 4½ × 2 miles in extent. On these estates were built great houses of the traditional New England pattern with gambrel roofs—the utmost development in *size* which this architectural type ever reached. Most of them are still standing; some in good condition, and a few still inhabited by descendants of their builders. The Casey house in Kingston burned down in 1763, reducing its occupant (my great-great-great-grand-uncle Samuel Casey) to a relative poverty which drove him into *crime*—the rather common and winked-at crime of counterfeiting. He had been an accomplished silversmith in addition to his agriculture, (specimens of his work are in both the Boston Museum of Fine Arts and the Metropolitan Museum in N.Y.) and he now—alas—turned toward the manufacture of Portugese moidores and Spanish milled dollars—abetted by all his respectable neighbours! In 1774 the long arm of the law nabbed him, and he was sentenced to be hanged—but one night a party of planters blacked up as negroes stormed His Majesty's Gaol at Little-Rest Village (now Kingston Village) and liberated the culprit; so that he rode out of Rhode Island annals toward the west on a white horse in the dark small hours, with coat-tails flapping behind him! Other Casey descendants have proved more law-abiding. Gen. Silas Casey, author of a standard textbook on military tactics, fell at the battle of Chapultapec.[3] Another designed the Washington monument, and the living architect Edward Pearce Casey designed the Congressional Library. This is the line descended from the O'Neills—they use the bloody hand of the O'Neills as their coat of arms. In the old Narragansett houses slaves were generally quartered in the attic or in lateral wings attached as in old Maryland and Virginia houses. The Hazard house had one slave wing with a great fireplace inside which all the pickanninies could sit at once. Almost without exception the blacks were well-treated, and once a year—on the 3d Saturday in June—the slaves of the whole county were granted a kind of celebration of the Saturnalian order, in which they dressed up in their master's clothes and elected one of their number to the mythical post of "Black Governor". Rivalry for this post was strong among the blacks, and they spent the pre-election weeks in busy political campaigning on behalf of their favourites—"parmenteering", as they called it. Our negroes were whimsically named much like those of the south—classical and bible and pastoral names predominating. Once in a while freak names would persist—like "Cuddymonk", the servant of a prominent physician, and "Jack Jibsheet" and "Cuffee Cockroach"—the last two being owned by a Bristol sea-captain who took them along as cabin-boys on his privateering voyages. The end of slavery in R.I. was gradual. In 1774 the importation of slaves was forbidden, and in 1784 general emancipation was declared—but this "emancipation" was virtually a meaningless thing, since all the Narragansett negroes were more than glad to keep right on "working for their keep". It meant nothing to them that they could leave if they *wanted* to. In most cases negroes stuck with families as long as the families themselves, amidst those troubled times, had resources enough to maintain them. When the old estates began to break up, and the younger generation struck northward to the Foster region of smaller farms, many of the blacks went along too—glad of the harbourage in exchange for rustic labour. As late as 1820 black servants on the farms were common, though they began to vanish as the era of manufacturing set in. The last lineal ancestor of mine who had one was Stephen Place—my great-grandfather who died in 1849. His last negro Moses is buried on a hill not far from his farmhouse. In this early period, the only Rhode-Islanders who had any violent sentiments about "abolition" were the Quakers. Later on, of course, some echoes of the Bostonian hysteria got across the border and influenced our "idealist" element, but in the main we were content to let Nature and social evolution take their course. But we'll never have another Old Narragansett! Those days were too good to last; and all they have left, in the main, is a body of tradition and a point of view which differentiate the King's County Rhode-Islander from other Yankees in general and from Massachusetts Puritans in particular. The bulk of the people were either Episcopalians or Quakers—the former being the most influential. Their best-loved rector, by the way, was a Celt—the Rev. James MacSparran,[4] from Ireland, who presided over old St. Paul's Church (built in 1707, and in 1800 moved from the open country—where it stood in the fields like a Virginia parish church—to the village of Wickford) from 1721 to his death in 1757. The church, lately repaired, is still a Wickford landmark; and "The Glebe", Dr. MacSparran's parsonage, also remains—though untenanted and in poor condition. Social customs were almost precisely like those of Virginia—hospitality, fox-hunting, horse-racing, etc. being proverbial. Literary taste, under the Newport influence, probably excelled that of Virginia; gentlemen (including the Hazards above-mentioned) being inclined toward philosophy and the arts. What especially stimulated this intellectual activity was a pleasant link with the old world supplied in 1729 by the presence of that distinguished Irish cleric (not a Celt, but at least the product of a Celtic scene) George Berkeley, then Dean of Derry and later Bishop of Cloyne. This famous philosopher (author of the widely-quoted line "westward the course of Empire takes its way")[5] came to America to establish a college for Indians in Bermuda—which he failed to succeed in doing—and during a three-year stay at Newport (near which he built a fine country-seat, "Whitehall", still standing in good condition) participated in the town's intellectual life to the fullest extent. He brought with him many many artists and men of learning, and influenced the nascent cultural life of the place to an astonishing degree. He founded a philosophical society, fostered the art of painting, promoted the idea of a library which took shape some years later, and so raised the standard of architectural taste that soon afterward Newport secured the finest architect available (Peter Harrison) to erect her new public buildings . . . . an architect so famous that Boston and other towns clamoured for his work. (It is a happy fact that every building Harrison ever erected is still standing. They range from the classic Redwood Library—1749—to the Jewish Synagogue—1763. Harrison also designed King's Chapel (1749) in Boston and Christ Church (1760) in Cambridge, Mass.) In 1760 or 1765 Newport was a far more cultivated town than New York, and in all the colonies could have been surpassed only by Boston, Philadelphia, and Charleston. Its houses were tasteful, its churches splendid, and its waterfront prosperous. About this time the Narragansett planters began to build fine gambrel-roofed mansions (unlike the square Georgian mansions favoured by urban Newporters) for town houses along the water's edge well to the north of the commercial wharf district. Those were great days! Today nearly all of these colonial scenes remain unchanged—old houses, narrow streets, Trinity steeple (1726), Colony-house (1739) and all—preserved as if by magic to shew the 20th century what an 18th century Yankee seaport was like. This is the one beneficent feature of the commercial decline which seized the town about 1765 and was made complete by the Revolution—a decline which checked the encroachments of trade and discouraged building-replacement and civic modernisation. Fashionable summer-resort Newport lies to the south, hardly touching the old town at all. And U.S. Navy manoeuvres (the town is an important naval base and seat of a training station) serve rather to prolong maritime memories than to destroy colonial quaintness. I love Newport, and almost wish I lived there—though it has not the *scenic* beauty and *late*-Georgian architectural richness of Providence, but has been so well preserved by stagnation that is *seems* infinitely older.

What commenced Newport's ruin was the rise and rivalry of Providence, whose position on the mainland at the head of the bay placed it on land trade routes without making it any less excellent a seaport—an economic advantage that foreordained it for ultimate supremacy. I can view this rivalry with personal impartiality, since although most of my R.I. lines come from Newport and Narragansett, I have 3 Providence lines—Field, Whipple, and Mathewson—and am myself a native and lifelong resident of this town. Our Providence shipping began in 1681, and had so steady an increase that the town began to approach Newport in wealth and power by the decade of the 1750's.

Providence taste and cultivation, however, did not equal Newport's; and the feeling between the two, both political and social, was extremely bitter. In 1760 this town consisted mostly of small wooden houses and modest churches huddled along the shore line east of the bay's head, and gradually climbing the half-perpendicular precipice to the plateau above—together with similar buildings on the marshy flats and islands on the bay-head's west side; a region linked to the east side by the Great Bridge at the civic centre. I have a picture on my wall which shews the scene vividly.

At this juncture, however, we see the beginning of efforts to make Providence a seat of culture commensurate with its new material dignity. Many of the best citizens frequented the artistic and philosophical circles of Newport, and naturally brought back influences which spread. Then—say from 1750 onward, the intensive cultural "drive" led by Governor Hopkins (who had met Dean Berkeley in 1732) begins.* This city owes more to Stephen Hopkins than to any other one person except Roger Williams, and I do not wonder that his house (built 1742) is preserved to this day as a public shrine and museum. At Hopkins' agitation the Providence Library was founded in 1750, and in every way he promoted taste and education both public and private. Luckily he succeeded in interesting the great local shipping family of Brown in his projects—and indeed, under his influence one of the Browns became a celebrated dilettante in the arts and sciences. Fine public buildings began to appear, (most, I am glad to say, still standing) and in 1762 the Providence Gazette was founded. Houses in an improved taste replaced the old ones, (that is why Old Providence now reflects the late 18th instead of early 18th century) and the college now known as Brown University was established on the crest of the great plateau. Many of the steep hill streets still reflect the aspect of that period. Our colony and court house of 1761 is still in fine shape—likewise our college edifice of 1770 and our Market House of 1773. In 1775 there was built the splendid 1st Baptist Church, with a steeple designed by Wren's pupil James Gibbs—to this day the finest Georgian church on this continent.[6] Artistic and scientific life picked up. Telescopes and microscopes, books and globes, became common. Streets were paved and coaches made their appearance. Brick supplemented wood in building, and wholly reigned in public structures. Public education grew, and a tradition of mellow culture like Newport's sprang up. Then the Revolution came and completed the overturn. Newport, hard hit by the war and occupied in turns by the armies of both sides, lost all its commerce and never recovered it. Providence, far behind the lines, remained peaceful and made fortunes in privateering and profiteering. In the young republic Providence was definitely

*N.B. Berkeley wrote his "Alciphron, or the Minute Philosopher" in Newport; much of it in a favourite outdoor spot where a great rock overhangs a road near the shore. This locality is unchanged today, and I have often sat in the Dean's chosen seat.

the R.I. metropolis, and it has ever remained so. A generation after the Revolution the new Providence culture began to age and mellow, till by the 1830's it was as ingrained and traditional as Newport's own. It became the "town" for all the remaining planters of any consequence, and acquired all the sober graces of a social capital. When Edgar Allan Poe knew it in 1848 it was as delightful a seat of elegance and civilisation as one could ask . . . . and it has not essentially changed with the years. The now-filled-in marshes of the flat "west side" have become the business section and taken care of the vast foreign element, leaving the old steep hill section as quaint and unchanged as Charleston or Newport or Salem. The same houses and streets and steeples, and pretty much the same sort of people—so that one who lives on the hill has the queer position of seeing quiet village quaintness around him, yet looking off to the west over a vast lower town 300 feet below, and bristling with modern domes and skyscraper towers! I live just over the crest of the hill—in a sedate backwater of old houses that you'd swear couldn't be in anything larger than a city of 3000. Glancing westward—past an overtaken farmhouse and yard antedating the eastward creeping of the city over this spot—one sees Barnes St. end between two old gardens in the blank, mysterious sky . . . but walk a block to the crest and look off, and the outspread modern metropolis will spring into view. That vista is by no means ugly, for it includes the splendid marble dome of the State House, and the gothic towers of some fine churches. All told, Providence is the most beautiful city I know, except Quebec. In quaintness it is surpassed only by such towns as Salem, Newport, and Charleston. I think its old houses are what really made me a natural antiquarian. They affected me strongly as early as my fourth year—especially the houses on the steep hill, with fanlighted doorways and double flights of railed steps rising from the old brick sidewalks. When I came to choose a bookplate I rejected the conventional coat of arms, and chose a typical old-Providence doorway as the most individually expressive and symbolic of all possible devices.[7] I'll enclose a specimen (which you needn't bother to return) to shew you what I mean. Certainly, the 18th century has never died so far as I am concerned!

As for Rhode-Island—shipping declined after the Embargo Act and War of 1812, and manufacturing took its place—bringing countless foreigners and destroying many of the quaintest and loveliest spots in the state. Now manufacturing, in turn, is apparently on the wane—though certain specialised manufactures and general land commerce keep urban Providence prosperous and on the increase. What the future holds, socially and politically, no one can tell; but we may at least boast that we have had a picturesque and distinctive past, with as individual a civilisation as if we were (like yours) the largest state instead of the smallest. In individualism we have been almost a separate nation. We were the last to ratify the constitution in 1790, and even then did so in the face of a rural mob which almost threatened physical violence to the advocates of union. Only South Carolina can match us in ingrained separatism. One interesting effect of Rhode Island's non-Puritan history is the scarcity among us of the bizarre and jawbreaking Bible names which make most New England genealogies look so grotesque—the Abimilechs, Sheerjashubs, Melchisideks, Ahabs, Jedediahs, and so forth. Just across the line in Massachusetts, of course, they flourished in all their barbaric splendour; but we had only pale echoes of them. Setting aside such names as Benjamin, Samuel, Daniel, etc., which are really naturalised into the English tradition, Rhode Island nomenclature probably had no more than 10 or 15 per cent of the Old Testament freaks—where Mass. and Connecticut probably ran as high as 75 or 80 per cent. In my own ancestry this kind of thing is limited to one Jeremiah, one Asaph, and two Enochs—the rest are plain Johns, James's, Richards, Thomases, and so on. In female nomenclature the Quaker tradition had some effect, giving rise to names like Hopestill, Freelove, Charity, Deliverance, etc.—though the Quakers seemed content to name the boys in the plain old English way. Quakerism, by the way, has almost died out in the last hundred years; so that the remaining handful of Friends are selling their ancient meeting-houses (that in Newport, built in 1698, is now a municipal community building) one by one, and erecting tiny chapels in their stead. That in Providence—built in 1745[8]—is now for sale—though Providence has a more enduring Quaker landmark in the large Friends' School for boys, still administered by the waning sect, but of course now drawing its clientele from all denominations. The main hall of this institution was built in 1819.[9]

Your local murder-ranch ought to make good fictional material with proper treatment. I certainly mean to tackle the old Narragansett legendry some day—though as I said before, I shall brighten up the tone a bit. Some of the old tales were fantastic and gruesome enough, and would have been terrifying if white people had really believed them—but it's just this matter of belief and seriousness which distinguishes liberal and sceptical Rhode Island from sombre and Puritan Massachusetts! There are many places in North Kingstown which the Indians and negroes used to point out as the site of witch conclaves—Hell Hollow, Park Hill, Indian Corner, Kettle Hole, and Goose Neck Spring being among them. At Indian Corner is a large rock which was reputed to *bleed when the moon shone on it*—surely an idea for some ingenious fantaisiste to use! Witch Rock, near Hopkins Hill, is the site of a cabin where a monstrous old witch dwelt in the 1600's, and the ground around it is so accursed that it is impossible to plough it. If anyone tries to trace a furrow, the ploughshare is mysteriously deflected. The old witch, incidentally, still skulks nearby in the form of a black crow or black cat—her present abode being an underground burrow. Block Island, off the coast in the open ocean, has a select store of marine legends—including a ghostly light which dances off shore. This island was once infested by wreckers who lured richly laden merchant ships to their doom through false lights for the sake of the plunder.

But as I have said, it is the night-black Massachusetts legendry which packs the really macabre "kick". Here is material for a really profound study in group-neuroticism; for certainly, no one can deny the existence of a profoundly morbid streak in the Puritan imagination. What you say of the dark Saxon-Scandinavian heritage as a possible source of the atavistic impulses brought out by emotional repression, isolation, climatic rigour, and the nearness of the vast unknown forest with its coppery savages, is of vast interest to me; insomuch as I have often both said and written exactly the same thing! Have you seen my old story "The Picture in the House"? If not, I must send you a copy. The introductory paragraph virtually sums up the idea you advance.

There is genuine grisliness, all apart from the supernatural legends, in the inside chronicles of Massachusetts. It begins to appear as early as 1642, when the correspondence of Gov. Bellingham with Gov. Bradford[10] of Plymouth reveals a genuine alarm on the part of both executives regarding the wave of utterly abhorrent and unnatural crime—very different from the ordinary offences common in England, and today classifiable as extreme forms of sadism and other pathological perversions—which had sprung up among the more ignorant orders of the people. "It may bee demanded how it came to pass," writes Bradford, "yt soe many wikked persons and prophane people shou'd soe quickly come over into this land, and mixe them selves amongst them? Seeing it was religious men yt began ye work, and they came for religions sake."[11]

Well—although he doesn't know it—Bradford really gives part of the answer in his own question. The very preponderance of passionately pious men in the colony was virtually an assurance of unnatural crime; insomuch as psychology now proves the religious instinct to be a form of transmuted eroticism precisely parallel to the transmutations in other directions which respectively produce such things as sadism, hallucination, melancholia, and other mental morbidities. Bunch together a group of people deliberately chosen for strong religious feelings, and you have a practical guarantee of dark morbidities expressed in crime, perversion, and insanity. This was aggravated, of course, by the Puritan policy of rigorously suppressing all the natural outlets of exuberant feeling—music, laughter, colour, pageantry, and so on. To observe Christmas Day was once a prison offence, and no one permitted himself a spontaneous mirthful thought without afterward imputing it a "sin" of his soul and working up a veritable hysteria of pathological self-analysis as regarded his possible chances of "salvation". To read of the experiences of the Rev. Cotton Mather, and of his precocious little brother Nathaniel (who virtually tormented himself to death with hysterical emotional "soul-questioning") is to witness genuine tragedy—the tragedy of ignorance and superstition. Poor little Nat died at 19—I have seen his gravestone in the old Charter St. Burying Ground at Salem. His fortunate escape from life came in 1688, and his epitaph (a tribute to his prodigious learning) reads with unconscious pathos—"An Aged Person who had seen but 19 Winters in the World". Bradford—a Plymouth Pilgrim outside the worst pest-zone of Massachusetts mania—is not without some appreciation of the situation in this respect; and remarks with unusual penetration for his age—"An other reason (for the wave of morbid crime) may be, yt it may be in this case as it is with waters when their streames are stopt or dam'd up, when they get passage they flow with more violence and make more noys and disturbance, than when they are suffered to rune quietly in their owne chanels. Soe wikedness being here more stopt by strict lawes, and ye same more nerly lookt unto, soe as it cannot rune in a commone road of liberty as it wou'd, and is inclined, it serches every wher, and at last breaks out wher it gettes vente". Good old Bradford! But the real Puritans couldn't see it his way; hence (since they were forced to recognise the extent and unprecedented morbidity of the increasing crimes around them) there gradually grew up the commonly-accepted doctrine that the devil was making a special war on Massachusetts because of the holy purpose to which that saintly colony was dedicated by the Lord's Brethren. The Bradford-Bellingham correspondence was in 1642. Exactly fifty years later the Salem witchcraft affair broke out. Can anyone doubt what prepared the masses of the people to regard the matter seriously? As a sidelight on the nearly-unendurable strain to which Massachusetts theocracy subjected the nerves of its victims, we may note the vast numbers who withdrew to Rhode Island soil. It is much less known that really considerable numbers *went over to the Indians*—"went native", as modern slang would put it. This condition was much more frequent in the Puritan zone than anywhere else in Anglo-Saxon America. Authorities say that 100 times more whites were Indianised, than Indians were Europeanised. One Massachusetts man—the Rev. William Blackstone,[12] who had been the first settler on the Boston peninsula—became a hermit; taking his books and family and building a home in the wilderness in 1635, on territory later part of R.I. He said, "I came to Mass. to escape the Lord's Bishops, and now I leave it to escape the Lord's Brethren".[13] Blackstone was really the first white settler in R.I., but because he did not found a colony he is not considered a rival of Roger Williams as the local pioneer. After Providence was founded, he used to ride in on a white bull and pay visits to Mr. Williams and other friends. It was he who introduced the apple-tree to this colony. He was a great friend of the Indians, and it is merciful that he died in 1674, before King Phillip's War convulsed the colony. His house and books were burnt by the Indians two years after his death.

But there was still another reason for Massachusetts crime and abnormality—a reason rather embarrassing to many upholders of the myth that Mass. blood is a kind of unofficial patent of nobility. This was the rapid importation, after 1635, of a vile class of degenerate London scum as indentured servants. We escaped this in R.I., since at first we were too poor to have many servants at all, and later used Indians and negroes (we imported the latter in small numbers from the West Indies before our own "triangular trade" began) instead of low-grade whites. But Mass. needed servants sooner, and did not have our penchant for exotics; hence (in addition to enslaving some local Indians, and importing a *few* negroes and Carib Indians from the West Indies) went in on a large scale for "bound" English labour—paupers, convicts, "floaters", and so on. They had not learned the lesson that more actually anti-social perversion occurs amongst the decadent scum of a high race, than amongst the mentally and physically sound types of an inferior race. We can picture the result of bringing this warped, inhibition-stunted, free and easy degenerate element under the domination of the ironclad Puritan theocracy and moral strait-jacket. Repression and explosion—just as intelligent old William Bradford of Plymouth saw. 'Wikedness more stopt up by strict lawes . . . . . breaks out wher it gettes vente.' It is interesting to see how this same custom of importing inferior Englishmen worked out in less repressive colonies. Virginia had tried it prior to the beginning of the African trade in 1619, and the wretched mass of scum resulting therefrom was gradually settled on small farms. There was never any violence or well-defined clash with authority, and not a trace of any epidemic of morbidity. The inferior whites gradually retreated toward the backwoods, becoming in the course of time that "mean white" or "white trash" element so well-known to sociologists. One may add that an analogous phenomenon ultimately occurred in New England, small colonies of inferior or decadent stock springing up on the fringe of settled regions and receiving such names as "Hardscrabble", "Hell's Half Acre", "Dogtown", etc., etc. In N.Y. and New Jersey, too—where the mean whites mixed with negroes and Indians and still survive as wretched semi-barbarians in the Catskills and Ramapos. But this segregation did not occur in Massachusetts till after the decadents had made many complications in the general situation.

Another and highly important factor in accounting for Massachusetts witch-belief and daemonology is the fact, now widely emphasised by anthropologists, that the traditional features of witch-practice and Sabbat-orgies *were by no means mythical.* It was not from any empty system of antique legendry that Western Europeans of the 17th century and before got their *significantly consistent* idea of what witches were, how they made their incantations, and what they did at their hideous convocations on May-Eve and Hallowmass. *Something actual was going on under the surface,* so that people really stumbled on *concrete experiences* from time to time which confirmed all they had ever heard of the witch species. In brief, scholars now recognise that all through history a secret cult of degenerate orgiastic nature-worshippers, furtively recruited from the peasantry and sometimes from decadent characters of more select origin, has existed throughout northwestern Europe; practicing fixed rites of immemorial antiquity for malign objects, having a governing system and hierarchy as well-defined and elaborate as that of any established religion, and meeting secretly by night in deserted rustic places. It has no inclusive name recognised by its own adherents, but is customarily called simply "the witch-cult" by modern anthropologists. Evidences of its persistent existence and unvarying practices are revealed by multitudes or trials, legends, and historic incidents; and by piecing these together we have today a very fair idea of its nature and workings. Originally it seems almost conclusively to have been simply the normal religion of the prehistoric Mongoloids who preceded the Nordics and Mediterraneans in northwestern Europe. It is based on the idea of fertility, as worshipped by a stock-raising race of pre-agricultural nomads, and its salient features from the very first were semi-annual ritualistic gatherings at the breeding seasons of the flocks and herds, at which primitive erotic rites were practiced to encourage the fecundity of the stock—much as certain savages practice such rites to this day. This religion was once dominant throughout Western Europe; but was naturally pushed to the wall when the Aryans conquered the land and brought in their own infinitely more refined, evolved, and poetic polytheism. It could not stand up against Druidism or the Northern religion of Asgard and Valhalla, so sunk (like the Mongoloid "little people" to whom it belonged) to the position of a subordinate and despised cult. It was probably never persecuted under the supremacy of the Celts and Teutons, but on the other hand no doubt gained converts from among the degenerate elements of these conquering races. The coming of the Romans—who generally disliked furtive, orgiastic religions, and had suppressed certain Dionysiac and Cybele cults in Italy as early as the 3d century B.C.—somewhat changed the complexion of the matter, and tended to drive the vestigial religion to cover. Yet it seems to have obtained degenerate Roman converts, and was probably carried into the British Isles (where the Mongoloids never were) by the Romans rather than by either Mediterraneans or Celts. It is possible that Sylvanus Cocidius, whose worship the Britanno-Romans discouraged, was connected with this cult. The semi-annual orgies (April 30 and Nov. 30) were what came later to be known as *sabbats.* In the main, they consisted of dances and chants of worshippers—mostly female, but presided over by a male hierophant in shaggy animal disguise, called simply "The Black Man". The conclusion of the ceremony was obscene to an extent which makes even Juvenal's sixth satire seem milk.[14] The cult as a whole was subdivided into local units called *covens,* each with its "black man", and all joined by a common body of tradition and system of passwords and nomenclature. Every member was given a new mystic name for use within the cult. Originally, the distinctly *malign* features probably did not exist; the religion being merely emotional and sensual. When, however, the dominant races began to oppose and persecute it, it began to strike back and specialise in bringing evil to its enemies. This doubtless caused an emphasis to be laid upon the supernatural powers conferred on its devotees by their communion with the gods of Nature through the ritual of the sabbat. Little by little the idea grew up—accepted both by the half-crazed devotees and by the outside world—that the cult was a device for giving people a supernatural means of working evil. When Christianity made its appearance, the persecution of the cult became infinitely strengthened;

since this new faith had so fanatical a hatred of everything pertaining to eroticism. For the first time, in all likelihood, the cult became *wholly secret and subterranean*—and correspondingly, the general fear and hatred of it, and the tendency to regard it as a link with nameless powers of darkness, no doubt vastly increased. Once driven to cover, it seems to have stayed put fairly well, and it probably died out in many places—including Britain. Conquests by Gaels and Saxons finished any remnants of it which may have been left. From the late Roman period to late in the Middle Ages there are only glancing evidences of it, although it certainly maintained a steady existence on the continent of Europe, recruiting many degenerate and discontented people since it promised them so many more simple, understandable, and available boons than did Christianity. It was always waiting, ready to catch anybody who grew tired of the ethics and aesthetics of the ruling European civilisation—just as the Indians were always waiting to take in anybody who sickened of Puritan life in early Massachusetts. The big recruiting came in the 14th and 15th centuries, during that period of despair, degradation, and recklessness following the ravages the Black Death. This is the period, you know, when the sardonic conception of the "Dance of Death", as exploited by Albrecht Dürer, gained form. Dissatisfied with all that civilised life gave and promised, thousands undoubtedly went over to the witch-cult (a gesture by this time identified with the conception of "selling oneself to Satan") and extracted from its mummeries and its Sabbats what pleasure and excitement they could get. Nor could this be kept wholly secret on so vast a scale. For the first time the cult began to be generally known and feared and identified with the worship of Satan. (Its connexion with the Black Mass would be a good subject for learned research.) Undoubtedly, it would have virtually wrecked European civilisation if left unopposed, for it fostered a spirit of seditious malignity aimed against all existing institutions. Let us appreciate, therefore, that the first mediaeval opposers of witchcraft were *not* mere fanatics fighting a shadow. They were deluded in that they thought themselves to be fighting something supernatural, but they were most certainly right in believing that they were fighting a genuine menace. Of course, *reports of* witchcraft far exceeded the actual number of instances of its practice; so that many individual witch-condemnations were indeed unjust. Also, the legend of witch-ceremonies undoubtedly spread far beyond the actual areas in which the real cult had its activities. For some reason or other, *Germany* was the scene of the most actual cult-doings, though covens undoubtedly extended into France and Scandinavia and perhaps as far south as Italy. The cult does not seem to have crossed into Britain till late in the 15th or early in the 16th century; and it there found its chief seat in Scotland. It entered Wales, but never seems to have had any foothold in either England or Ireland. From the time of Pope John XXII's bull against witchcraft in the first half of the 14th century, the war of civilisation against the cult gained headway. In 1484 Pope

Innocent VIII launched the most tremendous campaign of all—the one during which the Germans Sprenger and Kramer prepared their famous treatise on witchcraft and witch-finding: "Malleus Maleficarum".[15] Nor was it any phantom that Church and State alike were fighting. On the contrary, the degenerate cult gained strength, struck back, and increased in malignancy, until it seemed to be almost beyond control. In southern Germany it attained such magnitude that the wholesale collapse of civilisation seemed to be threatened; hence—amidst the impotence of all legal agencies—many fearless noblemen organised a wholly extra-legal society for detecting and punishing cult-adherents; a sort of mediaeval Ku Klux Klan called the "Holy Vehm",[16] which seized miscreants, tried them at dead of night in lonely forests, and saw that they never appeared again if judged guilty. This very practical "malleus maleficarum" really worked, hence after 1500 cult witchcraft was never a real menace. The scare, however, continued; and prosecutions and executions by both Church and State were exceedingly numerous until far into the 18th century. In Britain the chief witch fright occurred during the reign of James I—early in the 17th century—and was undoubtedly based on actual cult activities in Scotland. The last witch-trial in England occurred in 1712, though such things lasted on the Continent till the beginning of the 19th century. The witch-cult itself is probably now extinct, but no one can say just when it perished—for of course the rumour and legend-form must have persisted long afterward. It is the opinion of most, that no actual coven-meetings or sabbats occurred after the beginning of the 18th century—if indeed after the middle of the 17th. Interestingly enough, the existence of this cult was not suspected by moderns till late in the 19th century; the previous opinion of students being that all witchcraft scares were pure hallucinations. Arthur Machen made splendid fictional use of the discovery before it became widely known or universally accepted.[17] Not until 1921, however, was the matter systematically presented—honour for this step being due to Prof. Margaret Alice Murray of London University, author of "The Witch-Cult in Western Europe".

And now—getting back to the main topic—where does all this hitch on to the history of witch-belief in colonial New England? Well, we may see at once that all the colonists had minds well prepared by historic experience to believe in the possibility of diabolic manifestations. They knew all about incantations and sabbats, and had had enough glimpses of actual cult-practices to take such things pretty seriously. Naturally—since the cult was always concealed, and never fully admitted by everybody to exist—there were many sceptics about the whole matter; and of course, there were also many well-balanced people who, although admitting witchcraft to be possible, were nevertheless in no danger of imagining cases of it where no true ground for suspicion existed. This latter type probably predominated among the American colonists as a whole. Since they believed in orthodox religion, it was not extraordinary that they should believe in other forms of the supernatural; but they were hard-headed enough not to apply their theoretical speculations to the actual world around them. Not so, however, with the Puritans. The whole nature of their theology taught them to be on the watch for manifestations of the devil; whilst the epidemic of morbid crime and perversion in their midst was to them unmistakable evidence of a Satanic siege. Many believed the swart Indians of the black woods to be diabolic allies of a sort—and of course the customary life of cheerless repression, rustic solitude, wintry cold, and hysterical religious introspection and espionage, all tended to make the population jumpy, and eager to seize on any unusual symptom as an indication of unholy magic. Then, once witchcraft was indicated, there was no choice about a course to follow. Did not Jehovah thunder forth the inexorable command, "Thou shalt not suffer a witch to live"?[18]

To me, this background seems to explain all the New England witch trials (the first was in 1648) up to the time of the Salem scare. The witch-cult was not here, but its echoes and traditions were. Trials were by no means numerous, and executions very few. Then came Salem with its 50 trials and 19 executions, and with the strange parallelism of testimony in many cases, which profoundly impressed some of the most scholarly men in the Province. Cotton Mather—a learned man who was no fool for all his extravagant Puritanism—heard and sifted the evidence, and egged on the prosecutions with all his power and influence, believing some new and definite Satanic attack to have been made upon Massachusetts. What is behind all this? Merely a natural outburst and culmination of the mood which produced the early sporadic trials—or something new and systematic and tangible?

Well, we shall never know. Miss Murray, the anthropologist, believes that the witch-cult actually established a "coven" (its only one in the New World) in the Salem region about 1690, and that it included a large number of neurotic and degenerate whites, together with Indians, negroes, and West-Indian slaves. Of this coven, she maintains, the Rev. George Burroughs was probably the leader or "Black Man"; (detailed legend, testimony, and anecdote certainly prove him by no means saintly!) so that this hanging was perfectly well merited. Of the other victims, some were probably guilty of cult-participation whilst others were innocent and accused only through malice. Thus conjectures the learned author of "The Witch Cult in Western Europe"—though of course without definite proof. Others—Americans who have possibly examined the Salem records more closely than she—think it improbable that any formally organised cult-branch could have been concerned; though all agree that the answers to trial questions shew a vast familiarity with cult-institutions—more than could easily be accounted for by common legend, or by any sort of leading questions. For my part—I doubt if a compact coven existed, but certainly think that people had come to Salem who had a direct personal knowledge of the cult, and who were perhaps initiated members of it. I think that some of the rites and formulae of the cult must have been talked about secretly among certain elements, and perhaps furtively practiced by the few degenerates involved. I would not be surprised if Burroughs were concerned—and also the West-Indian slave woman Tituba, who started the scare in the first place by telling tales to neurotic children. Most of the people hanged were probably innocent, yet I do think there was a concrete, sordid background not present in any other New England witchcraft case.

Puritan witch-belief by no means ended with Salem, although there were no more executions. Rumours and whispers directed against eccentric characters were common all through the 18th and into the 19th century, and are hardly extinct today in decadent Western Massachusetts. I know an old lady in Wilbraham whose grandmother, about a century ago, was said to be able to raise a wind by muttering at the sky.[19] Nothing of all this, however, reached Rhode-Island. With our colonists witchcraft was always a remote thing—at most, a whimsical thing to joke about or scare children with. Whatever real belief existed here, was confined to Indians and negroes. No witchcraft trial ever took place within our boundaries.

About whippoorwills as psychopomps—I *think*, but can't be sure, that the idea is peculiar to the New World; although other living creatures, as well as the north-wind, are accorded similar functions in the oldest Aryan legends. I had never heard of this particular legend till 1928, and certainly do not think it exists in Rhode Island.

What you say of your ancestry is extremely interesting, and I think it is a great asset from the standpoint of fantastic literature to have so predominant a share of Celt. I have often thought, in surveying the trends of literature and socio-political organisation today, that the Celtic group is really the only *young* and unspoiled race left on the planet. All the rest of the white race has passed the naive and adventurous and life-loving stage of its evolution, and has reached that prosaic, urbanised, social-minded, unimaginative condition out of which vivid art finds hard work in growing. Only the Celt, I sometimes reflect, continues to think and feel spontaneously in poetic fashion—that is, in terms of symbolism, pageantry, dramatic contrast, and adventurous expectancy. In him we see the strongest remaining manifestation of the pure Aryan spirit—the spirit of the natural bard and fighter and dreamer as opposed to the merchant, the builder, the administrator, and the instinctive city-dweller. Very early in life I had an opportunity to see the Celtic poetic imagination at its very best, for my mother was a friend of the late Louise Imogen Guiney,[20] a poet of pure Irish blood who now ranks among the really major figures of American literature. When I was three years old we spent a whole winter at the Guiney home in Auburndale, Mass., and I can still recall how the poetess used to teach me simple rhymes which I would recite standing on a table! Another Celtic sidelight of my youth was still nearer home—my next-door neighbours and best playmates being three brothers whose relation to the Irish stream might be said to be your own, *reversed*—that is, they were descended from a line of Irishmen given to marrying Rhode Island Yankees, so that although they were about 80% Anglo-Saxon, they considered themselves heirs to the Irish tradition through descent in the male line and the possession of the name of Banigan. Their family always made it a point to travel to Ireland as often as possible, and were great collectors of Celtic antiquities. Their grandfather had a veritable museum of prehistoric Irish artifacts—indeed, I wish I knew what has become of that collection now that the family has left Providence and the brothers are all dispersed! Observing my admiration for these reliques of unknown yesterdays, they gave me two little greenish figures of a sort quite numerously represented in the collection; figures which they held to be of vast antiquity, but concerning which they admitted very little was known. Some seem to be metallic, whilst others are clearly carved of some light sort of stone. Their average length or height is only an inch and a half, and they are all overlaid with a greenish patina. They are grotesque human figures, sometimes in conventional poses and with curious costume and headdress. Their vast age is held to be indicated by the prodigious depth at which they are found in ancient peat-bogs. My two—one stone and one metal—have always appealed prodigiously to my imagination, and have formed high spots of my own assortment of curiosities. I think I will try to sketch them here, and see if your Celtic researches can throw any light on them. My friend Bernard Dwyer—pure Irish and 3 generations from the old sod—cannot explain them, but it is very possible that actual archaeologists have long known and described such things. Their outlines and features, unfortunately, are exceedingly chipped and worn down. But here they are—exact size and all. What are they? Were they ancient and buried and forgotten when Partholan first sighted Iërne's strange green shore? Did some Atlantean colonist, remembering strange secrets from hoary Poseidonis, fashion them in the light of primordial dawns? It's really a wonder that I haven't asked museum authorities about them long ago—but perhaps I dread being disillusioned and told that they are either fakes or something relatively recent! Sooner or later I shall probably get one or more tales out of them—for they certainly possess the most fascinating possibilities. [Lovecraft's illustrations][21]

It would be interesting some day to try to figure out just how much Celt I have in me. The Casey line gives me a Gaelic touch, and Cymri crop out constantly in my paternal ancestry—which is closer to Britain than my maternal, since my great-grandfather Joseph Lovecraft did not come to American till 1827, four years after being wiped out territorially and financially on his hereditary Devonshire soil. His fourth son George, born in 1815, is my grandfather, and my last forbear to see the light of day on ancestral acres and within ancestral walls. The old place, Minster-Hall near Newton-Abbot, is said to be no longer in existence. It is a great hope of mine, though, to visit around there some day and poke among gravestones and parish records, and at least get the feel of the landscape. My grandfather married an Allgood (a *Northumberland* line, whence I may get some Dane and Viking) whose mother was a Morris of Claremont, Glamorganshire, Wales. *Her* mother was pure Cymric; a Purcell, whose mother was in turn a Rhys. And her father, though of a Norman line, had one Cymric grandmother—a Jenkins whose mother was a Parry claiming descent from Owen Gwynnedd. This same father—the Rev. Thomas Morris, who died in 1799—was very interestingly connected through his mother, a Musgrave of Edenhall, Cumberland. This is the line that owned the celebrated fairy cup of legend—a glass goblet stolen from the fairies, who in revenge declared that disaster would overtake the house if it was ever broken. This cup, called "The Luck of Eden Hall", is now in the S. Kensington Museum, London.[22] I must see it if I ever get across, for it represents the only weird legend in my lineal ancestry! The Allgood-Morris connexions give me all the Welsh I have except a thin Carew link, but through earlier Lovecraft links I get some Cornish—and probably a great deal of Celtic Devonian, since sources prior to the Norman Conquest are misty and chaotic. Through a cousinly marriage I get two Edgecumbe great-great-grandmothers, and their mother was a Cornish Carew whose mother was a *Trefusis*. Could anything be more Cymric than this last? There is also more Cornish in the Carew line, which I can't keep straight in memory. Sooner or later I shall have to find a way of getting overseas and absorbing some of the colour of the immemorial past. I long to see Stonehenge, and to wander in some haunted oak wood where the trees arch overhead and attain an unbelievable girth! Such oak forests have haunted my dreams ever since I can remember.

That "Sky-high, caney" legend certainly has a tremendous force, and could be used with great effectiveness in fiction. Evil recluses high up among lonely hills always appeal to the imagination, and this tale is full of vivid and blood-curdling moments. References to the Blue Ridge would seem to argue a crystallisation of the tale's present form in Western Virginia. I have seen the Blue Ridge mountains, and can well testify to their wild picturesqueness. Their western slopes face the mysterious and cavern-honeycombed Shenandoah Valley—where in 1928 I obtained my sole glimpse of the primordial underground world; viz., the Endless Caverns near New Market, Va.[23]

As for the foreign overrunning of America—that is certainly the most tragic event in the continent's history. The very essence of a real civilisation is the continuous dwelling of generations on the same soil in the same manner; so that race becomes fitted to landscape, and a body of stable, genuine traditions and folkways grows up to give each new generation a sense of comfortable placement and interest and significance. Such a thing was well started in America by the first colonists, so that by 1700 there was a clearly-defined local fabric and feeling based on the Northern European temperament and heritage in conjunction with the given climate and topography. The thing had sharply crystallised, so that it could no longer be said that the land was an open country ready to receive all comers as material for a future civilisation.

You will hear this claim made by advocates of the foreigners, but it is pure sophistry. A compact and coherent Nordic English culture had established itself, and very obviously the only suitable new material was that having marked similarities and a consequent capacity for perfect absorption—namely, the vigorous stock of Northern Europe, with the characteristic instincts, tastes, standards, habits, and historic memories of the breed. English, Scotch, Irish, Germans, Huguenots from Northern France—all up and down the Atlantic coast these closely-related and psychologically sympathetic elements had settled down into one increasingly homogeneous mixture; approaching the problem of pioneering in the same general way, and thus building up a common fabric of experience and achieving a common stock of memories, loyalties, and customs. And for more than a century and a half after that the same process went on—new arrivals coming largely from the same kind of blood in the Old World, and fitting excellently into the expanding bulk of the new, even when (as in the case of the Germans and Scandinavians) there was a linguistic difference. Altogether, we may say that for *250 years* a sound, compact Nordic-English culture existed in America undisturbed and unthreatened, with only such accretions as it could ultimately use advantageously in preserving the pattern. As late as 1880 there was no dispute as to what constituted the American type, or any doubt about the permanence of that type. New immigrants were all *assimilable*—joked about for their dialect during one generation, but with children who entered the native pattern and became the jokers instead of the joked-about.

Then—through a false and sentimental policy of ignoring ethnic lines and minimising heritage—the complexion of immigrants began to change. Economic rapacity demanded cheap labour, and the popular industrial policy was to rake in any sort of human scum with a low living-standard and correspondingly low wage-demands. Nordics of so squalid a sort couldn't be found, so Latins and Slavs were imported. The powers who started this, of course, had no idea of ever treating these immigrants like white people. What they wanted was a kind of serf just a stage above the slave-labour of former times—but they miscalculated the social forces involved, and did not understand that white races, however humbly represented, have a restless expanding power which makes it impossible to herd and segregate them absolutely at will. It was inevitable that the importation of millions of dissimilar aliens should cause a repercussion on the national fabric and create the nucleus for a body of thought and aspiration antagonistic to the established order. And so indeed it turned out. The brighter and stronger foreign elements acquired resources, influence, and spokesmen, and gave birth to the dangerous false ideal of "the melting-pot". Forgetting what a well-defined and compactly crystallised thing the old-American civilisation was, they set up the familiar cry that "everybody's equally a foreigner except the Indians". As if the conquerors and builders of the nation were on a par with the latest lousy Lithuanian dumped on Ellis Island! At present, there is a kind of awakening to the true situation—hence the various regulations lately imposed on immigration. All these restrictions are in the right direction, and we may only hope that they have not come too late to preserve the original culture. Not all the country is as badly overrun as New England and the New York City area. Up in New York State the countryside is largely in hereditary hands, and south of the Potomac the population and folkways are surprisingly American. Charleston, S.C. is virtually as homogeneous and colonial as it was a century ago. The future will witness a grim and dramatic battle between influences. Can the foreigners be knocked into the traditional Nordic pattern in time, or will the pattern itself become impaired before it can accomplish such a conquest? I can feel no interest in the heterogeneous, traditionless industrial and mechanical empire which this nation threatens to become. Such a thing would not have enough coherence, continuity, memory-appeal, or identification with the historic stream to give me any satisfying sense of placement, interest, meaning, or direction. It might make a great nation—another Babylon or Carthage or Rome—but it wouldn't be my nation. What I belong to is the old English Colony of Rhode Island; and when that shall cease to have a cultural and psychological prolongation, I shall be a man without a country. I am too much of an antiquarian ever to feel a citizenship in a swollen, utilitarian national enterprise whose links with the past are cut, and whose instincts and sources have to do with scattered and alien people and lands and things—people and lands and things which have no connexion with me, and can have no interest or meaning for me.

I had heard that Louisiana was Italian-ridden, but did not realise that Texas also suffered from immigration. The Mexican is probably as much of a problem as the low-grade European, but I can see that he would not be likely to be quite so irritating, since he really belongs by heredity to the landscape. There is always something redeeming about any race *on its own soil*—where it is fitted to the landscape and possesses settled ways and traditions. The remaining white Spaniards of old Tejas, Arizona, and Nuevo-Mejico must be rather a picturesque and attractive element. I think I have heard that quite a number exist in New Mexico. Isn't that state still officially bi-lingual, with Spanish as one of the legal tongues? In New England our closest approach to this sort of semi-foreigner is the omnipresent French-Canadian from across the line in the province of Quebec. These people, on the average, have been in the New World longer than ourselves—the bulk of them having lived for 10 or 11 generations in a region not 400 miles from where I am sitting. You can hardly say that they immigrate consciously, as to another kind of life. They merely overflow the border and sift and filter down into New England, following the great rivers with their manufacturing centres. Some of them are of excellent racial stock, and about half come from classes whose hereditary living standard is scarcely different from the humbler American standard. In Quebec city, the better classes are *exactly* like the best Americans except in language, and the lower classes are not *nearly* so bad as our foreign slum-denizens. These people would be welcome and assimilable if they did not voluntarily hold aloof—but unfortunately (since they feel no sense of tradition in their short trip from ancestral soil) they are resolved at all costs to remain French in language and tradition. The British rulers of Quebec allow them to do so, they argue, so why can't we? In R.I. they are overwhelmingly numerous, some of our cities being as wholly French as Quebec. If your New Braunfels is another Potsdam, then our Woonsocket is another Amiens or Rouen or Cherbourg!

But I must cease wearying you with my rambling! Just finished a 69-page typing job[24] and got it out of the house, hence dropped into a sort of loquacious vacational mood as a reaction!

Best wishes, and thanks for enclosures. Most cordially and

sincerely yrs—

H P Lovecraft

Notes

1. I.e., REH's King Kull stories.

2. But see letter 46.

3. Silas Casey, *Infantry Tactics* (1862; 3 vols.).

4. James MacSparran (1693–1757), Episcopal minister, author of *America Dissected: Being a Full and True Account of All the American Colonies . . .* (1753).

5. George Berkeley (1685–1753), "On the Prospect of Planting Arts and Learning in America," l. 1.

6. The Old State House (Colony House) at 150 Benefit Street was constructed in 1762, replacing the 1732 Colony House that had burned in 1758. A tower was added in 1850–51, another addition in 1867–68. The College Edifice (University Hall) on the Brown University Campus was erected in 1770. The First Baptist Meeting House (1775) at 75 North Main Street was founded by Roger Williams in 1638.

7. HPL's celebrated bookplate, designed by Wilfred B. Talman, depicted a typical colonial doorway with fanlight.

8. HPL mistakenly dates the building to 1745. The Quaker Meeting House was at the corner of North Main and Meeting streets (thus, the reason Gaol Lane was renamed Meeting Street in 1772). For a time, town meetings were held there, and until the Moses Brown School was built in 1819, a school was there. In 1843 the building was moved to 77–79 Hope Street. A larger building, since razed, was constructed there. A new meeting house was built in 1953 at 99 Morris Avenue, adjacent to the Moses Brown School.

9. The Moses Brown School at 250 Lloyd Avenue.

10. Richard Bellingham (1851–1672), deputy governor of the Massachusetts Bay Colony; William Bradford (1590–1657), a framer of the Mayflower Compact and governor of the Plymouth Colony for 30 years.

11. Presumably quoted from Bradford's *History of Plymouth Plantation* (1856; not in *LL*).

12. Rev. William Blaxton (also Blackstone) (1595–1675) was the first European to settle in what is now Boston and lived in what is now Rhode Island. Ordained in the Church of England, he conducted the first Anglican services of record in Rhode Island, and his collection of books was probably the largest private library in the British colonies at the time.

13. Actually, he said he "'left England to escape the arbitrary conduct of the lord bishops; and Massachusetts, to be free of the rigid discipline of the lord brethren.'" In Alden Bradford, *History of Massachusetts, for Two Hundred Years: From the Year 1620 to 1820* (Boston: Hilliard, Gray, & Co. 1835), p. 20.

14. Juvenal (D. Junius Juvenalis, 60?–140? C.E.), author of fourteen *Saturae* (satires), the sixth (and longest) of which is a vicious satire on women.

15. Jacobus Sprenger and Henricus Institor [Heinrich Kramer], *Malleus Maleficarum* [*Hammer of Witches*], published in Germany c. 1486 as a guide to inquisitors in detecting, examining, and punishing witches.

16. A reference to the *Vehmgerichte,* secret courts in medieval Germany (chiefly in Westphalia), largely operated by knights with the tacit approval of the Holy Roman Emperor, that tried cases of perjury, violence, and heresy. They fell into decline by the end of the fifteenth century.

17. HPL alludes to Machen's tales of the "little people," which HPL (but not Machen) believed to have anticipated the ideas in Margaret Murray's *Witch-Cult in Western Europe.*

18. Exod. 22:18.

19. I.e., the grandmother of Edith Miniter (1869–1934). HPL had visited Wilbraham in 1928 and incorporated various scraps of legends encountered there into "The Dunwich Horror."

20. Louise Imogen Guiney (1861–1920), essayist and poet. HPL's account of spending the winter of 1892–93 in Guiney's home in Auburndale has not been verified, but in the absence of contrary evidence it can be provisionally accepted.

21. HPL had drawn the two figurines he is discussing. They were retraced in AHT, but so faintly that reproduction is impossible.

22. See *SLL* 2.184–85 The "S. Kensington Museum" is the Victoria and Albert Museum. Much of HPL's information regarding his paternal ancestry cannot be confirmed and is now suspect.

23. See HPL's "A Descent to Avernus" and "Observations on Several Parts of America."

24. "The Whisperer in Darkness," the composition of which was completed on 26 September.

[14] [nonextant letter or postcard by HPL]

[15] [TLS]

[c. October 1930]

Dear Mr. Lovecraft:

It is with greatest delight that I learn Mr. Wright has accepted "The Whisperer in Darkness" and I look forward to its appearance with highest anticipation. If I had never read any of your work, the weird and cryptic fascination of the title would intrigue me, and as it is, knowing the high quality of your tales, I know that that title is a true indication of a superb piece of bizarre artistry. I only wish that the story appeared in the next issue of the magazine.

Thank you very much for "The Recluse". I have read and re-read your article with the utmost interest.[1] You handle the subject in a clean-cut and highly intelligent manner, and certainly no one in the present literary world is more capable of dealing with that subject. I certainly wish you would enlarge this article into book form. I must admit my ignorance—the majority of the stories you mention I have never read—some I had never before even heard of. I have read most of Poe's work, a good deal of Bierce, some of Machen, Dunsany, etc., but I do not think that I ever read a line of Blackwood, for instance. I am, frankly, not at all widely read.

I am very sorry to hear that Mr. Cook has had a nervous breakdown[2] and trust he will soon be in better shape. I will indeed appreciate your obtaining Mr. Munn's sketch for me.

I am very glad that you liked "Red Thunder". I wrote it one midnight when distant thunder was rumbling through the high heaped clouds of the dark. I highly appreciate your comments on the rhyme; I neglected to tell you that I meant you to keep the copy, as well as the Alamo picture; I have several more. I intend some day to bring out a book of verse, but I doubt if it will be very soon.[3] Some time ago I ceased sending my verses to various poetry magazines: my best efforts were usually returned with lines by the editors, expressing appreciation for the rhymes, but requesting me to contribute verses less bitter or rebellious. My answer generally was that I refused to emasculate my stuff—poor as it was—for the empty honor of seeing my name in print. If poetry magazines paid for contributions it would be different. I find Weird Tales much more liberal regarding verse than most poetry magazines.

I'm sure you would enjoy San Antonio. Its not like any other Texas city—more like New Orleans in general color, but with a flavor distinctly its own. The little San Antonio river adds to its picturesqueness, being crossed in the main part of town by no less than sixteen bridges. The visible population is largely Latin, leisurely and old-world-like. You can go for blocks and never hear a word in English. Great numbers of Chinese settle in the purely Mexican quarters and amalgamate with the Latins, as well as negroes and a goodly number of Italians. The town being primarily Catholic, many old and picturesque cathedrals abound there, and just out of town are a number of old missions, some of them built before the Alamo, partly with material brought from Spain. Some of these missions are still in use. Living conditions are naturally low in San Antonio and a great deal of lawlessness exists. "The lower country" as it is called here in West Texas, swarms with mixed breeds of various nationalities who, mixing with the old lawless Scotch-Irish Texas stock, produce desperate characters. Consider the condition: the first of the

Nordic breed to invade that part of Texas were pioneers in the true sense—traders and buffalo hunters pressing westward. They found colonies of Spaniards who had already merged into the Mongoloid-Indian population and become what we know as Mexicans. These first pioneers mated freely with Indian and Mexican women and spread their offsprings wide. Then followed the cattlemen—always a lawless race in whatever country they are found. These, like the hunters, were mostly of English, Irish and Scotch-Irish stock, and came from the Southern states. Then, just about the time that the ranchmen were being pushed out of East Texas by the advance of the squatters—small farmers—some German prince, whose name I have forgotten, dumped a great conglomeration of Teutonic immigrants on the Texas coast. He left them to starve but the Indians fed them and they eventually founded the town of New Braunfels.[4] A constant stream from Germany has poured into the lower country for over half a century and of late years Slavs and Latins from eastern and central Europe and Italy and Scicily have swarmed to its shores. Immigrants from the British Isles and the Scandinavian countries have been comparatively few, though many Swedes and Danes have settled on the wide plains of Northwest Texas. Forty or fifty miles west of this locality the country swarms with Swedes.

But to return to the lower country—you can see what amalgamation of the various breeds would produce in many cases: where the mixture is of Indian-Mexican, pioneering British stock, German, Polack, and Latin. Of course many of the older families, both American and German, have held themselves apart from the rabble and intermarried with their own race and with each other, but the later arrivals from Europe tend to mix and mingle without rhyme or reason.

I am much taken with your suggestion for tying up the Etruscans with an Elder World civilization and mean to have a fling at it some day, though my notions about them now are so hazy that it will require a great deal of study of their ways and customs before I would be able to write intelligently about them.

I am inclined to agree with you that the Assyrians and Phoenicians were of Alpine-Semitic stock, also about the Jews. It is evident that the present day Hebraic race has little in common with the original wandering, fighting type. I wonder if that Alpine type could have been the result of admixture with Turanian races? It is said that the Assyrian's physiognomy was much like the present day Russian Jew's, and we know that the Jews of Russia and Poland have a great deal of Mongoloid blood in them—descendants of those Turanian Khazars with whom numbers of Jews settled and mixed in the Middle Ages.

Islam under the Arab caliphs certainly was superior to contemporary western civilizations, from all I have read, and had it not been for the unstable nature of the Semite, would surely have developed eventually into a civilization far surpassing our own, today. But it seems Semitic nations cannot stand the test of time. The caliphates were crumbling to decay when the Seljuk Turks overran and assumed leader-ship of Islam. Then cultural progress ceased; the Turk never built anything; his mission in life has been to destroy. He is in many ways, the counterpart of the Dane of Viking days, who, incapable himself of creating, nipped the growing culture of Saxon-England in the bud and almost totally blotted out civilization in Ireland. The Turanian has always, it seemed to me, been the man of action rather than the man of study and art. He has been, and still is, bold, adventuresome, capable and unsentimental, brutal and domineering; in creative genius he is infinitely inferior to the Semitic race. It would have been bad for the west had Martel lost at Tours; it would have been infinitely worse if the Occident had fallen before the hordes of Attilla, Genghis Khan or Timur-il-lang.

The Orient was early an enthusiasm of mine, though for some years I lost all interest in it. This interest was revived by the appearance of Mr. Wright's Oriental Stories Magazine, to which I have contributed a number of tales. I, frankly, have never even set foot on the east bank of the Mississippi River,[5] but if popular fiction writers wrote only about countries with which they were actually familiar, the fiction supply would be enormously limited! By the way, if you chanced to read my "The Voice of El-lil" in the first issue of Oriental Stories, I wish to say that that line mentioning the "pre-Aryan people of Connaught and Galway," represents a mistake of the printer. I wrote "Connaught and Galloway," meaning of course, the district in Scotland.

I found your chronicles of Rhode Island most fascinating and realize more than ever my vast ignorance of American history. You are right in saying that the average American knows only his own district. And then usually very imperfectly; I know only a skim of the history of Texas, and I daresay that the number of Rhode Islanders who are as well acquainted with the chronicles of the state as you are, are comparatively few. The average man does not concern himself much with history. America is entirely too big; too big to hold together long, especially with the invasions of unsavory hordes of foreigners. I sympathize with your interest in Colonial days; I myself find it difficult to co-ordinate myself with the age in which I live. I have often wished strongly that I had lived on the ancestral plantations in the Deep South, in the days before the Civil War! I particularly wished this in earlier days, when dragging a cotton-sack through the morning dew or swinging an axe in the face of a blue blizzard.

You Rhode Islanders reached your Golden Age earlier than the people of the South did, and your description of life in the old Narragansett plantation country makes my mouth water for mellow old days now gone forever. It is the fashion of the democratic modern age to jeer loudly at the old aristocracy-ruled days, but I'll be damned if I see anything particularly inspiring about the present-day trend—I see in this age neither a dignified civilization nor a clean, virile barbarism capable of producing a later culture. It seems merely a wallowing chaos with all lines down, a senseless commercial scramble in which all ideals are lost sight of.

The shipping era of your state was a virile and inspiring phase, and the picture you suggest of slave-ships sailing up unknown rivers and stumbling on ancient secrets is highly fascinating. The very phrase: the slave trade, conjures up intriguing pictures. That time has been neglected too much by fiction writers, rich as it is in dramatic possibilities. The linking of distant coasts by trade and exploration is a fascinating thought, anyway. The names and phrases: Slave Coast, Old Calabar, Bonney, Ashanti, Dehomey, Black Ivory, Bight of Benin, have always touched responsive chords in me. And consider the contrast—clean-cut clipper ships, manned by hard-headed, clear-eyed Yankee sailors, racing from the high, pure wind-swept coasts of New England, to the sullen, dank, devil-haunted swamps of the Slave Coast, with its abhorrent secrets, night-black jungles, squalling, teeming life, where fires flared and tom-toms thundered through the thick, musky night and black naked figures leaped and howled before blood-stained idols.

What a black and bloody land the West Coast of Africa is! The chronicles of the fleeting black empires read like nightmares. I tried, in "Red Shadows" to create a slight sense of the bestial inhumaneness of the country, but failed utterly. It must be something that a man must see in order to get a complete idea of it. Some day I intend to go and see it at first-hand.

If climatic and topographical conditions had been different, I wonder what the result would have been; for the majority of our negro slaves were of a comparatively low order of being. Living in the swamps and jungles they could not have been otherwise. I believe that if the American negro was a descendent of the more advanced Kaffir tribes of the south and east, his progress since emancipation would have been much more rapid.

Rhode Island has certainly had a vigorous and healthy history and I hope it will escape the swamping by foreigners that seems to have overtaken so many old American localities.

The legends you cite are extremely interesting, especially the one about the rock which bleeds in the light of the moon. That is a particularly fantastic touch, so strangely fantastic that it must have some basis of fact, though doubtless the fact is far removed in substance from the details of the myth. It seems to me that the more wildly fantastic a tale is, the more likelihood there is for its being grounded in reality one way or another. The average human is so unimaginative that the highest flights of fantasy are beyond his power to create out of nothing. The bleeding rock reminds me of a similar Irish legend, that of Raimreach Ruadh, wife of Goban Saer, in Bantry.

Speaking of witches reminds me of an old woman I knew in my early childhood in the "piney woods". She went bare-footed, was generally accompanied by a large flock of geese, gathered up manure to fertilize her garden, in her bare hands, and was generally looked on as a witch—tolerantly, to be sure, but the niggers were much afraid of her. One day she put a death-curse on a playmate of mine and nearly frightened him into a fit. And perhaps it was as well for her that superstition was not as rife as in former ages, because shortly afterward the child died.

As to the murder-ranch I mentioned, such ranches were fairly common in Texas during an earlier day. The owners would keep a cow-puncher working for perhaps a year without pay, then when he demanded his money, he was driven away; if he showed fight, he was shot down and his body thrown into a gulley or an old well. This particular ranch lies some miles west of this town and is now in different hands. The old man who owned the ranch, was, I have heard, of particularly repellant aspect and more dangerous than a rattlesnake. His worst crime, at least I consider it was, was the murder of a servant's baby; its noise irritated him and he dashed its brains out against the ranch house wall. He lived to be very old and was doubtless partly insane in the latter part of his life.

His son now has a ranch some hundreds of miles west of here, and some twelve or fifteen years ago killed a Mexican, sewed the corpse up in a cow-hide and flung it out on the prairie to rot. The Cattlemen's Association sent out a detective—just why so much trouble was taken about a Mexican I cannot understand, unless he was some way connected with the Association—and this detective, playing the part of a deaf mute, worked for months on the murderer's ranch and finally got full evidence. No one would have thought of looking into the cow-hide, for it merely appeared that a cow's carcass was rotting out there on the plains. The killer was brought into court and got a sentence of two or three years, though I cannot say as to whether he ever served his time or not. The last I heard of him, he was prospering in the western country.[6]

I agree with you that Puritanism provides a rich field for psychological study. I have never had the fortune to read your story, "The Picture in the House" but would most certainly like to.

I have noted the prevalence of perversion and unnatural crime in Puritan annals, and understand how it could have hardly been otherwise, since, as you remark, all natural instincts were strangled and strait-jacketed.

I found your remarks on witch-craft highly interesting. It was not until a few years ago that I realized that such a cult really did exist in former times—discovered this by reading an article by Joseph McCabe[7] on the subject. Your comments threw a good deal more light on the subject. A wealth of fiction could be written about it—especially about the time that European civilization seemed on the verge of crumbling before its insidious undermining. You are probably right in believing that the New England witch-craze was caused by members of the cult—probably trying to revive the old ways in the New World.

What you say of the youth and enthusiasm of the Celtic race is true, but I fear the good points of the race are balanced by points not so good. Celtic treachery is as well established as Celtic mysticism; Celtic dissention, jealousy and fickleness brought the English into Ireland and kept them there. The Gaels have never learned to act with each other; in later years many of the great leaders of Irish independence have been Celtized Englishmen. Why, it was only a part of the Irish who broke the Danes at Clontarf, and Mac Gilla Patrick not only refrained from aiding his countrymen, but actually attacked the Dalcassians as they returned and dogged their trail clear into Clare. And the great Brian Boru won the crown from Malachi by treachery. The history of the Irish race is one of betrayals, and only the incredible vitality of the breed has allowed it to exist at all.

Celtic nature has its moments of spontaneous gaiety and good nature, but it has depths of dark brooding and unexpected cruelty. It is wayward and uncertain as the wind; as water that flows to the sea and the grey waves of the sea. The Celt is oppressed by the everlasting sadness of the world and the fleeting shadows of this ephemeral dream we call reality. He is a primitive creature of rivers and shadows and dreams that can instantly turn to nightmares. He is moved and shifted by all winds that blow; his actions are determined by moods that pass over his soul like the shadows of wind-blown clouds across the grass. He fights the wars of all peoples and wins all battles except his own. He builds colossal cities and shivers in their streets, a beggar. He watches, unmoved, the slaughter of thousands, and breaks his heart over the falling of a leaf. He gives his coat to a stranger and robs his brother. A word can make him swear friendship for his enemy, and a word can make him turn against his best friend. He is Ishmael and his brothers are the Sons of Hagar. I am going to venture to quote here a rhyme of mine, of little worth, but in which I tried to create, in my crude way, some hint of the restlessness and discontent that is the heritage of all men of Gaelic blood.

Rueben's Brethren

"Unstable as water, thou shalt not excel".[8]

Drain the cup while the ale is bright,
    Brief truce to remorse and sorrow!
I drink the health of my friend tonight,—
    I may cut his throat tomorrow.

Tonight I fling a curse in the cup
    For the foe whose lines we sundered—
I may ride in his ranks when the sun comes up
    And die for the flag I plundered.

Kisses I drank in the blaze of noon,
    At eve may be bitter as scorning—

And I go in the light of a mocking moon
To the woman I cursed this morning.

For deep in my soul the old gods brood—
And I come of a restless breed—
And my heart is blown in each drifting mood
As clouds blow over the mead.

I am highly intrigued by the drawings of the images but am unable to give you any information about them. It might be possible that the works of P. W. Joyce[9] might throw some light on them, though Joyce was more of a historian than an archaeologist. However, his works are veritable store-houses of knowledge, and it is possible that his "The Story of Ancient Irish Civilization" might contain references to the origin or use of such images. This book is printed by The Talbot Press, Dublin, and published by Longmans, Green and Co., 39 Paternoster Row, London.

For my part, I am too little versed in antiquities to even offer an opinion, but I am inclined to think that these figures represent a pre-Christian age and have some phallic significance. I am especially inclined to this view by the consistent use of triangles in the stone figure. Phallic worship was very common in Ireland, as you know—the legend of Saint Patrick and the snakes being symbolical of the driving out of the cult—and in almost every locality where phallic worship thrived, small images representing the cult have been found, in such widely scattered places as Africa, India and Mexico. Though of course the workmanship of the images differs with the locality and I have never seen or heard of, figures just like these of your's. At any rate, they are fascinating and open up enormous fields of dramatic conjecture. I am sure you could build some magnificent tales out of them.

Your remarks on your ancestry interest me very much, more especially as the study of genealogy is one of my hobbies, or rather, would be, if I had time and opportunity to pursue it. Its interesting to trace back American families and learn just what part of Europe they came from. Its a queer thought to think that Americans are transplanted Europeans, somehow; after a race has lived in a locality five or six generations, its members tend to unconciously consider that the race has lived there always—it really takes some concious thought to realize that its otherwise!

You evidently have a great deal of Cymric Celtic in your veins. The modern Welsh are fully as imaginative and mystic as the Irish and in many ways are more steadfast and trustworthy, seeming to lack much of the Gaelic fickleness.

I have heard of the famous "Luck of Eden Hall" and would like very much to see it. In my early childhood I memorized Longfellow's poem about it.[10] How do you suppose the legend started? Was the cup taken from a rath, where it formed part of the loot of some forgotten king, do you suppose?

Like you, I would like very much to see Stonehenge and the Druidic forests. I can never quite bring myself to believe the tales of Druidic atrocities and debased worship. Most of such tales were spread by the Romans, who always accused their victims of hideous deeds mainly to excuse their own cruelties.

Stonehenge is supposed to be a pre-Druidic ruin, is it not? At any rate, it has always puzzled me as to how primitive men erected such things. Admitting the possibility of rearing great slabs of stone upright by sheer man-power, how could slabs of almost equal size be lifted and placed on top of the upright slabs without the aid of machinery? It looks impossible, unless the ancients built some sort of a mound up which they dragged the slabs. All in all, such edifices create a slight disquietude when considered thoughtfully, a faint feeling as if they had been erected by giants or creatures whose developement lay along other lines than those of ordinary humanity!

I agree with all you say about foreign immigration. "The melting pot"—bah! As if we could assimilate all the low-lived scum of southern Europe without tainting the old American stock. And that stuff they pull about "everybody being foreigners except the Indians," makes me fighting mad. Then the Indian is a foreigner too, because he was preceded by the Mound-builders. And the Gaelic-Irishman is a foreigner because the Picts came into Ireland before him. And the Anglo-Saxon is a foreigner in England because the Cymric Celts were there when he came. No—the true facts are this—after our ancestors had conquered the Indians, killed off the wild animals, levelled the forests, driven out the French and Spaniards and won our independence from England, a horde of lousy peasants swarmed over to grab what our Aryans ancestors had won.

Once it was the highest honor to say: "I am an American." It still is, because of the great history that lies behind the phrase; but now any Jew, Polack or Wop, spawned in some teeming ghetto and ignorant of or cynical toward American ideals, can strut and swagger and blattantly assert his Americanship and is accepted on the same status as a man whose people have been in the New World for three hundred years.

I would limit immigration in this manner: I would open the doors wide to all people of the British Isles. Let the other nations howl about discrimination. Why should we not discriminate? Did the Italians, the Russians, the Liths settle and conquer and build this country? Did the ancient Greek colonies welcome Egyptians and Phoenicians as citizens, or did they proudly remain Hellenes? Why should we open the doors to strangers? Britons settled this land and I would always welcome Britons. The rest, with exceptions among the higher class Scandinavians and French, I would bar completely.

Well—I cant say that I've added anything to the greatness of the nation, but I at least come of a breed that helped build up the country, which is more than can be said today by any number of Hebraic-Slavic-Latins running around and calling themselves "Americans".

My branch of the Howards came to America with Oglethorpe 1733 and lived in various parts of Georgia for over a hundred years. In '49 three brothers started for California. On the Arkansaw River they split up, one went on to California where he lived the rest of his life, one went back to Georgia and one, William Benjamin Howard, went to Mississippi where he became an overseer on the plantations of Squire James Harrison Henry, whose daughter he married. In 1858 he moved, with the Henry's, to southwestern Arkansaw where he lived until 1885, when he moved to Texas. He was my grandfather.

The Eiarbhins, or Ervins, to give the name its present Anglicized spelling, came to America a very long time ago; just when I am not sure, but it was before 1700. The family was originally Scotch and there is a legend to the effect that the name was once "Mac Conaire." How that name came to be Eiarbhin is more than I can say, but descent from Conaire, ard-righ of Erin is claimed, which, if true, shows that the clan went into Scotland at a comparatively late date.

At any rate, it was a wild Highland clan in the days of Robert Bruce and because they followed him and were granted favors by him, it is a tradition in the family that a male child in every generation be named Robert. My great grandfather was Robert Ervin, and my great-great grandfather the same; my grandfather, by some chance, was named George Washington Ervin, but he named his youngest son Robert, and I have several cousins of that name.

However, the Eiarbhins went westward early, and had been in Ireland for generations, before they came to America. My grandfather Colonel G. W. Ervin highly resented any attempt to attribute Scotch characteristics to him.

In 1800 the family was well established on [a] large plantation in North Carolina, but moved to Mississippi in the early 1840's. The Civil War ruined the plantation system and Colonel Ervin came to Texas in 1866.

The Henry's were the last of my various lines to arrive in the New World, being deported from Ireland a few years before the Revolutionary War because of rebellious actions against the English government. My great-great grandfather, James Henry, was born on the Atlantic ocean on the way over. He eventually settled in South Carolina where Squire James Harrison Henry was born.

So I really have no connection with the early history of Texas, though I was born here. Still, because of birth and environment I feel more closely knit to Texas than to the Old South. And it must indeed be said, that though most native Texans are of Southern blood, there is a great difference between them and natives of the Old South. I notice it every time I go to Lousiana or Arkansaw. We think of ourselves, and really are, not Southerners nor Westerners, but Southwesterners. Our accent is more like the South than the North or the Middle West, but it differs greatly from the true Southern accent. We constitute an empire of our own, and should never have entered either the Union or the Confederacy. With the great tracts of land we then owned and the possibilities we possessed, we had the makings of a vast and mighty empire. And it should have been so; America is too huge, too unwieldy; I fear it cannot long stand.

I have but recently returned from a trip to the great northwest plains which, beginning about the 33rd parallel run on up into Oklahoma and Kansas. Texas is really, especially in the western part, a series of plateaus, like a flight of steps, sloping from 4000 feet in the Panhandle to sea-level. You travel for a hundred or so miles across level plains, then come to a very broken belt of hills and canyons, then passing through them you come on to another wide strip of level country at a lower or higher elevation according to the direction in which you are travelling—and so on, clear to the Gulf. I was on the Llano Estacado, or Staked Plains, so called from the fact that Spanish priests, crossing the plains long ago, marked the way with buffalo skulls stuck on stakes. Twenty years ago most of that country was cattle-range; now the great majority is in cultivation. The Llano Estacado is the last stand for the big-scale Texas farmer. Farms of a thousands acres, every inch under cultivation, are not uncommon. A farm of that size requires a tractor and a veritable herd of work horses to cultivate it properly. During busy seasons the work goes on day and night; they work by shifts and labor from sunrise to sunrise. The average elevation is better than 3000 feet and the country is perfectly flat. You can see for miles in every direction; there are no trees except such as have been planted. Its a great, raw, open new country with mighty possibilities, but I'd go dippy living there. I was born and mainly raised in the Central Texas hill country and I have to have hills and trees!

The Llano Estacado is largely in the hands of native Texans of old American stock. You see, its really a pioneer country. The European scum sticks to the lowlands and the Gulf coast, waiting for the Old Americans to open the country up and get it going—and paying. THEN they'll swarm in and take it over.

I hate to see all the good ranges being broken up into farms. Once this country here on the Callahan Devide was a great cattle country with wide sweeping ranges, clear cold springs and streams and rich grass waist deep. Then the inevitable farmer came in droves, with his mule and his plow and his drove of offsprings. They fenced the land and the grass died; shinnery and mesquite and scrub oak sprang up and choked the springs; the streams ceased to run and the country dried up. The farmers wore out the soil. Thats the way they always do in a big country. They wear out a field, and simply move over and clear out another field. Eventually they run out of fields as the country fills up.

The oil booms came along and ruined what agriculture was left. Now this country is poverty ridden and worn out. The old rocky, clayey farms wont produce anything, what with the drouths, and the oil has just about played out; or else the big companies have bought out the smaller ones and shut down the works, to cut expense or to freeze somebody out. But now this country is drifting back to cattle and sheep and goats again. Its still a great country; it just needs a little intelligence. All over the older settled parts of Texas, the trend is away from agriculture and back toward stock-raising.

But is it any wonder that thrifty, hard working foreigners overrun the land when the descendents of the sturdy pioneers are in so many cases so shiftless and stupid and lazy?

Texans are naturally nomadic. Its difficult to find an old man who has grown old in the locality in which he was born. This extends to tenant farmers who often shift every year from one farm to another. And not farmers alone.

Why, by the time I was nine years old I'd lived in the Palo Pinto hills of Central Texas; in a small town only fifty miles from the Coast; on a ranch in Atascosa county; in San Antonio; on the South Plains close to the New Mexican line; in the Wichita Falls country up next to Oklahoma; and in the piney woods of Red River over next to Arkansaw; if you'll glance at a map of Texas you'll note that covers considerable distance, altogether; and I didn't mention a few short stays in Missouri and Oklahoma. I've lived in land boom towns, railroad boom towns, oil boom towns, where life was raw and primitive, and all I can say is: Texas is just too big for me to grasp. A better man than I will have to write her history.

I've seen towns leap into being overnight and become deserted almost as quick. I've seen old farmers, bent with toil, and ignorant of the feel of ten dollars at a time, become millionaires in a week, by the way of oil gushers. And I've seen them blow in every cent of it and die paupers. I've seen whole towns debauched by an oil boom and boys and girls go to the devil wholesale. I've seen promising youths turn from respectable citizens to dope-fiends, drunkards, gamblers and gangsters in a matter of months.

But the old Texas is gone or is going fast. All the plains are fenced in, where in my childhood I've ridden for a hundred miles without seeing a foot of barbed wire. I cant remember when I've heard a coyote. And one of my earliest memories is being lulled to sleep in a covered wagon camped on the Nueces River, by the howling of wolves.

When they built Crystal City twenty years ago in Zavalla county, some forty miles from the Mexican Border, the wolves came howling to the edge of the clearings. The woods were full of wildcats, panthers and javelinas, the lakes were full of fish and alligators. I was back there a couple of years ago and was slightly depressed at the signs of civilization which disfigured the whole country.

Well, it's not all civilized. There are places left where a man can get out and take a deep breath. In the hundred mile stretch from Sonora to Del Rio on the Border, there's not even a cluster of Mexican huts to mar the scenery and there's just one store, a sort of half-way place. The rest is just—landscape! Wild, bare hills, with no grass, no trees, not even mesquite; not even cactus will grow there—only a sort of plant like a magnified Spanish dagger, called—I believe—sotol.

And I have an idea that the plains south of the Llano Estacado are more or less wide open. A land boom flopped there quite a number of years ago and the railroad to the town where I lived a while was discontinued. I was very young and my memories are scanty; but I remember illimitable plains stretching on forever in every direction, sandy, drab plains with never a tree, only tufts of colorless bushes, haunted by tarantulas and rattlesnakes, buzzards and prairie dogs; long-horn cattle, driven in to town for shipping, stampeding past the yard where I played; and screeching dust winds that blew for days, filling the air with such a haze of stinging sand that you could see only for a few yards.

Judas, what a country! People came out from the East and filed on government land; and they went broke and went back home, or they went crazy and blew their brains out. Not many native Texans could stand it, even. People lived in tents, shacks, dug-outs—then they left, cursing the country and the old cattle-men watched them go and grinned in their whiskers. Though how even a Texas steer could live in that country is more than I can see.

But of all lousy lands, the Wichita Falls country takes the cake to my mind. There the plains are of white alkali and the glare nearly blinds you. The climate is treacherous. You ride out in the morning in your shirt sleeves, admiring the dreamy slumber of the plains, with the birds singing in the one tree the county boasts, and the heat waves shimmering in the distance; you see a coyote loping along with his tongue hanging out in the heat—and then by noon, maybe, a blue blizzard comes howling over the prairie and freezes your gizzard. Before they got gas wells in that country they burned corncobs; I've seen stacks ten feet high in people's back yards. Before they could ship corn in or raise it, cowpunchers burned dried cattle dung and before them the hunters and traders and Indians burned buffalo chips.

No, I don't care to live on the Cap-rock. This Cap-rock is the name of the rim of the highest plateau in Texas—the edge of the Staked Plains; at a distance it looks like low-lying clouds along the horrizon; then it appears to be an unbroken range of hills; then you ride up on it and see that its really a sort of cliff, marking the plateau and extending for more than a hundred miles.

But in a little town on the plains I met a figure who links Texas with her wild old past—no less a personage than the great Norfleet, one of modern Texas' three greatest gunmen—the other two being Tom Hickman and Manuel Gonzalles, captain and sergeant of the Rangers respectively. Norfleet is not unknown in New York and Chicago and a few years ago gained national fame by tracking down a band of con-men who had swindled him out of considerable money; he landed them all in the pen, instead of shooting them.[11] An interprizing firm published a book of his experiences, which reached an enormous sale.[12] He is now a United States Marshall and his latest exploit was in Chicago where he killed two gangsters who had the drop on him. He is a small, stocky man, about five feet four, I should judge, of late middle age, with a scrubby white mustache and cold light blue eyes, the pupils of which are like pin points. He is a very curteous and soft spoken gentleman and I could not help but notice, as I shook hands with him, that his hands are not of the type usually found in men who are quick with weapons—his hands being very short and blocky in shape. Nor did he have that quick, nervous grip in handshaking that I have noticed in killers. His nerves are in perfect control but in his quick movements he reminds one of a cat, and like all gunfighters, he keeps his hands in constant motion and never very far from his gun.

Though a very respectable and law-abiding citizen, Norfleet is as quick on the draw and as deadly a marksman as Billy the Kid, John Wesley Harding, Sam Bass, Al Jennings or any of the other old time Texas warriors.

The old-time gunmen of the west are passing fast, and when I say gunmen, I do not refer to the cowardly scum of the modern cities who disgrace the term by calling themselves gun-fighters.

Some ten years ago one of the greatest passed over the ridge—Bud Ballou, once a Ranger, whom Tom Hickman killed in the Wichita Falls country.

Of course, real gunfighters were comparatively rare, even in the old days, despite lurid western literature to the contrary, which literature would make appear that every man was then a walking armory and spent most of his time practicing the draw from all positions and shooting from the hip, the knee cap, and the collar button! Most men carried guns, but few were expert in their use. Just as in medieval times most men carried swords but the majority were neither duelists nor skilled fencers. It is surprizing the number of men who have been shot at and missed, in the west. But a strange thing seems to be, that a woman seldom needs any practice to get her man! They have a natural killer's instinct that sends their shot home. How often do you hear of a woman shooting at her husband and missing him?

A great majority of the killings in the old days were done with a shotgun from behind a rock fence. Killers generally show a preference for catching their man unarmed and then shooting him in the back.

But the real gunman scorned such subterfuges generally and was passionately proud of the notches on his gun.

A bold man was Dock Holder, who held forth in East Texas in the '80's and '90's. A gunman named Jackson shot him down, and Holder's sister lifted him and held him up while he killed Jackson. Of such stuff were Texas women made! Holder survived his wounds and lived until several years ago when one Jerome Persons got the drop on him and finished him with eight bullets through the body.

But for cold steel nerve no man ever surpassed that showed by old Judge

Jarrell in his street-fight with the Harris boys in Waco.[13] The Judge was an intellectual old man, but very radical in his views, a Civil War veteran and a gentleman of the old school. The Harris boys were news-paper men and they caught him in a cross-fire. J. W. Harris was standing in the door of his newspaper building firing, while across the street diagonally his brother J. F. Harris had his stand. Judge Jarrell walked swiftly yet deliberately across the street toward J. W. Harris, holding his fire. Something about that steady advance shook J. W.s nerve and his shots went wild. J. F., after missing repeatedly, came running across the street, firing as he came. At less than twenty feet a bullet shattered Jarrell's arm and the Judge fired for the first time, killing J. W. Harris. Then the Judge turned to meet the remaining brother who rushed in and attempted to grapple. Another man somehow ran between them and all three went down in a heap; and there the Judge, as cool as steel, reached his pistol-arm over the man between them and blew out J. F. Harris' brains. Two shots and two killings! He lost his arm but his foes lost their lives.

The Judge was a close friend of Bran, the Iconoclast, who was keeping Texas in an uproar, and this shooting occurred not long before Bran and Davis shot each other to death on the streets of Waco.[14]

Texas, all in all, has had a history of almost unbelievable violence and bloodshed. As late as the '80's it was not uncommon for some gunman to shoot down another in the streets of some western town and not allow anybody to touch the body—sometimes the corpse lay in the streets for days.

Well, it could hardly be otherwise, considering the powers that went to make up the history of the state. Our southern neighbors added considerably to the general disorder. For years we carried on an unofficial and unrecorded border warfare with Mexico and even today, the road between the Border towns of Eagle Pass and Del Rio, which follows the Rio Grande, runs along the rim of the valley, out of sight of the river. Once it followed the bank of the river but so many white people were shot by Mexicans across the river, the road was changed.

Thanks very much for letting me see the articles about Providence, also the splendid poem, "The East India Brick Row." I enjoyed scanning them all, particularly your poem, which is as fine as any of its kind I ever read. Its a pity that the old landmarks had to be torn away; modern America seems blindly bent on wiping out all vestiges of her glorious past.

What you say of the neighborhood in which you live is peculiarly fascinating; like living in a sort of mystical dream-town above and aloof from the rush and hurry of work-a-day world. You are very fortunate, I think, in your environments. In such a place one has time and inspiration for study and deep contemplation, I should think. Man is greatly molded by his surroundings. I believe, for instance, that the gloominess in my own nature can be partly traced to the surroundings of a locality in which I spent part of my baby-hood. It was a long, narrow valley, lonesome and isolated, up in the

Palo Pinto hill country. It was very sparsely settled and its name, Dark Valley,[15] was highly descriptive. So high were the ridges, so thick and tall the oak trees that it was shadowy even in the daytime, and at night it was as dark as a pine forest—and nothing is darker in this world. The creatures of the night whispered and called to one another, faint night-winds murmured through the leaves and now and then among the slightly waving branches could be glimpsed the gleam of a distant star. Surely the silence, the brooding loneliness, the shadowy mysticism of that lonesome valley entered in some part into my vague-forming nature. At the mouth of the valley stood a deserted and decaying cabin in which a cold-blooded and midnight murder had taken place; owls called weirdly about its ruins in the moonlight, and bats flitted about it in the twilight. I well knew, in later years, the man who committed that murder, and he never dared ride past that ruined cabin by night-time.

But I have rambled on long enough—too long. Again I must express the utmost delight to learn that another of your marvelous tales is to appear in print. I look forward to its appearance with the keenest relish, and hope that the day is soon when my library will be graced by the presence of your stories in book form. That will indeed be a treat of rare enjoyment.

By the way, I recently sold Weird Tales a short story, "The Children of the Night"[16] in which I deal with Mongoloid-aborigine legendry, touch cryptically on the Bran-cult, and hint darkly and vaguely of nameless things connected with Cthulhu, Yog-Sothoth, Tsathoggua and the Necronomicon; as well as quoting lines from Flecker's "Gates of Damascus"[17] and lending them a cryptic meaning which I'm sure would have astounded the poet remarkably!

But I hope I haven't bored you too much with my maunderings.

Very cordially yours
Robert E. Howard

P.S. Thanks for the copy of your bookplate; its a clever idea.

Notes

1. I.e., "Supernatural Horror in Literature."

2. W. Paul Cook suffered a series of breakdowns, aggravated by chronic appendicitis, following the death of his wife in early 1930.

3. REH never did publish a book of verse, although several have been published since his death: *Always Comes Evening* (1957; rpt. 1977); *Singers in the Shadows* (1970); *Echoes from an Iron Harp* (1972); *Night Images* (1976); and *The Ghost Ocean* (1982). REH had submitted the ms. of *Singers in the Shadows* to Albert and Charles Boni in early 1928, but the book was rejected. He also had intended to compile a book of poetry entitled *Echoes from an Iron Harp* (see letter 42), but the intended contents of that book are unknown.

4. Prince Carl of Solms-Braunfels (1812–1875), a member of the Prussian "Society for the Protection of German Immigrants in Texas." It was not Indians who "saved" the colonists, but Prince Carl's deputy, Otfried Hans, Freiherr von Meusebach (or "John

Meusebach," as he came to be known), whose industry and business acumen led to the establishment of the German colony centered about New Braunfels. See T. R. Fehrenbach, *Lone Star: A History of Texas and the Texans* (1968), pp. 291ff.

5. REH overlooks six weeks in 1919 when he lived in New Orleans, on the eastern bank of the Mississippi, while his father took a course at the Tulane University Graduate School of Medicine. See letter 12.

6. Jack Scott, longtime Cross Plains newspaperman, does not recall having heard the stories REH relates here. REH may be relating tales he had heard or read in some other context, transplanting them to his own locale for HPL's benefit. Stories of ranchers driving off cowhands without paying for their services, however, are common all over the western United States.

7. Joseph McCabe (1867–1955), former Franciscan clergyman, was an extremely prolific freethinker who wrote fifty Little Blue Books and forty Big Blue books for the publisher E. Haldeman-Julius, such as *New Light on Witchcraft*, Little Blue Book No. 1132 (1926). He was also the author of *The Evolution of Civilization* (1922).

8. Gen. 49:4.

9. REH owned Joyce's *A Short History of Gaelic Ireland* (1924); REHB 119.

10. "The Luck of Edenhall" (1842).

11. James Franklin (J. Frank) Norfleet (1865–1967) was a Texas cowboy and successful rancher. When he was swindled out of $45,000 by five confidence men, he spent $75,000 of his own money and traveled more than 30,000 miles in relentless pursuit of them. Armed with a commission in the Texas Rangers and the power to arrest, he tracked down all five and saw them safely behind bars. He was also instrumental in running down at least 75 others in associated confidence rings. He wrote a book about his experiences and starred (as himself) in a never-released motion picture about the chase.

12. This could be *Norfleet: The Actual Experiences of a Texas Rancher's 30,000 Mile Chase After Five Confidence Men,* by Norfleet himself (Fort Worth: W. F. White, 1924), or *Norfleet: The Amazing Experiences of an Intrepid Texas Rancher with an International Swindling Ring,* by Norfleet "as told to Gordon Hines" (Sugar Land, TX: Imperial Press, [c. 1927]).

13. REH must have heard an oral version of this story. The Judge's name was G. B. Gerald, and the Harris brothers were J. W. and W. A. Their gunfight on a downtown Waco street took place 19 November 1897.

14. William Cowper Brann (1855–1898), known as the "Iconoclast," became a newspaperman after moving to Texas from his home state of Illinois in 1886. After working at several papers, he founded *The Iconoclast,* "a monthly publication through which he proposed to combat hypocrisy, intolerance, and other evils." By 1897, monthly circulation in the U.S. and abroad had climbed to 98,000. Brann's attacks on the administration of Baylor University proved unpopular in Waco, provoking partisan violence. As he was preparing to leave on one of his frequent lecture tours, he and T. E. Davis mortally wounded each other in an encounter on a Waco street on 1 April 1898.

15. Dark Valley is a small community in Palo Pinto County, roughly 5 miles west of Graford, on the banks of Dark Valley Creek.

16. The story was based on comments made by HPL on Mongols in letter 4.

17. James Elroy Flecker (1884–1915), English poet, dramatist, and civil servant. His poem "Gates of Damascus" can be found in his *Collected Poems* (1916).

[16] [nonextant letter by H. P. Lovecraft]

[c. November 1930]

[17] [TLS]

[c. December 1930]

Dear Mr. Lovecraft:

As always, your letter proved highly enjoyable. I did indeed find the Recluse article most fascinating and instructive and look forward [to] its enlarged and republished form. Nothing that anyone else could write could possibly be better or more comprehensive in its scope. I highly appreciate your offer to lend me the Blackwood books and intend to take advantage of your kindness at some future date when my plans are not quite so uncertain as they are now. Thank you very much for the magazine with your story; I am certain that "The Picture in the House" will prove a real treat.

You're quite welcome to the "Red Thunder" business. I appreciate your comments on my verse and most certainly agree with you regarding the conventional unconventionalism of modern poets. Thats a point I've maintained for years—that these supposed exponents of radical freedom of thought and expression are serfs of conventions even more hide-bound and narrow and despotic than the old line. I am acquainted with a certain young and as yet unrecognized Texas poet whose work is superb—in spite of his views, I maintain, and not because of them—and this attitude is apparent in his every action; an excellent fellow when he forgets his superiority for a little, he is so infernally afraid that he'll appear human, he often makes himself obnoxious.[1] One shining example of tolerance and broad-mindedness among the moderns is my friend Ben Musser, a poet of no small note. Well—my rhyming isnt of sufficient importance for me to take it seriously, or to bind myself to any school or rule. I'm no poet but I was born with a knack of making little words rattle together and I've gotten a bit of pleasure from my jinglings. I'm willing to let the real poets grind out their images with blood and sweat, and to go through life piping lustily on my half-penny whistle. Poetizing's work and travail; rhyming's pleasure and holiday. I never devoted over thirty minutes to any rhyme in my life, though I've spent hours memorizing the poetry of other men.

I'm sure you would like San Antonio. I hope to spend a few months there and if I do I'll send you a lot of pictures of the place and the country thereabouts. The old Buckhorn Saloon is worth a trip to the city. Its full of heads and horns of buffalo, long horn steers, deer, elk, moose, rhinos, javelinas, walruses—every imaginable species. But the most interesting items are the snake rattles. It includes the biggest collection of rattles in the world. The counters and walls are decorated in designs made entirely of gilded snake rattles—literally thousands of them. Did you ever hear a rattler sing at you in the dark or among bushes, where you couldnt see him but knew he was somewhere within striking distance? Its the most blood chilling sound on earth. But the old Buckhorn—I can remember the days when it was in a big building and they sold hard liquor over the bar—it grates me now to see a Heinie behind the mahogany purveying kosher sandwiches.

Yes, the lower country is filling up with Latins and Polacks and even the Mexicans resent that fact. I remember the conversation of a certain Spanish-Italian desperado, one Chico the Desperate, whose real name was Marcheca, on the road to San Antonio, a few years ago. Chico was suspicious and reticent at first but soon warmed up and narrated his crimes with a gusto that kept me roaring with laughter. He was either a monumental liar or the most atrocious rogue unhung. But what amused me the most was his violent denunciations of the foreigners who were stealing the country! He was in favor of deporting all Germans, Polacks, and yea, even Italians! who had come over within the last generation and giving their land to natural Americans—including himself. He explained that the deportation of foreigners would not touch him, for though he was but one generation removed from Spain on the one side, on the other hand the Marchecas had been settled in America for three generations. Well—I'll freely grant an Englishman, Scotchman, Irishman or Welshman the right to become an American the instant his foot touches American soil, but as far as I'm concerned a wop or a Slav cant become American in five hundred years. But as for Chico's Spanish affinities, I dont believe I ever heard a Mexican admit he was anything but pure Castilian or Aragonese. His hair may be kinky or he may have the copper skin of a Yaqui but he will assure you that at least one of his very recent ancestors first saw light in Barcelona, Valladolid or old Seville.

A bull-fight was going to be broadcast today from, I think, Rio Nosa; thats one form of amusement I've never been able to induce myself to watch. I could stand the slaughter of the bulls but the disembowelling of the wretched worn-out horses would sicken me. The only inducement that would make me attend a bull-fight would be an absolute assurance that the bull would toss, rip open and dash the brains out of three or four spig toreadors. I would welcome such a spectacle with sincere gusto. There's a rotten streak in a nation that enjoys bull-fights. The Greasers come back with an indictment of prize-fighting and cock-fighting, but there is a difference. There is no comparison between pugilism and bull-fighting, and as for cock-fighting—well, its a fighting cock's nature to rip and kill, and a scrap between two well matched game chickens, armed with gaffs is comparatively short and painless—I've seen more sickening mutilations in barn-yard brawls than is usual in the fighting pit. But I am not upholding cock-fights; the law against it is one law I'd like to see enforced in Texas. But I do say its not as bestial as bull-fighting. Another thing that points to a weakening in the moral fibre of the American people is the interest which folks on the Border have been taking in such things of late—women as well as men, and not alone the idle rich. A bull-fight across the line draws crowds of eager Americans. And I note that certain adventurous Americans and Englishmen are going into the business—bad cess to them.

You are right in your denunciations of unrestricted immigration. I am sorry to hear that the old sturdy New England stock has been so swamped with aliens, and am glad to know that certain sections have held their own. You are fortunate in having lived in a district apart from the mongrel swarms. Your remarks about the eastern cities are highly interesting. My ideas about them, are of course, very vague, but I had noticed that in news items and the like pertaining to Philadelphia, Irish and English names seemed to predominate. I had heard, too, that the Old South is fairly free of foreign taint and am whole-heartedly glad to know that the homeland of my ancestors has escaped the overwhelming flood of alienism. I have never seen the South—the Deep South, beyond New Orleans, but I hope to visit it some day and to settle there, perhaps, and I would hate to see it swarmed over and violated by a low-browed foreign herd. I am sure Charleston is a beautiful city and would be a splendid place to live. I share your dislike for cold weather. So much so that I find this part of Texas unsuited for me. That is why I want to go to San Antonio—its two hundred miles south of here and much warmer. This Callahan Devide country isnt as cold as it is on the Plains, but its colder than I like. I'm not sure I'll ever be content this side of Mexico City. If I had my choice of residence, it would be there. I've never seen the place, but I've heard so much about it, the prospect is alluring.

As you say, the cases of Rome and America are curiously parallelled in regards to the foreign invasion, and your remarks on the subject made me realize that fact more than ever. When the barbarians finally broke into the empire, they found an unwieldy, cumbrous hulk, without identity or union, ready to topple at the first vigorous shove. Fortunately the tribes who finally trampled the crumbling lines, were of a young, vigorous race, capable of rebuilding what they had torn down, along more sturdy lines, perhaps. But now—where in all the world is there an unspoiled, hardy race of clean-blooded barbarians, fit to take the reins of the world when the older peoples decay? That great reservoir of strong, fresh races is exhausted; it seems to me that the last Aryan tribe to come into its own—the Russians—must eventually repeat the pages of history and conquer the civilized world, as all rising Aryan powers have done in the past. But it is a possibility which I contemplate with scant relish. There is too much Mongol blood in the veins of Russia for me to regard that nation as anything but alien.

Your contrast between Greece under Roman rule and the French-Canadians interested me very much. I had no idea the French in the New World had so completely resisted the advance of English culture and ideas. The people of Quebec must be a fascinating study.

I was also much interested in your remarks pertaining to the Assyrians and Turanians. True, the Assyrian nose is non-Turanian, and you are probably right in assuming that the resemblance between the Assyrian of yesterday and the Russian Jew of today can be traced to the Semitic relationship. The truly Semitic Jew is doubtless superior to the Mongoloid Jew in moral and cultural respects. However, the Mongoloid type seems to be the more aggressive of the two, judging from the great swarms of Jews now swamping the ranks of pugilism. Most Jewish fighters seem to have been born in Russia or Poland, or to have ancestral linkings with those countries, and they make, on the whole, skillful and courageous fighters.

I imagine that combination you mention—Semitic nose, Mongol eyes, Aryan hair, etc., produces a weird effect, even more so than the red headed niggers you occasionally see in the South. The most inhuman hybrid I ever saw was standing in the door of a laundry shop not far off Canal Street, in New Orleans. He—or it!—was as black as any negro I ever saw, but had the slant eyes and broad features of a Chinaman. He even wore a pigtail and had his hands in the wide sleeves of a typically Chinese outfit.

Your comments on the Carthaginian-Jewish subject proved most instructive to me, as it presented a phase of history entirely new to me. I have badly neglected informing myself on that subject and didnt even know that the Carthaginians became Judaised. If I had thought at all about it, I would have vaguely supposed that the Romans completely exterminated the Punic race. The Arab too, as you say, is doubtless of mixed breed; it seems to me as if the men of Yemen claim descent from conquering Persians of Cyrus' time, do they not? The Moorish subject too, is a fascinating one, and it is no doubt that their culture was of a high quality. And the Berbers—there's an interesting race, and an ancient one. Somewhere I seem to have read that their ancestors were fair haired and light eyed and lived in caves along the coast country of what is now the Barbary States.

I think Wright's "Oriental Stories" bids fair to show more originality than the average magazine dealing with the East, though the initial issue was, to me, slightly dissappointing—not in the appearance of the magazine but in the contents. However, with such writers as Hoffman-Price, Owens and Kline, I look for better things. I particularly hope that you will find it convenient to contribute to the magazine, since with your magnificent talents and your sincere interest in things Oriental, you should turn out some splendid work. Mr. Wright tells me that my "Voice of El-lil" has so far tied another story for first place. I hope you like the tale.

Mr. Wright tells me that the issuing of "Strange Stories" is being delayed because of Macfadden's disputing the right to the title. Several months ago he accepted a couple of my tales for the magazine, one of them dealing with the Bran-cult,[2] and I would like to see the publication on the newsstands.

Doubtless you are right in your theory that the easy life of the tropics contributed to the negro's lack of progress. As we know, the tropical countries can play havoc with the higher races, and make a beach-comber out of an aristocrat sometimes. Returning to the Eastern question, I too have been somewhat disgusted at the efforts of various writers to portray a conventionalized Orient. Especially the occultism of the East; Kipling, Mundy, a few others, they can write convincingly of Oriental mysticism; not many others that I have read after. For my part the mystic phase of the East has always interested me less than the material side—the red and royal panorama of war, rapine and conquest. What I write for "Oriental Stories" will be purely action, and romance—mainly historical tales. And I greatly fear that my Turks and Mongols are merely Irishmen and Englishmen in turbans and sandals!

Speaking of Arabian Nights, one of my first books was a copy of that great work—I was six, I believe.

The civilization you mention on the African east coast must have been a very mixed one—possibly an invading settlement of Hamitic conquerors, with a substratum of black aborigines; the whole modified more or less by a filtration of Semites from the east. What noble speculations the matter brings up! With a mingling of such passionate bloods as these, what violent intrigues, what plots and counter-plots, what savage crimes and what dark murders must have shaken the walls and palaces of that vanished civilization! I agree with you in doubting that the seeds of cultural development are present in the negroid race as a whole. They can ape and copy but that they could build a civilization on their own, I doubt.

Returning to the non-negroid blacks of East Africa, is it not supposed that the Elamites were an Australoid or negroid type? If so, is it not possible that they represented a branch of that East African amalgamation—perhaps a mixed race of Australoid and Hamitic or Semitic blood. Or they might have been a distinct type, approximating the black skinned, thin lipped, highly developed type you describe—Dravidian, perhaps, since I believe certain authorities tend toward the theory of a wide drift of Dravidian peoples extending from India to Egypt in very early times. Well, I'm not well enough informed in these matters to speculate, but I heartily agree with your remark that Africa offers a rich field for fantastic fiction.

The image you sketched is most intriguing in its implication of antiquity and its prehistoric possibilities, and I hope you'll make a story of it some day.

The legend of the bleeding rock in Ireland, is briefly, that Saint Moling changed the wife of Goban Saer, and a companion into stones; these stones are pointed out in Curraun townland, parish of Saint Mullins, in the barony of Bantry, County Wexford, and are known as Raimreach Ruadh; once, it is said, a blacksmith cut three grooves in the larger stone to blast it, whereupon blood oozed from the grooves, and the people decided that Red Raimreach was still alive and her blood circulating through the stone to which she had been changed.

The corpse in the range-cow's carcass was a ghastly business. I have not read the books by Gorman you mention[3] but the titles sound intriguing. The witch-cult offers great possibilities, in itself, and a writer need not tie himself down to the actual limits of the thing. Why should the cult be merely a fertility worship?—Why should it not have deeper, darker significance, dating from pre-human memories?—In fiction, at least!

Your analysis of the Celtic nature is correct, as far as I can see. After all—where does reality quit off and unreality begin? We know that we cannot trust our external senses—why should we imagine that we can trust our inner promptings, impressions and senses? When we are dead it is as if we have never lived, therefore, how can we be sure that we live? I remember a most curious dream I had when a child that I have remembered long after I have forgotten the tang of stolen fruit and the feel of the morning dew on my bare feet. I dreamed that I slept and awoke, and when I awoke a boy and a girl about my age were playing near me. They were small and trimly shaped, with very dark skin and dark eyes. Their garments were scanty, and strange to me, now that I remember them, but at the time they were not strange, for I too was clad like them, and I too was small and delicately fashioned and dark. I had been sleeping on a sort of couch, richly made, which stood on a wide porch or room—I am not sure now. But if it were a room it had many wide windows without panes, and it seems that there were large columns. The room or porch looked out over a green and beautiful landscape of trees and grass grown hills sloping to a wide bay, glittering blue in the sunlight. Now, as I woke in my dream, this scene was fully familiar to me, and I knew that the boy and the girl were my brother and sister. It was not as if I had gone to sleep and awakened in a strange world; it was as if I had merely wakened from a sleep, returning to my natural, work-a-day world. And suddenly in my dream, I began to laugh and to narrate to my brother and my sister the strange dream I had had. And I told them of what—if there is any truth at all in reality—constituted my actual waking life. I described to them, as a vivid dream, my waking life, but could not put it clearly because it seemed dim and vague, as a dream seems dim and vague when one awakes. I told them that my dream had seemed so vivid while dreaming it, that I had actually thought it to be real, and believed myself to be a stocky blond child living a waking life, without knowledge of any other. And I said that I was glad I had awakened because that dream life had not been a good one, but full of strange barbarisms and roughness. Then they laughed and I awoke in reality—or slept again, I have occasionally wondered which! On which side of the gulf of dreams do we walk, and do we sleep when we think we wake?

But even when all life seems like a dream to us, the unreality of our triumphs and pleasures, which fade like autumn clouds, cannot soften and blunt the sharps pains of life—it is in pain that the material hard cold reality of the universe is most plain to us. What if we are but things of mist and shadow? Because we can suffer so, our pains are real, and we might as well be solid fleshly things such as the realists tell us we are. There is no refuge in idealism.

I am glad you liked "Reuben's Brethren." It has never been published save in a small privately circulated paper.[4]

I am glad too, that you are so well inclined toward the South. Her past and her traditions are close to my heart, though I would be a stranger within her gates. But my people settled and helped build her greatness and they shared her fall and ruin. Blood like that in my own veins was spilled like water from Manasses to Appomattox, and I still have kinsmen scattered all over the old states.

I am glad that there is a revival of genealogical interest in New England. In these days of Slavic-Latin invasion the old stock does well to turn an eye toward the land from which they came and remember the royalty of their breed. You say that most of the people of Rhode Island came from Lincolnshire, I believe—a shire that has always sent out sturdy sons. And your people came in 1630—you certainly have a right to call yourself an American, if anyone does! Exactly three hundred years since your family settled in the New World.

I have read of Albert Marbin and his heroic expedition.[5] In those days men put honor above their lives and he well knew that to enter the Alamo meant his doom. But he went clear-eyed to his fate, and died like a true Aryan, taking more than a life for a life. There were more than a few sons of New England who helped bring into birth the Republic of Texas—Stephen F. Austin,[6] for instance, who in his way did as much for the struggling nation as Sam Houston did.

Speaking of Stonehenge, doubtless the Celts did erect it, but as you say, we need not confine ourselves to actuality in our dealings with it.

You are certainly correct about the standardism of America, and the merging of local individualisms. The great majority of people seem to look on this standardization with complacent approval. Not me; I seem to see the country assuming a drab and colorless uniformity without even a distinctive dialect—unless it is the Yiddish oi oi babble. But I think that even so the country will prove too unwieldy to survive. One part of the nation is exploited by men who live in another part. As the southwest has for years been exploited by oil companies and cattle and grain companies whose heads are located in New York or Chicago. Such concerns drain the money out of the country and bring nothing in. Oh, they pay wages of course, but in the case of the oil companies, a great majority of the workers are not native Texans, but Pennsylvanians, Kansans, and Indianans brought in by the promoters. This was especially so in the early days of oil development. Recently I seem to sense a slight stirring of sectional feeling; a certain class is growing in the southwest, not determined by race or business, which centers a real dislike upon the capitalist city of New York, and this dislike is growing into a real hatred. A small beginning, it is true, but it looks like a beginning to me. You see, for instance, men leave their farms and go work in the oil fields; the first wells drilled are almost invariably the property of small promoters; the big companies wont take any risks. They leave the wildcatting to the little fellows. Then when the field is going in full blast, they come in and start grabbing. Maybe there is an oil war on, or they want to freeze somebody out. They shut down the field and leave hundreds of men out of a job. The farms have been ruined by the oil boom and there's nothing to do but pack up and move on to some other field. This is the ruination of this country.

Then the juggling of the wheat and cotton and beef markets works real hardships on the farming class. All these things are beginning to be ascribed, more or less correctly, to Wall Street and New York.

Personally, I believe it would have been better for America to have been devided into several parts; say four sections, compromising the South, North, Northwest and Southwest. They could have been closely united by treaties and affinities of language and racial stock, so as to offer a compact front to any European invader, while developing each along its own natural lines. By the medium of trade, money would have flowed freely back and forth across the frontiers, stimulating prosperity, and one section would not suffer from asinine laws passed in another. Oh well, I dont know enough economics and politics to venture such propositions. But that dream of a Southwest empire from Blanca Peak to Panama makes my mouth water.

No, the founders of Texas had little idea of making a separate Republic out of the vast lands they wrested from the Latins. Old Hickory sent Sam Houston to Texas to add that country on to the United States, and most of the Texans clamored for admittance into the Union. But some of the far-sighted ones, Houston among others, held in their minds that lost dream of empire—well, it wasnt to be.

You are right—economics will have to [be] revolutionized entirely if the nation is to continue, and the choice seems to lie between fascism and communism—both of which I utterly detest. And doubtless the world will eventually, as you say, sink back into barbarism—if any humans are left alive after the next war. And since the inevitable goal of all civilization seems to be decadence, it seems hardly worth while to struggle up the long road from barbarism in the first place.

I'm glad you found my ramblings regarding Texas not too boresome. It is almost an empire in itself, and I look with real fury on the suggestion of dividing it into several states, though probably it would be an advantage to the Southwest politically. There are so many different kinds of landscapes in the state, though I must admit that a great percent of the scenery is utterly drab and without interest. Still, there are contrasts, and I can think of no more striking one than the sight that meets one's eyes when entering the Rio Grande valley on the Falfurrias-Edinburg road. The way lies seventy miles through level monotonous waste-land—an arid, sandy desert, grown scantily with grease-wood bushes and chaparrel, unrelieved by any hill, tree or stream—then without warning you ride out of the desert edge into the irrigated belt. Abruptly the whole scene changes; green fields, with broad irrigation ditches winding through them lie smiling in the sun, and blossoming orange-groves wave in the soft breeze; the road becomes an avenue of palms, flanked on either hand by the tall straight trees with their broad leaves whispering in the wind—and the little towns are so thick you can see from one to the other, almost, looking straight down the unwinding road—at least, that was the valley six years ago. I hear it has changed a great deal since then, but I am sure that the great floods of people pouring in, have not changed the general scenery much. Gad—I realized when I first saw it, how the Israelites must have felt when they first looked on Canaan after their wanderings in the desert.

There is another interesting but rather depressing phase of Texas in that region between San Antonio and Eagle Pass. In a certain section they raise little but onions and they plant onions as upper country farmers plant cotton—by the hundreds of acres. They have no water on top of the ground and a great many small oil promoters from my part of the country have gone there with their "spudders"—movable rigs for shallow wells—and made a bit of money drilling for water for irrigation. Ye gods—what a country! It isnt exactly flat, but rather rolling and bald as any desert, minus the sand. You can stand on a slight rise and see exactly the same thing stretching out to the horizon on every hand. It creates a most bewildering impression—its surprizing how easily you can get turned around and completely lost, in a country where you can see for forty miles. Its worse than a level desert; besides it all looks just alike—you get mixed up in directions and things you see at a distance dont turn out to be where they seem. No fences, no trees, no cattle; just a few houses here and there baking in the hot sun and a few rigs pounding away—it gives an impression of utter desolation, worse than a desert, because buzzards fly over a desert and horned toads and snakes wriggle in the sand. Yet almost all of that dreary and lonely land is sown with onions! They werent up when I was there and the landscape didnt look like any human being had ever laid a plough to it. There a mesquite tree looks like an oasis.

There are so many different phases of the state that people living in part of it are almost like foreigners to those living in another part. For instance, many folks living in East Texas regard West Texans much as, say, a New Yorker regards the people of Colorado and consider them to be a sort of cross between a cowpuncher and a Comanche. I travelled a couple of hundreds miles east of here since writing you before, and a citizen of the locality learning where I was from, he gazed on me with great interest exclaiming that I was indeed from the wild and woolly west! It seems that East Texans tend to roam east and south, and West Texans mainly travel westward—while a great percent of the population wanders all over the state and spills over into New Mexico, Arizona and California. I have never been to California but I hear that there is a great deal of prejudice in that state against Texans, just as there is in Kansas and Oklahoma—Kansas prejudice dating back to the days when Texas cowboys took the big trail herds up the old Chisholm to Abilene, and shot up the town to celebrate. Well—it wasn't such a hell of a town that the Kansans had to get snooty about it. Admitting that the Texas puncher of the old days was a dangerous and boisterous varmint, still when the boys had hazed a herd of longhorns up from the Border, through flooded rivers, blizzards, deserts and hostile Indian country, it was natural that they'd want to blow off steam. Abilene owes its very existence to the big Texas herds that flowed through it to the markets of Chicago and the East.

One branch of the old Chisholm trail ran within about thirty miles of this town, and the early squatters in this country subsisted mainly on strays that somehow got left in their brush corrals after the herds had gone on. But it was dangerous business; the punchers disliked having their steers swiped and they didnt like squatters anyhow. But gad, everybody stole cows in those days. All the big ranches were built or at least aided materially with running irons and mavericks. The big cattlemen who hanged rustlers were generally just as much thieves as the men they strung up; it was big business devouring the little, and the small-time promoter paying the penalty for his puniness.

The fiercest fights were between sheepmen and cattlemen and later between the small farmer and the ranchmen. That last was a bitter war, carried on with neither honor, mercy or human consideration. Ranchmen cut the squatter's fences, burned his buildings, and frequently wiped out whole families, men, women and children with no more hesitation than Comanche Indians would have shown. In return the squatter stole the ranchman's cattle and killed them on the sly, fouled the springs, dammed up the streams, dynamited dams on ranchmen's property, ambushed cowboys and shot them out of their saddles—and made laws. Thats the way they licked the cattlemen—by legislation. They simply swarmed in and took the country, swamping the original settlers just as they, in turn, had swamped the Indians in an earlier age. One of the worst of all cattlemen was an Englishman who lived in Concho country; his worst—and last—crime came about this way; finding that a young man he didnt fancy, was writing letters to his daughter, he took a crushing revenge and killed the postman who delivered the letters! He made a sweeping gesture of it by sending word to the sheriff, who was kin to the slaughtered postman, that he intended killing him too, on general principles—a bad move—the sheriff killed him instead. That all happened only a few years ago.

One could write a book from the tales told of Sonora alone, a sleepy little town of a few hundred inhabitants lying in the hills about a hundred miles from the Border. For instance, a good many years ago, a young cowpuncher went on the rampage up in Wyoming and started smoking his way to the

Border. I dont know what started him on the tear—maybe a girl went back on him, or red liquor ran him crazy—anyway he came south like a sandstorm, leaving a trail of shot-up towns and bullet-riddled marshals and sheriffs behind him. That went alright as long as he was in Wyoming, Colorado and New Mexico, but the Texans of that day were a hard, hard breed. He rode up on the hills about Sonora one day and started throwing rifle bullets into the streets. Everybody scattered, not thinking much about it, but supposing it was just some local puncher in on a tear. But he got hold of somebody and sent word that he would ride into the town at a certain hour for supplies and he ordered the stores left open and the streets deserted—he would kill any man, woman or child he saw in the town. And he most certainly meant it. At the hour named he rode down the street and saw no living soul. The stores were open but they were deserted. He dismounted and entered. No one behind the counters. He began filling his saddle-bags with groceries—and the town marshal appeared at one door and the county judge at the other. When the smoke cleared away all three were down—the Wyoming man stone dead and the other two badly wounded, though they recovered.

Then once, up in Oklahoma, a young puncher stole an old ranchman's daughter and they rode hell-for-leather for the Border, with the old man hot on their heels. Another hundred miles and they might have been safe, but the old man caught up with them and killed them both just outside Sonora.

With the passing of open range one picturesque type has practically vanished—the range tramp. He was indeed a hobo but a more cleanly type than the ordinary wandering Willie. He worked for his living, but he did not need much nor did he work long or stay long in any one place. He drifted up and down the ranges from Mexico to Canada, and from the Canadian River to the Coast; his sole belongings were a broom tailed broncho, a worn old saddle and the clothes he wore. There were no fences to bother him and he need not stay in beaten trails. He grazed his mustang in the tall lush grass and slept under the stars. He was sure of a meal for himself and the bronc at any ranch-house he stopped at, and when he needed a little money he stopped a few days and lent a hand at round-up or corral-building. He gambled a little, drank a little, played the painted ladies a little, but his love for these things could never make him settle down to the thirty-a-month grind of the average cowhand. He shunned trouble but was generally deadly when cornered. He drifted across the ranges, a lazy and good-natured ghost that came at dusk and went at dawn, and he never settled down until the coyotes picked his bones. He was not troubled with policemen and vice squads; he was not forced to tramp through dusty highways, or ride the rods, or gorge on mulligan in a lousy, vermin-ridden jungle. He had it over the modern city-going tramp a hundred ways and when I reflect on his nomadic and care-free life, I wish I had been born forty years ago.

Well, Texas is swiftly becoming modernized to suit the standards of big business; very seldom you even hear any of the old range songs any more—"Sam Bass", "The Killing of Jesse James", "The Old Chisholm Trail", "Utah Charlie", "San Antonio", "The Ranger."

But Texas was never as prolific in the matter of songs as Arkansaw, for instance. In the Scotch-Irish settlement of Holly Springs where William Benjamin Howard settled in 1858, they still sang songs that carried the tang of the heather, though the singers were generations removed from the old country. Forty years ago such songs were popular there, as "Barbary Allen", "William Hall, a young Highlander", "The Wearin' of the Green", "Little Susie, the pride of Kildare", "Shamus O'Brien", one the name of which I forget but it had to do with the elopement of "pretty Polly" with one "Lord Thomas" who had drowned "six king's daughters", "Caroline, the Belle of Edinburgh-town," and one which began

"Young Johnny's been on sea,
Young Johnny's been on shore,
Young Johnny he's in New Orleans
Where he has been before."

Narrating the triumph of a prosperous young sailor over an avaricious landlady. Then there was another, the name of which I do not know, but it contained the lines

"Oh, come to me arms, Nora darlint,
Bid your frinds and ould companions good-boi,
For its happy we will be in thot dear land
av the free,
Livin' happily wid Barney McCoy."

Then there was one which must be very old, dealing with "Fair Elinor,[''] "Lord Thomas" and "the brown girl". Lord Thomas married the brown girl because of her wealth, but invited Fair Elinor to the banquet, where the jealous brown girl killed her with "a wee pen-knife." Thus the horrific climax!:

"Lord Thomas having a Hielan' sword,
It being sharp and small,
He cut off the brown girl's head
And threw it against the wall!"

But doubtless you know the old ballad. Such were the songs sung by the people who came from Mississippi and the Carolinas and Georgia to build a homeland in the piney-woods of southwestern Arkansaw. Squire James Henry was among the first to hew a clearing and build a house, and after him came the Howards, the Laffertys, the Burkes, the Houses, the Sinquefields, the Goodgames, the

Goings, the Drakes, the Hulsemans, the Proctors, the Sullivans, the O'Briens, the Ellises, the Deans, the Hastings—southwestern Arkansaw was a virgin wilderness in the 1850's—thick pine woods that had never known an axe, rich land beneath them, bear and deer in plenty. The settlers were responsible to no one. A few like Squire Henry had money in Arkansaw's one bank, in Little Rock. Most of the rest seldom saw a coin. They didnt need it; they raised or took from the woods what they needed. Waves of war washed back and forth across the piney-woods, and nearly devastated the country, but it recovered from the devastation quicker than other parts, because the people were more hardy and primitive. Forty years ago they were giving "sheep saffron" and "chicken saffron" for "aggers" in Arkansaw—tea made from dried sheep and chicken dung. Fires were banked in the wide fireplaces at night to keep the coals glowing, for matches were practically unknown.

Lumber mills came at a comparatively late date; when my grandmother came to Texas in '85 she sold large tracts of fine pine land for fifty cents an acre and thought it a good bargain. The buyers have become rich from it. The first usage of the land was agriculture; the larger cotton raisers like my great-grandfather, Squire Henry, took their cotton down to New Orleans on steamboats by way of the Ouachita, the Red River and the Mississippi. The Squire didnt share in the general ruin of Southern planters because, after he was discharged from his regiment in the first year of the war because of old age and wounds, he came to Texas with his niggers and for three years he raised and stored cotton. After the war was over, he went back to Arkansaw and went into business with the money resultant from the sale of that cotton. He slipped one over Abe Lincoln that time, because the emancipation meant nothing to his niggers and they didnt get their freedom till after the war was well over, and they'd already built the foundations of the Squire's fortune. But if he drove them like a madman, he protected them, and years afterward, when he was past seventy, he fought one of the most desperate men in the country with his naked fists, for bullying his niggers.

Probably the most picturesque figure in the Holly Springs country was Kelly the "conjer man",[7] who held sway among the black population in the '70s. Son of a Congo ju-ju man was Kelly, and he dwelt apart from his race in silent majesty on the river. He must have been a magnificent brute, tall and supple as a black tiger, and with a silent haughtiness of manner that included whites as well as blacks. He had little to say and was not given to idle conversation. He did no work, nor did he ever take a mate, living in mysterious solitude. He always wore a red shirt, and large brass ear-rings in his ears added to the color of his appearance. He lifted "conjers" and healed disease by incantation and nameless things made of herbs and ground snake-bones. The black people called him Doctor Kelly and his first business was healing. Later he began to branch into darker practices. Niggers came to him to have spells removed, that enemies had placed on them, and the manner of his removal must have been horrific, judging from the wild tales that circulated afterwards. Consumption was unknown there, almost, among whites, but negroes had it plentifully and Kelly professed to cure such victims by cutting open their arms and sifting in a powder made of ground snake-bones. At last negroes began to go insane from his practices; whether the cause was physical or mental is unknown to this day, but the black population came to fear him as they did not fear the Devil, and Kelly assumed more and more a brooding, satanic aspect of dark majesty and sinister power; when he began casting his brooding eyes on white folk as if their souls, too, were his to dandle in the hollow of his hand, he sealed his doom. There were desperate characters living in the riverlands, white folks little above the negro in civilization, and much more dangerous and aggressive. They began to fear the conjure man and one night he vanished. Nor is it difficult to picture what happened in that lonely cabin, shadowed by the pine forest—the crack of a shot in the night, the finishing stroke of a knife, then a sullen splash in the dusky waters of the Ouachita—and Kelly the conjure man vanished forever from the eyes of men.

Arkansaw had many noted fighting-men in those days, who fought for the fun of it, as bears fight, making a carnival of blood-shed at every log-rolling, dance or frolic, but as it happens, the greatest fighting man of southwestern Arkansaw was not a native of that state—he came into Holly Springs one day, bare-footed, black-bearded, limping from a bullet-wound in his leg—a present from certain revenue officers who objected to his brewing of mountain-dew on his own land at Sand Mountain, in Georgia. He married a second cousin of mine and to the best of my knowledge there never was a man that licked him, even when he had a gallon of whiskey in him. He was nearly seven feet tall and built in due proportions. By trade he was a wagon-maker and his labor with the mallet gave his huge arms a hitting power that was far too much for the kicking and gouging of the ordinary rough-and-tumble fighter.

And speaking of mountain-dew, again we have big business devouring the small-scale producer. Why did the revenue men go into the hills and hunt down men who were merely seeking to augment their fearfully barren lives with a little hard money on the side? To protect the big liquor corporations! Why, the white liquor made by Southern mountaineers was generally far superior to anything the bar-keep shoved across the bar, but the makers seldom had the money to buy any sort of a license to manufacture or sell whiskey. Not infrequently the best customers the moonshiners had were owners of saloons. The mountain-men would raft their produce down to the river towns—corn, a little cotton maybe, coon and possum and wolf and bear skins—an innocent looking cargo, and certainly no room on a flat raft to conceal contraband. But underneath the raft, fastened firmly to the bottom, were kegs and barrels of good white corn liquor. By day the "upper" cargo was unloaded and sold, and late that night the "lower" cargo was slipped ashore to the saloons on the river bank. The liquor was carefully concealed, allowed to age a few months, colored, bottled and sold across the bar as labelled Bourbon, Haig & Haig, Scotch, or what have you! And at about three hundred percent profit for the saloon man. But the customers werent cheated; it was good, pure whiskey, not to be compared for an instant with the muck modern bootleggers make.

You're right about oil booms—they bring a lot of money into the country and take more out, as well as ruining the country for other purposes. This might offend men in the oil business, but its the truth that I've seen more young people sent to the Devil through the debauching effects of an oil boom than all the other reasons put together. I know; I was a kid in a boom town myself. The average child of ten or twelve who's lived through a boom or so knows more vileness and bestial sinfulness than a man of thirty should know—whether he—or she—practice what they know or not. Glamor and filth! Thats an oil boom. When I was a kid I worked in the tailoring business just as one terrific boom was dwindling out, and harlots used to give me dresses to be cleaned—sometimes they'd be in a mess from the wearer having been drunk and in the gutter. Beautiful silk and lace, delicate of texture and workmanship, but disgustingly soiled—such dresses always symbolized boom days and nights, to me—shimmering, tantalizing, alluring things, bright as dreams, but stained with nameless filth.

The shimmer and the filth were lacking in the old days, when men and women were more or less clean-lived and primitively-hardy. Some day I'd like to write a chronicle of the Southwest as it appears to me, but I don't suppose I could handle the thing properly. Well, if I never write it, at least people of my blood had a hand in making it—which is infinitely better than unromantically writing down the deeds of other men. Kinsmen of mine were among the riflemen at King's Mountain, and with Old Hickory at New Orleans; I had three great-uncles in the '49 gold rush—a Howard and two Martins—the Howard settled in Sonora, California, and one of the Martins left his bones on the trail—both my grandfathers rode for four years with Bedford Forrest, and I had a great-grandfather in the Confederate Army too, as well as a number of great-uncles—one died in a nameless skirmish in the Wilderness and another fell in the battle of Macon, Georgia; my grandfather Colonel George Ervin came into Texas when it was wild and raw, and he went into New Mexico, too, long before it was a state, and worked a silver mine—and once he rode like a bat out of Hell for the Texas line with old Geronimo's turbaned Apaches on his trail; an aunt of mine married and went into the Indian Territory to live years before the government ever opened the land for settlers; and one of my uncles, too, settled in what is now Oklahoma, in its wildest days, when it swarmed with half-wild Indians and murderous renegades from half-a-dozen states.

Colonel Ervin once owned a great deal of property in what is now a very prosperous section of Dallas, and might have grown with the town, but for the whippoorwills. They almost drove him crazy with their incessant calling, and though he was a kindly man with beasts and birds, and killed men with less remorse than he killed animals, in a fit of passion one night, he shot three whippoorwills; it was flying in the face of tradition and he quickly regretted it, but the damage was done. According to legend, you know, human life must pay for the blood of a whippoorwill, and soon the Colonel's family began to die, at the average of one a year, exactly as the old black people prophesied. He stuck it out five years and then, with five of his big family dead, he gave it up. No one ever accused him of cowardice; he hacked his way alone, through a cordon of Phil Sheriden's cavalry-men; but the whippoorwills licked him. He sold his Dallas property for a song, went west and bought a sheep-ranch. Of course, Dallas was a swamp then, and very sickly. Still, its not wise to kill a whippoorwill. Screech owls are about as bad; but you can stop a screech owl's screeching by taking off your left shoe, turning it upside down, and then putting it back on at once. A funny thing, but it works every time. Of course, the owl only screeches so long, and by the time you've made up your mind to try the old superstition, and have done it, the owl is through and flown off.

I've received the magazine since writing the first part of this letter, and have read your story and article with keenest interest.[8] The tale lives up to my expectations; indeed you have never, in any later story, I think, created a more masterful atmosphere of almost intolerable ghastliness. I cannot praise the story too highly; it shows, as do all your tales, the master's touch. And I enjoyed your philosophical article very much. I am hardly capable of judging it, since I never devoted any study to theology, philosophy or science, but I do not think that anyone could have handled the subject in a more masterly manner. I particularly like the point you made in that truth and necessity not always coinciding, some religion is necessary for the masses. I have always maintained this, myself. As for myself, neither idealism nor materialism appeals to me greatly. That life is chaotic, unjust and apparently blind and without reason or direction any one can see; if the universe leans either way it is toward evil rather than good, as regards life and humanity. That there is any eventual goal for the human race rather than extinction, I do not believe nor do I have any faith in the eventual super-man. Yet the trend of so many materialists to suppress all primitive emotions is against my every instinct. Civilization, no doubt, requires it, and peace of mind demands it, yet for myself I had rather be dead than to live in an emotionless world. The clear white lamp of science and the passionless pursuit of knowledge are not enough for me; I must live deeply and listen to the call of the common clay in me, if I am to live at all. Without emotion and instinct I would be a dead, stagnant thing.

A materialistic resignation to unalterable laws is sensible but repellant to me. I will freely admit the necessity and desirability of such a resignation which is no more than recognizing natural laws—if such things be. A man who does not resign himself is like a caged wolf who breaks his heart and beats his brains out against the bars of his cage. Yet I must admit that such a course appeals to me more than that of calm submission. Foredoomed to failure, a man can still snarl and tear. Many and many a time, when one is reeling and dizzy and sick at heart and soul, broken and tossed by the blows of fate or destiny or whatever it is that makes life a hell on earth, one may wish for the ability of philosophic resignation; but with a slight renewal of strength the old blind fighting lust comes surging back and makes him break his fangs on the iron bars anew.

I'm no philosopher, but resignation isnt in my blood. I wish it was. It isnt necessarily a hope to win that makes a man rebel against the infamies of life, vainly. Defeat is the lot of all men, and I come of a breed that never won a war. Men and women too, of my line have fought for hopeless lost causes for a thousand years. Defeat waits for us all, but some of us, worse luck, cant accept it quietly.

Life reminds me of a fight I had, when a kid, with a heavyweight prize fighter. Round after round I rushed savagely and futiley, mad to come to grips and smash his ribs in, but hitting only the naked air. It was like fighting a shadow that wielded clubs; at the end of the fight I was swaying on the ropes groggy and dizzy, with my nose broken and my face cut and bruised, sick with a feeling of utterly helpless futility. Thats Life—its full of things that punish you fiercely and that you cant come to grips with. Punishment isnt so bad if you're handing it out at the same time. The other fellow may be strangling the life out of you, or ripping your ear off with his teeth, but if you're driving your knee to his groin, sinking your fists in his belly or have your thumb in his eye, you can stand the punishment. The hell of it comes when you're up against a battler you cant hit, or are licked and down in the muck with the other fellow stamping your guts out or grinding your face in with his hob-nails. Thats Life—fighting shadows; taking lickings that you cant return.

But here I'm rambling on and on without coherency or connection. Thanks very much for giving me the tip about Talman.[9] I cant place Frio Canyon just now, though it seems I've heard of it. It's probably in the Davis Mountain country; I've never been in that part of Texas.[10] Your comments on your early environs—thickly settled district on one hand and country-side on the other—intrigue my imagination; it must have been much like living on the threshold of the older and newer ages, with a clear insight to both. You looked back into the pioneering youth of the country and forward into its maturity. And the cultural history and architectural age of your environments has undoubtedly contributed to your splendid literary back-ground. I envy you them.

Best wishes—cordially yours,
Robert E. Howard

P. S. I've received a letter from Talman, regarding contributions to his paper; he says you suggested my name to him, and I wish to express as much as I can, my sincere appreciation of that fact. I am indeed deeply grateful to you. I'm glad you liked "Kings of the Night", also; I hope that your "Whisperer in Darkness" will be swiftly followed by many other tales; I can hardly wait for it!

Notes

1. Probably REH's friend Tevis Clyde Smith.

2. "The Dark Man," accepted for the magazine, finally appeared in *WT* (December 1931).

3. Probably Herbert S. Gorman (1893–1954), literary critic and biographer, and author of the weird novel *The Place Called Dagon* (1927). HPL was not in the habit of recommending other titles by Gorman.

4. *The Junto.*

5. Albert Martin (1808–1836), of Rhode Island, a defender of the Alamo.

6. Stephen F. Austin's father, Moses, was born and reared in Connecticut, where Stephen, born in Virginia and raised in Missouri, attended private schools for four years.

7. Kelly was the subject of REH's article "Kelly the Conjure-Man." REH had written it for the *Texaco Star* but it was rejected; see n. 9 on "The Ghost of Camp Colorado," which the magazine accepted. Kelly was the basis for Saul Stark in REH's "Black Canaan."

8 "Idealism and Materialism—A Reflection," published in the same issue of the *National Amateur* ("July 1919") that contained "The Picture in the House."

9. The "tip" (see postscript) regarded the *Texaco Star*, the house organ of the company for which Talman worked. This led to the publication of REH's article, "The Ghost of Camp Colorado" (April 1931), and to a continuing correspondence between the two men.

10. The canyon of the Frio River is located southwest of San Antonio, not in the Davis Mountain country of far West Texas.

[18] [non-extant letter by H. P. Lovecraft]

[late 1930 or early 1931]

1931

[19] [TLS]

[c. January 1931]

Dear Mr. Lovecraft:

As always I found your recent letter most interesting and instructive. Your comments on pioneering gave me a new and fascinating slant on the thing as a whole, making me realize that after all, the pioneering and settling of a new wild country is a reversion to the primitive Aryan type of life. This fact is obvious, yet I had never so fully realized it before. Since reading your letter I realize too how closely New England and the South are knit to England. It is a rather fascinating thought somehow, to think of men in England planning and mapping out towns across the ocean in a wilderness they never looked on. Doubtless the West has passed through a more truly primitive pioneering epoch, but you folks of the New England states and the South had the enormous advantage of an epoch we have not had and will not have. You had the advantages of a settled and mature cultural civilization before the rise of the present machine-ruled age. You had a period of cultural developement during which your ships plied the high seas bringing the wealth of foreign ports, and the arts of poetry, literature, architecture and so on, acquired solid foundation and had the opportunity to flourish and blossom. Even now, in this helter-skelter age, I believe that New England, as represented by its older and purer element at least, presents a more firmly grounded bulwark of the deep solid principles and ideals that once characterized this Anglo-American civilization, than can be found anywhere else, and will resist the senseless wholesale exploitation of mechanized modernism longer than any other part of the country. I may be wrong, as I have never had the opportunity to observe conditions first hand, but that is the impression I get.

The Southwest and West on the other hand, have never had the time to develope a cultural civilization of their own. The transition from primitive pioneering times to the machine age is almost unbroken. Westerners have not had and will not have time to develope any real civilization, founded on cultural ideals and principles, before the rise of the mechanized epoch. What past of that sort the Southwest and West can boast, is now symbolized by the crumbling walls of old Spanish missions—mute reminders of the lazy, colorful and romantic days of Spanish rule in California and Texas, when gay clad caballeros diced and flirted and raced horses and duelled in the shadow of those missions, and within their cool drowsy shelters, monks and priests toiled at neatly written manuscripts, and decorated the walls with delicate hand-painted and hand-carved patterns. No, pioneer life was somewhat inspiring, was hardy and clean, but it was fiercely barren, too, and had the effect of making men and women so brutally practical that most of the latent poetry and artistic instinct was ground out of their souls—and then before their descendents could develope, as you all in New England developed, a cultural civilization with distinctive standards, the machine age was—or is—dominant.

I am very glad you liked The Voice of El-lil and sincerely appreciate the kind things you said about the tale. You're right, of course, about the Asia Minor business. Using the term to designate Mesopotamia was sheer carelessness in me. I'm afraid you'll find my work riddled with errors like that. I have a slovenly way of not stopping to look up references when I'm writing. But my erroneous use of Asia Minor was really inexcusable and I'm glad you called my attention to it. By the way, what is your opinion about the origin of the Hittites? My ideas about this race is very vague; I seem to have a dim impression that they inhabited most of what's now Anatolia, and that after fighting back and forth with the Egyptians and Assyrians for many centuries, they were finally conquered and Aryanized by the Phrygians who preceded the main body of Hellenic conquest. And I seem to have read that these Hittites employed large bodies of Amazons in their armies. But possibly my data is all wrong. If you can cast any light on this ancient people, I'd highly appreciate it.

Mr. Wright informed me of his plan to make Weird Tales a bi-monthly and I'll admit I dont like the idea.[1] It cuts down the market too much. I dont believe the change will be very popular with the readers, either. Like you, I hope the magazine isnt discontinued. Its the only magazine in the world, so far as I know, in which the writer can give full sway to his imagination. Yet there is one advantage in the bi-monthly idea—I'll get to read your "Whisperer" all at once, without having to wait a month for the last installment. Mr. Wright told me he was pretty well stocked up on Weird Tale stories, and that fact, together with the fact that no more serials will be used, caused me to abandon a sequel I was writing to Skull-Face.[2]

Speaking of rattlesnakes, in the Spring when the varmints come out of their lairs I'll try to get you some rattles. They make rather interesting items in a collection of curios, and as this is a snake country through here, I ought to be able to secure some good ones. I remember one time when I was about twelve years old, a friend and I were trapping in the Coleman county hills, and one warm day in early Spring we went looking to our traps. It was just such a day when snakes, half blind and sluggish from their long sleep, crawl out and sun themselves on rocks in the lee of a hill. We were on the south side of a good sized hill, and my friend climbed down a big rock to examine a trap set back under it in a sort of a cave. Carelessly bending down on all fours to look under the rock, he set his bare hand within a few inches of a four-foot diamond-back rattler that lay sunning himself. I'll never forget that. My friend gave a howl and came floating back up the cliff like a wind-blown wisp of fog; I presume he climbed somehow, but his ascent gave the impression of a squirrel-like scamper straight up the sheer rock. I was laughing so, and he was so weak from fright that our well-meaning stones went wild and the snake crawled sluggishly back under the rock. He was really too lethargic to bite anyone. And I'm not likely to forget the time that I, climbing up a creek bank, guilelessly and trustfully took hold of a water mocassin thinking it was part of a tree. In the east part of this town the country is sandy and copperheads used to abound. A few years ago a big snake of that species bit a child, striking her with such force he knocked her down, and then biting her repeatedly while she was on the ground. Big spots came out all over the child, but these West Texas kids are as hard to kill as cats. She nearly died, but eventually got over it. A mad snake is the devil's own; he wont quit striking you until he is dead or you, and I've heard of snakes continuing to strike the corpse of a man they'd killed, until their venom sac was completely empty. Not long ago they passed an ordinance prohibiting hogs from running wild in the Austin hills, and now I hear that the snakes are increasing at an alarming rate and even wriggling down into the city itself. Hogs eat snakes and so do chapparal birds—Indian runners or sage-hens they call them in the West—and I used to have a tomcat that killed snakes of all sorts and devoured them with gusto. A rattler can bite a hog all day without hurting the hog.

Bullfighting is indeed a reversion to Roman amphitheater days. I have an idea that the Mediterranean peoples have practiced it in some form or other every since the days of Crete, where it flourished, according to paintings on vases and the like. You're right about athletics; more and more the tendency is to watch the professional perform rather than to indulge one's self. Organized athletics are having an effect on the schools which I do not believe is good. When I was a country schoolboy there was little systematic and competitive athletics, but all engaged in some playground form of amusement—baseball, snap-the-whip, wolf-over-the-river, wrestling, all hard strenuous games inclined to toughen and strengthen the participants. Now, certain groups of pupils play football and basket-ball and compete in track events, and the great majority stand about and watch them. It seems to me that organized sport is tending to create a powerful and athletic minority and a soft-bodied and sluggish majority. Take the average high school. Ten, or perhaps fifteen percent of the pupils go in for the grinding grill of competitive athletics; the rest do nothing in the way of building their bodies, or dissipating their natural animal spirits in wholesome ways. No wonder drunkeness and immorality are so prevalent among students. To the average boy or girl the accumulation of knowledge isnt enough to spend their energy on—they can learn only so much, anyhow, and the Devil himself couldnt teach the average pupil, with his undoubtedly limited capacity, very much, anyway. They must have a physical outlet, and since systematic sport denies this to all but a chosen few, the rest naturally turn to amusements less wholesome. This seems to be the trend of modern life, to me.

Thanks very much for the statistics-paper. It seems in truth that only Americans are dying in New York and only Jews are being born. It seems certain that in a generation or so, New York will be a full fledged Hebrew city, 100 Yiddish. Yet I am less sorry to see this happen to New York than I am to note the inroads of the aliens into New England, though I'm sure that wops and Polacks are preferable to Jews. I can understand how the French you mention are to be preferred to the rest; as you say, they have some right on this Continent. I was much interested by what you say of the Fiji Island colony.[3] Ye gods, what next will be dumped on the shores of this long-suffering land? They must present an interesting study, at least. You are probably right in assuming them to be of Australoid-Dravidian stock, with a liberal mixture of pure negroid from prehistoric times.

I'm afraid that in a few generations Texas will be over-run with mongrels. Looking at the state as a whole: the great bulk of the population is of Anglo-American stock, mainly with Southern ancestry, but with quite a goodly proportion who trace their lines back to the Mid-West or New England. Central Texas is more dominantly Anglo-Saxon and Scotch-Irish than any other portion. On the Border there is a large Latin element, and on the coasts swarms of foreigners. The inevitable Jew infests the state in great numbers. You can hardly find a town of three thousand or more inhabitants that does not contain at least one Jew in business. And the Jew almost invariably has the country trade. It is a stock saying among rural Texans that if the Jew cannot sell his stuff at his price, he will sell it at yours. What they cannot seem to realize is that at whatever price he sells his shoddy junk, he is making a bigger profit than the legitimate merchant can make. No Aryan ever outwitted a Jew in business. I used to work in a Jewish dry-goods store. Before each sale—and Jewish sales go on forever—I would "mark down" the goods according to his instructions. For instance, the regular retail price of a pair of trousers would be $5.00. I would mark in big numbers on the tag—$9.50, then draw a line through that and mark below, $5.50. Thus the duped customer, noting the marked out price and comparing it to the new price, would consider that he was getting a bargain, whereas he was in reality paying fifty cents more than the regular price of the garment. But you cant make the average countryman believe that he's not saving money and getting gorgeous bargains by trading with the Jews.

But to return to the foreignization of the state. Houston, the largest city, has a vast alien population—Jews, Slavs, and Italians, the last drifting up from New Orleans. Dallas fairly swarms with Jews, in ever increasing numbers. In fact, the term "Dallas Jews" is applied indiscriminately to inhabitants of the city by spiteful people. Dallas also has numbers of Greeks, Russians and Italians and quite a few Mexicans. San Antonio has a large population of Mexicans, twenty or thirty percent of the entire population, and the usual quota of Jews, Italians and Slavs. Of the remaining population, a large percent is Germanic. Fort Worth, thirty miles west of Dallas, and originally settled by cattle-men, is overwhelmingly American; the foreign percentage is very small. Waco, in central east Texas, has, in addition to a vast negro population, a steadily increasing foreign element. The Jew is there, but not many Italians, their place being taken by Poles, Bohemians, Czechs and Magyars. In contrast to most of the rest of the state, the rural element about Waco is strongly alien in flavor, immigrants from eastern and central Europe having swarmed into the country a generation or so back, and slowly pushed out the original Anglo-American farmers. There were several waves of immigration. The Scotch-Irish and Anglo-Saxon farmers followed the cattle-men, then a host of Germans came up from the coast, and later, after them came a swarm of Poles and Bohemians who now seem destined to eventually take over the country. In some places, a "white German" even with a strong Deutch, accent seems like a brother, among the swarms of "black Germans"—dark haired Poles and Slovaks. Even there, there is still a substantial base of Anglo-Americans but I cannot say what a few more generations will do. Austin, the capital city, set among picturesque hills, is mainly free from aliens, but Galveston and Corpus Christi swarm with Italians, South Americans, Cubans, Filipinos, Slavs, Jews—the usual population of sea-port towns. As for the Rio Grande Valley, the alien population is immense, some towns, I hear, being almost entirely composed of Latins and Jews, aside from their natural Mexican element. A broad belt of coast country from Port Arthur to Matagorda is dominated by the usual swarm of Poles, Swedes, Slavs, Latins, Germans—etc. West of Cross Plains, the fertile grain country is inhabited thickly by Swedes and Germans, and this is the case with most of the richest parts of the state. The American farmer cannot compete with the low living standards and close economy and wheel-horse work of the alien farmer. He is slowly but surely being pushed off the best land, into the cities or on to worthless farms. Just now his last stand is on the great plains of western Texas, and he is supreme there, because its a big country, and a hard country, and no place for weaklings, and un-developed as yet. And for enduring hardships and taking big chances, for guts and stamina and man-killing work in huge, dynamic bursts, there never was and never will be a race to compare with the American of old British stock. Its not the fierce hardships that ruin the race—they can overcome any obstacle, so long as its big enough and hard enough to grip and trample; but the long, monotonous, grinding toil with a far-distant goal to view, the scimping, and petty economy, the saving the pennies and living on bacon-rinds, the use of every inch of land, every blade of grass, every hog's bristle, all that whips the Anglo-American, viewed as a whole, while such things are second nature to the peasant from Europe. America must learn the secret of concentrated farming before her sons can compete with the scum of Europe. But who in the Devil wants to succeed by the bacon-rind and hog-bristle route?

Let the wops live on a penny a day and grow rich selling garbage crumbs. Havent I seen Joe Rizza and his wife, stand day after day, seven days in the week, behind a counter shucking oysters and waiting on trade as if their lives depended on it, and he worth maybe a hundred thousand dollars and the owner of a whole chain of Italian restaurants and fish houses? And my French landlady, bewailing the ancient glories of French New Orleans, would wrathfully repeat the tale of how Joe Rizza had landed in America fifteen years before with not even a nickel to his name. Gad—how she hated the Italians! And how all the Creoles hated them. It was my fortune to be acquainted with some elderly maiden ladies by the name of Durell—gentlewomen of the old school living in semi-seclusion and striving to maintain the standards of a faded aristocracy, and reconcile their natures with the necessity which forced them to run a rooming house. They talked French among themselves and though born and raised in New Orleans, spoke English with a very distinct accent. They talked a great deal of how the rising wave of Italian immigration had swept the original French inhabitants away; and I have seen the old Durell mansion in the heart of the Old French Quarter—now the Latin Quarter—once a stately, century-old, residence, built with characteristic French style—now a hovel housing half a dozen squalid Italian families, with goats browsing and ragged children playing in the weed-grown, filth-strewn court-yard. In justice to the Italians, I must say that the scum that overflows New Orleans really originates mainly in Scicily. There are many very decent Italians in the city who look down on and despise these Scicilians as fiercely as do the French. But to get back to Joe Rizza and his oysters—the only sign of wealth sported by the Rizza family was the large gold rosary worn by his wife, the sight of which always sent my French landlady into tremors of wrath. She resented the fact that a wop's wife could wear a rosary such as she, whose ancestors once ruled New Orleans, could not afford. But no other sign was given by the Rizzas than that—to the casual eye they were hounded by the dogs of starvation whose fangs they could only hope to avoid—by shucking oysters seven days out of the week, from early morning to late at night! And I'm sure they lived on just a few cents a day, just as they had in the days when they really were poverty-stricken. I've heard that wops haunt the garbage piles for their food, and I'm prepared to believe it. Well, let Americans watch closely the Jewish-Italian way of making money, let them take the lesson to heart and go and do likewise, if they wish to compete with them—but I'm willing to bet my hat that the average American would rather hang or starve all at once than to drag out a slow starvation of body and soul over a long period of years, merely to acquire the empty honor of dying a rich man.

Your vivid and fascinating descriptions of the South fill me with a great desire to visit there. Every word of it was deeply interesting and instructive to me, as my ignorance of that country, geographically and historically, is abysmal. I was particularly enthralled by your descriptions of Virginia, and

Charleston. It must be fascinating to watch the remodeling of Williamsburg. When it is completely restored it should prove a veritable paradise to lovers of the old days and old ways of Colonial America. You know, I find it almost impossible to vizualize a long-settled country-side. I always think of large cities in connection with long settlement, which is natural considering the fact that such cities as San Antonio and New Orleans have always represented old established occupancy to me, and the Cajun and nigger teeming swamps of Louisiana gave me no real impressions on the subject. Born and bred in the newer lands as I was, it is hard for me to visualize a country-side peopled by folk who have lived there for hundreds of years. Here in Texas, in this part particularly, a farm-house fifty years old is considered remarkably ancient. Fifty years ago the danger of Indian raids was scarcely past. The thought of a farm that has been passed down from generation to generation, through perhaps a hundred and fifty years is most strange to me. I must see the Eastern states before I can formulate any logical impressions on the idea. Dialects always interest me, and I appreciated very much your comments on Charleston accent. In keeping with my ignorance of the South in general, it was news to me, that citizens of this city spoke with a different accent from the rest of the South, and I am sure that the reasons you put forward for this difference are correct.

Your letters are certainly broadening my views and store of knowledge; they give me a conception of the country east of the Mississippi, which has always been a great vague land of mist in my mind. How few people give any thought to the history of even their own locality! Why, it was from the Concho River, only about a hundred miles from here that John Chisum started to New Mexico in 1868, with his herd of ten thousand cattle, his caravan of waggons and his army of hard-bit Texas cowpunchers, yet his name is hardly known in this country. John Chisum was born in Tennessee and grew up in East Texas. He was an empire builder if one ever lived. To read New Mexican history of the 70's it would seem that he supported the territory—people either worked for John Chisum or stole cattle from him! In the days of his greatest power his herd numbered more than a hundred thousand head. The Long-rail and the Jingle-bob were known from Border to Border. He always kept open house; there any man could stay and eat his fill as long as he wished and no questions were asked him. Breakfast, dinner and supper places were set for twenty-six at the table in his big adobe house and generally all places were full. He was a figure of really heroic proportions, a builder of empires, yet he was by instinct merely a hard headed business man. Nothing dramatic about John Chisum, and maybe thats why history has slighted him in favor of fruitless but flashing characters who blazed vain trails of blood and slaughter across the West. John Chisum never even buckled a gun on his hip in his life; he was a builder, not a destroyer. He did not even take the war-path in that feud known as the bloody Lincoln County war. Have you ever read of it? There's drama! There's epic and saga and the red tides of slaughter! Heroism, reckless courage, brute ferocity, blind idealism and bestial greed. And the peak of red drama was touched that bloody night in the shuddering little mountain town of Lincoln, when Murphy's henchmen crouched like tigers in the night behind the flaming walls of McSween's 'dobe dwelling. Let me try to draw that picture as it has been told and re-told in song and story in the fierce annals of the Southwest—the greatest fight of them all.

The night is forked with leaping tongues of crimson flame; the bullet-riddled 'dobe walls have crumbled; the fire has devoured the west wing, the front part of the building, and now licks greedily at the last room remaining of the east wing. The walls are beginning to crumble, the roof is falling. Hidden behind wall and stable, eager and blood-maddened, crouch the Murphy men, rifles at the ready. For three days and nights they have waged a fruitless battle with the defenders; now since treachery has fired the adobe house, their turn has come at last. They keep their eyes and rifle muzzles fixed hard on the single door. Before that door, in the red glare of the climbing flames lie McSween, Harvey Morris, Semora, Romero and Salazar in pools of their own blood, where the bullets struck them down as they rushed from the burning house; four dead, one—Salazar—badly wounded. O'Folliard, Skurlock, Gonzalez and Chavez have made the dash and somehow raced through that rain of lead and escaped in the darkness. Now is the peak of red drama, for in that blazing snare still lurks one man. The watchers grip their rifles until their knuckles show white. McSween's right hand man has yet to dare that lead tipped gantlet—Billy the Kid,[4] that slim nineteen year-old boy, with the steel grey eyes, the gay smile, the soft voice and the deadliness of a rattler. The flames roar and toss; soon he must leap through that door if he would not be burned like a rat in a trap. Bob Beckwith, whose bullet struck down McSween, curses between his teeth and trembles like a tensed hunting hound in his eagerness. He and his comrades, hidden by wall and semi-darkness, are comparatively safe—but no foe of the Kid's is safe within gun-shot range. Scarce ten yards away the soaring flames will etch their prey mercilessly in their rifle sights—how can the best marksmen of the Southwest miss at that range? Bob Beckwith curses and his eyes dance with madness. He killed McSween; now to his everlasting glory he must kill Billy the Kid, and wipe out the stain of Murphy blood—Morton, Baker—victims of the Kid's unerring eye and steady hand. A shower of sparks—the roofs falls in with a roar; as if the happening hurled him from the building, a figure leaps through the door into the red glare. A mad rattle of rifle-fire volleys and the air is filled with singing lead. Through that howling hail of death the Kid races and his own guns are spurting jets of fire. Bob Beckwith falls across the wall, stone dead. Two more of the posse bellow as the Kid's bullets mark them for life. Slugs rip through the Kid's hat and clothes; death sings in the air about him—but he clears the wall and vanishes in the darkness. His time is not yet come and there still remain further red chapters to write in that red life. The Murphy men come from their coverts to roar their triumph, and while fiddles are brought and set going, the victors drink and shout and dance among the corpses in the light of the flaming embers, in a wild debauch of primitive exultation. But the Kid is fleeing unharmed through the night and he wastes no time in cursing his luck; plans for swift and gory vengeance occupy his full thoughts.

Truly the bloody Lincoln County war is the saga of the Southwest; glory and shame and murder and courage and cruelty and hate flaming into raw, red primitive drama, while through all stalked the gigantic shadow-shape of Billy the Kid, dominating all—as if that crimson feud were but the stage set for his brief stellar role—his star that flamed suddenly up and was as suddenly extinguished.

Mongolization is certainly going on among the Russians to a larger extent than I had realized. The cases you mention, of Mongols taking Russian names and settling among Europeans, surely would seem to prove that the eventual trend of the Russians was toward complete Orientalization. Probably it will take a long time, but with the increasing rousing of the East, and the westward drift of Mongoloid peoples, I fully expect that some day the typical Russian will be slant eyed. That negroid-Jew you speak of must have been a grotesque and amusing spectacle. Amalgamation produces curious results. I imagine those Cape Verde Bravas are bad hombres. There are several of them who have gained some prominence in the ring, and they have an untamed look about them.

What you say of the Carthaginians interested me very much. I have noted the quick and complete absorption of the Vandals on the site of their ancient empire. Those Aryan barbarians must have practically vanished in a comparatively few generations. The further south Aryans wander the more swiftly they are absorbed it would seem, and this fact makes me lean to the theory that Africa has in prehistoric and semi-prehistoric times swallowed up completely, unrecorded drifts of white tribes, both Aryan and Semitic. It seems logical to me that some white races might have wandered down into Africa either across Suez or the Straits of Gibraltar, and forging into the interior, mingled with the dusky natives and eventually vanished. It would not take many centuries to breed out a white strain almost entirely, and I have repeatedly read of vague rumors of red-haired niggers occasionally occurring in the interior of the Continent.

Speaking of Oriental Stories, I'll admit I was dissappointed in Owens' story in the first issue.[5] He seemed to have written it hurriedly and without making much attempt at realistic portrayal. I've never read the novel you mention by Benoit.[6] And I must admit that the prehistoric South African race is news to me too. What you say of them interests me most intensely and I would appreciate it sincerely if you would tell me all you know of them. I look forward to the time when you will find it convenient to write an African tale, for in this barren period of literature, such treats as this is bound to be, are few and far between. I've never read "Facts Concerning the late Arthur Jerwyn and His Family", but I'd certainly enjoy doing so, if you have a spare copy or one you can lend me. I entirely sympathize with you in your irritation at the editor's changing the title.[7] The original title certainly was far superior in originality and interest.

In your remarks on prehistoric races you certainly present a clear picture of the various theories of anthropologists and historians, and one which helps me to straighten such theories up in my mind. I must devote some study to these subjects, as they are of intense interest.

Thanks very much for sending me the articles on Druidic remnants. What strange and misty speculations are brought up by the thought of those gaunt and brooding columns! What curious and fantastic rituals of worship were there enacted, and what invokations of what monstrous gods? I am almost consumed by curiosity concerning the immemorial past, and irritated beyond measure to think that that curiosity will never be satisfied!

The dream you described is most fascinating, particularly the names, etc., and the culmination.[8] I remember reading the incident in Long's serial, which, by the way, is the best thing appearing in Weird Tales since Mr. Wright published your last story.[9] Long lacks something of your own master touch, but he is a good craftsman and this story is splendid. Wandrei's dreams of Druidic forests are interesting also. I believe that many dreams are the result of ancestral memories, handed down through the ages. I have lived in the Southwest all my life yet most of my dreams are laid in cold, giant lands of icy wastes and gloomy skies, and of wild, wind swept fens and wildernesses over which sweep great sea-winds, and which are inhabited by shock headed savages with light fierce eyes. With the exception of that one dream I described to you, I am never, in these dreams of ancient times, a civilized man. Always I am the barbarian, the skin-clad, tousle-haired, light eyed wild man, armed with a rude axe or sword, fighting the elements and wild beasts, or grappling with armored hosts marching with the tread of civilized discipline, from fallow fruitful lands and walled cities. This is reflected in my writings, too, for when I begin a tale of old times, I always find myself instinctively arrayed on the side of the barbarian, against the powers of organized civilization. When I dream of Greece, it is always the Greece of early barbaric days when the first Aryan hordes came down, never the Greece of the myrtle crown and the Golden Age. When I dream of Rome I am always pitted against her, hating her with a ferocity that in my younger days persisted in my waking hours, so that I still remember, with some wonder, the savage pleasure with which I read, at the age of nine, the destruction of Rome by the Germanic barbarians. At the same time, reading of the conquest of Britain by those same races filled me with resentment. Somehow I have never been able to concieve fully of a Latinized civilization in Britain; to me the struggle has always seemed mainly a war of British barbarians against Germanic barbarians, with my sympathies wholly with the Britons.

But my most vivid dreams have been of Indian wars. The last Indian raid in Central Texas was in 1874 when Big Foot and Jape the Comanche left their reservation and swept through Texas, leaving a trail of fire and blood. The Frontier Battalion—Rangers—trapped the war-party on Dove Creek perhaps a hundred miles west of here, and both war-chiefs went to the Happy Hunting Ground at the muzzles of Texan rifles. But the old people of this country have many tales of Indian terrors, and I have listened to many such stories, particularly when I was a child and very susceptible to such things. So the Indian wars seem even more realistic and actual than even the World War. When old timers have told of red skin raids, the telling, even of a halting illiterate style, has seemed so vivid to me, that sometimes it seems as if I, too, must have really lived through those times. Even now, the tale of a massacre and scalping that occurred perhaps seventy years ago seems more real and horrifying than the horrors of the Great War little more than a half score years ago.

And I've often relived those days in my dreams. I have known the lurking stillness about a lone cabin, broken suddenly by the nameless rustle of leaves and underbrush—the tense waiting in the darkness, eyes straining into the shadows for the crawling foe—the quavering call of the wolf, and the sudden horrified realization that it was no beast that gave tongue in the night—the glimpse of vague shadows flitting among the trees and underbrush—the sudden, blood-freezing clamor of madly exultant yells and the rain of arrows and bullets against the cabin-logs—the vain and frenzied firing at mocking, darting shadows—the cold clammy sweat of fear, and fingers clumsy with haste fumbling with powder horn, wadding and bullet pouch—the arching, comet-like flight of flaming shafts into the roof and the terrorizing smell of smoke—the ghastly realization that the ammunition is exhausted—the new tenor of the war-whoop as the savages find their shots are unanswered—the rush across the clearing in the moonlight and the shattering strokes of rifle stock and tomahawk on the splintering door—the futile efforts to hold the door, in a shower of flaming embers from the burning roof—the deluge into the room, over the ruined door, of fiendish painted faces and brawny arms, polished bronze in the red glare of the flames—the frenzied swinging of the broken rifle stock at narrow, shaven heads in the strangling smoke—the gleam of tomahawks in lean hands—then red chaos and oblivion. All this I've known in my dreams. They always get me, the red devils!

It was the Comanches and Kiowas that raised particular Cain in Texas; in earlier days the Wacoes, Tonkawas—cannibals, and supposed connected with the Caribs—and other small tribes made some raids, but they never amounted to much. The Comanches were devils. Blood kin of the Mescalero Apatches, too. Once, long ago, Comanches and Apatches were one tribe, but during a big drouth and famine, the ancestral tribe split up, one half taking to the plains, the other to the mountains. For mutual welfare, the mountain people agreed to eat no buffalo or other plains creatures, while to the plains people the mountain animals were taboo. The mountain men became Apatches, short, stocky, with unusual strength and endurance, while the men of the plains became tall, rangy, powerful and magnificent horsemen, and were known as Comanches. The greatest chiefs of the Apatches were Mangus Colorado and, of course, Go-yat-thi-lay, known as Geronimo. Petah Nocona was the last and greatest war-chief of the Comanches while his half-breed son, Quanah Parker, is one of the stock folk-lore characters of the Southwest and as smart a horse thief as ever rode off with a rancher's hoofed stock. All Comanches prided themselves on their horse-thieving ability.

You are right in saying that America's main struggle is between the individualist and the corporation and I suppose nothing can stop the present cultural and industrial trend. Doubtless in a few more generations all the United States will present one uniform pattern, modeled on the mechanized fabric of New York. I have seen pictures of the new architecture; it certainly is in keeping with the growing spirit of the Age, and would seem to conform to the strictest ideas of standardization. If the Colonies had never separated from England, many of the tangles confronting the people might, as you say, have been more readily adjusted. At least, America would not have been deluged by a horde of non-British immigrants as it has been.

Your comments on the New England-Canadian question presents a thought entirely new to me. I had not realized to what an extent the New England states and Canada were connected, geographically and economically. I sympathize with your dream of political connection as well, and believe, with you, that such a step would be of benefit to both New England and Canada. It would certainly mean a revival of old thought-ways and ideals—a sort of British Colonial renaissance with the accompanying gain in literature and art. Why, the thought is really a wonderful one, with gigantic possibilities. British New England might well become the seat of learning and culture for the world, a sort of modern Athens, or rather, a Mermaid Inn for a modern Elizabethan Age. It would receive, not only the best minds of Canada and its own domains, but to it, from all the rest of America, would flock folk in whom Colonial traditions and ideals still live. Well, it rouses splendid speculations, even if it never comes to pass.

I am glad my comments on the Southwest interest you, and I feel most highly honored, indeed, at the kind things you have said about my descriptions, etc. Kelly the conjure-man was quite a character, but I fear I could not do justice to such a theme as you describe. I hope you will carry out your idea in writing the story you mention, of a pre-negroid African priest reincarnated in a plantation negro. As for me handling this theme better than yourself, it is beyond the realms of possibility, regardless of any first-hand knowledge of background which I might possess. I lack your grasp on cosmic thoughts, your magnificent imagination, your command of rhetoric and vocabulary, your power to invest the unreal with a grisly reality—in short, I am a mere novice where you are a master. I hope you will write this story some time, and if any of my anecdotes of pine land and negro lore can be used in any way, or give you any ideas, you are more than welcome to them.

I hope to some day write a history of the Southwest that will seem alive and human to the readers, not the dry and musty stuff one generally finds in chronicles. To me the annals of the land pulse with blood and life, but whether I can ever transfer this life from my mind to paper, is a question. It will be years, at least. Much of the vivid history of the Southwest is lost forever and the breed growing up now looks toward, and apes, the East, caring nothing at all about the traditions and history of the land in which they live. How many know anything of Lucien Maxwell?[10] Yet in his day he owned a Spanish land grant bigger than whole Eastern states, containing more than a million acres. This was in New Mexico in the '70's and '80's. In his mansion he kept royal style, with places for two dozen set at his generous table; the dishes were of solid silver, the wine goblets of solid gold. He sold his holdings for $7,50,000, and the buyers sold for nearly twice that amount. He died a poor man. How many know of Captain King, who owned the biggest ranch the world has ever seen?[11] It stretched from inland rivers to the Gulf of Mexico and when the country was settled up, it was devided into whole counties. I have seen the old ranch house which cost nearly a million dollars to build, and it looks more like a castle than an ordinary house. How old it is I cannot say, but the great stone stable has a date of 1856 carved over the door, and once cannons were mounted about the building to resist Indian attacks and Mexican raids. It lies adjacent to the little town of Kingsville, a most beautiful town—the prettiest I have yet seen in Texas. The worthy ranchman was an old sea-captain and I have heard it hinted that, if he followed the same tactics on sea that he did on land, he must have been a pirate. Years and years ago he was killed by a Mexican vaquero who worked for him, and who, it is said, carried out his orders regarding various men who owned ranches the captain desired. Be that as it may, they died and their ranches were engulfed in the ever growing boundaries of the great ranch. Giant fortunes are not built without intrigue and bloodshed, whether those fortunes be land or gold, or both. And John Chisum, who built the Texas town of Paris, and who owned more cattle than any other man in modern times—he is almost forgotten. And Pat Garrett, who ended the blazing comet-trail that was the life of the Billy the Kid. Garrett was an Alabama man, but he grew to manhood in Texas. And Sam Bass, of whom the old song narrates:

"Sam Bass was born in Indiana, that was his native home,
And at the age of seventeen, young Sam began to roam.
He first came out to Texas, a drover for to be,
And a kinder hearted fellow, you seldom ever see.
Sam used deal in race stock, one called the Denton Mare;
He matched her in scrub races and took her to the Fair.
Sam used to coin the money, and he spent it just as free,
He always drank good whiskey, where-ever he might be."

Sam's exploits shook the country, but he fell at Round Rock, outnumbered and surrounded by a vengeful posse, and already his fame has faded. And Pat Couglin of New Mexico,[12] cattle-king in his day, and John Slaughter of Texas,[13] who moved his herds into the naked lands and fought Indian raider and Mexican bandit alike, and later white rustlers and renegades. He is forgotten. And Willie Drenon, whom I saw wandering about the streets of Mineral Wells, twenty years ago, trying to sell the pitiful, illiterate book of his life of magnificent adventure and high courage; a little, worn old man in the stained and faded buckskins of a vanished age, friendless and penniless.[14] God, what a lousy end for a man whose faded blue eyes had once looked on the awesome panorama of untracked prairie and sky-etched mountain, who had ridden at the side of Kit Carson, guided the waggon-trains across the deserts to California, drunk and revelled in the camps of the buffalo-hunters, and fought hand to hand with painted Sioux and wild Comanche. One of the last of the old scouts he was, this pioneer, whom Kit Carson picked up, a lost and bewildered French immigrant boy, wandering about the wharves of the port where he had landed, and his neglect by the country and the people he served is but one case in many thousands. Always the simple, strong men go into the naked lands and fight heroical battles to win and open those lands to civilization. Then comes civilization, mainly characterized by the smooth, the dapper, the bland, the shrewd men who play with business and laws and politics and they gain the profits; they enjoy the fruit of other men's toil, while the real pioneers starve.

Well, they have gone into the night, a vast and silent caravan, with their buckskins and their boots, their spurs and their long rifles, their waggons and their mustangs, their wars and their loves, their brutalities and their chivalries; they have gone to join their old rivals, the wolf, the panther and the Indian, and only a crumbling 'dobe wall, a fading trail, the breath of an old song, remain to mark the roads they travelled. But sometimes when the night wind whispers forgotten tales through the mesquite and the chapparal, it is easy to imagine that once again the tall grass bends to the tread of a ghostly caravan, that the breeze bears the jingle of stirrup and bridle-chain, and that spectral camp-fires are winking far out on the plains. And a lobo calls where no wolf can be, and the night is dreamy and hushed and still with the pregnancy of old times. But gone are the days when the prairie schooners carried their cargo of empire into the sunset lands and gone the reckless, roaring days when the trail herds went up along the old Chisholm. The old time cowboy with the Spanish mustang and the longhorn steer has followed the raiding Comanche, the buffalo hunter, the whole-sale cattle rustler and the old scouts into silence and oblivion.

But I've rambled enough, and I hope I havent bored you. I'm sending you some stuff under separate cover which I hope may be of interest. These are some snap-shots, a magazine containing a story by me, and a tale of A. Merritt's which recently appeared in Argosy.[15] My story hasnt any particular merit but it may serve to amuse an idle hour. The magazine containing it, and the pictures are your's to keep, and there's no hurry about returning the Merritt yarn.

With best wishes,

Most cordially yours,
Robert E. Howard

Notes

1. For economic reasons, *WT* became a bimonthly for the issues of February/March, April/May, and June/July 1931, thereupon resuming monthly publication.

2. The unfinished story, "Taveral Manor."

3. Cf. HPL to Lillian D. Clark, 15–16 August 1930 (ms., JHL): "Our drive to Onset [on Cape Cod] was uneventful—though it was interesting to have Belknap point out a colony of *Fiji-Islanders* near Onset." The matter is glancingly mentioned in "The Shadow over Innsmouth" (1931).

4. Billy the Kid, byname of Henry McCarty (1859–1881), who seems to have adopted the name William Bonney, Jr., after arriving in New Mexico. From this and his youth sprang the name "Billy the Kid." He was one of the most notorious outlaws and gun-fighters of the American West, leader of the McSween forces in the "Lincoln County War," reputed to have killed at least 27 men before being gunned down at about age 21. REH owned *The Saga of Billy the Kid* (1926) by Walter Noble Burns (1872–1932); REHB 22.

5. Frank Owen, "Singapore Nights," *Oriental Stories* (October–November 1930).

6. Pierre Benoit, *Atlantida.* A novel about Atlantis.

7. HPL, "Facts concerning the Late Arthur Jermyn and His Family" appeared in *WT* variously as "The White Ape" and as "Arthur Jermyn."

8. HPL's account of his famous Roman dream does not survive in the transcripts of his letters to REH, but see the published accounts in letters to Bernard Austin Dwyer (in *Dreams and Fancies* [1962]) and Donald Wandrei (in *MW* as "The Very Old Folk").

9. REH refers to FBL's *The Horror from the Hills,* which incorporated verbatim HPL's description of his Roman dream as written in a letter to FBL of November 1927.

10. Lucien Bonaparte Maxwell (1818–1875) was a rancher and entrepreneur who at one point owned more than 1,700,000 acres—the largest private landowner in U.S. history.

11. Captain Richard King (1824–1885) and Gideon K. Lewis (ca 1823–1855) started a cattle camp on the banks of Santa Gertrudis Creek in South Texas in 1852; the ranch eventually expanded to 825,000 acres, the largest in the U.S.

12. Pat Coughlin (1822?–after 1910) (or Coghlan, or Coughlin), the self-styled "King of the Tularosa," and an associate of Billy the Kid. Billy and his gang would steal cattle, and Coughlin would sell them to buyers far from the ranches they were taken from. Coughlin was arrested by John W. Poe, but escaped prosecution when the only witness against him was killed.

13. John Slaughter (1841–1922), cattleman and lawman. In the late 1890s he bought a large area of land in southern Arizona which became known as the San Bernardino Ranch. The ranch house straddled the U.S.–Mexico border, half the house being located in each country. It is now a National Historic Landmark.

14. William F. Drannan (1832–1913), *Thirty-one Years on the Plains and in the Mountains; or, The Last Voice from the Plains* (Chicago: Rhodes & McClure, 1903, 1908); or *Capt. W. F. Drannan, Chief of Scouts, as Pilot to Emigrant and Government Trains, across the Plains of the Wild West of Fifty Years Ago, as Told by Himself* . . . (Chicago: Rhodes & McClure, 1910). Most authorities consider these "memoirs" spurious, if not outright fabrications.

15. REH, "Alleys of Peril." The Merritt story apparently is an installment of "The Snake Mother," a sequel to "The Face in the Abyss" (later combined as the novel *The Face in the Abyss*) that began a seven-part serialization in the *Argosy* on 25 October 1930.

[20]

10 Barnes St.,
Providence, R. I.,
Jany. 30, 1931.

Dear Mr. Howard:—

[. . .] Your rattlesnake anecdotes are surely interesting in the extreme; and I shall of course be tremendously appreciative of any rattles which may come my way—though you must not go to the trouble and peril of stirring up a nest just on my account. By the way—is it a fact that the corpse of a person repeatedly bitten by snakes swells and bursts? A revision client of mine in Kansas City had a plot-germ based on that idea, and I worked up a story from it—"The Curse of Yig", which you may recall in W. T. It made good fiction, but I have always wondered just how much truth there was in the original notion. What you say of the natural enemies of snakes interested me greatly. Hogs and sage-hens seem to be the Texas counterparts of the East-Anglian mongoose, which kills cobras. The mongoose, however, is *not* immune from snake poison; contrary to popular legend. He gets the cobra through agile dodging—causing the snake to strike again and again, hitting nothing but empty ground and finally emptying its sac. Then, when the cobra is temporarily harmless, the mongoose darts up and bites him in the neck.

It would be interesting to see whether bull fighting could trace any subterranean folk-connexion with ancient Crete. Owing to the fact that the very existence of the Cretan civilisation was forgotten in classical times, the link must be very slender; yet it would be too much to claim that the particular cult of the bull did not linger on somehow along the North African littoral, cropping out later in a preference for bull-fighting over other Roman arena sports. That the Apis bull of Egypt had some Cretan connexion seems highly probable—and from this link a prolongation might well exist. Come to think of it, there's another possible link, too—for bull-fighting seems to have had a vogue in Thessaly, in northern Greece, quite independently of the Roman arena. This, of course, is a long way from Crete, but that means nothing, since outposts of Minoan culture existed all over Greece and the coast of Asia Minor. Indeed—upon reflection, I'd venture to guess that this Thessalian link stands more of a chance of being the real one than any in North Africa. Certainly, the cult of the bull was tremendously grounded in the very ancient world, so that the later ancient world had much to remember. As for the modern attitude toward athletics—I agree wholly with you. To despecialise and de-commercialise sport and restore it to the majority after a long period of showy exploitation is a task worthy of any sociologist.

Yes—New York is pretty well lost to the Aryan race, and the tragic and dramatic thing is the *speed* with which the change occurred. People hardly past middle age can still recall the pleasant, free and easy New York which really formed an American metropolis, and in which there was nothing more foreign than the wholesome, cheerful immigrants from Ireland and Germany. As late as 1900 this old New York was still the visible state of things on Manhattan Island—but then the packed East Side, which had been silently filling up with Russian and Polish Jews since 1885 or 1890, began to disgorge its newly prosperous foreign-born and first active generation. In 1905 certain troubles in Russia sent over countless hordes of cringing Jews; and by 1910 people began to notice the overwhelmingly Semitic tinge of the crowds on all the New York streets. In 1917 the draft statistics shewed what New York had become—so that "Kemp Uptown, by Lunk Islunt" housed an array which had the facial aspect, though hardly the martial spirit, of the hordes of Sennacherib and Nebuchadnezzar! And now the vital-statistics pages of the papers tell their own story. Ultimately, if the pest doesn't spread over the surrounding terrain, this exotic population may make New York a strangely interesting place which outsiders can view with more curiosity than repulsion. Even now—when one doesn't have to live there—there is a sinister fascination in the swarthy, alien faces that mill through the shadows cast by topless towers. One feels as one might in Bombay, or Bagdad, or Babylon—or in some forgotten city of Atlantis or Valusia! But it sure is hell on the native New Yorkers who remember and love the city that used to be. They are like the Indians now—spectators of a new and unaccustomed order on their ancestral ground. No—it isn't quite as bad as that in New England, for the Slavs and Latins at least come from Aryan backgrounds, and do not push so quickly to the fore. By the time a Dago gets to be a professional man or city official he usually has something of his native peasant crudeness rubbed off—and that crudeness was a good deal tempered by affability and taste-capacity to start with. But the Jews manage to get money and influence without losing a particle of their hard realism and unctuously offensive rattiness. They push brazenly ahead—in the intellectual and aesthetic as well as the practical field. Right now their control of the publishing field is alarming—houses like Knopf, Boni, Liveright, Greenberg, Viking, etc. etc. serving to give a distinctly Semitic angle to the whole matter of national manuscript-choice, and thus indirectly to national current literature and criticism. It will be curious to see what 3 or 4 generations of good living and power will do to the New York Jew. Many of the ratty, furtive traits will certainly tend to disappear, so that there will arise a wholly new species of polished Oriental. But the social pressure of the Aryan hinterland will probably encourage many of these Jews to adopt Aryan ways and fuse themselves with Aryan blood, so that the local culture will always have a sort of hybridism and uncertainty about it. The better Jews are gradually shedding the most obvious externals of their shady sharpness; so that their great department stores can really be depended upon not to fleece one. In New York the lesser ones impose on Americans in the approved Dallas way; but as their clientele becomes more and more like themselves, this game rather fails them. It's one thing to sell John Smith or Patrick O'Brien ah nize pair uff $5.00 pents for $10.00 a'ready, but somethink else again to try det same beezness on Jakey Cohen or Ikey Finkelbaum! Oy, soch a beezness!! But all the same, don't try to buy anything at a marked price even in a Jew-clientele district—for the customers *don't expect* to pay the marked prices! With them, it's a case of waving palms and back-and-forth haggling—such as an Aryan hates, but which among virtually all Semites (and many non-Semitic Orientals as well) is not only the normal type of negotiation but has a positive intrinsic pleasure. It is the tale of the Bagdad bazaars all over again.

It really astonishes me—as I think it would astonish any untravelled Easterner—to hear how extensively Texas is foreignised. We still think of the historic pioneer Texas here—or if we stop to realise its growth, we carelessly couple it with the Old South, of which it seems to us an extension. The rural-foreign sections are probably much like our Slav-peopled Connecticut Valley, and such other New England areas as the French-Canadians have taken. Some Italians also seek the land. In western Rhode Island there is also a rural *Finnish* element. Well—you're lucky to have some areas and towns dominantly American. In Rhode Island there is only one city really American, and that is Newport; but as I have said, the residential part of Providence, on the steep hill, is a purely American oasis in the midst of cosmopolitanism—so that this letter is being written in an immediate milieu as Yankee and colonial as it was in 1831 or 1731. As you say, the secret of foreign progress is willingness to accept a low living standard; and that is assuredly a hard enemy to beat. What the country will look like in 2031 is more than I would care to picture! New Orleans must have undergone a painful transition—and I don't wonder at the disgust of the old inhabitants. The French people would probably find Quebec a congenial haven, with much that they miss still flourishing—if they could stand the climate in winter, which is more than I could do.

Glad you found my random travel-observations on the Old South of interest, and hope the pictures and printed matter proved even more so. Too bad I didn't get word sooner that the latter were to keep—but as I said before, just let me know if you want these things for your files, and back they'll come! As for an *ancient countryside*—it never occurred to me before that many people perfectly familiar with *old cities* have very slight acquaintance with the rural scenes of corresponding periods. Yet that is very natural if one travels mainly among railway routes or crowded main highways. Typical old rural scenes of the past lie along the unfrequented byways—and I can assure you that both north and south have a rich variety of regions, of every degree of rusticity, which still look much as they did before the revolution. Different sections of the old colonies had different types of farm buildings, just as they had different types of town houses. Manor-houses or sumptuous country-seats also differed. I have not seen many of the rural places of the Carolinas because of the wildness of the routes traversed; but the Virginia countryside is extremely familiar to me. The great colonial plantation houses (see sketch) were generally of brick, with steep roof and chimneys, and with kitchen and house-servant quarters on either side in the form of symmetrical buildings following the general plan of the house in miniature, and connected with it by means of brick arcades. They were usually secluded in large grounds. The more popularly known type of plantation-house, with great pillared portico, is of later date—usually 1800–1850—and a result of the classical influence introduced by Thomas Jefferson. Smaller Virginia farmhouses are of wood, with steep roof and end chimneys. Most of the Virginia country is very gently rolling, so that one may see many of these farmhouses at once, with yellow clay roads winding past them, and tilled fields divided by zigzag rail fences stretching far in the rear. These fences are highly typical of Virginia—though one finds them also in French Quebec. The old rural parish churches—invariably Episcopal—occur in the wildest parts of the open country, with no houses near them, since their parishioners were generally planters coming from neighbouring estates. They are usually very plain—of Georgian design with peaked roof but without a steeple. Some are *very* old—going back to *original* (not revived) Gothic in architecture. It is one of these—St. Luke's in Isle of Wight county—which constitutes *the oldest edifice of English origin in the Western Hemisphere*—dating from 1632 and being 4 years older than the second-oldest Anglo-American edifice. (the Fairbanks farmhouse in Dedham, Mass., between Providence and Boston)[1] These churches are, for the most part, obsolete as houses of worship, owing to the urbanisation of modern life. They are, however, well cared for by the Society for the Preservation of Virginia Antiquities. Small Virginia villages generally cluster around the brick county court houses, and are named for them—as, for instance, Fairfax Court House, Amelia Court House, and Halifax Court House. The houses are generally of the small-farmhouse type, though in the larger villages more urban buildings are seen. Near the coast, there are some gambrel roofs of the New England type in many villages—perhaps a result of sea trade with New England. In the few Virginia cities, the colonial houses were usually of the small brick, slant-roofed type derived from England and characterising all American cities except Charleston and the wooden-housed cities of New England. Virginia villages are still very primitive in aspect, and seldom have paving or sidewalks. The inhabitants—like Virginia farmers in general—have a much stronger flavour of the soil than in the north, and are very leisurely in their ways. They are fond of lounging in crowds around the court houses. Except in the coastal area, negroes are not at all common in rural Virginia. They were, in the old days, largely confined to the great plantations; small farmers seldom owning more than one or two. Occasional nigger farms exist, but by no means as numerously as in the Carolinas or farther south. Near the coast, though, they thicken—and there is one village near Yorktown—called Lackey—populated wholly by them. Maryland is very much like Virginia. In Pennsylvania, however, we encounter a wholly different order of things—being now in a region where German and Welsh influences are paramount. The Welsh buildings have heavy overhanging cornices—always carried around the gable end of the house—and are generally of brick or stone. The German houses are almost invariably of stone—plain, with peaked roofs and doors horizontally divided. Sometimes one will see these influences fused in a German stone house with a Welsh cornice crossing the gable end. Some public buildings—churches and schools—shew strong German influences, such as slender belfry and very small dormer windows. These old Germans were a sturdy and enterprising lot—the first ones coming with Penn in 1683. One of them printed the first Bible ever printed in America. The city of Philadelphia, though lightly touched by Welsh influence, shews nothing of the German; and had become thoroughly English-Georgian by 1750 or 1760. Brick is the dominant construction material for colonial houses, and gambrel roofs are frequent. The English country-seats near Philadelphia—mostly built of stone—are held to be the finest examples of their kind in America. They follow the British Georgian manor-house type quite faithfully. Ascending into New Jersey, we no longer see the Pennsylvania type of houses, but a new milieu altogether. *Dutch* influence is perceptible in the presence of a porch, and of a row of low, broad, attic windows above it. A typical feature of the flat New Jersey landscape is the *red clay* as distinctive as the yellow clay of the South. Villages tend to retain the farm type of house, while the towns run to wooden gambrel roofed houses. Churches are usually Georgian with tall steeples—as indeed are the English churches of colonial Philadelphia. Good country-seats of Georgian design exist. In New York state the colonial countryside shews Dutch influence on every hand. The Dutch town houses of New York and Albany had stepped gables in the old Holland style, but none now exist. The farmhouses, at first steep-roofed stone affairs like the Pennsylvania German houses, soon acquired a very distinctive style of their own—with gambrel roof of short upper pitch and long *curved* lower pitch—the latter carried out over a wide porch on one or both sides of the house. The lower stories were usually of stone, the upper of wood. On Long Island, however, where stone was rare, all-wooden construction predominated. English colonial farmhouses of this region do not posses the Dutch porch or curved roof line, but adopt the Dutch gambrel proportions with short upper pitch. English had Dutch country seats tend to be of stone, and of square, plain architecture. Dutch churches were plain and peak-roofed, with belfry. English had Georgian steeples. One also finds in N.Y. many of the farmhouses of the New Jersey type—so many, indeed, that one must really deem the style as belonging to N.J. and N.Y. in common. The older Dutch type—stone, with peaked roof—is found mostly in the up-Hudson region; Kingston and vicinity being an ideal centre. The landscape there is very beautiful. On Long Island it is flat and salt-marshy, like the landscape of Old Holland. Crossing into New England, the one outstanding feature of the ancient landscape is the rambling stone wall—as typical of Yankeedom as the zigzag rail fence is of Virginia. The country is rocky and markedly rolling, with the giant elm as the characteristic tree. It is the abundance of rock which made stone walls so common. These walls are of loosely heaped field stones of large size—never dressed. Wall-making was a real art in colonial times—and in Rhode Island was usually left to negro slaves and Indian servants. Elsewhere the farmers themselves were expert. Farmhouses tended to be low—a story and a half or 2 stories—and had either a gambrel roof with equal pitches or a plain slant roof—never even nearly as steep as a Virginia farm roof. As elsewhere north of Maryland, central chimneys outnumbered end chimneys—serving better for heavy winter heating. The very old farmhouses faced south and had roofs sloping down in the rear almost to the ground. In the towns the earliest houses were of the medieval European type with many gables, diamond paned windows, and overhanging upper stories. Several of these still remain, especially in Salem. A New England town of 1680, with bristling gables and stack chimneys, must have looked very much like the Old World—but most of the houses were altered when the square-paned window and gambrel roof came into fashion between 1700 and 1730. About this time, also, Georgian architecture came into vogue with its classical ornamentation—giving rise to the typical "Colonial Doorway". In the towns, a variety of Georgian designs came in, and tall Georgian steeples arose on all the churches both urban and rural. Gentlemen's country seats were square and spacious, with exquisitely carved doorways but a plainer general finish than Middle-Colony houses. In the old Rhode Island Narragansett Country, where (as I once mentioned) there was a patriarchal plantation life like that of the South, the demand for large houses arose before the evolution of the Georgian mansion type; and was met by a spacious enlargement of the simple gambrel roof farmhouse type. Nowhere else in America was the gambrel roof design used for such large and elaborate houses. Details of design varied greatly in different parts of New England—there being, for instance, a whole Connecticut-Valley school of architecture now well exemplified by the village of Deerfield, Mass. Wood was always the favourite construction material, though brick invaded some of the larger town in the 18th century. On the farms, toward the end of the 18th century, it became usual to link the barn and other buildings to the house by means of arches suggesting those of Virginia plantation-houses. Arrangements like that shewn in the sketch are very typical. These rows of buildings on a winding grey road, with stone-walled rocky pastures undulating off to the edge of a forest, and hillside apple orchards with gnarled boughs rising in the rear, present about as perfect a picture of a long-settled countryside as anything in North America. The structures fit the landscape so well—and both are so unique and distinctive and graceful—that artists never tire of painting the idyllic ensemble. Add to these things a background of tall ancient elms, an old mill by a reedy stream, and a vista of a distant valley where the massed foliage is pierced by the roofs of a village with characteristic white-steepled New England church, and you get an impression of stable antiquity and tranquil beauty not excelled by anything else this continent has to offer. Not even the South can approach this—the greater taste of our countryside being due to the fact that the farmers were largely prosperous yeomen (and even small gentry) with an eye for neatness and beauty, whereas the small farmers of the South were a humbler class, subordinate to the planters on their vast estates. Also, the New England topography with its rolling terrain, picturesque rocks, splendid trees, and exquisite rivers and valleys, is absolutely unapproachable from a scenic standpoint. In Southern New England the landscapes are beautiful in a gentle way; but in Vermont and New Hampshire the presence of mountains adds a kind of weird grandeur. The ancient *seacoast*, with old ports and wharves, and memories of whaling and East-India trade, has a flavour all its own—Marblehead, Mass. being an ineffably glamourous place hardly changed since 1700 or 1760. I am well situated to enjoy all types of New England antiquities; for by going just north of Providence I can tap the region of hills and forests, whilst by going south down either shore of Narragansett Bay I can get at the colonial seaports and fishing villages—Pawtuxet, Apponaug, and Wickford on the west shore, and Warren and Bristol on the east shore. And by taking an hour's coach trip—or a two-hour sail down the bay—I can reach ancient Newport with its winding lanes, colonial public buildings, and typical 18th century waterfront. Possibly it is this environment which made me such a natural antiquarian. The *mills* of old New England deserve especial mention. Many are in excellent condition, though of commercial use only in Vermont and New Hampshire. Standing beside some ancient stream with mossy banks, venerable dam, and glassy mill-pond above, they recall pictures of the Old English countryside as their ponderous old wheels grind on. In flat regions devoid of good streams—like Cape Cod, the island of Aquidneck, (on which Newport is situate) and other seacoast areas, there used to be numerous old *windmills* with flailing arms—some of which can still be found; at least 2 on Aquidneck, and many on Cape Cod. Another typical landscape feature surviving from fairly old days (the 1820's) is the *covered bridge*—a veritable tunnel so built to protect the roadway from the weather. These are rapidly disappearing, and are now wholly absent from Rhode Island—though I recall two or three hereabouts in my youth. They are still quite numerous, however, in Vermont; and a few survive on central and western Massachusetts. One odd thing about them is that, in winter, the farmers have to shovel snow on the roadway to provide a passage for sleighs and sleds—which still exist in Northern New England, though long gone from these parts. Yes—New England is a great old country, with 300 years of continuous settled life behind it; and it'll take the machines and the foreigners a long time to tear the whole of it down! There is a real and inimitable beauty in the marks of continuous habitation lingering about a place like this—a beauty that can't be duplicated by any amount of raw modern "landscaping" and scenery-building. I hate to see the old landmarks go, one by one, for with them goes a great deal of the very essence of the world I grew up in. And I shall be very melancholy about leaving if ever the bitterness of the winters drives me south—though of course I shall find an equal antiquity awaiting me in the Charleston region. Still farther north, Quebec topography is much like that of New England, save that the vegetation is thinner, and that great treeless areas occur. The French farms have barns much like those of New England, save that they have small belfries or cupolas and tiny steeples atop them. The farmhouses are very different, following ancient French lines and having steep roofs curved *at the eaves only*. These roofs overhang the cottages considerably. In the early 19th century another type with gambrel roof having a long, very steep lower pitch was devised—though this type is more common in towns and villages. Houses are commonly of stone, and are almost universally surrounded by flower gardens. The countryside as a whole is notable for such typical features as zigzag rail fences of the Virginia type, *very small* haystacks of a sort never seen in the U.S., wayside shrines with images of Christ or the Virgin Mary, small milk or produce carts drawn by *dogs*, and quaint villages with clustering roofs surmounted by the inevitable tall French steeple of the all-powerful Catholic Church—a type of steeple more ornate and grotesque than the tastefully simple Georgian spires of New England. All buildings have French casement windows with cross bars instead of the small square panes of English colonial windows. Church steeples and urban roofs are frequently *tinned* in order to produce a silver-like lustre—the effect (especially in Quebec City) being ineffably picturesque. The city itself is the most gloriously picturesque sight on this continent, with myriads of silvery belfry-steeples, and steep slant roofs of characteristically French design. The houses are tall, with broad end chimneys and high doorways. An unique feature is the prevalence of 2 attic stories—involving double rows of dormers. One finds these especially marked in the ancient stone public buildings. Other odd things are the half-opening blinds on the windows—the top halves remaining closed while the bottom halves are thrown open. Streets with steps, vast flights of stairs from lower town to cliff-perched upper town, wide vistas of river, countryside, lower-town roofs, and distant Laurentian mountains from the upper town or the still loftier citadel—all these things are typical of urban Quebec.

Needless to say, I enjoyed your Texas anecdotes tremendously. In time, I think your region will become very well represented in literature; for I notice an increasing number of books dealing with it—books which I hope to get time to read some day. For example, there is a history of the Chisolm Trail—allusions to which were doubly interesting because of my having heard about it more directly in your letters. John Chisum was a truly feudal figure—a fact which is not lessened by his hard-headedness, since many of the actual leaders in feudal times were undoubtedly just such steelly business-men. But for sheer drama it would be hard to beat the Lincoln County War you so vividly illuminate. I have of course heard of "Billy the Kid"—in fact, there is a book about him, though I have not read it—but I never came across any specific account of his battles. You certainly shed an epic light on the McSween farmhouse battle—again emphasising the veritable Iliad atmosphere of early Southwestern history. Most assuredly you must write that history of the Southwest. No one with your keen knowledge of the subject, and your positively genius-touched ability to "put it over", has any right not to!

There seems to me no question but that the future of Russia is Oriental. The Mongol element is one influence, and the strongly Oriental Iranian elements—Georgians, Caucasians, etc., form another. The present dictator Stalin is from Georgia, and you can see the East written all over him. Then, too, it is very probable that the Russian people will eventually assimilate all of their enormous Jewish element.

I feel sure, as you do, that Africa has swallowed many a white tribe both Aryan and Semitic—to say nothing of Hamites, Dravidians, and Australoids. The vast variability of the present black population is beyond all possible variation within the true negro race. The actual negro base in undoubtedly very primitive and apelike—best represented by the tribes of the west coast—but on this has been superimposed all sorts of unknown stocks, European and Asiatic, so that in the East we see such relatively superior tribes as the Kaffirs and Hottentots. An old negress who occasionally works for my aunt claims to be a Hottentot, and I can well believe it from her general practical intelligence as compared with the usual nigger level. All I know of the Boskop race—in fact, that *anybody* knows of it—is that around Cape Town there have been found skulls of a race utterly unlike any other known; with *the largest cranial capacity of any human stock*.[2] It must have been white, but it was not civilised at the period of these skulls, since only primitive artifacts (say of about the Cro-Magnon—Aurignacean—grade) were found associated with the latter. If it had any known affiliations at all, these must have been with the Cro-Magnons. Probably it was surprisingly recent in time—perhaps 5000 to 10,000 years back, or even less. When the deposits are better examined geologically, more can be told. The discovery is very recent, and was made by amateurs—a couple of railway employes, father and son. Anthropologists, in comparing the skills of surviving African tribes with the excavated specimens, think they can trace faint evidences of the strange old blood in some of the southeasterly Bushmen. An idea quite prevalent is that this old race formed the aboriginal stock of the Cape of Good Hope region, and that the negroes did not penetrate the district till late in history. Perhaps there were no blacks even in Rhodesia when the Semites came down the east coast and founded Zimbabwe—it may have been these mysterious elder people whom they found. Apparently they were peaceful and artistic—intelligent and sensitive, but without any especial wish to found a formal civilisation. They seem to have lacked both aggressiveness and defensive skill, so that they fell an easy prey to the savage blacks who eventually arrived. Whatever be the case, it is clear the African ethnology and history are a tangled and obscure affair; involving many a dramatic surprise for the future historian and archaeologist. It is not for nothing that Africa has been labelled a continent of mystery.

As for dreams—you will see more of my Romano-Hispanic specimen as Long's novel advances. He has taken a good deal of my own wording in describing the annihilation of the cohort. Your visions of the primal north are surely notable in the extreme, especially in view of your lifelong environment; and argue a personality and imagination of the most distinctive sort. They contrast strongly with my own pseudo-memories, for I must admit—despite your dislike of Rome—that I have never found it possible to feel like anything but a Roman in connexion with ancient history. The moment history gets behind the Saxon conquest of Britain, my instinctive loyalty and intangible sense of personal placement snap south from the Thames to the Tiber with startling abruptness—so that I cannot help thinking of "our" legions, "our" conquests, "our" flashing eagles, and "our" melancholy coming fate as foreign blood dilutes the old hawk-nosed stock and weakens our fibre in the face of barbarian invasion. I have a profound subconscious Roman patriotism which takes hold where Anglo Saxon patriotism leaves off; so that my nerves tingle curiously at such images or phrases as S. P. Q. R., Alala!, the Capitoline Wolf, Nostra Respublica, mare majorum, consuetudo Populi Romani,[3] the toga, the galea, the short sword, the aquilae, or *any* really Roman place or personal name—Brundisium, Mediolanum, Genua, Florentia, Forum Julii, P. Cornelius Scipio, Q. Antistius Labeo, Cn. Pompeius, and so on. I find myself (*despite my* **conscious** *intellectual and aesthetic preference for them*) despising Greeks as effeminate—parvuli Graeculi—barbatuli—and deploring the influx of barbarian blood, especially Eastern, (eheu, Syrus Orontes in Tiberium defluxit!)[4] into Roman veins. Still more in detail—I find myself disliking the later Empire and longing for the simpler days of the ancient Republic of Cato and the Scipiones. Toward the western barbarians (my own real blood ancestors) I find myself holding sentiments of mixed fear and respect. I recognise their Roman-like strength and aggressiveness, and fear they will retain them longer than "we" (the Roman people) can manage to do. Whenever, for instance, I think of the Teutonic folk-hero Arminius—(or Herrmann) it is with grudging admiration and melancholy; for did he not annihilate "our" three legions under P. Quintilius Varus?[5] "Vare, Vare, legiones redde!" And I thrill with pride at the later defeat of the Germans, and the recovery of Varus' lost eagles, by that hero of heroes, Claudius Drusus Germanicus. S. P. Q. R.! ROMA! I have had dreams of the Gallic War—but always as a Centurio or Legatus in the camp of C. Caesar. I do not, in these dreams, view the Galli with disrespect; but my prime wish concerning them is simply to bring them under our Roman Imperium. My sentiments toward Caesar are usually divided—I admire his genius, and am loyal to him in the interest of the Republic, but I do not personally like him, and am disturbingly well-disposed toward Cn. Pomeius and the Senatorial Party. My image of myself in all these dreams is of a man of early middle age and typical Roman physiognomy—the image having never varied from boyhood to the present. My name, however, does very widely—L. Caelius Rufus, M. Valerius Messala, C. Hurunculeius,[?] P. Cornelius Lentulus Crus, T. Fulvius, P. Licinius, etc. being only a few among many. It is not too much to say that I am compelled to view all the ancient world through Roman eyes. It is honestly *difficult* for me to think of regions like Graecia, Aegyptus, Palaestina, Hispania, Gallia, Illyricum, Mesopotamia, Carthago, Cyrenaica, Athenae, &c. &c., by other than their Roman names. My *subconscious* image of Babylon, for instance, is far from what a devotee of El-Lil would expect. To me—instinctively—it is a strange great ruin in the country of the Parthians, lately conquered by our arms under M. Ulpius Trajanus, and described in the history of Q. Curtius Rufus. A desolate, vine-grown place—which the Parthians use as a quarry in getting building and repairing materials for their capital Ctesiphon. My image of the Caledonian tribes, too, is simply that of a dangerous menace to be pushed back. If we can't defend the Vallum Antonini, along the line betwixt the Clotae Aestuarium and Bodotriae Aestuarium—the line first fortified by Cn. Julius Agricola and restored by C. Lollius Urbicus,—we can at least hold the Valla Hadriani et Severi, betwixt Itunae Aestuarium and the mouth of the Tina. This old Britannia is to me a place of strange woods and fields traversed by our roads and dotted with our towns and camps—Eboracum, the capital—Isca Silurum, capital of Britannia Secunda,—Lundum, Camulodunum, Durovernum, Durobrivae, Venta, Caeva, Isca Dumnoniorum, Glevum, Aquae Sulis with the balneae, Deva, and so on, and so on—stone streets with drains in the centre, stone and stucco houses, marble temples, amphitheatres, country villas—Italia under northern skies, with more and more of the natives adopting Roman names and joining us in the towns and the army. And always the great oak woods looming and brooding in the offing, and holding one knows not what horrors. The great stone circles, reared by unknown hands—the barbarous Druidae, whose black linkage with the unknown makes necessary their destruction for the sake of the Republic's safety, just as in Italia, in the time of M. Cato and P. Scipio, we had to suppress the dark enormities of Bacchic worship by means of the Senatus Consultum de Bacchanalibus. And so on—and so on. Yet as a matter of fact I have not a drop of blood in my veins other that Teutonic and Celtic; and am a lanky, Anglo-Saxon featured specimen 5 feet 11 inches tall, with a chalk-white complexion which tans only with difficulty, and bleaches again with almost Scandinavian facility. Though I have brown hair and eyes, there can't be more than a slight trace of any but a Nordic heritage in me. Physically, my ancestors were the Germanic hordes of Arminius who annihilated "our" legions, and the very Celtic barbarians whom "we" had to hold in check at the Valla Antonini et Hadriani. Yet some odd quirk has put my wandering imagination on the other side of the fence, and made it take its stand utterly outside my line of blood. If I believed in hereditary memory, I'd say that some Roman legionary must have been among the pre-genealogical forbears on my Welsh side—but if he was, he left little enough trace in my looks! That dream-face I spoke of is about as unlike my real one as a white face well could be! I realise that the Romans were an extremely prosaic race; given to all the practical and utilitarian precepts I detest, and without any of the genius of the Greek or glamour of the Northern barbarian. And yet—I can't manage to think behind 450 A.D. except as a Roman! Can you beat it? Your Indian War dreams are surely realistic enough! I never had anything like that, though I constantly dream of being in the 18th century . . . . both in England and in these Colonies. In such dreams I look more like myself—and this dream-self has come to represent me so perfectly that in waking hours I sometimes feel odd for lack of my three-cornered hat, powdered periwig, satin small-clothes, silver sword, and buckled shoes. Probably this 18th century personality is even stronger than the Roman one—indeed, it has coloured my writings and point of view from the very first. As a small child I used to find a strange fascination in the steep colonial hill districts of Providence, and in the older books of the family library—the 18th century ones with the long "s". I began using the long "s" myself in writing—when I was about 7—and aped the prose of Addison and Johnson, and the verse of Pope, Thomson and Goldsmith. In a way, the key to my whole personality can be found in my ineradicable spiritual membership in the 18th century. Possibly even my weird tastes spring from subconscious effects to defeat the objective natural laws which have placed me physically in an age not psychologically my own. When I come to think of it, some of my earliest sensations of weirdness were derived from my contemplation of the old Georgian hill streets and the archaic New England countryside, and my imaginative certainty that I was somehow closer to these things than to the fin-de-siecle world into which I was corporeally born.

I don't agree that you couldn't do justice to Kelly, the Conjer-Man, and his Atlantean antecedents, in a story—and you will try it some day. I have a whole book full of idea-jottings which I could never write up if I lived to be a thousand—indeed, I sometimes lend it to other writers and invite them to borrow from it. That's where, for instance, Long got the idea of his Black Druid. Just now I'm lending it to Whitehead.[6] If you ever want to see it, let me know. Not that it's really worth anything. By the way—you mentioned not having seen "Arthur Jermyn". Here it is—my only copy aside from my W.T. file; hence to be returned ultimately, although there is not the slightest hurry about it. Hope it won't bore you—it is a product of 1920, and perhaps has some crude or naive spots which contemporary works wouldn't have.

I read your fight story with keen interest and enjoyment, and believe you succeeded admirably in its creation. It hangs together finely, and has enough varied turns and incidents to satisfy the most exacting popular craving for action. It is lifelike, too, despite the necessary strain on probability, and gives one a real sense of the breathless adventure in unknown and sinister labyrinths. Steve is a likeable chap,[7] for all his simian resemblance; and the reader ends up with three cheers for his indomitable spirit! I never heard of Fight Stories before—surely the "pulp" magazine world is going in for intensive specialisation! I wish I could write more *variedly*—heaven knows I need the money—but when I get off of weird stuff I am always abominably uninspired. That is rather bad luck for me, since of all possible markets, the weird one is about the narrowest. Do you go in much for "scientifiction"—the "voyage to Mars" stuff? There is really quite a market for that—at least three magazines. Clark Ashton Smith is invading that field with some degree of success.

Thanks for the Merritt yarn—at which I haven't yet had time to glance, but which I shall read with interest and return very carefully. Merritt has great stuff in him, but has unfortunately succumbed to the popular magazine formula to some extent. His best work was, I think, his very first—the original version of "The Moon-Pool" (before he added a sequel and changed the early part to match) as published in the old All Story Magazine some time in November 1918.[8] That story had *genuine atmosphere* of a sort seldom found in magazine fiction. The unholy archaism of the Pacific Islands, and the hints of pre-human monstrosity in the vast Cyclopean masonry on Ponape . . . . . agh! I can even now feel the authentic kick it gave me when I read it for the first time! Merritt knew, in those days, how to hint at elder aeons and cosmic linkages too terrible and intangible to define—but latterly, alas, the glib and unctuous formula of commercial cheapness has "got" him. Another fine old piece of Merritt's—considerably shorter—was "The People of the Pit"—reprinted a few years ago in Amazing Stories. I shall certainly be glad to see how he is writing today—I don't believe I've seen a thing of his since the obviously machine-made "Ship of Ishtar", which was republished as a book.

Well—let me thank you again for all the items—"Alleys of Peril", the pictures, the Merritt loan, and above all the magnificent epic glimpses of primitive Texas. Hope you found the antiquarian travel matter enjoyable—and again let me urge you to send for it again if it would be of the least use to you in your permanent files. Hope the present rambling hasn't bored you too extensively. The things I have to tell of the Old East seem not so full of action as of tame description. Not that there haven't been stirring events hereabouts—Indians, privateering, the expeditions against New-France, the Revolution, and so on—but that my specialty seems to be the assimilation of mere visual impressions of survival, which stand as symbols of the historic pageantry stretching behind. Customs, institutions, perspectives, national moods, etc. etc. stick in my memory and imagination as tenaciously as do the events of actual conflict. But you can imagine your own fights against the merely scenic and architectural background I suggest.

Best wishes—

Yrs most cordially and sincerely—

H P Lovecraft

Notes

1. See HPL's "An Account of a Trip to the Fairbanks House" (1929).

2. The Boskop is a region in the Transvaal of South Africa. Boskop Man was once thought to be a unique and ancient hominid genus that lived in southern Africa probably between 30,000 and 10,000 years ago. The genus was based on a hominid skull discovered in 1913. The skull was 30 percent larger then the modern human skull. The term "Boskop Man" is no longer used by anthropologists, and its supposedly unusual characteristics are considered to be a misinterpretation. HPL undoubtedly had Boskop Man in mind when he alluded to "great-headed brown people who held South Africa in B.C. 50,000" in "The Shadow out of Time."

3. S.P.Q.R. = *Senatus Populusque Romanus* (The Senate and the People of Rome); *Alala!* = a Graeco-Roman battle cry; *Nostra Respublica* = our republic; *mare majorum* = the sea of our ancestors (i.e., the Mediterranean); *consuetudo Populi Romani* = the custom of the Roman People.

4. "The Syrian [river] Orontes empties into the Tiber." Juvenal, *Satires* 3.62. Juvenal's text reads: "Syrus in Tiberim defluxit Orontes."

5. P. Quintilius Varus, a Roman general, suffered a disastrous defeat in 9 C.E. at the hands of the German barbarians led by Arminius at the Saltus Teutobergiensis (Teutoberg Forest) in northwestern Germany. Three entire Roman legions were annihilated.

6. HPL refers to his commonplace book. FBL's story "The Black Druid" (*WT*, July 1930) derives from one entry; Henry S. Whitehead's story "Cassius" (*Strange Tales*, November 1931) from another.

7. I.e., Sailor Steve Costigan, one of REH's series characters.

8. A. Merritt, "The Moon Pool" (*All-Story Weekly*, 22 June 1918). HPL ranked this version (not its subsequent incorporation with its sequel, "The Conquest of the Moon Pool," as the novel *The Moon Pool*) as one of his ten favorite weird tales.

[21] [TLS]

[c. January 1931?]

Dear Mr. Lovecraft:

This is rather a belated letter thanking you for the cards and literature you sent me. They certainly constituted a wealth of interest and information, and looking at the views of the old houses and reading the descriptions made me determine more strongly than ever to cross the Mississippi some day and see these things for myself. I am particularly glad to hear that efforts are being made to reconstruct Colonial survivals. The old houses, landmarks of past grandeur, and so utterly different from the architecture to which I have always been accustomed, particularly intrigued me, and gave me the sensation of gazing at views of an entirely different country, rather than a different part of my own native land. Indeed, I cannot but believe that were it not for a common tongue, America would be a land of many different countries, as divergent and unalike as, say, Holland and Hungary. I am fascinated by your New England scenery and would like to take a walking tour from Rhode Island to Maine; indeed I am determined to do so if I ever come East. I would like to go along the old Mohawk Trail at sunrise, a trail which must be frought with the ghosts of the past and the memories of stirring events in the dim yesterdays. By the way, what is the average altitude of the New England states? I suppose it varies greatly from point to point, owing to the great number of mountains. This part of Texas where I live has an altitude of about 1700 feet and I find I feel better at a somewhat higher level, as a usual thing. That's one thing I have against the coast country—lower altitudes do not seem to agree with me.

I presume you will have gotten the package of cards etc., by the time you've received this letter. Please look them over and see if anything is missing. The package was opened by mistake before I brought it home, and while I do not think such a thing occurred, it is possible that something might have been dropped out. I am very sorry this happened, and if anything is missing, I will do all in my power to recover it and return it to you.

I'm enclosing a post card folder of Texas which I hope you may find of interest. You neednt bother to return it. Its not very complete and gives scant idea of the state as a whole; you'll note that nearly all the views are laid in

South and East Texas. But its West Texas that's the coming empire, however much the Easterners of Red River and the lower Brazos may slight that fact. El Paso and Amarillo are the only towns of any size west of the Colorado but thats no drawback to my mind. And some day the Llano Estacado will team with great cities—not in my day, though—thank the lord. You'll note in these views, the oleanders in bloom in Galveston; the flowers and palms of the streets are the best features of a rather dingy old town, fading as a sea-port since they brought deep water up to Houston.

Again thanking you for the opportunity of studying the views and scenic literature, I am,

Yours most cordially,
Robert E. Howard

[22] [nonextant letter by H. P. Lovecraft]

[c. February 1931]

[23] [TLS]

[c. February 1931]

Dear Mr. Lovecraft:

I highly appreciate your intention for me to retain the antiquarian literature, and would indeed like to have it for my permanent collection, since you say you have duplicates to all the material you sent me, though I feel it would be an imposition on you to ask you to go to the trouble and expense of sending the package back. As I remarked in my last letter, I found the views and descriptive matter most fascinating and received the impression of life lived in a spacious, mellow and solidly founded age so utterly different from the plane of existence I have always known.

I can imagine your fatigue after revising an entire book of verse—it must be a task that exhausts one's energies; however I know that you did a first-class job on it; you could not do otherwise.

Glad you found the folder and pictures of interest; I should have a vast collection of snap-shots, considering the extent of landscape over which I've carried a kodak. But sometimes I've been too lazy and sometimes I've found to my disgust that I was out of films. One time I remember I visited the old Santa Gertruda Rancho (Captain King's South Texas hacienda) and there remembered I'd carelessly left my kodak at the little town of Bishop a good many miles away. When I went up on the Plains last fall, I took along my kodak for the purpose of securing some snap-shots for you, of the Caprock and the canyons—and it was cloudy and rainy practically all the time. Of all the pictures I took, not one was any account at all.

I am glad to learn that New England is resisting the modernistic movement, and that the South also is not following the new trend so much. Chicago—the Middlewest—its to be supposed that they'd fall for the futuristic hokum. Chicago must be a lousy dump from all I've heard. Here in the Southwest, as I see it, at least, modernistic architecture and the like is resisted to a large extent by a Spanish style, tradition, culture or whatever it might be called, though I suppose the eventual result will be a weird blending of the styles. I hope not, though. I particularly like the old "Mission" form of architecture and if I ever build me a house, it will be as much like a hacienda of Spanish days as possible. The furniture too, of high-class Mexicans has a certain richness and attractiveness seldom met with in American homes, whatever their wealth—Mexicans, that is, who have not adopted American ways too wholly. Altogether, Mexican tastes as a whole, appeal to me, though I cannot say that the Mexicans themselves do.

Thanks for giving me the data on the Hittites; most of it was news to me, as my historical education is extremely sketchy and I havent kept up with researches and archeological discoveries, though they fascinate me. If I was wealthy I'd never do anything but poke around in ruined cities all over the world—and probably get snake-bit.

No, I hadnt heard anything about Weird Tales going monthly again, but I'm glad to hear it. My magazine-market is slender enough as it is, without reducing that part of it. I'll probably try to write the "Skull-Face" sequel as I intended.

Glad you found the snake-yarns of some interest. The Southwest has been so long noted for its crop of truly mastodonic lies about reptiles that I find myself hesitant to discuss serpents at all, lest I be placed in the same category! I remember the "Yig" story; it was a good one and I thought at the time that I could detect the touch of your master-hand here and there. I should think it quite likely that a rattler-victim might burst if bitten a great many times. One bull diamond-back carries enough venom in his fangs to kill almost anything smaller than an elephant, except those animals which seem to be immune from such venom. I remember once seeing in a moving picture, a fight between a mongoose and a cobra. The scene wasnt faked, but was a German-issued news-reel spliced into the main picture to lend atmosphere to an Oriental locale. The fight, with the accompanying Oriental music, was most weird. I must say I was surprized at the appearance of the mongoose which I had pictured as something like a mink. He was of a very deceptive appearance; he looked clumsy and slow but he was so quick it was hard to follow his motions. He made no waste movements whatever and his timing and judgment were absolutely wonderful; he would feint with his nose in a way that was science itself and his counter-spring was nothing short of marvelous. If I were managing a boxer, I'd buy him a mongoose and make him study it hours each day. This mongoose, by the way, got his snake.

To return to snakes; this may sound like a regular Texas snake-lie, but I had (and may still have, for all I know) a curious ability to sense the presence of a snake, particularly a rattler, before I saw, smelt or heard him. This ability was very strong in me during the ages of nine, ten and eleven, and gradually dwindled as I grew older, though its never failed me entirely—yet. I may walk blindly into a whole den of the scaly beasts some day, like a cryptic joke of the gods, but so far some obscure instinct has kept me off snakes, even when I couldnt see them. I cant explain this instinct—I cant begin to. But I know that in the past, particularly during the ages I've mentioned, I've suddenly felt cold shudders run up and down my spine, have been shaken with deep nausea, and looking about, have discovered a rattlesnake coiled somewhere out of sight, or sunning himself. It hasnt worked every time. Sometimes I've been only a foot or so from the varmint when I felt the warning, involuntary shudder and nausea. The first time I ever experienced this, was when I was very young, and out in the pastures on a school picnic. We came out of a scrub of woods and went down a slight slope into a sort of wide meadow. I was walking across a fairly large rock, intending to step down off it, when suddenly the sensations described took me, with a blind and sudden panic, and instead of stepping down from the rock, I leaped as far out as I could, and even as I leaped, I heard the blood-freezing whir of a rattler. He was coiled at the base of the rock, and if I had stepped, I'd have stepped right into his coils. As it was I sprang over him and landed out of his reach. This instinct may be a common one for all I know, and I believe any man can feel a rattle-snake's eyes fixed on him, if he isnt completely absorbed in something. That they have hypnotic power is well known. Squirrels, prairie dogs and birds are unable to flee when transfixed by the baskilisk power of the serpent's stare, though they may leap up and down, flutter wings or limbs, and give vent to the most pitiable outcries. I hate snakes; they are possessed of a cold, utterly merciless cynicism and sophistication, and sense of super-ego that puts them outside the pale of warm-blooded creatures.

Its a pity the Yids have taken New York. I imagine the mongrel population does present a bizarre aspect—I remember with what deep interest and absolute fascination I read your story, "He," with its setting in the mysterious labyrinth of New York's alleys and secret ways. I cannot praise that tale too highly; the impelling sweep of its power held me positively enthralled and spell-bound.

I must say that you have done what no one and nothing else ever has done—aroused in me a spark of interest in New York. Until reading your observations on the city, I cannot truthfully say that I ever felt any real desire even to visit New York. I always wanted to see New England, but New York never interested me. But what you say of the dark aliens, towering buildings, labyrinthine alleys, etc., and your comparisons of the city with Babylon and the dark towns of old, rouse in me a sense of exotic strangeness, mystery and weirdness, as in the shadow-haunted, black-spired cities of lost empires.

I agree with you that there is far too much Semitic control of publication and I view this fact with deep resentment. If American literature cant somehow shake off the strangle-hold the Jews seem to have gotten on it, I believe its doomed. Not denying that the Semitic race is capable of producing fine work itself; but to each race its own literature. I dont want to control the artistic expression of the Jews, and by God, I dont want them to control and direct the expression of my race.

You're right about the haggling and noise accompanying commerce among the Orientals. In New Orleans all this noise and argument isn't confined to the Semites alone. I used to pass the Old French Market and hear the Italian women screeching and squabbling over pennies, and see them grabbing and snatching in shameless greed until I was sick and ashamed of the whole human race. That kind of stuff absolutely physically nauseates me. I realize that in the slums its a struggle to live and conditions make people fight over pennies, but plenty of the people I saw screeching and scrapping in the markets were not slums-rats. The Continental European peasant seems to have inherited an innate spirit of hard, shameless avarice, difficult to get rid of.

I have read and re-read, with the utmost interest, your comments on Colonial architecture and wish to thank you for going to so much trouble of detail and explanation, for it has been a veritable education for me. My ideas of early architecture have been so very vague—based mainly on Spanish missions, old adobe houses, and a few plantation houses with great pillars, on the banks of the Mississippi. I wish to express my admiration for your knowledge of the subject, which is certainly deep and vast. I hope you will be able the make the trip to Europe which you mentioned once, because, from what I've read of old castles and buildings in general there, they must furnish a veritable paradise for an antiquarian. Looking over your descriptions and the drawings—and you are an illustrator of no small talent—I find a curious fact in regard to architecture of the Southwest—It is, largely, a queer conglomeration of the styles you depict, together with many features either evolved separately or imported from Mexico and Southern Europe. I have seen nearly every feature you mention in one way or another, but cannot remember having ever seen any house that represented entirely, any one of the types you show. The New Jersey house with its porch seems more familiar than any of the others you have sketched, though without the attic windows.

One feature that the older houses of the Southwest had—after log-cabin days—was the porch. Almost invariably there were deep, wide porches, front and back; sometimes one porch which went clear around the house. These were necessary for coolness; milk and ollas of water were kept there where the breeze could blow on them and at the same time remain in the shade. And people sat there and rested in the evening. But now porches are vanishing. People dont sit on them like they used to; they're out gadding about. Old ranch houses used to have a wide open hall running through them—or rather the house itself was devided into two parts connected by a roofed hallway open on both sides. Generally the family slept in one part of the house and cooked and ate in the other part.

I'm surprized to hear the Virginians still use rail fences; they went out of general use in Texas years and years ago. In fact, they never were used in the western part very much—there wasnt enough trees. Rail fences were used in Arkansas—my grandmother—born in Alabama and raised in Mississippi and Arkansas—used to say that she'd never heard of barbed wire till she came to Texas in 1885.

You find the most un-American looking houses in South Texas, where Poles, Swedes and Germans have built homes, following old country styles. I particularly remember an old Swede who lived about seventeen miles inland from Galveston who lived in real old-country style—if that means living like a hog. He lived in a queer two-storied house with a very steep roof and small windows, and the stairway on the outside. He lived in the second story; the lower floor was a stable wherein dwelt horses, mules, cows, hogs and chickens. He lived in America for a good many years but never took out naturalization papers. At last he sold out and went back to Sweden with all the money he'd hoarded. And he found that he was no longer a Swedish citizen. They shot him back to the U.S. and the U.S. didnt want him either. He wasnt a citizen and he got into some kind of a jamb by lying, somehow, I heard, to the customs officials. They booted him back to Sweden and the last time I heard of him, he was being kicked back and forth like a football. Nobody wanted him; and if you'd ever smelt him, you wouldn't wonder why.

Your sketch of the New England stone walls reminds me of the stone fences, sections of which I've tumbled down in search of gold popularly supposed to have been hidden under them by Mexican outlaws—in the Palo Pinto country. Stone fences were common there, among the hills and when I contemplate the work they represent, it always fatigues me.

It is a beautiful and alluring scene that you draw in your vivid description of New England landscape with its ancient farm-houses, streams and dreaming valleys and I can understand your attachment for it and sympathize with your feelings at seeing the old landmarks give way to the rising tide of modernism—well, may they not all go, and may the Colonial traditions still stand for many years to come!

I'm glad you find my rambling comments on Southwestern history and tradition not too boresome. Yes, I think the section is at last coming into its own in literature. A vast lost empire has been slumbering here for a hundred years, waiting for some skilled pen to wake it into life. I think that writers are beginning to realize that fact now. More, I think that at last, the bulk of people are beginning to weary of sophisticated trash, novels dealing with perverts and half-baked pseudo-artists, and are turning toward the more wholesome phases of American life—toward the clean, clear cut epics of pioneering and settlement. Well, the past is dreaming in the Southwest, high endeavor, stark cruelty, red war and heroism—material for a thousand books and chronicles. An empire dreams between Red River and the Rio Grande—

Here men and women were confronted, in the very recent past, by conditions that had been forgotten east of the Mississippi for centuries. When men began to write of the West, it was to exploit its more lurid aspects for sensational purposes. Hence, rose the "cowboy" tradition, the "Wild West" tradition—an absolutely criminal distortion of the literary growth of the region and traditions that made a vulgar jest out of what should have been one of the most vital and inspiring pageants of American history. What the ignorant and blundering pens of sensational yellow-backed novel writers failed in doing, the pens of sophisticated arm-chair critics completed. Really good writers, with a few exceptions, shied away from the Western tale, lest they be branded with the yellow-backed dime novelist. It seems to me, from what I've read and heard, that most people who have never seen the West, are devided into classes—the class that believes the West swarms with movie-type cowboys and Indians where bullets whiz continually—and the class that lifts the lip in scorn and rejects all the tales of the West as mere drivel. The truth, as of course you realize, not belonging to either of the above mentioned classes, lies about half-way between. Men didnt go about with guns slung all over them, shooting at the drop of a hat, hanging rustlers to every tree, chasing Indians twenty-three hours of the day, but life was a fierce and hard grind, and murder and sudden death were common. Now thinking people all over America are beginning to realize the truths of the pioneer West, with the resultant boom in good Western literature—which I hope spells the doom of the Wild Bill dime-novel.

Referring to the Chisholm trail, which I've mentioned before, I was born almost on it, as the main branch passed very close to the little town where I first saw the light of day. That branch went up into Oklahoma and Kansas. The western branch went into New Mexico and on up into Canada. Think of hazing a herd of longhorns from the Rio Grande to Canada! Yet it was done occasionally; it took a year at the least estimate.

Yes, John Chisum was a giant figure of the early days—much, as you suggest, like the hard headed and hard handed barons of medieval days—with the exception that he never did any of his own fighting himself!

Thank you very much for the kind things you said in regard to my efforts at depicting the Lincoln County war; I appreciate them very highly indeed, coming as they do, from a man of your literary ability and artistic education.

Yes, the Lincoln County war was a dramatic and bloody episode. Wherever the Aryan race reverts to its early history in thought and mode of living, fierce feuds arise and are fought out to the bitter finish. Witness the feuds of the Virginia and Kentucky hills; witness the short, ferocious feuds of early Texas; witness the "wars" of New Mexico, Arizona, Colorado and California.

Western feuds have generally been fought over land—cattle—sordid commercial wrangles in outward appearance, but with the underlying reasons of stubborn independent pride. More men have been killed in Texas over fences than for any other one reason. When two men own each thousands of acres, it seems foolish for them to shoot each other to death because one insisted on setting his fence forward a foot or so, doesnt it? But its the old story of "the principle of the thing." And after all, a man cant be blamed for defending what he thinks is his, or taking what he thinks is his. Say you and I own adjoining ranches and I claim that the fences werent run according to the survey. I claim a strip of your land four feet wide and half a mile long. You are just as certain that it dont belong to me. I come in the night and set the fence up four feet. You are patient and not quarrelsome, so you come back the next night and set the fence back where it was. I come again and start moving that fence once more. Well, there's nothing left for you to do but take your Winchester and start throwing lead in my direction and you're quite right, too. A man has a right to defend his property. Its not the money value or the grazing value of the land; its the sturdy resolve of the Anglo-Saxon or the Scotch-Irish-American not to be bullied out of his natural rights. And when both contestants are of the same breed, and both absolutely certain they're right, well, by-standers might as well start ducking, because there's only one way to settle a row like that, and if its taken to court, it wont do any real good, but merely make feeling more bitter on each side, which-ever way the decision goes.

The Lincoln County war began in a cattle row. Thieves were stealing John Chisum's cows and being acquitted in the courts. Dolan, Reilly and Murphy were merchants in the town of Lincoln and all-powerful. Murphy ordered his lawyer, McSween, to defend certain rustlers against the charge brought against them by Chisum. McSween refused and Murphy fired him. McSween was engaged by Chisum, prosecuted the rustlers and sent them up the river. Then McSween, Chisum and an Englishman named Tunstall went into partnership and McSween opened a big general store in Lincoln. He grabbed most of the trade and Murphy saw he was being ruined. McSween won a suit against him and for reasons too complicated and lengthy to narrate here, Murphy got out a writ of attachement against McSween's store and Tunstall's ranch—the last an obviously illegal movement, since Tunstall owned his ranch apart from the partnership and had nothing to do with the law suit. A posse of some twenty men rode over to attach Tunstall's ranch. They overtook him in the mountains, shot him down in cold blood, beat out his brains with a jagged rock and left him lying beside his dead horse. That was the beginning of the Bloody Lincoln County War.

Billy the Kid was working for Tunstall as a cowboy. The Kid's real name was William Bonney; he was born in the slums of New York, the son of Irish emigrants. He was brought west when a very young baby and raised in Kansas and New Mexico—mainly the latter. Pancho Villa killed his first man when he was fourteen; Billy went him one better; he was only twelve when he stabbed a big blacksmith to death in Silver City, New Mexico. That started him on the wild life. When he drifted into the Lincoln County country, he already had eleven or twelve killings to his name, though only nineteen years old—that isnt counting Mexicans and Indians. No white man of that age who had any pretensions to gun-fame counted any but the regal warriors of his own race and color. The Kid had probably killed ten or fifteen men of brown and red skins, but he never considered them worthy of mention, though he was considerably proud of his white record.

The Kid was a small man—five feet eight inches, 140 pounds, perhaps—but he was very strong. But it was in his quickness of eye and hand, his perfect co-ordination that made him terrible. There was never a man more perfectly fitted for his trade.

The Kid had been living by gambling and rustling until he started working for Tunstall. At the time of the latter's brutal murder, he was making an honest living as top-hand on the Rio Feliz rancho. Had the Englishman lived, the redder phase of the Kid's life might well have never been written, for Billy liked Tunstall almost well enough to go straight for him.

But the murder of his friend drove him on the red trail of vengeance. McSween organized a posse to arrest the murderers, and had Dick Brewer, foreman of the murdered Englishman, sworn in as a special constable. They rode out after the killers and caught two of them in the Pecos Valley—Morton and Baker—former friends of the Kid. On the way back to Lincoln the Kid killed both of them, supposedly when they tried to escape. One of the posse, an old buffalo hunter named McCloskey, was killed by Frank McNab when he tried to protect the victims.

The next victim was a Murphy man named "Buckshot" Roberts, a Texas man whom it had once taken twenty-five Rangers to arrest. He was so full of lead that he couldnt lift his rifle shoulder high, but shot from the hip. Thirteen McSween men cornered him at Blazer's Mill on the Tularosa river, led by Dick Brewer and the Kid. Bowdre, the Kid's closest friend, shot Roberts through and through, but before the old Texan fell he wounded Bowdre, John Middleton and George Coe, and as he lay dying he shot off the top of Dick Brewer's skull.

The next episode took place in the town of Lincoln. Judge Bristol dared not open the regular session of court there and sent word for Sheriff Brady—a Murphy man—to open court and adjourn it as a matter of routine. On his way down the street to the courthouse, the Sheriff and his deputies were ambushed from an adobe wall by the Kid, Bowdre, O'Folliard—a Texas man—, Jim French, Frank McNab and Fred Wayte; and Sheriff Brady and Deputy Sheriff Hindman were killed. McSween was enraged by this cold blooded murder and threatened to prosecute Billy, which he probably would have done had events allowed. A very religious man was McSween and no more fitted for the role in which Fate had cast him, than a rabbit is fit to lead a pack of wolves. However, he felt that he was in the right, and did his best. Following the murder of the Sheriff, he elected—by force of his gunmen—a fellow named Copeland to the office. Murphy appealed to Governor Axtell, who removed Copeland and appointed George Peppin in his place.

Peppin immediately organized a posse and rode out after McSween's men, killing Frank McNab. Then followed the famous battle of the McSween House. The clans met in Lincoln and in the fighting that followed, Morris, Romero, Semora, and McSween were killed on the McSween side, and Salazar, and Gonzalez were wounded, while on the Murphy side, Crawford was killed by Fernando Herrera, and Lacio Montoya was wounded by the same man. Bob Beckwith was killed by the Kid who also wounded two others.

That was the end of the Lincoln County war, proper. Murphy had died, a broken man, a crownless monarch, and the rest were ready to throw down their guns and call it a draw. All except the Kid and his immediate followers. But from that point, Billy's career was not that of an avenger, fighting a blood-feud. He reverted to his earlier days and became simply a gunman and an outlaw, subsisting by cattle-rustling. There was one other incident of the war, after peace had been declared; one George Chapman, a lawyer from Las Vegas, hired by Mrs. McSween, was murdered wantonly and in cold blood by a Murphy man, one Richardson, a Texan.

Emigration to that part of New Mexico had just about ceased. The tale of the Kid's reign of terror spread clear back east of the Mississippi. President Hayes took the governorship away from Axtell and gave it to Wallace—who, by the way, while writing "Ben Hur" had to keep his shutters close drawn lest a bullet from the Kid's six-shooter put a sudden termination to both book and author. John Chisum, the Kid's former friend, and others got together and elected Pat Garrett Sheriff. Garrett was a friend of the Kid's and knew his gang and his ways. He, himself, was Alabama born, Texas raised—a man of grim determination and cold steel nerves.

Meanwhile the Kid went his ways, rustling cattle and horses. One Joe Bernstein, clerk at the Mescalero agency, made the mistake of arguing with the Kid over some horses Billy was about to drive off. A Jew can be very offensive in dispute. Billy shot him down in cold blood, remarking casually that the fellow was only a Jew.

Several times Garrett and his man-hunters thought they had their hands on Billy but he eluded them. Once they cornered him at a roadhouse, but he killed Deputy Sheriff Jim Carlisle—again in cold blood—and escaped. At Fort Sumner he killed one Joe Grant, a Texas bad man who was after the reward offered for the Kid.

But Garrett was on his trail unceasingly. The Kid's best friends were Bowdre and O'Folliard. At Fort Sumner Garrett killed O'Folliard and at Tivan Arroyo, or Stinking Spring, he killed Bowdre and captured the Kid. Billy was tried in Mesilla and sentenced to be hanged for the murder of Brady and Hindman. He was confined in Lincoln and kept chained, watched day and night by Deputy Sheriffs Bell and Ollinger.[1] He killed them both and got clean away. But love for a Mexican girl drew him back to Fort Sumner when he might have gotten clean away into Old Mexico.

I think the very night must have ceased to breathe as the Kid came from Saval Guierrez's house through the shadows. Surely the nightwind ceased to rustle the pinon leaves and a breathless stillness, pregnant with doom lay over the shadowy mountains and the dim deserts beneath the stars. Surely the quivering mesquites, the sleeping lizards, the blind cactus, the winds whispering down the canyons and the 'dobe walls that glimmered in the starlight, surely they sensed the passing of a figure already legendary and heroic. Aye, surely the night was hushed and brooding as the Southwest's most famous son went blind to his doom. He crossed the yard, came onto the porch of Pete Maxwell's house. He was going after beef, for Celsa Gutierrez to cook for a midnight supper. His butcher knife was in his hand, his gun in his scabbard. Pete Maxwell was his friend; he expected no foes. On the porch he met one of Garrett's deputies, but neither recognized the other. The Kid, wary as a wolf, flashed his gun, though, and backed into Pete's room which opened on the porch. There he halted short—in the shadows he made out vaguely a dim form that should not be there—someone he knew instinctively was neither Pete nor one of Pete's servants. Where was that steel trap will of the Kid's that had gotten him out of so many desperate places? Why did he hold his fire then, he who was so quick to shoot at the least hint of suspicion? Azrael's hand was on him and his hour was come. He made his last mistake, leaping back into the doorway where he was clearly limned against the sky. He snapped a fierce enquiry—and then Death bellowed in the dark from the jaws of Pat Garrett's six-shooter. They carried the Kid into a vacant carpenter shop and laid him on a bench, while the Mexican women screamed and tore their long black hair and flung their white arms wildly against the night, and the Mexican men gathered in scowling, fiercely muttering groups.

The Kid was twenty-one when he was killed, and he had killed twenty-one white men. He was left handed and used, mainly, a forty-one caliber Colt double action six shooter, though he was a crack shot with a rifle, too. That he was a cold blooded murderer there is no doubt, but he was loyal to his friends, honest in his way, truthful, possessed of a refinement in thought and conversation rare even in these days, and no man ever lived who was braver than he. He belonged in an older, wilder age of blood-feud and rapine and war.

Yet to compare him with such brigands as Jesse James, Sam Mason,[2] the Harpes,[3] etc., is foolish. The Kid was an aristocrat among his kind, and as far above torture, needless brutality and senseless slaughter as any man might be. It took the slums of the great cities, the blind, bloody chaos of Border warfare and the gloomy shadows of the thick forests to produce the really inhuman criminals. It was the wilderness that bred Mason, the Harpes and John A. Murrell.[4] Just as the gloom and silence of the New England hills brought forth the lurking shadows in the souls of the Puritans, so the grim deeps of the wilderness brought forth the slumbering atavism and primordial instincts of inhabitants, and made ordinary men into monstrosities from whose foul and abhorrent image the mind shrinks aghast.

And what a grisly fantasy was John A. Murrell's imperial dream and what a strange and ghastly empire he planned! Surely in that man slept the seeds of greatness, overshadowed by the black petals of madness.

The shadow of John A. Murrell and the shadow of the threat of his outlaw empire still hovered over the pine woods and the river lands in the 1850's when my great-grandfather, Squire James Henry, came west along the Wilderness Road with fifty head of fine cattle, a drove of horses, and five big wagons loaded with his family, slaves and belongings.

They were in Murrell's country, and though he had recently been released from prison and his planned slave-uprising had been nipped in the bud, his name was still one to conjure shudders. And in the sunset they came to a wild, frothing river, lashed to frenzy by the flooding rain, and saw, on the other side, a man sitting on a log beneath the forest branches. Something about his posture fired grisly recognition in the mind of a man traveling with the wagon-train and he paled and cried out that it was John A. Murrell who sat on the opposite bank.

I wish I could find words to paint that picture so that you might see it in your mind. The rain had slackened, the clouds were breaking away, rolling sullenly back, shot with blood. On all sides loomed the great trees of the wilderness, monstrous, grim, and pregnant with evil. On the eastern bank the wagons were halted, mired with the ooze and mud through [which] they had toiled since dawn. Before them the nameless river frothed and leaped and raced like a living, malevolent thing, howling among the rapids. On the further bank sat that still figure, like an image, unmoving, a symbol of unamed threat and lurking horror. Behind him the sun was setting, like a ball of blood, glimmering evilly through the black trees and sending somber shafts along the dark and dripping branches that deepened into night-like gloom in the depths of the forest.

The women of the party blenched and the black slaves wailed their terror in a wild death-chant—all except Wyatt, the "outlaw", who feared not man nor demon. The women begged Squire Henry to turn back, or to camp on the east bank, but the Squire merely cursed. He rode into the foaming flood on his great black horse, old Proctor, and the hounds of the flood caught him and shook him like a rat in their teeth. But he battled his way back to the bank and he bound the wagons strongly together. Then he struck into the stream again, with the horses swimming and the wagons floating, and he and Wyatt riding along-side to steady them against the sweep of the current as much as they might. They gained the western bank, and the Squire and Wyatt rode back after the cattle and the horses. The beasts plunged and screamed their fear and the river tore at them white-fanged; and the Squire was threatened not alone by the roaring white water; he saw in Wyatt's murky eyes and in the set of the thick lips, the thought to strike him from his horse and drown him in mid-stream. But he devided his attention between the slave, the river and the beasts, knowing that Wyatt would not dare attack him except from behind; and lashing, battling and cursing, he swam the beasts across and came out safely on the western bank. Then he remembered the man on the log.

He reined about and looked for him; the man still sat in the same posture in which they had first glimpsed him. Apparently he had not moved. The Squire rode up close to him and spoke aggressively and harshly, leaning out from his saddle. The man made no reply; his hands lay listlessly at his side, and vacant eyes gave back an unseeing stare. The squire saw and realized what broken ambitions and ten years in a prison dungeon had done to the man. His face was worn and lined and prematurely old. From beneath wispy white hair, pale, glassy eyes stared through the Squire and far, far beyond him. A rifle lay by the log, like a forgotten bauble. There he sat, in a cloud of lost dreams and dim red visions, the King of the Mississippi—who had worn his crown and pressed his regal seat only in mad visions—the monarch that was to be, in that mad, black kingdom of death and destruction, whose plan was conceived in insanity and crushed in blood and terror. His face was old beyond the ken of men, his eyes were those of a ghost—and his slim white hands that had ripped so many shuddering souls from their fleshly bodies, lay limp on the log that was his final throne.

And so the curtain of iron laughter rings down on the red comedy, and the gods cut the string on which their puppet dances, flinging him into the pit of lost desire. And the red dream of glory and power and gilded empire ended on a rotting log by a nameless river where frogs croaked from the mud and the rain dripped drearily from the shaking branches, black against the sunset. Something about the thing slightly awed the wild Irish planter, and without a word he reined away, gesturing for the wagons to follow. They took up the long westward trek again, lumbering away through the trees; and still John A. Murrell sat upon his log, hearing naught, seeing naught, lost in the shadows of old dreams, and night fell over the wilderness.

Thank you very much for loaning me the manuscript (which I'm returning in this letter). I found it fascinating, with its horrific hints of semi-human monstrosities, and Elder cities set in dark, grim jungles. Its the sort of horror story I like, with its weird foreshadowings and grisly climax—above all, the shadowy web-work of dark implication lying behind the visible action of the tale.

I'm glad you found the prize-fight story of some interest. Its one of the least machine-made of the tales I've been supplying that magazine for the past couple of years. As you say, the pulp magazines are specializing to an alarming rate—western stories, fight stories, air stories, gangster stories—for instance—Wild West Weekly, Battle Stories, Gangster Stories, Two-Gun Stories(!), Wall-street Stories, being a few of the titles of magazines now seen on the news-stands. I've never tried the pseudo-science field—I'm so grossly ignorant of mechanics and science it would be virtually impossible for me to write convincingly in that line. Have you ever tried Argosy? I believe you could sell them some weird stories—they gobble up Merritt's stuff and you have him beat seven ways from the ace. Not that Merritt isnt good; he is. But his work lacks the sheer, somber and Gothic horror of your tales. A touch of mere fantasy sometimes mars his work, whereas your horror-tales are built starkly of black iron, with no slightest hint of tinsel—and therein lies their greatness. I've been reading your tales over again, in the old magazines—The Unnamable, The Temple, He, The Terrible Old Man, The Silver Key—and I hope that Farnsworth will see his way to publish all of them in book form soon—together with "The Festival" and "The Music of Erich Zann" both of which I missed, somehow. These must have been published in the old Weird Tales. By the way, did the old magazine go bankrupt or was it in good shape when Mr. Wright took it over? I seem to have heard from some source that it was in pretty rotten shape when he took it.

If you havent seen the latest Oriental Stories, let me know. I have some extra copies. It contains a story by Tevis Clyde Smith and me, which you might possibly entertain an idle half-hour with, though I fear it isnt anything to brag about.[5]

I'm sending you some stuff in a separate envelope which I hope you'll find interesting.

What you say of the pre-historic African race is most interesting and thought-inspiring, and I hope future research throws more light on the past. I feel a deep pity for that people—living in peace and friendliness—an unwarlike and pastoral race—and suddenly confronted by a horde of black slayers as rude and merciless as they were strong. It must have been a slaughter rather than a war, and its a damned pity that the Boskop people didnt have some Aryan traits to stiffen their spines and train their hands in fighting. I hate to think of white people being wiped out and enslaved by niggers. How do you suppose these people got there in the first place? Did they wander down the coast until they came to a country that suited them, or do you suppose their trek took many generations as they slowly shifted southward?

I've read the concluding chapters of Long's story—a splendid tale and very well written. The narration of the dream was the high spot of the whole story, and to my mind, exceeded the final climax. The language used in the whole chapter of the dream, is nothing short of pure poetry and I have reread it repeatedly, and with the utmost admiration. The finely worked plot with its shuddery hints and horrific climax in the night-mantled hills is an absolute triumph in Gothic literature—a story within a story.

I can hardly find words to express the extent to which I was fascinated by your comments on your Roman subconscious and dream-life. As you say, one's instincts and fancy take strange quirks. I envy you your deep and profound knowledge of history and familiarity with classic names and places. I fear I've merely skimmed my historical studies, culling disconnected bits here and there.

But (to omit all mention of American instincts and subconscious sense of personal connection), my strongest instinctive leanings are toward the more ancient cities. I somehow feel more a sense of placement and personal contact with Babylon, Nineveh, Askalon, Gaza, Gath, and the like, than I do with Athens or Rome. I know nothing of the ways and customs of those ancient cities, cannot even form a clear mental picture pertaining to them, yet when I think of the ancient world, my thoughts leap instantly and subconciously to the valley of the Tigris and Euphrates and the fertile lands of Mesopotamia, in the early days of the Semitic kingdoms. I can form no mental picture of Asia Minor of that day—I instinctively think of it merely as a waste of enemies and barbarians. Egypt is a land of brooding mystery that from time to time sends swarming hordes of war-chariots sweeping from the south to ravage and destroy. My real interest and sense of personal placement ceases with the establishment of the Mede-Persian empire. I feel no real kinship with the Semitic races of that day, and I do feel a personal connection with the Aryan Medes and experience a sense of gratification at their victory; yet from that time on, or at least until the Crusades and the invasions of the Mongols, the Near East holds no particular interest for me. Nor, until many centuries later do I feel any clear sense of personal connection with any age or any locality, until my sense of placement settles on the British Isles.

I feel more of an instinctive interest and loyalty toward individuals rather than nations, races or countries; as for instance, and especially, King Saul, King Arthur, (whether historical or legendary), Joan of Arc, Robert Bruce, Brian Boru and Hugh O'Neill. And to a lesser extent, Hannibal, Arminius, King Penda of Mercia, Alfred the Great, Richard the Lion-heart, Bertrand du Guesclin, Edward Bruce, Shane O'Neill, Hugh Ruadh O'Donnell, William Wallace, Patrick Sarsfield, and The FitzGerald.

I have always felt a deep interest in Israel in connection with Saul. Poor devil! A pitiful and heroic figure, set up as a figure-head because of his height and the spread of his shoulders, and evincing an expected desire of be[ing] king in more than name—a plain, straight-forward man, unversed in guile and subtlety, flanked and harassed by scheming priests, beleagered by savage and powerful enemies, handicapped by a people too wary and backward in war—what wonder that he went mad toward the end? He was not fitted to cope with the mysteries of king-craft, and he had too much proud independence to dance a puppet on the string of the high priest—there he sealed his own doom. When he thwarted the snaky Samuel, he should have followed it up by cutting that crafty gentleman's throat—but he dared not. The hounds of Life snapped ever at Saul's heels; a streak of softness made him human but made him less a king. He dared too much, and having dared too much, he dared not enough. He was too intelligent to submit to Samuel's dominance, but not intelligent enough to realize that submission was his only course unless he chose to take the ruthless course and fling the high priest to the vultures and jackals. Samuel had him in a strangle-hold; not only did the high priest have the people behind him, but he played on Saul's own fears and superstitions and in the end, ruined him and drove him to madness, defeat and death. The king found himself faced by opposition he could not beat down with his great sword—foes that he could not grasp with his hands. Life became a grappling with shadows, a plunging at blind, invisible bars. He saw the hissing head of the serpent beneath each mask of courtier, priest, concubine and general. They squirmed, venom-ladened beneath his feet, plotting his downfall; and he towered above them, yet must perforce bend an ear close to the dust, striving to translate their hisses. But for Samuel, vindictive, selfish and blindly shrewd as most priests are, Saul had risen to his full statu[r]e as it was, he was a giant chained. David he knew was being primed for his throne—under his very feet they pointed the young adventurer for the crown. Yet I think he was loath to slay the usurper, because he felt a certain kinship with him—both were wild men of the hills and deserts, winning their way mainly by sheer force of arms, forced into the kingship to further the ends of a plotting priest-craft. To one man Saul could always turn—Abner, a soldier and a gentleman in the fullest sense of the word—too honorable, too idealistic for his own good. Saul and Abner were worth all that cringing treacherous race to which they belonged by some whim of chance.

David was wiser than Saul and not so wise, caring less for the general good, much more for his own. He was the adventurer, the soldier of fortune, to the very end, whereas Saul had at least some of the instincts of true kingship in his soul. David knew that he must follow the lines laid out for him by the priests and he was willing to do so. A poet, yes, but intensely practical. When he heard of the slaying of Saul and Johnathan, he composed a magnificent poem in their honor—but first he gave orders that the people of the Jews should practice with the bow! He knew that archery was necessary to defeat the Philistines, who were evidently more powerful in hand-to-hand fighting than the Israelites, and were skilled in arrow-play. He had a long memory and his enemies did not escape—not even Joab, who did more to win David's kingdom for him than any other one man.

I cannot think of Saul, David, Abner and Joab as Jews, not even as Arabs; to me they must always seem like Aryans, like myself. Saul, in particular, I always unconciously visualize as a Saxon king, of those times when the invaders of Britain were just beginning to adopt the Christian religion.

Another Hebrew who interests me is Samson, and this man I am firmly convinced was at least half Aryan. In the first place, he had red hair or bright yellow hair; I feel certain of this because of his name, and the legend concerning his locks. His name referred to the sun, always pertaining to redness, brightness, golden tinted, in any language; his strength lay in his hair; I connect his name with his hair. What more natural than a superstition attached to the red hair of a child born in a dark-haired race? And that angel in the field—well, in the old, old days of Ireland, there was a legend that the old gods had fled into the west, from which they occasionally emerged to bestow their favours on some lucky damsel. Many a wanderer from the western hills assumed the part of a god. I am convinced that the "angel" was a wandering, red-haired Aryan, and that Samson was his son.

The strong lad's characteristics were most certainly little like those of the race that claimed him. He wouldnt even associate with his people. He feasted and revelled with the lordly Philistines, and his drinking, fighting and wenching sound like the chronicles of some lad from Wicklow or a wild boy from Cork. He was a great jester, a quality none too common in his supposed race, and in the end he displayed true Aryan recklessness and iron lust for vengeance. When, in history, did a true Semite deliberately kill himself to bring ruin to his enemies? The big boy was surely an Aryan.

My antipathy for Rome is one of those things I cant explain myself. Certainly it isnt based on any early reading, because some of that consisted of MacCauley's "Lays of Ancient Rome" from which flag-waving lines I should have drawn some Roman patriotism, it seems. At an early age I memorized most of those verses, but in reciting, changed them to suit myself and substituted Celtic names for the Roman ones, and changed the settings from Italy to the British Isles! Always, when I've dreamed of Rome, or subconsciously thought of the empire, it has seemed to me like a symbol of slavery—an iron spider, spreading webs of steel all over the world to choke the rivers with dams, fell the forests, strangle the plains with white roads and drive the free people into cage-like houses and towns.

Its difficult for me to visualize a Romanized Britain. I know it is there, with the villas and towns you dream of, but I've always instinctively connected myself with the untamed tribes of the West, or those of the heather. The great oak forests are friendly to me, in my dreams, giving me shelter, food and hiding-place. And its almost impossible for me to visualize a Druid as anything but a tall, stately old man, white robed, having golden buckled sandals to his feet and a staff to his hand, with a long white beard and very kindly, very wise eyes. I've never been able to think of the cult as any other than white bearded sages, wise in astronomy and agriculture, very close to Nature. Its difficult for me to think of them in connection with human sacrifices and I've never been able in writing to lend an air of mysterious horror to Druidic-worship. I may some day, but it will be in direct violation to my instincts on the matter. My sense of somber mystery and elder-world horror centers on the worship and priest-craft of the little dark people who came before—the Mediterranean race which preceeded the Celts into Britain. I can experience a real shuddery sense of black magic and devil-worship when I contemplate these little stone age men, with their dark spirits and their bright spirits, their human sacrifice and their polished weapons and implements, the uses for some of which are not now known.

And just as you consciously prefer the Grecians and instinctively lean toward the Romans, I consciously despise the Stuart kings, and instinctively defend them. If there's anything in ancestral memory, this is natural, for to the best of my knowledge, my ancestors on both sides of the Irish Sea fought for those kings. Indeed, one Sir Robert Howard spent seven years in the Tower on their account and was freed only at the Restoration. Always, when I read anything against the Stuarts, I unconciously find myself defending them, even though I may conciously heartily endorse everything said in their disfavor. I reckon I'm just naturally a Jacobite by instinct—why, the Devil knows, because I detest the line consciously. I feel a real personal shame in regard to the Boyne Water. A pity that Shamas a cacagh had not at him even a wee bit of Patrick Sarsfield's spirit. Monmouth was the best of that line, to my notion, and even he ran like a scared rabbit.

Let me again express my admiration for your drawing ability; your pictures of the Roman and the cavalier are strikingly vivid, and I share your dissatisfaction with drab modern mode of dress. I think I'd feel more at home in a suit of chain mail and a surcoat myself! Men's styles have certainly come upon colorless and uninteresting ways.

But now I've rambled on: I only hope I haven't bored you to the point of nausea. I never seem to be able to find a stopping place. Thanking you again for the architectural sketches and descriptions, the loan of the ms. and the antiquarian literature, I am, with best wishes,

Cordially,

Robert E. Howard

Notes

1. Robert A. Olinger (1841–1881), a bad-tempered gunfighter, was serving as one of Pat Garrett's deputies when he was killed by Billy the Kid.

2. Sam Mason (d. 1804) is the earliest bandit associated with Cave-in-Rock, c. 1797. He later removed to the Natchez Trace, where he continued to lead a gang of thieves. He met his end in 1804, but there is some doubt whether the bounty-hunter who killed him was indeed "Little" Harpe.

3. Micajah (1768?–1799; known as "Big Harpe") and Wiley (1770?–1804; known as "Little Harpe"), believed to have been brothers, are considered by some to be the nation's first serial killers.

4. John A. Murrell (1806–1844) was arrested after boasting, to a traveler he had just met, of his plans for leading a slave revolt to establish himself as ruler of Mississippi and Louisiana. Imprisoned in Nashville c. 1834, he was released in 1842 and disappeared.

5. REH and Tevis Clyde Smith, "The Red Blades of Black Cathay."

[24] [TLS]

[c. March 1, 1931]

Dear Mr. Lovecraft:

I'm writing this letter only some two hundred thirty-odd miles from my home town, yet its like being in a different state, so much difference exists in climate, topography and inhabitants. Its spring here, with birds chirping, roses and smaller flowers in bloom, deep fresh grass, palm trees, banana trees, date and fig trees adding to the effect. Only the Mexicans hurry here, ordinarily; the white people go leisurely. Tomorrow begins a week-long fete marking the opening of the old Spanish governor's palace, closed and vacant for generations.[1] Thousands are expected; Cardinal Patrick Hayes of New York is to be the special speaker. San Antonio's strong for fiestas, fetes, bailes, etc.

This town is about the only place in Texas that takes much stock in history; the city itself is like one vast museum of old times.

There is, of course, a great percentage of unmixed American population, but a vast number of San Antonio's people are a welter of mixed bloods of many nations: Indian, Spanish, French, German and Polish. Mexican blood tinges the social order up and down the scale. You will find it in the veins of aristocratic American families, and in the veins of mixed-breed negroes. Not many negroes here though; low class Mexicans crowd them out or absorb them.

Rather too cosmopolitan for my tastes. My natural homeland is Central and Western Central Texas, which localities (with the Great Plains region) are freer from foreignization than any of the rest of the state. I'll add the piney woods of East Texas to that list, though the great new oil fields of that regions are likely to bring in a foreign element. But East Texas swarms with negroes, of which there are but few in Western Central Texas. Neither are there many Mexicans in the latter province, the land being almost entirely in the hands of small independent farmers and resident ranchers. Absentee ownership will eventually prove the ruin of South Texas just as it was the ultimate ruin of Ireland. In my part of the country, the Latin element is small. Here it predominates. The oil booms brought swarms of people from other states into Central Texas and many of them were of foreign parentage, but in almost all cases they were German, Scandinavian and Irish extraction. The Latins dont follow the oil trail much. These Nordic strangers are easily assimulated and absorbed by the native population. Not so easy to absorb strangers from Southern Europe. Its more likely to work the other way round. The percentage of brunets in this city is infinitely greater than in my homeland. The streets swarm with flashing black eyes and black locks, whereas in Central Texas blue and grey eyes and light or only mediumly dark hair are overwhelmingly the rule. A couple of weeks ago I was in a boxing arena in Fort Worth, watching a bout between the welter-weight champion and a lad who was a high school kid with me once, and I noted the predominance of white men in the crowd, which filled the great building to full capacity. Outside of a very few Mexicans, I did not see a single person who was not an unmistakable American of Nordic descent. Of course, there doubtless were a few foreigners but the percent was negligible. Fort Worth is certainly a white man's town—one of the few so remaining. It lies 165 miles east of my home-town, and San Antonio is only some 70 or 80 miles further away, south, south-east. You can travel clean across the state from east to west and find little change in the nationalities of the natives, but a hundred miles north or south makes a lot of difference.

San Antonio certainly offers a colorful and interesting spectacle, not to be duplicated anywhere in the New World. I'm sending you some views which I hope may be of some interest. The colored pictures I got in the Buckhorn Saloon and the uncolored Mexican views I obtained in a little curio shop down on Houston Street, which deals exclusively in Mexican things.

Best wishes and most cordially,
Robert E. Howard

Notes

1. The Spanish Governor's Palace officially opened 4 March 1931.

[25] [nonextant letter by H. P. Lovecraft]

[April–May 1931?]

[26] [ANS][1]

[Postmarked Saint Augustine, Fla.,]
n.d.; c. May 1931]

Well—I've struck your ancient Spanish country at last—oldest city in U.S., & site of Ponce de Leon's quest! This is really my first taste of the actual sub-tropics, for I can now see that Charleston was merely an adumbration. I've sent you folders of Charleston & St Augustine—trust they arrive safely. The climate braces me up like a tonic, & I hate to think of returning north. Have a balconied room fronting the Matanzas River—only $4.00 per wk. owing to poor tourist season. Of course, St Augustine has lost much naive quaintness through catering to tourist traffic; yet a good deal of the old visual atmosphere is left. There are many houses built in the late 1500's—the typical form being a coquina (coral stone) lower story & wooden upper story. No adobe construction—indeed, I think the western Spaniards must have picked that idea up from the Indians. There was no Indian influence here. The dense green twilight of tropic palm vegetation fascinates me—though just now I am on the sun-drenched parapet of ancient Fort San Marcos. On my way down I

stopped in Charleston, & will do so on the way back. After all, nothing can even approach that for pure traditional survival. Best wishes—
H P L

Notes

1. Front: Entrance to St. Augustine, Fla.

[27] [ANS from HPL, nonextant]

[postmarked Dunedin, Fla., c. 31 May 1931?]

[28] [TLS]

[c. June 1931]

Dear Mr. Lovecraft:

I didn't take much of a trip after all. I had vague ideas of drifting down to New Orleans when I started out, but they didnt materialize. I merely went to Fort Worth, about 165 miles east of here, and then down to Waco, which lies about a hundred miles south of Fort Worth, then on a small health resort about thirty miles east of Waco where I spent a week.[1] I came back through the Central Texas black-land belt and I never saw finer prospects for crops this year. All over Texas, for that matter, the land is a riot of wheat and oats. Whether they'll be able to sell it, the Devil who rules the Southwest only knows. Times are fiercely hard, even though the mild winter saved the cattle and stock, and the people are restless and getting mean. There's been more shooting scrapes and cutting affrays around here in the last few months, than there has been since the early days.

Thanks very much for the package of views and literature, also for the folders of Florida.[2] That must be an exotically beautiful country, and I'm mighty glad you got to make the trip. Charleston must be a most fascinating place; I am enthralled by the pictures of it you sent me. Many of the views of San Augustine seem familiar to me, because of their resemblance to the Spanish architecture of Southern Texas. Especially the patio of the "oldest house" which much resembles the Governor's Palace in San Antonio, snap-shots of which I'm enclosing. But that trick of building the upper part of the house with wood, is new to me. You are right about the western Spaniards borrowing ideas from the Indians. You'll notice, in some views I sent you of New Mexico, the simularity between the ancient pueblos and the Spanish buildings.

I'm very sorry to hear that you've been suffering with eye-strain. It seems most writers are afflicted with that complaint, more or less, as is natural, I suppose. My eyes are bad; especially my left, which has stopped some savage blows in bygone days that didnt do it a lot of good.

I'm delighted to hear about your new story—the antarctic horror[3]—and sincerely hope that you found a market for it. Literature, at a low ebb generally, is enriched by every stroke of your pen. I most certainly hope that Putnam & Sons have decided to bring out your work in book form—both for your own sake and for the sake of American literature as a whole.[4] I look forward to the appearance of the volume with eager anticipation, and hope I can have the honor of being the first to review it for the Southwestern papers.

I have read and re-read with the most intense interest, your descriptions of rural Rhode Island, and I am amazed to learn of the wide unfrequented stretches. With my hazy knowledge—or rather my complete lack of knowledge—of the area, I had vaguely supposed all of the Eastern states to be thickly settled, as in the case of some of the Middle-western states. How I would enjoy gazing on some of the contrasts you so vividly depict! I must visit the Atlantic sea-board some day, though the Devil only knows when it can be.

The population, as you describe it, aside from the older Saxon communities, must be bewilderingly cosmopolitan indeed. I imagine that your French element must be about the most desirable of all the alien stocks. France is not particularly well represented in Texas, though of course quite a number of persons with French blood in them have drifted in from Louisiana, and most of them are so long Americanized they differ but little from the Anglo-Americans.

I can appreciate your feelings toward New York, as a Nordic city engulfed by alien hordes—much the same process must have taken place in Rome, in the days of the later empire. I can imagine a Roman patrician of the old pure stock feeling much the same toward later Rome, as you feel toward modern New York.

Yes, I intensely enjoyed your descriptions and drawings of colonial architecture. The picture of 'Clivesden'[5] was most interesting. American architecture has certainly fallen far from the taste and artistry of the Colonial types as far as I can see. The most radical change I've noticed in Texas architecture is in the type of court-houses. All over Texas they are replacing the old buildings with a very modernistic type—I'll try to get you some pictures of the new and the old, for comparison.

Its a dirty shame that the Polacks are selling those fine old stone walls and replacing them with wire fences. Another proof that traditions mean nothing to these aliens, who bring their own traditions with them and callously trample on those of the land they pollute by their presence.

I'm glad you found my ramblings about State history and legendry of some interest. My mind is a kind of jumbled store-house of tag-ends—snatches of history, incidents in the lives of gunfighters and outlaws, anecdotes, myths, legends of the country, and the like. I could fill a thick volume of such disconnected bits and still not exhaust my chaotic store.

John A. Murrell was a hell-bender, in Southwest vernacular. He planned no less than an outlaw empire on the Mississippi river, with New Orleans as his capital and himself as emperor. Son of a tavern woman and an aristocratic gentleman, he seemed to have inherited the instincts of both, together with a warped mind that made him as ruthless and dangerous as a striking rattler. He must have murdered at least a hundred niggers in his time, yet they trusted him, and even when he was in prison, they were ready to rise in the revolt he had plotted and destroy their masters, had not chance intervened. It reminds me of the revolt old Colonel Leopard the carpet-bagger planned in East Texas. He stirred the niggers up and was going to lead them to a bloody victory. He was holding forth in a meeting place in the woods, with the fires blazing, and hundreds of blacks howling like fiends, and Leopard roaring and shouting as he goaded them to frenzy—urging them to march on Waco and slaughter every white man, woman and child in the place. And about that time old Captain Wortham and his bushrangers opened fire from the bushes and they dropped eight niggers at the first volley. The rest scattered and the worthy Colonel led the flight.[6] The Texans hunted him clear across the state with blood-hounds and while he was licking his sores in Old Mexico, a letter came from his wife telling him a daughter had been born to them. He wrote back and told her to name it Coyote, because, he said, the Texans had hunted him across the state like a coyote. And Coyote they named the child.

I'm surprized that Argosy rejected your stories,[7] especially in the old days, when the magazine was superior to the present one. But what can you expect from any standardized publication? They'd turn down the masterpieces of all the ages, if they chanced to depart slightly from the regular pattern. I've made Argosy once, with a prize-fight story;[8] they've rejected stacks of my stuff, and in my case, I reckon the rejections were justified. I must admit most of my junk is deserving only of rejection slips. And by the way, I want to thank you again for suggesting my name to Mr. Talman as a possible contributor to the Texaco Star. I'm sending you a copy of the publication, containing my article on old Camp Colorado, which Mr. Talman tells me recieved quite a bit of favorable comment from the moguls of the company. I've had time only to work up the one article, but hope to be able to place more of them soon. And I have you to thank, for had you not suggested me to Mr. Talman, I'd never have placed the article.

Awhile back Street & Smith suggested I supply them with a series of prize-fight stories; they snapped up three yarns,[9] but I dont know how long I'll be able to keep selling stories of the ring. I've written so blamed many I'm hard put to work up new plots and situations—particularly as its a rather narrow field in its dramatic possibilities. Well, I repeat that I hope to soon see your work in book-form; I dont know of any literary event which could give me more genuine pleasure.

Yes, I got quite a kick out of Long's story, and wrote to Mr. Wright praising the author's work and urging him to use more of the same sort. I have not seen the unfavourable comment on his work you mentioned—in fact, I'm not familiar with the Editor magazine—but I cannot see how any sincere objection to his style could be made. I like Long's work, and if anything I can do, can help offset the criticism you referred to,[10] I'll be more than glad to do it. Yet, though the whole story was excellent, in my honest opinion, your interwoven dream was the high spot.

What you say of the unfortunate Boskops interested me greatly, also your remarks about the Wegener theory.[11] I first heard of that theory about three years ago—or perhaps it was a different theory based on similiar principles—I had gone up to Fort Worth to see the Doss-Chastain fight[12] and the college professor with whom I stayed talked quite a bit about the theory of land-driftage, and suggested I write a story based on it. But I lack your cosmic sweep of style and imagination, and I never attempted it. I'd forgotten all about the theory until you mentioned it in your letter. It is indeed a fascinating thought, and I am anxious to see how you have handled it in the antarctic tale.

Fantastic linkings with by-gone ages are certainly curious. I must confess I lean toward the theory that racial memories are transmitted from ancestor to descendent, though I am not prepared to offer any argument upholding it. I have wondered at times if I number some Babylonian or Chaldean among my ancient ancestors, so strong at times have I felt a connection between the ancient East and myself—for it is only with the Mesopotamian countries that I feel any sense of placement. My only sensation of the East beyond the rivers of that day is but a dim haze of unknown lands and half-mythical races. Yet I certainly show no trace of Oriental blood—thank God. Strangely enough, something like you mentioned I feel a dim sense of a vast epoch lurking BEHIND the East of the early ages—a sort of huge lurking night behind the dawn represented by Egypt and by Babylon—a dim sense of gigantic black cities from whose ruins the first Babylon rose, a last mirrored remnant of an age lost in the huge deep gulf of night. I have touched on this briefly in a story titled "The Blood of Belshazzer" which Mr. Wright accepted for Oriental Stories.

Regarding the various interests in time-cycles and individuals—to me history seems mostly a chaotic jumble, through which move certain fairly well defined streams and currents, but which is mainly too tangled for my comprehension. As I have said, I lack your universal and cosmic scope and comprehension. From contemplation of history as a whole, my mind retires bewildered and baffled and fixes on various figures which rise here and there momentarily above the general drift. It is the individual mainly which draws me—the struggling, blundering, passionate insect vainly striving against the river of Life and seeking to divert the channel of events to suit himself—breaking his fangs on the iron collar of Fate and sinking into final defeat with the froth of a curse on his lips.

As for Biblical history, my real interest begins and ends with the age of Saul, outside of snatches here and there, as in the case of Samson. I'm sure you're right in your theory that numbers of Aryans must have drifted into the near East of that age, and as far as I can see, the days of Saul and David represent an Aryan phase in the racial-life of Israel. With the passing of David, my interest fades. The history of Judea sinks back into the general aspect of a truly Semitic court and dynasty, with a typical Oriental ruler in Solomon.

Another thing difficult to understand is my aversion toward things Roman. As you say, Rome made no attempt to destroy the folk-traditions of her subjects; life in the Roman republic and early empire must have been far more desirable than life in the later feudal age. Rome built system and order out of chaos and laid down the lines of a solid civilization—and yet the old unreasoning instinct rises in me and I cannot think of Rome as anything but an enemy! Maybe its because Rome always won her wars until the very last days, and my instincts have always been on the side of the loser—Celtic instincts again, I suppose.

It is quite possible that you have a trace of Roman blood, from Romano-Cymric ancestors, especially since your Welsh lines were in such close proximity to the centers of Roman occupation. I hope you will soon be able to gratify your wish to visit your ancestral home, and I am sure that in the shadows of the Druid oaks and ancient Roman ruins, you will realize your fullest expectations of atmosphere, sleeping racial memories and ancestral traditions.

My sense of placement, as I've mentioned, is always with the barbarians outside the walls. Indeed, when I look upon the picture or drawing of some old walled city, and try to imagine myself in that setting, I always have the sensation of standing on some wooded hill or in the desert without, gazing over the walls, rather than of being inside the city. You mentioned your vivid dreams of a Roman personality; in my dreams of old times, I am always a light eyed, yellow haired barbarian, resembling my real self but little. And yet it is evident I have quite a wide strain of Mediterranean blood in my veins, for though I am long-headed and blue-eyed, my hair is dark, and so is my skin which does not blister in the sun, but burns so brown that I have a few times been mistaken for a Mexican, though my features are certainly not those of a Latin, thank God. When I was a child I was a pure Saxon in type, with curly yellow hair and very fair skin, but as I grew older I grew darker, taking after a line of black Irish ancestors.

Another instinctive feeling of mine is that of kin-ship with the Scandinavian peoples of my English line, rather than the Anglo-Saxon stock. I suppose that any man with English blood in him has a good deal of the Saxon in his veins, yet I have never felt any kin-ship with the Juts, Angles and Saxons who made the first Teutonic invasion of Britain. My sense of personal placement in the Isles centers mainly in Ireland and Scotland; what connection I do feel with England begins with the Danish invasions. Nor is this feeling perhaps unnatural for my very name is not the modern form of the Saxon Hereward or Hayward, but is the Anglicized form of the Danish Havard.[13] And some recent ancestors of mine, though greatly mixed with Irish blood, still had more of the look of the Scandinavian than of the Saxon; with their high, rather narrow heads, blue eyes and dark hair and beards, they must have looked much like the Vikings of the Dubh-Gall who swept the Isles in the old days of plunder and conquest.[14]

I remember the first story I ever wrote—at the age of about nine or ten—dealt with the adventures of one "Boealf" a young Dane Viking. Racial loyalties struggled in me when I chronicled his ravages. Celtic patriotism prevented him from winning all his battles; the Gaels dealt him particular hell and the Welsh held him to a draw. But I turned him on the Saxons with gusto and the way he plundered them was a caution; I finally left him safely ensconced at the court of Canute, one of my child-hood heroes.

I'm glad you liked "Children of the Night". Some remarks of your's in your letters regarding the Mongoloid aborigines gave me many of the ideas. As regards my mention of the three foremost weird masterpieces—Poe's, Machen's and your own—its my honest opinion that these three are the outstanding tales.[15] Though I consider your "Dunwitch Horror", "Horror at Red Hook" and "Rats in the Walls" quite worthy of ranking alongside Poe and Machen, also.

I've received your letter from San Augustine since writing the above and have read it and re-read it with the most intense interest; your observations on the city and country have been a real education for me, since my ideas about Florida have been about as vague as they are about China. Thanks very much for the postcards, folders, booklets etc. I am repeatedly impressed by the tropical beauty of the scenes they show; a tropical atmosphere not even equalled by any of the scenes in extreme South Texas. I envy you your travels! And I hope you got to take that excursion to Miami and Key West which you mentioned. I'm sorry to hear that Whitehead is in poor health, and hope for his speedy recovery.[16] I'm glad to hear that Long and Dwyer have found my work interesting, and I very much appreciate their kind comments.

Glad you enjoyed the cuttings etc. I sent you. The Austrian architectural survivals of the "little people" were new to me; I'd never heard of them before either. Great fictional possibilities there! By the way, I learn that the Clayton people are about to bring out a new magazine on the order of Weird Tales;[17] the address is Harry Bates, Editor, Clayton Publications, 80 Lafayette Street, New York, in case you care to try them. They're also contemplating bringing out a magazine dealing entirely with historical tales—cloak-and-sword romances, etc.[18]

Well, I knew there was a catch in it somewhere—the grain crop, I mean. At the beginning of this letter I mentioned the fine prospects for wheat and oats. Now the insects have attacked the grain and are stripping it; farmers are cutting it green in self-defense, and still the worms eat it. Threshing it is all that will stop them, and its too green to thresh, mostly. Of course further south the grain is more forward, and most of it will be saved. Besides that, some terrific hail-storms have damaged the crops. Its always something in

Texas. And even if a huge wheat crop were made, the farmers wouldnt get any price for it. Always a mild winter is followed by an insect plague. Prospects look good for cotton this year, but I know, almost, that there will be a swarm of grass-hoppers. They'll strip the fields over-night. In a life-time spent in the Southwest, I've seen perhaps a half-dozen full crops made. Drouth, floods, hails, sand-storms, boll-weevils, worms, grass-hoppers—all take their toll. Some people accuse the Southwest of being backward—God, if we are, we have reason to be. This is a fierce, barren land; a hard, drab land, where all the elements are set against the hand of man.

And confound it, it seems as if most of the farmers wont use what sense they have. Take this land around here; most of it isnt worth anything. Yet forty years ago, it was rich and fertile. But the men who farmed it knew nothing about crop-rotation, fertilizing the land, or anything else. They planted cotton till they wore the land out. Drouths baked all the moisture out of the soil and floods washed it away. This land washes amazingly in rainy seasons. Terracing would have saved it—would have kept the fat dirt from washing away and held the moisture in the land. But its only recently that any terracing has been done and now its too late. Of all the land in Texas that needs it, only about 10 percent is being terraced. Now they're wasting time and money terracing bare yellow clay from which the richness has long been washed, while out west of here, on the fertile Coleman prairie, the same old thing is in process—the land's washing away and nobody turns a hand to stop it. Maybe in a few years when the fields are practically worthless, some one will begin to make terraces. Most of the best farmland in Texas is in the hands of Germans, Bohemians and Swedes—especially that rich Black Land belt above Austin; nearly all that rich, waxy black country is being owned and worked by Swedes. The old Texas stock has been crowded off into the bare clay hills and sand roughs. But the first Texans were following grass and they rode over the rich farm-land and left it to the European emigrants who came later. And many Anglo-American families have left the farms and moved into the cities. Another thing that rasps me is the failure of most farmers to raise any of their own food. They plant cotton—grain, some corn perhaps—most of them never have a garden, raise no chickens, turkeys, ducks or geese—have few cows, or none. A farmer is supposed to be at least partially self-supporting. Many of these farmers come into town to buy their vegetables at the stores. Of course, that isnt the case among all of them. But one reason the farmers are in such bad lines today, is their failure to raise poultry and vegetables at home. Well, its none of my business, of course, but I hate to see individualism fade out entirely.

But times are changing fast. And just now I am thinking, for no particular reason, of a picturesque but rather lousy phase of Southwestern life which has practically vanished in the past ten or twelve years.

Several years ago it was the custom in West Texas towns to set aside a certain day in the month known as "trade's-day." In this town it was the third

Monday of the month and was referred to variously as "Third Monday" "Trade Monday" and "Horse Monday." On that day the streets and alleys were full of men swapping horses and mules. For three or four days before "Trade's Day" the roving brotherhood would begin to arrive—the people who went about making their living by horse trading. They were generally a seedy and disreputable lot, who moved about in wagons, with a string of lean, mangy cayuses, lived from hand to mouth and camped wherever night found them. Trade's Day would find them camped at the edge of town, sometimes a dozen families together, and they would plunge into the business at hand. Farmers would come to town with equally worthless nags and the noise of arguments, assertions and refutations must at times have equalled the clamor in an Oriental bazaar. How anybody ever made anything out of most of the swaps, is more than I can see. It always looked to me as if both parties got gypped.[19]

The wandering horse-traders were more or less of a nuisance; they were thievish, quarrelsome—though not particularly courageous—and the men would invariably get drunk and beat their wives so the women would howl until it was a scandal to hear. After prohibition came in their favorite drink was fruit extracts and the amount they imbibed was a caution to behold. I used to work in a grocery store and the amount of lemon extract etc., I've known some of them to buy in one day, would startle one. I particularly remember a couple who were generally together most of the time: a big red-whiskered brute and a horrible hunchback, a stunted monstrous giant, of the most sinister aspect I ever saw in any man. He seldom talked, and I never heard him speak above a menacing whisper. Generally Red-whiskers did all the talking for the pair, prompted by the hunch-back's uncanny whispers.

I remember once I heard a most outrageous outbreak of noise and clamor—howls, blows, bellowings and the drum of flying hoofs—and saw Red-whiskers careering down the street in high state. He was lying hog-drunk in the bed of a wagon, roaring at the top of his voice and slashing at his son—a kid of ten or twelve—with a rolled-up slicker. The kid was screaming at the top of his voice, standing upright and pouring leather into the mules. The old man was beating the boy, the boy was beating the mules, and the mules were at a dead run. Why the wagon didnt come to pieces, I dont know, for it was just hitting the high spots.

What became of the horse-traders, the Devil only knows. Maybe they all drank themselves to death. With the stuff the people drink these days, it would not be an impossibility. American taste in liquor has sure degenerated—of necessity, of course. Bootleggers take no pride in their work. When I used to work in a law-office I saw a good deal of good whiskey, but for the past few years it's been getting rottener and rottener until its risky to even smell a cork. The stuff dont make men drunk; it maddens them.

I remember a wild night I passed on an isolated ranch in mid-winter, several years ago;[20] one of the party was wild drunk on beer and another was stark crazy on raw jamaica ginger, with the obsession that he was a werewolf. One of the bunch was a young German who didnt drink, and wasnt used to the violent drunks common to Americans; he backed up against a wall and I couldnt help laughing at his expression when the jamaica victim began to smash the furniture, gallop about on all-fours and howl like a mad-dog. About midnight a howling blizzard came up to add to the general lunacy. Gad, it makes me laugh to think about it now.

I have—since writing the above—received your card from Dunedin, and repeat I envy you your sojourn into Florida. The scene on the card strongly reminds me of pictures I've seen of the South Seas. I'm glad you like the old Gulf; I feel as if she's a part of Texas—and God knows, she's taken enough Texans and their work into her bosom. She's treacherous as a Mexican dance-hall girl; not only broken ships sleep in the slimy ooze of her deeps, and the bones of sailormen—walls and columns and shattered dwellings of landsmen lie there strewn among the bones of their builders. Galveston—Rockport—Corpus Christi—she broke their levees and foamed over their walls and the people drowned like rats.[21] They say the sea-wall at Galveston is safe; I say—not publicly, but to you—that no wall is sufficient to hold back the Gulf when she shakes her mane; and that as the pirate Lafitte once drove his ships across the howling waves that hid the island, so again the Gulf will claim her own at will. Once the sea rolled over these hills and plains, and I believe at no distant date, as the history of the planet is measured. And I believe that some day the Cap-rock will again be the shore of the Gulf, and that Houston, Galveston, San Antonio, even Fort Worth and Dallas will sleep untold fathoms beneath the foam. For I have found petrified deep-sea shells hundreds of miles inland, and it is always said that the sea eventually claims her own again.

I'll most assuredly watch for Whitehead's new story;[22] and I appreciate his salutation on the card. I hope that his ill-health has not seriously impaired that remarkable muscular development of his which inspired so much admiration among the people of the West Indies; did he show you his feat of tearing a pack of cards into halves and quarters with his bare hands?[23]

I've been reading over the Eyrie of the latest Weird Tales, and am gratified to note with what enthusiasm the readers hail your forthcoming tale—"The Whisperer in Darkness". Their enthusiasm for your work denotes a real appreciation of genuine literature—an appreciation which is, alas, too often lacking in the reading public. As for myself, I can hardly wait for the story to appear.

I also note with considerable amusement that a rumor has been circulating pertaining to me being a professor in the University of Southern California.[24] It was, it is true, only a freak of chance that kept me from being a Californian. Had not cholera struck the camp of William Benjamin Howard and his band of '49ers on the Arkansas River, reducing their number from nineteen to seven, and weakening their leader so he was forced to turn back, I, his grandson, would have undoubtedly been born in California instead of

Texas. But as for being a professor of history in a great university, that's beyond the pale of possibility—I never even attended college as a student.[25]

Its been some weeks since I wrote the first part of this letter, in which I commented on the grain crop. Since then a bumper crop has been assured. Hail did damage in some sections, but not as much as was expected. And—in this locality at least—the invading horde of army-worms which was stripping the oats, was devoured by an army of bugs following close on its heels. The insect world has its migrations and tribal drifts, its wars and its massacres, just the same as the world of humans. But the grass-hoppers are swarming in and if something radical isnt done, they'll eat the cotton before it can bloom. We lack not insect scourges here. I've seen the ground so thick with big, fuzzy, horned caterpillars that one could not walk without crushing them. And grass-hoppers—Lord! I remember one particular scourge that ate not only the cotton but the very leaves off the trees. About the only person that really enjoyed that plague was my pet raccoon who ate those big jumbo grasshoppers till he could hardly waddle. Of course the coyotes always thrive likewise.

So Texas has a big grain crop this year—particularly a big wheat crop. God knows what we'll do with it. The kind, benevolent gentlemen on Wall Street have juggled the prices down until the wheat will hardly be worth the gathering. And our Bolshevik brethren are considerately glutting the market, so as to ruin what remains. Dear little Russia, with her American-made machines, she will see that the grain farmers of America are ruined, if others fail. Well, I reckon we can always eat the damned stuff ourselves and feed it to the stock. Next year we'll have a drouth, and those who store grain now will be wise.

I notice a slight—oh, a very slight—trend back to the soil. A few people are leaving the city, under the press of present economic conditions; going back to the farms their parents left, or that they left in their youth. After all, there remains in our weak veins, some slight trace of the sturdy blood of our pioneer ancestors, that revolts against working for some other man forever. On all hands I hear the announcement—"I'm getting tired as Hell working for the other man." There is freedom of a sort on the farm, though it may be purchased with grinding toil and barreness of existence.

Well, Aryans were not made to coop themselves in walls. This fact is brought strongly to my mind each time I go to Fort Worth. There, of all Southwestern cities, is the last full stronghold of the Anglo-Saxon. Almost everyone you meet has some pristine feature—blue or grey eyes, yellow hair, fair skin—one or more pure Aryan feature. Yet they seem stunted—stocky, but undersized. I notice this fact more than in any of the more cosmopolitan cities. Why, I am not a particularly large man, judged by Oil-Belt standards; I weigh 200 pounds in good condition, but am only 5 feet 11 inches tall, yet when I walk the streets of Fort Worth I fairly tower above the crowds. I take this to show that the Anglo-American race deteriorates in cities. In Houston, Dallas, San Antonio, you will meet giant Italians, Hebrews, Greeks, Slavs. But the Saxons can not, as a whole, stand city life and keep their original statu[r]e, I believe. Of course, there are always exceptions. But West Texans seem to be a taller and stronger race than their East Texan brothers, though this may be an hallucination on my part. Of course, all through the Oil-Belt you will see hordes of Middle-westerners—big men, mainly of Germanic or Scandinavian blood, from Kansas, Nebraska, Illinois, the Dakotas. Tall mountain men from Kentucky and West Virginia. These, with the native giants form an impressive part of Oil-Belt population. In this town and about its not uncommon to see men over six and a half feet tall. I believe the finest built big man I ever saw—barring Tiny Roebuck, the giant Indian wrestler[26]—was a huge Viking of a man from somewhere in the Middle West. He was an oil driller, and he spoke of Manchuria, Sumatra, Persia, China, as familiarly as the average man speaks of the streets of his home-town. He stood some six feet and eight inches, weighed about 270 pounds, and there was no fat on him. He was no victim of abnormal glands—neither his jaw, hands nor feet were out of proportion. He was simply a natural giant, blue eyed and with a shock of flaxen hair. He moved with a certain aloof dignity, like a lion, and continually cursed the Catholics—why, God knows.

These men from the Middle-west—oil field workers at least—are generally a turbulent race, ready to fight at the drop of a hat, with their fists, but generally not so quick to draw knife or gun, as the fighters of the Southwest. And I notice a racial difference here, not as applied between Middle-westerner and Southwesterner, but between white men as a whole, and Latins. The Mexican is quick and deadly with a knife, but his instinct seems to be to slash his foe to ribbons, while the instinct of the Anglo-American seems to be to thrust—to drive the blade in straight with terrific force. One of the cleanest stab-wounds I ever saw was in the body of a young cowpuncher who'd had a row with another cattleman. A long-bladed stockman's knife had been driven nearly to the hilt between the sixth and seventh ribs and left sticking in the wound. The victim had removed it himself, drawing it straight out. Had the wielder twisted it, it would have made a nasty wound. As it was, though dangerously near the vitals, the young fellow recovered quickly, and lived to be shot down by Mexican bandits south of the Border.

Another friend of mine got one of those long stockman's knives rammed into him—the blade went in under the collar bone and went nearly through him, just missing the arch of the aorta. Such power had the wielder of the knife put behind the blade, the sheer force of the blow knocked the victim down. He recovered after quite a long period, during which he imagined in his delirium that he had slain his foe and had his severed head under the bed to gloat over. Thinking perhaps that the victim might seek to put his dream into reality, the man who had stabbed him carried an automatic shotgun for years. He put it aside at last, and not many weeks ago his eldest son put it into play again—it figured prominently in an informal shotgun duel in which its wielder came out victorious, though he failed to finish his man.

Shotguns had their part in the winning of the West; yea, verily, and even today the humble scatter-gun is generally the ace when the last hand is dealt in the feuds of the brush-wood—which, mark ye, have not attained the publicity given the feuds of the mountain-laurel, but lack not in the essentials of sortie, surprize and sudden extinction. If they are shorter, they are more suddenly deadly. Only a few months ago a shotgun, crashing from the brush-wood, put a period to an old hate that has been smoldering in the sand-roughs only a few miles from this town; a hate that began when the present victim's brother died in Arizona and his chaps and spurs were sent back to his people to quarrel over. So a very brave man has gone over the ridge, and his grand-nephew has begun a forty-year term in the penitentiary. Thirty years—from real or fancied partiality of a kinsman, to a shotgun thundering in the twilight.[27]

I remember another shotgun victim who lived among the hills quite a number of miles south of this town. His waylayer aimed too low; the victim—a friend of mine—escaped with his life, but I counted twenty-seven buckshot in his leg the next day. And his horse's shoulder was badly torn, which was a dirty shame. I believe that incident soured my friend, for only a few years later he figured in another shotgun jubilee, with the exception that this time he was at the other end of the gun. His target was the man whose daughter he had married, and he did not miss—either time. In fact, he killed his victim deader than a cooked goose.

But lord, lord, here I am rambling on and without rhyme or reason. If I seem drowsy and lacking in connection, please blame it on the heat and langor of spring. My laziness always increases in warm weather, and for the past days I've sort of let things slide. In the past three weeks I've managed, by sheer force, to pound out four prize-ring short stories, an adventure short, a Western short, a fact article and a long historical novelet, and the effort has been about as much physical as mental. My indolence has always handicapped me.

Again I thank you for the wealth of material you have so kindly sent me—the package of pictures and literature, the cards, views and folders of Florida and the South; I value them all highly and they form an important part of my collections.

Cordially,
Robert E. Howard

P.S. I'm venturing to include a rhyme of mine here, which is doubtless entirely without rhythmic or literary merit, but which does, I feel, in some slight way describe the sensations one recieves while traveling that savagely barren country between the little town of Sonora and the Border.

The Grim Land[28]

From Sonora to Del Rio is a hundred barren miles
Where the soto weave and shimmer in the sun—
Like a horde of rearing serpents swaying down the bare defiles
When the scarlet, silver webs of dawn are spun.

There are little 'dobe ranchos brooding far along the sky,
On the sullen dreary bosoms of the hills;
Not a wolf to break the quiet, not a desert bird to fly
Where the silence is so utter that it thrills.

With an eery sense of vastness, with a curious sense of age,
And the ghosts of eons gone uprear and glide
Like a horde of drifting shadows gleaming through the wilted sage—
They are riding where of old they used to ride.

Muleteer and caballero, with their plunder and their slaves—
Oh, the clink of ghostly stirrups in the morn!
Oh, the soundless flying clatter of the feathered, painted braves,
Oh, the echo of the spur and hoof and horn.

Maybe, in the heat of evening, comes a wind from Mexico,
Laden with the heat of seven Hells,
And the rattlers in the yucca and the buzzard dark and slow
Hear and understand the grisly tales it tells.

Gaunt and stark and bare and mocking rise the everlasting cliffs
Like a row of sullen giants hewn of stone,
Till the traveler, mazed with silence, thinks to look on hieroglyphs,
Thinks to see a carven Pharaoh on his throne.

Once these sullen hills were beaches and they saw the ocean flee
In the misty ages never known of men,
And they wait in brooding silence till the everlasting sea
Comes foaming forth to claim her own again.

Notes

1. Marlin, Texas, where REH's mother was a sometime patient at the Torbett Sanatorium.

2. HPL was on an extensive tour of the Eastern seaboard, including St. Augustine, Dunedin, and Key West, Florida; Savannah, Georgia; Charleston, South Carolina; and Richmond, Virginia.

3. *At the Mountains of Madness,* written in January–March 1931. HPL completed preparing the typescript on 1 May. It was submitted to *WT* later that year but was rejected.

4. Putnam's turned down the collection (see *SLL* 3.395–96).

5. Cliveden, also known as the Benjamin Chew House (1763–1767), is a historic mansion in the Germantown district of Philadelphia. It was the scene of some of the bloodiest fighting in the Battle of Germantown, fought in 1777 during the Revolutionary War.

6. This story seems to have provided the basis for REH's "The Hand of Obeah" and may have inspired elements of "Black Canaan" as well.

7. *Argosy* rejected "The Rats in the Walls" in October 1923 (see *SLL* 1.259).

8. "Crowd-Horror."

9. *Sport Story Magazine* had written REH ca. January 1931 wanting to take over the Steve Costigan series, which had been running in *Fight Stories* (see *CL* 2.163). REH replied that *Fight Stories* would probably want to keep that series (later confirmed, apparently; see *CL* 2.188), but that he would be happy to write a new series. The three stories mentioned here, all Kid Allison tales, were the only ones accepted and published by *Sport Story*: "College Socks" (25 September 1931); "Man with the Mystery Mitts" (25 October 1931); and "The Good Knight" (25 December 1931).

10. In the article "The Use of Ambiguous Words," by E. Irvine Haines, *Editor* 92, No. 3 (17 January 1931): 46–48, FBL's *The Horror from the Hills* is taken to task for ambiguity of language (FBL is never mentioned by name). Haines writes, in part: ". . . it has an excellent plot, is full of action, has plenty of mystery, and holds the interest of the reader, but—ambiguity runs through it with a vengeance. Because the author likes high-sounding words and phrases he makes his characters appear unnatural and nonsensical. Perhaps a few thousands of years hence ordinary mortals may speak in such language as he uses but not in this age of slangisms" (p. 46). Haines goes on to single out several passages for their use of unusual words.

11. A reference to the continental drift theory propounded by Frank Bursley Taylor (1860–1938), Alfred Lothar Wegener (1880–1930), and John Joly (1857–1933), cited in *At the Mountains of Madness.*

12. Jack Doss, of Lampasas, Texas, and Clyde Chastain, of Dallas, fought in Fort Worth on 16 December 1927, and in Dallas on 20 January 1928.

13. In a letter to Tevis Clyde Smith c. 4 March 1931, REH mentions learning from genealogy books that his name derives from Hereward the Wake—perhaps he got this information on "Havard" as he continued his reading in the library at San Antonio.

14. REH thought his Walser forebears were Danish; Patrice Louinet has conclusively shown they were Swiss.

15. "'But in such tales as Poe's *Fall of the House of Usher,* Machen's *Black Seal* and Lovecraft's *Call of Cthulhu*—the three master horror-tales, to my mind—the reader is borne into dark and *outer* realms of imagination.'" "The Children of the Night" (*BMM* 219).

16. HPL visited with Henry S. Whitehead at his home in Dunedin c. 21 May through 5 June. Whitehead suffered from a persistent stomach ailment. (See *SLL* 4.115–17, 120–21, 126–27, 148–49.)

17. *Strange Tales* (September 1931–January 1933). REH had two stories published in the magazine. HPL repeatedly submitted stories, but none was accepted.

18. Initially advertised as *Torchlights of History* but published as *Soldier of Fortune;* the magazine lasted only a few issues. REH submitted his story "Spears of Clontarf," but it was not accepted.

19. Cf. William Faulkner's humorous account of such horse trading in "Fool about a Horse" (*Scribner's Magazine,* August 1936), later incorporated into *The Hamlet* (1940).

20. An evening with Tevis Clyde Smith, Truett Vinson, and Herbert Klatt at Smith's uncle Ben Stone's ranch, after Christmas 1925. See Glenn Lord, "Herbert Klatt," *The Dark Man* No. 1 (1990): 25–26. REH fictionalized the episode in *Post Oaks and Sand Roughs* (81–85).

21. REH is referring to cities devastated by hurricanes: Galveston in 1818, 1867, 1900 (when the city was virtually wiped out, and after which the seawall was built), 1915; Rockport and Corpus Christi in 1916 and 1919.

22. Perhaps "Black Terror" (*WT,* October 1931).

23. REH probably learned of this from Whitehead's letter to *Adventure,* published in the 10 November 1923 issue. REH quotes it at length in his letter to HPL of 6 March 1933.

24. In "The Eyrie" (*WT,* June–July 1931), Earl Morgan of Detroit posed several inquiries about *WT* writers, including, "Is Robert E. Howard a professor of history at the University of Southern California (I have heard he is)?" Farnsworth Wright replied that REH was not a professor of ancient history, and lived in Texas rather than California.

25. REH had attended the Howard Payne Academy, which offered certificate courses in typing, bookkeeping, etc., not the College.

26 Theodore "Tiny" Roebuck (1906–1969), a Choctaw Indian, was a boxer, wrestler, and actor.

27. Apparently a reference to the killing of Bob Ensor, cut down by a shotgun blast from ambush on 28 March 1931 as he opened a gate in a field near his home. Ensor's great-nephew, Jerry Kent, was convicted of the murder. He was said to have been angry that his car had been searched for stolen goods by police in Cross Plains several months before and thought Ensor, a former deputy sheriff of Callahan County, was responsible. He was sentenced to forty years in prison. There is no mention in contemporary news accounts of a thirty-year-old feud, though of course this does not preclude the possibility. See REH to AWD, 4 July 1935 (*CL* 3.335).

28. Cf. "Sonora to Del Rio," *HC* (Summer 1961); in *EIH,* which lacks the second and third stanzas of "The Grim Land."

[29] [nonextant postcard by H. P. Lovecraft]

[Key West, Fla.,
c. 11 June 1931]

[30] [TLS]

[14 July 1931]

Dear Mr. Lovecraft:

Just a line to congratulate you on "The Whisperer in Darkness." I stopped work right in the middle of a rush job and went thirty miles to get the new magazine, and didnt do a lick of work until I'd thoroughly read your tale. To say I enjoyed the story would be putting it lightly. Your subtle handling of the difficult theme again proves your mastery of the bizarre branch of literature. The subtle threading through shadowy mazes of horror, the dark implications, the tensing trend toward the horrific climax, marks this story as one as far above the general ruck of weird literature as any finished work of art is above the efforts of tyroes. The final implication, that the mask etc., MIGHT NOT BE OF WAX, was almost intolerably grisly, with the demoniac shadowy vistas of ghastly speculation at which it hinted. Thanks very much for including Kathulos and Bran in your dark references.

I suppose you're back in Providence now, after your delightful journeys. Talman mentioned that the Kalem Club would convene upon your arrival in Babylon—I believe Kalem was the name.[1]

I trust you're not bothered with the heat-wave. In the Southwest and Midwest the sun's been bowling them over regular. So many poor devils have been driven to jobs of manual labor who never worked outdoors before, and they cant stand the pace. An indoor worker cant concieve the power of the sun on laborers, especially in the great fields of grain, which seem to absorb and generate more heat than is believable.

Right here, right now, its cool. A sandstorm just passed over and the atmosphere is still rather dusty along the horizons, though clearing rapidly. Just a flurry. We dont have sandstorms like we did when I was a kid, when they used to blow three days and nights without a let-up. The Panhandle's settling up, and the land's under cultivation that was bare prairie when I was a child. At least that's the reason generally given for the decreasing number of sandstorms. But nobody can explain the drouths! Best wishes.

Cordially,
Robert E. Howard

Notes

1. The Kalem Club was an informal band of friends in New York City, of which HPL was the central figure, most of whose names started with the letters K, L, or M. Members included George Kirk, Rheinhart Kleiner, Arthur Leeds, FBL, Everett McNeil, James F. Morton, and later such figures as Vrest Orton and Wilfred B. Talman. The club's heyday coincided with HPL's New York period (1924–26), but even long after, HPL continued to refer to the New York gang as the Kalem Club.

[31]

10 Barnes St.
Providence, R.I.
August 6, 1931

Dear Mr. Howard:—

I trust you have not wholly given me up for lost despite my protracted silence. You doubtless received my postcard from Key West, and deduced therefrom how keenly I enjoyed my taste of the semi-tropics. K. W. is the most southerly point in the U.S., and is only about one degree of latitude above the Tropic of Cancer. It is warm all year round—so that the houses have no steam heat—and its old-fashioned white cottages, balconied and set in groves of palm verdure, suggest the West Indies in many ways. The population is about half Cuban—but no other foreigners exist there, and the black element is not large. I did not care greatly for Miami, which is thoroughly modern and urban. On side-trips from there I saw a Seminole Indian Village at the edge of the Everglades, and a remarkable growth of marine flora on the submerged coral reef—the latter viewed from a glass-bottomed boat. The Miami region is very poor scenically, but the city and its suburbs have been made into a pleasant tropical jungle by means of expert landscape gardening. Key West is about the only place on my itinerary where tropical vegetation is a natural feature. The subtropical belt of live-oaks and Spanish moss—which begins in South Carolina—ends at about the middle of Florida, giving place to a zone of sandy barrens with scrub pines and anaemic palms. On the outer keys, however, we begin to get the full tropical scenery which one associates with the Indies and other realms of glamourous tradition. Of all these types of scenery, I most like the live-oak and moss species—which includes St. Augustine and Dunedin. This type, I believe, also characterises New Orleans and perhaps parts of Texas. Of the various towns I saw, St. Augustine is by far the most interesting—for there alone has history flowed on for centuries. Next comes Key West—founded in 1822 and almost unaltered since then. In some ways Key West may be said to excel St. Augustine—especially as regards the absence of modern hotel and resort features. It is, of course, isolated from the outside world to a phenomenal degree—having only one train and one motor-coach per day—and was even more isolated before the railway and highway were laid across the keys. The railway extends without a break, but highway travel still has to submit to two long ferry trips—each of two hours' duration. These sea voyages, though, are not without their charm. The water is shallow and greenish, and the air abounds with exotic tropical birds. Even the cloud formations are fantastic and unusual.

From Key West I returned up the East coast to St. Augustine, where I spent another week. I then proceeded to Savannah—being very glad indeed to reënter a region of Anglo-Saxon traditions and behold the familiar colonial designs in steeples and doorways. Savannah is a fine old town, though not comparable to Charleston in quaintness and antiquity. It was a pleasure to get back to old Charleston itself, and I lingered there for half a week,—obtaining some more views for you, which I'll send along as soon as I can find them among the tangle of material left from my journey. I then went up to Richmond—very reluctantly leaving behind the live-oak vegetation I had become so used to. Here I visited my favourite spots—including the boyhood haunts of Poe, and the exquisite gardens of Maymont which I think I have described to you. My next stop was ancient Fredericksburg, and after that came Philadelphia—where I explored the entire length of the Wissahickon Valley, besides taking in the picturesque antiquities of quaint Germantown and Philadelphia proper. Finally came the jump back to N.Y.—where I visited a week and a half with Long and another week and a half with Talman. I reached home July 20—and have since been trying to catch up with accumulated reading and correspondence. As usual, I do as much as possible of my reading and writing in the open air—in fact, I am now seated in the woods some 5 miles north of the city. The Metropolitan Park Commission has preserved a great deal of Rhode Island woodland and farm land in its ancient condition, so that my present surroundings are essentially those of the rural 18th century. Weather has been warm—85° to 93° lately—but at no time too warm for my taste. I don't know what it is to be too hot, though the least touch of cold puts me completely out of business. By the way—my trip seems to have cured that strain on my left eye which troubled me last winter. It began to diminish as soon as I stopped reading the daily paper, and disappeared altogether during my Dunedin stray. So far, no reappearance—though I'm reading the papers again.

Glad you liked "The Whisperer in Darkness"—which reminds me that I extracted a splendid kick from your recent tale of the immemorial African tomb and That Which Dwelt Within.[1] As to my new stuff—uniform bad luck. Wright turned down the antarctic tale, and Putnams rejected the bunch of original MSS. they asked for in the first place.

I appreciated tremendously all the old-time Texas material—letters, snapshots, cuttings, illustrated folders, cards, etc., and that marvellously interesting book by Tevis Clyde Smith.[2] Some of the pictorial material was forwarded to me in Florida, and it was interesting to compare the Spanish architecture of the Southwest with that of the Southeast. The governor's palace in San Antonio must be a highly impressive place—indeed, I must some time see this, as well as other historic scenes and objects in the Texas region.

About the Boskops of South Africa—I saw them referred to only the other day, in connexion with the possible ancestry of the Bushmen or Bosjesmans of the Orange Free State—a small, intelligent, copper-coloured race akin to the Hottentots and sharply differentiated from the thick-lipped gorilla-like West African blacks. Certain comparisons of cranial measurements suggest that at least a small strain of the Boskop blood has survived in these superior natives—whose qualities have hitherto been attributed to an Asiatic origin.

Pseudo-racial memories are certainly highly interesting things, though I doubt greatly if they have any basis in fact. When we consider the vast *number* of our distant ancestors—the almost *infinite* extent to which our heredity is divided and subdivided as it recedes in time—we can see how slight an effect on us is exerted by any one ancestor or even by any especial group of ancestors—in the ages behind recorded history. Nothing of a personal or individual nature is likely to be inherited through many generations—for what happened to any *one* progenitor simply fades into relative nothingness amidst the vast bulk of experiences inherited through the geometrically multiplying array of other lines. A grandparent is only a fourth of us—a great-grandparent an eighth, a great-great-grandparent a sixteenth, a great-great-great-grandparent a thirty-second, and so on. It makes me laugh to hear of a person boasting of a remote forbear, as if he inherited anything more from that forbear than do the thousands or perhaps millions of others who also descend from the same source even though they do not bear the same name. Heredity counts only when one has behind one a *very large proportion* of the same kind of blood—blood which represents a certain definite type of experience or natural selection. Thus it means nothing whatever to be "descended from Charlemagne". Probably every living Anglo-Saxon is! Nor does it mean anything in particular to have had one or two celebrated ancestors in the Elizabethan or Jacobean—or even the Georgian—period. But it *does* make a difference whether the *bulk* of one's ancestors have been men accustomed to power, freedom, and a high intellectual and aesthetic standard of living, or men accustomed to subservience, manual labour, and a low level of mental and artistic life. Differences of this kind in the bulk of one's recent and fairly recent ancestors undoubtedly involve elements of natural selection favouring the scion of the freer and more cultivated stock so far as tastes, sensitiveness, and cerebral capacity are concerned. Our likes or dislikes for types and periods in ancient history are undoubtedly matters of accidental sentiment wholly unconnected with our blood stream. Early tales and reading—chance impressions from pictures, plays, or conversation—all these things generally lie behind such inclinations concerning ancient races or personalities. Of course, the fact that we generally hear most about our ancestors causes us to incline in most cases toward their cause in history. This, however, is a matter of traditional culture and not of blood heritage. If educated from infancy among another group of similar physique and biological disposition—as an English boy among the Dutch or north Germans, or a Spaniard in Italy—anyone would naturally feel all the 'hereditary' loyalties of the environing groups. Thus I haven't the faintest idea that any possible Roman ancestor has anything whatever to do with my instinctive feeling of being a Roman. I may indeed have such an ancestor amidst the Cymri of my Welsh lines—but if so, he would have no chance of transmitting any recognisable inclination to one, 1600 years or so later, in whom 53 or more generations have implanted such an overwhelming preponderance of non-Roman blood that the single Roman strain must necessarily be reduced almost to a mathematical nullity. The amount of cell-matter inherited from any one ancestor 1500 years or more in the past cannot possibly have any biological influence—and it's just as well that this is so, for when we think of the thousands of *niggers* all over the Roman Empire who disappeared into the general population we hardly feel we'd like to know about *every possible progenitor* in the year

A.D. 150 or 50 or so. Of course, this latter point chiefly concerns the Mediterranean regions where Nordic replacement least occurred—but when we think of the scum and riffraff sent to Britain with the legions, we feel like emphasising the purely Celtic and Teutonic sides of our ancestry! The chances are that every Englishman has at least one Greek or Syrian or some such person among his lineal ancestors from A.D. 50 to A.D. 410 or so—for the combings of the whole earth were assembled at the camps all over the island and before Hadrian's Wall. However—this hasn't hampered the British people very much in their adherence to a dominantly Teutonic pattern of aspect and folkways.

I was interested in your drawing of your Viking dream-self . . . . . a sturdy soul, who I hope will never catch my Roman self in any shadowy oaken wood far from the camp of the legion![3] Actually, we must both have a slice of Mediterranean; for my maternal grandfather's line is black of hair and eye, though three of my grandparents were blue or grey-eyed, and I was blue-eyed and yellow haired myself till about 5 years old. Or rather, I was blue and violet eyed till 2½, and yellow-haired till 5. My hair darkened steadily till I was 20 or more—and then began to acquire a sprinkling of grey at 26. But my complexion has always remained chalk-white, since I have not been constantly in the open air. I burn easily, but tan only with great difficulty—and even the deepest and hardest-won coat of tan is soon lost. The best coat of tan I ever had was during this recent trip, when Key West and Miami added to the acquisitions of St. Augustine and Dunedin. I might have put up a bluff at being a Cuban if I had had the lingo—but it took only about a fortnight in the north to peel the whole business off!

About shadowy epochs behind the East—there is good fictional material there, and one does not need to violate the probabilities of history to use it. Latest researches seem to establish the priority of Tigris-Euphrates cultures as compared with Egypt's, nor have any excavations disclosed any Chaldaean remains other than civilised. In a word, there is no visible archaeological evidence that the population of the Babylon-Ur region, whether Sumerian or Semitic, were ever other than reasonably civilised in institutions and manner of living. Where, then, were these folkways worked out? On the spot after all? Or in other, remoter cities of Cyclopean megaliths high amidst the plateaux of Central Asia, whence the coming of drought and sandstorms drove the inhabitants at a time when the Neanderthalers still roamed Europe and the Mediterranean shore? Who can say? Or what is to prevent the fictionist from assuming what he chooses?

I imagine that your instinctive self-placement among antiquity's hardy barbarians is due to your early familiarity with an environment in which many of the conditions and values of primitive times were reproduced. It is likely that your preference for the Danes over the Saxons springs from the fact that Scandinavians have figured more largely in glamourously recorded exploits. I have never had much choice among the various Nordic elements extending behind me, and have never stopped to figure out whether Saxon, Norman, or Dane preponderates in my Teutonic lineage. The Lovecraft line is Saxon; but a great number of contributory lines have Norman origins, whilst my father's mother's line—the Allgoods of Northumberland—come from a region where Danish blood preponderates. Incidentally—this region (near Hexham) is also very rich in Roman antiquities, being close to Hadrian's Wall. I have a great admiration for the Scandinavians, since the bulk of them kept to their ancient ways much later than any other Teutonic race. They are a link between our present and our past, whether we be one of themselves or of a Teuton tribe whose absorption and conversion came at an earlier date. Thor, Odin, Freyer, Asgard, and Valhalla are behind us all—even though our Saxon side broke away sooner than our Danish side. I can still get more of a kick out of the names and deeds of the old Northern gods than out of any other religion. As a Roman, I am a philosophic sceptic just as in actual modern life. The religion of Greece and Rome, though a thing of exquisite beauty, grips only my aesthetic emotions; as indeed was the case with most Romans of mature cultivation in the late republican age. The frosty blond deities of the north, on the other hand, seem to my mind to be curiously woven into the elements of terrestrial and celestial Nature; so that the sound of thunder evokes images of a great blue-eyed being in Berserk fury, whilst a cold winter twilight calls up all sorts of images of shadowy shapes marching imperiously in some Northerly middle region just beyond the Earth.

About magazines—I heard of the Bates-Clayton venture, and sent in some stuff—only to have it rejected.[4] Recently, though, Bates wrote me that restrictions against purely atmospheric stories are being abandoned. I may try this magazine yet, when I have something new ready—though without any especial expectation of success.

Glad to hear of the triumph of the grain crop over all its obstacles, and wish there were a more assured market for it. Too bad the agricultural process of Texas lags so far behind its needs—but that is the way with most phases of human endeavour.

Your account of "Trade Monday" and the odd element creating it is vivid and interesting indeed. I trust this phase of local sociology is properly recorded in history and literature—it is the business of the pen to preserve all such things for the eye of the future. Yes—it does seem as if the Gulf of Mexico created a sort of natural link between Spain's two North American realms. I felt very much impressed by my first sight of it—and by virtue of the Key West ferry can say that I have sailed upon its surface. Hope it won't try to reconquer its lost Texan domain in too much of a hurry. As for shells—one can sometimes find such traces even on the highest mountains, where strata have been upheaved. *All* land was once under the sea, so that it will take quite a bit of conquest on Neptune's part to get back the full extent of his primal domain.

Hope the slight movement back to the soil will be a permanent and increasing one—though many signs point discouragingly in the opposite direction. What you say of the relative height of Anglo-Saxons in pristine and rural milieux is very interesting to me in view of an almost opposite opinion I have gained from local observation. Among the better classes of the North—both New England and the West—I have *seemed* to notice a positive *increase* in the average height of young men. The number of six-footers among my young friends is so great as to seem to me more than a mere coincidence. Talman is 6 feet tall, Wandrei the same or a little over, Alfred Galpin is 6 feet 2 inches, and so on. I have thought that this may be the result of the more scientifically balanced diets of today—for height depends largely on glandular secretions which are in turn determined rather largely by the proportion of different vitamines assimilated. In the north, of course, such things as Anglo-Saxon masses can hardly be said to exist—since all the plebeian population is more or less alien. It is possible that if vast numbers of our stock were to be herded in towns like the Italians and Portugese and French-Canadians, living under equally squalid conditions, a decrease in average height would be observed. However—I can't say that I notice any particular shortness in the urban population of Richmond, Charleston, Jacksonville, Winston-Salem, Charlotte, Miami, and other sizeable Southern towns where the native stock persists. It must be remembered that our ancestors were by no means uniformly gigantic. They varied according to source of origin in the British Isles—men of Yorkshire and the north generally tending toward considerable height, whilst those of the south—Kent, Surry, Devon, etc.—were fairly short until the belt of giant Cymri in Cornwall and western Devon was encountered. Old suits of clothes in local museums prove that the average New Englander (usually of East Anglian derivation) did not average more than five feet 10 or 11. I am 5 ft. 11 myself—and weigh 145—having poor muscular development because of invalidism in youth which precluded exercise. Here, by the way, is a snapshot of me which Talman took last month, and which conveys a rough idea of what I look like. You needn't bother to return this. Any time you have a spare snap of yourself to send, I wouldn't mind seeing it.

By the way—I don't think we have as many big foreigners up here as you do in Texas. Southwestern soil and air must agree with them. Our Providence Latins tend to be very undersized, so that the old Nordic stock still towers physically over all comers. However—in western Massachusetts the Slavs are rather tallish as well as thick set. Generally, the peasant races of Central and Southern Europe tend to be thicker—chunkier—than we, although not so tall. They have thick necks, wrists, and ankles where ours are thin—though they do not exceed us either in height or in breadth of shoulder. That's a curious contrast which you point out in connexion with Latin and Nordic knife-fighting. Doubtless each of the two tendencies is deeply bound up in some transmitted racial tradition. Our northern Italians used to be great stabbers, but under the

Capone influence they are now turning to the use of machine guns from ambush—the progress of urban civilisation! It is really surprising to the northerner to learn how much shotgun and other fighting still goes on in the southwest. I must say that this epically primitive system appeals far more strongly to me than does the northern underworld system of furtive gang murders.

Your verses "The Grim Land" gave me a tremendous kick, and I hope to see them in print some day—if they haven't already achieved that distinction. I can't think of anything to pick up except the second line of the 5th stanza, where the metre is incomplete—and I have an idea that this may be a slip in *copying* rather than in *composing.* (There are no other metrical breaks in the whole poem) The line calls for six trochaic beats—5½ feet—whereas one is missing in the text.

´ ˘ ´ ˘ ´ ˘ ´ ˘ ´ ˘ ´

Laden | with the | | hēat of | sēven | hells[5]

Just fill up that blank, and you're all right. Also—I assume that in the next line you inadvertently left the final plural "s" off of *rattlers*—the verbs in the next line calling for a plural subject. That poem certainly captures the spirit of the Southwest—as I understand it from various sources—about as well as any equally compact specimen could; and I congratulate you most heartily upon the achievement.

Let us hope that your new stories will all find congenial and remunerative placement. You surely have an enviable fund of energy in order to turn out as much material as you do. I am enclosing a couple of odds and ends of possible interest—an account of the aërolites in the Am. Museum of Natural History, and a picture of the old stone mill at Newport, (where I was last Tuesday) which has been attributed (on the flimsiest of romantic pseudo-evidence) to our friends the Vikings.[6] On the strength of this thing they have named Newport's leading hotel "The Viking"—though serious archaeologists remain unimpressed.

Hope you can pardon the heterogeneous chirography of this epistle. I am trying to settle on a new fountain pen, and have trouble in deciding among several candidates. My hand is very hard to suit—I want an easy pen that works with light pressure, yet can't bear a stub that makes a line like a paint brush. I wear a pen out discouragingly soon—since I use it incessantly, never touching a typewriter except when absolutely compelled. I hate machines like poison!

Best wishes, and apologies for delay.

Yrs most cordially—

H. P. Lovecraft

Notes

1. REH, "The Footfalls Within."

2. Tevis Clyde Smith, *Frontier's Generation.*

3. Reproduced in *LC* 381 as "R.E.H. as mythical Dane Dream character Hrobjart Havard's sen."

4. Including at least "Beyond the Wall of Sleep" and "The Nameless City."

5. REH seems not to have made the correction suggested by HPL.

6. HPL refers to the Old Stone Mill in Touro Park, Newport, the remains of a windmill probably built by Benedict Arnold (colonial governor of Rhode Island, 1663–66, 1669–72). Longfellow wrote a poem about it, "The Skeleton in Armor" (1842), hinting of Norse origin.

[32] [TLS]

[c. week of 10 August 1931]

Dear Mr. Lovecraft:

You must indeed have had a delightful journey and I envy you your invasion of the semi-tropical haunts, which evidently must be far more exotic and dream-provoking than anything we have in Texas. I very much appreciated the views, folders, etc., you sent me, and read your descriptions of the country with the greatest interest. I was also interested in what you said of Savannah, the more so because my branch of the Howards landed there when they first came to America, in 1733, I believe it was.

Yes, I did indeed like "The Whisperer in Darkness", and appreciate the kind things you said about "The Footfalls Within", which I feared failed miserably in creating the atmosphere I was striving after. I speak with full sincerity when I say I am bitterly disappointed that the Putnams rejected the mss. they were considering—disappointed not alone for your sake, but for the sake of literature as a whole. However, though set-backs and disappointments are part of every man's life, the power of your work will eventually over-ride all obstacles. You cannot fail of eventual recognition, and with it the fame and monetary remuneration you so richly deserve. I am also very sorry that Mr. Wright rejected the antarctic story, and hope by this time you've marketed it else-where; if you should fail to sell it, I would like very much to read it sometime in manuscript form, if it isnt asking too much.

I'm glad you found some of the Texas material of interest. Yes, the old Governor's Palace in San Antonio is most interesting, having been restored with the utmost care; it has the atmosphere, somehow. To add to the interest, the woman in charge is a direct descendent of the Canary Islanders who, arriving in San Antonio de Bexar in the early 17's, practically created the city; it was then only a cluster of missions and a military post. If anyone has a background of inherited traditions, she has, for her people have lived in, and governed the city since its birth; her brother was mayor for years. The changing fortune of the city is somehow symbolized in her, for only in her eyes does she show her Latin strain, just as San Antonio becomes yearly more and more Americanized and modernized.

I've wandered about a little in the last few months, though my journeys are hardly worth the name, since I havent left the state; you can cover a good deal of territory, though, and still stay in Texas. I went into Central East Texas, into the edge of the Bohemian settlements, and am again impressed by the fact that the average native American cannot hold his own with these invaders. They are industrious, law-abiding, hard-working and unusually intelligent. They are also clannish and help each other. In a day when most farms are mortgaged and remortgaged to the hilt, practically all Bohemian farmers are free from debt. Nor are their activities limited to rural pursuits. They come into towns and make shrewd, conservative business men, and fine professional men. They are less like us than are the Germans, but are less quarrelsome, and apparently less inclined to drunkeness. I see little chance of their being absorbed in the native population, since they tend to cluster together in communities and to intermarry with each other. At the same time they send a continual flow of young men and women out into the more purely Anglo-American localities, and some of these marry Americans. In other words, the extensive Bohemian settlements seem to me like a clump of luxuriant grass which is slowly spreading over the surrounding country. In a few generations, we may note a distinct Bohemian influence in the main blood-stream of Texas, though on the other hand, I may attach too much significance to this trend. The dominant Bohemian type seems to be dark, though often with fair skin and blue eyes. I have seen a few who looked distinctly Celtic, while others show unmistakable traces of Turkish blood. There is some friction between them and the native Americans, though as a whole these Bohemians are a peaceable race and seem to mind their own business pretty well. While I was in Temple this friction was evident in a row which took place in a Bohemian community a few miles from the town. Conflicting stories were told and the true details will probably never be known, concerning the trouble between the Bohemian and a native American—but the Bohemian was dead, with a bullet in his back and nine gashes in his head—still clutching his pistol, which was, however, unfired and still in its holster.

Later, I went to Fort Worth—the Mecca of all West Texans—and returned through the land of my birth—for the first time since early childhood. The country seems to be changed little—except that it is even less thickly inhabited than formerly—it passed through an era of extensive farming which proved more or less of a failure. Many of the farmers left and the country settled back to its natural destiny of cattle-and-sheep-raising. The tide of progress seems scarcely to have touched Peaster, the tiny village where I was born—as then the few stores are kept by old ranchmen too old for riding and roping—tall, bent old men with flowing white moustaches and keen blue eyes who sit and dream of old times.

A student of early Texas history is struck by the fact that some of the most savage battles with the Indians were fought in the territory between the Brazos and Trinity rivers. A look at the country makes one realize why this was so. After leaving the thickly timbered litoral of East Texas, the westward sweeping pioneers drove the red men across the treeless rolling expanse now called the Fort Worth prairie, with comparative ease. But beyond the Trinity a new kind of country was encountered—bare, rugged hills, thickly timbered valleys, rocky soil that yielded scanty harvest, and was scantily watered. Here the Indians turned ferociously at bay and among those wild bare hills many a desperate war was fought out to a red finish. It took nearly forty years to win that country, and late into the '70's it was the scene of swift and bloody raids and forays—leaving their reservations above Red River, and riding like fiends the Comanches would strike the cross-timber hills within twenty-four hours. Then it was touch and go! Much as one may hate the red devils one must almost admire their reckless courage—and it took courage to drive a raid across Red River in those days! They staked their lives against stolen horses and white men's scalps. Some times they won, and outracing the avengers, splashed across Red River and gained their tipis, where the fires blazed, the drums boomed and the painted, feathered warriors leaped in grotesque dances celebrating their gains in horses and scalps—some times they did not win and those somber hills could tell many a tale of swift retribution—of buzzards wheeling low and red-skinned bodies lying in silent heaps.

But that was in the later days. In the old times the red-skins held the banks of the Brazos. Sometimes they drove the ever-encroaching settlers back—sometimes the white men crossed the Brazos, only to be hurled back again, sometimes clear back beyond the Trinity. But they came on again—in spite of flood, drouth, starvation and Indian massacre. In that debatable land I was born and spent most of my early childhood. Little wonder these old tales seem so real to me, when every hill and grove and valley was haunted with such wild traditions! The very county of my birth—Parker—got its name from old Colonel Parker,[1] who spent actually years haunting its hills and valleys in search of the daughter stolen from him by the raiding Comanches—Cynthia Ann Parker. How many long lonely danger-frought nights he lay alone in the wilds, hunting out his foes, spying on their camps, trailing their hunting parties and their war-parties—hoping, yearning for some sign to show the child he sought lived—it was not granted to him, though I'm sure—and hope—that many a painted brave rode the fading trail to Ghostland to pay that debt. There is an aching sorrow about the tale of Cynthia Ann Parker, a terrible pathos that takes a man by the throat. Flung between red men and white, driven along a trail black with hate and red with blood, to this day the memory of Cynthia Ann Parker lingers and haunts, like a pitiful ghost crying in the night.

I saw Dark Valley again, which I think I've mentioned to you before. Dark Valley—now hardly worthy of the name, to the casual glance, since many of its trees have been cleared away, and the road, which used to follow the bed of the winding creek, now passes along high up on the ridge. But down in the valley the untouched wilderness still waves—there the trees grow taller and thicker than anywhere else in Texas, I believe—their rank growth is almost sinister—suggesting something malevolent, somehow. The country is still very sparcely settled, and of the two-roomed cabin on the creek bank, where I lived, no trace now remains.

Not long after returning from this trip, I took a somewhat longer one in the other direction—to San Angelo, about a hundred miles southwest from this place, one of the most promising town west of Fort Worth, and the greatest wool and mohair market in America. Its fine rolling prairie country, with some hills. The entire population of the county is about 38,000, of which 25,000 live in San Angelo, which leaves a rather light population to be distributed over 1454 square miles of rural territory. I went south about eighty miles to Sonora, an old frontier town abounding in virile traditions, then turned east about sixty-five miles to Junction, county seat of Kimble, a county which has an area of 1301 square miles, and a population of 3581. There isnt a railroad in the county but some fine roads. And beautiful mountainous scenery. Then from Junction I went to Kerrville, a rather noted health-and-pleasure-resort among the mountains about fifty miles southeast of Junction; after a couple of days stay at Kerrville I went on to San Antonio, seventy miles to the south, then continuing south to George West, about a hundred miles from San Antonio—turned east again there to Beeville, and back home by way of Goliad, Victoria, Gonzales, Austin and Brownwood. It wasnt really much of a trip, as it extended only over about a thousand miles altogether and I was gone only a week. But I rather enjoyed it, though I'd been over most of the country before. South Texas is the portion of the State vibrant with early historical tradition—there the first colonies were planted and there were fought all the battles of the Revolution. I believe Goliad, Vitoria and Gonzales are, in many ways, the most picturesque-looking small towns I've ever seen in Texas. Many of their buildings are very old, and the towns are laid out on the old Spanish style, with broad plazas. The population is now largely mixed with German, especially in Victoria, and as many of these Teutonic emigrants came in the '80's and '90's, and even earlier, they have added their part to the German influence. After their stirring history most of these southern towns seem sleeping—quiet and drowsy, they live in dreams, while the frontier has moved on, with it the sweep and change of progress and events.

No doubt you're right in deciding that racial memories are a myth. As you point out, a distant ancestor could hardly have much influence on the life and ideas of a present day descendent. Yet it might be possible that atavistic forces might reproduce, to a certain extent, a shadowy ancestral shape in modern form. We know that cases exist in which a person bears a striking resemblance to a grand-parent or even a great-grand-parent, and this might occasionally be extended further into the past. I believe that one certain ancestor may sometimes exert a stronger influence on his descendents than former or later forbears. For instance there is an extensive family here who numbered, among their not very recent ancestors, a full-blood Portuguese. The present representatives of this family cannot have a very broad strain of Portuguese in their blood now, in fact, the added strains of British blood must have almost drowned it out—yet practically all of them to this day, show unmistakable Latin features and characteristics, and some of them, even of the youngest generation, would easily pass for full-blooded Portuguese. I do not maintain that they have inherited any racial memories—in fact, I feel certain of the contrary—but the fact remains that that one thin strain of Latin blood has proved stronger than all the Anglo-American blood since acquired. And if that one Latin has transmitted his racial tendencies and features throughout all the line of an otherwise British-American family, it seems that the case might be reproduced elsewhere, when the influence of one particular ancestor, or group of ancestors, might be felt for generations.

I was very much interested in your remarks about the coloring of yourself and your various ancestral lines, as noting the hue of eyes and hair and complections of people is one of my hobbies. Not that I have any particular reason for it, since I do not hold with the theory that a man's character etc. is shown by his coloring; in fact I have very little faith in the study or theories of physiognomy. I have seen pure blonds and pure brunets who had instincts and natures almost exactly alike.

I was also very much interested in hearing about the researches in the Near-East. The Sumerians must have evolved their civilization somewhere, as you point out, and the question of where? evokes almost limitless realms of speculation. What are your own theories on the subject?—I mean where do you suppose these tribes worked out their problems of progress? Perhaps the ever-rising sand-ocean of Turkestan hides the ruins that might tell of their march upward from the ape. Or—it seems somewhere I've read of a theory that the Mediterranean shifted her bed within the life-time of mankind and drowned great areas of level sea-land. Is it possible that in these sunken lands the ancestors of the Sumerians attained mind and culture—and that in tales of that inundation grew the legends of the Flood?—and of lost Atlantis? And since the Tigris-Euphrates civilization is now believed to have preceded the Egyptian, is it now the theory that from the Sumerian culture the Egyptian grew, or that these civilizations evolved along different, separate lines?

It may be, as you say, that my preference for the Danes over the Saxons comes from reading Norse sagas—though the first Nordic folk-tale I ever read was Beowulf. It may be rooted in an old hostility to the word "Saxon"; in my childhood and early boyhood I hated every thing English with a deep and abiding hate, and the terms Sassanach and Saxon represented to me the objects of my hatred. Even now I prefer to think that my English strain is rather Danish than Sassanach, since as near as I can learn my distant English ancestors came from the old Dane-lagh. But its really not worth considering, since any Saxon strain in me must necessarily be very small, and the same goes for the Danish, though one of my great-great-grandfathers came directly from Denmark. Yet I believe that every Englishman, Irishman or Scotchman, or person of such descent, has more Norse blood in his veins than is generally realized, considering the extent to which the Norse over-ran the British Isles for centuries. I know that with practically all of the people I know: they jest and joke a great deal, and laugh easily, but get them alone and scratch the surface and you find the almost fatalistic pessimism and gloomy philosophy generally attributed to the Scandinavian peoples. It may be Celtic, I dont know; but I do know that our German neighbors seem more innately cheerful and optimistic than do we of the old stock.

Like you, the sagas of Norse gods and heroes fascinate me. Their mythology seems more characteristically Nordic than any other—naturally, of course. I still feel a deep resentment toward Charlemagne for his bloody conversion of the Nordic pagans—and while I do not consider that it was in revenge for his ruthless crusade that sent the more remote Norsemen sweeping down to ravage the south—it was more likely a natural result of growth and expansion and press of population—still I can appreciate the feelings of those Odin-worshippers who destroyed shrine and monastery and burned the priests in the ruins of their altars. They had little reason to love Christians, with the Great King's example before them. I like to feel that Karl realized, before he died, that doom was bursting on his borders, and that retribution was sweeping on his vassals, if not on himself. And it is pleasant to reflect on those Vikings who stabled their horses in his palace.

I'm surprized to learn that the Claytons rejected your stories. I notice that many of the old Weird Tale writers have found a berth there. The editor rejected a couple of my yarns; he gave no reason for the rejection of one, but he objected to the other on the grounds of thin plot and light action. Later Mr. Wright accepted this yarn for Weird Tales, though he had formerly rejected it. I'm glad Bates is abandoning the restrictions against atmosphere stories. In a letter to me, some months ago, he said they preferred stories with a good plot and about three climaxes, I believe it was. Of course, he knows what the readers want, and I dont blame him for trying to supply the demand. But as far as I'm concerned, a plot is about the least important element in a weird story.

Yes, we made a big grain crop, after all. We have no market to speak of, but the people are storing it, and will have feed for their stock this winter, which is what they didnt have last. I hear that on the Plains they're burning wheat for fuel. Crops over Texas are rather spotted. In South Texas, with the exception of the Rio Grande valley, the cotton crop has been practically a complete failure. Insects destroyed the bloom. The stalks are tall and strong, but they have no cotton on them. People from this part of the country used to go south to pick cotton; it looks like it will be the other way this year. Yet I see that parts of South Texas are calling for cotton-pickers. This shortage of labor is not so much because of a bumper crop, as because of the exodus of Mexican workers, who have been flocking back into Old Mexico by the thousands. North and West Texas seem destined to raise fine cotton crops, but it wont be worth picking. In South Texas over a week ago, cotton was selling for a little over five cents. By the time its ready to pick on the Plains, it wont pay for the labor. Maize was blighted, also, in South Texas, because of too much rain, though they made a good corn crop. In fact, the corn has been good all over Texas, just about. You should see the people laying in provisions for the winter! Right around here there's a distinct movement back to the farm, and this fact, coupled with the scientific methods which are beginning to take root among the younger generation of agriculturists, causes me to believe that the country will pull through, if given half a break. Canning machines are working over-time, as the native Americans are following the example of their German neighbors, who have been putting up their own food and raising their own vegetables for generations. I look forward to feasting on canned stuffs myself, this winter, though the spoiling of six dozen cans of fresh corn has rather disgusted me. Fruit, vegetables, and meat are being put up—young bulls going into cans at a remarkable rate—heart, liver, tongue, and all—every thing but the horns and hoofs! Its a pipe-dream, but I'd like to see the day when Texas would be independent as in the old days—at least as far as food-stuffs go.

Glad my remarks on Trade's Day were of some interest. As far as I know, no one has ever chronicled it and its followers at all. Many phases of the Southwest have been neglected or ignored entirely.

The old Gulf is interesting, as you say. But repellant too, at least to me. She's too treacherous. It sickens one to think of the horrors that she has shaken from her white mane—when people died screaming at Galveston—Corpus Christi—Port Aransas—Indianola—oh, the list is far too long. Texas has no coast; when the waves rise and roll inland there is nothing to break their force. The whole state is a series of steppes—plateaus that descend like stairs from 4000 feet elevation to sea-level. The counties that line the Gulf range in elevation from sea-level to perhaps fifty feet. During a bad storm, the waves rush inland with nothing to stop them. Once a railroad train was washed off the track nearly twenty miles from the coast. Even now many of the houses a considerable distance inland are anchored to the ground with heavy iron cables set deep in concrete, and are furnished with thick shutters, against the wind, which during those tropical storms, rises to appalling proportions. Towns, once thriving and prosperous, have been crippled and forever ruined; others have been wiped out—destroyed. Such as Indianola, the City of Bagdad, Clarkesville, of which its said no slightest trace now remains to mark that once important port.

Relatives of mine were in Galveston when it was washed away in 1900, but fortunately all were saved, though many of their friends were drowned. One of their friends, having been out of the city at the time, hastened back to find that his whole family had perished. He fell like a dead man and when he recovered conciousness, days later, his hair was white as snow. Aye, men's hair turned white then, and the hair of young men and the soft locks of girls. And there was a woman who walked across an ironing board from one crumbling building to another, stronger one, with a child in her arms, and the black night howling over her and the screams of the dying in her ears—the black waves foaming and lashing under her feet and the corpses wallowing and bumping against her feet. And just as she stepped into the comparative safety of the other building, the walls she had left collapsed and thundered into the raving waters and screams of her friends were drowned—with hundreds of others, their bodies were never recovered. Many were swept out to sea; the salt-marshes were littered for many a mile. And strange to say, a babe in a cradle was washed far inland and lived when so many died—people found her floating in her cradle among the debris and they took her and raised her, not knowing her name or anything about her, but she lives, a woman in South Texas, to this day.

God, what black horror must have gripped the hearts of the people, when the doom of winds and waves struck them in the night—when they rushed from their houses with the thunder of the crumbling sea-wall in their ears, and were caught in the black madness that thundered over the doomed city—that shattered their walls, broke their roofs, swept their houses away like straw and strewed dead bodies for a hundred miles among the marshes. Who was spared when the tide broke? Old crippled men cried in vain for aid; the babe at the breast was torn away to drown alone; women whose hour was upon them were hurled out on the breast of the black horror, and their shrieks of agony were choked by the clamor of the waves—aye, babes struggled into birth in that horror, meeting death instead of life. The very tombs were broken open and moldering shapes floated among the living and the newly dead. Trains, halted by the rising water on the mainland, were deserted by their frenzied passengers—and these passengers told tales of corpses floated up to the windows that seemed to fumble at the panes with dead fingers.

Galveston must have seemed like a city of the dead when the tide abated. And thirst and hunger and the black horror of madness fell upon the survivors stumbling among the ruins where ghouls ran looting the dead, hacking off the fingers to get the rings.

God grant no such fate befalls the city again. But in the old days before the city was, the pirate Lafitte drove his ships right across the island in a storm.

Texas, at least the southern part, was under water at no greatly distant date, as the age of the earth is reckoned. Even now one can trace in the hills, the old lines of the ancient shore—promontories, indentations and harbors.

Such a great expanse of the state, bordering the Gulf, is only a little above sea-level, it would take no impossible convulsion of Nature to drive the waters a hundred miles inland—an earthquake or a volcano in the Gulf. Such things have occurred. I dont know what the scientists say about it—whether the water-line receded because of some natural shifting, or because of the drying up of the Gulf. But we have no protection in the way of cliffs or mountains against a tidal-wave and I do not intend to ever make my permanent home on the Gulf-coast.

It may be my imagination that Americans in cities are shorter than formerly—and really, I have no right to make any sort of an assertion concerning city-people, since I so rarely visit cities. However, it is the truth that the larger towns and cities of Texas swarm with folk of very medium statue, particularly in Fort Worth, compared to the people of the rural localities, especially in the Oil Belt and the western area. It may be that people are really growing taller—indeed, a study of athletes would tend to prove it. The heavyweight champions are a pretty good index, I should think. The present day fighters seem to be taller. Going a good way back, Jem Figg—1695–1734—was six feet tall, but Jack Broughton—1704–1789—was five feet-ten; Jack Slack—17—–1778[2]—while weighing over two hundred pounds, was five feet-eight; Bill Stevens, Bill Darts, Tom Faulkner, Ben Brain, Tom Spring, Gentleman John Jackson, Jem Mace, Tom Sayers, not one of them was six feet tall. The great Bendigo was five-nine, Daniel Mendoza was five-seven, Yankee Sullivan was five-eight. These were all Englishmen, of course. John L. Sullivan, first American champion, was a little over five-ten. Succeeding champions were mainly taller. Fitzsimmons was five eleven and three-fourths. Corbett, Jeffries and Dempsey were each six one and three fourths; Burns was short—five feet-seven. Jack Johnson and Gene Tunney were each slightly over six feet. Willard was a giant, six feet six and a half. The present champion—so-called—Max Schmeling, is six feet one. The ring is at present full of giants, mostly foreigners. Primo Carnera of Italy, Jose Santa of South America, Pat Redmond of Australia, Vittorio Campolo of Argentine, all of these are nearly seven feet tall. Then we have Babe Hunt of Oklahoma—the list is too long. Dempsey could have whipped the entire gang in one ring when he was in his prime.

Present day Texans seem shorter and bulkier than formerly. If there ever was a typical type of Texan, he was tall and rangy. Their mode of life made for such a build. Most of the earlier settlers, too, were of Scotch-Irish descent and I believe—though I may be wrong—that the Scotch-Irish leaned to height and ranginess in build. I was interested in what you said about the heights of Talman, Wandrei etc. My friends are mostly of good size, and strongly built, since most of them are men who make their living by the work of their hands. By a peculiar coincidence, the majority of my friends have been, and are, of a uniform height of five-feet eleven-inches—which is my own height. I have noted this time and again. Some are taller; Tevis Clyde Smith, co-author of "Red Blades of Black Cathay" is six feet one; another friend by the name of Vinson is six feet two. Both live in Brownwood, forty miles south of Cross Plains. Of my five special friends here, four are five-feet-eleven. One—a Kansan of German descent—is six-feet one. However, he is lighter than the others.

Speaking of the contrast between Nordic and Latin knife-play: I dont know whether the slashing habit is an Indian or a Spanish instinct. If Spanish, it may be a survival of Moorish influence. As of course you know, the Oriental nations favor curved blades, and generally slash instead of thrusting. The early Nordic warriors hacked too, but they used straight swords, depending on the weight of the blade and the force of the blow, whereas the Orientals curved the blade to gain the effect. But the early Greeks and the Romans understood the art of thrusting, as witness their short swords. And the rapier was created in the West. I am not prepared to say whether the Spaniards borrowed any ideas of weapons and their use from the Moors, but I will say that Mexicans swords are generally more curved than those used by Americans. I noted this recently during a trip to the battlefield of Goliad where Fannin and his men were trapped by the Mexican army. I saw two sabers—a Mexican arm and an American—both of which were used in that battle. The Mexican sword was curved far more than the Texan weapon—in fact, it would be almost impossible to thrust effectively with it. Blade, hilt and guard were all made in one piece of steel, and I could hardly get my hand inside the guard to clutch the hilt; some grandee wielded it, no doubt, some proud don with blue blood and small aristocratic hands—well, I hope he got his before Fannin surrendered, and gasped his life out in the mud of Perdido with a Texas rifle-ball through him.

Glad you liked my verse—which, like most of my stuff, hasnt been published and probably wont be. Thanks for pointing out the break in metre. I'd never have known it, otherwise. Scanning verse—outside of iambics—or is it pentameter?—I never can remember which is which—is something that's entirely beyond me. I know nothing at all about the mechanics of poetry—I couldnt tell you whether a verse was anapestic or trochaic to save my neck. I write the stuff by ear, so to speak, and my musical ear is very full of flaws.

Thanks for commenting on my energy in writing—but honestly, I'm provokingly indolent. I work in bursts and spurts. I may turn out a month's output in a few days, and then loaf for weeks. I sell so little, though, that I have to produce a great deal in order to make a living at all. Just before Mr. Wright left on his vacation he took a long story for Oriental's, which he had requested—a yarn dealing with Baibars the Panther.[3] The readers seem to like my historical tales, for some reason or other, and I'm duly grateful, for I love to write historic fiction, puerile though my efforts may be.

Thanks very much for the material, especially the snap-shot of yourself, also for the post-card view, and the literature about the meteorite. I remember, very faintly, the fall of a meteorite in South Texas, many years ago. I was about four years old at the time, and was at the house of an uncle, in a little town about forty miles from the Mexican Border; a town which had recently sprung up like a mush-room from the wilderness and was still pretty tough. I remember waking suddenly and sitting up in bed, seeing everything bathed in a weird blue light, and hearing a terrific detonation. My uncle—an Indian—had enemies of desperate character, and in the excitement it was thought they had dynamited the house. There was a general leaping and snatching of guns, but nothing further occurred. Next day it was learned that a meteorite had fallen. People who saw it described it as being about the size and shape of a barrel, and averred it burst twice before striking the ground, making a loud explosion and shedding that strange blue light over everything. No trace of it was ever found.

And speaking of natural phenomena, an occurrence has taken place in Texas which is without precedent. We have had an earthquake. Faint tremors have been recorded in El Paso before, probably echoes of California quakes, but not within the memory of white men has Central Texas felt a tremor. It seemed to center in Valentine, in the Sierra Viejas, but was felt all over West and Central Texas. Since the first jar, several other quakes have been felt at Valentine, and the people have been sleeping outdoors mostly, I hear; the Mexicans particularly being terrified. Their adobe houses fell down like stacks of cards, though no one was hurt, it seems.

The quake was very apparent in this part of the country, and many of the people, never having experienced anything of the sort before, were completely mystified. Of course, I had to sleep through it, to my disgust. I'm a rather sound sleeper anyhow, and that night several of us had been out on a small party; for the first time in years, I was slightly intoxicated when I retired, besides being tired from wrestling with the huge foreman of the local ice factory. So I slept more soundly than usual and knew nothing at all about the earthquake until next morning. A rather amusing incident was attendent to the quake—one of my friends, who was one of the party before mentioned, drank considerably more than I did, and awakening in the midst of the quake, thought he was in the grip of delirium tremens or some other mysterious malady connected with the intoxicants he had imbibed. He was sleeping in an upstairs room and felt the shaking very plainly indeed. He was extremely relieved to find it was only an earthquake.

Nothing of the sort has ever happened in Texas before, to the best of my knowledge. I'm sending you some clippings, and with these comments you have a first-hand account of Texas' first earthquake, from a participant—though the participant ingloriously slept through the entire excitement!

I cant sleep through a thunder-storm, but I can sleep through almost any other sort of disturbance. It would take quite a bit of shaking up to waken me, ordinarily. And being wakened by shaking is something I always despised. I remember when I was a kid of eighteen, the owner of a boarding house where I stayed always woke us up by trying to shake the liver out of us, regularly at six o'clock. He seemed to think it a great joke and some of the boys learned to wake up as he entered their room, and leap out of bed in a hurry. I protested in vain, and one morning when I was awake, I heard him ascending the stairs, and I lay still, feigning sleep; as he bent over the bed and laid hold of me I gave him a smash under the heart that nearly laid him out and after that, when he wanted to wake me up, he did so by calling from outside the doorway.

Well, the oil war rages. Doubtless you've heard some echoes of it, on the East Coast. The Oklahoma City Oil Field is under martial law, and so is the great East Texas field.[4] A thousand men of the National Guard are patrolling East Texas and they have Hickman and his Rangers there—to protect the National Guard, I reckon. Ordinarily I am rabidly opposed to any sort of martial law, but this time I believe its a good thing. The big oil companies are strangling the very life out of the industry.

I havent visited the East Texas field but I hear its a hummer. Several former law-officers of this section of the country served there for awhile in one capacity or another. But there seemed to be considerable prejudice there against West Texans, especially as officers, and this was probably increased when the former marshall of this town killed a man at Gladewater in a raid. Shortly afterwards an East Texas officer ran amuck and killed a Ranger, narrowly missing several other officers, before he himself was killed by one of them.

But there'll never be another boom like Ranger had. Ranger lies about fifty miles east of this town, on the Fort Worth road, and there's little about it now to suggest the wild and lurid glamor of its past. This town too, like most towns of this region, had its booms and echoes; millions of dollars have flowed through it; men have come here paupers and left millionaires, and vice versa. Particularly vice versa.

To get back to the oil situation etc., it looks as if some radical step must be taken if the independents are not to be ground down entirely. I note that Kansas is considering a shut-down. Good enough. I hope its a step she takes. Of course nothing can be expected of Pennsylvania and California, but Texas, Oklahoma and Kansas can do a lot, if they stick together and stand by their guns.

States rights seem to be fast fading into non-existence. Laws have become props to uphold big criminals and heels to grind down petty violators. Most of the present contempt for law seems to be the result of corrupt law-enforcers—graft, fraud and injustice run rampant. A big shot can get away with anything while ordinary men are ruthlessly trodden into the mire. There was more justice in the old days when each man packed his law on his hip. Men—at least in the West—recognized the rights of the individual, which are now ignored. Nowadays a man isnt supposed to have any heart, guts, brains, blood or honor. He's supposed to crawl on his belly and lick dirt before the fetish of that vast, vague and uncertain idol Society—while the big ruthless ones trample that same idol with perfect impunity. I say Society is founded on individuals who have individual rights. This was once recognized. An uncle of mine, a gambler who was well known in the Southwest in the '80's, when on the witness stand, knocked down a domineering prosecuting attorney who was attempting to badger him. The judge only mildly reproved him, recognizing the fact that a man has individual honor apart from his obligations to "the Mass" and a right to resent insults, on any and all occasions.

But now—damn such a stinking age. If I could choose the age in which I was to live, I can think of no better epoch than this: to have been born about a hundred years earlier than I was, to have grown up on the Southwestern frontier, to have fought through the Texas Revolution and taken a part in San Jacinto, to have served as a soldier in the war with Mexico, to have gone to California with the '49'ers, and to have fallen in some great battle of the Civil War. If I could have grown up and lived in primitive virile surroundings, if I could have taken part in stirring events, if I could have shot straight, lived like an Indian, run like a mustang and fought like a grizzly, I would not care whether I could read a line or write my own name. And here I am, fat, slothful, un-warlike and short-winded!

Your mention of Latins reminds me of a question I have intended asking for some time—are the New England wops as criminally inclined, and as well organized in crime as the Italians of Chicago and New York? I suppose a great deal of killing goes on among them, where-ever they are, as that seems to be a characteristic of the Latin races. Our most turbulent element is the Mexicans, of course, who slaughter each other with energy and consistency. Yet it isnt fair to blame all their lawlessness on the Latins, since there is so little actual Spanish blood in most of them. San Antonio leads the rest of Texas cities in crime a long way. In the three weeks I spent there last winter there must have been half a dozen murders, at least—all Mexicans. And a daily and nightly tale of sluggings, robberies and hold-ups; burglaries and thefts. Occasionally a Mexican kills a white man. Naturally, the closer to the Border, the more such crimes occur. The most recent atrocity was when a Mexican wood-chopper raped and murdered a little white girl and fled from San Antonio south across the Border. The Mexican government refused to give him up for punishment. Well, I know what would have happened in the old days.

In Northwest and West Texas, the Mexican population is very scanty and of course the crimes are fewer. Though not altogether unknown. A year or so ago some Mexicans murdered an officer in Mason county, for which they went to the chair. And a few years ago, further west, a young Mexican was guilty of a most detestable crime. He had married a white woman, who being a bed-ridden invalid and having a baby about two years old to support, probably turned to him in desperation, having no means of support. For some reason or other he became angered at her, and to torment her, tortured the child before her eyes for hours in the most hideous manner, and wound up by beating out its brains with a rat-tail file. But they got that spig.

Some years ago in this country two Mexicans came to a lonely ranch-house to rob a white woman—but she killed them both with a butcher-knife. And again a young Mexican, in the town of Brownwood, evidently went crazy over brooding about Pancho Villa who was raising Hell down in Mexico. He'd been raised by a family who treated him like a son—but he attacked the woman who'd raised him, and her young daughter, one morning about dawn, and slashed both of them badly before they could take the knife away from him. He ran then, but he didnt run far. Pursued by a mob of wrathful whites, he gained the open country, and tried to shoot a rancher as he ran by the man's place. But his gun snapped and the rancher sent back an answering bullet that dropped him dead in his tracks. In his pocket they found an unmailed letter addressed to his brother in Villa's army, in which he swore to come and join the bandit, and to kill all the white people he could on the way. Poor devil, its just as well for him that the rancher's shot killed him quick. That was an easy death.

I note that another book of ghost-lore has blossomed from the pen of Montague Rhodes James[5]—of whom I had never heard in my life before I read your fascinating article on horror-literature in The Recluse. I would like to read some of this gentleman's work. Could you tell me what company handles his stuff, or where I could obtain it?

My reading has been and is, indeed, deplorably scanty. I find, looking over the tales you mention in your article, that I have read only a very small percent of them. Sometime I hope to be able to take off about a year and catch up with some reading. Your splendid article—which I have re-read repeatedly—whets my appetite for the bizarre. Some day I must read "Melmoth"[6] and the tales you mention by Blackwood, Chambers, Machen, etc.

I read Whitehead's "Black Beast" and wrote him my appreciation of the tale.[7] By the way, while you were in Florida, did you hear anything of "the Old People"? According to Hugh Pendexter, old chronicles of the country speak of ruins of roadways, fortresses and buildings, supposed to have been erected by some pre-Indian race. In his serial recently appearing in "Adventure"—the first installment of which appeared in the same issue as "The Black Beast"—"Devil's Brew" he strikes some really convincing notes of lurking horror and sinister speculation with his mysterious sunken city, brooding beneath the sullen waters of a swamp-land lake, with its serpent-guardians and cryptic golden, headless and winged images, hinting uncanny origin and meaning.[8] If you havent seen this tale, I'd be mighty glad to lend you the magazines containing it.

I note with delight that you have a story appearing in the next Weird Tales.[9] I await it with impatience. By the way, E. Hoffmann Price writes me that he and Mashburn are attempting to promote a sort of anthology of weird tales—or rather a collection of ten selected stories, which includes your

"Pickman's Model" and my "Kings of the Night."[10] I'm all for it, myself. Have they mentioned anything about it to you? I think it would be great.

I'm glad to hear you've gotten over your eye-strain. A writer with bad eyes is like a fighter with crippled hands. Doubtless your trip gave your eyes a needed rest.

And speaking of trips, I hope you'll find it convenient to come to Texas some of these times. For nearly a year, my plans have been very chaotic and uncertain, and I've hardly been able to outline my life from one day to the next. Even now I cannot predict with any certainty where I'll be tomorrow or the next day. But its possible that by next summer I'll be in a more settled and tranquil state of existence, and if so, I'd like very much to entertain you to the best of my ability.

There are parts of the state I'm sure you'd find interesting, and if things work out like I hope they will, I'll show you all of it, with some of Oklahoma and New Mexico thrown in. Much of the territory is monotonous and possessed of a sameness, but a lot of it is fascinating, especially the hill countries. I often wished you were with me on my recent short trip through the southwestern hills, especially along the Old Spanish Trail, winding in and out among the vast, thickly timbered slopes and along the rivers, through deep cool valleys. There is a slumberous quiet among those hills, where the occupancy of man has scarcely made itself evident. Big wild turkeys flew across the road, so close that I could have dropped them with a pistol-shot—but I'm no hunter. It will take a hundred years to settle up the wilder portions of the state. I know of few greater pleasures than to drive over the long dreaming miles with the towns left behind and scarcely even a ranch-house or a wandering traveller to break the primeval solitude. And further west it is even wilder and less frequented. There is Brewster County with its area of 5,935 square miles, and its population of 6,624; Crockett area 3,215 square miles, population, 2,590; Pecos, area, 4,134 square miles, population 7,612; Terrell, area, 2,635, population, 2,660—one human per square mile; Maverick, area 1,251 square miles, population 6,120. And etc., etc., also etc.

Its rather foolish to make plans far ahead—and by next summer I may be in Oklahoma, China or Hell—but if I am settled as I hope to be, I'd feel honored by a visit from you.

Best wishes.

Cordially,
Robert E. Howard

P.S. Glancing over this letter, much of it seems rather morbid. If I'm too prone to linger over subjects of gory or gloomy trend, I really must beg your pardon. We of the Southwest—of the old stock, at least—are inclined to be a gloomy race. Our folk-songs reflect our natures. The greater majority of the songs and ballads which grew up in, or were favorites in the early Southwest, dealt almost exclusively with battle, murder and sudden death. Listen to some of the lines of a few:

> "As I rode by Tom Sherman's barroom, Tom Sherman's barroom, so early one day,
> "I saw a young cowboy, so young and so handsome, all wrapped in linen, as though for the grave!"[11]

And:

> "Twas in the merry month of May, when all sweet buds were swelling
> "Sweet William on his death-bed lay, for the love of Barbara Allen."[12]

And:

> "One morning, one morning, one morning in May,
> "I heard an old soldier, lamentingly say—"[13]

And:

> "Come all you punchers and listen to my tale,
> "While I tell you of my troubles on the Old Chisholm Trail—"[14]

And:

> "Oh, beat the drum slowly and play the fife slowly,
> "And play the death-march as you bear me along!
> "Take me to some green valley and lay the sod o'er me,
> "For I'm a young cowboy and I know I've done wrong!"[15]

And:

> "He had wasted in pain, till o'er his brow
> "The shades of death were gathering now.
> "And he thought of his home and his loved ones nigh
> "And the cowboys gathered to see him die!"[16]

And:

> "Early in the morning, in the month of May,
> "Brady came down on the morning train,
> "Brady came down on the Shining Star,
> "And he shot Mr. Duncan in behind the bar!"[17]

And:

> "Oh, once in the saddle I used to go dashing,
> "Oh, once in the saddle I used to look brave,
> "I then got to drinking, and then took to gambling,
> "Got into a fight, and now for the grave."[18]

And:

> "Oh, put me in that dungeon, oh, put me in that cell—
> "Put me where the north wind blows from the southeast corner of Hell!"[19]

And:

> "The dogs they did howl, the dogs they did bark,
> "When Stackerlee the murderer went creeping through the dark—

"Everybody talk about Stackerlee!"[20]

And:

"Come all of you my brother scouts,
"And listen to my song;
"Come let us sing together
"Though the shadows fall so long."[21]

And so on. The list is endless. These songs were the natural outgrowth of the country and the country's people, and reflect the spirit of the people far more accurately than can any work of educated poets and writers. Some of them were old Scotch-Irish ballads twisted about and changed to suit the times, the surroundings and the listeners. Others grew like mesquite grass, from the soil and the settlers. They dealt with violence, misfortune and doom, for the frontiersmen encountered such things far more often than they encountered cheer and good ease. And if I am boresome with my gloomy tales and incidents and observations, please pardon it. Its a racial tendency.

R.E.H.

[P.S.] By the way, I'm sending you a Sport Story magazine containing a yarn of mine, the first of a new series, the continuance of which I have an idea will depend a great deal on the expression of the readers' opinions.[22] If you like the yarn, I'd be greatly obliged if you'd drop Street & Smith a line saying so, that is if it isnt too much trouble. If the publishers receive some letters approving my work, they'll be more likely to continue buying stories of the series. Also by the way, here's a snapshot of me for your private rogue's gallery—dont judge me too much by my looks; I'm really not as scoundrelly as I look.

P.S.S. I just finished reading your latest story in Weird Tales, and am fascinated by its beauty and mystic depths. It calls to mind "The White Ship" and "The Silver Key"—shimmering etchings of pure beauty. And well do I recall the Terrible Old Man who talked with haunted pendulums. I hope you will use him again.

R.E.H.

Notes

1. REH errs in believing Parker County to be named for the father of Cynthia Ann Parker. She was the daughter of Silas Parker, who was killed during the Comanche raid on Fort Parker in which she and her brother John were captured. It was her uncle, James, who spent years searching for her. The county was named for another of her uncles, Isaac Parker (1793–1883), a state legislator who introduced the bill that established the county.

2. Jack Slack, the "Norfolk Butcher," lived from 1721 to 1768 (some accounts say 1778).

3. REH, "The Sowers of the Thunder."

4. The East Texas Oil Field was discovered in 1930 and quickly proved to be the largest field known in the world at that time. By the end of 1931 it had produced over 100 million barrels of oil, and land speculation and drilling were frenzied. Because of the enormous quantities being produced, the price of crude oil dropped from $1.10 to 10 cents per barrel. To shore up prices, Governor Ross Sterling in August 1931 declared martial law, ordered all wells to shut down, and sent in National Guard troops to enforce the order and the proration decrees that followed. When the field reopened on 5 September, the reduced allowable and corresponding price jump led to the running of "hot oil" (i.e., oil produced illegally or beyond the allowable limit for a well). In February 1932 the state Supreme Court found the governor's martial law declaration unconstitutional, but the last troops did not leave until December. Meanwhile, control of the field passed to the state's Railroad Commission, which sent in special investigators to enforce proration decrees and stop hot oil production. As was inevitable where so much money was involved, corruption among the investigators was rampant. While Sterling had to rescind the order that REH mentions here, his successor, "Ma" Ferguson, at the request of the Railroad Commission, sent in a large force of Rangers in February 1933.

5. *The Collected Ghost Stories of M. R. James* (London: Edward Arnold, 1931).

6. Charles Robert Maturin, *Melmoth the Wanderer* (1820).

7. Henry S. Whitehead, "The Black Beast" (*Adventure,* 15 July 1931).

8. Hugh Pendexter (1895–1940), "The Devil's Brew" (*Adventure,* 15 July, 1 August 1931).

9. HPL, "The Strange High House in the Mist."

10. The book never appeared.

11. "The Dying Cowboy" (also known as "The Cowboy's Lament" and "The Streets of Laredo"); based on an Irish song "The Unfortunate Rake" of the late eighteenth century.

12. "The Ballad of Barbara Allen."

13. "The Rebel Prisoner"

14. "Old Chisholm Trail."

15. "The Streets of Laredo."

16. "Oh, Bury Me Not on the Lone Prairie."

17. In REH, "Boot Hill Payoff."

18. "The Streets of Laredo."

19. "Frankie and Johnny."

20. Known variously as "Stagolee," "Stackerlee," and numerous other variant titles.

21. William F. Drannan, "The Old Scout's Lament."

22. REH, "College Socks."

[33] [ANS][1]

[Postmarked Plymouth, Mass.,
24 August 1931]

New England's oldest! Having a great time.
Regards—
H P Lovecraft

Notes

1 Front: Unknown.

[34]

Providence, R.I.
September 12, 1931

Dear Mr. Howard:—

[. . .] As for atavism and racial memory—of course, the two are quite distinct. Undeniably, heredity occasionally reproduces a physical and perhaps mental structure after the lapse of a few generations; (just how far this can be carried is still an open question) but the reproduction of the acquired mental images of that structure is something far different and probably impossible. The most atavism could do is to duplicate a general temperament and set of inclinations. Concerning heredity in general—it is curious how a dark strain will persistently crop out among a blond stock, whereas a blond strain is completely lost among a dark stock. This proves that the dark type is by far the more basic and normal in the species, and that the Nordic is the product of an exceptional and tenuous specialisation—whose results are insecurely lodged in the race, and always ready to be overthrown by any influence favouring the original arrangement. Facial features, I think, are more malleable—more affected by climatic and cultural changes—than matters of pigmentation and skeletonic proportion. This is natural, since the contours of flesh and fat, nerve and muscle, are largely dependent on temperature, moisture, respiration, nourishment, and personal experience both objective and emotional. It is probably a fact that the 2nd and 3d generations of alien immigrants' descendants are less foreign and aberrant in facial aspect than their European forbears.

As for the ultimate origin of civilisation—I don't believe any sort of theory could amount to more than a guess. That the human race started on some plateau in central Asia is almost certain; hence the natural inference is that settled agricultural life probably began in some fertile river-valley south of that mid-Asiatic upland terrain. Archaeology is still too incomplete to afford an answer, hence imagination is free to speculate over the whole of Mesopotamia, Persia, India, and kindred regions. Possible source-regions extend as far north as the Black and Caspian Seas. The Mediterranean has indeed undoubtedly changed its bed, but it is not likely that civilisation began so far west. Still, without doubt vast Mediterranean areas once peopled and civilised—probably with the Cretan culture in its early stages—are now submerged. The Flood-legend may be connected with this subsidence, though modern research favours a more local explanation. Inundations in the Tigris-Euphrates region, due to the bursting of glacial dams, are now considered the sources of the Flood-tradition—which is thought to have been carried by word of mouth to widely distant realms.

Possibly your Danish preference is due, as you suggest, to an early dislike of the Saxons. Just how extensive the Norse element is in British veins can never be accurately determined—and it must be remembered that the underlying Ragnarok-melancholy can come through Saxon as well as Scandinavian sources. Originally, all the Nordic or Germanic races were one, and shared the same myths and feelings. Angles and Saxons, no less than Jutes and Danes, were heirs to the gloomy and heroic legacy of Odin and Asgard.

Clayton rejections are hard to explain—but the underlying principle is that the Bates-Clayton standard is the purely conventional one of mechanical plot and aimless action for action's sake. It may be that experience will cause them to broaden their policy—as indeed they have already begin to do—but it will be a long time before they would care for anything of mine. Atmosphere, not plot, is the heart of a weird tale; indeed, I think that all highly complex plot is more or less artificial and meretricious.

Economic matters are certainly in a tangle these days; and in Texas, where one encounters raw materials on a vast scale, the essentials of the drama stand out with especial vividness. I wish that the present crisis might pave the way for at least a partial return to self-sufficiency on the part of small units. There is something ironic in the thought of a farmer starving in the midst of plenty, because he can't sell the fruit of his land for a high enough price to keep him in canned meat and vegetables! It is a hopeful sign when the raising and canning of food for one's own use begins.

You make the precarious physical situation of East Texas very vivid—indeed, I had never before fully realised the extent of the grim old gulf's latent menace. I well recall accounts of the Galveston flood, and have often wondered about the possibility of repetition. Surely that was a time of unrelieved horror—a horror which you reflect with vast macabre potency in your descriptions. Nature, after all, has been only fractionally conquered by mankind—and it is an unfortunate fact that some of the generally pleasantest regions of the globe have violent physiographical drawbacks—earthquakes, hurricanes, and the like. The present Belize disaster is a good illustration.[1] But for hurricanes, the West Indies would be an earthly paradise—indeed, some of them seem to get off lightly enough to merit that designation as it is. Whitehead swears by the Virgin Islands as about the ideal spot on the globe—he'd be back there now if he didn't feel that he ought to be near his elderly father, who insists on staying in St. Petersburg, Fla.

Changes in national physique come so slowly and gradually that it is hard to say what trend is prevailing at any given time. Probably America is too large to develop any one uniform type—though the increasingly migratory nature of the people would seem to promote that end. Sir Arthur Keith[2] maintains that the typical modern American is shorter and heavier than the Colonial American; but he allows for the effect of blood admixture, and does not attempt to consider the pure American of unmixed British ancestry. Nourishment, exercise, and other factors play a vast part. It seems to me that the more favoured classes tend to increase in height, while the urban and underexercised masses stagnate or decrease. My own height is exactly the same as yours—5 feet 11 inches in shoes with ordinary heels. This was also the precise height of my maternal grandfather, whom I greatly resemble.

Your verses are splendidly vivid—and so generally accurate and regular that I am astonished by your disclaimer of metrical knowledge. Your case would seem to be an argument that good versifiers are such by instinct rather than by acquisition—"poeta nascitur, non fit"[3]—a conclusion which I had almost reached from a precisely opposite angle—i.e., the difficulty of making many persons able to create smooth and vivid lines even with the most careful instruction. But I think, none the less, that you would find certain rules and principles of assistance in composition. Read Brander Matthews' "Study of Versification"[4] or Gummere's "Handbook of Poetics". There are several basic metres, and many modifications of them. Iambic verse is that in which there are alternate short and long stresses—like this—

˘ ´ | ˘ ´ | ˘ ´ | ˘ ´
Behold | the trees | of yon | der vale

Each pair of stresses—short and long—is called a "foot". The most common iambic measures are tetrameter—four feet, like the specimen just given—and pentameter—five feet, like this:

˘ ´ | ˘ ´ | ˘ ´ | ˘ ´ | ˘ ´
Achill | es' wrath, | to Greece | the dire | ful spring[5]

Verse of this last kind is the standard English epic measure, and is called "heroic" verse.

Trochaic verse is the opposite of iambic—i.e., the feet have a long syllable followed by a short—like this

´ ˘ | ´ ˘ | ´ ˘ | ´ ˘
Tell me | not in | mournful | numbers[6]

Anapaestic verse is a light, tripping measure in which each foot has 3 syllables—two short followed by a long—thus:

˘ ˘ ´ | ˘ ˘ ´ | ˘ ˘ ´ | ˘ ˘ ´
Oh, believe | me, if all | those endear | ing young charms[7]

The opposite of this is *dactylic*—with a long syllable followed by two shorts—thus—

´ ˘ ˘ ´ ˘ ˘ ´ ˘ ˘ ´ ˘ ˘
Mystical | memories | beating un | endingly

I envy you your sight of a meteorite's fall—or rather, the blaze and report incidental thereto. Visitors from outer space always fascinate me, and I always pause reflectively in the hall of the American Museum in N.Y., where many giant specimens are ranged about on pedestals. It is enthralling to the imagination to lay actual hands on a piece of material substance from *Outside*.

I was also vastly interested in your account of the earthquake, and sorry you could not have witnessed the experience. Your friend's reaction was surely amusing enough—and ought to keep him away from the bottle for a full day or two! I have had two sizeable tremors in my vicinity—only one of which I could feel. That was the shock of Feby. 28, 1925 which I use in my story "Cthulhu". I was then living in Brooklyn on the second story of an old brownstone house; and the tremor rattled dishes, skewed pictures, rocked chandeliers, and produced a perceptible feeling of swaying in the house. My friend George Kirk, who had a room on the floor above me, felt it even more violently according to his description. The other shock was in Providence, several years later, which shook up the downtown section quite a bit. I missed it, however, because 10 Barnes St. is on the crest of a 150-foot near-precipice of solid granite, which seems not to have taken part in the general sliding. Earthquakes are very rare in the East, and never violent in New England. The only really considerable earthquake recorded on the Atlantic coast is that of 1886, which shook up my favourite city of Charleston, S.C., causing much damage. Thanks for the newspaper account of the unique Texas phenomenon.

Yes, the oil situation must seem very close and dramatic in Texas—even in parts not reached by the industry. Here again we see the economic tangle of the present age—the way civilisation has tied itself up into a knot of complexities which nobody knows how to untie. Certainly, it will take entirely new principles of legislation to deal with matters of this kind—and one may only hope that the situation can be tolerably eased over with various palliatives until a rational quasi-permanent system can have time to develop.

Undoubtedly the independence and self-sufficiency of the individual states is shrinking as life becomes more and more involved in nation-wide economic and industrial arrangements, and daily living-conditions become more and more standardised. Sectional needs and habits and speech and thoughts and feelings grow more and more alike with each new generation—and industry concentrates more and more in chains and monopolies with capital, executives, and layout indifferently scattered without regard for geographical boundaries. Any political unit as small as a state necessarily has less and less actual practical significance under the new order—and since that order is an inevitable consequence of the equally inevitable invention of machinery, the outlook for political and economic localism is not bright. Probably the tendency of the remote future will be to ignore historic state boundaries and divide the nation into centrally controlled administrative units based on industrially significant climatic and topographical considerations. Preservation of local heritages must be a cultural affair—and I am glad to see the rise of a new regional consciousness to offset the opposite political trend. Both Vermont and the Southwest seem to be making efforts to confirm a local culture which shall outlast the political isolation of the respective regions. Meanwhile, though, the individual indubitably suffers—and it is a brain-racking problem to try to get him back his lost status amidst the growing and apparently unavoidable control of government by large-scale industry. Most attacks on the present system of government and industry aim only at conditions which would make it even worse for the individual—as in Bolshevik Russia, where the independent mind is utterly and ruthlessly crushed into the preconceived, unnatural mould of so-called "proletarian ideology". I don't think there is any real solution for the problem of civilisation. Machinery is triumphant, and human folkways will have to be bent into conformity with the new condition. All we can hope for is some degree of palliation—to be achieved through antiquarian scholarship, and a steady resistance to any forces seeking to curb the field of individual human research and artistic expression. The one redeeming point in the new order is its increased leisure—and the big fight will be for the right to spend that leisure as one pleases.

Your choice of an age and place to live in is very dramatic and appropriate, and I feel sure that you would have done justice to such a strenuous setting. I think my own choice would be England of the 18th century—to have been born in Devonshire in 1690, just two hundred years before I actually saw the light in Providence. Of course, there are many things about that period which I would not have relished—but one can't find *all* that one wants in any *one* age. 18th Century England probably averages as high as any combination of time and place for a person of my particular psychology. I would have lived as a country squire of liberal tastes, visited London occasionally, fought on the government side in 1715 and 1745, and been a Tory in politics. If living at the time of the American war, I would have advocated liberal measures with the colonies, but stern military measures once they actually repudiated their rightful sovereign. My second choice of a living period and place would be the Roman republic about the time of the third Punic War—the age of Cato, Laelius, and Scipio Aemilianus. I would have welcomed the less decadent features of Greek culture while exulting in the acquisition of Grecian territory and would have tried to participate in the reduction of the ancient African enemy. The conquest of Spain, too, would have thrilled me—how inspiring to have been with Scipio under the walls of stubborn Numantia!

S.P.Q.R.—Alala! But pardon me—I am aware that my ancient choice of nationality is one in which you are not likely to concur!

Speaking of Italy, but descending from her ancient to her modern representatives, I doubt if New England dagoes are as well organised in crime as their New York and Chicago kinsfolk; though they certainly lead all other elements among us in crimes of intelligent and foreplanned violence. They are the natural leaders in all forms of systematic viciousness, even when not managed as compactly and effectively as the minions of a Capone. Providence has its share of this kind of thing—so much so that a murder on Federal Hill (the solid Italian quarter) is never good for more than a half-column of space on the inner pages of the newspapers—yet we also have a higher-grade Italian element which ought not to be confused with the criminal scum. Immigration conditions have brought Providence several streams of blood from small Italian towns which assay much higher than the stock of the wop-warrens in Boston and New York, so that certain Italian sections here are fairly free from the extreme squalor and malodorousness of Salem and Mulberry Streets. Many small professional men, well-educated in Italy, have come to Providence; so that we have a sprinkling of Italian doctors, lawyers, teachers, etc., who form real assets in the community. One of the Justices of our Superior Court—Antonio A. Capotosto—is an Italian of tremendously high character and ability. Rhode Island has always had a liking for Italy because of especially close artistic and scholastic relations. Our leading artist, H. Anthony Dyer,[8] practically lives in Italy, and has been given every possible decoration by King Victor Emmanuel and Mussolini. And the late Prof. Courtney Langdon of Brown was a translator of Dante and lover of the Florentine Renaissance.[9] Nowhere else, I think, have Italians been taken with less friction into political and professional life of an American community. But that doesn't lessen the trouble caused by the criminal scum—and we surely wish that some miracle could wipe Federal Hill clear of its jabbering and predatory denizens! The only way to like a typical Federal Hill dago is to range him beside a typical South Main St. Portugese . . . . in which case contrast gives us a new perspective! Portugese and Poles are the most *stupidly* anti-social elements among us. The Italians are *intelligently* anti-social. Your Mexicans must be quite a problem—perhaps like our Portugese, though their ancient occupancy of the land doubtless makes them less unnatural and repulsive. We have almost no Spanish-speakers in New England, though New York has large Porto-Rican sections. In Southern Florida, Cubans are quite numerous; though they do not seem to present any unusual problems in law-enforcement. Key West is fully half Cuban, and some of the Latins there seemed very prepossessing—infinitely better than the swarms of Italians in the north. Nevertheless, the average Floridian wishes there were less. Just now there is much regret at the way they are trickling into Miami—hitherto all-Nordic.

I'll get you the address of M. R. James' publisher from Derleth.[10] The new collected edition has all the tales in the older books, plus two or three new ones. Glad you liked Whitehead's "Black Beast". No—I never heard of any Florida legends of "Old People", and would be interested to learn more on the subject. The story you mention must be highly interesting—I'd like to see it some time, though I hate to ask you to ship a whole stack of magazines. I did not keep the July 15 *Adventure*, but tore the Whitehead tale out for preservation. Thanks anyway for the suggestion.

This proposed Price-Mashburn anthology is a new thing to me—I have had no word from either of the twain. I'd be glad enough to have them use "Pickman's Model", which was included in the British "Not at Night" series,[11] but has not seen book publication in America. Glad your "Kings of the Night" is also considered.

So far no return of the eye-strain, for which I'm profoundly thankful. Summer always sees me all in! Just now I'm doing virtually all my reading and writing in the open fields and woods—though the season for such sessions will soon be over.

I wish I could get out to Texas—and I most heartily appreciate your offer of guidance in such an event. Certainly, no more capable pilot to the historic wonders of the region could possibly be found! With me the great travelling drawback is lack of cash—the same lack which kept me from Havana last spring, and has so far kept me from seeing New Orleans. Cheap 'bus service, however, has helped to open up far territories for me—and a jaunt across to the Lone Star State is by no means an unthinkable feat. Perhaps I shall try for it when I attempt New Orleans—since that will have taken me so far westward. Your description of the still-unsettled counties is alluring in the extreme—and I'd certainly want to see a bit of New Mexico; especially Santa Fé. Well—we shall see what fortune holds—and meanwhile I must repeat my grateful appreciation of your suggestion!

Don't worry about the gloomy events chronicled in your letters. The author of "Pickman's Model", etc. isn't looking for overdoses of wholesome sunshine! I can well understand the persistence of a macabre and melancholy strain in the folklore of a strife-ravaged region, and have noted the tendency many times in collections of cowboy ballads. The citations you give are highly interesting and illuminating.

I haven't done much travelling of late—except for one-day jaunts to sundry ancient and historic spots. Doubtless you received my card from old Plymouth—which retains an enormous amount of archaic colour. It is, of course, the oldest permanent white settlement in New England; (1620) but its surviving antiquities now suggest the 18th rather than the 17th century. There are some marvellous tangles of steep, narrow, unpaved hill streets just south of Burial Hill.

I greatly appreciated the prepossessing snap-shot of yourself, which reveals an athletic solidity to which I can never aspire. It has been carefully filed in the choicest section of my gallery of notables!

By the way—did I mention before that both Long and I are to be represented in the coming weird tale anthology "Creeps by Night"—edited by Dashiell Hammett and published by the John Day Co.? Long's tale will be "A Visitor from Egypt", and mine, "The Music of Erich Zann". I'm glad of that latter choice, for "Zann" is one of my favourites among my own stuff.

Weather here has been remarkably warm for the last four days—94.2° yesterday. This puts me in my very element, though others complain of the heat. It's the coming autumn and winter that I dread.

I'm anxious to read "The Gods of Bal-Sagoth", but so far haven't had time to glance into either the new W.T. or *Strange Tales*. Doolin has given you what looks to me like a fine illustration, though it remains to be seen how well it fits the story.

Well—I must get back to the revisory drudgery! With best wishes, and hoping that no unexpected earthquake may swallow you up, I remain

Yrs most cordially and sincerely,

HPL

Notes

1. Belize City, the capital of the country of Belize (formerly the colony of British Honduras), suffered serious damage in a hurricane and tidal wave on 11 September 1931, in which 200 to 400 people were killed and damage estimated at $7,500,000.

2. Sir Arthur Keith (1866–1955) was conservator of the Hunterian Museum of the Royal College of Surgeons in London (1908–33) and a leading anthropologist and ethnologist of his time. His speculations on American ethnography can be found in *The Antiquity of Man* (1925) and *New Discoveries Relating to the Antiquity of Man* (1931).

3. "A poet is born, not made." An ancient Latin proverb.

4. HPL recommended this treatise in several essays on poetry; e.g., "Notes on Verse Technique" (*CE* 2.145).

5. Alexander Pope (1688–1744), *The Iliad of Homer* (1715–20), book 1, line 1.

6. Henry Wadsworth Longfellow (1807–1882), "A Psalm of Life" (1838), l. 1.

7. Thomas Moore (1779–1852), *Irish Melodies* (1808–34), "Believe Me, If All Those Endearing Young Charms," l. 1 ("Believe me" in Moore).

8. Hezekiah Anthony Dyer (1872–1943), Rhode Island artist known for his landscapes and coastal views.

9. Courtney Langdon (1861–1934), *The Divine Comedy of Dante Alighieri;* the Italian text with a translation in English blank verse and a commentary by Courtney Langdon (Cambridge, MA: Harvard University Press, 1918–21).

10. See letter 7, n. 7.

11. Christine Campbell Thomson, ed., *By Daylight Only*.

[35] [ANS][1]

[No postmark
c. mid-October 1931]

Dear R E H—

Here's a new tale which Talman asked me to send you, for subsequent return to him.[2] Very good for a short item, I think.

When I got home from the Boston region I had to start at once for Hartford to consult about a book editing job; & on the return trip I made a detour through an exquisitely beautiful part of Connecticut I had never seen before—hilly, & full of magnificent vistas. Paused to explore the ancient town of Norwich, which is built on the steep terraces rising above the river Thames. Fascinating place—narrow, winding streets, & occasional winding steps between different levels. Now I'm dead to the world for a week or two—frightful job of editing a long (500 p) history of Dartmouth College.[3] May have to go to Brattleboro Vt. for another consultation after it is done. Having delectably warm weather.

Best wishes—H P L

Notes

1. Front: School House Founded by Dr. Daniel Lathrop 1783. Joseph Carpenter Store Built about 1772.

2. It is not clear what story is referred to. In late October, HPL made reference to Talman's "Van Kampen story"; again in March 1932.

3. Leon Burr Richardson (1878–1951), *History of Dartmouth College* (Hanover, NH: Stephen Daye Press, 1932; 2 vols.). The Stephen Daye Press was managed by HPL's friend Vrest Orton.

[36] [TLS]

[October 1931]

Dear Mr. Lovecraft:

Thanks for the post-card views. The Lathrop school and the store are certainly quaint and fascinating looking old buildings. I wonder if American barns werent copied on the style of these old-time houses. I've seen numerous barns in this part of the country that looked something similiar, especially the sloping roof.

Congratulations on the story, "In the Vault". I hope Mr. Wright publishes it soon.[1]

I envy you your visits in the New England hill country. I know you enjoy these trips immensely—just as I know I would. I enjoyed Mr. Talman's stories greatly. And especially liked the one in the current Weird Tales.[2] I sympathize with you in your job of editing the College history. That must be a wearing task.

Its hard for me to keep at my typewriter days like this—and this day is a delightful change from the weather that's been prevailing here. Its been abominably sloppy and nasty, following a short drouth. The other night it rained over eight inches, which is very unusual for this part of Texas, and I was out in the worst of it.

Somewhat past midnight, at the height of the down-pour, I sallied forth to rescue a small but pestiferous pig from the flood which was threatening to drown him in his pen. Did you ever pursue a yammering pig around a muddy pen at midnight, with the rain driving down in torrents, the wind howling in gusts, and the thunder and lightning splitting the heavens? If the pen had been larger I dont suppose I'd ever have caught the little wretch, and when I did, he yelled bloody murder all the way to the barn where I dumped him into a shed with the greatest of disgust. The old sow woke up—its not her pig but she seems to think she's responsible—and she tried her best to tear down her pen so she could get out and rip me up, and as I plodded back through the mud and rain, I'll admit I was completely disgusted with live stock in general. The next day my rheumatism got in its licks and that didnt sweeten my disposition any.

I'll admit I'm naturally leary of pigs. My distrust of them dates back to an episode in South Texas when I was a very young child. A little girl in the vicinity fell into a hog-pen and the hogs dismembered her and had her half-devoured before anybody could come to the rescue.

The sow I mentioned before—a big, mean, chicken-killing, fence-breaking old outlaw—has it in for me, anyhow. Nearly every time I've gone into the lot its been a scrap. Talk about an elephant's memory! I was gone for several days and when I got back, the misguided old heathen was waiting for me at the lot-gate, and I had to fight her off with a club. Yesterday she got me hemmed up against the barn and came for me, roaring like a wild beast, champing and snorting, and if there hadnt been a section of iron pipe handy, one of Mr. Wright's contributing gang would have been minus a good leg or so. A fighting sow can tear a limb off a man with little effort. I bent the pipe over the old fool's back and sold her the idea of retiring, but she retreated sullenly. I hate to manhandle animals, but it was she or me. She may get me yet, but I hope to dine on roast pork eventually.

But, heavenly days, how I'm rambling, without rhyme or reason. With best wishes,

Cordially,
Robert E. Howard

Notes

1. Farnsworth Wright rejected the story in November 1925. AWD had retyped it in late 1931 to replace HPL's tattered typescript. At AWD's urging, HPL resubmitted

the story and it was accepted. HPL may have mentioned it in one of the postcards REH refers to.
2. Wilfred B. Talman, "Doom Around the Corner" (*WT*, November 1931).

[37] [non-extant letter by Lovecraft]

[October 1931]

[38] [TLS]

[mid-October 1931]

Dear Mr. Lovecraft:

I intended to answer your very interesting letter sooner, but I've been up to my ears in work. I'm glad you found the views of some interest; if I had had more time as I passed through the countries where these were taken, I might possibly have gotten clearer pictures, since in many cases I didnt have the sun right. Thank you very much for the nice things you said about "College Socks" and thanks very much indeed for the letter to Street & Smith, which I know will help me along a great deal with the editors.

I hope Mr. Wright will reconsider and accept the antarctic tale, but if he shouldnt, I'd like very much to read the ms. Yes, I did indeed like "The Strange High House." Its pure poetry of the highest order, and like all great poetry, stirs dim emotions and slumbering instincts deep in the wells of conciousness. I like the illustration, and like you, think that Doolin is a splendid addition to Weird Tales. By the way, I wonder what ever became of Rankin?[1]

Speaking of Bohemians, what are they, anyhow? I know of course that they are Slavic in language and lineage, but what I'd like to know, is where they came from, and how they got there? Were the Czechs a Slavic tribe drifting off the main Slav stem who wandered into Bohemia following the westward drift of the Teutons, or were they the Dacians etc., of Roman times—did they follow the Germans across the Danube or were they already there when the Goths started westward? Was Bohemia originally a province of Germany or did the Prussians wrest it from some more Slavic kingdom? And didnt Bohemia form a part of the Ottoman empire for some time following the conquests of Suleyman the Magnificent, or did it? My ideas about the history of Eastern Europe are vague in the extreme.

Yes, the region between the Trinity and the Brazos saw many a red drama enacted. I remember an old woman, a Mrs. Crawford, whom I knew as a child, and who was one of the old settlers of the country. A gaunt, somber figure she was behind whose immobile countenance dreamed red memories. I remember the story she used to tell of the fate of her first husband, a Mr. Brown, in the year 1872.

One evening some of the stock failed to come up and Mr. Brown decided to go and look for them. The Browns lived in a big two-storied ranch-house, several miles from the nearest settlement—Black Springs. So Brown left the ranch-house, hearing the tinkling of a horse-bell somewhere off among the mesquite. It was a chill dreary day, grey clouds deepening slowly toward the veiled sunset. Mrs. Brown stood on the porch of the ranch-house and watched her husband striding off among the mesquites, while beyond him the bell tinkled incessantly. She was a strange woman who saw visions, and claimed the gift of second-sight. Smitten with premonition, but held by the fatalism of the pioneers, she saw Brown disappear among the mesquites. The tinkling bell seemed slowly to recede until the tiny sound died out entirely. Brown did not reappear, and the clouds hung like a grey shroud, a cold wind shook the bare limbs and shuddered among the dead grasses, and she knew he would never return. She went into the house, and with her servants—a negro woman and boy—she barred the doors and shuttered the windows. She put buckets of water where they would be handy in case of fire, she armed the terrified blacks, and led them into the second story of the ranch-house, there to make their last stand. She herself went out upon the balcony of the second story and waited silently. And soon again she heard the tinkle of a horse-bell; and with it many bells. Cow-bells jangled a devil's tune as the mesquite bent and swayed and the riders swept in view—naked, painted men, riding hard, with cow-horns on their heads and cow-tails swinging grotesquely from their girdles. They drove with them a swarm of horses, some of which Mrs. Brown recognized as her own property, and at their saddle-bows swung fresh crimson scalps—one of these had a grim familiarity and she shuddered, but stood unmoving, starkly impassive. Inside the house the blacks were grovelling and whimpering with terror. The Comanches swept around the house, racing at full speed. They loosed their arrows at the statue-like figure on the upper balcony and one of the shafts tore a lock of hair from she head. She did not move, did not shift the long rifle she held across her arm. She knew that unless maddened by the death or wounding of one of their number, they would not attack the house. That one arrow flight had been in barbaric defiance or contempt. They were riding hard, spurred on by the thought of avengers hot on their trail, light-eyed fighters, as ferocious as themselves. They were after horses—the Comanche's everlasting need—they had lured the rancher to his doom with a tinkling horse-bell. They would not waste time and blood storming the ranch-house. They did not care to come to grips with that silent impassive figure who stood so statue-like on the upper balcony, terrible with potentialities of ferocity, and ready to spring and die like a wounded tigress among the embers of her home. Aye, they would have paid high for that scalp—there would have been no futile screams of terror, no vain pleas for mercy where no mercy ever existed, no gleeful slitting of a helpless soft throat; there would have been the billowing of rifle-smoke, the whine of flying lead, the emptying of saddles, riderless horses racing through the mesquite and red forms lying crumpled. Aye, and the drinking of knives, the crunching of axes, and hot blood hissing in the flames, before they ripped the scalp from that frontier woman's head.

Silent she stood and saw them round up all the horses on the ranch, except one in a stable they overlooked—and ride away like a whirlwind, to vanish as they had come—as the Comanches always rode. They came like a sudden wind of destruction, they struck, they passed on like the wind, leaving desolation behind them. Taking the one horse that remained to her, she went into the mesquites and some half a mile from the house she found her husband. He lay among the dead grasses, with a dozen arrows still protruding from him, his scalped head in a great pool of congealed blood. With the aid of the blacks who had followed her, wailing a wordless dirge of death, she lifted the corpse across the horse and carried it to the ranch-house. Then she put the black boy on the horse and sent him flying toward Black Springs, whence he soon returned with a strong force of settlers. They saw the dead man and the tracks of the marauders; the wind blew cold and night had come down over the hills, and they feared for their own families. Mrs. Brown bade them go to their respective homes and leave her as a guard in case of the return of the slayers, only Captain McAdams, with whom, she said, she would feel as safe as with an army. So this was done, but the Comanches did not return. They swept in a wide half circle like a prairie fire, driving all the horses they found before them, and outracing the avengers, crossed Red River and gained their reservations and the protection of a benevolent Federal government.

Mrs. Brown was Mrs. Crawford when I knew her. A strange woman, and one whom the countryside looked on as a "medium"; a seer of visions and a communer with the dead. After she married Crawford, he went forth one day to look for his horses, just as her former husband had. Again it was a cold drear day, gloomed with grey clouds. Crawford rode away awhile before sundown and she heard his horse's hoofs dwindle away on the hard barren ground. The sun sank and the air grew cold and brittle. On the wings of a howling blue blizzard night shut down and Crawford did not come. Mrs. Crawford retired after awhile, and as she lay in the darkness, with the wild wind screaming outside, suddenly a strange feeling came over her which she recognized as the forerunner of a vision. The room filled suddenly with a weird blue light, the walls melted away, distance lost its meaning and she was looking through the hills, the long stretches of mesquite, the swirling blue distances and the night, upon the open reaches of prairie. Over the prairie blew an unearthly wind, and out of the wind came a luminous cloud and out of the cloud a horseman, riding hard. She recognized her husband, face set grimly, rifle in his grasp, and on him a blue army coat such as she had never seen before. He rode in utter silence; she did not hear the thunder of his ride, but beneath his horse's hoofs that spurned the hard earth, the dead prairie grass bent and the flints spat fire. Whether he rode alone she could not tell, for the luminous cloud closed in before and behind and he rode in the heart of the cloud. Then as a mist fades the vision faded and she was alone in the dark room with the wind screaming about the house and the wolves howling along the gale. Three days later Crawford came home, riding slowly on a weary horse. The blizzard had blown itself out; the cold sunlight warmed the shivering prairies and Crawford wore no coat, as when he had ridden away. He had not found his horses, but he had found the tracks of the raiders who had taken them, and while examining them, a band of settlers had swept past on the trail, shouting for him to follow. And he had followed and in the teeth of the freezing blizzard they had harried the marauders to the very banks of Red River, emptying more than one saddle in that long running fight. She asked about the coat, the blue army coat she had seen in the vision, and he replied with surprize that he had stopped at a settler's house long enough to borrow the coat, and had returned it as he rode back by, returning from the chase.

Many a time, as a child have I listened to her telling strange tales of old times when white men and red men locked in a last struggle for supremacy. I wandered around her old ranch-house in awe. It was not the memories of Indian forays that made me shiver—it was the strange tales the country folk told—of doors in the old ranch-house that opened and closed without human agency, of an old chair rocking to and fro in the night in an empty room. In this chair Crawford had spent his last days. Men swore that the chair rocked at night, as he had rocked, and his old spittoon clinked regularly, as it had clinked in his life-time when he rocked, chewing tobacco, and from time to time spat. Mrs. Crawford was a true pioneer woman. No higher tribute could be paid her. I liked and admired her, as I admire her memory. But to me as a child, she was endowed with a certain awesomeness, not only as far as I was concerned, but to the country-folk in general.

Any touch of supernatural always effected me as a child. But my ghosts—which I did not believe in, but which caused me goose-flesh in the dark—were always white ghosts or black ghosts. I never even considered a red ghost. I never thought of being haunted by Indians, even though I knew at times I might be walking over ground which held hidden the moldering bones of great chiefs and mighty warriors. I examined and handled bones taken from an Indian mound and the only feeling they aroused in me was a desire to have a collection of Indian teeth and finger-bones for a necklace. Even when ghost tales told by an old negress sent me shuddering and shivering to bed, I could have lain down near a collection of Indian skulls and slept soundly, untroubled by ghostly or demoniac speculations. I would have feared living Indians; extinct red-skins held no terrors for me.

But the traditions of the Palo Pinto hills: there it was that Bigfoot Wallace[2] slew his first Indian. Have you heard of Bigfoot Wallace? When you come to the Southwest you will hear much of him, and I'll show you his picture, painted full length, hanging on the south wall of the Alamo—a tall, rangy man in buckskins, with rifle and bowie, and with the features of an early American statesman or general. Direct descendant of William Wallace of Scotland, he was Virginia-born and came to Texas in 1836 to avenge his cousin and his brother, who fell at La Bahia with Fannin. He was at the Salado, he marched on the Mier Expedition and drew a white bean; he was at Monterey. He is perhaps the greatest figure in Southwestern legendry. Hundreds of tales—a regular myth-cycle—have grown up around him. But his life needs no myths to ring with breath-taking adventure and heroism. On his first adventure into the wilds he was captured in the Palo Pinto hills by the Keechies and was tied to the stake to be burned, when an old squaw rescued him and adopted him in place of a son, slain recently in a fight with another tribe. As an Indian Wallace lived for three months, hunting with them, riding with them on their forays against other tribes and against the Mexicans. Once with them he drove a raid into Mexico and in desperate hand-to-hand fighting with the Mexicans, won his name as a warrior. But he wearied of the life, and escaped to his own people again. He was scout, ranger, hunter, pioneer and soldier. When he settled on a ranch in the Medina country, he made a treaty with the Lipans that they would not steal his cattle. They kept that treaty until they decided to move westward. When they moved, they took Bigfoot's stock with them—every head of it. Bigfoot was slow to anger; he was swift in vengeance. He went to San Antonio and was given charge of a ranger company of some thirty men. With them he hunted the thieves to the head-waters of the Guadalupe River. In the ensuing battle two white men bit the dust, but forty-eight red warriors went to the Happy Hunting Grounds, and the Lipans dwindled from that day, and in a comparatively short time, were but a memory of a once-powerful tribe.

Tales, and many tales, are told of his adventures as a scout, a ranger, a soldier and a stage-driver from San Antonio to El Paso, but the tale I like best is the tale of his battle with "the big Indian", the epic combat of all the Southwest.

The rangers had trailed the Indians to the head-waters of the Llano. They went into camp, seeing at sundown the signal-smokes going up. Bigfoot was restless; that turbulent, individualist spirit of his would not let him lie down and sleep quietly with the enemy near, while other men stood guard. A few hours before dawn he slipped out of the camp and glided through the mesquite and chaparral like a ghost. Daybreak found him traversing a steep narrow canyon, which bent suddenly to the left. As he made the bend, he found himself face to face with a giant painted brave. In fact, they caromed together with such force that both were thrown to the earth by the compact. Simultaneously they bounded to their feet and for a flashing instant stood frozen, the grey eyes of the white man glaring into the flaming black eyes of the Indian. Then as if by mutual consent, each dropped his gun and they locked in mortal combat.

No white man in the Southwest could match Wallace in hand-to-hand fighting, but this red-man was quick as a cougar and strong as a bull. Not as heavy as Wallace, he was nearly as tall, and, clad only in a loin-cloth, and covered with bear's oil, he was illusive and hard to grapple as a great serpent. It was man to man, blade to blade, the terrible strength and ferocity of the giant white man matched against the cruel craft and wiry agility of the savage, with all his primitive knowledge of foul crippling holds and twists. Back and forth they reeled, close-clinched; now rolling and tumbling on the ground, tearing and gouging; now staggering upright, locked like bears. Each was trying to draw his knife, but in the frenzy of battle, no opportunity presented itself. Bigfoot felt his wind failing him. The iron arms of the grave bent his ribs inward and threatened to shut off his breath. The grimy thumbs with their long black nails gouged cruelly at his eyes, ripping the skin and bringing trickles of blood; the steely fingers sank deep in his corded throat; the bony knees drove savagely for his groin. Shaking the blood and sweat from his eyes Wallace reeled upright, dragging his foe by sheer strength. Breast jammed hard against breast, they leaned against each other, gasping wordless curses. The great veins swelled in Wallace's temples and his mighty chest heaved; but he saw in the red mist the sweat beading thick the redskin's face, and the savage mouth gaping for breath. With one volcanic burst of superhuman effort, Wallace tripped his foe and hurled him backward, falling on him with all his great weight. The Indian's head struck crashingly against a sharp-pointed rock and for an instant his dazed body went limp. And in that instant Wallace, with a desperate lunge, snatched out his knife and sank it to the hilt in the coppery body. As a dying tiger bursts into one last explosion of terrible power, the Indian started up convulsively, with a terrible yell, throwing off the giant white man as if he had been a child. Before Wallace could recover himself the Indian's hand locked on his throat, the brave's knee crashed down on his breast, and the knife in the red hand hissed down. In that flashing instant Wallace looked death stark in the face—he thought agonizedly of his childhood home and a girl who waited him at the settlements—he saw the black eyes of the Indian "gleaming like a panther's in the dark"—the knife struck hard—but only into the earth beside Wallace and as the knife came down, the Indian fell forward with it, and lay dead on the breast of his foe. And Wallace said that a grim smile curved the warrior's lips, as if, dying, he believed he was sending the white man to blaze the ghost trail ahead of him.

Shaken with the titanic upheaval of that terrible battle, Wallace rose, gazing dazedly down at the silent form of the conquered. His knife was still sheathed in the Indian's body. The point of that knife was in the red-man's heart and the wonder of it is that the brave, after recieving that terrible wound, lived long enough to all but slay his foe as he died. Such vitality, surely, is possible only to beasts and men bred close to the red throbbing heart of the primordial.

Wallace looked down at his foe and in his heart rose the respect of one warrior for another. He did not scalp the big brave; he arranged the stiffening limbs and piled rocks above the corpse to make a cairn and protect the body from the ravages of buzzards and coyotes, and beside the brave he laid the knife, and the Indian's rifle, broken to pieces—weapons for a warrior to bear to the Happy Hunting Ground. And I think of Wallace standing alone and sombrely beside that rough cairn as the sun came up over the wild tree-clad hills.

Your comments on the possible locale of early mankind proved of great interest to me; as indeed I always find your remarks regarding history and historical theories of most vivid interest. I wonder what new discoveries the next century of research will bring forth? There is, to me, an awesome and enthralling fascination about historical research—groping in the dark dusty corridors of the past and dragging forth nameless and cryptic shapes to light. I'd like to accompany some research party or expedition some time—some where—it doesnt particularly matter where.

Concerning Saxon and Danish descent, how do historians etc., explain the difference between Saxon and Scandinavian tongues? I mean, was the Saxon language—as spoken in the days of the conquest of Britain—closer to the Nordic root-stem than the Scandinavian, or vice versa? I presume that the division between Saxon and Norse occurred before the fall of the Roman empire—or am I wrong, as usual? What made the Saxon language so much softer than the Norse? Was it a modification of the original Nordic tongue, and did this modification take place in Germany before the conquest of Britain, or in the latter country after the conquest? Or was it the Norse tongue which was modified by some cause or other? In other words, was Saxon a branch of Norse, or was Norse an off-shoot of Saxon? I suppose that the Jutes, Angles and Saxons all spoke the same tongue with different dialects, just as later the people of Norway, Sweden and Denmark spoke one language. I said that Saxon was softer than Norse; that is my own idea and may have no basis in reality, since I know nothing of either language. But Saxon seems softer to me, with its "ceorl" and "eorl" compared to the Norse "carl" and "jarl". I'd appreciate any information regarding these matters.

Yes, economics are in a mess, as you remark. Economic problems were always a hopeless jumble to me, from which my baffled mind recoils to contemplate less complex situations of past ages. Maybe that's why I like the study of history so well—I'm unable to orient myself with this complicated age and understand it.

Nature is a grim old mistress, as she has proved time and again, in Galveston and elsewhere. Storms and inundations have always sent shivers along my spine, even in the contemplation of them. Anything you cant fight is horrible. You cant shoot or cut a hurricane nor brain a flood with a bludgeon. All you can do is die like sheep—a most detestable end. I wouldnt live on the coast for that reason—although destructive wind storms are not uncommon in this country. I have noted a tendency to resent remarks concerning the possibility of future catastrophes, among the people of the Coast. Just as Californians speak of the earthquake as "the big fire" and resent comments regarding earthquakes. I remember a night I spent at Rockport, a little port not very far from Corpus Christi. I stayed in a big rambling hotel close to the water's edge, and learned that in one of the more recent hurricanes—one which did great damage in Corpus Christi—a derelict hull rammed the hotel and almost demolished one side of it. But the proprietor of the hotel waxed irritable at the suggestion that the town might fall prey to another hurricane some time, and he said that Rockport was in no more danger from the elements than any other town in the country. Not wanting to antagonize the man, I agreed with him, commenting on the peril of oceanic inundation of Denver, Colorado, and the risk of tropical storms run by the inhabitants of Butte, Montana, and Madison, South Dakota. But he seemed to suspect a hint of irony in my innocent remarks, and thereafter treated me coolly.

Doubtless you are right in saying America will probably not develop a uniform type of size, owing to the vast extent of the country, and the diversity of racial blood-strains. Doubtless Sir Arthur Keith is correct in his theory that the size average of Americans as a whole is shorter and thicker, considering the vast numbers of stocky foreigners who have poured into the country of late years. Whether Americans of British descent tend to grow shorter, I am not prepared to say, though it seems to me that modern Texans are, as a whole, shorter and stockier than their earlier ancestors, though I may be wrong. For myself, at least, that is true; I am of squat build compared to my grandfathers, both of whom were six feet two inches tall, my great-grandfather Ervin who was six feet four inches, my great-grandfather Henry who was about the same height, and my great-grandfather Howard who was six feet eight inches. Some of my great-uncles were nearly seven feet in height. None was abnormal; they were simply big men, well proportioned and powerfully built. My grandfather George Ervin was accounted the strongest man in his regiment and one of the strongest men in Forrest's command. He could cleave a man from shoulder to waist with a single stroke of his saber. He owed his life to his great strength on at least one occasion, when he was captured by a band of guerrillas—thieves who preyed on both armies. They bound him on a mule and were taking him into the thickness of the forest to do away with him, when, as they were passing through a dark thicket, he suddenly snapped the cords with which he was bound, and seizing a revolver, leaped into the thicket and invited his foes to come in and take him. But they declined and made a hasty retreat, like the dirty yellow cowards they were. These ancestors of mine were taller and rangier than I, generally; some were as heavily built as I am, but all were taller. If I ever have a son, I have a feeling he'll be shorter and stockier than I am. In fact, I look depressedly down the long vistas of descent to the time when my descendants, having grown shorter and heavier in each generation, eventually resemble toads and go hopping drearily through life, croaking praises of the lost tallness of their ancestors.

I greatly appreciate the kind things you said about my verse, and thank you very much for the information regarding various forms of poetry, and the scanned examples you gave, and which I have studied long and closely. As I said before, I never studied verse-forms; I always was fascinated by poetry, and have always intended to learn something about the mechanics of it, but somehow the time or opportunity never presented itself. I can make a stab at scanning iambics, but as I said, the rest is Grecian to me. Thanks for the tip about the poetry-books to study; I intend to follow your advice regarding them when I get the time. The main trouble with writing verse is, there is so little money in it. I never felt I could afford either money or time in studying a subject in which there was such slight monetary recompense. Some time when I have more time and money—if that time ever comes—I'll make a close study of mechanics and forms, and try to versify a little for my own amusement and satisfaction.

There is a fascination about meteors, one of which is on display among the trophies of the Perdido Battlefield. They rouse fantastic speculations as to their former state—also as to what might happen if one of them crashed through a roof instead of falling in a field or pasture.

I remember the earthquake used in "Cthulhu", that is, I remember you using it, though of course, the actual shock was not felt in the West. It must have been an eery experience. With my usual ignorance of occurrences east of the Mississippi, I didnt even know South Carolina experienced a shock in 1886. Earthquakes seem to occur in all parts of the country, without any particular choice of locality.

Yes, state's right and individuality seem doomed, just as the individual seems doomed—except, of course, the individual who is rich and powerful enough to make his own laws and ride on top of the cheat and hallucination of mass-rule. Standardization is crushing the heart and soul, the blood and the guts, out of humanity and the eventual result will be either complete and unrelieved slavery or the destruction of civilization and return to barbarism. Once men sang the praises of ephemeral gods carved out of ivory and wood. Now they sing equally senseless praises to equally ephemeral and vain gods of Science and Commerce and Progress. Hell.

I would rather have lived in the pioneering age I mentioned—but the trouble is that in whatever age I lived, I would doubtless be as slothful, timid and disinclined to strife and violent action as I am in this age. If I could change my nature to suit the epoch, I can think of several ages in which I had rather live. Your choice of 18th Century England is quite interesting, and I reckon that particular age was wholesome and sound, and agreeable to a thinker and practical philosopher. I am even more interested in your choice of a Roman environment. Dont worry about my instinctive distrust of Rome! Though somewhere in this life or one previous, I have picked up a decided personal antipathy for things Roman, I have no quarrel with anyone's preferance for those things. In fact, I am highly interested in your Roman leanings, and would like to know more about your feelings for that age and empire, and your instinctive placement therein. As far as that goes, I wouldnt mind to have been a British or Gothic mercenary in the Roman army in the days of the later empire, when political graft and corruption made possible the acquisition of large fortunes quickly. I would like to have been stationed somewhere in the Orient, rather than in Germany or Britain, where there was less chance of acquiring treasure than there was of acquiring a split skull. I would like to have had control of some rich territory or city, and after a few years spent in systematic plunder, to have retired to a large villa in southern Italy, to spend the rest of my life in idleness and luxury, honored and respected by all. Roman civilization must have been paradise to such barbarian warriors as entered the ranks of her legions and acquired wealth and power. Superior in vitality and vigor to the degenerates about them, they coped successfully with the heirs of the waning empire in war and intrigue, gathering unto themselves treasures of the ages, which they had not been at trouble to create or collect, and their iron frames allowed them heights of debauchery impossible to the weaker and softer Romans.

Italians—and especially Scicilians—seem to lead all immigrants in crime, all over the country. It may not be strange, considering the heritage of bandit and piratical blood in Scicilian veins—the admixture of Grecian, Roman, Phoenician, Illyrian, Vandal, Arab, Norman, Italian—there's a good argument for the law-abiding instincts of a pure race, considering the criminality of the Scicilians compared to that of the Swedes, who are probably the most law-abiding elements America recieves from Europe. Texas has a number of Italians, who mix in readily with Spanish and Mexican elements. Portuguese are less in number and seem to stay more to themselves. Poles, which you mention as numerous in New England, constitute a considerable percentage of aliens in the Southwest, though less in number than Bohemians and Germans. My main irritation at all these races, is their clannishness and their general refusal to contribute anything to the welfare of the country, beyond that which will rebound with advantage to themselves. There was trouble among the German settlements during the Civil War. Germans were about the only aliens in Texas in those days, and they didnt think they ought to have to fight in the Civil War. Well, I can understand their viewpoint. Many of them had only been in this country a few years. They owned no slaves, had no quarrel with the Federal Government, and had only a vague idea of what the war was about anyway. Just the same, they were thriving and growing fat off the country; they had the same advantages and rights as the natives, and it looks like they should have shared some of the responsibilities. At least, that's what the Texans thought and those lean bronzed frontiersmen were in the habit of backing up their opinions with Colt and Bowie. The German settlers would not go to the war, so the war was in a few cases brought to them, suddenly and violently, after the fashion of early Texans. Besides, the Irish have never been noted for their love of the Dutch, and most of the Texans were of Irish or Scotch-Irish descent. Some of the Germans hid along the rivers and some got over into old Mexico. One group of eighteen started, but the Texans got wind of their intended flight to avoid military service, and came up suddenly with them on the Guadalupe River. Those were savage and ruthless days. The fight was short and terrible. When it was over eighteen Germans lay stretched silent in their own blood and their conquerors were riding back to their own settlements. To the more civilized people of this day and time, the early history of the Southwest seems incredible violent and blood-stained. But it was the characteristic of the frontier, and in the Southwest the pioneers, reverting by necessity to the barbarism of their ancestors, merely duplicated the colonization epoch of the East, a century or so before.

There was a good deal of pro-Germanic sympathy in this part of the country during the last war, nor was it always limited to people of pure German descent. However, many Germans were as staunchly patriotic as any American, and I noticed that the most truly American were generally those who had been born in Germany and had known something of that country before they came to America. Quite a pro-German feeling existed among some of the second and third generation, who, knowing nothing about the land of their ancestry, imagined it a glamorous realm of beauty and justice and ancient culture. A local editor refused to publish a rhyme of mine during war-time for fear of offending the German element of the population—I'm glad he did because the rhyme was a work of childhood and amazingly rotten, even for a child. But it shows how strong German sentiment was in parts of Texas. There was some talk of holding a pro-German rally and raising the German flag at a picnic, but it was abandoned, partly because none of the patriots could procure a flag and partly because the Anglo-Saxon population was prepared to scatter Teutonic remnants all over the landscape by the means of shotguns and high-powered rifles.

The main thing I dislike about Mexicans is their refusal to speak English. Most of them can speak our language—at least they can, but they wont. Of course, numbers of Mexicans will answer questions to the best of their ability, but lots of them—and especially when you get south of San Antonio where they swarm—seem to think they are subtly insulting a white man by denying all knowledge of the English language. Ask one of them something and very often he'll look at you stolidly—"No sabe Englese." You know he's lying, but there's nothing you can do about it. You restrain your impulse to strangle him, and go on. The average Texan knows as little about Spanish as the average Mexican claims to know about English. I guess its the Indian blood in them that makes them so confoundedly stolid and reticent.

I ran onto a white renegade once, though, that made me madder than any Mexican ever did. He was a white-bearded dissolute looking old scoundrel, clad in the slouch hat and boots of a cowboy, and he was apparently living in the Mexican quarter of a little South Texas town, not so very far from the Border. He refused to talk, also, or to answer a simple, civil question, and a fat Mexican woman leaned out of a window, squealing an hilarious string of Spanish, at which the brown-skinned loafers chortled and looked superior. I thought yearningly of San Jacinto, and left. Its bad enough for a greaser to retire behind a masquerade of ignorance in order to avoid answering a civil question regarding directions, etc., but when a white man sinks so low he consorts with the limpid-eyed heathen and pulls that "no savvy" business, it rouses thoughts of massacre and sudden immolation.

I'll appreciate the address of M. R. James. I'm sending you the issues of Adventure containing Pendexter's yarn. No hurry about returning them. I'm very glad that "Pickman's Model" has been used in a British publication, and will gladder when it appears in American covers. Price said in his last letter that he and Mashburn had not had an opportunity to go further into the business of getting the anthology going, but that they intended to see about it eventually.

Glad your eyes are holding up well. My own optics have been giving me a good deal of trouble. I ought to wear glasses all the time, but I dread the idea. There's always so much chance of somebody smashing them in your eyes. Glasses are a distinct disadvantage in every-day life, though I'm grateful to their aid in reading and writing.

I hope you can come out to Texas some time. I'm sure you'd enjoy New Orleans and the Louisiana swamp-country, as well as the more westerly regions. There is, of course, little difference between western Louisiana and western Arkansas and the eastern-most part of Texas. After you get to Forth Worth you begin to see the real Western Southwest. I hope some day I can show you around over the state. There are numbers of places unknown and unvisited by the great mass of tourists which I believe you would find interesting.

I'm glad my sombre narrations havent proved too boresome. Western folkways and traditions are so impregnated with savagery, suffering and strife, that even Western humor is largely grim, and, to non-Westerners, often grotesque. Of songs sung on the Western frontier, most of them, especially cowboy songs, originated in Texas, since that state was the first Anglo-American region to truly deserve the designation "West" in the proper sense. Texas songs went up the Chisolm with the longhorn herds and spread all over the West, being changed in other states to correspond with the locality in which they were sung. Other songs—hunter's and rivermen's—came through the Middle-West. A few originated in America, most were old British ballads changed by ignorance or intent, taken from, and added to, to suit the minstrels' notions. Its strange how old some of those songs are, and how long the old ballads lingered. For instance, "Barbara Allen" at one time [was] sung all over the South and Southwest. Its age can be calculated when it is known that the last stanza of the original version—which stanza I have never heard sung, is as follows:

"But by and rade the Black Douglas,
"And wow, but he was rough!
"For he tore up the bonny briar
"And threw it in Saint ——'s Loch."

I've forgotten the name of the Loch and so leave it blank. And then there was an old drinking song very popular in taverns a generation ago:

"Old Compass lies dead and is under the ground,
"Ho, ho! under the ground!
"A green apple-tree grew over his head,
"Ho, ho! over his head!"

The revellers had long forgotten who or what "Old Compass" was, but, in correspondence with Gordon, the ardent collector and student of folk-songs,[3] I learned that this was a distortion of an old English song of the days of the Commonwealth, and that "Old Compass" was none less than the bloody hypocrite himself, Cromwell. But this song was never popular in Texas; it flourished in the Irish communities of Arkansas.

I recieved your card from Plymouth and was fascinated by the view of the old house. Indeed, the very picture of the ancient building seemed to breathe the spirit of the Colonial days. And thank you very much for the generous material from Charleston. The pictures are very clear and vivid and most fascinating, and they suggest a leisurely artistic age of mellow culture and tradition, alien, strange and intriguing to me—contrasting strangely with the restless background of the Southwest. I have found Arkansas and Louisana alien to me—I am sure I would find the deep South even more alien and fascinating.

I am most delighted to hear that Long's story and your "Erich Zann" are appearing in book-form. Let me know when the book appears; for I most certainly will enrich my book-collection with a copy. What makes me more eager for it, is that I've never read "Erich Zann" and look forward to a rare literary treat.

I hope you liked the "Bal-Sagoth" yarn. As for "The Black Stone" my story appearing in the current Weird Tales, since reading it over in print, I feel rather absurd. The story sounds as if I were trying, in my feeble and blunderingly crude way, to deliberately copy your style. Your literary influence on that particular tale, while unconscious on my part, was none the less strong. And indeed, many writers of the bizarre are showing your influence in their work, not only in Weird Tales but in other magazines as well; earlier evidences of an influence which will grow greater as time goes on, for it is inevitable that your work and art will influence the whole stream of American weird literature, and eventually the weird literature of the world. I do not say this in flattery, but because I know it to be a truth. If you and I were stepping off the paces of a life-and-death duel, I would still say the same thing, because it is an inevitable truth.

By the way, I have been recently corresponding with Bernard A. Dwyer—a most interesting correspondent, whose letters hold a touch of true Celtic mysticism.

But I've been rambling on long enough. Hope I havent bored you too much. And thanks again for the pictures. Best wishes.

Cordially,
Robert E. Howard

P.S. I have recieved and read Talman's manuscript and think it splendidly done; I suppose it will appear in Weird Tales.

By the way, if you like a good tearing smashing game of football, you might drop around to Cambridge the 24th of this month, when the Lone Star State makes her first invasion of the East. The University of Texas plays Harvard then, and a special train carries thousands of Texas fans to the game. Eastern sports-writers underrate the power of the Texas team, champion of the Southwestern Conference, and as strong or stronger than last year, when it easily conquered S.M.U. of Dallas, the one Southwestern team recognized by national sports-writers as a whole. S.M.U. gave Notre Dame her hardest fight, swamped Indiana University and routed the Navy with ease, but fell an easy victim to the thundering attack of the Longhorns. Last week Texas defeated the University of Missouri 31–0, and they're coming East with the intention of giving their best. They are big, powerful men with a line like a stone wall and a ramming, bone-crushing attack, mixed with crafty aerial tactics. I believe it will be a game you would enjoy.

R.E.H.

Notes

1. Joseph Doolin and Hugh Rankin were *WT* illustrators in the 1920s and early 1930s. Of Rankin, HPL said he "really had the most genuinely fantastic imagination of any W.T. illustrator" (HPL to RHB, 16 November [1931]; *O Fortunate Floridian* 14).

2. William Alexander Anderson (Bigfoot) Wallace (1817–1899) came to Texas from Virginia in 1836 to avenge the deaths of a brother and cousin, killed by the Mexicans in the massacre at Goliad during the Texas Revolution. He fought in several skirmishes with the Mexicans while Texas was a republic (1836–45), served with the Texas Rangers against Indians and during the Mexican War, and commanded a Ranger company against Indians and border bandits in the 1850s. Wallace loved to tell exaggerated stories of his exploits and, even during his lifetime, became a larger-

than-life, legendary hero. REH owned *Adventures of Bigfoot Wallace* (1860), by John C. Duval (1816–1897); REHB 73.

3. REH corresponded with the early collector of folk songs, Robert Winslow Gordon (1888–1961), during the period Gordon edited the "Old Songs That Men Have Sung" department for *Adventure* magazine. Gordon was the first head of the Library of Congress folk song archive and traveled the country collecting songs from 1917 to 1933. REH contributed the song "Sanford Burns" to that department in the issue for 1 March 1927. The surviving REH–Gordon correspondence dates from 1925 to 1927.

[39] [TLS]

[c. October 1931]

Dear Mr. Lovecraft:

Many thanks for the opportunity of reading your magnificent "At the Mountains of Madness". This story certainly deserves publication in book form and I hope some day to see it so published. There is not, as far as I can see, a single false or unconvincing note in the whole; the entire story has a remarkable effect of realism. And I marvel once more—as in so many times in the past—at the cosmic sweep of your imagination and the extent of your scientific and literary knowledge.

When Mr. Barlow sent me the ms. he did not mention whether it should be returned to him, or to you, so I am sending it to you, as I suppose it was intended that I should.

Cordially
Robert E. Howard

[40]

Banks of the Seekonk—
October 30, 1931

Dear Mr. Howard:—

[. . .] As usual, your Texas reminiscences proved especially fascinating, and I followed the stormy tale of Mrs. Crawford with keen interest. She must have been a strange and impressive figure in her later years—with her claims to spectral divination, and her sombre and spirit-haunted house. Surely her history and personality fit in well with the grim and steely tradition of the southwest. Curious that your ghost ideas in youth excluded the Indian while including the negro. For my part, though, I can't feel much weirdness in connexion with any but the white race—so that nigger voodoo stories very largely leave me cold. The exception is where *fabulous antiquity* is concerned. I can feel weirdness in connexion with any *lost* race—any builders of primal masonry of which faint ruined traces are found in remote and desolate jungles, and so on.

No—I never heard of Bigfoot Wallace before, and am certainly glad to get an idea of such a leading figure in Southwestern folklore. His fight with the Big Indian surely deserves to rank among the celebrated single combats of literature, like that of Achilles and Hector, or of Aeneas and Turnus. Probably it will in the course of time, for the old Southwest seems to be receiving more and more literary attention.

As for Saxons, Danes, etc.—there is no real blood difference between any of the Teutonic barbarians of the 5th century A.D., though separate habitation had created linguistic variations. I think that the old Saxon—a Low-German dialect—was closer to the original Nordic language than the Scandinavian, since the Low-Germans appear to have had the stablest history, inhabiting the forests of north Germany continuously while the Scandinavians and High Germans were offshoots to the north and south respectively. The Jutes were probably more like the Scandinavians than like the Saxons, since they were contiguous to the Danes. What caused linguistic changes among the Germans who left north Germany is of course open to conjecture. Perhaps contact with other languages had a good deal to do with it—for the High Germans came into contact with Celtic-speakers, while the Scandinavians encountered the Mongoloid Finns and Lapps. The amount of blood admixture in each case is also problematical, though it has no especial biological significance in the case of the early High-Germans, since the Celts were virtually identical in race-stock. Later, though, Slavic blood entered the High-Germans. In the case of the Scandinavians, there must have been a slight admixture of Mongol, much as one may hate to admit it. It may, though, have been confined to the lower orders. Brachycephalic[1] types are not uncommon among low-grade Swedes and Norwegians—and of course the Finns are a complete mixture, though with Nordic blood predominating despite the use of a Mongoloid language.

By the way—Whitehead gave me quite a disconcerting light on the modern Danes last spring, shewing that they have undoubtedly taken in a distinct (though invisible) amount of *negro* blood as a result of their long ownership of the Virgin Islands. There is no colour line in the Islands, and the Danes of position—and even of title—have legally married women of mixed blood there while in commercial or administrative service, later taking their families back to Denmark to merge into the general mass of the Danish people. After more than two centuries of this slight but steady infiltration, it would be almost impossible to tell just who has and hasn't a subtle, imperceptible touch of the tar-brush.

About modern economics—I'm not sure but that a good deal of my own antiquarianism comes from lack of interest in a present world so tangled up in complex and prosy laws of industrial relationship. Certainly, the springs of action in the modern world are wholly intertwined with intricate financial and economic principles, so that the traditional liberal education of former generations gives one a very poor idea of what is really going on. It has come out so strongly since the war that I feel like a veritable illiterate when discussing contemporary politics. And of course recent college curricula are seeking to catch up with the times by giving economics (which was almost unknown as a definite educational subject in the past) a greater and greater place among other studies. But I don't see how anything so indirect—so far removed from the simpler emotions—can ever be of very acute intrinsic interest. The world can't help growing duller as it grows more complex.

As to the size of Americans—Keith thinks that the native stock tends to grow shorter and stockier even when unmixed with later elements, though as I have said, my personal observation has led oddly in the opposite direction. You certainly have an impressive array of giants in your heredity—and it is only by comparison with them that you need feel at all diminutive yourself. 5 ft. 11 passes for a pretty good height—at least in the east. It is my own height in ordinary heels, and I am usually called "tall". I doubt if your departure from the ancestral height is necessarily the beginning of a continuous downward trend. Talman is taller than any ancestor whose height is recorded, and towers high over his own father. Wandrei is also a record-breaker for his line. In a less altitudinous sphere, I am myself as tall as any ancestor of recorded height, though I do not exceed any.

It would certainly pay you to go through a few books on poetical technique, for you have a gift splendidly worthy of development. Not but that most of your verses are all right as they are—but the more you know of the established laws the better you will be able to polish your final versions. I don't know that I ever encountered a better natural ear for rhythm than yours. To follow the swing of one of your average poems one would imagine it composed with a full knowledge of all the technical principles involved. Some can study for years without ever achieving such a rhythm.

Yes—the Charleston earthquake of 1886 was quite an historic event. It shook down the pillars of many public buildings, almost destroyed two or three steeples, upheaved the pavements, and wrecked many private houses. Up to last year a gatepost in one of the side streets was left tilted as a souvenir of the catastrophe. I saw it in 1930, but this spring noticed that it was gone. However, the Atlantic coast is not often severely visited. The last great quake before this one was exactly a century behind—in 1786, when the Connecticut Valley in New England was heavily shaken. Hanover, N.H.—seat of Dartmouth College—felt that upheaval most severely. There are certain probabilities regarding earthquake occurrences, based on the structure of the earth's crust at different points, which geologists can map out in a general way, though one could hardly call any region totally immune. Belts of great earthquake frequency are usually near where great mountains have been thrust up, or where the neighbouring sea-bottom contains a geological "fault".

As for my feeling of instinctive placement in ancient Rome—anything as subtle as that is hard to define. It began very early, when I read about Rome in connexion with its mythology, and also heard of it from another and unfavourable angle in Sunday School. In the first case, after reading of Arabia and Greece with a sense of only objective interest, I felt a sudden surge of *personal connexion* when I stumbled on Roman names and Roman pictures and events of Roman history. I began to have pride and exultation in all Roman victories, enmity toward all foes of Rome, and deep melancholy at the downfall of the Roman world. Also—the mere sound of a sonorous Roman name (*any* name, such as Cnaeus Ventidius Bassus, Aulus Domitius Corbulo, Lucius Pomponius Mela, and so on . . .) gave me a peculiar thrill of almost indescribable quality. Typical place names like Tiber, Sabinum, Ostia, Tibur, Veii, Reate, Baiae, etc., also awaked odd feelings of affectionate psuedo-memory. And I could not avoid pseudo-patriotic feelings at *symbols* linked with Roman glory. The she-wolf, the eagles, the initials S. C. or S. P. Q. R., the battle-cry of Alala! or Venus Victrix!—and later (when I began to study Latin) certain phrases characteristic of patriotic Roman writers—non esse consuetudinem Romanorum—mare nostrorum majorum[2]—etc., etc. Moreover, Roman architecture fascinated and tantalised me ineffably—beckoning me, as it were, to vast imaginary vistas filled with lordly domes, towering Corinthian columns, and titanic arches surmounted by spirited equestrian groups. I also found the Roman physiognomy peculiarly homelike and attractive, alien though it is to my own. It never seemed foreign—and I felt a paradoxical resentment at its dilution and disappearance in the imperial age, even though that dilution brought it nearer to my own racial type than it was before! When Rome was presented to me from the second and unfavourable angle—the Sunday-School horror of Nero and the persecution of Christians—I could never sympathise in the least with the teachers. I felt that one good Roman pagan was worth any six dozen of the cringing slum riffraff who took up with a fanatical foreign belief, and was frankly sorry that the Syrian superstition was not stamped out. I didn't admire the Emperor Nero personally—but that was because he was not of the good old Roman type. When it came to the repressive measures of Marcus Aurelius and Diocletianus, I was in complete sympathy with the government and had not a shred of use for the Christian herd. To try to get me to identify myself with that herd seemed in my mind ridiculous. My own sense of placement lay unerringly and unchangingly with the Romans and the general Roman civilisation. My chief loyalty, though, concerns a day before there were any Christians—for it is the old Republic that captivates me. My favourite period is that of the later Punic Wars and the conquest of Spain and the East—say backward from 100 B.C. But any period fascinates me potently enough, and there is of course a profound charm in the Imperial age when the Roman civilisation began to extend to the land and races connected with my real blood ancestry. Roman Britain has a magical spell all its own—I can imagine myself a centurio in the Second Legion at Isca Silurum, or a retired provincial quaestor with a villa on the outskirts of Eboracum. But oddly, my instinctive imaginary picture of myself is never that of a British or Gothic Roman. It is always that of a hawk-nosed member of the old Latian and Sabine stock from the Tiber and the slopes of the Apennines.

But I'd hate to have anything in common with the mongrels who represent the Italian peninsula in Rhode Island! As you say, they are an inextricable admixture of all the races who successfully swept over the south of Italy and the island of Sicily—and of all their strains of blood the Roman is probably the least. In the first place, their region was never really Roman or even widely Latin-speaking in the best days of Rome. It was Magna Graecia—an outpost of the Hellenic race, and virtually a conquered a province in the days of the republic. Tarentum, Syracusae, and Neapolis were all Greek cities—and it is from the neighbourhood of Neapolis—Naples—that most of our Dagoes come. I think the Arabic strain is strong in all Sicilians—indeed, some of the most typically Semitic faces I have ever seen have been on Italians of this type. Of our foreigners, Italians seem to be at once the most intelligent and the most anti-social. One class of them produces more high-grade professional men than any other foreign element in the state can boast—while another class has a corner on all the organised law-breaking in sight. The better-grade Italians here have a great deal of public spirit, and have served really notably in the Providence city government. The Poles and French-Canadians, however, act only in blocs for the furtherance of their own racial interests. That is, the bulk of them do—although individual high-grade French-Canadians have held with honour the highest positions in the state. Our present junior U.S. Senator—Felix Hébert—is one of the latter, and is always eager to discourage the anti-assimilational activities of his narrower kinsfolk.[3] The Portugese are a total loss—though a higher-grade Portugese element of maritime origin exists on the coast of Massachusetts. We have a small and orderly Swedish element, but no German element as such. The few Germans who come here mix quickly with the old stock, so that the World War brought none of the problems met with in Wisconsin and elsewhere in the west. Your Texas trouble in the Civil War had its northern counterpart in the New York draft riots of 1863, also started by recent immigrants. The mobs in N.Y. refused to be drafted for federal service, and battled the police and militia for days—likewise wrecking all the nigger dwellings they could. They were finally put down and dealt with firmly but not over-severely.

The Mexican habit of denying knowledge of English undoubtedly has its roots in an age-old peasant tradition—that of a furtive defensiveness which feigns ignorance and stupidity. It crops out in all well-marked peasant elements, and the peon psychology of the low-grade Mexican no doubt accentuates it to its highest possible degree. I can well imagine that the acme of exasperatingness in this line is reached when a white man "goes native" and adopts the "no sabe" pose himself.

....

With every good wish—yrs most sincerely,
H. P. Lovecraft

Notes

1. Dolichocephalic means "long-headed," brachycephalic "short-headed." The terms were used in the now discredited practice of measuring the length of the head to establish racial distinctions. As early as the late 19th century anthropologists determined that skeletal remains of various racial groups did not fit conveniently or consistently into these rubrics.

2. S. C. = *Senatus Consultum* (decree of the Senate); *Venus Victrix* = Venus the conqueror; *Non esse* . . . = It is not the habit of the Roman people; *Mare nostrorum majorum* = the sea of our ancestors (i.e., the Mediterranean).

3. Felix Hébert (1874–1969), a Republican in the U.S. Senate, served from 1929 to 1935. Born near St-Hyacinthe, Quebec, he came to the U.S. when his parents returned in 1880 and resumed residence in Coventry, Rhode Island.

[41] [TLS]

[9 December 1931]

Dear Mr. Lovecraft:

I would have answered your letter long ago, but the fact is, I spent some time in East Texas, and am just now catching up with my correspondence. Thank you very much for the cards, etc., some of which were forwarded to me in East Texas. I found the views, as always, most fascinating, especially the beautiful old New England doorways, and the streets of Portsmouth. More and more I am realizing what a domain of tranquil beauty the ancient landscapes and towns of New England must be.

I'm glad the publishers appreciated your work on the book you spoke of, and that you are to have their business in the future.

Too bad Rankin had to be let go. As you say, he put more weirdness in his illustrations than any of the Weird Tales artists. Too bad the liquor threw him. Its a hard horse to ride. I know. I like Doolin, especially like his ability to depict the muscular development of his subjects—a department of the game at which Senf[1] is deplorably weak.

Thanks very much for the information regarding the Bohemians, which proved quite an education for me. They seem to have been a liberty loving and independant-minded race, which probably accounts for their superiority over other Eastern European races. As you remark, they must be greatly mixed—their types, I have noted, run from pure blonds of Nordic aspect to swarthy brunets with distinctly Turanian features—despite their resistance of

Turkish conquest there must have been considerable mixing of bloods along the borders; or perhaps some Turkish blood got into the main stream through Serbian channels. Most of the Bohemians I have noticed seemed to have round or mesocephalic heads, but a few were long-headed. I cannot say I like them as a race, though I am not particularly prejudiced against them, any more than I am against any alien swarm. The coach of the Cross Plains high school football team is a Bohemian, and Bohemian names appear more and more in various sections all over the state.

Yes, Bigfoot Wallace was really a gigantic figure in the old days of the Southwest, when individual prowess and courage meant so much in the development of the frontier. Wallace was well qualified to rank with the more widely known Indian fighters, such as Wetzel, Kenton, Boone, Kit Carson, and Buffalo Bill—if you might call the last an Indian fighter, one of the most over-rated and over-advertised figures west of the Mississippi. If there ever was a greater Indian fighter than Wallace it was Wetzel,[2] and the only reason for that is that Wetzel was a monomaniac and lived only to take Indian scalps. By the way, I once was acquainted with a descendant of that grim warrior, and no more striking example of the change a few generations make in a line, could be imagined. This Wetzel was a harmless giant, good-natured and rather simple-minded, no more like his ferocious ancestor than an ox is like a tiger. Yet the poor devil came to a violent end, when he was shot down by an enemy on the streets of Brownwood a few years ago.

I was much interested in your comments on the Danes and Saxons, and would like your aid in untangling a question about which I have always been vague. Just what is the exact difference between the High Germans and the Low Germans? Were the Goths, Franks, Vandals, etc., High Germans, or had the separation between High and Low occurred at the time these tribes began their wanderings? I agree with you heartily that there is a distinct Mongol strain in the Scandinavians, else whence these round heads, which have caused the Swedes etc., to be referred to generally as "square-heads"? In fact, most of the Swedes that I ever saw were brachycephalic, though it was generally in the case of peasant immigrants.

Whitehead's information about the negroid strain in the modern Danes struck me as rather ludicrous. That's mating of Poles with a vengeance! The Scandinavian and the nigger, the extremes of development! Well, its glad I am that my Danish great-greatgrandfather was so fair-skinned, blue-eyed, and red-haired-and-bearded that no one could mistake him for a Virgin Islander!

Economics is a study I loathe and about which I am completely ignorant. I cannot help but feel that there is an artificial something in a world so completely dominated by present principles, a rotten trunk in the mushroom growth, that will some time bring the whole bloated structure crashing down, or explode it like a bubble.

Your remarks regarding the sizes of Talman, Wandrei, etc., remind me of a question I've been intending to ask for some time, regarding Wandrei, whose poems I have often read with great appreciation in Weird Tales. Of what nationality is he, and does he devote all his time to literature, or if not what sort of business is he in? I realize that none of these matters is any of my business, but his verses have created an interest in him, and they seem to indicate a close study of literary forms and styles.

I appreciate very much indeed, the kind comments you made regarding my efforts at verse. I am determined to some day make a study of the art of poetry, so as to try to hammer the kinks out of my meter, rhythm, etc. Though when I'll have the time and money, I cant say. By the way, I recently took the liberty of using your mythical "Arkham" in a single-stanza rhyme which Mr. Wright accepted for Weird Tales, and which fell far short of doing justice to its subject. Here it is:

Arkham.

Drowsy and dull with age the houses blink
　　　　On aimless streets the rat-gnawed years forget—
But what inhuman figures leer and slink
　　　　Down the old alleys when the moon has set?

Your instinctive placement with the Rome of antiquity is, as I've remarked before, most interesting, and I found your narration regarding this fascinating beyond measure. Some senses of connection with past ages seem so unerring, so strong and so instinctive that I sometimes wonder if there is a bit of truth in the theory of reincarnation. It is difficult, I admit, to concieve of any sort of an after-life, yet the light of human knowledge casts its gleams such a short distance, the abysses of the unknown are so vast, that it might be that there are grains of truth in even such a fantastic belief as reincarnation. And if so, perhaps dim shadows of memory might accompany the ego upon its travels down the centuries.

Perhaps you were an armored Roman centurion and I was a skin-clad Goth in the long ago, and perhaps we split each others' skulls on some dim battle-field!

Roman Britain! There is a magic charm to the phrase—the very repeating of which brings up in my mind vague images, tantalizing, alluring and beautiful—white roads, marble palaces amid leafy groves, armor gleaming among the great trees, blue meres set in the tranquil slumber of waving forests, strange-eyed women whose rippling golden hair falls to their waists, the ever-lasting quiet of green hills in the summer sun, standards gleaming with gold—though it is always as an alien that I visualize these things. It is as a skin-clad barbarian that I stride the white roads, loiter in the shade of the green whispering groves, listen to the far elfin echo of the distant trumpet call, and gaze, half in awe and half in desire, at the white-armed women whose feet have never known the rasp of the heather, whose soft hands have never known the labor of fire-making and the cooking of meat over the open flame. I am of Britain, but it is the Britain of the Pict and the Gael.

I sympathize with New England's Italian problem. So far, the wops havent come into Texas in such large numbers as to constitute much of a problem, though with the departure of thousands of Mexicans, who are swarming back into Old Mexico, I wouldnt be surprized to see their place taken by Italians. Already in some parts of the state there seems to be a movement on to bring in hordes of Latins and Slavs from the Eastern cities.

Glad you liked the Pendexter story. When I was reading it, I had an idea that he'd reveal the haunting horror to be a reptile of some sort, and wished that you were writing it, for I knew you'd make the climax fit the atmosphere in a much more shuddersome and imaginative manner.

Glad you found my recent efforts in Weird Tales of some interest.[3] I've been trying to make the new Clayton magazine but don't seem to have much luck in that direction.

As for the Texas-Harvard game—the next time I start bragging on a football team, do me the favor of knocking me in the head with the barrel of your pistol. Of all the ignominious, utterly disgusting upsets, that took the cake. I hope the next time this state sends a team East, it'll send one of the strongest—not one of the weakest. But I wasnt the only one fooled; most of the sportswriters in the Southwest predicted a banner-season for Texas University, and proclaimed the power of its team far and wide. Yet it failed to make good in almost every instance. Shortly before the team came to Cambridge, it barely nosed out Oklahoma, and was defeated by Rice Institute, one of the weakest teams in the Conference. So after all, the defeat by Harvard was not such a great surprize as it might have been, though the large score certainly was. I am not seeking to take any of the glory from the Harvard players. They were a great team, they played magnificent football, they deserved to win. Yet it was not the strongest team in the Southwest they were pitted against, though it might be that had they been, the result would have been the same. After the Harvard game Texas University was defeated by S.M.U., and by Texas A & M.

I'm not a fanatic on sports, I hope, but I'll admit, I get a good deal of enjoyment out of certain kinds. Boxing is my favorite, next to it football, and wrestling, when its on the level. I enjoy games that are mostly contests of brawn and endurance, with a certain amount of personal conflict a definite element, as in boxing, wrestling, and to a somewhat lesser extent, football. I never had the opportunity to play football—when I was a kid it wasnt played in the country—but my favorite games were always of the rougher sort. I remember once I tried out for basket-ball, and quit in disgust during the first practice because I was repeatedly reproved for roughness. I kept instinctively tackling the ball-carrier, after the manner of a football player, though I'd never seen a game of football in my life. Such games as basketball, tennis, golf, and the like interest me not at all. I like to watch a good game of base-ball or polo, but no game can interest me much unless there is plenty of violent action in it, the hurtling of man-power against man-power, muscular force pitted against muscular force. I like to watch a powerful, fiercely-driving, bone-crushing football team in action, plunging the line. There's a player on the team of a small college in Brownwood whose play is replete with real drama—a big Indian, whom it would warm your heart to see the way he rams the opposing linesmen in the belly with his head. I didnt intend to ramble on this way.

Best wishes.

Cordially,
Robert E. Howard

P.S. I'm enclosing an amusing clipping, narrating a characteristic incident in the robust days of Fort Worth, twenty years ago.

Notes

1. C. C. Senf, *WT* illustrator, noted for his careless representations of items to be illustrated. HPL characterized him as "impossible": "I could disembowel that brainless ass Senf for the hash he made of the illustration. Good god, can't the idiot read? Look at the nice, pretty Jumbo he has drawn on its pedestal, & then note Belknap's description of the loathsome & unutterable hybrid-thing that is dreaded Chaugnar Faugn!!" (HPL to Wilfred B. Talman, 10 December 1930; *SLL* 3.239).
2. Lewis Wetzel (1763–1808), frontiersman and Indian fighter in Virginia (where Wetzel County is named for him) and Ohio.
3. Probably "The Black Stone" (November 1931) and "The Dark Man" (December 1931).

[42]

10 Barnes St.,
Providence, R. I.,
Dec. 26, 1931

Dear Mr. Howard:—

Your interesting letter duly arrived, and I was glad to learn that recent antiquarian postcards have proved of interest. New England is certainly a treasury of visible reminders of the past. Nowhere else, probably, can be found so many villages with the earmarks of the centuries plainly upon them—the reason being that compact settlement was more pronounced here than elsewhere in the colonies. Whereas in the south the first-comers largely spread over the land with plantations, New England filled up more solidly and less extensively—being a virtual overflow from Old England, with handicraft and commercial elements as proportionately abundant as the agricultural. This gave rise to urban and semi-urban life, with an abundant sea trade, at a very early date. By 1660 or so the leading seaports—Boston most of all—were busy places; with clusters of peaked gables and stack chimneys rising above wharves and winding, unpaved lanes. Most of those old houses have gone, but the next wave of building—which gave birth to the typical gambrel roofs of 1720 or thereabouts—still survives extensively here and there. By 1720 our large seaports had extensive tangles of narrow streets, (a few of them paved) steepled churches of good size, ornamented doorways, occasional brick public buildings, and in general most of the characteristic aspects still preserved by places like Marblehead. After 1750 finer public buildings and a really classic school of architecture began to appear; the great late-Georgian mansions of the early 1800's forming the finishing touch. A finer sight than one of these old towns about 1820 (just before the decadence began to set in) would be hard to imagine.

Yes—the Bohemians have surely had a varied history, and today are about the best of all Slavs. It is easy to notice the rational management of their present republic—Czecho-Slovakia—as contrasted with the turbulent doings in all other Slavic countries—Russia, Poland, Jugo-Slavia, etc. Of course, America gets the very poorest of the stock; since the superior elements have less reason to emigrate. This is true also of most other modern arrivals.

About High and Low German—these terms really have no *racial* significance, except so far as *modern* replacements within the German nation may or may not have altered the character of certain local regions—and even then, the changes would not be apt to coincide with definite High or Low German areas. The expressions have reference purely to *linguistic* distinctions (and thence to *residential* distinctions of lesser definiteness) which did not originate until the early middle ages and which were probably only barely perceptible in Charlemagne's time. They arose, probably, from the contact of the groups speaking the given dialects with groups speaking other dialects or languages; and involved no change in the race-stock. Moreover—the cognate dialects known as High and Low German are restricted to the regions now known as German-speaking, and do not include any of the other Teutonic dialects or languages recorded in history. The number of Teutonic sub-dialects has always been great, and as some die out others subdivide to form new ones. The ancient Goths spoke a language radically unlike the one which later split up into High and Low German—a language more like the Scandinavian than any other surviving speech. The Vandals, so far as we can judge without direct evidence, were closely allied to the Goths in speech. It is not known what differences, if any, existed between the speeches of the Ostrogoths (who invaded Italy) and the Visigoths (who invaded Spain). In general, the Goths lost both their language and racial identity through mixture with the vastly larger Roman or Romanised populations whom they conquered. A small isolated group in the Crimea retained a corrupt form of the Gothic language until the 16th century, but this speech disappeared shortly thereafter. Incidentally—it may be remarked that many of the older writers classed Gothic with Low German because the latter differs from High-German *in the direction of* Gothic. The fact is, I suppose, that Low-German represents the kind of non-Gothic and non-Scandinavian German *which was most affected by* Gothic-Scandinavian speech. However, Low-German differs from Gothic-Scandinavian *so much more* than it does from High-German, that we cannot but consider it a variant of the latter, influenced by the former, rather than a variant of the former influenced by the latter. The earliest division of the Teutonic races of which we have any knowledge is into Eastern and Western Germans; the former corresponding to Goths and Scandinavians, and probably representing the original homogeneous Teuton stock (at its first prehistoric splitting off from Celtic-speakers) more closely than the latter. Later we find the Western Germans subdividing into two dialectic divisions, with one roughly predominating in the north and west, (later to become Low German, Frisian, Dutch, Saxon, and Anglo-Saxon) and the other (later High-German) in the South and East. As just remarked, the northern and western tribes or nations within this general western group were probably influenced more or less by contact with tribes or nations of the general Eastern group—Scandinavians on the north, and Goths in the southwest where the Frankish and Visigoth kingdoms were neighbours. Just how much the southern and eastern tribes or nations of the western group were influenced by other languages I am not certain—but they were certainly exposed to considerable Slavic contact—just as both groups were exposed to considerable Celtic contact. It would perhaps be difficult to say at the present time just which dialect—Low or High German—most closely represents the original speech of the Western Teutonic group. Low German, on the surface, is more like the Gothic-Scandinavian speech which we consider most primitive; but as we have seen, this is perhaps due to the historically late influence of Gothic and Scandinavian neighbours. On the other hand, it is conceivable that the original Western German speech differed less than we think from the Eastern (Goth-Scand.) speech, and that High-German represents an alien influence while Low-German represents merely a passive adherence to the earlier form. Many advocate this theory—who shall decide when doctors disagree?[1] Some, I think, believe there were more than two definite Teutonic groups; and that the Frisian type of speech was always intermediate between eastern and western. It's a confused mess, and I fear my attempt at exposition may sound like a sorry muddle indeed. Let's see what a diagram will do:

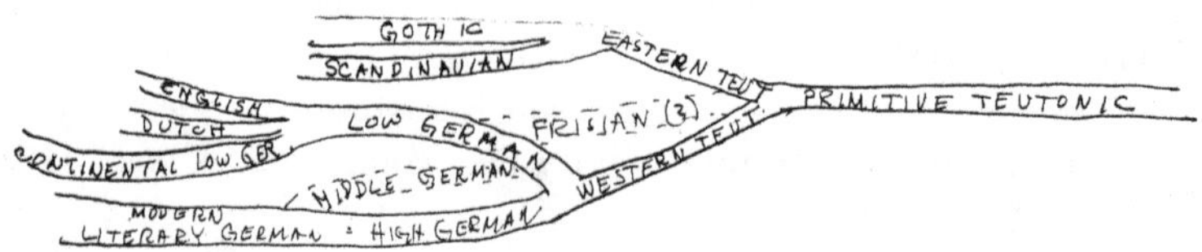

The Franks at the time of Clovis probably spoke in a Western German idiom antedating the division into High and Low—even though by that time the Western Germans around the North Sea had begun to feel Scandinavian influence and to assume rudimentary Low-German characteristics. Later the Franks seem to have become divided in speech; those toward the north tending to Low-German while the bulk farther south assumed High-German characteristics. Those in Gaul, of course soon became Latinised and evolved the French language. Taking German districts and other Western Teutonic nations today, we may class their basic folk idioms (as distinguished, in some cases, from their literary languages) as follows—largely ignoring the exact division of general High-German into *Middle-German* and High-German proper:

Low German	*High German*
Upper Rhine Provinces	Saxony (mid. Ger.—tho' old Saxon was Low)
Westphalia	Hessia
Hamburg	Franconia
Friesland	Thuringia
Oldenburg	Silesia
Hanover	Bavaria
Belgium (Flemish)	Austria
Holland	Switzerland
England and America (though of course our vocabulary has become so Latinated that the language can only be called *grammatically* Teutonic at the present time.)	Swabia Pennsylvania (Colonial German areas) Yiddish speaking areas of Jews

In England and America prior to the 19th century a very erroneous use of the terms High and Low German (or "Dutch", as the word *Deutsche* was usually Anglicised) was followed, which finally came to the classification of all Germans proper as "High Dutch" and of Holland Dutch as "Low Dutch". It is from this usage that the misleading term "Pennsylvania Dutch" (applied to the Colonial High-German stock from the Palatinate) arose. As most are aware, the literary language of modern Germany and Austria—what is now commonly taught and recognised as plain "German"—is due to the example set by Martin Luther in his translation of the Bible, and is essentially a High German of the Middle-Germanic type. Specifically, Luther chose the law-court speech* of Franconia (he was himself a Thuringinian of roughly cognate dialect) as the best sort of "happy medium" for a book which would be studied alike by Low and High Germans. The dialectic differences (prefixes, consonantal usages, etc.) are in all cases largely overlapping, so that certain middle dialects—what might be called the "Lower" forms of High-German—might be read after a fashion by almost all the people of the German States (though probably not by the Frieslanders) from the Low-German Westphalians and Hamburgers to the ultra-High Austrians and Bavarians. Of course, the Middle High Germans—Franconians, Hessians, Thuringians, Saxons, etc.—were in luck, since their dialects were pretty close to the artificially chosen norm; while the Low-Germans of the north probably had the hardest time of all. The importance of the new Scriptures at the time of the Reformation made Luther's choice of language very far-reaching in effect; and its endorsement by two eminent grammarians—Sebastian Franck in Luther's own generation and Johannes Clajus in the next—conclusively established it as *the* German language; thenceforward to be taught in schools and to become the universal speech of all urban and literate Germans. From 1600 onward, we may ignore all German dialectic variations except when dealing with peasant speech. As for race-stock—the Low-German division of the Teutonic people probably represent the original strain about as well as any. Southern and Eastern Germans have suffered vast admixture with brachycephalic Slavs; while as previously mentioned, the northern Scandinavians have undoubtedly picked up some Lapp-Finn blood. The West Indian negroid strain in Denmark must of course be very slight—and confined largely to the minority of families who had connexions with the Virgin Islands. It impressed Whitehead because he came up against many concrete cases—negroid families in the Virgins who had relatives married into certain noble and aristocratic Danish houses. The negroid aristocrat of the West Indies is a peculiar phenomenon causing infinite embarrassment to visiting Americans. It would be impossible, on West Indian soil, to regard as 'just a nigger' a light tan man who carries a Danish coat-of-arms on his coach panels, who lives like a feudal lord and sends his sons to the University of Copenhagen, and whose ancestors—coffee-coloured for perhaps 5 or 6 generations and blond white in the paternal line before that—have always been cultivated, respected, and absolute masters of wide acres and hundreds of tenants. The American in the Virgin Islands finds dozens of men like this moving freely in the very circles—composed of British and French residents of fine family and education—which he is expected to enter; and if he tries to draw a colour-line he is regarded with amazement and disapproval by the very Englishmen and

*these so-called "chancery" idioms were devised in the 15th century to make legal notices more widely intelligible than they would be if adhering precisely to any one local dialect.

Frenchmen he really wants to know. Whitehead finds that most Americans—even Southerners—tend to compromise after the first few weeks; especially since there is a sharp local line between these "gentlemen of colour" and the out-and-out blacks. He himself—although of an old Virginian family—frankly regards as friends several coloured planters of this description; although he owns he would not wish many persons in the U.S. to know it. He once advised a man of that element (wholly indistinguishable from a pure Caucasian) not to send his daughter to a fashionable American school—and although the man had hard work understanding the American attitude, he did not think it important enough to feel offended about it when he did understand it. Instead, he sent his daughter to a Copenhagen school—and she later married a Danish baron and became the mother of the present heir of a large Danish estate. On another occasion Whitehead met a "coloured gentleman" who was furiously angry because his daughter was determined to marry a pure white Dane whose coat-of-arms did not have a sufficient number of quarterings! This tan-hued patrician was of all-noble descent except for one slight fraction of mixed blood. Probably this business started in the 17th century with the usual crude concubinage betwixt plebeian Danes of the clerk or overseer class and coal-black negresses—or perhaps a Spanish mulatto figured to some extent. At any rate, but the middle of the 18th century there had arisen a large element of mixed-blooded Virgin Islanders, reared carefully enough by their left-handed fathers or grandfathers to be considered eligible for social recognition; and including young women of sufficient attractiveness and accomplishments to be wooed for legitimate wedlock by Danes of the highest ancestry and position.

About Wandrei—he is mainly Anglo-Saxon, with just the one German strain (the 1848 Midwestern stock) to give him his odd name. He is a tremendously brilliant kid of 23, who graduated from the U. of Minnesota at 20, and is now an English instructor there. I enclose his picture—which I'll ask you to return at your convenience, though there's no hurry about it. Wandrei is the author of two privately printed books of bizarre poems—"Ecstasy" (1928) and "Dark Odyssey" (1930)—the latter illustrated by his still-younger brother, who is a fantastic artist of great promise. All of Wandrei's time outside of college hours goes into literature. He is now finishing a long novel of cosmic horror which will soon be tried on the publishers. Commercialism is anathema to him. He came to New York when just out of college and obtained a fine advertising position with the Dutton publishing house, but was so disgusted with business psychology that he chucked the job within a year and went home. After some post-graduate work at the U. of Minn. he obtained his present instructorship. He's really a marvellous boy, and would undoubtedly appreciate hearing from you. In the summer of 1927 he visited the East, staying in Providence two weeks and letting me show him around the various scenes of antiquarian interest here and in the Boston zone. He lives at 1152 Portland Ave., St. Paul, Minn.

My attitude toward economics is an exact duplicate of your own, though I realise nowadays that one can't expect to understand contemporary history—or speculate on future history—without some grounding in the subject. The one book which I imagine might give a layman a fair general outline of the basic principles is that new thing by H. G. Wells[2]—which I want to get hold of sooner or later. As a matter of fact, economics as a major determinant of history seems to mark a later and complex—and perhaps decadent—stage in the life of a civilisation; when the retreat from primitive barter has gone so far that all exchanges of commodities and services are tangled up in endless labyrinths of intangible intermediation. Artificial values spring into being, so that the principle of simple supply is wholly submerged; and whole fortunes are made through the involved manipulation of commodities which no party to the transaction ever sees or cares a hang about. Oswald Spengler, in "The Decline of the West", associates this phenomenon definitely with cultural senility; and I imagine he is not far wrong.[3] Complex flimsy structures of this sort sooner or later collapse with their own weight—and if the western world is wise, it will at least attempt a general unscrambling of matters before it is too late.

Your "Arkham" stanza is splendid, and I feel honoured that my imaginary city of brooding horror should have evoked such an image. Glad Wright took it, and hope you'll have more verse for him before long. You certainly have the gift; and with the added technical study you plan, your poetry is likely to be even more vivid and notable than it now is—although, as I've said, it is tremendously powerful in its present form.

As for my instinctive Roman placement—biology doesn't make reincarnation or hereditary memory a very likely thing; and I'm much more inclined to lay such phenomena to especially powerful unconscious impressions—pictorial, literary, or conversational—received in early childhood. In my early years I was always digging around among books and pictures, and antiquity was my favourite theme. My chief wish seems to have been to project myself into the ancient world, and very naturally I would choose that part of it to which entrance seemed easiest—the part of antiquity that used our alphabet, had many words sounding like ours, and had an architecture with the arches and Corinthian columns made familiar by modern public buildings. Then again, I picked up a lot of travel information from my grandfather, who had travelled in Italy, but not in Greece or the East. Of all the cultures of antiquity, Rome had the most links with the scenes and ways about me—hence was the most natural for me to turn to when sheer ancientness for its own sake became my object. Your vision of Roman Britain sounds very vivid indeed—perhaps I saw you many a time as I rode through the fields and woods during my service in Britannia under P. Ostorius Scapula!

I hope the departure of Mexicans from Texas may not invite a wave of Slavs and Latins. In itself, I imagine that the exodus must have been something of a relief—but if it brings worse consequences, it will be a dearly bought boon. The Mexicans were at least natural denizens of the general region—adapted to the soil, and presenting no new or far-reaching problems of adjustment.

Sorry the Texas-Harvard game was such a disappointment to southwestern hopes. My lack of interest in games—sedentary as well as athletic—is a rather curious phenomenon in view of the wide diffusion of the competitive instinct. I enjoy the idea of great conflicts of force when they are natural—not prearranged—and involve actual historic issues, but my symbolising power seems to be too weak to give me a comparable thrill from isolated or artificial combats as represented by sports. I'd think my early ill health had something to do with it if it weren't that my indifference to sedentary games is just as great. A Brown-Dartmouth football game and a Lenz-Culbertson bridge contest leave me equally unmoved. Thanks for the cutting, which certainly reveals a vigorous and untrammelled pioneer milieu. It is hard to realise that such frontier moods existed as lately as 20 years ago—yet I suppose it is really only the immediate post-war period which has so thoroughly standardised and toned down the whole country.

I shall be looking for your new work in W.T., and hope that before long you'll find a new opening in the Clayton market.

Wishing you a Happy New Year—

Most cordially and sincerely yrs—

H. P. Lovecraft

Notes

1. "Who shall decide, when Doctors disagree . . .?" Alexander Pope, *Moral Essays* (1733–34), Epistle 3, l. 1.

2. H. G. Wells, *The Work, Wealth and Happiness of Mankind.*

3. Spengler's treatise was a major influence on HPL's later political and cultural thought. See S. T. Joshi, *H. P. Lovecraft: The Decline of the West* (Mercer Island, WA: Starmont House, 1990; rpt. Berkeley Heights, NJ: Wildside Press, [2001]).

1932

[43] [ANS][1]

[No postmark][2]

Behold the neo-Georgian splendours of Old Cambridge! A warm & rainy New Year's enabled me to get down to Boston for a week-end with W. Paul Cook, & we are devoting all our time to museums. Saw 5 in Cambridge to-day—Germanic, (both Low & High!) Semitic, (including *Hittite* bas-reliefs & *Sumerian* artifacts) Peabody, (anthropological—with everything from every-where except Valusia, Bal-Sagoth, Atlantis, & Lemuria!) Agassiz (Nat. hist.) & Fogg (art). Tomorrow we explore the good old Fine Arts & the Gardner Renaissance place in the Fenway. Regards—H P L

Your last I have read is The Dark Man, which I enjoyed hugely.
W. Paul Cook

Notes

1. Front: Possibly the Lowell House, Harvard University, Cambridge, Mass.; HPL sent several such cards at this time.

2. HPL and Cook made their museum visits on 2 January 1932.

[44] [ANS][1]

[Postmarked Providence, R.I.,
9 January 1932]

Thanks tremendously for the varied material. Texas certainly upholds its san-guinary record! ¶ That old knife may easily have been an heirloom of some German immigrant of the 19th century, but it's interesting for all that. Those Thevenin articles are fascinating—although they represent a sort of wild speculation with not much behind it.[2] The representation of Saturn is clearly a decorative coincidence, for the ring as shewn is unlike Saturn's ring. All told, it isn't likely that any civilisation existed before 12,000 or 15,000 B.C., or elsewhere than in or near Asia. From that the others spread or descended. Just how early accurate astronomical knowledge arose is debatable—but there is no real evidence for a falling-off from some primal state of vast erudition. Still—the fictionist can weave his own fables!
Best wishes—H P L

Notes

1. Front: Unknown.

2. René Thévenin (1877–1967), French author of works on mythological animals, American Indians, legendary places, and other matters; also author of science fiction

and fantasy novels. His "A Race of Supermen Who Disappeared 20,000 Years Ago?" appeared in nine installments of *American Weekly* (16 November 1931–10 January 1932.

[45] [TLS]

[c. early January 1932]

Dear Mr. Lovecraft:

Yes, I enjoyed the postcards very much. As you point out, the case of New England's settling was certainly unique among the colonies, inasmuch as it was a whole-sale transplanting of English life into the New World—though sure I'd never realized it until you pointed it out. I've learned a great deal more from your letters about the Atlantic sea-board than I've ever learned from histories and the like. And from my correspondence with Talman I'm getting a lot of interesting lights on the early Dutch occupation of New York—or Niew Amsterdam, if that's the way its spelled.

Thanks very much for the generous amount of information regarding High and Low German, which seemed to cover the subject in a very clear and concise manner. I especially liked the chart which I have studied with great interest. I reckon its difficult to trace a modern word or term to its exact source, especially when that source is non-Latin. For instance its long been my whim to discover the original form of my first name. Dictionaries give it as a High German name, arguing an eastern European origin; yet it appeared in Saxon England as "Redbriht" and among the Scandinavians as "Hrobjart". The Normans, among whom it was a favorite name, having adorned some of the most infamous scoundrels in history, seem to have introduced it into the British Isles in its present form. Do you have any idea as to what the confounded cognomen was originally?

I've noticed the American term you mention in regard to "Pennsylvania Dutch". This race has swarmed into Texas in large numbers, following the oil fields, and most of them are easily recognized by their large noses and dark, almost—and sometimes—swarthy skins. Was that their original complection, or have they mixed with some Latin or Slavic invader since coming to America?

The color-condition in the West Indies was news to me, but I do not think it would cause me any particular annoyance, in case I should ever be so fortunate as to visit these islands. Manners and mode of conduct depend, of course, on custom, habit, etc., and I hardly think I'd feel any embarrassment at social contact with such persons as you mentioned—the cultured aristocratic ones, of course. Though if any should seek to pay court to a sister or daughter, I'm afraid I'd resort to primitive Nordic tactics, regardless of the suitor's quarterings. Somehow that reminds me of the breeding of negro girls for concubines which was once practiced in New Orleans and doubtless elsewhere, though possibly never on a very extensive scale. Their owners had an eye to posterity and mated them with as much care as they might have given to the breeding of their race horses. The girls were raised with only one idea in view—the pleasure of their masters—and were often well educated and refined. After a few generations such girls, the vestige of negroid blood in their veins scarcely discernable, carefully raised, well taught in the arts of love, knowing no will save that of their masters, made mistresses and slaves not excelled by any Eastern seraglio. They brought fancy prices, and they were worth it.

Thanks very much for the opportunity of seeing Wandrei's picture—which I'm returning. He seems to enviably tall, and certainly has a fine head. I have often admired the depth of his imagination, both in his prose and his verse. I had no ideas he was as young as he is.

I hope some steps will be taken in America before the whole damned structure falls to pieces. But I have no faith in the leaders of the country. The United States might pull out of this depression, but right now the country is faced with a war for which its not prepared. Some time ago I predicted that Japan would ignore the protests of the League of Nations; that having secured Manchuria she would move to China proper; that American businesses in Manchuria would put up a howl and the American government would become embroiled; and that the European nations would back out, leaving America holding the sack. A great deal of this has already happened.

I realize that possession of Manchuria is vital to Japan, with her ever-expanding population. She can not let go her grasp. On the other hand, even if this situation is smoothed over without war, we will be forced to fight her sooner or later. With room and resources by which to expand—all of which Manchuria furnishes—in thirty years Japan will be the most powerful nation in the world. And developement and power mean conquest to any Oriental nation. Its my belief that Japan will sooner or later clash with Russia, who can hardly allow an Oriental empire to grow up beside her—but it would not surprize me, for the present, to see Russia and Japan allied against America—which will play hell getting help from any European nation.

I love peace, yet I wouldnt mind a war right now such a hell of a lot, if the country was prepared; but it isnt. Japan knows it; that's why she thinks she can kick the flag around, beat up American officials, and get away with it. I wish to the devil the country was prepared. I wish warfare was on its older, simpler base. Though I'm far from war-like, yet I've always felt that with the proper training, I could learn to be fairly annoying to the enemy with a bayonet or rifle butt, but this new-fangled chemical warfare would make me a total loss. What's the glory in pushing a button and slaughtering men fifty miles away, or flying over a city and spraying the noncombatants with liquid hell? When they traded the warhorse for a submarine, they ruined the blasted business as far as I'm concerned. That's what science has done for the world. Ruled by scientists on one hand and big business on the other, the average man has about as much chance as a beetle in a chicken-yard. Admitting that scientists have made the world a much easier place to live in, what's the use, if they're preparing to blot all life from it by their hellish inventions?

But that's none of my business. Fellows like me are not the ones interested—not the ones who plan and direct the wars; only the ones who get slaughtered. Well, whatever the cause of war, once its started, the only thing to do is to fight like hell, and if the country was prepared, I wouldnt kick. I'm not saying, keep out of wars; I'm only saying, always be ready in case of war.

Referring again to your sense of placement with Rome—which is a subject so interesting to me I can hardly keep off it—your explanation is logical and without doubt correct. My sense of placement among the various western barbarians can doubtless be explained as logically. But there is one hobby of mine which puzzles me to this day. I am not attempting to lend it any esoteric or mysterious significance, but the fact remains that I can neither explain nor understand it. That is my interest in the people which, for the sake of brevity, I have always designated as Picts. I am of course aware that my use of the term might be questioned. The people who are known in history as Picts, are named variously as Celts, aborigines and even Germans. Some authorities maintain they came into Britain after the Britons, and just before the coming of the Gaels. The "wild Picts of Galloway" which figure largely in early Scottish history and legendry, were doubtless of a very mixed race—probably predominantly Celtic, both Cymric and Gaelic, and speaking a sort of bastard Cymric, adulterated with elements of Gaelic and aborigine, of which latter strain there must have been quite a percentage in the blood of the Picts. There might have been considerable Germanic or Scandinavian mixture, as well. Probably the term "Pict" was properly applied only to the wandering Celtic tribe which settled in Galloway and persumably conquered and was absorbed by the aboriginal population. But to me "Pict" must always refer to the small dark Mediterranean aborigines of Britain. This is not strange, since when I first read of these aborigines, they were referred to as Picts. But what is strange, is my unflagging interest in them. I read of them first in Scottish histories—merely bare mentionings, usually in disapproval. Understand, my historical readings in my childhood were scattered and sketchy, owing to the fact that I lived in the country where such books were scarce. I was an enthusiast of Scottish history, such as I could obtain, feeling a kinship with the kilted clansmen because of the Scottish strain in my own blood. In the brief and condensed histories I read, the Picts were given only bare mention, as when they clashed with, and were defeated by, the Scotch. Or in English history, as the cause of the Britons inviting in the Saxons. The fullest description of this race that I read at that time, was a brief remark by an English historian that the Picts were brutish savages, living in mud huts. The only hint I obtained about them from a legendary point of view, was in a description of Rob Roy, which, mentioning the abnormal length of his arms, compared him in this respect to the Picts, commenting briefly upon their stocky and ape-like appearance. You can see that everything I read at that time, was not calculated to inspire an admiration for the race.

Then when I was about twelve I spent a short time in New Orleans and found in a Canal Street library, a book detailing the pageant of British history, from prehistoric times up to—I believe—the Norman conquest. It was written for school-boys and told in an interesting and romantic style, probably with many historical inaccuracies. But there I first learned of the small dark people which first settled Britain, and they were referred to as Picts. I had always felt a strange interest in the term and the people, and now I felt a driving absorption regarding them. The writer painted the aborigines in no more admirable light than had other historians whose works I had read. His Picts were made to be sly, furtive, unwarlike, and altogether inferior to the races which followed—which was doubtless true. And yet I felt a strong sympathy for this people, and then and there adopted them as a medium of connection with ancient times. I made them a strong, warlike race of barbarians, gave them an honorable history of past glories, and created for them a great king—one Bran Mak Morn. I must admit my imagination was rather weak when it came to naming this character, who seemed to leap full grown into my mind. Many kings in the Pictish chronicles have Gaelic names, yet in order to be consistent with my fictionized version of the Pictish race, their great king should have a name more in keeping with their non-Aryan antiquity. But I named him Bran, for another favorite historical character of mine—the Gaul Brennus, who sacked Rome. The Mak Morn comes from the famous Irish hero, Gol Mac Morn. I changed the spelling of the Mac, to give it a non-Gaelic appearance, since the Gaelic alphabet contains no "k", "c" being always given the "k" sound. So while Bran Mac Morn is Gaelic for "The Raven, Son of Morn", Bran Mak Morn has no Gaelic significance, but has a meaning of its own, purely Pictish and ancient, with roots in the dim mazes of antiquity; the similarity in sound to the Gaelic term is simply a coincidence!

But what I intended to say was, I am not yet able to understand my preference for these so-called Picts. Bran Mak Morn has not changed in the years;[1] he is exactly as he leaped full-grown into my mind—a pantherish man of medium height, with inscrutable black eyes, black hair and dark skin. This was not my own type; I was blond and rather above medium size than below. Most of my friends were of the same mold. Pronounced brunet types such as this were mainly represented by Mexicans and Indians, whom I disliked. Yet, in reading of the Picts, I mentally took their side against the invading Celts and Teutons, whom I knew to be my type and indeed, my ancestors. My interest, especially in my early boyhood, in these strange Neolithic people was so keen, that I was not content with my Nordic appearance, and had I grown into the sort of a man, which in childhood I wished to become, I would have been short, stocky, with thick, gnarled limbs, beady black eyes, a low retreating forehead, heavy jaw, and straight, coarse black hair—my conception of a typical Pict. I cannot trace this whim to an admiration for some person of that type—it was a growth from my interest in the Medditeranean race which first settled Britain. Books dealing on Scottish history were easier for me to obtain than those dealing with Irish history, so in my childhood I knew infinitely more about Scottish history and legendry than Irish. I had a distinct Scottish patriotism, and liked nothing better than reading about the Scotch and English wars. I enacted these wars in my games and galloped full tilt through the mesquite on a bare-backed racing mare, hewing right and left with a Mexican machete and slicing off cactus pears which I pretended were the heads of English knights. But in reading of clashes between the Scotch and the Picts, I always felt my sympathies shift strangely. But enough of this; it isnt my intention to bore you.

I'm afraid the moving out of the Mexicans will bring in a good many Slavic and Latin emigrants—or immigrants, I can never remember which way to spell the infernal word. I'd rather have the Mexicans. They kept their place and offered very little social problem. The high-class Mexicans, mostly Spanish in blood, are generally accepted socially, though much less in Texas than in New Mexico, Arizona and California. The lower class keep to their place, mainly. But a European peasant, after learning the English language and picking up a little Americanization, sees no reason why he shouldnt immediately be given the president's daughter for wife, and a job running the government. Least ways, that's the way it appears to me.

Of course, most of the immigrants I've known have been Germans. And a more excitable, easily-unbalanced race I never heard of, unless its the Swedes. I've heard a lot about Germanic stolidity—well, maybe these Texas Swedes and Germans are different from most. But these can go crazier quicker over less than any Celtic or Latin race I ever heard of. The Swedes are always bumping themselves off. During the war there was an old German who lived not far from this town—a fine old man, too, by the way—who, in spite of long residence in America, had failed to take out naturalization papers. Well, to show his patriotism, which was the real article, alright, he applied for citizenship, and worried for fear lest his American neighbors might despise him as an alien. Assurances to the contrary failed to reassure him, and some slight hitch came in the getting of his citizenship; it didnt amount to anything, but he blew his brains out with a Winchester. Then, not long ago, a woman in the western part of the state killed her three children and wounded herself, because she said the children were taking up American ways. But she was a Russian. And then again, in one of the foreign communities which are slowly increasing in the western part of the state, as elsewhere, a Swede was alone in his shack and it caught on fire. He ran to put out the fire and his foot broke through the floor and got caught. Well, with typical coolness, he at once set to work cutting off his leg at the knee! The fire went out before it reached him, but he died from loss of blood, having cut his leg about half-way off with his pocket-knife, before he was found. When a German gets something on his mind, he broods and broods until it assumes such monstrous proportions he goes clean crazy.

And why is it, when the English and Germans are to supposed to be of practically the same race, why is it that English literature reflects, in the main, such a sturdy optimism, and an opinion that all is well in spite of hell, while German literature seems so gloomy, melancholy and assured of the futility of human vanity? Which was the original Nordic instinct? And another thing; I do not question the stubborn courage of the German people, but in this country at least, Germans are more peaceable than people of English descent, generally less ready to fight at the drop of the hat. Whence this more belligerent nature of the Anglo-Saxons?

I'm a lot like you in regard to card games and the like. Maybe if I had more luck, I'd feel differently, but I doubt it. It makes me as nervous as hell to sit still for hours at a time and shuffle and deal bits of cardboard, and I've neither the skill nor the luck to make any money at it. I havent the analytical mind it takes to be a good card-player. I used to play seven-up a lot, and occasionally enjoy a game now, but as for bridge, poker and the like—I work too hard for my dough to throw it away. I played fan-tan half the night once and didnt win a penny. And even if I had luck and sense enough to win, I'm no gambler. I dont like to risk money I worked hard to get. I was never a very welcome guest in the gambling houses of Mexico, for I was merely a looker-on. Well, the sharks arent all in Mexico; I remember one night in Texas, when I foolishly allowed myself to be gotten soused in one of these innocent, "friendly drinking bouts" and when I was so biffed I couldnt tell a trey from a king, the serpentine suggestion was made for a gentlemanly game of draw poker. My reply was a mocking and bibulous laugh; I'd have to be drunker than that to forget the thin strain of Scotch blood in my veins.

But physical sports, especially the strenuous kinds, have a definite interest for me. Despite the tinsel and show, the artificial adjuncts, and the sometimes disgusting advertisement, ballyhoo and exploitation attendant upon such sports as boxing and football, there is, in the actual contests, something vital and real and deep-rooted in the very life-springs of the race. Competitive sports are essentially Nordic in their nature, and if the Central Eastern European countries would devote as much time to such sports as do America and England, I think less wars, bickering and intrigues would result. Football, for instance, is nothing less than war in miniature, and provides an excellent way of working off pugnacious and combative instincts without bloodshed. Just now there is a great uproar because nearly fifty players were killed this year. The total is appalling and unusual, but it seems incongruous for so much racket to be raised over the taking of fifty lives, when wars that blot out men by the millions are looked on as necessary. God knows I'd rather die on a clean football field, playing a clean game, than to die like a rat in the muck and slush of a bloody war, the reasons for which I was only dimly aware.

Football is essentially Anglo-Saxon. The Juts, Angles and Saxons brought the game to Britain with them. The present style of football, as played in this country, is a distinct evolution, entirely in keeping with the American nature. It is a far faster, more bruising and more complicated game than the English branch. Next to boxing, it is the most difficult of all sports to master, since to be a skillful player one must combine speed, unusual strength, toughness, intelligence, co-ordination, foresight and generalship. It is not, as so many people seem to think, a mere senseless mauling match. It contains strategy, science, and the elements of psychology. A good football player must be a good judge of human nature, he must be quick and strong, a quick thinker and a clean player.

Wrestling, of course, is the most savagely brutal of all sports. Professionall wrestling must of necessary be framed, since if the contestants went in with the intention of battling on the level, nearly every bout would be accompanied by a fatality, or a crippling for life. Professional wrestling now is a good show, no more.

Boxing, now on a slump, partly because of the general depression, partly on account of the poor talent, but mostly because of the avarice of the managers and promoters, and their nauseating exploitation of the game, is more primal, more fundamental, than even football. A football game can never attract me as does a really good prize-fight, but perhaps my instincts are more primitive than most. A well-trained fighter can take an astounding amount of punishment, and what seems frightful brutality to the casual looker-on, really is not. The most disgusting part of pugilism is the crowds. I know of no more nauseating sight than to see some pot-bellied, flabby-muscled, hog-jowled imitation of a man sitting in a ringside seat and squealing insults at some kid who is taking a beating that would kill the squealer and all his yellow-gutted brothers. But sometimes the fans act funny. I remember one time in Fort Worth I was watching a scrap between Kid Dula and a set-up called Racehorse Rogers. There was a Jew sitting beside me who had bet five dollars with a big fireman that Rogers would stay the limit. Rogers stayed and the Jew won the bet, but the fight was harder on him than on Rogers. As Dula would drive Racehorse across the ring, slugging him savagely, the Jew would leap up and wave his arms wildly, shrieking for Rogers to clinch!—hold!—stall!—do anything! As the gong would end the round, the Jew would shriek that Rogers was saved by the gong and would fall limply back into his seat, in a state of collapse.

The real hilarity comes at a wrestling match. Everybody, except the most rabid fans, knows that the outcome has already been decided and agreed upon before the warriors enter the ring, but its a good show, if the boys know their stuff. Good wrestlers will bellow, make terrible grimaces, bite and claw, kick each other terrifically in the pants, pull hair out, throw each other out of the ring, etc. Its almost hysterically funny to see such showmen perform, and to see the frothing fury that the fans who take their wrestling seriously, get into at the abuse of their favorite.

But football; that's straight, clean and Homeric. I've seen no less than heroism on the football field. I remember a halfback who used to play in the small West Texas college where I took a business course. He was a giant blond with an Irish name. He was forbidden to play the game because of a weak heart, but he faked a physical examination and got on the team. I never saw a man who played with such utterly reckless fury. Almost every game he knocked himself senseless. I remember once when he entered a game with three broken ribs and his heart nearly twice its normal size. He tore in with such berserk fury even his team-mates were appalled. Three times I saw him take the ball, hurl himself headlong at the opposing line, carrying the whole forward wall with him, and lie senseless where he went down. He knew that each charge might be his last, and he might be carried lifeless from the field. Foolish, perhaps; yet no more foolish than the soldier who plunges headlong upon the bayonets of his enemies. They're all games, only in some the penalties are greater. But I'll wander on indefinitely at this rate.

I mentioned to you before the tendency of the people of Texas to live at home. This of course has been a necessary move, but its a good one, I believe. I never saw so little money and so much food in the country in my life. Most of the barns and granaries are filled with grain, and the cattle are fat. Of course, the catch in that is so much land, crops and livestock are mortgaged, and so many bank failures have caused the collection of notes and debts and the like. Still, some of the farmers are developing a shrewdness in law and an ability to prevent themselves being stripped of everything. And the canning machines have been working overtime. Not only in the country, but in towns.

We are not farmers. We live in a small town and have only a very small piece of land, but we have enough to keep a little stock and raise a garden. Right now we have far more than we need of greens, radishes, turnips, and the like. We have been taking cattle, hogs and canned stuffs on debts, as well as grain and feed. We have a good supply of hay, oats, cotton-seed, maize, and corn, and we have meal and flour ground from corn and wheat we got the same way. We have milk from our own cow, and plenty of meat. We had a whole calf canned—its surprizing how much meat a good fat calf makes—cans of steak, roast-beef, soup, hash, chili, liver, heart, tongue—everything but the hoofs. And you ought to see the pork we have—huge sides of bacon, yard-long sacks of sausage, hams so gigantic they have to be cooked in the vat used for rendering lard. We dont have to pay out much money for food. And we've done quite a bit of trading in a small way—trading canned meat and lard and feed for work, and other things. I just mention all this to show the present trend, even in the towns.

I hope the times get better, but I hope people will continue to live at home as much as possible. Its the only way for independence. They're building a huge dam in Brown county, at a cost of several million dollars, where a couple of rivers join and run through a broad, steep-walled valley. It will be the biggest artificial lake in Texas, with a shore-line of 145 miles. A huge area will be irrigated. I want to get a few acres of land on the shores of that lake, and raise vegetables and a little stock. Its only nine miles from Brownwood, one of the best trade centers in Central West Texas, but I wouldnt be raising the stuff primarily for market purposes, but mainly for home use. When anyone has his own meat, eggs, butter, milk and vegetables and doesnt owe any money, he can tell anybody to go to hell. That country where the lake is to be hasnt been much account, because of the lack of rain. Its mostly rugged hill-country, rocky, barren or grown with drab post oak thickets. But irrigation will make the valleys bloom like a rose, or something.

Thanks for the view of Harvard. The buildings are certainly stately and possessed of a colonial grandeur. I envy you your so-journ in Boston and exploration of the museums. How I'd love to get among such relics of antiquity as you mention! Most of the antiquities I've had the opportunity to examine in Southwestern museums have been those of Indians and Aztecs, which dont have quite the kick, somehow, that Asiatic and African relics have. Please extend to Mr. Cook my greetings and best wishes, and my appreciation for his kind comment on my story. I hope both you and he like my latest pipe-dream.

And so, with best wishes, I am,

Cordially,

R. E. H.

P.S. I almost forgot to tell you that I finally made Clayton's Strange Tales with a yarn called, "The People of the Dark" a tale of reincarnation, pre-Roman Britain, Mongoloid aborigines, yellow-haired Britons, Irish pirates, and anything else I could lug in; I hope you've also made this market, and certainly, no weird magazine is complete without your magnificent tales.

Notes

1. The first story in the series was "Kings of the Night."

[46]

Providence, R.I.

January 16, 1932

Dear Mr. Howard:—

I'm glad my discourse on High and Low German proved more informative than tedious—for the subject is certainly complex enough! I don't know much about the early development of Teutonic proper names, hence couldn't say what the earliest form of "Robert" is. Undoubtedly it goes back to the earliest times, since it is shared by all branches of the Germanic race in one form or another—Rupert and Rupprecht being variants of the same name. I would be inclined to think that the Scandinavian form was the most primitive, since Eastern Teutonic speech is usually held as more basic than the Western.

The Pennsylvania Germans are certainly an odd lot—their backwater culture in the Lehigh Valley (dating from 1700 or thereabouts) retaining many unique and primitive features to an astonishing degree. They are tremendously tenacious of their dialect and traditions, so that the former is still generally spoken despite two or three generations of English public schooling. Their odd customs and witchcraft superstitions are a subject of wide anthropological study and wonderment, and I want to explore their region some day. I have two correspondents in Allentown, Pa. who shed a great deal of light on the local folkways[1]—and what they tell is certainly remarkable. Generations of magical belief have made the natives as acutely suggestible as Polynesians, West Indians, or Africans in matters of necromantic ritual, so that the "hexes" are able to produce startling phenomena of a probably hypnotic nature. They profess to inflict injuries by the stabbing of waxen effigies in the traditional way, and doubtless cause many an illness through fright. Farmers paint strange symbols on their barns to keep their malign influences away from the horses and cattle. Temperamentally the Pennsylvania Germans are inclined toward secretiveness and taciturnity, and both of my correspondents (though belonging to the stock themselves—in one case wholly and in the other partly) profess to see something almost sinister in the rural bulk of the population. They come largely from the Pfalz district along the Rhine—the dialect of which, a variant of High German, remains dominant—but accessions from Switzerland and Moravia have been absorbed. There has been no foreign admixture since their arrival in Pennsylvania, and any non-Nordic characteristics must be attributed to *Indian* blood, of which considerable seems to have filtered into part of the population—especially toward the north. One of my correspondents speaks of having an Indian great-great-grandmother. Just why the Pennsylvania "Dutch" differ so much from other Germans is still a problem. For one thing, they probably represent a more uniformly peasant origin than other German immigrant elements—urban middle and even upper classes being included in the N.Y., Ohio, and Wisconsin German influx. The peasants of Germany are noted for superstition and conservatism, and were dangerously involved in the witch-cult movement of the 15th century—so that a sort of medieval Ku Klux Klan called the "Holy Vehm" had to be organised to check the spread of diabolism amongst them. Then again, I fancy their main locale in Pennsylvania made for isolation and seclusion from broadening contacts. Those who settled on the edge of the

English districts never developed any eccentricities, but became quickly Anglicised. Indeed, some of the best Pennsylvania families—Sauer, Wister, Harbough, Eberlein, etc.—trace a connexion with the stock. I am very fond of visiting Germantown, on the outskirts of Philadelphia, which was settled by Germans and still contains a vast amount of their solid stone architecture of the 18th century. It was here that the first Bible was printed in North America (in German) by Christopher Sauer about 1750. But the back country—including the cities of Lancaster, Pottstown, and Allentown—is said to shew surprisingly little assimilation, and to harbour all sorts of strange customs and survivals. Even the English spoken by the younger urban generations is very queer, and the subject of many jokes in English Pennsylvania. For example, one hears a story of the householder whose doorbell was out of order and who marked it with a note reading "Bump—bell don't make." According to another version the note read "Bump—button don't bell." It is from the Pennsylvania Germans that the slang word "dunk" (meaning to dip a doughnut or other baked article in coffee or some other fluid at a meal) arose—it having been common in the Lehigh valley long before it gained general popularity. Streams of Pennsylvania German stock have branched out into Delaware, Maryland, southern Ohio, and the Shenandoah Valley of Virginia, and have played considerable part in history. President Hoover represents a strain which went still farther afield. The dialect has not, however, moved with them permanently—except in Virginia, where a very decadent form of it is now dying out. The architecture of the Pennsylvania Germans is very solid, distinctive, and quaint—I have seen such specimens as are near Philadelphia, including some specimen interiors in the art museum. They built almost wholly with stone, and often left exteriors in rather a rough state, with the ends of beams visible in the masonry. They had horizontally divided doors like the real Dutch in Nieuw Nederland, and their public structures had steep roofs with tiny dormers and tapering-steepled belfries. In southern Penna. their structures were modified by a Welsh influence—manifested by heavy cornices and cornices carried around the gable ends.

As to why Continental immigrants of Nordic stock seem more unbalanced and excitable than British settlers—I fancy the reasons are two in number. First, the historic experience of the British races has bred a characteristic national attitude of pride, confidence, and self-sufficiency which is independent of biological stock. The Briton of today represents a definitely conquering stock like the Roman of yesterday, and this fact reaches the consciousness of all classes and gives them a certain unmistakable pattern of feelings. Just as every Roman felt strengthened and buoyed up from his ability to say "civis Romanus sum",[2] so does the holder of Anglo-Saxon traditions feel personally stimulated by the knowledge that he represents the dominant language and folkways. This sense of pride and power is very efficacious in keeping down the mercurial emotional fluctuations which seem to be universal in mankind except where special influences (as with Spartans, Romans, Indians, British, etc.) impose other patterns. But secondly—the continental immigrants represent a more uniformly peasant stock than do the British. The bulk of the old-Americans were restless rovers, hardy yeomen, or bold gentlemen-adventurers—the most self-sufficient, combative, and confident elements that Europe could furnish, and comparatively untouched by the submissive fatalism and timid excitability of the peasant who always feels at the mercy of others. Some of the lower peasantry in Great Britain would probably exhibit the poorly-balanced qualities found here only in continental immigrants.

As for the original Nordic instinct—I think that a fierce pride and combativeness, underlaid by a strong fatalistic melancholy, is the general racial norm. The German and Scandinavian is closer to type that we are, since we have been bolstered up by the experience of representing an imperial and conquering civilisation. It is in the earliest folk tales and religious myths that we must look for primal racial feelings, and here we find the substratum of pessimism and melancholy very marked. In our religion the conception of Ragnarok—the fall of the gods—bulks very large, while many folkways attest the dominant conception that life is really worth very little. In the devastating drinking traditions of the Teuton we see the continual quest for oblivion as the supreme end. But of course we carried our pessimism differently from the way the Slav carries his. He allows his sense of futility to paralyse coördinated action, whereas with us the same conviction produced a wish to seize immediate things, coupled with an easy recklessness regarding death.

To sum up—the old American is buoyant and belligerent because he represents a dominant civilisation and a proud and free stratum of society; while the continental immigrant is melancholy and timid because he represents a less distinctive civilisation and an oppressed, timid stratum of society. Add to this one more thing—the Briton in America has the easy sense of placement and confidence which results from being on his own soil, where his own speech and traditions are dominant; whereas the continental, speaking another language and often harbouring a somewhat different set of traditions, feels all the bewilderment of a stranger who is at a disadvantage.

Colour in the West-Indies is certainly an odd thing from the U.S. standpoint. In many of the islands the lower-grade blacks are very respectful, but in certain of the British possessions—especially Barbadoes and Jamaica—there is an insufferably insolent type of urban nigger who goes about with a chip on his shoulder and the phrase "Ah's a British subjeck!" in his mouth. New York gets quite a number of these cocky Aethiops, and they are a very long time in learning their place. They generally become hall-boys and elevator-boys in apartment houses. I had heard of the carefully cultivated negresses of New Orleans, but hardly realised that their training was so well-defined and traditional. Are there not a considerable number of French-speaking mixed families in Louisiana at present, with some vestigial remnants of cultivation? One reads of them occasionally in fiction.

Wandrei is a great kid—and I have just had the pleasure of reading his long novel—"Dead Titans Awaken"—in manuscript.[3] This book mounts to great cosmic heights in its second half—certain horrors centreing in Easter Island. I doubt if he can land it with a publisher in these depressed times, but hope that Wright or somebody will accept it as a serial. Incidentally—have you heard of the new magazine of weird fiction to be issued by *Carl Swanson, Washburn, N. D.*? I don't believe the remuneration will be very high, but it might prove a good market for things rejected elsewhere. I've sent in two old stories of mine—though they may not be taken.[4] Congratulations, by the way, on your entrance to the Clayton market! I haven't tried this any more, for I feel convinced that Clayton (if not Bates) is temperamentally opposed to material of the mood and style I produce. Possibly I may try again later if I can get time to produce a greater variety of material. And this reminds me to remark how much I enjoyed "The Thing on the Roof". That carried the sort of kick I enjoy! Before long I mean to quote Justin Geoffrey and von Juntz's "Black Book" in some story of my own.[5]

As for national prospects—I don't pretend to be an informed or intelligent analyst, but I suppose that sooner or later some clash with Japan over Pacific rivalries is bound to occur. And yet I doubt whether the present Manchurian affair will precipitate any such thing. America would have a hard time getting any amount of public support for a war waged over a remote issue of interest only to a few investors, and any attempt to apply coercion might start a long-smouldering social rebellion. Just now the whole western world (except for France and Italy) is so flagrantly unprepared for fighting that I fear Japan can get away with almost anything. And in any case, as you point out, there is very little chance for stimulating combat in the traditional sense. Today a war means large-scale slaughter and destruction at long range, with the victory assured to the nation with the most money or natural resources and the most advanced technology. Japan's first major conflict, I think, will be with Russia—and it would really be hard to take sides in a war where both parties are potentially hostile either to our race or to our social order. I'd hate to see a strengthened Russia as badly as I'd hate to see a strengthened Japan—and wish the two could fight each other into a state of mutual feebleness!

Your instinctive sense of placement with the Picts is certainly a most puzzling and unusual phenomenon, though I dare say a psychoanalyst could unearth at least a few significant clues from your fund of early impressions. For one thing—I believe we all have a certain half-latent yearning toward that which is *most unlike* ourselves; a wistful exoticism based on man's natural revolt against the accustomed and the commonplace. Just as we fly to fantastic fiction to escape a sense of the limitations of life, so do we often like to merge our imaginations with some stream of life other than that which monotonously engulfs us. Of course, we don't look too far afield, since beyond certain limits alien races and cultures have too few points in common with ours to give us any sense of real life. But we do like to think ourselves now and then into some exotic milieu which is as far away as possible without forfeiting some illusion of similarity. Thus many boys lead a dream-life as Indians—the idealised and sympathetic sort popularized by Cooper;[6] who represent an opposite racial type, yet who also represent the familiar American landscape and the familiar noble sentiments put into them by novelists. I've known many boys (who never saw a redskin except in the circus) who try their best to merge themselves into the stream of Indian traditions. Then again—how many young dream-Arabs have the Arabian Nights bred! I ought to know, since at the age of 5 I was one of them! I had not then encountered Graeco-Roman myth, but found in Lang's Arabian Nights a gateway to glittering vistas of wonder and freedom. It was then that I invented for myself the name of Abdul Alhazred, and made my mother take me to all the Oriental curio shops and fit me up an Arabian corner in my room. Had I not stumbled upon Graeco-Roman myths immediately afterward, my sense of dream-placement might easily have been with the Caliphate of Bagdad. As it is, I still retain just enough of half-placement to feel a certain homelikeness in Saracenic art and ways, whereas other Oriental ways seem wholly alien. In the Crusades, I find myself often siding with the Saracens instead of with my own blood ancestors—for were not the Saracens the kin of my old friends Haroun al Raschid, Ali Baba, Nouredin, and so on? Still—I concede that this semi-Arabism of mine is not as remarkable as your Pictism. But the basic principle is probably not dissimilar. In the Picts you found a rallying-point for an imagination eager to escape the usual, yet demanding a certain residue of the familiar. They represented a blood and history wholly different from yours, yet also represented a scene of action and general tribal organisation more or less congenial to you through your general love of Celtic antiquity. It is something like the young Eastern boy's cultivation of Indian loyalties and pseudo-memories. Your account of the name Bran Mak Morn is exceedingly interesting. I can't quite recall where I did get *Abdul Alhazred.* There is a dim recollection which associates it with a certain elder—the family lawyer,[7] as it happens, but I can't remember whether I asked him to make up an Arabic name for me, or whether I merely asked him to criticise a choice I had otherwise made. Your hero Brennus has always been one of my ogres; for as you know, we view Gallo-Roman affairs from opposite angles! My heroes are old M. Papirius, who struck the Gaul who touched his white beard; Pontius Caminius, who carried the Senate's massage to Veii; the Sacred Geese, who roused M. Manlius from sleep and saved the capitol; and M. FURIUS. CAMILLUS, who drove away the enemy when Brennus had thrown his sword into the ransom-weighing scales and uttered his famous aphorism "Vae victis!"[8] Yea—and

T. Manlius Torquatus, who took the golden chain from the Gallic giant he slew; and M. Valerius Corvinus, upon whose helmet a raven perched as he fought and conquered a titanic Gaul . . . Alala! S. P. Q. R.—but pardon the outbursts of an enemy!

Your remarks on games and sports interested me greatly, and I certainly agree that football is a highly strategic and intellectual as well as physically daring sort of contest. My interest in things of this kind might have been much greater had my health in youth been such as to permit my participation—for I share your disgust at mere spectatorship and vicarious fortitude. I suppose my primary coolness toward games lies in the fact that they are only symbolically connected with any larger end. Probably I lack the primal zest for struggle *per se*—for I always want a conflict to decide some historic issue. I take a delight in thinking of a Greek at Marathon hacking away at a Persian, for that represents the upholding of the Aryan West against the Asiatic East; but when the pair are transferred from the battlefield to a prize ring where nothing but a purse is decided, I find my interest in the combat rapidly waning. I can thrill when a splendidly marshalled Roman legion outmaneuvres the Macedonian phalanx of a Pyrrhus—for that means the assertion of ROMAN supremacy over a decaying Hellenistic world; but when the affair is moved to a stadium with the legion called Harvard and the phalanx called Yale, I can't keep up an abstract zest for the adroit tactics and intrepid alertness. That is a typical defect in my personality—doubtless arising from the fact that while I have always had an active imagination, I have never had any surplus (or even sufficiency till I was over thirty) of physical energy. In youth—between breakdowns—I had just about energy enough to keep on my feet and no more; hence all emotions based on an exuberance of physical energy could be known to me only objectively. Historic imagination lent a glory to battles waged for definite racial or national issues; but only a "sporting sense"—a sense of abstract competition*—could have lent a similar glory to athletic sports. And that sporting sense was left out of my emotional composition. With such a dual lack—of physical energy on the one hand and of competitive interest on the other—I probably came to regard sports as a sort of wasteful use of energies which could better be applied to real issues. I realised only objectively, and could not feel subjectively, that they actually had a symbolic function to fulfil and that they often furnished excellent training both physical and psychological for the real contests of history. But I think I always respected athletics more than sedentary games, for I recognised their place in history as attributes of all the great civilisations, especially the Greek. Sedentary games I have always regarded as squandered time and mental energy—and the more intellectual they are, the more I regret the cerebration wasted on them. In a world full of unanswered questions and significance

*or perhaps a very strong symbolic sense

aesthetic media, I have never understood what is meant by "spare time" or "time to kill". For my part, the great tragedy of existence is that I haven't a fraction of the time or brains necessary to answer the questions about the past, the universe, and the laws of nature which provoke my curiosity. If I have any time, I'm sure the one sensible use to put it to is in reading or reflection on some congenial theme, or in writing out some thought or image I may happen to have on my chest. And if I have any mental energy to use, I'm sure the sensible place to exercise it is in coping with the problems of science, philosophy, or history, which interest and baffle me. God knows I'm no such mental giant that I can solve all the riddles of human knowledge and thus have enough excess cerebration left over to throw away on the meaningless moves of chessmen or the irrelevant shufflings of bridge cards. I concede the intellectual nature of the games—but what is the use of intellect when it functions toward no correlated and satisfying end? This feeling doubtless illustrates my general lack of interest in any process, mental of physical, which is detached from the context or general pageantry of life and knowledge. I seem to care very little for individual things; acquiring interest only when they become parts of a dramatic and unfolding panorama. Possibly this is typical of those who are primarily imaginative rather than intellectual, emotional, or physical.

I certainly hope that the self-educated economics of Texas may become a permanent institution. A whole nation organised like that could escape most of the devastation of the financial cycle. That Brown County lake will undoubtedly be a marvellously helpful thing—though I hope it won't obliterate any well-loved or historic countryside. That's the great tragedy of all the great reservoir projects in the East—they wipe out and inundate lovely valleys and white-steepled villages where people have lived for 200 or 250 years. The breaking of ties and the sacrifice of a native scene are often pathetic in the extreme.

Weather here has been delectably warm, but colder conditions are now threatened.

Best wishes—Yrs most sincerely—H P L

Notes

1. Carl Ferdinand Strauch (1908–1989) and Harry Kern Brobst (b. 1909).

2. "I am a Roman citizen."

3. Revised as *The Web of Easter Island* (Sauk City, WI: Arkham House, 1948). The original version was titled *Dead Titans, Waken!*

4. "Beyond the Wall of Sleep" and "The Nameless City." Both were accepted, but the magazine, *Galaxy,* never appeared.

5. In "The Thing on the Doorstep," HPL wrote of the "Baudelairian poet Justin Geoffrey, who wrote *The People of the Monolith* and died screaming in a madhouse in

1926 after a visit to a sinister, ill-regarded village in Hungary" (*DH* 277). HPL referred to the "Black Book" in "The Dreams in the Witch House," "The Thing on the Doorstep," "The Shadow out of Time," "The Haunter of the Dark," and two stories he ghostwrote for Hazel Heald, "The Horror in the Museum" and "Out of the Aeons." To give the book an authentic-sounding German title for REH's *Nameless Cults,* HPL consulted with August Derleth, who came up with the name *Unaussprechlichen Kulten.* In correspondence, HPL jokingly provided the first name "Friedrich" for von Junzt, but it was never used in print by either HPL or REH.

6. James Fenimore Cooper (1789–1851), author of the novels of frontier adventure known as the Leatherstocking Tales.

7. Albert A. Baker (1862–1959), HPL's legal guardian during his minority.

8. "Woe to the conquered!" See Livy 5.48.

[47] [ANS][1]

[Postmarked Providence, R.I.,
26 January 1932]

Thanks for the final Thevenin article. Of course real anthropology—& geology too—shows all this speculation to be flimsily chimerical, but it's interesting for all that. It is just possible that a continent did exist in the Indian Ocean at a relatively late date; but comparison of fossil remains on all the shores of the Atlantic, & on islands like the Canaries, West Indies, &c., proves that although these regions were indeed once connected, that connexion was during an early geologic period when man could not possibly have existed. There are no recent forms of fauna & flora in common—only tertiary & pre-tertiary fossils.

Best wishes & renewed thanks—

H P L

Notes

1. Front: A Shady Walk, Roger Williams Park, Providence, R. I.

[48] [ANS][1]

[c. February 1932.]

This isn't to flaunt my homely countenance, but to serve as an illustration of the luxuriant plant-life in South Texas; note rubber-plant, cactus, hibiscus, and banana-tree all growing together.

Notes

1. The front of the card is a photo of REH standing under a banana tree, next to a white frame house.

[49] [TLS]

[2 March 1932]

Dear Mr. Lovecraft:

I'm finally getting around to replying to your letter of Jan. 16.

I was extremely interested in your comments on the Pennsylvania Dutch. I'd heard, of course, of their witch-craft ideas, hexes, etc., but had no idea their backwardness and peculiarity was so extensive. There seems great material for a weird tale there, and I hope some day you'll find it convenient to write such a story, as I know you could lend those primitive hill people as sinister a glamour as you have lent the witch-haunted settlers of New England in tales laid in that locality. I'd like to make some explorations in their country, myself.

No doubt you are right in attributing the excitability of the Continental immigrant to his lack of racial experience in freedom, and his peasant origin. Strangely enough, Latins, that is Italians and French, while apparently more excitable on the surface, seem, beneath their exterior, to be more practical-minded and better balanced than the average Swede or German. At least that's been my observation. I believe the Latin races are really the most cynical, practical and materialistically minded people in the world.

Concerning families of mixed blood in New Orleans, I understand that there are such families as you mention, speaking French and retaining vestiges of past culture.

I certainly hope Wandrei places his novel, which, judging from such of his work as I have had the pleasure of reading, I am sure is splendid. By the way, what luck did you have with Swanson's new magazine? I hope you placed the stories you sent him. I havent tried him with anything myself. In fact, I havent done much work of any kind for longer than I like to think of. I'm glad you liked "The Thing on the Roof" and appreciate your kind comments about it. I'll feel greatly complimented to have you allude to Justin Geoffrey and Von Junzt in your work.

I'm rather surprized to learn that there's no attempt at recruiting in the East. Here in the Southwest war is looked upon as practically inevitable. Of course many men out of work look on recruiting as a superior alternative to starving. But another thing that possibly makes Westerners and Southwesterners look on the Far East situation with keen interest, is the fact that the West would bear the brunt of a Japanese invasion. It doesnt seem very far out across the Pacific to the big guns of Nippon! Not with the modern type of ships and war-planes. Along the Border there is a definite undercurrent of expectation, or at least apprehension, of Mexican invasion in case of war. There has been a persistent rumor, every since the last war, of the mysterious presence of vaguely sinister activities of a hundred thousand Japanese in the interior of Mexico. It is well known that in several cases of bandittry, the Mexican outlaws were led by Japanese. Possibly these Orientals were mere renegades—possibly not. Of late there has been some bandit activity in the Rio Grande valley, just west of the thickly settled citrus-fruit district. Mexico has unofficially declared that she will stand by the United States in case of war. But the memory of Mexican treachery is still too fresh in the minds of Texans—the betrayals and massacres at Goliad, Mier, and elsewhere—for them to take much stock in such declarations. Doubtless the government would keep its pledges. But Americans along the border seem not inclined to trust their southern neighbors overmuch. During the last war there were the usual rumors of a Mexican invasion which never materialized. But this is somewhat different. There were not enough Germans in Mexico to bring such a movement about. We dont know how many Japanese there are there. I wonder if the recent movement on the part of the Mexicans to drive the Chinese out of Mexico was prompted by Japanese? I wouldnt want to say, lacking all accurate knowledge. Possibly it was only a natural part of the recent nationalist movement in Mexico, a movement in which I am heartily in accord. Mexico has been a grab-bag for foreign exploiters long enough. I'd be glad to see them take hold of their country and make something out of it—if they can, which is rather doubtful.

Concerning the Chinese—the average Mexican is no match for him in business competition. The Chinaman is more industrious, more progressive and more intelligent. I dont know whether they've run the Chinese out of Piedras Negras or not. When I was there a few years ago—its the town opposite Eagle Pass, Texas—it was largely dominated by Chinese. They owned small irrigated farms along the river, and ran most of the best cabarets and saloons in the town. In contrast to the Mexicans they were clean and prosperous—well, in contrast to almost anybody they were. There were first-class saloons and cafes where only Chinese or white men were allowed to enter—no Mexicans were admitted—and that in Old Mexico!

I'd prefer Chinese immigrants to Japs. From what I hear of the Japs, they're the original freeze-out artists. For instance, I've heard of their activities in the fruit-country of California. They would come in, I've heard, as laborers. They'd work for much less than white fruit-pickers and packers could afford to work for. After awhile, they'd have forced the white laborers out entirely, and the work of the groves and orchards would be in the hands of Japs altogether. Then they'd form unions and begin to raise the price of labor. Eventually the owners of the fruit would find themselves facing ruin because of these cut-throat methods. They'd be forced to sell out, and the Japs would buy, at less than the property was worth. Soon they'd be owning whole fruit valleys. Their eventual aim, was, I suppose, to control the whole fruit market. Well, they'll never get a foot-hold in the citrus-country of South Texas. Mid-Western Germans seem to have most of that.

But returning to the war; I had an experience while in San Antonio the other day which gave me a slight—oh, a very slight taste of what modern warfare would be like, and also served to show how uppermost the idea of war is in the minds of the people of the Southwest. It was a cloudy, rainy day, as so many days in Texas are, and have been for the past few years; walking along the street in the broad plaza in front of the municipal building, I suddenly was aware of a stinging, smarting sensation in my eyes, and noticed other people rubbing their eyes and shaking their heads. Men stopped each other and asked the meaning of the phenomenon. There was no smell, no sign other than the almost intolerable smarting in the eyes. I saw people involuntarily glancing up at the cloudy sky—I myself did this. The same thought had entered all minds, and one man put it in words—"By God," he shouted, "I believe the damned Japs are droppin' gas on the town!" But no plane showed among the clouds. There was a restless jerky feeling in the air—as if it wouldnt take much to start a blind panic or a senseless riot. The fire-companies were called out and the police began searching the source of the mysterious gas. As for myself, having ascertained that the low-hanging clouds were not masking an invading air-fleet, I concluded that a gas-bomb had been released somewhere near-by in some gang or racket activity; theaters have been bombed in San Antonio in the past, and as far as I know, other businesses as well. I entered the municipal building, interested myself in examining an exhibition of Chinese curiosities, and forgot all about the mystery. It was not until later that I learned the source of it. Three miles from the city, the soldiers of Fort Sam Houston had been experimenting with a smoke screen, laden with tear-gas. A shift of the wind had blown it down on the city. I was only in the fringe of it; in other parts it was experienced far more thoroughly—the smoke settled like a dark fog, and the gas almost blinded people, temporarily. There was almost a near-riot. It was significant to note that people's minds leaped instantly to the thought of an air-attack. That seems foolish perhaps—but firmly rooted in the average Texan's mind is the conviction that anything can come up out of Mexico—and in such a case, San Antonio would be one of the first objectives.

Well, if England will stand firm with America, I dont fear Japan. But I wish the Japs and Russians would cut each others' throats, if there must be a war. As you say, neither is a friend of ours'.

As to my feelings toward the mythical Picts, no doubt you are right in comparing it to the Eastern boy's Indian-complex, and your own feelings toward Arabic things. My interest in the Picts was always mixed with a bit of fantasy—that is, I never felt the realistic placement with them that I did with the Irish and Highland Scotch. Not that it was the less vivid; but when I came to write of them, it was still through alien eyes—thus in my first Bran Mak Morn story—which was rightfully rejected—I told the story through the person of a Gothic mercenary in the Roman army; in a long narrative rhyme which I never completed, and in which I first put Bran on paper, I told it through a Roman centurion on the Wall; in "The Lost Race" the central figure was a Briton; and in "Kings of the Night" it was a Gaelic prince. Only in my last Bran story, "The Worms of the Earth" which Mr. Wright accepted, did I look through Pictish eyes, and speak with a Pictish tongue!

In that story, by the way, I took up anew, Bran's eternal struggle with Rome. I can hardly think of him in any other connection. Sometimes I think Bran is merely the symbol of my own antagonism toward the empire, an antagonism not nearly so easy to understand as my favoritism for the Picts. Perhaps this is another explanation for the latter: I saw the name "Picts" first on maps, and always the name lay outside the far-flung bounds of the Roman empire. This fact aroused my intense interest—it was so significant of itself. The mere fact suggested terrific wars—savage attacks and ferocious resistance—valor and heroism and ferocity. I was an instinctive enemy of Rome; what more natural than that I should instinctively ally myself with her enemies, more especially as these enemies had successfully resisted all attempts at subjugation. When in my dreams—not day-dreams, but actual dreams—I fought the armored legions of Rome, and reeled back gashed and defeated, there sprang into my mind—like an invasion from another, unborn world of the future—the picture of a map, spanned by the wide empire of Rome, and ever beyond the frontier, outside the lines of subjugation, the cryptic legend, "Picts and Scots". And always the thought rose in my mind to lend me new strength—among the Picts I could find refuge, safe from my foes, where I could lick my wounds and renew my strength for the wars.

Dont think I'm fanatic in this matter of Rome. Its merely a figment of instinct, no more connected with my real every-day life than is my preference for the enemies of Rome. I can appreciate Roman deeds of valor and no one gets more thrill out of Horatius's stand on the Roman bridge, than I do. I am with the Romans as long as their faces are turned east. While they are conquering Egyptians, Syrians, Jews and Arabs, I am all for them. In their wars with the Parthians and Persians, I am definitely Roman in sympathy. But when they turn west, I am their enemy, and stand or fall with the Gauls, the Teutons and the Picts. Fantastic, isn't it?

I regard the Roman hero Camillus with the respect one must give a bold and resourceful foe. I favor Brennus, of course, but must admit he was not the Roman's equal in strategy and tactics. By the way, aside from instinctive feeling and tribal placements, I wonder how the world's history would have been written had the Gauls pushed on after their defeat of the Romans at Allia, and destroyed completely the budding Roman civilization?

And I sometimes wonder if the chaos of the Middle Ages was not the result of the barbarian tribes seeking to adapt themselves to an alien civilization instead of building up one of their own? I wonder if, had Rome been completely destroyed by the Goths, Franks and Vandals, all traces of Roman culture wiped out, if, after a longer time, the Germanic nations would have emerged from barbarism by their own efforts and with a culture more suited to their particular nature? However, this practically occurred in Britain, when the Saxons swept the land clean of Roman civilization, and progress seemed to have practically ceased in England prior to the Norman conquest. Though, there, as in Ireland, the growth of civilization had been halted by the invasions of the Danes. Doubtless I am wrong, but I somehow feel that the Roman culture—especially the latter-day type, mixed with the decay of Greece and the Orient—was not suited to the straight-forward western barbarians. At any rate, I'm enclosing a rhyme which I wrote when younger than I am now.[1] Its crude, no doubt, but I rather like it. There's no hurry about returning it, though I'd like to see it eventually.

That's one of a number of rhymes I hope some day to bring out under the title of "Echoes from an Iron Harp". But the devil knows when I'll get to do it. Most authorities consider the Cimbri were Germans, of course, and they probably were, but there's a possibility that they were Celtic, or of mixed Celtic and German blood, and it gratifies my fancy to portray them as Celts, anyway.

Well, the big guns are booming in Shanghai, and the Chinese are putting up an unexpected resistance. More power to them. I'd like to see them beat the hell out of Japan. Though, if they do, its remotely possible that it might be the beginning of the end of foreign domination in China. Remote, but possible. A victory over Japan would undoubtedly stir the Chinese, and might lead to a far more aggressive assertion of national rights. It seems hardly possible that China could win, lacking a strong central government, proper equipment, etc., and with her vast unwieldy armies controlled by separate—and mercenary—war-lords. But you cant tell. I hear on good authority that many German soldiers of fortune, from the old Prussian armies, are in the Chinese forces. I note that in Germany, by the way, the citizenship of Hitler has been questioned to the extent of forcing him to withdraw from the presidential race. I hope Von Hindenburg carries the election. During war days I would cheerfully have lighted a torch to burn him at the stake, but now I think he is one of the strongest stabilizing factors in Europe, and that his re-election would be to the advantage of not only Germany, but the entire world. He was doubtless the ablest general of any nationality in the Great War, and now seems to be about the most level-headed statesman on the Continent.

I expect the disarmament conference to come to nothing,[2] and am in favor of that result, if the alternative means shearing more claws from our already depleted national defense. The outlawry of war is proven to have been an empty thought. I believe that the next few generations will see a continual series of wars, and the best thing to do, is to be prepared. America has no friends in Europe, or in Asia, or in the world. It seems to me that conditions are somewhat similiar to those which produced the feudal age. The only nations which are likely to survive the dawning Age of Iron, are those which adopt a powerful military form of government. This style of government is not the kind to endure in such an age, because big business has its finger too much in the pie. It seems we must choose between a strong soviet government, and a strong dictatorship on the fascist style. Just as in the feudal days, men chose a strong baron or count to serve, for mutual protection. Personal liberty, it would seem, is to be a thing of the past. Individualistic independence must be sacrificed for national security. We must throw off the idealistic cloaks we have partially donned during the last generation or so, and recognize the naked bestiality of life. There is no question of right or wrong, but simply of necessity and survival. The strong will win, and might will rule, as it always has, and there need be no hypocricy about it. Right or wrong, for instance, has little to do with the present Japanese-Chinese-Manchurian affair, as I see it. It is necessary to the existence of the Japanese nation that they expand into Manchuria, and eventually into China. It is necessary to the existence of other nations—America, for instance—that they are not allowed to expand. I am in sympathy with China, because the more Japanese forces they shatter, the less Americans will have to face when the eventual war comes. I am all for the building up of the armies and the navy, for the equipment of the forces with the most modern type of arms, and, if it seems necessary, of compulsory military training. The naked facts are—we must grind or be ground.

I am no student of events, but I consider at least these wars inevitable: a Russo-Japanese war; an American-Japanese war; a Russo-American war; a French-Italian war; and possibly a war in which Russia will be pitted against the foremost European powers. The world is a seething volcano.

Glad you found the postcards of some interest. The extreme south of Texas is really very interesting, and full of strange contrasts. For instance, the Lower Rio Grande valley, that is, the well irrigated citrus belt from Brownsville to Mission, is thickly settled, with broad, well kept roads, lined with palm-trees so that the highways are like boulevards, dotted with prosperous, thriving towns set close together, and covered with beautiful luxuriant groves of golden fruit.

But west of Mission, the country changes with startling abruptness. It changes from an almost perfectly flat plain, to a rolling, brush-wood country, broken by low hills and dry arroyos. The brush is not tall but it is incredibly thick and dense. And everything seems to grow thorns—there is one plant, the name of which I forget, which grows nothing but thorns—neither leaf, bloom nor fruit. The mesquites are much thicker than they generally grow in West Texas, though perhaps not quite so tall. Prickly pears and cacti grow so thick you wouldnt believe me if I told you. Prickly pears, which in West Texas seldom grow four feet tall, stand in tree like clusters, sometimes as high as ten feet. It was in that country that chaps and hooded stirrups originated; without them a vaquero would be torn to pieces, rounding up cattle in the brush. It amuses me to see movie cow-boys, supposedly of Texas in the old days, portrayed with sheep-skin or woolly chaps. If one of these gentlemen would start chasing a saber-horned steer through the South Texas brush, he'd leave tufts of wool on every mesquite and huisache and prickly pear he passed.

But to return to the population. In the citrus belt proper the Mexican is being gradually thrust out. Many of them are returning to Mexico, many are going up the river into the broken ranch country. Starr County, which lies west of Hidalgo County, is Mexican to an astonishing extent. In Rio Grande City, the country seat, for instance, a town of 2283 inhabitants, there are scarcely a dozen white families. A man said to me, "There's too much law in the settled part of the valley; west of Mission the only law is the will of the Mexican czars." That's exaggerating of course, but the rich Mexican land owners in Starr County do wield enormous power. As a contrast, the Lower Valley is settled largely by people from the Midwest who seem so law-abiding that they ring themselves round with ordinances and rules that the people in my section of the country dont think about.

Wondering about the future of the valley, I venture a comment: the people now settling, mainly prosperous Midwesterners looking for climate and rich land, are pushing out the Mexicans. It takes a lot of work to run a grove. The owners arent going to do the work. If they push all the Mexicans out, they'll have to import laborers. Prices have always been low in that country, and it isnt likely that they'll ever raise them enough to attract white laborers from other sections of the country. As a result, a generation or so will probably see the groves being worked by Slavs or Italians—most likely Italians. These, being a thrifty and industrious race, will soon be owning groves themselves. If valley industry follows the trend of American industry as a whole, the big corporations will soon begin to freeze the independent fruit-growers out of business. Raising taxes and holding down the price of the fruit will do the job. I seem to see, in the future—perhaps twenty, thirty, forty years—the Lower Valley groves owned almost exclusively by big corporations, and settled and worked by Italians. All this is not for publication. Its none of my business—I dont own a foot of land in the world, or a blade of grain, or the bark on a mesquite tree. But I've seen the big cattle corporations crush out the small ranchmen, and the big oil companies freeze out the independent oil men. Its the trend of the times.

But to get back to the Valley. Its more historical than most people realize. There, for instance, were the famous ports of Clarksville and Bagdad, at the mouth of the Rio Grande; Bagdad, founded by the Spaniards about 1780, reached the pinnacle of her lurid glory during the Civil War, when the trade of the world flowed through her fingers—cotton, armaments, slaves. It was on the Mexican side of the river, Clarksville on the American. There were more than fifteen thousand people in Bagdad when the thirsty gulf rose and drank her, and her sister city, in a single night. When the dawn rose calm and clear over the waves, it was as if the sites of those river towns had been swept with a titanic broom. So a Catholic priest had prophesied, for men said it was the wickedest city in the world, with its criminals, cut-throats, pirates, smugglers, renegades and the scum of the Seven Seas. That was in 1867.

Steamboats used to go up the river as far as Rio Grande City, but not any more. Too much water is used in irrigation. Of course, there's no particular reason for steamboats to ply the Rio Grande now.

I talked to an interesting person while in San Antonio—a high caste Indian, who, though born in Calcutta, had spent most of his life in China. His wife was half Hongkong Chinese and half Calcutta Indian herself, and I wish you could have heard her play on a contraption she called a yangchin, or something that sounded like it.[3] You've probably seen them, though I'd never even heard of such a thing. It had strings and she played it by tapping the strings with a limber strip of bamboo in each hand. The man interested me much. I'd never seen a high caste Indian before, and I may have embarrassed him by my close scrutiny of his head and features—for skull-formations interest me intensely. He was—as I suppose all high caste Hindus are—decidedly dolichocephalic, with a high narrow forehead and regular features. But for his color, which was very dark, he might have been an aristocratic American. He was a man of evident culture and intelligence, and I was interested in his views regarding the Jap-Chinese situation.

He maintained that no nation would ever conquer China, which he said was far too large. He said that the last census was taken in China over thirty years ago, and that the actual population far exceeded the generally accepted figure. He said that there were at least eight hundred millions natives in China, and the population was growing rapidly and steadily. Their very number may constitute a threat to white races in the future—my thought, not his. He disagreed with Ghandi's idea that a revolution could be achieved by peaceful means, but was quite evidently in full accord with the idea of self-rule in India, as elsewhere in the Orient. He was, I should say, a sort of Oriental nationalist; he spoke of "we" "us" and "our", regardless of what Eastern race happened to be his subject—identifying himself with the Indians, Chinese, Japanese, irregardless. His sympathies seemed to be with the Chinese in their present war, however.

He was a delver in religions and cults, and said that he was a firm believer in the theory that Christ spent several years in India—a theory which he had for years been seeking to prove by searching old books and manuscripts.

As I listened to him, I was fascinated less by what he said, than by what he represented—the long pageantry of wars and conquests of which he and his kind are the eventual result. I was thinking that in spite of his dark skin, the dominant line of his ancestors sprang from the same stock as mine, in the dim dawn years of lost eons. But his wandered south, down through the snowy passes of the Himalayas, and mine—and your's—went westward, over the river-slashed steppes and the rolling hills, until they came upon the sea-plains and heard the roar of the North Sea. I was thinking how those south-farers wandered, and what wars they waged, and what mud-walled villages they sacked and burnt; what nameless rivers they crossed, and what tribes fled before them. Until they came to a land that was pleasant to them, and a dark-skinned, primitive people who bowed prostrate before them; and they dwelt there as lords, with their loves and their wars, their hunting songs and their drinking horns, until the centuries wrought curious changes in their blue eyes and yellow beards, and their slaves became at last their conquerors by virtue of their primal blood, so that when the sons of their ancestors, who had wandered into the west, came across the sea, these did not recognize their kin.

But I've rambled around long enough. I'm sure the poetry lecture by Benet was very interesting. If I'd stayed another day in San Antonio, I'd have gotten to hear a lecture on the ruins of Zimbabwe by Miss Theckla Hall, whose father's ranch (two and a half million acres, I heard, but I'll swear that sounds like a hell of a ranch) was adjacent to the mysterious locality, and contained quite a few of the ruins. I'd have enjoyed the lecture, I'm sure, for its a fascinating subject. Best wishes. And bohut salaam. (That's some kind of a Hindu salutation, though I'm a bit hazy about it.)

Very cordially,
R E H.

Notes

1. "An Echo from the Iron Harp" (also known as "The Gold and the Grey").
2. The League of Nations sponsored a Disarmament Conference in Geneva, beginning in February 1932, chiefly to resolve military tensions between France, Italy, and Germany, specifically in regard to the size of the German army. Although a pact allowing Germany greater leeway for expanding its army was signed on 7 June 1933, the agreement was undermined by Hitler's secret plans for a massive rearmament.
3. Yang-ch'in: a Chinese dulcimer in which tone is produced by striking the strings with bamboo beaters covered with rubber or leather. The vibration of the strings is transmitted to a trapezoidal wooden soundboard by bridges, over which the strings are stretched.

[50] [nonextant letter by H. P. Lovecraft]

[c. March 1932]

[51] [TLS]

[c. April 1932]

Dear Mr. Lovecraft:

At last I've gotten around to answering your most welcome letter. Thanks very much for the kind comments you made on the Cimbric rhyme; I appreciate them highly, and am encouraged towards further efforts.

I hope you can before long explore the Pennsylvania Dutch regions, where I'm sure you'll find splendid material for stories. I'm sure the young man you mentioned—Brobst—must be quite interesting, with his first-hand knowledge of the ways and customs of the people. I am very gratified to hear that he has read and liked my yarns.

I have read and re-read your comparison of southern and northern Aryans, which is the most vivid and powerful thing of the sort I ever read, and goes deeper in the matter—to the very roots of cause and effect, and race consciousness and memory. I have vaguely felt much of what you describe with such power and clarity. Here arises a question of reality—which is real, the firmly founded security of the Latin's defined and measured universe, or the chaotic, unstable, wind-torn cosmos of the Nordic? I feel that in his aborted gropings, in his pessimisms and distrusts of security, the Nordic strikes nearer at reality than his more practical brother. What is this universe, but clouds that break up under our feet, as we stand precariously poised upon them, hurling us into the abyss of howling chaos?

I was especially interested in your remarks concerning the effect of northern skies on our barbarian ancestors. I have mentioned to you the predominance of cold grey overcast skies in many of my dreams. I hate cloudy weather, and no one appreciates the clear bright skies of the south more than I, and yet, the sight of a cold northern sky, piled high with grey winter clouds, stirs indescribable feelings in the very pits of my soul, and there is a sensation of vague familiarity, rooted deep. The cloud effects in this part of the southwest are remarkable; a cousin of mine, who has travelled widely in the western part of the continent, from the Great Lakes to the west coast, says that nowhere has he seen such sunsets, and cloud formations as in this locality. On this high devide the clouds blow up from the gulf, and they roll down from the high backbone of the continent, across the endless plains, meeting and mingling. Of all the sunsets, I believe the most impressive are those in which the whole sky seems flecked with gold, great rifts of flaming gold that sweep from horizon to horizon, with spaces of gleaming blue between. Strange that such magnificent wealth should stretch over so dreary a country of sand-drifts and post-oak hills. But when the blizzards sweep down the rolling grey clouds from the high plateaus, misty, gigantic and fantastic, fold on misty fold, rolled and tattered like grey flowing banners, it is then that all the latent instincts of my race stir in me, and I am filled with a vague desire for snow-clad mountains, shimmering expanses of cold blue water, and frosty shores lapped by icy waves.

Swanson's venture seems rather amateurish, but he may make something of it. I let him have a yarn, "The Hoofed Thing" which Bates had previously rejected.[1] I am very glad to hear of your new stories, and hope that they will find the market they deserve. Your latest story in Weird Tales is as grim and gripping a tale as I ever read.[2] The lending of common-place, every-day things and events a macabre and soul-freezing significance is the most difficult of all literary feats, it seems to me, and you are the more to be congratulated because you succeed in this so splendidly.

I feel honored that you should refer to Von Junzt's accursed document, and thanks for the German of "Nameless Cults", which I'll use in referring to it. Though I've lived adjacent to Germans for many years, I know nothing of the language—and neither do a lot of them. The Book of Eibon is properly noted.[3] Smith has come along in his prose fiction at an astonishing rate. In fact, I consider him second only to yourself in the weaving of fantastic tales. He has a classic back-ground so many of the younger writers lack—myself, for instance. I dont wonder that you recieve letters inquiring about the Necronomicon. You invest it with so much realism, that it fooled me among others. Until you enlightened me, I thought perhaps there was some such book or manuscript sufficiently fantastic to form the basis of fictionized allusions. Say, why dont you write it yourself? If some exclusive house would publish it in an expensive edition, and give it the proper advertising, I'll bet you'd realize some money from it.

I've been working on a new character, providing him with a new epoch—the Hyborian Age,[4] which men have forgotten, but which remains in classical names, and distorted myths. Wright rejected most of the series, but I did sell him one—"The Phoenix on the Sword" which deals with the adventures of King Conan the Cimmerian, in the kingdom of Aquilonia. I also placed another yarn with Strange Tales—"The Valley of the Lost"—a horror tale in an early Texan setting.[5] I'm trying to invest my native regions with spectral atmosphere, etched against a realistic setting; "The Horror from the Mound" in the current Weird Tales was a feeble effort of the sort. And now I'm working on a mythical period of prehistory when what is now the state of Texas was a great plateau, stretching from the Rocky Mountains to the sea—before the country south of the Cap-rock broke down to form the sloping steppes which now constitute the region.[6]

I read with interest your comments on the Eastern question, and agree with you that Japan should be kept out of China, at least. With millions of Chinese trained into the Nipponese military machine, there'd be hell to pay.

Just now my interest in the Far East is centered on that trial in Honolulu, which makes me ashamed of my own race.[7] How a white man can stand up in court and prosecute a white woman, before the scum of the Orient, with

Orientals on the jury, is more than I can understand. I consider it a blot on the country's flag and honor that the case was ever brought to court; at least she should have been honorably acquitted without delay. Why, good God, what's the Caucasian race coming to? Is a white individual not allowed to protect or avenge the members of his or her family? What ever they do to the defendants, any way, they cant resurrect that damned yellow-belly they killed. He got it easy; good thing for him it wasnt Texas. Men have been burned alive at the stake here for less than he did.

I fully agree with you concerning the chimera of disarmament, also as to limiting international commerce. Let the nation be as self-supporting as possible. I consider the only eventual salvation of America will be a close Anglo-American alliance, which I hope to see some day. God knows, we'd have more personal liberty today if we had never broken away from the empire, and doubtless be better off in every way. If those ancestors of mine who helped mow down the red-coats at King's Mountain, could have looked forward a few centuries, I wonder if they'd have been as whole-hearted in the slaughter—possibly so, since they were Scotch-Irish refugees from the isles, and bitter. But maybe the Revolution was a mistake, anyway. If there'd been an Englishman on the throne, instead of a damned Hanover—oh, well, what the hell. I'm like you, in preferring a Fascist rule to a Commune—as the lesser of evils. Judas, Sovietism would be like being suddenly bounced onto another planet.

The afore-mentioned Hindu was, as I said, very interesting. I recognized his distant kinship to our own tribe, but in so many ways his thoughts and ideals were so alien—it was really strange. If he'd been round-headed and slat-eyed, it would have seemed natural. But somehow, even with his very dark skin, it seemed queer to encounter so many non-Aryan traits in him, when his features were so like those to which we are accustomed. For instance, he spoke of the ghastly tortures of the Orient with evident approval, as the only curb for lawlessness. And he mentioned seeing scores of Chinese Communists beheaded on the open streets, with a pleasant smile, and a manner too casual to have been feigned. The mere thought of such a spectacle slightly nauseated me. On the other hand, had we engaged in a political argument, and I had forgotten myself to the extent of knocking him bow-legged with a clout in the mush, I have no doubt that he would have considered this perfectly natural act as the nadir of abysmal barbarism. They have drifted far from the Aryan stem.

I read with much interest and appreciation your speculations on the possible trend of history, in the event of the destruction of Rome by the Gauls; they seem to have considered all possible angles. Continuing with these theoretical wanderings: suppose that Martel had not stopped the Arabs at Tours? Or that Tamerlane or Genghis Khan had conquered Europe? Or, speculating from the other way, suppose that Alexander the Great had conquered India, and pressing on, subjugated the Cathayan empire? Would the East have been Aryanized, or the Western races sunk that much quicker in a mire of Orientalism? And suppose the Black Prince had carried out his dream of Oriental conquest? He was probably the only Western general of medieval times capable of holding his own with the great Eastern conquerors. In fact, I am convinced, that, with his English archers, he would have proven more than a match for Tamerlane, Genghis Khan, Baibars, Subotai, Saladin, or any of the rest. The main reason that the Crusaders and other western armies were so repeatedly defeated and overthrown by the Moslems and Mongols was partly because of the extreme mobility of the Oriental armies, partly because of the incredible inefficiency of the western kings and generals. By the way, Wright thought well enough of my yarn, "The Sowers of the Thunder" published in the current Oriental Stories, to advertise it in "Asia". It deals with Baibars the Panther, and the overthrow of the last Christian army in Outremer: a magnificently dramatic historical episode which I fear I have failed by a long way to do justice. I'll swear, I've written of Christian armies being defeated by Moslems until my blood fairly seethes with rage. Some day I must write of the success of the earlier Crusades to gratify my racial vanity.

History fair drips with blood. Its a marvel to me how the race has survived all the wars, pestilences, famines and massacres which have been so generously bestowed upon it since the beginning of time. Yet its always seemed much of a miracle to me that the average child lived to be grown. Youngsters of this generation seem not quite so hazardous except in the way of mechanical speed, bad liquor and venereal diseases. But when I was a kid growing up in the country, it seemed their natural instinct to risk their necks on every occasion. And when the hazards of this younger generations—speeds, machines, poison liquor, vamps, etc.,—are balanced against the hazards of outlaw horses, wild steers, rivers in flood, rattlesnakes, accidental discharges of fire-arms, rotten tree-limbs, and the savage gouging, tearing, knifing fights that were an every-day occurrence with the youths of the last generation, the balance, if anything, is on the side of the latter. When I was a kid it was a common thing for youngster to be killed or maimed by falls from horses, or the half-grown steers they rode for sport, to be hurled to their deaths by the breaking of pecan-tree limbs—the most treacherous of all woods—to be accidentally shot while hunting, drowned, or to meet crippling or death in various other forms. One of my first playmates, when I was about three years old, and he was the same age, came to a violent end from one of the above mentioned causes—got into the corrals in his play and a killer mule stamped his brains out.

Why, I always led about the most quiet hum-drum life imaginable, and took as few risks as can be imagined, yet when I recall some of the narrow scrapes I had, I can scarcely understand how I escaped death or being maimed permanently. Among those I vividly recall at present, is that of having a horse fall down a steep bluff with me; having a horse throw me and then crash down on me with her hoofs, barely missing my head, and literally crushing the flesh on my arm; getting my hand split open in an impromptu brawl while knocking the knife out my antagonist's hand, the gash missing a large vein by a hand's breadth; having the point of my own hunting knife driven deep into the inside of my knee, close to the great artery that runs there; having a horse turn a complete somersault with me, landing fairly on her back, so that all four hoofs waved for an instant in the air—gad, that was close! It was just chance, that threw me headlong out of the saddle as the mustang fell, that kept me from being crushed to a pulp, as I've known others to have been crushed. And leaping through a solid glass window at about three o'clock of a morning was not a hazard to be passed lightly, considering that I crashed through pane and screen, and fell some five or six feet to the hard ground, side-ways—when I took inventory my underwear was soaked with blood from head to foot, but, except for gashes on my arm and a triangular wound that laid bare my shoulder bone, and bruises on my ankle, knee, hip, shoulder and arm, from the fall, I was unhurt. These trivial matters stand out in my mind, because my life was so placid and devoid of adventurous risks, and yet I knew plenty of youngsters to whom such affairs—minus, perhaps, the window-leaping episode—were every day occurrences, too common for notice or recollection—they broke wild horses and swam rivers in flood, neither of which I ever attempted; they took all kinds of risks at climbing; they were reckless with weapons, with which I was always extremely careful; some of them broke their necks, got drowned, shot or crippled, but the great majority grew to maturity unscathed. Add to those risks as well, the vicious environs of a wildcat oil boom. Yet they thrived and grew fat. Verily, though the individual human is easy to slay or maim, the race as a whole is as tenacious of life as a barrel-full of cats. Man has not yet exterminated rabbits; neither has Nature exterminated men.

Chance again is a titanic factor. It is a well established fact that a comparatively light blow on the head may often result in a fatality. Men have been killed by a stroke from a bare fist. Yet, again, the human skull may stand up under incredible battering. I remember seeing an oil field worker shortly after he'd been hit over the head half a dozen times with a Stillson wrench. You'd think a crack from a ponderous implement like that would have caved his skull in; his scalp was laid open in half a dozen places, he was bloody as a stuck hog, yet he was able to walk, supported by his friends. Nor was his skull even slightly fractured! And I saw Red—well, a noted oil-field bully, brought from Ranger to "clean up" Cross Plains, a short time after he'd begun his campaign; he was lying senseless on the floor of the jail, whither he'd been dumped, bloody as a butchered steer, with his scalp laid open in eight places. He looked like he was through; it looked as though even the redoubtable Red had reached the end of his lurid trail; while he was strangling the city marshall, the marshall's deputy had repeatedly smashed his gun-barrel over Red's head—had in fact beaten him into insensibility, so complete they had to drag him to the jail by main strength; he was out cold. He remained out, while the woman who ran the place which the officers had been raiding when Red attacked them, stood outside the jail, and harangued the crowd which stood about, trying to stir up a mob to rescue Red and avenge her insult—gad, I was in my early teens, and I remember that scene vividly—the throng milling about the tiny, one-roomed jail, glaring avidly at the blood-stained, senseless body of the bad man—the tall, slender, well dressed woman, with her hard, intelligent features over-cast with anger, standing flanked by several of her hard-faced girls, the motley crowd, huge drillers and roustabouts in their grimy, oil-stained working clothes, hatchet-faced gamblers, hard-eyed, quick-fingered thugs—honest laborers and the scum and scrapings of the oil fields—gradually they drifted away, and left her still holding forth wrathfully. But what I started to say was, that Red not only lived after that terrible beating, but was as good as new, as soon as his scalp was sewed up. Though he took a hurried departure, and made no more attempt at cleaning the town.

For the past few weeks there has been one sandstorm after another. It looks like the beginning of a big drouth. If the people in this country dont raise a good grain crop this year, and there's no winter grazing, suffering among men and animals will be intense next winter. The only thing that's kept the people from starvation so far has been the stuff they raised. Well, sandstorms are unhealthy, nerve-racking and disagreeable; and yet, for my own personal preference, I prefer them to rain. I cut my teeth on sandstorms, and I spent most of my life in dry countries; I've never gotten used to incessant rain. Continued cloudy rainy weather is about the most damnable stuff imaginable. These sandstorms are drab, raw and without esthetic value, and yet, there is sometimes a weird beauty about them. When the sun sinks like a great red ball, veiled in the reddish dust that all but obscures the sky, there is a feeling of unreality somehow, to be able to gaze directly at the sun without being dazzled. Then sometimes, between sandstorms, when one has blown itself out, but left a vague sifting of dust in the air, or when another is just faintly beginning, sometimes the whole sky has a silvery sheen, and the few clouds that appear are like delicate silver traceries.

I'm glad you found the South Texas views of some interest. I do not believe that cocoanuts thrive anywhere in Texas. As to the abrupt contrasts in the lower country, you can meet with them driving along paved highways. A great deal of the country is furnished with good roads, and even when they are not paved, as in many cases they are, they can be traversed with comfort most times of the year. Tourists swarm into South Texas by the thousands, and many naturally find their way into the less settled areas. But there's still plenty untouched, and if you ever get out here to Texas, I'll show you places no tourist has ever seen—less interesting from a scenic standpoint, but rich in tradition. I'm enclosing a post-card view of a grotto, built in imitation of the famous one of Lourdes,[8] the work of a very interesting character in Rio Grande City—the Rev. Gustav Gollbach,[9] of the Oblate Fathers. I found him a remarkably interesting man, of unmistakable culture and eruditon. He is a native of Hesse—a province against whose inhabitants I always had an instinctive prejudice, from memories handed down since the Revolution. I can remember when "that old Hessian" was a term of anathema in the Southwest. But my prejudice—which after all was active only in my extreme youth—did not extend to the Reverent Gollbach. He was dolichocephalic, typically Nordic, with light blue eyes and fair skin. He has thirteen thousand Mexicans under his spiritual guidance, and body and soul they are much the better for his aid. Although the Catholic religion is fast losing power in Old Mexico and along the Border. Ten years ago the priest was all-powerful among our southern neighbors. Now he is as likely to get a bullet in the back as a layman. I have an idea that a priest on this side of the Border really wields more power than one in Mexico.

But I know this rambling missive is trying and boresome. I must really beg your pardon; I've filled it with trivialities and maunderings, without rhyme or reason. I'll try to do better next time. I've been unwell for some weeks—a condition extremely rare for me—and my physical condition always reacts on my mental condition. When I'm not fit bodily, my mind is sluggish and stupid.

Tomorrow, if nothing happens, I start for the East Texas oil fields; I hope also to go into Louisiana. I have no zest for the trip, and would not go if it were not for business reasons. If I get into any interesting countries, I'll send you some views. Thank you again for the kind things you said about the rhyme, and my ability as a rhymer. I appreciate them the more, coming from one whose artistic ability I so highly admire. And so I close this tedious letter, hoping that next time I'll be able to put more snap into my correspondence.

Cordially,
R.E.H.

P.S. Wright took another of the Conan the Cimmerian series, "The Tower of the Elephant", the setting of which is among the spider-haunted jeweled towers of Zamora the Accursed, while Conan was still a thief by profession, before he came into the kingship.

Notes

1. Original title of REH's story "Usurp the Night."
2. "In the Vault."

3. The Book of Eibon (or Liber Ivonis) was invented by CAS (see "The Door to Saturn" [*Strange Tales,* January 1932]). HPL first alluded to it "The Thing on the Doorstep."

4. As articulated in REH's essay "The Hyborian Age."

5. The story had been accepted by *Strange Tales,* but the magazine folded before the story could appear. See letter by Harry Bates to REH (4 October 1932) concerning the failure of the magazine and the return of the copyedited ms. (*LC* 375).

6. "Marchers of Valhalla."

7. The notorious "Massie case," in which Mrs. Grace Fortescue, the mother of Thalia Massie, Lt. Thomas Massie, Thalia's husband, and two sailors were tried for the murder of Joseph Kahahawei, one of five men who had been accused of raping Thalia. When a jury deadlocked in the trial of the five men, Mrs. Fortescue, her son-in-law, and two of his sailor friends kidnapped Kahahawei, attempted to beat a confession out of him, and shot him. They were caught with his body in their car as they sought to dispose of it, so their guilt was not in doubt; the defense sought to portray their actions as justified. Clarence Darrow served on the defense.

8. In 1858, from 11 February to 16 July, Bernadette Soubirous, a 14-year-old girl, had numerous visions of the Virgin Mary in the nearby Massabielle grotto in Lourdes in southwestern France. The visions were declared authentic by the Pope in 1862, and the cult of Our Lady of Lourdes was authorized. The underground spring in the grotto, revealed to Bernadette, was declared to have miraculous qualities. Lourdes has since become a major pilgrimage center.

9. Gustav Gollbach, O.M.I. (1878–1955), a native of Germany, was ordained a priest in the Oblates of Mary Immaculate order on 21 April 1906. He immigrated to Texas soon after his ordination and served churches in Del Rio, Castroville, Mercedes, San Benito, and Ballinger before coming to Rio Grande City in 1924. He built a replica of the grotto shrine at Lourdes, using petrified wood and native stone from the Roma area, dedicated in 1928.

[52] [nonextant postcard by HPL, W. Paul Cook, H. Warner Munn]

[Boston,
c. April 1932]

[53]

Providence, R. I.
May 7, 1932

Dear R E H:—

Your interesting letter, the note, the postcard, and the copy of *Oriental Stories* all duly received and appreciated. Thanks in abundance! I enjoyed "Lord of Samarcand" tremendously, and congratulate you on the vividness with which you mirrored the colour, pageantry, and feelings of the East. I must get hold of the earlier issue with "Sowers of the Thunder"—glad Wright showed such appreciation of it. I can understand how galling it must be to record an endless succession of Saracen and Tartar victories, and hope you'll soon get around to the more pleasing task of writing up those crusades in which the Western world came out—for the nonce—on top. Incidentally, I was greatly interested in your 'might-have-beens' touching medieval history. This period touches the weakest spot in my historic knowledge (for I can't seem to feel any substance or reality in anything but the Graeco-Roman and modern Europaeo-American worlds), yet I know enough of the bare outlines to appreciate the dramatic factors involved. It is my opinion that a *Saracen* conquest of Europe would have ended the Western World and established a dominant Moslem Empire, for the Arabs at their height were more civilised than we were at the same time. Had they conquered us physically, they could certainly have imposed their culture on the land—as indeed they did for centuries in Spain. On the other hand, I doubt if the *Tartars* were civilised enough to do it. I think they would have become half-Aryanised—and heaven only knows what sort of a mongrel culture would have resulted. As for the reverse possibilities—Aryan conquests of the East—I agree that under the right leader the united forces of the West might have mopped up the Saracens during the Crusade period. How far they could have pushed their conquest, and what effect it would have had on the west's civilisation, is for better imaginations than mine to deduce. Going back to antiquity—it is certainly fascinating to speculate on the possible results of a conquest of India and China by Alexander. Undoubtedly some Hindoo and Chinese traits would have struck back into Greek life, while it is certain that Greek cities would have sprung up in India and the Far East, creating peculiar types of Indo-Hellenic and Sino-Hellenic life. Probably Hellenistic dynasties—as in Egypt and Syria—would have ruled for a time in India and China, but I believe they would eventually have been swamped by the local cultures. The Greek culture would never have really permeated the farther East, any more than it did Egypt—for as in Egypt's case, there were competing civilisations too long-seated, powerful, and utterly alien to yield to any new conquering influence. Syria became half-Hellenised because the dominant Persian culture was so antipodal to Hellenism. The Persians were Aryan by blood, to begin with; and they had also long been in touch with Greek influences through the Greek and half-Greek settlements and kingdoms in Asia Minor. By the time of Alexander the Hindoos were too thoroughly de-Aryanised to be anything but alien to the Greeks. I doubt if Greek culture-centres like Alexandria could have survived very long in the farther East, because communication with the Mediterranean world would have necessarily been so difficult. Alexandria remained Greek despite its unhellenised hinterland only because of its close proximity to other firmly-established centres of Greek life—which permitted a constant interchange of Greek population. Also—its favourable economic position gave it a prosperity which deliberately attracted the best blood and minds of the Hellenistic world to it.

Thanks for the offer of the new *Strange Tales,* but I have a copy. Your "People of the Dark" is indeed fascinating, and admirably well handled. But I must praise in particular your "Horror from the Mound" in last month's W.T. That is a magnificent piece of work, and gave me a shiver of the genuine sort which is not often obtainable from popular magazine material. The suspense and atmosphere are admirable—a brooding charnel pall seems to hover over the whole scene. That and Smith's "Yoh-Vombis"[1] are the high spots of the issue.

As for this Olson—I haven't ever been honoured by his direct attention, but I have seen some of the letters with which he has been pestering poor Whitehead during the last few months.[2] It appears that he is quite a notorious nuisance among 'scientifiction' writers, especially those contributing to the Clayton magazines. He is—in the opinion of Bates, Whitehead (who has had some experience as a psychiatrist) and myself—a genuine maniac; though we don't know whether or not he is under actual restraint. He may be a relatively harmless case living with his family—though none the less wholly demented in certain directions. He has been giving Whitehead long and frantic lectures on "vectors", and "A, B, and C-space". It seems there is something especially sinister and menacing about C-space—so that it will bring about the end of the world very shortly unless all living sages get busy and call in the aid of the "vectors". Olson also has some startling and unique biological theories. According to him, the blood is not the life but the death. It is our blood which makes us die—and therefore, since food makes blood, the one simple way to become immortal is to discontinue the use of food! Poor devil—I suppose he is an ignorant, weak-brained fellow who saturated himself with odds and ends of popular occult and scientific lore either before or after the crucial thread of sanity snapped. As Whitehead says, there is nothing to do but ignore the letters of a case like that. Another case—probably closer to extreme eccentricity than to actual dementia—is that of an old chap named William Lumley of Buffalo, N.Y., who got hold of me through W.T. He claims to have travelled to all the secret places of the world—India, China, Nepal, Egypt, Thibet, etc.—and to have picked up all sorts of forbidden elder lore; also to have read Paracelsus, Remigius, Cornelius Agrippa, and all the other esoteric authors whom most of us merely talk about and refer to as we do to the Necronomicon and Black Book. He believes in occult mysteries, and is always telling about "manifestations" he sees in haunted houses and shunned valleys. He also speaks often of a mysterious friend of his—"The Oriental Ancient"—who is going to get him a forbidden book (as a loan, and not to be touched without certain ceremonies of mystical purification) from some hidden and unnamed monastery in India. Lumley is semi-illiterate—with no command of spelling or capitalisation—yet has a marvellously active and poetic imagination. He is going to write a story called "The City of Dim Faces", and from what he says of it I honestly believe it will be excellent in a strange, mystical, atmospheric way. The fellow has a remarkable sort of natural eloquence—a chanting, imageful style which almost triumphs over its illiteracies. If he finishes this tale I think I'll help him knock it into shape for submission to Wright. There is real charm—as well as real pathos—about this wistful old boy, who seems to be well along in years and in rather uncertain health. He obviously has a higher-grade mind than Olson could ever have had—for even now there is a certain wild beauty and consistency, with not the least touch of incoherence, in his epistolary extravagances. Young Brobst (as I told you, a nurse in a mental hospital) thinks a touch of real insanity is present, but I regard the case as a borderline one. I always answer his letters in as kindly a fashion as possible.

What you say of your dreams of cold, grey skies—and of the actual skies and sunsets in your part of the world—interests me vastly. I am myself extremely susceptible to sky effects, particularly gorgeous and apocalyptic sunsets. Sunsets arouse in me vague feelings of pseudo-memory, mystical revelation, and adventurous expectancy, which nothing else can even begin to conjure up. They always seem to me to be about to unveil supernal vistas of other (yet half-familiar) worlds and other dimensions. I am also ineffably fascinated by the golden light of late afternoon which somewhat precedes the sunset. Any sort of scene bathed in this unearthly splendour—with tinges of crimson and long, fantastic shadows—seems to my fancy part of a strange, ethereal realm of wonder and beauty but faintly allied to anything in the domain of prosaic reality. I think the tropics fascinate me more than the north—although, paradoxically no spot on earth holds my terrified imagination more potently and breathlessly than the aeon-dead, unknown reaches of the great white antarctic.

As possibly you have learned directly by this time, Swanson's plans for any kind of publication are now definitely abandoned. He plans to return my two stories shortly. I am sorry to see any market disappear, even though this one never promised to be very important. Another blow to the weird writer is the retrenchment policy just adopted by Clayton, whereby S.T. becomes a quarterly whilst *Astounding* becomes a bi-monthly. These are certainly lean days for the publishing business, as for other businesses! As for writing the Necronomicon—I wish I had the energy and ingenuity to do it! I fear it would be quite a job in view of the very diverse passages and intimations which I have in the course of time attributed to it! I might, though, issue an *abridged* Necronomicon—containing such parts as are considered at least reasonably safe for the perusal of mankind! When von Junzt's Black Book and the poems of Justin Geoffrey are on the market, I shall certainly have to think about the immortalisation of old Abdul! Your mention of a new series of tales dealing with the "Hyborian Age" arouses pleasant anticipations, and I also look forward to the tale of early Texas. My admiration is about evenly divided betwixt tales which are utterly cosmic and exotic, and those which grow realistically from the soil and possess all the atmosphere and colour of their locale.

The East is certainly a complex and worrisome problem. My reaction toward the Hawaiian case is much the same as yours, and it seems to me a vast mistake that a grand jury indictment was ever returned against the defendants. When a region is unwilling or unable to enforce a code of law adequate to the protection of a dominant race, there is certainly no alternative for that race but to maintain its integrity through the primitive and extra-legal processes of the frontier. Thus during the disgraceful period of so-called "reconstruction" after the Civil War the Southern states could not possibly have withstood the malignant barbarism of ignorant adventurers and politically exploited blacks except for the salutary purgation afforded by the original Ku Klux Klan. In the Hawaiian instance, the primarily regrettable thing is that the avengers did not get all five of the mongrel offenders instead of only one. Even now, if the surviving miscreants are not properly punished in their second trial, I hope that navy men or other Americans will see that these dogs drop permanently and abruptly out of sight, one by one. The commutation of sentence extended to the avengers was the very least that could be expected in view of American public opinion, and ought soon to be followed by steps to restore full civic rights. But the real mistake was in bringing them to trial at all. In my opinion Hawaii is too mongrelised and exotic and region—to full of unsettled and de-traditionalised mixed blood—to warrant the status of a self-governing territory. It ought to be administered directly by the navy department, with a naval officer responsible to Washington as governor.

Your Hindoo acquaintance must certainly afford an interesting study in contrasts. To hear the basic Asiatic perspectives expressed by a straight-featured, dolichocephalic speaker surely upsets one's superficial conceptions of fitness—though of course we realise scientifically that regional attitudes are vastly more cultural than biological in their origins.

I was extremely interested in your dramatic enumeration of the hazards of Southwestern life in the past—and agree that the human stock must be pretty tenacious to allow men to grow to maturity under such conditions. It is scarcely any wonder that those who did survive the weeding-out process are a hardy, active, and fearless breed—a selected element whose contempt of danger and injury is almost incomprehensible to the descendants of long-sheltered lines. Certainly, we pay a high price for the securities of a settled civilisation; for under such a regime the native hardiness and resourcefulness of the race quickly declines—except when artificially sustained in individuals through camping experiences and other voluntary returns to the primitive. What you call a 'quiet, humdrum youth' would seem to an Easterner active and violent beyond all non-fictional conception! "Red", the oil-field 'bad man', would be promising raw material for epic treatment.

Your sandstorms are something I can picture only through imagination, for they have no equivalent here. I hope the recent ones are not in truth the harbingers of a famine-breeding drought. Their atmospheric attributes—red sun and red dust—must surely have much impressiveness. They remind me of what Wandrei writes of the curious sky-effects seen at rare intervals in Minnesota when that region receives the tail end of some sweeping prairie dust-storm. He will never forget one red, ominous sunset in St. Paul, when the earth seemed almost convulsively in the grasp of unknown forces from Outside.[3]

South Texas must surely be an alluring place, and I hope I can see it some day. Thanks exceedingly for the view of the synthetic Lourdes—which surely attest the cleverness and perseverance of your new sacerdotal acquaintance. Father Golbach must be a highly versatile and interesting character, and I hope he may escape a violent end despite the waning hold of his church on the Mexicans.

Hope your trip proved enjoyable even though you held no high anticipations about it—and I certainly trust that your health is now fully back to par. I am just now recovering from a racking and devastating cold.

You doubtless received the Boston postcard signed by W. Paul Cook, H. Warner Munn, and myself. Munn—of Athol, Mass.—and I were Cook's guests for five days, and we had an excellent and varied time. Since Munn did not know the city very well, Cook and I acted as his guides to museums and historical antiquities. Among other things we climbed Bunker Hill Monument—my first ascent since I was 7 years old. The view, though, is always a disappointment—no open sea or green countryside, but only dull urban roofs and squalid factory chimneys. You would have enjoyed many things in the museums—especially the imagination-stirring *Hittite* inscriptions and bas-reliefs from Corkemish. I don't believe there are any things like that in any museum in New York. One afternoon we went to the ancient suburban town of Medford, where colonial houses survive in abundance, and absorbed goodly slices of the past. Enclosed is a card of the principal old mansion we saw. This is a good example of a New-England Georgian manor house of the earlier 18th century—the seat of Isaac Royall, an Antigua planter who moved up to the Massachusetts-Bay in the 1730's. The smaller building housed the slaves. Royall's son—Isaac Jr.—founded the first law professorship in Harvard University. In 1775 he was loyal to the King and government, hence suffered exile and the confiscation of his property by the revolutionists. The family, however, still flourishes in England—and some if its blood in the female line remains in Massachusetts.

Pretty soon I hope to get off on some kind of a real trip, though bad finances make matters still rather vague. I had hoped to reach New Orleans, but am now rather doubtful about it. But in any case I shall visit Long in N.Y., and get up the Hudson to the wild domes hills and hanging woods of

Ulster County to see Bernard Dwyer. Dwyer is now back on his ancestral farm after a winter in Kingston.

Tardy spring has come to the north at last, and there are flowers and feathery-leafed trees on every hand. One or two days have been warm enough to let me take my work out to the woods and fields.

With all good wishes—

Yrs most sincerely—
H P L

Notes

1. CAS, "The Vaults of Yoh-Vombis" (*WT,* March 1932).
2. See *SLH* 2.17, 18.
3. See Donald Wandrei to HPL, 6 April 1927; *Mysteries of Time and Spirit* 72.

[54] [TLS]

[24 May 1932?]

Dear Mr. Lovecraft:

Glad you liked the Oriental story, and thank you very much for the kind things you said about it. Its always with misgivings that I submit an Eastern yarn to the magazine, for I never know how many glaring errors and mistakes I've made. My knowledge of the Orient is extremely sketchy, and I have to draw on my imagination to supply missing links which I cant learn in the scanty references at my command. Price and Miller,[1] however, are a big help in the matter of Arabic names, grammar, etc.

I read with much interest your comments regarding theoretical conquests of the West by the East, and vice versa. As you say, the Arabs, at their height, were far more highly civilized than we, and an Arabic conquest—had it not been for the fundamental difference in nature—might not have been so bad—though the mind revolts at the thought. I agree with you that a Mongolian conquest would have been a mess. It seems to me that the Mongol tends to degenerate even quicker than the Aryan, when thrown from his nomadic pristine existence into luxurious environments, and more completely—as witness the decay of the Seljuks in Asia Minor, whose magnificent empire went to pieces scarcely more than fifty years after they swept out of High Asia. And look at the static condition of the Ottoman today—however, the Ottoman is a mongrel of the most tangled type, and he was never a Turk, anyhow, in the true sense of the word. If we'd been over-run and conquered by Turks or Tatars, I imagine the present-day western world would present a bewildering and paradoxical picture—probably with names like Yaruktash McDonald, Genghis O'Brien, or Tughluk Murphy.

Alexandria must have presented a gorgeous pageantry of splendor and colorful contrasts. I'd never thought much about it, and hadnt realized that it kept its Grecian character so long. We are of the West are well mixed, but the natives of the Mediterranean must be mongrelized beyond all reckoning.

Thank you very much for your comments on "People of the Dark" and "The Horror from the Mound." Your remarks concerning the latter story especially encourages me. I'd begun to fear it was a complete wash-out, seeing that Bates originally rejected it, and some of my friends were'nt much impressed with it. But your kind comments revive my confidence. Please extend my heartiest thanks, also, to Mr. Cook and Mr. Munn, both gentlemen for whose literary talents I have the sincerest regard. I fear my demoniac Black Book scarcely deserves Mr. Munn's high compliments. I am sorry that his work does not appear more often in Weird Tales. I remember his "City of Spiders" as one of the most striking and powerful stories I have ever read;[2] and his "Tales of the Werewolf Clan" had the real historic sweep.[3] He is evidently a deeply read student of history.

Poor Olson—what you say of him clinches my conclusion that he is completely insane. I first heard from him a long time ago when he wrote commenting on my "Hills of the Dead"; favorably, by the way. "The Horror from the Mound" seems to have enraged him. He hasnt pulled any "C-Space" or "vectors" on me, though he has had considerable to say about "Ramas" A, B, C, etc. Neither has he given me the secret of immortality, though he has hinted darkly at it. I've never answered any of his letters, though the impulse has been strong to reply with a missive that would make his ravings sound like the prosaic theorizings of a professor fossilized in conventions. But it would be a poor thing to make game of the unfortunate soul.

I was much interested in what you said of the man Lumley, of Buffalo. He must be indeed an interesting study; possibly of such a sensitive and delicate nature that he has, more or less unconsciously, taken refuge from reality in misty imaginings and occult dreams. I hope he completes his story, and that it is published. Do you believe the "Oriental Ancient" has any existence outside his imagination? There is to me a terrible pathos in a man's vain wanderings on occult paths, and clutching at non-existent things, as a refuge from the soul-crushing stark realities of life. One of the tragedies of Man, mounting to almost cosmic heights, it seems to me, would be for a human, having spent all his life groping in the shadows, to realize on his death-bed, that his gropings and imaginings were vain, and that his visions of "something beyond" were mere self-induced phantasies—to have all his props and stays of mysticisms and dreams and fancies and beliefs, blown suddenly away like smoke before the hard wind of reality, leaving him writhing feebly on the jagged rocks of materiality, dying as any other insect dies, and knowing that he is no divine spirit in tune with some mystic infinity, but only a faint spark of material light, to be extinguished for ever in the blackness of the ultimate abyss.

I had realized, from your writings, something of the fascination sky-effects have for you, and your remarks pertaining to this subject are really poetic in vivid beauty. Like you I am moved by the golden glory that foreruns some sunsets; and then, in the long summer days, when the skies are cloudless, I am stirred by the dreamy magic of slumbering twilights, between the set of the sun, and the gathering of night. At such times familiar sights somehow take on an alien and glamorous aspect; gables of houses, wood-clad hills, even figures of people moving through the twilight. Somehow, when I see high-ridged houses blocked out darkly against the deepening blue of a western twilight sky, a vagrant thought enters my mind, a dim semi-expectancy, of fantastic winged monsters dropping from the sky and lighting on the dusk-etched roofs, folding their great wings and crouching there gargoyle-like, their chins resting in their cupped and taloned hands.

I mentioned the cloud-effects on the Callahan devide. Some are tenuous and beautiful as golden webs of silver fleece. More are lurid, sinister, menacing and grim. This strip of country is known as the cyclone-belt, and terrible storms have wrought havoc in the past. When a funnel-shaped tornado tears across the country, men are utterly helpless. They can but crawl into cellars, if they have time, and listen to their property being blown away and destroyed, and thank the Powers if they escape with their lives. The utter helplessness of mankind before a storm is a terrible sensation. You can not strangle the lightning with your hands, you can not riddle the clouds with bullets, and you can not hack the wind with a knife. If you die, you die like a sheep, and if you live, it is by the whim of chance or the Prince of the Air. Outside of actual wind-storms, this country is much subject to terrific thunder-storms, floods of rain, hail-storms, and in drouths, sand-storms, which, of all the atmospheric disturbances I have mentioned, I much prefer. Among my earliest recollections as a child, scarce out of infancy, is that of crouching in dank, dark, or dim-lit, and sometimes reptile-haunted, cellars, while outside the wind shrieked and raved through the night, ripping the branches and leaves from the trees, while rain fell in mad foaming torrents, crashes of thunder shook the very earth, and blinding, insane rips of lightning gleamed through the cracks of the cellar-door.

Sorry to hear Swanson has had to give up his "Galaxy". As you say, the game was given a sock below the belt when Claytons changed the appearances of their Strange Tales and Astounding Stories. The change in Strange Tales hit me viciously in the pocket-book, because I'd apparently just got started good with them. Another of my regular markets—Fight Stories—was taken out of circulation entirely recently. I like the idea of an "abridged" Necronomicon. After all, it wouldnt be a good idea to let the general public in on ALL the dark secrets of antiquity! Besides, you might later, in a discreet way, bring out the suppressed chapters of the demoniac work, and cash in again. If you were careful enough to word these secret chapters so nobody could possibly understand the text, the average reader would lay it down with the feeling that he'd been dipping into genuine inside dope of the cosmos, his admiration for the author would mount to heights of actual worship, and I bet half a dozen new secrets cults and occult societies would spring up like mushrooms. As regards the hellish Black Book, if I can find some well-educated maniac, who hasnt been crammed with conventional occult hokus-pokus, I may have him write it for publication. If not, I may shoot myself full of dope sometime, and write it myself.

That Hawaii business is a rotten reek in the nostrils of decent men. I agree with you in believing that the island should be put under military or naval rule, and in hoping that the dirty yellow-bellies that committed the crime will be put away properly. I know what would have happened to them in Texas. I dont know whether an Oriental smells any different than a nigger when he's roasting, but I'm willing to bet the aroma of scorching hide would have the same chastening effect on his surviving tribesmen. Yet I consider the actual perpetrators of the crime more decent and honorable than the attorney who prosecuted the avengers, and the jury—supposedly composed largely of white men—which convicted them. I guess outside pressure was brought to bear on the jurymen—I understand Hawaii is controlled by Oriental interests. Instead of a boycott, a noose should have been used wholesale. As for the attorney, for any white man who is low enough to crucify an outraged child of his own color before a mongrel swarm, a roll down a hill in a barrel full of safety-razor blades is too good for him. It is my ardent hope that he will come to his end at the hands of some of his yellow-bellied pets, and that his demise will be neither swift nor painless.

I hope the boycott will continue, but it is a poor revenge, and shows to what depths of powerless cowardice American manhood has sunk, when they leave the settling of a case like that in the hands of their women. American men had better give the government over to the women, for the men have become the most spineless, yellow, cringing cowards the world has yet seen. I'm thinking of writing to my congressman to put a bill before the House recommending that men be exempt from active service in the next war, so that the women may do the fighting. If its left to the men, America will get the hell kicked out of her. I am unable to decide whether the deterioration of the American man is a result of his domination from birth by women, or whether that domination is a result of his damned spinelessness. If this degeneration continues, damned if I dont move to the Irish Free State. Those cut-throats seem to have a good deal of manhood left. And judging from the riots and gang-fights in Australia, there are plenty of white men left in that part of the world. Australia may be the last stand of the Aryan race.

Returning to Hawaii—which I would like to do with a squadron of bombing-planes—I heard the war-correspondent, Floyd Gibbons, talk over the radio after his return from that part of the world.[4] According to him, forty percent of the Hawaiian population are Japanese; control of the island has passed into the hands of Orientals—I guess American politicians cater to their votes and power, just as certain politicians cater to the Mexican vote along the Border—and Americans are about as safe there, and get about as much justice, as they would in a purely Oriental government. More, he did more than hint that in case of war with Japan, a concerted uprising, with arms furnished by the Japanese government, would rob America of her western-most defense, and leave her coasts open to attack. Which seems reasonable enough, and is all the more reason for putting the cursed island under a naval authority. I hope Hoover or somebody restores full citizenship to the defendants. It was a dirty black shame they were ever convicted, or even indicted.

As regards that Hindu, I only saw him once. Since the Hawaiian affair, I've had a bad taste in my mouth for all Orientals, Aryan or otherwise. I'd have been interested in his view-point on the affair—but it would have probably been just the opposite of mine, in which case I might have crowned him in the heat of the moment, at least immediately after the verdict of guilty was rendered, which shocked and infuriated me beyond measure.

As concerns the hazards of existence in the Southwest, anybody would think a virile, intensely hardy people would be bred thereby, and in some parts of the state, and in many individual cases, that is true. But here, as elsewhere, the old stock is degenerating, despite everything. Ignorance, poverty, undernourishment, and other things are destroying the descendants of the pioneers. Through this part of the country especially, the poverty, and illiteracy, of the rural population is depressing. Crowded out of the fertile parts of the state by Bohemians, Poles and Germans, the American country-people are in many parts sinking into utter degeneracy. The old free independant spirit of their ancestors seems lost entirely. In some cases, that spirit never existed anyway. Many of the inhabitants of Texas, especially in these parts, are sons and daughters, or grandchildren of poverty-stricken tenant farmers from the clay hills, sand drifts, and creeks of Georgia, Tennessee, Alabama, and other southern states—poor white trash, they were called there. They were never slave-holders, never owned the land they worked, and therefore never tried to improve their state, and they brought their characteristics to Texas. When land was cheap and plentiful, they did fairly well, according to their lights—moving onto another strip, when they had worn out and exhausted the original farm. Then land ceased to be free and plentiful, and they were stuck on the side of some alkali hill, or in the midst of a waste of sand drifts or post-oaks. There they stuck, those who had progressed enough to own their own land. Generally their sons sold it for what it would bring, and again took up the existence of tenant farmers—and nothing is more devitalizing to the land and the man. Why waste more work than necessary on land you'll never own? Texas was ruined when the squatters swarmed in and made an indifferent agricultural state out of a magnificent cattle-empire.

As regards that bould bucko Red, of the sledge-hammer fists and adamantine skull, he was merely a higher developed example of a type most common in all oil fields—a slugger, a bully, a swash-buckler, possessed of small mentality and great animal courage in certain ways. He was imported from Ranger by the gang of thugs which was then trying to run the town; after Red failed to turn the trick, the city-marshall was framed by them on a bootleg charge and lost his job, whereupon the more boisterous element held high revel day and night. Where Red came from, I dont know. Oklahoma, some said, but I'm more inclined to think he was originally from Pennsylvania or West Virginia. I never heard of him using a weapon of any sort in his scraps, and most of the Oklahoma toughs I've seen—and that state has sent more bad men into Texas oil fields than any other state in the Union—were handy with knife or gun.

At present Oklahoma is being ravaged by a thug called "Pretty-boy" Floyd, who seems to be a reversion to the old-time outlaw type.[5] He has eleven men to his credit, seven or eight of which are officers of the law, which probably accounts for the failure of the authorities to apprehend him. Its a lot easier to beat a confession of some sort out of some harmless poor devil than it is to nab a young desperado who wears a steel bullet-proof vest, and draws and shoots like lightning with either hand.

He's being touted as a second Billy the Kid, but deadly as he undoubtedly is, I doubt if he has quite the ability of that young rattlesnake. I consider the Kid the greatest gunman that ever strapped a holster to his leg, and that's taking in a lot of territory.

If I expressed my opinion as to the three greatest gunmen the West ever produced, I would say—and doubtless be instantly refuted from scores of sources, since you cant compare humans like you can horses—but I'd say, in the order named, Billy the Kid of New Mexico, Wild Bill Hickok[6] of Kansas, and John Wesley Hardin[7] of Texas. The Kid killed twenty-one men in his short eventful lifetime; Hardin had twenty-three notches on his pistol-butt when John Selman shot him down in an El Paso saloon; how many men Wild Bill Hickok killed will probably never be known; conservative estimate puts the number at fifty-odd. But Wild Bill had a somewhat softer snap than the Kid, since the quick draw had not attained its ultimate heights when he was at his best. As for the famous fight with the McCandlas gang, on which much of Hickok's fame rests—in which he is supposed to have killed seven or eight of them in hand-to-hand combat, unaided, I've heard on pretty good authority that he had plenty of help, and that far from being an open, stand-up fight, Hickok and his friend way-laid the McCandlas's and mowed them down with shot-guns, and that some of Wild Bill's lady friends aided in the fray by beating out their victims' brains with hoes and mattocks, while they lay wounded on the ground. But that Wild Bill was a master killer can not be denied; differing from most gun-men, who generally aimed at the body, Wild Bill usually shot his victims in the head.

But some-how I've wondered off the subject, which was oil-field bullies. The fightingest son-of-a-gun that ever came into the Callahan oil-fields was a full-blooded Irishman from the Pennsylvania hill-country. He wasnt an unusually big man, as they go, but he was built up like a brick-house. He was steel cords and lightning—strong as a bull, with a blinding, steel-trap co-ordination that made him supreme among the general run of lumbering, slow-witted sluggers. He used to wrap his wrists and arms half-way up to the elbows with adhesive tape—to keep them from shattering under his terrific blows—and then invade the toughest joint he could find and go to the mat with the entire attendance. I've heard he licked eleven men in one day, but cant verify that statement. But he would have been a champion, if he'd gone into the ring. He fought for the sheer fun of it, and laughed all the time he fought. He wasnt a bully, in the accepted sense of the word; he never picked a fight with a peaceable man; his meat was the swaggering brawlers who thought they were tough. Its a wonder somebody didnt kill him. But he lived to die young, in a natural manner. At least, in a manner so common to oil field workers that it might be considered natural, since it was syphilis that mowed him down. It affected his mind long before it touched his magnificent body, and he lost the use of his vocal cords. He used to come into the drug-store where I worked, quite often, and he always wanted me to wait on him, since I was the only one who seemed to have sense enough, or was sober enough, to understand his signs. He couldnt speak articulately, but made noises like an infant, though he never entirely lost his sanity. And this is strange—long after he lost the power to speak ordinary simple words, he could still pronounce oaths and profane phrases. At last he died, and for months before death came, he was like a skeleton, with a hairless, parchment-like yellowish skin stretched over his skull like a death-mask.

I've seen some human ruins in my time, from venereal disease, liquor, dope—paragoric was a great favorite with certain types. It used to make me gape, the amount an addict could store away at a time. But it knocks them quicker than other kinds of dope. Of all the paragoric-fiends that used the haunt the place I where I worked, the only one that's still alive—at least he was alive the last time I heard of him, and he must have gotten off the stuff—is an ex-vaudeville actor. He used to do clog-dances for us, after the crowd had gone and we were ready to close the joint for the night. He must have been good, before he hit the toboggan, for he still had a nimble foot.

Small things turn a man from his road into by-paths and blind-alleys, sometimes. I believe the average wretch, instead of being booted onto the road to ruin with some gigantic overwhelming cataclysm, is helped gradually, a push here and a shove there, until he's well on the down-rush, and the hob-nails of a tender-hearted humanity shower joyously on his bleeding head, and hurl him headlong on his way in a blaze of glory and cat-calls.

If mankind's affairs are tinkered with from Outside, it must be with malicious intent. If a man walks across a ten-acre tract in the dark, with one rock in it, he'll invariably bust his toe on that rock. If there is one weak spot in the ice on a frozen river five hundred miles long, he'll find it and fall through. If he is confronted with seventeen roads, one of which leads into a cactus-bed and the other sixteen to his destination, he will inevitably select the one wrong road. With seven doors leading out of an unlighted room, he will blunder into an open closet and stick his toe into a mouse-trap. I remember the heavy sign-board on a store next to the place I worked, which swung to and fro in a hard wind all night, and nearly worked loose. Everybody said it was going to fall, and the natives of the town walked shy of it. Scores of people passed and went around it. Then, just as I glanced out of the drugstore where I was working, I saw a smart dressed young salesman, a stranger in the town, advancing briskly, and knew that he was going to walk under the signboard. I didnt have time to warn him, but I knew the board would fall, the instant he got under it. It did, and crashed on his head with what sounded like a whoop of delight, smashing his hat and laying his scalp open. He came into the drugstore bleeding like a stuck hog, and everybody surveyed him gloomily, as another example of the capriciousness of chance. I'm beginning to doubt the element of coincidence; it looks like a systematic plot to make life miserable for humanity, and the next time I fall over a chair in the dark, that shouldnt be there, I'm going to look under it for a gnome, or an elf, or some other varmint from Outside!

I remember various galling experiences, where the random-element, or the law of averages, or something, came up behind me and kicked me in the pants with a hob-nailed boot, and one as galling as any, that still makes me writhe and mutter profanely when I think of it, happened when I was a kid of ten or eleven, in a country school. I was stockily built and fairly proficient in the brutal and unscientific style of wrestling then prevalent in the country, which depended less on speed and skill, than on strength and endurance. One day the teacher came out of the school-house to watch us play—a rare event. I happened to be wrestling with a friend of mine, and they stopped to watch us. I wished to make an impression on them—to show off, in other words. I wished for a worthier opponent—since I had thrown this particular friend forty or fifty times. And while I was wishing, suddenly and stunningly I found myself thrown! It never happened before, and it never happened again—at least, with that boy. I was shocked, humiliated, well-nigh maddened. I urged a renewal of the strife, but the teachers laughed mockingly and withdrew into their sanctum. I withdrew from public view, and broodingly contemplated my shameful defeat. I sought soothing of stung vanity by vanquishing my conqueror, but it did not rob my original defeat of its sting. The teachers did not know I had been thrown by chance; they thought my friend was the better man. They probably think it to this day. I plotted a return match, some day when the moguls should again emerge to watch the antics of the herd, but it was not to be. A few weeks later the boy I wrestled went to his last reward with a bullet through his heart, and I never got to vindicate myself in the sight of those awesome and superior beings, the Teachers.

Another thing that discourages me, is the absolute unreliability of human senses. If a hunting hound's nose fooled him as often as a human's faculties betray him, the hound wouldnt be worth a damn. The first time this fact was brought to my mind was when I was quite small, and hearing a cousin relate the details of a camping trip, on which one Boy Scout shot another through the heart with a .22 calibre target rifle. I was never a Boy Scout, but I understand that they are trained to be keen observers. Well, there were about twenty looking on, and no two of them told the same story in court. And each insisted that his version was the correct one, and stuck to it. And I understand that this is common among all witnesses.

I devoutly hope I'll never be a witness in a court-trial, because I'd probably be so muddled, and make so many contradicting statements that my testimony would land ME in the jug, instead of the defendant.

Its amazing how twisted a story can get, after passing through the mouths of even three or four people. There seems to be a perverse obstinacy in the human critter that prevents him seeing or realizing the true facts of a case. I remember once when I was working in an automobile agency during a town-site oil boom; I was alone in the place, when I heard a groaning and cussing on the outside and saw one of the town's would-be bad men approaching the joint, using a repeating shot-gun for a crutch. From the way he stumbled along, and the noise he was making, I thought maybe he'd accidentally shot himself and was bleeding to death. But when I hopefully questioned him on the subject, he replied profanely and with many racking moans, that he had re-hurt an old strain. He was barely able to walk. I helped him into a chair and leaned his gun against the wall, while he sat and pitied himself, nearly weeping as he spoke of the pain of his hurt. Like all synthetic bad men, and most of the real article, he wasnt endowed with a great deal of guts when it came to enduring pain himself. That breed is strong on dealing misery, but not so strong on taking it. After awhile I went out, leaving him still sympathizing with himself in the chair, and started across the street to a drugstore. As I crossed the street, an auto came careering down on the wrong side, and I jumped out of the way, startled and angry. But there was a man slumped down beside the driver, and from the ghastly pallor of his face and the limp way his head rolled, I knew that he was dying. I went on into the drugstore and later, while I was getting a drink, a fellow came in and asked who it was that had gotten shot. Another fellow came in and said that it was Bill D. I here spoke up and told them that Bill D. was still in the land of the living and had only strained a tendon. They looked at me unbelievingly, and one of them said that was hokum; that Bill D. was the man, because he saw him limping along on his shot-gun, groaning like a man in his last throes. I answered that the man who had been shot, had not been able to limp; that I had seen him as he was rushed to first aid; and that if they doubted my word, let them go over and personally inspect Bill D. whom they would find sitting in a chair in the auto agency. By this time their eyes were flashing and their jaws were setting with the perverse instinct of the human who thinks his word is being doubted. Its quite possible I might have had a most unwelcome fight on my hands, when another party entered who confirmed my statement, and told them that it was another man than the afflicted and disputed Bill D. who had blown half his foot off climbing through a fence with a shot-gun, and bled to death before he could be given proper treatment. The debaters grudgingly let themselves be convinced, but I doubt if either of them ever had any use for me after that.

Your mention of Wandrei, in connection with Minnesota dust-storms, reminds me to ask about the book-length weird story he was writing. Has he finished it yet, and if so, has he found a buyer? I hope he has, or will be able to market it. His work shows a deep imagination, and a delicate touch in plot-development. His state is one—in fact, the only one—in the Mid-West, which touches my fancy somehow, the northern-most of all the states, where surely some traditions of the pioneer West must still be alive. When I try to visualize it, I merely get a mixed-up impression of vast plains covered with waving grain, cold gigantic blue skies, huge football teams, and Scandinavians with mystic blue eyes and yellow moustaches. The state must be a veritable power-house of virility.

Strange to say, the sandstorms stopped abruptly some weeks ago, and since then the whole state has been flooded with rains. There was a heavy rain last night, with some hail, and it has been cloudy today, though it seems to be clearing now. There is, in the southeast, a great heap of fleecy white thunderheads exactly like clouds in a Doré illustration. From behind them, and partly veiling them, sweeps a fan-shaped drift of light grey cloud, little heavier than mist, covering a quarter of the sky, and sharing the young dim moon in its feathery fringes. There may be hail and wind tonight, and men and their works be swept into Eternity, but just now the whole sky is soft and beautiful with sunset.

There have not been, in years, sandstorms such as the country used to know. As more and more of the Panhandle and upland plains are being put in cultivation, the drift of the sand is checked to some extent. I remember how they used to come up—sometimes suddenly, with driving clouds, a spatter of rain, and then a gust of wind-swept dust that swept the skies clean of all else. But often their coming was somewhat in this fashion: The sun would rise red and hot, in a clear breathless sky. There were no clouds, but a sort of breathless tenseness. Even in the early morning, the scanty flowers wilted with the heat, and the young leaves drooped on their stalk. Then the wind began to rise, in fitful gusts that rose and ceased suddenly. In the northwest a long low black line appeared, that grew with appalling speed. It rose steadily, seeming to climb into the sky, though its lower edge never left the earth. At first it seemed like a hideous black cloud. On it swept, towering higher and higher; now it reared its awesome crest hundreds of feet in height, and was like a black tidal-wave—an onrushing basaltic wall, stretching from east to west—a black wall five hundred feet high and ten miles long. Black dots whirled above it, which were quickly seen to be buzzards and birds of prey, flying hard before it. Now it loomed half-way to the zenith, and an awesome roar filled the air. Yet suddenly the terror of it was gone; it was no longer black but reddish-brown, and then with a rush and roar, the sand-particles were whirling past, and the wind was howling through your hair, and the sand-storm was on. It might last for days, sinking to a whisper at night, perhaps, to roar with renewed vigor at dawn. There would be no clouds, only driving, pelting, whistling sand—sand—sand! which found rest in your eyes, ears, nostrils, mouth, hair; which filtered through window frames in steady streams, and sifted under doors until a passing foot left a clear imprint. You found sand in your bed, in your clothes, your shoes, your food. When you opened your mouth to curse it, you felt grit between your teeth. At midday you could look unwinking into the sun, which hung like a pale yellow ball in a reddish flying drift. At night you might glimpse a few stars high in the dim hazy sky, lent a strange alien silver by the dust-laden atmosphere, or a moon, surrounded by a pale yellowish glow, might glimmer through. For a day or so after the wind had ceased blowing, the dust still veiled the skies, lending everything a strange unnatural quality, an aspect of illusion and witchery.

I'm sorry to hear you've been under the weather, and hope that by now you've made a complete recovery. I didnt go to the oil fields, after all. I got no further than Fort Worth, where the condition of my health caused me to abandon my plans. I remained there a few days, and then returned to Cross Plains. My health seems to have suddenly gone on the rocks, caused, I think, by strain and too close confinement. My occupation causes me to spend too much time indoors, and allows me too little time for exercize; but there is no help for it, and the shrinking of my markets force me to increase, rather than diminish, the length and intensity of my working hours. I am not worrying; I've been on the verge of a complete break-down half a dozen times before, and my bull-like physique and vitality has always pulled me through.

Thanks for the post-card views, which, as always, proved most interesting. I envy you your visit into Massachusetts. The museums must be fascinating, and I would have enjoyed examining the Hittite relics, I know—not that I know much about such things, but remains of the Hittite and Babylonian civilizations have a peculiar fascination for me. Assyrian, also. Something that strikes me as strange, is the fact that Assyria's rule was a never-ending series of wars to put down revolts, which threatened her domination to the very end of her empire. There was scarcely a year that did not see some of her various provinces in rebellion, and the more savagely the Assyrians punished rebellions, the more fiercely the rebels rose. Those ancient Semitic nations must have been people of remarkable virility; and yet the Aryan Persians and Medes crushed these same nations easily, and had little trouble with the very races that had struggled, more or less successfully, against Assyria for centuries.

By the way, there is something I want to ask you, my own ideas on the matter being pretty vague. It is this: when you quote a bit of verse, or a few prose lines from some author, or use the same as a heading for a chapter, are you supposed to always get permission from the publishers of the original text? And when the stuff's been reprinted several times, how are you going to find out who holds the original copyright? Any information you could give me on this point would be greatly appreciated.

Another thing; I've recently joined the American Fiction Guild, which looks like a pretty good thing. If you are not already a member, and would care to look into it, I'll have them send you some literature regarding it.

I hope you'll get to take that trip you spoke of, and that it will come up to expectations. Your mention of Dwyer reminds me that I owe him a letter. He recently let me read his "Brooklyn Nights" which I found fascinating. He is a natural poet.

With best wishes,

Cordially,

R E H.

P.S. I just received the Whitehead letter. Thanks very much for forwarding it to me. I dont know how I managed to be so careless as to neglect to give Mr. Whitehead my address. I'd already decided not to make any contract with the agent in question, and had written him to that effect. Mr. Whitehead's letter certainly clinches the matter.

If you havent already obtained a copy of Oriental Stories, containing my "Sowers of the Thunder", I'll be more than glad to lend you mine.

I'm enclosing a rhyme induced by recent Asiatic affairs;[8] no hurry about returning it. Wright rejected the antediluvian Texas story;[9] not enough weirdness about it.

R.E.H.

Notes

1. E. Hoffmann Price and Warren Hastings Miller.

2. H. Warner Munn, "The City of Spiders" (*WT,* November 1926).

3. H. Warner Munn, all in *WT:* "The Werewolf of Ponkert" (July 1925); "Return of the Master" (July 1927); "The Werewolf's Daughter" (October, November, Decem-

ber 1928); "The Master Strikes" (November 1930); "The Master Fights" (December 1930); and "The Master Has a Narrow Escape" (January 1931). Included in *Tales of the Werewolf Clan* (West Kingston, RI: Donald M. Grant, 1979; 2 vols.).

4. Floyd Gibbons (1887–1939), war correspondent for the *Chicago Tribune* during World War I. In the 1920s and '30s, he was widely known as a radio commentator and narrator of newsreels, for which he received a star on the Hollywood Walk of Fame.

5. Pretty Boy Floyd, byname of Charles Arthur Floyd (1901–1934), American gunman whose run-ins with police and violent bank robberies (he had adopted the machine gun as his professional trademark) made newspaper headlines.

6. James Butler (Wild Bill) Hickok (1837–1876), legendary Western hunter, lawman, gambler, and Wild West show performer.

7. John Wesley Hardin (1853–1895), born in Bonham, Texas, was (with Billy the Kid) one of REH's favorite subjects in correspondence. An outlawed killer from age 15, he ranks second only to Jim ("Killer") Miller in number of "confirmed" killings by a gunfighter. Convicted in 1877 of murdering Sheriff Charlie Bell, he was sentenced to 25 years in prison. While there he studied law. Pardoned in 1894, he practiced law for short periods in Gonzales and Junction, then opened an office in El Paso, where he began associating with a hard crowd and drinking heavily. John Selman shot and killed Hardin on 19 August 1895.

8. Possibly the poem "John Kelley," a diatribe against the prosecutor in the Massie case; in *CL* 2.345.

9. I.e., "Marchers of Valhalla."

[55]

Hotel Orleans,
New Orleans, La.,
June 8, 1932

Dear R E H:—

Well—I'm writing you from a considerably lesser distance than I've ever written from before, and only wish I had the cash to complete the journey and see old Texas![1] Your letter of recent date was duly forwarded to me, and I have read it with the keenest interest—also the delightfully spirited poem, which I am returning in case it is an original copy destined for your files or for submission elsewhere.

I left home May 18, and stopped a week in N.Y. with Long—likewise seeing others of the local crowd. Then, on the night of the 25th, I hopped off on the trip proper. For the first time in my life I traversed the entire length of the Shenandoah Valley—Winchester, Staunton, Lexington, Roanoke—and was utterly knocked out by the beauty of the Blue Ridge landscape. Then came Knoxville, Tenn., and a ride across country to Chattanooga. Here once more I was reduced to gasps of breathless admiration; for the beauty of the Cumberlands—and of the river-bluff environs of Chattanooga in Lookout Mountain [line of text dropped] and revelled in the marvellous view of the outspread river, town, countryside, and hills—and also descended into the mountain's vast chain of caverns, including the great vaulted chamber (discovered 1930) wherein a 145-foot waterfall roars ceaselessly amidst eternal night. Another object at Chattanooga whose interest was more historic than natural was the old Civil War locomotive "General"—preserved in fine shape in the old (1858) Union Station—which in one exciting day was captured from its civilian crew by the Federals, and then chased and captured by the Confederates.

The ride from Chattanooga to Memphis (my whole trip is by 'bus) took me through a continuation of this mountainous wonderland—along what is locally called the "Grand Cañon of the Tennessee". At Memphis I saw the lordly Mississippi for the first time, and was duly impressed. Then "down the ribber" through the flat Yazoo delta cotton country and finally up the bluffs of picturesque and historic Vicksburg. Between there and Natchez I began to encounter signs of the really far south—gnarled live-oaks with tangles of Spanish moss, and similar forms of luxuriant vegetation.

In general, I think the Natchez country has the finest subtropical scenery I have ever beheld. It reminds one of the landscapes delineated in the "Atala" of Chateaubriand—who indeed once visited in Natchez.[2] The roads, owing to the soft and friable nature of the local yellow clay, are all deeply sunken below the level of the surrounding terrain; and present a weirdly impressive appearance with their high vertical walls overrun by vines and the roots of ancient oaks and cypresses. These great trees, arching overhead and draped with grotesque festoons of Spanish moss, keep the scene shrouded in a perpetual green twilight.

Natchez itself is a stately old town where the past still lives—a quiet backwater with but little physical change since the early 19th century. Few places can be more fascinating to the historically-minded. The settlement was founded by the French (under the Canadian-born leader Jean-Baptiste Le Moyne, Sieur de Bienville, who two years later founded New Orleans) in 1716, as the military and trading post of Ft. Rosalie. Ruins of the fort—that is, old earthworks—still exist on the high bluff. In 1729 the Natchez Indians massacred all the garrison, but the post was regarrisoned and maintained. In 1763, by the treaty of Paris, the whole region passed to Great Britain as part of the new Province of West-Florida, and Natchez became Ft. Panmure. In 1799 the Spaniards under Don Bernardo de Galvez (Governor of La. and son of the Viceroy of Mexico) took advantage of the American revolution to invade West-Florida, and seized Natchez among other towns—holding them by force till 1798, even though the treaty of 1783 very clearly assigned the northern part of West Florida to the nascent U.S. Many surviving houses of Spanish design attest the solid nature of the Spanish occupation. When the Americans finally got the territory and flocked in—organising the State of Mississippi—the great days of Natchez began. It was a logical port for the abundant cotton of the newly-developed delta country, and the rising Mississippi traffic made it a predestined commercial focus. It became, likewise, a town centre for the rich and cultivated Louisiana planters across the river. From about 1810 onward, Natchez filled up with stately mansion-houses of the pillared classic-revival type—most of which remain to this day in every state of preservation from perfect maintenance to utter ruin. The town proper lies atop the great bluff, while on the narrow shore strip at the base of the 200-foot precipice are the wharves—not quite deserted yet, since steamboats can still carry cotton more cheaply than railways can. Around the wharves cluster the ancient brick houses of what is called "Natchez-Under-the-Hill"—once a roaring haunt of roystering boatmen, but now a squalid abode of niggers, occasional mills, and desolation. I spent two full days in Natchez, thoroughly absorbing its atmosphere and hating to leave it when the time came. Finally, however, I had to continue "down de ribber".

I suppose—from various references of yours—that you know Louisiana fairly well, hence will not waste space on needless descriptions. The first thing which struck me was that this state is flatter than the Mississippi bluff country, and that its soil is grey instead of yellow. I did not pause at Baton Rouge, for this town—the LA. state capital—has been disconcertingly modernised.* South of there the ground falls to river level and below—giving me my first glimpse of the vast levee system.

At length New Orleans was reached—and after settling down at a modest hostelry (the Orleans, at 728 St. Charles St., where I got a room and bath for $7.00 per wk.) I proceeded to explore the town and its environs. As you know, the cream of everything centres in the Vieux Carré or original Creole town—outside which the modern American town grew up. The great fire of 1788 destroyed nearly all of the old French houses, but the area was at once rebuilt—very solidly, and in a predominantly Hispanic style—with the aid of government engineers. It is this really Spanish town of arcaded, galleried brick houses with inner courtyards or patios which survives to this day, almost unchanged materially, as the "Vieux Carré" or "old French quarter". Really, it is a perfectly preserved 18th or early 19th century city, vying for architectural honours with Charleston and Quebec. In its day, of course, it has been a slum, and it is now slightly touched with the Greenwich-Village atmosphere—studios and antiques shops. For this reason it has not quite the utter charm of quiet Charleston and Quebec, which are still leading their simple old lives in unbroken organic continuity with the past. But for all that, it's a great old place. From having seen it, you can judge roughly what Charleston and Quebec look like. Imagine the old houses farther apart, with extensive outdoor walled gardens at one side instead of central patios, and you have Charleston. Cut out both the balconies and the walled gardens, and you have Quebec. I'm certainly having the time of my life drinking in the archaic col-

*The new skyscraper State House—semi-modernistic design—is an insufferable eyesore.

our and getting set on my feet by vitalising tropic warmth. My hotel—as its address reveals—is outside the Vieux Carré, but I spend each day in that centuried backwater—wandering through the narrow old streets with no modern impressions intruding upon me, and doing my reading and writing on a bench in the old Place d'Armes—Jackson Square—where the silver chimes of the old Spanish cathedral float on the air each quarter-hour.

I notice, by the way, that New Orleans is markedly subtropical in its vegetation—being well below the 30th parallel of latitude. The change from Natchez is very obvious; for whereas that town has only a few tiny scrub palmettos carefully nurtured in gardens, New Orleans teems with tall Washington palms and flourishing Brazilian date palms.

I'm here for over a week, and have seen the modern as well as the ancient city. I have also looked up such old plantation-houses as are near to (or engulfed by) the growing municipality. Of these country houses, as you probably know, there are two general types—the older Creole sort with steep slant roof and dormers, and the early 19th century American type, massive in proportions and of pillared classic-revival architecture. Both of these types can also be found in and around Natchez. In the N. O. region I have seen such surviving places as Ormond, d'Estretan, Three Oaks, the Westfeldt ho., and the decrepit and slum-encompassed Delord-Sarpy house.

From here I shall go to ancient Mobile, Alabama, and after that my plans will depend upon finances. I have a vary faint—and diminishing rather than increasing—hope of getting to Charleston, which is still my favourite among towns. In N.Y. I shall probably stop a week with my friend Samuel Loveman, and if I have any cash left I shall try to get up the Hudson to see Bernard Dwyer.

Speculations on historic might-have-beens are certainly interesting in the extreme, and I imagine you are largely right about the probable effect of a Mongol conquest of the Western world. Today the basically Mongol stocks which (of course after much admixture) are classed as white are the Finns (whose Mongol heritage is residual and not a matter of conquest), the Magyars of Hungary, and the Turks. The Finns and Magyars have done pretty well in the matter of civilisation, but the Turks—in spite of Mustapha Kemal—remain to prove their capacity for Europeanisation.

Yes—Alexandria was thoroughly Greek to the last—that is, till the Moslem invasion of the 7th century—and was indisputably the successor of Athens as the cultural centre of the Hellenistic world. In the Hellenistic era Athens itself was out of the running except as a centre of rhetorical scholarship, and Antioch was a soft, decadent place—never a serious contender for cultural honours. The one possible rival of Alexander was Pergamum on the coast of Asia Minor, which developed a marvellous culture under the Attalid sovereigns. Ptolemy Philadelphus was so concerned over the rivalry of Pergamum that he forbade the exportation of papyrus thither—thinking to cripple the literary growth of the rival in a basic material way. The Pergamenes, however, got around the difficulty by using sheepskin for writing—so that to this day their name survives in almost unrecognisably corrupted form in the word *parchment.* Syracuse had a high Greek culture, but remained subordinate to Alexandria—many Syracusan men of science and letters moving to the great Ptolemaic capital when they became famous. The Alexandrian era was really a great age—although it was of course critical and scholarly rather than creative. The Arabs, although they seemed to destroy this mellow culture, really absorbed a lot of it—and transmitted it to us across those Dark Ages in which we ourselves had relapsed largely into ignorant barbarism.

As for the cracked and ubiquitous Olson—Clark Ashton Smith has been hearing from him now. He is fairly frothing at the mouth over what he considers Smith's disrespectful treatment of vampires—who, he argues, are the saviours of the world because they take away the blood which forms the death of us all! Obviously, the poor fellow's epistles admit of no reply. All one can do is to let him keep on writing—which doubtless relieves his agitated and disordered emotions. This fellow Lumley, on the other hand, is a really fascinating character—in a way, a sort of thwarted poet. It is very hard to tell where his sense of fact begins to give way to imaginative embroidery—but I think he usually enlarges on some actual nucleus. He has, I imagine, really knocked about the world quite a bit—hence his dreams of visiting Nepal, darkest Africa, the interior of China, and so on. I fancy there is some old fellow corresponding to his idealised figure of "The Oriental Ancient"—perhaps an aged and talkative Chinese laundryman, or perhaps even some "Swami" of the sort now found in increasing numbers wherever the field for faddist-cult organisation seems promising. Providence, for example, has several of these swarthy Eastern ascetics nowadays. Lumley is naturally in touch with all sorts of freak cults from Rosicrucians to Theosophists. I surely hope he will finish his "City of Dim Faces", for anything written uncommercially—from the pure self-expression motive—is a welcome rarity nowadays. There is surely, as you say, a tremendous pathos in the case of those who clutch at unreality as a compensation for inadequate or uncongenial realities. The fortunate man is he who can take his phantasy lightly—getting a certain amount of kick from it, yet never actually believing in it—and thus being immune from the possibility of devastating disillusion.

Your remarks on southwestern cloud and sky effects interest me exceedingly, and I know that you must appreciate such things to the full—both their weirdly beautiful and their menacingly macabre examples. Sandstorms are something of which I have always read, yet which I have never witnessed. They must have a majesty and terror all their own—as I may learn some day at first hand if I am able to keep on with my present expanding travel programme.

Too bad the magazine field is getting curtailed—but that's the universal story in depression days. I hope *Weird Tales* will be able to carry on. It ought to if any weird magazine does, for it is the first and most deeply entrenched of all the periodicals in its field. A discreetly abridged Necronomicon, Black Book, or Book of Eibon might be quite a thing if one had the energy and inspiration to go on about it in the right way. Put me down for a copy if there is ever a fresh edition of *Unaussprechlichen Kulten!*

Certainly, the recent Hawaiian affair shows a most singular lowering of racial morale on the part of local American officialdom. In fact, I have heard it stated that the Hawaiian Islands are developing a kind of soft, easy-going, laissez-faire American type prone to accept all sort of exotic conditions complacently, and more resentful of Washington oversight than of internal disorder of even the gravest sort. If this is so, then the only logical government for the island territory is a strict naval or military administration with orders coming from the mainland. I don't think Oriental interests actually *control* things, for the bulk of money power is centred in large American fruit interests; but the Oriental *population* predominates, and lax officials like to cater to it for the sake of popularity and easy management. Surely, the situation is repugnant enough to any American of the older school, and I doubt if the present incident could be parallelled in continental America despite all the undeniable softening everywhere observable. Of course, in a Japanese war Hawaii would be the second objective of the enemy—the Philippines being the first. That the vast horde of Japanese-Hawaiians would aid their ancestral country is almost beyond dispute—and I imagine that American military authorities would take extreme precautions with them the moment such a conflict became really imminent.

As usual, your observations on the Southwest and its people interested me extremely. The occasional decadence of the pioneer stock which you note has its parallel everywhere in the U.S.—especially in Rhode Island, which as early as 1905 it was stated by an historian that the rural population of some of the western townships were lapsing into the "poor white" state. In the east this apparent decadence does not so much imply a *decay* of the biological stock as it implies a *sifting*—with the poorer elements unfortunately predominating on the original soil whilst the sounder main stream lives elsewhere—in cities or in the west. Undeniably, the New England old stock has become almost exclusively urban except when wealth sends it back to the soil on summer estates. What is left on the farms—with a few happy exceptions everywhere, and with many exceptions in Northern New England—is a distinctly shiftless and inferior strain. When the urban trend began around the 1850's it was always the more alert and competent who went to the city and founded urban families, while the weaker brothers stayed behind and bred an increasingly decadent posterity. Then when the foreigners began to invade the countryside the native's doom was sealed. French-Canadians, Poles, and Italians can extract from the soil (by virtue of their peasant heritage and low standard of living) a livelihood beyond the power of New-Englanders to obtain—so everything is slowly passing into their hands. But just the same it is a mistake to say that the old Yankee stock has gone to seed. It hasn't—but it *has* gone to the city and to the west. In its new habitats it will be found just as sound as ever, and still displaying many of the especial aptitudes for which it has always been traditionally distinguished.

Too bad so many of the poorer whites have drifted into the southwest. Their biological heritage probably antedates their advent to this continent, for they seem to represent the London gaol-scourings sent over as indentured servants and later liberated on the land when black labor became universal. We had some of these types in New England—especially a lot sent over to Boston around 1640. They formed the subject of considerable lugubrious correspondence between the governors of Plymouth and the Massachusetts Bay.

Your mention of "Pretty Boy" Floyd both surprised and interested me, since I did not know that any of the old-time desperadoes were left nowadays! Such gentry have obvious enough faults, yet even so they shew up very favourably beside the modern product—the slinking urban gangster of South-Italian derivation—that has usurped their title of "gunman"! It is curious to see how the zones of physical violence and non-violence shade into one another as the west and east meet. In the east, as I have said, Anglo-Saxons hardly know what physical conflict is like. They are bred to certain inhibitions of order which prove really effective, so that the occasional infractions always seem startling in their crudity and savagery. Basically, this is the result of the triumph of the urban, upper-class ideal of good manners and discipline—made possible by the fact that the native rough and ready element is in a minority, being supplanted by foreigners in the north and negroes in the south. The instinctive code which has survived, therefore, is that of the city and the manor-house—not that of the frontier. There has been a return to the ancestral European attitude—the attitude of an old and settled civilisation rather than that of a new country. Personal differences are generally marked merely by severed relations—and of course the provocations for such differences are infinitely lessened under a settled social order with a deep-seated and valid code of manners. Unceremonious violence, far from winning approval here, is almost a cause for ostracism among gentlemen—although of course the challenge to a formal duel served as a safety-valve until about 1840 or 1850. Sometimes I am half-inclined to regret the total disappearance of the duel, since the lack of an organised outlet for violated feelings often works much psychological harm, and leads to indirect, sneaking types of revenge. But of course certain exceptions to the rule of non-violence do exist here. Extreme types of insult always call for a well-directed fistic blow—although the use of any but Nature's weapons would be frowned upon.* And

*Again, with the exception of certain grievous cases of unredressed personal wrong in which the use of the pistol has its apologists.

naturally, no man is expected to receive a physical blow without replying vigorously in kind. In general, however, violence and the use of weapons are left to the foreigner in the east.

Now it is interesting to see where this code begins to change, and give way to the frontier code in which lightning-quick struggle of the old Homeric order has a place. In general, I think that the *third* zone of settlement—the region populated from around 1770 onward—is the first district where, going westward, one finds a disposition to frontier methods on the part of the better-grade native population. But in the northern part of this zone the tendency has been obliterated through the intensive Europeanism brought about by commercial prosperity. You won't find the primitive spirit in western New York State, Pennsylvania, Michigan, Wisconsin, or northern Ohio, Indiana, and Illinois, but you *will* in *southern* Ohio, Indiana, and Illinois, and in Kentucky, Tennessee, Mississippi, and possibly Alabama and western Georgia. Even in this zone, though, there is no early-Aryan battle spirit to compare with that of the southwest. Still—the frontier trend is unmistakable. In Natchez I met a young civil engineer from Kentucky who spoke of the degree of physical violence to which he is accustomed in various Anglo-Saxon milieux, and who regards himself as exceptional because he always goes unarmed. He is probably a very good representative of the transitional type—a type whose pioneer instincts of direct physical struggle with nature and enemies are not yet subconsciously obliterated by security and the codes of settled civilisations. We of the east have probably lost something through the obsolescence of the ready combative instinct. This obsolescence admirably fitted us for the law-abiding conditions of the 19th century Atlantic seaboard, but it counts against us when we are suddenly faced by primitive menaces such as that presented by Italian racketeering. It would also count against us in the case of a communist uprising. However, it would be less of a drawback if our social system were *really* as mature as that of the old world; for in England the enforcement of law is so relentless and effective as to cover almost any possible situation. What a drama there is in this constant struggle of two groups of instincts—the egoistic and individual, and the diffusive and social! The dramatic quality is especially brought out when one single racial-cultural group, like the Anglo-Saxon, is spread out so widely and diversely that its members are divided between different zones of instinct. In New York a couple of weeks ago Long took me to see a cinema which displayed the Western psychology of violence very vividly—a film called "Law & Order", with Walter Huston in the leading role.[3] I wondered how authentic a real Westerner would find it—and finally decided that it probably was not an exaggeration, melodramatic though it seemed at the given time and place.

The career of that Pennsylvania Irishman in the oil country certainly teems with both drama and pathos. The paregoric-fiend, also, must have been an interesting specimen. I agree with you that most cases of human disintegration are the result of gradual chance incidents—little things acting on a more or less weak hereditary fibre—rather than the product of sudden and overwhelming disasters. As for the chances of mishap, as very graphically outlined in one of your paragraphs, I am inclined to think that you overstress the picturesque force of adverse fate just a trifle. Actually, Nature is supremely impersonal. The cosmos is neither for nor against the tiny and momentary accident called organic life, and the still tinier and more momentary accident called mankind. What happens to man is simply the result of chance—his environment is perfectly neutral, and aims neither to harm nor to help him. The environment does not take man and his needs into consideration at all—it is wholly man's own outlook how well he can fit himself to the general, unchangeable environment, and how much he can change the immediate details of the environment to suit his needs more closely. Turning to your illustration—for every man who stubs his toe on the single rock in a 10-acre tract at night, there are a dozen or two men who cross the same tract under similar conditions without stubbing their toes at all. There are hundreds of weak spots in the ice of frozen rivers where no one happens to be injured—and the man who falls in at last may have narrowly escaped a dozen times before. With a chance of 17 roads and only one wrong, the vast majority of travellers *will indeed* get a right road. When, according to the laws of chance, some poor devil actually *does* take the one wrong road out of 17, he naturally remembers and emphasises the fact—for it is always the *exceptional* which sticks in our consciousness. The incident of the signboard which you cite would seem externally to argue some malignant ruling power—but as a matter of fact these occasional coincidences can hardly count as evidence. That sign would have fallen just the same even if no natty stranger had been walking under it. There are thousands of times when objects fall with no one under them, and thousands of times when they don't fall with people under them. Once in a while a rare combination of falling and person beneath will occur—but no general law is deducible from this. Such cases are extremely exceptional, their very rarity being an indication of their lack of significance.

The incident of your boyhood fight is extremely interesting psychologically. There would seem to be but little doubt that your anomalous and unexpected defeat was due wholly to the *divided* state of your mind—your acute consciousness of the audience and your deep subconscious desire to make a good impression upon it. This distracting element unquestionably sapped away something of the complete single-minded devotion to the immediate fight issue which generally brings victory to a combatant. All of you was not in the fight. But it must have been an exasperating event for you, none the less. Sorry the other boy met such an untimely end.

Your observations on the unreliability of the human senses confirm a principle long pointed out by historians and folklorists. As a matter of fact, it is only with great difficulty and through a large amount of comparison and coördination that we are able to get any sort of a dependable picture of the external world which stretches around us. The moment we rely on one-man evidence—however bona fide—we are lost. The best illustration of this sort of thing is the vast body of perfectly honest testimony in behalf of occult phenomena collected by serious students like Chevreuil and Flammarion.[4] On its face, this testimony regarding haunted houses, premonitions of death, supernatural visitations, etc. etc. would be more than enough to establish the occult as a truth of science—yet we know that it does nothing of the kind among conservative scholars. As a matter of fact, each soberly related incident involves some basic error of perception, or some inventive magnification in the course of narration and repetition—so that any one of them ultimately boils down either to a misrepresentation or misinterpretation of something which did occur, or to an unconscious exploitation of a folklore pattern involving the serious assertion of something which never occurred. But there are many who cannot and will not take this unreliability of the senses into account. Among such stubborn persons is our youthful colleague August W. Derleth, who persistently believes in telepathy and allied phenomena on evidence which no scientifically-minded thinker could accept for even a moment.

As for Wandrei's weird novel—"Dead Titans Waken"—it was finished some time ago, and I read it before departing on my trip. It is really powerful and excellent—especially in its later chapters—but I doubt if its chances of publication are very good. Wandrei has submitted it to several publishers with only negative results. This is just as bad a time in the book world as it is in the magazine world. Yes—there must be a good deal of fascination in the Minnesota milieu, although St. Paul and Minneapolis are probably too metropolitan to be very colourful. That whole northwestern region has a definite atmosphere all its own, so far as I can judge from the outside, with Scandinavian influences always perceptible outside the larger towns. Minnesota—the Dakotas—Montana . . . . . but beginning with Idaho another regional culture, more purely Anglo-Saxon, seems to begin; the Pacific Northwestern culture which centres in Washington and Oregon. I used to hear a good deal about Idaho at second hand, because my maternal grandfather—with whom I lived—was Pres. and Treas. of the Owyhee Land and Irrigation Co., which had a dam on the Snake River and dealt extensively in irrigated Idaho fruit lands. He often visited the Company's holdings in Idaho, and used to bring back specimens of minerals, etc. which made me feel very close to that distant realm.

Hope your rains have by this time abated. I've had marvellous luck with weather during this trip. Straight sunshine till day before yesterday—and even then the occasional rains didn't wet me because of the almost universally arcaded sidewalks of New Orleans' Vieux Carré. Glad that increased cultivation of land is ridding Texas of its worst sandstorms—yet they certainly must have been stupendously impressive phenomena in their heyday. Your description of one is a masterpiece of vividness.

Sorry your health has been giving you so much trouble, and hope you can somehow manage to get more exercise and outdoor air despite commercial exigencies. Can't you do more of your writing in the open, as I do? I've probably mentioned before that no fine summer afternoon ever finds me under a roof. Current work and reading all go into a black leatherette bag, and accompany me to whatever neighbouring woodland retreat I choose. Likewise when I am away—I always choose some picturesque park or other outdoor spot to do my reading and writing in. Here in New Orleans, as I mentioned before, my headquarters is ancient Jackson Square—where I am at the present moment. But as for health—I'm only just on my feet again myself. I was slowly recovering from my April cold when I hit New York, but there the unheated condition of Long's apartment house gave me a hell of a relapse. I used 33 handkerchiefs in the course of only a few days, and could not smell or taste a thing from May 23 until 3 days ago! All my southward trip—enjoyable as it was—was made under the most distressing nasal and bronchial conditions, with a steady headache accompaniment! But the warmth of New Orleans is baking the venom out of me, and I feel better each day.

About *quotations,* I am no authority at all, but have an impression that copyrighted matter requires permission *if the extract is of any substantial length.* I don't think that a line or two as a motto would require such a formality—yet here again I can't be absolutely sure. If the stuff *is* copyrighted, you may be sure that the proprietor of the copyright will be designated wherever the substantial extract occurs. Absence of such information would imply that the material is not copyrighted, and that you are free to use it. I never heard of the Am. Fiction Guild, but would be interested to know what it's like.

Yes—Dwyer's "Brooklyn Nights" is real poetry of a sort. It is the only thing that ever made me able to see Brooklyn in a favourable light! I hope to see "Sowers of the Thunder" sooner or later—when I get home.

And so it goes. Wish I could piece out my trip and get into the Lone Star State, but financial limitations are adamant.

Best wishes, and hope the summer will bring you perfect health.

Yrs most sincerely,

H P L

Notes

1. Though in New Orleans, HPL was still nearly 700 miles away from Cross Plains.

2. François-Auguste-René, vicomte de Chateaubriand (1768–1848), French author and diplomat, one of his country's first Romantic writers. A fragment of his unfinished Indian epic appeared as *Atala* (1801), the story of a Christian girl who has taken

a vow to remain a virgin but falls in love with a Natchez Indian, and who poisons herself to keep from breaking her vow.

3. *Law and Order* (Universal, 1932), directed by Edward L. Cahn; starring Walter Huston, Harry Carey, Ralph Ince, Walter Brennan, Andy Devine. The film involves a Wyatt Earp–type figure who cleans up the crime-ridden town of Tombstone, chiefly by killing many of its citizens.

4. L[éon Marie Martial] Chevreuil (1852–1939) *Proofs of the Spirit World (On ne meurt pas),* tr. Agnes Kendrick Gray (New York: E. P. Dutton, 1920). Camille Flammarion (1842–1925), French astronomer and author, served at the Paris Observatory and the Bureau of Longitudes, and in 1883 set up a private observatory at Juvisy (near Paris). He was noted chiefly as the author of popular books on astronomy, including *Popular Astronomy* (1880; tr. 1907) and *The Atmosphere* (1871; tr. 1873). His later studies were in psychical research, on which he wrote many works, among them *Death and Its Mystery* (3 vols., 1920–21; tr. 1921–23). HPL owned his book *Haunted Houses* (1924; *LL* 319).

[56] [ANS][1]

[Postmarked New Orleans, La.,
14 June 1932]

Thanks profoundly for your unexpected & happily inspired act of telegraphing Price my N.O. address. I knew he lived here, but couldn't find him in the telephone book or directory. He called me up as soon as your message arrived, & we spent 25½ hours in continuous conversation—from 9:30 p.m. Sunday to 11 p.m. Monday![2] He is a delightful chap, with an inexhaustible flow of pleasant & intelligent conversation. We discussed & argued on every conceivable topic under the sun. He now lives in the Vieux Carré, but is about to move to quieter quarters outside—since he needs to concentrate on his new programme of purely literary activity. Incidentally, he has a most enthusiastically high opinion of you & your work. He wants to get out to see you, but is too broke for extended travel just now. Last week he went to Chicago to talk over the literary situation with Farnsworth Wright. I expect to see Price again tonight. Around Thursday I shall be leaving for Mobile. Thanks again, & best wishes. Damnably sorry I can't extend my trip as far as Cross Plains. Sincerely yrs—

H P L

Notes

1. Front: Chartres Street in New Orleans.

2. See E. Hoffmann Price, "The Man Who Was Lovecraft" (1949), in *Lovecraft Remembered,* ed. Peter Cannon (Sauk City, WI: Arkham House, 1998), pp. 288–92, for Price's account of the visit.

[57] [ANS][1]

[Postmarked Richmond, Va.,
21 June 1932]

Greetings from the old Confederate capital—now full of flags & stalwart veterans having their annual reunion. On account of early enlistments, some are not beyond their early 80's. ¶ Stopped a day in old Mobile, & only 2 hrs. in Montgomery, & not at all in modern metropolitan Atlanta. I love old Richmond—boyhood home of Poe—& hate like the devil to move onward. No use talking, the South is the only large area remaining which still represents the old American civilisation. Next on my programme come Fredericksburg, Alexandria, Washington, & Annapolis—all familiar ground to me, yet always delightful to revisit. ¶ The card-writing session with Price lasted till 6:10 a.m., & the next night we sat discussing fiction till dawn. A great chap—hope he can get out to see you!

Regards—
H P L

[P.S.] Poe's mother is buried in this churchyard.

Notes

1 Front: Old St. John's Church [Broad and 25th Sts., Richmond, Va.].

[58] [TLS]

[13 July 1932]

Dear Mr. Lovecraft:

It is with the utmost humiliation that I begin this letter. It had long been my intention, since you first mentioned, a year or so ago, your intention of visiting New Orleans, it had been my intention, I say, to meet you there and bring you on out into Texas. I wanted to meet you, and to show you my native country. I intended buying an automobile, and being able to show you the whole state, as I might have remarked. But circumstances prevented it; the failure of certain banks, the crumpling of fiction markets, and other conditions reduced me suddenly to that penniless condition out of which I had begun slowly and painfully to climb. Far from buying an automobile, I found myself unable even to secure a saddle-pony. I say all this without shame, since I am in no way to blame, but bitter regret, since I was unable to carry out former plans for your entertainment. Nor is it my intention of burdening your ears with my troubles, but because I owe you an explanation for my failure to meet you in New Orleans. I realize now the truths of certain old adages. A wasted youth is not to be made up for by the most intense application and the hardest work of the more mature years. Still, as hope springs eternally etc., I still look forward to some dim time when I'll be able to entertain you on my native heath as royally as I wish.

I'm glad you and Price had an enjoyable time. I could hardly have ventured to intrude my crude ideas in such an intellectual discussion as I know your conversation was, but I would have enjoyed intensely sitting and listening. Price was much impressed with you, according to his letters to me, and remarked that he had benefitted much by your knowledge of literary workmanship. I would be interested in your reactions (I believe that's the phrase) toward him. As you probably know, I've never met him personally, though I have a high regard for him, both as a workman, through his work, and as an individual, reflecting from his letters to me. I believe he has a great future as an author before him. In his last letter he said that he'd be probably unable to visit me any time soon. I look forward to meeting him. I had to decline a recent invitation from Kirk Mashburn of Houston, who wished Price and me to spend a week-end with him. Houston might as well be Kabul as far as my chances of going there, even on excursion rates.

I thank you very much for the intriguing views you have sent me, and which go into my permanent files—likewise whetting my desire to see those places first-hand. Your vivid descriptions of the Southern terrain I have read and re-read, getting a clearer idea than I ever got from study of text-books. Somehow it comes to me with a feeling of strangeness and unreality, the realization that my ancestors climbed those mountains, rode through those valleys, drank from those rivers, and trod those streets. Only some eighty years ago men of my name left the river-plantations and pushed southwestward, and yet it is difficult for me to realize that my family had its roots anywhere but in the land where I was born and came to manhood. Among these post-oak-covered hills and mesquite-grown plains my instincts seem to place my ancestry for a thousand years. And my instinctive urge is westward, not eastward. I feel a strong longing to visit the Old South and to linger among its mellow beauties, but only as a visitor. The pull from the other direction is stronger. I can not go east permanently; when I am able to make a move from this dreary country, I must go westward—to the Big Bend, to New Mexico, or Arizona. This is not a conclusion reached by any logical reasoning process; it is a natural instinct with me. For centuries my people have pushed slowly westward. It is not in me to change that trend. But I strongly desire to see all the vast land that lies east of the Mississippi; and hope to see it some day.

Speaking of Mongol stocks, I notice the Finns seem to be somewhat devided among themselves, even to the point of violence. But as you say, they and the Hungarians have adapted themselves to western civilization surprizingly well for Mongolians. I think the backwardness of the Turks can be laid partly to the fact that they have always been more or less of a conquering caste, with the resultant intolerance of change, and distaste of manual work. They came out of the steppes, wandering, fighting nomads, who gained their living by following the flocks and plundering their fellow-man. They imposed their will on hordes of country-folk who did their work for them. The Turk has always scorned all labor but that of war. And what fighters they are! They are the one people whom decay and degeneration has not robbed of their pristine warlike heritage. History does not show a race, not even Roman or Spartan, which can boast of such consistent courage. Clean or depraved, honorable or degenerate, proud or besotted, the valor of the Turk has remained forever constant, as if it were a natural characteristic shining apart, untouched by the other characteristics of the man or the nation. I can not find an instance in which Turks showed the white feather. I intensely admire their high courage, and I hope to live to see the day when the Ottoman empire will be finally and completely swept out of existence.

I was, as always, much interested in your remarks concerning the classical world, of which I know so little. What a city Alexandria must have been! I had no idea of the origin of the word parchment. As I've said before, your letters are an actual education for me. Some day I must try to study the ancient Grecian world. Its always seemed so vague and unreal to me, in contrast to the roaring, brawling, drunken, bawdy chaos of the Middle Ages in which my instincts have always been fixed. When I go beyond the Middle Ages, my instincts veer to Assyria and Babylon, where again I seem to visualize a bloody, drunken, brawling, lecherous medley. My vague instincts towards classical Greece go no further than a dim impression of calm, serene white marble statues in a slumbering grove. Though I know the people of the classic times must have wenched and brawled and guzzled like any other people, but I can not conceive of them. The first mythology I ever read was that of Greece, but even then it seemed apart and impersonal, without the instinctive appeal I later found in Germanic mythology. Once I tried to write polished verse and prose with the classic touch, and my efforts were merely ridiculous, like Falstaff trying to don the mantle of Pindar.

I stopped writing this letter long enough to listen to the final session of the Democratic convention, which I've been following over the radio to the extent of staying up all night to listen to the—I believe it was the sixth session. I was pleased that Garner got the nomination for Vice-president; John deserved it, because it was his votes that swung the nomination of President for Roosevelt. Its well said John is for the people; I lived three years in Red River County where he was born, and anyone born there is bound to be of the people. No bloated capitalists there, not in those days, anyhow. A lady in Mission, near which Garner owns a good deal of land, told me last winter that many a time she's seen him out in the pastures burning stickers off prickly pears for his cattle during drouths. A homely touch that I appreciate highly, because that's all that kept the cattle in this section alive during the big drouth of '17 and '18. Of course my favorite candidate was Bill Murray of Oklahoma, but I knew he didnt have a chance from the start.

Bill Murray has more solid timber in him than any other man in American politics. A certain news-paper man spoke rather condescendingly of him, over the air. Let no man be decieved by the fact that Bill scorns the dapper dress and airy ways so much thought of by some people. Bill Murray has more real education than any other man in politics today, and enough sand in his craw to make the Sahara Desert look like a piker. Ealy of Massachusetts—or however his name is spelled—spoke of Al Smith as a second Jackson. Ye gods! If there's a man in the world today that remotely resembles old Hickory, its Bill Murray. I'm proud to have been born in the same county as he was.

Anyway, I reckon Tammany will learn finally that they can't shove Al Smith down the gullet of the Democratic party.

Referring to "Pretty-Boy" Floyd, he's still at large, as near as I can learn, having recently shot his way out of a trap where the police had him surrounded. Its rumored that he was in the farm-house in Missouri the night the Young brothers massacred those six officers, and I think it quite probable. You know the Youngs were cornered in Houston and killed themselves.[1] I dont think Floyd will go out that way. He'll probably be shot in the back by one of his own gang who wants the big reward.

I was much interested in your remarks concerning the various zones of physical violence, and was considerably surprized as well, to learn that certain sections of the country are comparatively free from violence. I supposed that men quarrelled and fought with fists and weapons about equally all over the nation. While I never travelled much, I've been thrown in with men from many countries and states, in the cosmopolitan oil fields, and I've found them about uniform in regard to aggressiveness and courage, regardless of where they come from. Some were quarrelsome and pugnacious, some were retiring and peace-loving, and it seemed to depend entirely on the individual. With this exception—I dont believe I ever saw an Oklahoman who wouldnt fight at the drop of a hat—and frequently drop the hat himself. But in general it seems to me, from my observation, that the average man is opposed to violence, except as a last resort, and disapproves of it largely, regardless of where he comes from. Of course, the world is full of bullies, who strut and swagger and impose on quiet people, and is also full of raw young fellows who feel their oats, and while perhaps are not actually vicious, are always looking for an opportunity of giving their physical prowess free rein. Understand, I am not questioning your remarks concerning the zoning of American violence. Recently I have studied statistics, since reading those remarks, which bear you out surprizingly well. I can not understand it, for I dont believe the average Southwesterner is possessed of any more real warlike instincts or courage than the average American wherever you find him. I leave the explanation to smarter men than I am. I was interested in your young Kentuckian. Many Kentuckians have come to Texas, and I know several personally—"blue-grass men", mostly. That state must be the bloodiest in the union. One of my friends is a relative to the McCoys, of the famous McCoy-Hatfield feud, and the tales he tells of even modern Kentucky, can scarcely be touched by anything in modern Texas, unless it be found in some of the more primitive border sections. Another was a government agent who spied on the moonshiners, and from what he says, there is, or was, at least, a distinct feud between the mountaineers and the blue-grass people. The old hostility between the people of the barren mountains, and the people of the fertile valley. He is an old man now, and conditions doubtless have changed. But it would stir your blood to hear his tales of raid and counter-raid, flight, pursuit, and the stark savagery of bloody battles in the hills.

Returning to violence in the Southwest. I have seen a good many fights and brawls, and more have gone on without my having witnessed them, all about me, all my life. Judging from the number of such affairs, it would seem the people of this country were unusually quarrelsome. Yet these fights and feuds were in the main carried on by a small minority of people who were forever quarrelling and fighting with each other. The majority of people went about their business and seldom resorted to any kind of violence. For instance, in a country school I attended, when about ten or eleven years of age, there was usually a fight going on on the grounds, any time you looked around, yet these scraps were almost invariably between a group of perhaps half-a-dozen boys, whose main object in life seemed to be the mutilating of each others' features. They fought each other and it was very rare that any of the rest of us ever had any trouble, either with them or with each other. And these fights seldom amounted to anything. The real blood flew when the trouble lay between persons who were not generally quarrelsome. It stands to reason that a boy or man who fights all the time doesnt expect to take his average scrap too seriously. There are exceptions to this rule, but they frequently die young.

For myself, I can say, truthfully, that, with one exception, I always did my best to avoid trouble of all kinds, and never fought unless a quarrel was deliberately forced on me, and I had to act in self-defense. There is a sordidity and bestiality in the average alley-fight that is bound to repel any man of ordinary sensitivity. A friendly go with the gloves is different, or a clean fight in the ring, with no hard feelings. That's good and healthy. But a tearing, gouging, biting, kicking dog-fight, down in the muck, with a dirty crowd yelling and cursing—that's neither cleanly nor decent. Though many a bully is in his element there. There's much of the actor in the average bully, and he must have his audience. I take notice that if you challenge him to come away from his gang, out in woods or fields with only the naked earth and the sky to watch, and none to cheer him on and none to tear your fingers from his throat if the fight goes against him, very often he will decline the invitation.

Most of the people I know are like me—they hate trouble and avoid it as much as possible. Yet it does seem that there is a great deal of quarreling and scrapping going on all the time. I attribute this in part to the great numbers of bullies in the world. They wont let a man alone. This was particularly true during the oil booms, of course. But the country at any time is too much infested by such bravoes. The average bully is a creature of great muscular power and feeble intelligence, whose main object in life seems to be the imposing of his presence on less belligerent people. He swaggers and brags and talks loud, scowls and swears and blusters; his conceit is monstrous and often takes the place of courage, bolstering him up to acts, the guts for which he would otherwise lack. He assumes that he is greatly feared, simply because the average man would rather give him the path, and let him bellow, than to get into a fight or some other kind of trouble. Because a man gets out of a skunk's way is no sign he is particularly afraid of the varmint. But the professional bully is a thorn in the flesh of decent men. Once let him get the idea that you are afraid of him, and he grows drunk with egotism, and starts riding you. He seldom has sense enough to know when he's gone far enough, and I've known men to be driven to momentary madness—and murder—by the continual abuse of such a character. Its one of the many injustices—if that's a proper word—of this country and system. A bully doesnt generally start picking on you unless he is your physical superior. And he usually has a gang behind him. There are three courses open to you, and each is abhorrent. You can swallow his insults and indignities until your very guts revolt; you can resent them, and get beaten into a pulp, with perhaps your ribs stamped in and your teeth kicked out after you're down and out; or you can kill the bastard and likely go into court and listen to his pals swear your life away. Rats rally to one another's defense much quicker than honest men rally to help one another.

There is one consolation to a peace-loving man; the average bully doesnt last many years. He gets shot up or cut up, or he gets on the wrong man and has the devil beaten and stamped out of him, and mends his ways—sometimes. I've seen bad men, semi-bad-men and would-be bad men come and go, and it was a bear-cat that lasted over ten years.

Talking about Red, whom I mentioned in a previous letter, got me to thinking about a fellow who was probably the worst man, for all-around toughness, that this part of the country ever produced. The oil field didnt bring him in—he was born and raised down in Brown county, some miles south of this place. Now I think of it, I believe he had a harder head than Red. In his palmy days I never heard of anyone daring to tackle him with anything less than a club or a gun-barrel. He was tall, lithe, slit-eyed, wore a sort of sardonic half-smile on his lips usually, and walked with the springy tread of a big cat. And he was all bad. He used to come into the boom-town joints with a six-shooter in his hand and advise the customers to hunt the floor, because he was going to start shooting waist-high and at random. But concerning the adamantine quality of his skull—I dont know how many knocks it withstood in the course of his lurid career, but I do know of the following incidents: in the boom days of Desdemona, he stuck his head into a gambling dive and instantly somebody wrapped a lead pipe around it, fracturing his skull; he was laid up for weeks, but recovered; the city marshall of Cross Plains had him down in the street one night, hammering his head with a gun-barrel, when one of his pals knocked the marshall kicking from behind, and the tough customer departed, apparently none the worse for the battering; the proprietor of a hotel in the same town struck him over the head with a pistol-barrel, knocking him down a whole flight of stairs; none of these taps seemed to worry him a great deal. But years of dissipation and wild living finally told on him. He drifted away into other oil fields, and when he came back to this country, he seemed but a hull of a man. Men who formerly feared him, pummelled him with impunity. And his aborted sense of humor brought more trouble on his long-suffering head. In a poker game, for a joke, he reached across the table and cut one of the players from his shoulder to the hip on the opposite side. It wasnt a deep cut, just through the skin, but it bled like a butchered steer. The victim, a former school-mate of mine, thought so little of the jest, that he procured a rock and hammered the joker's scalp into a beastly mess, before he could be pulled off. I didnt see the incident, but I saw the joker some days later and damned if he didnt look like the last rose of summer. His scalp—which he never had bandaged—had mostly healed, but the terrible mauling had somehow affected his arm, and his legs. He held his arm in an unnatural manner, and walked jerkily. I dont believe the fellow's head will stand many more beatings without his mind being affected. He seems to have vanished again—off to the East Texas fields, I imagine. The last time I talked with him—several years ago—he'd been up in the hills of Arkansas, and evidently got into a crowd too tough for him, even. He said those benighted Arkansawyers were not civilized, and that he considered himself lucky to have escaped with his life, leaving behind his entire bank-roll. By which I deduce that he won their money with the cards, and they took it back—and his too—at the point of a gun; a custom not unknown in the oil fields.

By the way, one night a few weeks ago I was wakened from sleep by the crash of a .44 and a terrible cry that marked the end of one of the town's toughest characters.[2] You have doubtless noticed the inhuman quality in the last cry of a man stricken by death. I dont know which is the more nerve-racking—the death-cry of a man, or the screams of a woman over her dead. This was a freak-shot, in a way; it was fired at close range, and it seems as if it should have torn the whole top of the victim's head off, but the bullet, crashing through the rim of the temple, rolled around the inner curve of the skull, cracking it like an egg, and lodged in the back part of the head. The man lived some fourteen or fifteen hours afterwards, with his brains oozing out, but of course he never recovered anything like consciousness—only his incredible vitality kept him alive that long. I had known him for years, but not as a friend. He hated me, but left me severely alone, and that's all I ever asked of any man.

As regards the mysterious workings of adverse chance in regard to man, stumping of toes, breaking of ice, falling of sign-boards, etc., that was mostly in jest, of course. The universe was a whole is undoubtedly indifferent to man's and his paltry wishes and ambitions. Though I am by no means certain that unseen and only dimly suspected forms of life and energy do not impinge upon us from Outside. The universe as a unit is indifferent to man, true; but it is full of material, visible beings not indifferent to him and his works—mosquitoes, jack-rabbits, man-eating tigers. They prey on him or furnish him sustenance as the case may be. I am not certain that there are not invisible beings and forms of matter, above or below our senses of discernment, which are not altogether oblivious or indifferent to mankind. This is no question of the supernatural; there may be beings and forms of life natural enough in their sphere and plane, yet still intangible to us.

Yet for accidents, it is true that certain people seem targets for accidents, because of some lack in their make-up—some lack of coordination, concentration, or reasoning faculty, perhaps. I knew a fellow once who was a good example of that. This person, a class-mate of my earlier days, had scars all over him from various blunders and mishaps. He had scars from machinery into which he had managed to get his fingers; scars gotten from whitling, sawing, and driving nails; one scar, I regret to say, he'd gotten from my knife. But mishaps seemed to dog him continually, and it was my honest conviction when I told him that he was doomed to perish early in life. Nor had he been out of school many years, when, having climbed into a tree to help free an aviator whose parachute had caught in the branches, he fell from an upper limb and landed headfirst. He weighed 212 pounds, and he never recovered consciousness.

I dont know what's come over Texas. Instead of drouths, we have floods. Right now all the western rivers are on the rampage; the Colorado, the Frio, the Guadalupe, the Nueces, the San Antonio, and all the others. At least nine lives have been lost, and the damage to property runs into the hundreds of thousands of dollars. Highways and railroads have been washed out, bridges washed away. And naturally, humanity couldnt be content with the damage the elements were doing, but they had to war on each other. Guns barked in the flooded district to the southwest and a soldier out of San Antonio got a slug through his heart. All up and down the flooded area survivors clinging to trees and house-tops were taken off by the rescuers. Most of the damage to property was in southwestern Texas, but the water was higher in this part of the woods than I've ever seen it. Judas, what a rain! It started raining about midnight, and along towards dawn it turned into what almost amounted to a cloud-burst. I've seen it rain in Louisiana and the East Texas blacklands, but I never saw such a rain—and this section was almost on the fringe of it, the main bulk falling west of here. All the creeks and rivers rose out of bank, and the Brown county lake, which was estimated would be two years in filling, was flooded over-night; 145 miles of shore-line, and mighty deep, too. That was four days ago, and still the water is gushing over the spill-way, in spite of the fact that all flood-gates are being kept wide open, to take care of the surplus. Two main streams run into the lake—the Pecan Bayou and the Jim Ned, and the water in both streams is backed up for miles. I never saw so much water in West Texas in all my life. A new high-way, recently built by Brown county at much expense, was simply cut to pieces. The farmers along those streams are ruined; their whole crops swept down to the Gulf. Particularly those above the new highway that crosses the Bayou. Against the urgent protests of these men, the highway engineers built a dump or levee across the river bottom, more than half a mile wide—supposed to keep the highway above water. To the assertions that the flood-gaps were not large enough to accomodate the water at high-tide, they merely laughed. What do farmers know about road-building and bridge-building? So this flood ripped their fine levee to shreds, rushed over it and washed the highway down the creek; and what is much worse, the remnants of the levee backed the water up and ruined hundreds of acres of grain which otherwise might have escaped destruction.[3]

That's a typical example of scientific misrule. What does a farmer, who has only lived on the bank of a stream fifty or sixty years, know in comparison to a dapper young engineer, who has been out of a technical college for at least six months? The tyranny of science is beginning to irk the people. I could mention numbers of incidents, not in civil engineering alone, in which blunders cloaked in the name of science have been imposed on the people, over-riding the protests of experience and common judgment. Scientific methods are being made a fad and a fetish. I have no quarrel with true science; but I would suggest that the devotees of science realize that there may be sound sense in men who never went to college and to whom the technical jargon may be sheer gibberish. We have made gods out of our scientists; but they have no right to practice their theories on us. They presume too much; a club properly applied might bring home a realization of the rights of humanity, even unlettered humanity, to whom science is a closed book, and who know only what their experiences have taught them.

Ah, well, if our leaders will give us back our booze I will quarrel with no one. My entrails have been insulted with so many damnable concoctions for so many years, that I fear I may have lost the ability to appreciate good liquor—though on my pilgrimages to Mexico I find that knack unimpaired so far. I shudder when I think of the stuff I've put into my innards. Looking back, I find that drinking, in this country at least, has been divided more or less definitely into various epochs, in each of which a different brand of poison and hell-fire dominated the thirsts of the people. Right after prohibition came in, everybody drank a tonic known as Force, which bore a picture on its label of Samson tearing the lion—and its effect was similar; they alternated this with another tonic known as Lyko. Then followed a fruit extract period, until the companies began bringing out extracts without alcoholic content. I still recall the fervent and sincere bitter blasphemies of staunch souls who had quaffed numbers of bottles of extracts, before discovering their non-alcoholic nature. Then came the boom-days of jamaica ginger, which exceeded all epochs before and since. I doubt not that even now the mad-houses are filled with the gibbering votaries of jake. Legislation interfered with jake, and the makers of white mule, red eye and rot-gut came into their own. Of course, these drinks had been interwoven in all the other periods. Alternating poisons were hair-tonics, wood-alcohol and canned heat. I've seen old soaks who apparently preferred canned heat to anything else. Then there were other tonics—Sherry Bitters, Padres Wine Elixir, Virginia Dare. Virginia Dare tastes the best—that is to say, a strong man can get it down by gagging and holding his nose. A friend of mine and I stood one rainy night in the lee of the Brown county library wall, and strove manfully to get down a bottle of Sherry Bitters. Seasoned though we were on rot-gut, we ended by throwing the bottle over the nearest fence and drifting away on the bosom of the great, silent, brooding night. Padres Wine Elixir was a favorite of mine in my younger and more unregenerate days. It is bottled in California, and is merely a cheap grade of red wine, with enough drugs in it to make it nominally a tonic. Those drugs change it from a mere low-grade wine to a demon-haunted liquor. It never hits you twice the same way, and will eventually affect your heart. Pay no attention to the amount of alcohol stamped on the label; it varies from bottle to bottle. I have drunk three bottles and gotten no more cockeyed than I have with half a bottle on another occasion. If you keep it cold it tastes slightly better, but when its hot it has a more lethal kick.

And yet, when I look back over a sordid past, I find that the worst liquor I ever got hold of bore the government seal and stamp. It was prescription liquor and cost, altogether, seven and a half dollars a pint; more, it purported to be sixteen years old. It knocked me blind and kicking, and if it hadnt been for nearly half a pint of Canadian rye whiskey I drank at the same time, I believe it would have wound my clock. The rye fought the poison in the other stuff. Separately, either might have finished me; together, one counteracted the other. Judas, will I ever forget that debauch! It was colder than hell, one Christmas. There were three of us playing seven-up by a fire in the woods. When the deuces began to look like aces, I called to mind the feat of Rob Roy's son in driving a dirk through a board, and forthwith stabbed at the box on which we were playing, with my hunting knife. But the box was much lighter than the Highlander's board, and knife and fist as well crashed clear through it, ruining the game. The liquor was at all of us, and one was clear wild. In the grip of the obvious hallucination that he was John L. Sullivan, he began to swing hay-makers at me whenever I reeled into reach. He was six feet two in height and as broad as a barn-door; besides, he had heavy cameo rings on each hand, and these rings sunk into my flesh unpleasantly. So I avoided him and sought to go elsewhere; I must have merely revolved about the glade, because eventually I found myself back near the fire, with my misguided friend grunting and swearing as he flailed his long arms about my ears. In desperation I caught him under the heart with my right and down he went. I remember pulling him out of the fire; and then for hours I remembered nothing, while I lay blind and senseless. But I remember the dawn that broke, cold, grey, leaden—full of retching, disgust and remorse. Uggh—those drab, brittle, grey woods! When we went to the town, we found the countryside in an uproar; for while we lay drunk, the "Santa Claus" gang that had looted Southwestern banks for more than a year, had swept into Cisco, 35 miles away and in an attempt to rob the main bank, had raved into a whole-sale gun-battle that strewed the streets with dead and wounded. Two or three of them had gotten away into the brush and posses were beating the hills for them. To invitations to join the man-hunt, my friends and I laughed hollowly; we were in no shape to even lift a gun to our shoulders, much less confront a band of desperate outlaws.[4]

Gad, the country buzzed like so many bees! The authorities sent south for the great Ranger captain Tom Hickman, and Gonzaullas—"Lone Wolf" Gonzaullas—"Trigger Finger" Gonzaullas—"Quick Action" Gonzaullas—hero of more touch-and-go gun-fights than I know, and already almost a mythical figure in the Southwest.[5] But they were not needed; the fugitives staggered in and gave themselves up—haggard shapes in torn and muddy garments, caked with blood from bullet-wounds. It was the end of the last great robber-gang of Texas. Let me see; it was three—no, four years ago. It doesnt seem that long. All the Southwest rang with the news. Their names were on all men's tongues. Now I doubt not they are completely forgotten, except by the kin of the men they slew, except by the men who carry the scars of their bullets. Helms, the leader, went to the chair, roaring and cursing blasphemies, fighting against his doom so terribly that the onlookers stood appalled. Hill, the boy whose life was twisted and ruined in his boyhood when a ghastly blunder consigned him to a reformatory instead of the orphanage to which he should have been sent—he is serving a life sentence in the penitentiary, after an escape and a recapture. Blackie, the sardonic jester, dying with a rifle-bullet through him, gasped the names of respectable business men of Wichita Falls as his pals and accomplices, for a last grim jest. Ratcliff, who entered the bank clad in a Santa Claus robe and whiskers to avoid suspicion, feigned madness, killed his jailer, was shot down as he sought to escape by the jailer's daughter, and that night a mob tore him, wounded as he was, from his bunk, and strung him up to a near-by tree, to sway in the shrieking blizzard. Eh—life is a strange fierce thing.

Yesterday I spent most of the day in the flooded district south of here. In that flood, the worst ever experienced in Central West Texas, the devastation to crops and fields has been almost beyond belief. Along the rivers and creeks, the trees for miles are festooned with grain hanging to the stems and branches like Spanish moss. Thousands of bushels of wheat and oats were in the shock, having been cut but not thrashed, and the flood swept it all away. Fences were torn up for miles and washed clean out of sight, or left tangled among trees along the banks. I dont know how many cattle and horses were drowned. The most impressive sight, however, was the Brown County lake. I can not describe the sensations of seeing that gigantic body of water where for so many years I have been accustomed to seeing dry-creek beds, or semi-dry creeks, winding among arid post-oak ridges. It has changed the whole aspect of the country-side. Where fields parched and baked under a dry sun, now vast marshes stretch out. Hills have become islands and peninsulas. Where bridges and ranch-houses stood, water eighty feet deep ripples instead. It is so strange, seeing a big body of water in the midst of this drouth-haunted country of post-oak hills. Where the water is ninety feet deep now, I have seen cattle stagger and fall and and perish from thirst. I have seen whirlwinds of dust ripping among the withered mesquite where now the water stretches from brim to brim. It is but the work of men, who stretched a dam between the hills, yet it seems like a miracle. And more so when one recollects that it literally filled itself over-night. 145 miles of shore-line—and one torrential rain filled and overflowed it. For days the flood-gates have been left wide open, and still all the rivers leading into the lakes are backed upstream for miles. It is the greatest project ever put forward in this part of the country. If times ever pick up again, and men can take up work where they left off, that lake will make the surrounding country blossom like a rose. You can grow almost anything in this country if you have the water. Irrigation ditches will provide that, and from putting in huge fields of grain and cotton, people about the lake will begin the surer and in the long run, more remunerative, practise of intensive farming—raising vegetables [and] the like on smaller, well-watered patches. Intensive stock-farming will follow, and blooded cattle will replace the scrubs that now swarm the hills—though these have been steadily replaced, in many cases, with purer Herefords. Then the lake will become a pleasure-center; casinos, and places of amusement will grow up along the shore. Men will come there to hunt and fish; for in the shallow, warm marshes, fish will breed and spawn by the millions, and water-birds will come up from the gulf to prey on them.

Just now there is a great deal of resentment among the farmers and stockmen who live up the rivers, who consider the dam the main reason for their ruin in the flood, though in reality much of the damage would have been done, dam nor not. But they should be paid for their fields along the rivers, for with the lake full, any kind of a rise will back the water up over these fields again. There is much hard feeling, and talk of guarding the dam against possible dynamiting. Though I hardly think anyone would be mad enough to do such a thing. The town of Brownwood lies directly below the dam, only ten miles away, and should the dam burst, the havoc wrought there could hardly be conceived.

I'll bet, if prohibition still continues in force, that the moonshiners and bootleggers will swarm about the shores, because the whole lake is surrounded by rugged hills covered with dense thickets, and arms of the lake run up into gorges and inlets where boats of contraband could be concealed. I look for stirring times—and in the amusement centers along the shore, too, when the hill-people come down and get their first look at them. A little liquor to liven things up, and the knives are likely to start humming. If things pick up, some of my friends and I intend to put us up a shack on the lake-shore, in some more or less isolated spot, where we can fish, swim and drink without interference; I know of several good spots. I went over the ground and picked them out before the dam was completed.

An old custom is being revived this year—a two-days "picnic", with, no doubt, the usual attendant rodeo and carnival. Why they want to have the thing, with everybody broke, is more than I can see. Besides, the nerves of the people are on edge, their dispositions are bad, and theres likely to be trouble. There are usually a number of fights; some of the swiftest battles I've ever seen took place at these picnics. I havent attended these festivals very much for years, because I dont like trouble. However, I think I'll attend the political speeches this time.

Tom Blanton and Joe Jones are running against each other for congress, and they've had several clashes already. Tom called Joe a liar over at Cisco the other day, and they had to hold Joe's old man off him, I heard. I'm hoping they'll tangle at the picnic; but I havent much expectation. Politicians fight better with their mouths than with their fists. Then I hear a fighter is going to be imported to meet one of the local sluggers, and I want to see that. However it goes, I'll bet it ends in a free-for-all battle.

I was much taken with Wandrei's recent poem, "The Little Gods Wait".[6] It had a distinctly Celtic flavor; so much so that I would not have believed that anyone besides an Irishman could have written it. I have always highly admired Wandrei's work, and I believe I like that poem better than anything else of his I ever read. I have not yet read the latest Weird Tales, but can tell that Smith, and Derleth and Schorer, and of course, Price, have written splendidly. I deduce this by simply glancing over the pages. But I am always disappointed in not finding one of your stories in the magazine. I hope something of yours appears soon.

The revived question of prohibition has roused in my mind a question I've intended to ask you for some time; why, when the Saxons and Normans were of practically the same race, should they have differed so greatly in the matter of temperance? On the eve of the battle of Hastings we find the Normans passing the time in pious devotions and meditations, while the Saxons revel and feast and guzzle. Again, studying the customs of those ages, we find the Saxons heaping their boards with whole roasted hogs and oxen, eating and drinking enormously; while the Normans, while their meals consisted of many courses of food prepared in many fanciful ways—gilded meats, pastries carved in the shapes of castles, etc.—ate sparingly and were temperate in their drinking. Did they take up these ways from the neighboring French, or inherit them from their Scandinavian ancestors? On the other hand, the Saxons maintained that gluttony and drunkeness were introduced into England by the Danes—possibly by the followers of that Danish king—Harthaknut, I believe, who, like Alexander, drank himself to death, while toasting the guests of a wedding. The Danes always had a reputation for gluttony. Surely the Norsemen were not otherwise. Longfellow says of Olaf the Christian, that at banquets he was, "first to come and last to go,"[7] yet from other, and possibly more accurate sources, I hear that this same monarch detested over-indulgence, so that when one of his nobles over-ate, he compelled him to play the part of the fox, in the somewhat childish games of which Olaf was fond, and be pursued over the hills by the yelping nobles who enacted the role of the hounds. So the varying tastes of the Saxons and Normans remain a mystery, as far as I'm concerned. Can you throw any light on it?

I enclose a clipping concerning Japanese ambitions. I am no economist nor politician, yet I can not but feel that the western peoples do not attach proper importance to the powers rising in the East. My studies of history show that such has always been the case; blinded by their own affairs, the people of the west have ignored the hordes of Atilla, Tamerlane, Genghis Khan, Baibars, until those hordes were hammering their armies into bits. Now they ignore Tatar-Russia and Japan. The bodies have hardly rotted in Chapei, yet already Europe and America seem to have forgotten the incident. I can not but feel that European policies and squabbles are thread-bare and outworn; while the people wrangle, they are blind to the powers rising in the East that may some day overwhelm them.

I wish you were here to study folk-ways in the forthcoming picnic. I understand Jim Ferguson, our ex-impeached-governor, is going to speak in favor of his wife, who's running again for governor, having held that office once, herself; there's always fireworks when Jim speaks. In fact, I look for brisk times. Still and all, I repeat, I doubt the wisdom of holding this festival. Bad times and bad liquor; people dont give much of a damn whether they live or die; anything's likely to set them off. Knives may be out before the celebration's over. But I doubt if affairs reach the hilarious state of the cock-fight gatherings down along Pecan Bayou in the Holloway Mountains to the south. When the hill-country sportsmen gather to match their respective fighting roosters, its no place for a peaceful man. At these gatherings both blood and red licker have flooded freely, and the clashing of the gaffs have mingled with the rattle of sixshooters, knives, and brass knuckles. When you visit me, we'll try to take in one of these shebangs. The new Brown county road runs through a gap in the Holloways, though, and I reckon the country is going to get civilized past all interest. A lot of the old-timers have moved on up the creek.

I'm sorry to hear that your health hasnt been all it should, and hope it hasnt interfered with the enjoyment of your trip. Personally, I cant enjoy anything when I'm sick. I hope you've fully recovered by this time. I certainly envy you the magnificent journey you will have completed by the time you receive this letter, and hope next time you'll be able to extend your trip further westward. There's a weary lot of Texas that isnt at all interesting to a stranger, but there is also much that is fascinating. And of course New Mexico and the West are full of magnificent scenes.

Well, I've inflicted my aimless maunderings on you long enough; thanks again for the fine views, and I hope when next you ride westward, things will be better.

Most cordially yours,

Notes

1. Harry and Jennings Young fatally shot one another when trapped in a house by Houston police on 5 January 1932. They were wanted for killing six peace officers who had attempted to arrest Harry at a farm near Springfield, Missouri, on 2 January.
2. This is probably a reference to the killing of Arch Davidson on 11 June 1932 by cafe owner Walt Farrow. Farrow claimed self-defense: he said the Davidson brothers had created a disturbance in his cafe two weeks earlier, and the afternoon of the shooting he had ejected two of the Davidsons for causing another. He claimed that when Archie Davidson entered the cafe, "he looked like a wild man and I thought he was coming over the counter at me." He was convicted of "murder without malice" and given a suspended three-year jail sentence.
3. On 10 January 1931, work began on an earthen dam to impound a reservoir at the confluence of Pecan Bayou and Jim Ned Creek, just north of the city of Brownwood. It was estimated that, at the average annual rainfall for the area (25.9 inches annually), it would take three years to fill the reservoir. Around 20 June 1932, however, a low-pressure area stalled over the Hill Country of central Texas, resulting in record rainfall and serious flooding, as REH reports. A soldier from Randolph Field was shot 3 July at a filling station on the Laredo highway, at a point where a number of motorists were marooned by the high water. On the night of 3 July, torrential rains flooded both Pecan Bayou and Jim Ned Creek, with peak inflows into the newly created reservoir estimated at 235,000 cubic feet per second. The basin was filled to 150,000 acre-feet, covering more than 7,000 acres of land, in about six hours. REH's story "Wild Water" is based on this event.
4. The "Santa Claus Bank Robbery" took place 23 December 1927, so called from the fact that Marshall Ratliff, the leader of the gang, wore a Santa Claus suit during the robbery of the First National Bank in Cisco, Texas, just over 20 miles from Cross Plains.

5. Manuel Trazazas ("Lone Wolf") Gonzaullas (1891–1977) served as a Mexican army major at age 20, worked five years for the U.S. Treasury Department, and joined the Texas Rangers in 1920. During the 1920s and '30s, he enforced the law in the oil fields and on the border, pursuing bootleggers, gamblers, and drug runners alone.

6. Donald Wandrei, "The Little Gods Wait" (*WT*, July 1932).

7. Henry Wadsworth Longfellow, *Tales of a Wayside Inn* (1863), "The Musician's Tale: The Saga of King Olaf: II. King Olaf's Return," l. 72.

[59] [AH 17.11; *SL*555]

On the cliffs of old Newport—
Overlooking the boundless Atlantic.
July 25, 1932

Dear R E H:—

This reply to your admirably interesting and generously proportioned letter of the 13th is undoubtedly going to be wretchedly inadequate, since I have lately been under a severe nervous strain. I am sure, however, that you can excuse the fault in view of the circumstances. Toward the end of my long trip—as I was paying a final visit in Brooklyn—I was summoned home by a telegram of my elder aunt (age 76), long a semi-invalid, but the presiding genius and animating spirit of 10 Barnes St.[1] Arriving on the same day, I found the patient semi-conscious—and peaceful death occurred on July 3d. The resulting vacancy in the household is easy to imagine, and I can hardly adjust myself to the unwelcome change. Meanwhile there has remained the melancholy task of distributing my aunt's furniture, pictures, bric-a-brac, papers, books, and other effects (for she had an unfurnished room, just as I have, being in no health to keep house), so that the nerves of my younger aunt and myself (all that remain of the family) are worn almost to exhaustion.

This week—my surviving aunt being on Cape Cod on a tour of recuperation—I am taking advantage of the low steamboat rates caused by a clash of rival companies, and am sailing to ancient and picturesque Newport almost every day; picking up nearly as deep a tan as I acquired in Florida last year. The trip down green-shored Narragansett Bay is exquisite, while the old town itself is ineffably fascinating. Narrow, winding hill streets, tangles of gambrel and peaked roofs dating back to 1673, 1698, 1720, 1730, etc. etc., white steepled church of 1726, colony-house of 1739, classic library of 1749, city hall of 1760, Jewish synagogue of 1763—and so on. This was the greatest seat of culture in the north prior to the Revolution, and was visited by Dean Berkeley is 1729–32. He built a house called "Whitehall" (still in good shape) in the suburbs, and used it to sit on the great cliffs to read and write. In the decade 1760–70 Providence outstripped it as a commercial centre, and the Revolution ended its prosperity. Accordingly it still retains the houses and general physical aspect which it possessed about the revolutionary period—a veritable "Vieux Carré" of the North. I am always fond of visiting Newport, and with this 50¢ round trip rate (giving 6½ hours in the town) I am getting my fill—always taking along my current reading and writing, and working on the cliffs as old Berkeley did two centuries ago. Just now there isn't a thing but air and water between me and Spain. To the northeast, though, is the green Sachmesh peninsula, crowned by the magnificent Gothic tower (by Ralph Adams Cram)[2] surmounting the chapel of St. George's school. A glorious day—and I really hate to start for home!

There's certainly no need to apologise for not shewing Texas to me! Hades—but if you came to Rhode Island I couldn't do more than guide you around on the public conveyances . . . . which, by the way, I profoundly hope I'll have a chance to do sooner or later. If I'd had more cash myself, I'd have travelled into Texas anyhow—but necessity made me stick to a straight line, or something very like it. I do hope to see Texas some day.

Price proved delightful, and I am surely indebted to you for putting him in touch with me. He is a dark, handsome, rather small, wiry man of 34, with a small moustache, pleasant expression, and fluent, voluble, and musical speech. His affability and friendliness are tremendous, and our three sessions lasted respectively *25½,* 10, and 9 hours each. He is a model of intelligence and versatility—West Pointer, war veteran, Arabic student, Persian rug connoisseur, chess expert, fencing-master, abstruse mathematician, amateur coppersmith and ironworker—and what not! All in addition to his writing talent. He lost his job with the Prestolite Co. on May 1st, and has since been trying to adopt authorship as a sole source of income. That means a hard, uphill climb, and a considerable sacrifice of original creativeness to the idols of the market-place; but with his acute constructive intelligence I think he has excellent chances of success. Glad he found my suggestions useful. He has the most intense admiration for you and your work and regrets prodigiously the financial circumstances which have so far kept him from meeting you. Some day I hope that you, he, and Mashburn can have a long triangular conference.

Glad you enjoyed the views of old Southern towns, and surely hope you can visit the regions in question some day. There is always a deep and poignant satisfaction in visiting ancestral soil, and you would undoubtedly take delight in tracing your lineage backward through geography—first the great columned houses of the lower Mississippi region, settled in the early 1800's, and then the more ancient tidewater zone of Georgia and the Carolinas, where the earliest seeds of far Southern life were sown in the 17th and early 18th centuries. But I suppose the pull of your immediate personal environment is strongest of all, so that the real lure lies westward. I, on the other hand, have never left the region settled by my ancestors from 1630 onward; hence can't visualise the west as an actual reality. Around here there are too many memories of when the Connecticut River was the frontier, and when outposts like Deerfield and Haverhill were in constant peril of raids from the

French and Indians. The places I love to visit are the old places, and the land to which my imagination strays is Old England with her ivied towers, gabled villages, and parish countryside containing the bones of my forefathers.

We are precisely opposite in our reactions to the classic Graeco-Roman world, for it seems to me the *only* real and understandable period in history except the present. The Middle Ages, and the early Oriental cultures, seem very vague and unreal to me. The Greeks and Romans were, in the main, wholly modern in spirit. All that we are, except for certain impulses of Teutono-Celtic pride and mysticism, we draw from Greece and Rome. The Greek was an alert, intelligent, appreciative type of man; fond of argument and intensely proud of his tradition. He had the failings common to all men, though restrained from many extravagances by his innate taste and sense of proportion. His great virtue was his profound rationality; his great vice a tendency toward trickiness. He was a natural philosopher and scientist, and probably represents the highest biological organism developed on this planet. Under Roman rule he sank to humiliating depths of sycophancy and satellitism, becoming only a caricature of his former independent self. The name "Graeculus", or "Little Greek", became a term of contempt among the Romans from about the time of the Augustan age. Probably you wouldn't care for the Greeks extensively, since they were above all things urban and sophisticatedly civilised. They did not (after the Achaean or Homeric element had become absorbed in the Dorian (native Minoan) population) care for fighting on its own account, although they were conspicuously brave in battle whenever their civilisation and liberty were menaced—that is, until their decadent days after Roman conquest. They lacked political good sense, and always remained divided and mutually hostile city-states except for the brief period when Alexander welded together an Hellenistic Empire. Read the tragic writers Aeschylus, Sophocles, and Euripides, the comic dramatist Aristophanes, the historian Thucydides, and a few other representative classics (good translations are always available) in order to get a comprehensible "inside" picture of the Greek mind. The Roman differed widely from the Greek. He was cruder, more practical, less intellectual, subtle, sensitive, and aesthetic. He had a strong moral sense absent from the Greek, and a love of power for its own sake—plus a positive genius for order and organisation. He was less urban than the Greek, and made more of the country-gentleman type of life. He had a strict honesty not common among the rank and file of Greeks, but was deficient in humour. In war he was utterly bold and dominant—without fear and bent on sweeping all before him—though acting more from an intelligent desire to conquer than from the blind, joyous battle-impulses of our own Northern ancestors. Common life among the Romans was even more orderly than among the Greeks. Vice, though less frequent, was cruder and coarser. The Roman was more demonstrative in speech and gesture than is commonly supposed; though never as much so as the Greek. Contact with Greece softened the manners of the Romans, and gave them many of the rational, artistic, and cultivated characteristics of the Greeks themselves. At the same time this contact communicated many bad features, so that the fashionable vicious element acquired coarser habits of depravity than the Greeks had ever had. The old race-stock began to be vitiated by immigration and military colonisation as early as the 1st century B.C., and (according to the physiognomical evidence of realistic portrait busts) was thoroughly mongrelised by the 2nd or 3d century A.D. After the conquests of the Teutons in the 5th century A.D. and afterward, the "Romans" acquired a decadence not unlike that of the Greeks under the Roman rule, though less marked by tricky sycophancy and civility. It must be remembered, however, that these decadent "Romans" were not of the blood of Scipio and Caesar. In effect, they were the modern "wops" we know with such doubtful admiration.

Later—on the boat going home.

Penmanship is a bit shaky under the conditions imposed by navigation—but here goes for an attempt. I heard some of the Dem. convention speeches over the radio while in Brooklyn, but did not find them much different from the usual irrelevant campaign hokum. I imagine that Garner must be a very attractive character, and hope he gets the Vice-Presidency; although all parties are really irrelevant so far as the needs of the future are concerned. The blindness of conservatives to the coming social changes is appalling and incredible—they ought to read Randall's "Our Changing Civilisation" or Briffault's "Breakdown"—but one may hope that they will take a more analytical attitude before it is too late and a revolution of some sort is upon us. It probably matters very little what set of candidates gets in the White House next year—but one may hope the winners will be to some extent disposed to view realities and give archaic slogans a rest. Of Hoover and Roosevelt, I think the latter is preferable by at least a small margin; though he has his weaknesses.

I saw an item about Pretty Boy Floyd the other day, and recalled your mention of him. He surely is a breath from the past—and a far cry from the urban gunmen of today.

As for violence—it is certainly not common among the settled native population of modern England the Eastern U.S. The foreigners give us plenty, but not the Anglo-Saxon stock. Violence among modern Anglo-Saxons seems to occur only in regions of relatively new settlement (or where the traditions of new settlement are for some reason prolonged), or among the members of certain itinerant classes of physical workers—such as lumbermen, fishermen, etc. In regions of long settlement the various elements of a community are adjusted to one another through a course of age-long adaptations, so that occasions of mutual encroachment become rarer and rarer. People learn forbearance and order through the forces of custom, so that each has a profound innate sense of what forms his proper sphere of action, and what forms unjustifiable encroachment. Order being a deep Anglo-Saxon ideal, these tacit boundaries are taken for granted as important things, and the forces of government are expected to back up their maintenance. When government fails to fulfil this function—as in Chicago—criticism is always widespread. Such are the habits of mature Anglo-Saxons in the older regions, that relatively few occasions for mutual encroachment ever occur—hence there is no urge toward pugnacity. You can easily see that a race of urban dwellers, each with a specific function, is not likely to develop the causes of conflict which arise on a frontier of wide spaces, flexible occupations, and insufficient police protection. And the same holds good for a long-settled farming population such as New England used to have. Remember that the East *never had* a "pioneer" stage properly so-called. As I told you some time ago, the peopling of this region was so *thick* and *rapid* that it was in effect a bodily transfer of a bit of old England, with all of old England's settled ways and instinctive sense of order. Of course there has always been brawling among the lower classes, but this was generally of a mild, half good-natured order—and conducted with fists only. Now, of course, we have almost no native lower class; since all the menial functions are performed by foreigners in the north and niggers in the south. The "poor white" element of course brawls—but that is hardly reckoned a part of organised society. In New England a crime of violence by an American is so rare as always to command a front-page newspaper spread—while a double murder and suicide among the dagoes often gets only a single column on an inside page. All this, of course, refers to pre-war normal times. In these desperate days robberies and holdups by natives have shewn some increase—and *crimes passionels* are frequent. But on the whole, the Easterner of the old stock rarely has anything to do with violence. No person of my acquaintance has ever witnessed a death by intentional violence except in war. It is all a matter of deep psychological instinct—of ideology, as the modern sociologists would express it. For example—in the east a typical mining-camp bully would instinctively inspire two dominant emotions—ridicule, and a sense that the fellow ought to be locked up as a maniac. If a man started to shoot up a saloon in Boston or Providence, some one would tell a policeman, who in turn would telephone to the station from a corner box and bring four to six uniformed men in a fast motor patrol car. They would rush the maniac, probably using their guns, and quickly get him into the patrol and in a cell. Then he would be examined for sanity, tried, and placed either in an asylum or jail. The idea of allowing such a person at large would never enter anyone's head—and with the evidence at hand, no amount of pull could get him off . . . . except in certain cities at certain periods, and even then only if he belonged to certain gangs in with the police. Any person is absolutely safe on any central street of any Eastern city at any hour of the day or night, except for the relatively rare activities of motor bandits—who, moreover, never molest anybody save the known custodians of payrolls. In the thinly settled suburbs, of course, thugs and footpads are more numerous—but all these crooks are mainly Italians. It is notable that nearly all the little violence there is in the east is connected with crimes against property. Aside from the playful antics of college youths, there seems to be no motive for fighting except the unlawful seizure of property. Reprisal is always left to the law—for the simple reason that the law can always get better results than private agencies can. If our legal and police system were less effective that it is, there would undoubtedly be another story. By the same token, Canada and Great Britain, whose legal system is superior to ours, have even less violence than we. I have never seen a fight among adults, and probably never shall unless I get a chance to explore the west or live to see a social revolution. That is why the surviving pioneer conditions west of the Alleghenies and the Mississippi seem so exotic and glamourous to us here—because they correspond to absolutely nothing in our experience or even ancestral memories short of the robust Elizabethan age. I think the sense of innate law and order became universal among settled Anglo-Saxons toward the second quarter of the 17th century. The Puritan ideal had something to do with it, and the age of the Commonwealth clinched it at home. Over here, the widely spreading influence of the Puritan colonists played its part. Brawlers were whipped, dunked, and put in the stocks until they felt more pacific-minded. Undoubtedly the regions of Puritan settlement were freer of violence from the start than those to which this influence filtered at a later date. Another reason why brawling was always rare in the east is that we were almost always at war. Any excess energy of ours found vent against the French and Indians.

I note your observations on chance, and on the possible invisible but sentient influences operating from "Outside". Certainly, there is no proof that such entities do *not* exist—and for the purposes of fiction I am glad enough to acknowledge them . . . . from Tsathoggua to Cthulhu, and Kathulos to Yog-Sothoth! But in sober fact, there is not a particle of evidence to indicate that they *do* exist; hence it is rather fantastic and gratuitous to assume that they do. There is no evidence of their action, so why think that they are there? That goes likewise for all gods from Baal to Buddha and Jove to Jehovah.

I certainly hope your floods won't do any more damage than they've already done. It is surely singular for them to come when drought is expected. The filling of the new reservoir-lakes must have been ineffably impressive. In the east many reservoirs for city water supplies have been made in their way, but I don't recall any case of such sudden filling.[3] The new body of water will surely make a vast difference in the region, and I hope all your plans regarding it will mature successfully. Sorry the engineers made such a miscalculation about the new levee—but one really ought not to blame *science*. That was not *science* but merely narrow *technology*. True science weighs all the evidence at hand, and is always ready to modify its conclusions if any well-authenticated body of data points in a new direction. Folklore and tradition are always carefully studied, so that there is small chance of the 'wisdom of the Elders' going to waste. What sometimes messes up modern life is not *science,* but a narrow spirit of pragmatic technology which forms a psychological offshoot of a mechanical civilisation.

Your reminiscences of alcoholic vicissitudes are certainly colourful in the extreme—especially that of the Christmas party which coincided so infelicitously with the bandit raid. For my part, I've never been able to figure out why people seem to find artificial paradise of alcoholic excitation so necessary to their happiness. I'm 42—or will be next month—and have never touched alcoholic liquor in any form . . . . nor do I ever intend to do so. And yet I don't feel any dearth of colour or interest in the world around. My imagination seems to work in a fairly satisfying way without the aid of external impetus. I don't see anything at all graceful or attractive about the phenomenon of drunkenness, but on the other hand see in it considerable of an obstacle to the efficient administration of society. I was a prohibitionist until I saw that the law was not working, and I would be again if I thought there were any feasible way of really discouraging the habit of alcohol-drinking. As for the relative moderation of the Normans as compared with other Teutonic tribes—there is no question but that the cause was their assimilation of Latin civilisation in Gaul. Our forefathers were a gluttonous and bibulous lot, and exceptions like Olaf only emphasise the condition. What really civilised us was the coming of the Norman, who brought us again in touch with the orderly and cultivated heritage of Rome. But for the conquest our civilization would have been of slower growth—like that of the Germans and the Scandinavians. As it is, we are on the dividing line between the nations of direct Latin heritage and those which remained outside the charmed circle.

I read the Japanese article with much interest. While it is obviously a rather sensational and jingoistic treatment of the theme, it certainly has many elements of undeniable truth. Sooner or later some decision over paramount influence in the Pacific must be reached, and it will probably have to be by force of arms. When that time comes, I surely hope all the Anglo-Saxon nations will hang together and present a common front to the enemy.

I'm glad you liked Wandrei's poem—which really is a remarkable production. Why don't you write him about it? I've had no chance as yet to read the new W.T. or S.T. I fear it will be a long time before I have any work in any of the magazines. I'm not suiting the capricious editors these days. Your local picnics and cockfights sound like impressive events, and I shall surely have to see one of them if I ever get around to the Texas region. Possibly I can get in that way my first glimpse of violence among adult Anglo-Saxons! It would be interesting to have a first lesson in this vivid phase of folklore—perhaps emphasised by a fractured nose or skull or something equally picturesque. Hope the current picnic doesn't develop too much really serious trouble.

My health cleared up at once under the genial sun of New Orleans, so that I came home in fine shape. No question—I really need a warm climate although my attachment to my native soil will keep me settled here as long as I can possibly hang on. But winter certainly does raise hell with me—the only way I can drag through it is by staying inside a well-heated house. Temperatures of 14° to 17° have knocked me out completely—sending me unconscious, and affecting my heart action in such a way that my ankles swell up and stay swollen till a good spell of hot weather returns.

Have recently come into touch with the weird writer Hugh B. Cave, who is a delightfully pleasant chap. I suppose you know his work. He lives near Providence, but is now spending the summer in Boston. I haven't seen him in person yet.

Well—almost home now! Guess I'll conclude and mail this letter down town.

Best wishes—and hope you can excuse this dull letter and bad writing.

Yrs most cordially and sincerely—

H P L

P. S. Here are some Newport views.

Notes

1. Lillian D. Clark.
2. Ralph Adams Cram (1863–1942), a noted architect, was also the author of *Black Spirits and White: A Book of Ghost Stories* (1895).
3. HPL's "The Colour out of Space" (1927) tangentially concerns the creation of an artificial reservoir.

[60] [TLS]

[9 August 1932]

Dear Mr. Lovecraft:

I am very sorry to hear of your recent bereavement. There is very little one can say on such an occasion, but please accept my sincere sympathy. Such things are the most tragic phase of Life, which is in itself fundamentally tragic.

I am sure you find a certain ease and consolation in your ramblings among the quiet beauties of the scenes you have so well described for me in the past. Old Newport must be a fascinating spot, with its glamour of old times. Thanks very much for the pictures, which I found most interesting, as always with the views you have sent me from your native country.

I'm glad you enjoyed your meeting with Price. He is, indeed, a versatile chap, judging from his letters. I hope he wont find the writing game too hard going; and I'm sure he'll arrive on both feet eventually.

It would indeed be fascinating to trace the routes of my people westward, by going over those trails eastward, as you mentioned. That route would lead me from here to East Texas, then to Arkansas, then to Mississippi, then to Alabama—at last to Georgia, where the Howards landed in 1733. After that—quien sabe? Somewhere on the western coast of England, I imagine. Although because of the infusion of Gaelic blood in the strain after reaching America, I can't feel any real connection with England. From the Atlantic states I'd rather follow the strains that lead unerringly to the hills of Kerry and Galway.

As always, I read your remarks on Romans and Greeks with intense interest. I think no one has a keener and truer insight into those times and peoples than yourself. I'll admit that I derive much more knowledge and entertainment from reading what you write about them, than from reading about them in histories and the like. You infuse life and spirit into what otherwise seems dusty and inert. I have tried to study Greek and Roman history, but have found it dull and to some extent inexplicable. I can not understand their viewpoints. The Achaeans of the Heroic Age interest me, and to a lesser extent, the Romans of the early republic, when they were a struggling tribal-state, if they could be called that. But soon that interest dwindles. I attribute this, not to any real lack of interest those times contain, but to a defect in my own make-up. I am unable to rouse much interest in any highly civilized race, country or epoch, including this one. When a race—almost any race—is emerging from barbarism, or not yet emerged, they hold my interest. I can seem to understand them, and to write intelligently of them. But as they progress toward civilization, my grip on them begins to weaken, until at last it vanishes entirely, and I find their ways and thoughts and ambitions perfectly alien and baffling. Thus the first Mongol conquerors of China and India inspire in me the most intense interest and appreciation; but a few generations later when they have adopted the civilization of their subjects, they stir not a hint of interest in my mind. My study of history has been a continual search for newer barbarians, from age to age.

By the way, the study of the East Roman or Byzantine empire contains a certain amount of interest, what of their continuous wars and intrigues with the Moslems and barbarians Mongoloid and Aryan. What a strange mingling of voluptuous luxury and bloody conspiracy that empire must have been!

You are right, of course, about the relative merits of both political parties. I'll admit I got a big kick out of the Democratic Convention, but then, I'm so constituted that I get momentarily enthusiastic about nearly everything I encounter. I did think that they used the Prohibition question to befog certain more important issues. Roosevelt no doubt has his faults—as who hasnt?—but I'd cut my throat before I'd vote for Hoover. I agree with you that the Conservatives are blind—they ought to read the books you mentioned—but whoever heard of a politician reading anything? We need statesmen, not politicians—men like my revered ancestor, Patrick Henry. Instead we have Andy Mellon and Hoiby de Hoover.

Yes, Pretty Boy is still at large, and getting the blame for every crime committed in Oklahoma. The cops say he's a rat. I'd call him a wolf. The cops are all afraid of him, judging from the way they're not catching him; if he's a rat, what does that make them?

Concerning violence—I fear that I may have created an erroneous impression of Texas as a whole, by my maunderings and sordid reminiscences. I may have appeared to generalize, which one can't do with Texas; its too big. There are many phases of Texan life, and I represent only a few, and those the more primitive. In many parts of Texas there are centers of culture and refinement—but in those parts I have not lived. In such cities as Houston and Dallas, I imagine you would find much the same conditions as exist in Eastern cities of the same size. Texas is an empire within itself and culture and ignorance, sophistication and primitiveness exist, sometimes almost side by side. Each man is prone to present the side of the shield to which he is familiar, and often falls into the fault of presenting his portion, as the whole. A cultured and educated person in some of the cities of south-eastern Texas, would probably give you a very different view of Texas—but it would be, as applied to the whole, no truer than mine, applied to the whole. It is not the newer, modernized, cultured Texas that speaks in me—in me it is the backwoods that speak. I can scarcely imagine a wider gulf than I have found existing between myself and certain city-bred Texas acquaintances. The gulf between us is infinitely wider than that existing between them and the urban people of the North and the East—if such a gulf exists at all. Portions of Texas are almost earthly paradises, but I do not live in such places and never have. My lot has been for ever cast in the high barren ridges, the land of postoaks and sand-drifts, of feuds and drouths, of tenant farmers and small stockmen, where life at best is a drab, savage grind for a bare existence. So it is the more primitive phases of life of which I am a part, and of which I tell and write. You will no doubt find urban Texans who will laugh at me, and say that the tales I tell are impossible and lies; they lie in their teeth, or rather through their ignorance. I make no attempt to interpret their phase of life; let them keep their hands off mine. Pardon this seeming—and irrelevant—heat. I was just thinking of some friends—perhaps I should rather say acquaintances—young members of the intelligentsia, who have made no bones about referring to me as an uncouth barbarian and callous brute. I have no resentment in that direction, but I do resent their skepticism toward the tales I was fool enough to tell them pertaining to the people among which I've lived most of my life. I may be a yokel but I'm no liar.

Pardon the foregoing. I shouldnt inflict my personal conflicts on you. Its bad taste and has no bearing to the matter in hand. What I started out to say was that my remarks and conclusions concerning my native heath have to do with, mainly, my own primitive environments, and are not to be taken as generalities, though I don't doubt they sounded that way.

Concerning beings from Outside, I don't think I said that I assumed the positive existence of such things. My mind is open; I refuse either to deny or affirm. This is precisely my attitude toward questions mystical and theological. I have read a little in science—I used to be a violent admirer of Haekal,[1] though I don't remember much about him now—and I've listened to endless discussions by professors and men who were supposed to be scientists. I've never heard a theological argument which convinced me beyond the shadow of a doubt in the existence of a Supreme Being; nor have I ever heard a scientific argument that convinced me that such a Being did not exist. The most I've heard on both sides have been unprovable theories. The same way as regards life—if any—after death. I do not stand ready even to positively deny the existence of an orthodox heaven or hell. I have never believed in their existence, but wiser men than I have, and do. I have never been convinced that reincarnation is either a reality or a myth. I say, when it comes to such questions, that its groping in a darkness which neither the eye or science or of theology can discern more than shadows of their own pre-conceived ideas. I have no arguments to offer. I can not defend my position either against the theologist or the scientist. I know my arguments are painfully crude and naive. Anyway, I refuse to argue with either. I detest arguments. I never won a dispute in my life, save on a few occasions when fists took the place of logic—and not often then. Generally I'd rather agree with the other fellow, even when I know he's wrong. On the other hand, once I weigh evidence—or what passes for evidence—and fully make up my mind—as on a stand like this—no amount of argument can shake me. I do not reply, but I remain unmoved.

Regarding liquor—or licker, as we call it in this neck of the woods. I have no doubt that the absolute prohibition of the stuff would make for better conditions—especially among the upper classes, to whose ease the laborer could contribute the time he wastes drowning his sorrows in drink. Personally, I regret the noble experiment. I was once an ardent prohibitionist. I liked my dram but was willing to sacrifice my tastes for society—that is to say, the upper classes, who are society, as far as I can make out. Drunkeness makes for inefficiency; a drunken man can't contribute his best efforts toward the enrichment of his masters. As for reasons of drunkeness, they are varied and involved, I think. In my case they have been.

There are no doubt, men who are stimulated to the state of exaltation you spoke of, but I think they are comparatively few. I never found anything particularly exalting about a drink. In the first place, since having been repeatedly poisoned by bad licker, I can hardly abide either the taste or smell of even good whiskey, cognac, or wine. The stuff almost gags me with its nauseousness. Nor can I say that I really like the effect. It does not stimulate; it merely clouds the mind. During the earlier stages I have fits of jovial good-feeling, but soon follows a fierce melancholy, intensifying a naturally moody disposition beyond the understanding of a non-drinking man. A real drunk is followed by sickness of soul, mind and body, a savage disgust and a feeling of having wallowed in the filth with hogs and vermin.

In the interests of human research, and because it is the habit now to dissect all human habits by the medium of that half-baked arrogant conceit known as psychology, let me go into the winding and devious ways of drunkeness and drink. Please forgive me if I bore you, or disgust you. The ways of drink are fundamentally disgusting, none admits it quicker than I.

I was born with, not a hunger for liquor, but with a liking for it, and a discriminating taste for good liquor. That was my birth-right, about all the heritage my aristocratic ancestors bequeathed me. That I threw it away is neither their fault nor mine, but the fault of changing times and conditions—prohibition and poverty. My grandfathers, and my greatgrandfathers kept fine wines, brandies and whiskeys on hand and drank regularly and moderately. They looked on a drunken man as a thing lower than a wallowing hog—which he often is. They drank their liquor like gentlemen and took no harm. I came to drink mine like a beast. I have drunk until the moon and the stars crashed in a blinding blaze in my brain and I fell senseless. I make these remarks without pride and without the slightest shred of shame.

Undoubtedly it is a part of my Texas heritage. Early day Texans were much harder and fiercer drinkers than the people of the Old South. We—my friends and I—do not drink like our ancestors did. They took their liquors with their meals, in friendly converse at bars, and the like. We seldom touch it at all unless we have enough to throw us, and then we deliberately plan our drunks, and drink hugely and with no other end in view. Prohibition is partly responsible. If we could get it all the time in moderate amounts, few of us would ever really get drunk.

Jack London analyzed the liquor question far better than I, or any other man, can ever hope to do, in his book "John Barleycorn" which every man should read.[2]

Yet I will analyze my own part of the game for want of a more interesting subject. I am dull and stupid these terrific hot days and unable to carry on a really intelligent conversation.

I was a prohibitionist. I was very nearly grown before I was ever drunk, though of course I'd had drinks before then. At the time I was working in a drug store, in an oil boom. I was a work-horse. That sounds like a funny remark to make concerning work in a drug-store, doesn't? But ask any "soda-jerker" who ever worked through a boom. I worked seven days out of the week, no vacation, no time off, from about nine-thirty in the morning to after midnight—sometimes until two or three o'clock in the morning. It was a continual rush to keep up with the work. You have no idea how much ice cream and soda water a mob of oil-field workers can guzzle! Then I often had the whole store on my hands, especially at night, when the main rush came. The manager who was supposed to be helping me, would find the crowd too tough for him; when they started brawling among themselves and shooting craps on the floor, he generally sloped and left me to hold down the joint; to wait on throngs that absolutely crowded the store to capacity, to mix syrups, watch the cash register, sell patent medicines and "handle the front", wrangle with bellicose customers who wanted drink or dope and took refusal as an insult—to do the ten thousand things there is to do around a boom-town drug-store. At night I'd fall into bed and be asleep with fatigue before I landed, and the next morning I'd still be tired. I had no opportunity to rest.

I had no time to write, read, or think. I went to no shows, had no social intercourse except the rough badinage that passed back and forth across the bar, had no time for girls, books, ambitions—no time for even life. I developed varicose veins and my health went on the rocks, but the worst of it was the stupefying effect on my mentality. The last few Sundays I worked there, a couple of boys—young oil-field workers of the better class—brought beer to us. They made it themselves and they and their friends drank it. They liked the drug-store bunch, and they brought us beer in big gallon medicine jugs we furnished them. It was nauseous. They never bottled it—began drinking almost before it quit working. It was cloudy, green and sweetish. Gaggh! I always let my beer stand in bottles at least a week before I touched it. But we drank this while it was still warm from the fermentation. Sunday after Sunday I got drunk on it. It helped me pass the day. It put spring in my weary muscles, and a smile—vacuous no doubt—on my generally snarling lips. It put a little of the human touch back in life again. I thought of myself as a man once more, and not altogether as a work-horse. Life, under the illusive effects of the beer, took on a brighter aspect. Old dreams and ambitions woke in me. Life stirred in me anew. The men I served drinks seemed more jovial, more friendly; the girls seemed brighter and prettier. Sunday was always the worst day, culminating a week of frenzied labor. The beer made it endurable, and quieted nerves that were jerking and twitching maddeningly. The last Sunday—which was the last day—I worked at that job, I was so drunk I could hardly wait on the customers. So was the owner, the manager, the pharmacist, and the clerks; so were most of the customers. Why not? We were all work-animals, writhing in the mire below the foot of the social ladder. We were predestined before our birth to be beasts of labor; why should we not make ourselves beasts on our own account, if doing so would lighten our load any?

Rich men, people of the upper classes, mental workers—they have no need of liquor, and possibly no right to it. But I say that the work-horse, the laboring man, has a right to anything that will brighten his hellish existence a little, even though that brightening be the illusive and lying gleam of drink, and that no man and no class of men has any right to deprive him of it. Drowned in drink, he can forgot the miseries of the week past, and the miseries of the week and the weeks and the years to come. To say that men are born free and equal is merely one of the trite and inane epigrams of the ruling classes. Most men are caught in a triple-cinch before they're born. They can't better their lot. Then in God's name, let them forget it as much as they can.

After I left the drug store and entered less strenuous pursuits, I felt no need of liquor, and did not touch it for years. When I did begin to drink again, I had grown into manhood, in size at least; I was accepted as a worthy companion by men who would have formerly scorned me for my youth and literary leanings. They drank and so did I. It was part of our fellowship. I think in the last analysis, that is why I drink, and why most men drink. It is part of the social life of men, varying according to their occupations and social status. Right now there's nothing I enjoy better than to make one of a congenial crowd of five or six jovial souls, and sit around drinking beer, eating limburger cheese sandwiches, and throwing the bull till we all get comfortably soused. My distaste for whiskey does'nt include beer. My ancestors scorned that beverage, but to me nothing can compare to a foaming stein of the real stuff, so cold that it cuts your throat as it goes down. I dont know where I got my liking for it. The Irish don't drink it much, and it was practically unknown among the higher classes of the Old South. Maybe its because of my thin strain of Danish blood! Or perhaps because of the Germanic tinge of my environments.

I do not like to get drunk on beer. I drink it because I like the taste. But when I am drunk, I am not a picture to either amuse or disgust. I inherited the ability to handle my liquor, at least something like a gentleman. I am neither maudlin or quarrelsome, nor supersensitive. I do not cause any disturbance nor tell my troubles to strangers. Nor do I weave and stagger. When I can not walk a straight line, I can not walk at all. At my best I am a jovial companion, neither smart nor witty, but friendly at least; at my worst I am merely moody and taciturn, desiring only solitude in which to brood over the melancholy images which haunt a gloomy mind.

I reckon you're right about the Latin trend moderating the Norman instincts. I dont know what moderated the Celt. So far as I can learn, the Irish were never particularly gluttonous eaters, though great drinkers. The same applies to the Highland Scotch. Well, when it comes to eating I'm all Dane. Give me good beer and good food, and plenty of both, and the ruling classes will have no revolt out of me. (This confounded type-writer is jumping spaces.)

The Mongols and Tatars were great eaters and drinkers, and especially in their more nomadic stages. Easily seen why; they lived a strenuous active outdoor life, and then food was not always handy. When they had plenty, it was their instinct to gobble as much as possible, against the times when they might go hungry. I hardly see how the Mongols of the Gobi managed to live, when their food consisted almost entirely of meat and milk—cheese and butter, perhaps, and fermented mare's milk. They apparently had no grain, vegetables or fruit of any sort. At least not while they were penned in the wastes outside the Great Wall by the power of the Chinese. I'm all for the nomads when it came to wasting China. They'd had nothing but abuse from the Chinese for ages.

That reminds me—that business about Turanian drunkeness—that some of the readers took exception to my making Tamerlane[3] a drinking man. I expected to be attacked on other scores—on Bayazid's suicide, which of course never took place—about my version of Timour's death—more particular I expected to be denounced because of the weapon my character used in that slaying. There were firearms in the world then, and had been for some time, but they were of the matchlock order. I doubt if there were any flint-lock weapons in Asia in 1405. But the readers pounced on to the point I least expected—the matter of Muhammadan drunkards. They maintained that according to the Koran, Moslems never drank. Wright admitted in the Souk that the Koran forbade liquor, but went on to quote a long extract from Clivijo's memoirs[4] to prove that Timour and his Tatars drank to excess.

This writing of historical stories is hell in a way, though intensely interesting. Its so easy to make mistakes. For instance I noted in his book of travels, Bayard Taylor,[5] when speaking of his explorations in Vienna, mentioned Count Stahremberg as commanding Vienna in 1529, when, he said, Sobiesky rescued the city from the siege of the Turks under the Grand Vizier Muhammad. Stahremberg hadnt been born in 1529. Count Salm commanded then, and beat off, not Muhammad, who, with Sobiesky was still in the womb of the unborn, but Suleyman the Magnificent. It was in 1683 that the others played their part. And the Vizier was not Muhammad but Kara Mustafa.

And that reminds me—do you know what year the Danube Canal was constructed, the one that runs through Vienna, or was it a natural arm of the river? I've ransacked all the reference books in this part of Texas and can't find out. Evidently it existed in 1683, because Stanley Lane-Pool speaks of "the island suburb of Leopoldstadt";[6] that former suburb is now a part of the city under the same name, to the best of my knowledge, and is the only part of the city on the other side of the Canal from the Alstadt or old city, and lies between the Canal and the Danube proper. Yet I can find no mention of the Canal in the siege of 1529.

Lately I've been brushing up on my knowledge of Eastern Europe. I find it fascinating. And I see a certain parallel in the cases of Poland and modern America. The partition and destruction of the Polish kingdom were inevitable. All effort for centuries was toward the establishing of special privileges for the upper class, to the degradation of the lower classes—just as it is in America today. Nobles were free of taxes and heaped up enormous fortunes, while stamping out all vestige of liberty in the lower classes. Independant merchants were taxed unbearably. Independent farmers became peasants, then serfs. The elected kings were shorn of all power lest they take the part of the people against the nobles. Graft ran rampant—just as in America. Money raised to build forts and armies went into the pockets of unscrupulous nobles. The standing army was abolished because the ruling class was not willing to pay for its upkeep. Then when they needed an army, they paid the price of their swinish avarice and blindness. They had it coming to them. Austrian, Prussian and Russian overlords were no harder on the common people than their own lords had been. Likely they were easier.

But what a tangled mess and confusion Balkan history is! And what a mixture of blood-strains the average Balkan must be! Celtic, Roman, German, Slav, Greek, Mongol, Turkish—no wonder they're always ham-stringing each other. I understand that for some time in those smaller countries the Germanic strain, and culture, has been dwindling out and being replaced by the cruder and more primitive Slavic—which is bound to be well mixed with Turanian strains, considering the century-long raids and occupations of the Huns, Bulgars, Avars, Petchenegs, Khazars, Mongols, Tatars and Turks.

Outside Bohemians and Poles, there are not many representatives of the Slavic groups in the Southwest. These, I think, are the superior race—especially the Bohemians or Czechs, because of their long proximity to the German races, during which time, too, they were cut off from their southern kin by the Mongoloid Hungarians. But I understand that the eastern cities have large numbers of Balkan Slavs. I believe you've mentioned them, as settling in the New England valleys in large numbers along with the Poles.

I remember meeting one such person in San Antonio a year or so ago. He was a Communist organizer—a Slovene, I was told by my socialist friend who introduced me to him—the friend himself having been the Socialist nominee for lieutenant-governor of Texas. The Communist was about my own age—a trim dark young man, dolichocephalic, to my surprize, and rather handsome. Doubtless American girls found his dark, almost Oriental type of manly beauty extremely romantic. The crude blundering Saxon and the even more blundering Celt can't compete with the perfectly poised Latin and Slav in amorous skirmishes! They have us licked at the start, when it comes to the ladies. This young man had keen dark eyes and a highly intelligent type of face; nothing of the Slavic dreamer about him. He had a poise and an alertness, an air of versatility noways inferior to the Latin, yet definitely not Latin. A fantastic conceit came to me as our mutual friend did most of the conversing that passed among us. I thought of the alien hordes that swarmed into Rome before its fall, and who no doubt—at least those from the East—were as superior in adaptability and versatility to the native Romans, as these new aliens are superior to our native stock. Possibly this very chap's Dacian ancestors, mixed with Greek, were undermining the empire with their wiles from within, while our more straightforward ancestors—your's and mine—were smashing the lines from without and from the other direction.

We eyed each other as I imagine a native Roman of the old stock and an alien Greek might have eyed each other in Rome, in the later empire—with mutual distrust and lack of understanding; tinged with resentment on my part and a hint of contempt on his, which his perfect manners could not quite conceal. What, to him and his, were the traditions that lie behind me, and of which I am a part? How could the representatives of two such utterly separate stocks and traditions bridge the gulf between? It can not be bridged. Not in my life-time or his. What is Bunker Hill, Lexington and Paul Revere to him? What is King's Mountain, the Battle of New Orleans, the drift of '49, Gettysburg, Bull's Run, or San Juan? Nothing. A meaningless drift of words, talismans of a slow-thoughted breed, to him inferior, in his own mind. If the difference lay just in this country, it might be overcome. But it lies beyond that. What to him and his is Hastings, the Crusades, the Wars of the Roses, the Battle of Culloden, of Bannockburn, of Preston Pans, of the Blackwater? The Black Prince means nothing to him, nor Robert Bruce nor Shane O'Neil. The gulf will be bridged when our race—your's and mine—is destroyed by the rising tide of such as he, and a mongrel breed, lacking all sentiment and tradition, reigns over the land our ancestors bled and sweat for. And I suppose it will come to pass. I dread their adaptability, their versatility. I could have broken this fellow half in two with ease, but it was easy to see which of us had the quicker, more alert mind. In an intelligence test he would have led me in a walk and not half tried.

But I had to laugh at his efforts to organize the thousands of Mexicans in and about San Antonio. A Mexican of the lower order will promise you anything to get rid of you, but just try to get him to make good! This particular chap led a big parade of several thousand up to the very steps of the city hall, and there one of their own race met them, in some government capacity, and made them a speech in opposition to the Slovene's—full of flowery rhetoric and burning Latin phrases. The Communist demonstration turned into an anti-Soviet rally and the organizer had to run for his life. I still maintain that a Slav can't handle a Latin, especially when the Latin is about half Yaqui.

My Socialist friend spoke bitterly of the fickleness of the Mexicans—whose ignorance is so abysmal its almost impossible for a white man to comprehend it. That day the soldiers were out, parading down the streets—cavalry and infantry. My friend watched a regiment of cavalry canter past, sabers drawn, and assured me that they were being thus paraded in order to awe the multitude. I think he attached too much importance to his friend's endeavors. But it amused me to surprize a fleeting look of satisfaction on my friend's countenance. He evidently felt the cause was flattered by the appearance of the troops—though in reality it was just one of the ordinary parades and exercises common enough in the city.

Well, the picnic came and went, and no violence. That's the forty-ninth picnic of its kind to be held in this town, and if there ever was another one that didn't have a few fights, I never heard of it. Certainly I never saw one before so peaceful. But a lot of the old-time toughs were missing—some having left the country, some having previously stopped bullets, some in jail. Even at the boxing matches the crowd seemed to consist largely of youngsters, certainly less pugnacious than those of the previous generation. We stood packed like sardines in the outdoor make-shift arena and I don't believe the fighters suffered much more than the crowd did. One boy had a tough time—somebody kept appropriating the chair on which he was supposed to sit between rounds, and his seconds kept having to dispossess the occupant, who generally put up a resistance. And then somebody stole the kid's shirt which he'd hung up outside the ring for lack of a proper dressing room. The main bout was a flop. They brought a slugger from Fort Worth with a blare of trumpets and a ruffle of drums to fight a local boy called Kid Pancake—I dont know if that's his real name or what he is. He came from Oklahoma, originally, I think, and he looks more like an Italian than anything else. His real name may be something like Panciata. Scarcely had the fight started when the Kid leaped across the ring like the panther he is, shooting a murderous left hook to his adversary's jaw. The city boy went down like a butchered steer, his head lolling over the lower rope; he was carried out, his eyes shut, his limbs trailing limply. He was so unconscious he snored; I've seen many a man knocked stiff, but I never saw one snore before. I've heard of it, but never saw it until then. It was another triumph for the post-oak country over the more civilized portion of the state! The crowds at the fights were very orderly—oh, of course they whooped and yelled and cursed, but there was no fighting among themselves. The boys that felt the urge to scrap, got in the ring and fought it out with the gloves. One funny thing happened; numbers of young fellows tried to climb over the top of the roofless wall which surrounded the arena, and one of them, when the sheriff requested him to get off, replied with a crushing smash on the jaw that nearly laid the limb of the law among the daisies. Only a couple of fellows were thrown into the jug for drunken and disorderly conduct, though of course many more were soused. One drunk from down the Pecan Valley caused a good deal of annoyance to a political speaker who was boosting a gubernatorial candidate, by getting up on the speakers' platform, drinking the speaker's water, and resisting efforts to be dislodged. At last he got to raising so much hell they had to lock him up.

One reason there wasnt any violence of any kind, was the fact that the usual carnival was missing. There's a standing feud between country people and travelling carnivals, and I understand its not limited to Texas alone. To the yokels, carnival people are fair play and vice versa. I'll admit I have scant patience with the country folk in that connection. Their main squawk is the gambling games attendant to the carnivals. They say they're crooked. Well, hell, whoever heard of an honest gambler making a living? Of course they're crooked. They have to be. Nobody makes the countrymen play them. Its their greed as much as anybody's. They come in and try to get something for little or nothing themselves. They lose their money, and they send up a yelp—call a cop or more often try to take matters into their own hands. What did they expect? If I'm in a legitimate business and a man comes along and gyps me on what I was led to believe was legitimate—if he makes me believe that its on the level—reasonable returns for reasonable investment—and then skins me, why, maybe I've got a kick coming. A shyster gypped an uncle of mine that way once, and didnt live to see another sun rise.

But if I'm carrying on a crooked business, or if I try to make money out of a crooked deal, and get fleeced, then I've got no yell coming. And if I try to beat a gambling game and get skinned with marked cards, loaded dice or what-not, then I've no kick either. But the average fellow dont see it that way, of course. You'd be surprized at the venomous hatred many country people have for carnivals and carnival people. A friend of mine, for instance, a fine fellow, though a little rough in his ways, perhaps, knocked a carnival girl senseless with a baseball, and considered it a great joke. She worked at what is known as a "cat-stand"—where one throws a ball and tries to knock cats out of the rack. Instead of throwing at the cats, he threw at her, and they had to pour water on her to bring her around. That's just an instance of something that frequently happens. I may be a bit squeamish, but I really couldnt see any humor in the joke.

Maybe I'm prejudiced on that score, for I had the same thing happen to me once, though not with the same effect. I was working at a carnival, at one of those blasted cat-stands. I was behind the rack bending over to pick up a cat, when some bully let go with everything he had. I just got a glimpse of him out of the tail of my eye as he threw, and all I could tell of him was that he was a big florid man, weighing, I should judge, anywhere between two hundred and two hundred and fifty pounds, and he threw with all his might. I didn't have time to dodge and the ball caught me squarely on the ear. I was only about fourteen years old. You can imagine the effect of a throw like that, at perhaps twenty or thirty feet range, with the whole weight of a big powerful man's body behind it. It dazed me—almost knocked me down. It knocked me so dizzy I didn't even think of retaliation. And it knocked out of my head the ability to remember just how the fellow looked. I remember faintly hearing the woman I was working for, cursing him for crippling her hired help, and him laughing; but I wasn't crippled. I was just stunned and went on setting up cats kind of mechanically. The girl came up and put her arm around me and asked how bad I was hurt, and I pushed her away roughly like a kid will—embarrassed because everybody was laughing at me. I was tough as a boot—physically, I mean. But it was an hour or more before I could think straight. Then my pal and I went looking for the man that hit me, but I couldn't remember what he looked like—there were scores of big florid men there—and nobody would tell me who he was. Everybody that saw it, swore they didn't know the fellow. You know how that goes. But it irritated me. I know he did it just for a joke, and that there was nothing personal in it, but he might very easily have blinded me for life with his damned foolishness.

But anybody that works to amuse the public apparently is considered fair play. Prize-fighters, actors, clowns. The entertainer is generally far superior to his audience. Its the crowd that sickens me with such games as boxing. What does the crowd care for skill and courage? They want to see blood spilled—to see somebody hurt. Same way with acrobats. Half the people that go to acrobatic performances to secretly hoping to see one of the performers miss his grip and break his neck. Else why do they swarm out so when the performers act without a net? I had a cousin who pulled that stunt. He packed 'em in—not because he was one of the greatest acrobats west of the Mississippi, but because he never had anything between him and the ground. He was just twenty-one years old when he missed a flying trapeze in the old Delmar Garden in Saint Louis—he fell thirty feet and his back broke like a rotten stick. He always guaranteed the mob a thrill; I reckon the rats slobbered and slavered with joy over the last act he gave them. And the priests beggared my aunt for money for masses for his soul—by God, a man can't even escape the pack by dying.

I note that some indignation is being expressed over the country in regard to the detestable police practise of grilling prisoners. Its about time. I think police harshness is mainly because the people have become so cowed by the heel of the law, that they do not resent or resist any kind of atrocity inflicted on them by men wearing tin badges. In the old days we had a type of law-officers as much superior to the present type as the old-time gunfighter was superior to the present-day gang-rat. They were brave, honorable, and generally merciful when they had the edge. I can't imagine Pat Garret, Wyatt Earp or John Poe summoning his deputies to help him beat up a cringing prisoner in irons.[7] In the old days it was no light thing to arrest a man. Resentment and resistance was the order, not the exception. I noted your remarks as to the treatment of a theoretical bully on a tear in some Eastern city. That's precisely what would happen in any western city. A number of police would be sent to handle the disturber—or in Texas perhaps some Ranger like Gonzaullas might be sent to handle him single-handed—a much more manly procedure, to my mind. Though the other way is effective with the softer-fibred toughs of the present age. There's nothing particularly courageous in half a dozen men clubbing a single individual into helplessness. But I can think of no more rediculous and futile thing than half a dozen ordinary cops, East or West, rushing into a saloon to capture an old-time warrior of the type of Billy the Kid, John Wesley Harden, Ben Thompson or King Fisher.[8] All six of them would have been dead on the floor before they could lay hands on him. And if they elected to shoot it out with him, the result would have been the same, barring a lucky accident. Such types created special types of law-officers to deal with them. Instead of overpowering their prey by force of numbers, the old-time officer fought it out with the outlaws on more or less even terms—what odds existed were generally on the side of the disturbers of the peace. The modern officer, with a few exceptions like Norfleet, Hickman, Gonzaullas, and the like, would stand little chance under such conditions. Why, hell, the cops have had Pretty-Boy Floyd cornered more than once, and then failed to take him, when he came out shooting. Once a couple of them got the drop on him in a hotel, I believe it was. Lifting his hands, he casually removed his hat, flung it across the room, sardonically requesting them to watch it. Unconsciously their gaze followed the flying hat, and that instant of carelessness was all he wanted. In that flashing bit of time he drew, and before they could move, both of them were down—along with an innocent nigger who was hit by a stray bullet. And Floyd walked out unharmed.

John Wesley Harden was the prime law-killer of the Southwest. Conditions helped to make him a bad man, just as in the case of the James boys—I wont add Quantrell[9] as many do. That old tale you hear in the Southwest about the Jayhawkers of Kansas murdering Quantrell's brother, and leaving the poor young lad—Quantrell himself—lying naked and wounded on the prairie—having waylaid the boys on their way from Baltimore to California—that tale, I say, is a lot of baloney. Quantrell never had a brother, as far as I can learn. And he wasn't from Maryland; he was born in Ohio. He made up that yarn to tell the Southerners when he decided at last to toss his lot among them. He was a Jayhawker before he was a guerilla. And the man who says he held a commission in the Confederate army is a liar. The Southerners would have hanged him just as quick as the Federals would have. After being refused a commission by the Confederates, he preyed on both sides, and it was the failure of a raid into Texas that really started the crumbling of his band. I've known men who rode with him, and they gilded his memory with their admiration—but honestly he was a bloody-minded devil. But what the hell! I started talking about John Wesley Harden.

The carpet-baggers made a desperado of John. Outlawed at the age of fifteen for killing one of the swaggering black bullies that tried to rule the country after being freed, he was hounded from place to place by carpet-bag officers and negro soldiers. The fools kept sending nigger officers after him, and as regular he sent them back feet-first. After that first slaying, he ambushed three sent after him—a white man and a couple of niggers; again, after being captured by three more, he loosed his bonds and killed them while they slept—but I could go on almost indefinitely. He was, as far as I know, the only man to stand up to Wild Bill Hickok and live. Wild Bill had a standing feud with Texans. He was the most noted Kansas law, and many a battle he had with the wild boys who brought the big longhorn herds up the old Chisolm. He got the drop on Harden, but the Texan turned the tables on him—and then spared his life. I don't know how many officers, black and white, John killed. The score was a large one. At one time he was an officer himself, in Kansas—at the same time that a price was on his head in Texas, and Wild Bill had a warrent for his arrest, but refused to carry it out. Hendry Brown,[10] Billy the Kid's pal, was a law in Kansas, too—when they hanged him for robbing a bank in a neighboring town, he was still wearing his marshall's star. He's worth a book himself—a lean, lithe, blond devil, handsome as a classical young pagan, soulless and deadly as a rattler. Utterly without fear, he shot his way out of traps and confronted perils with heroism worthy to be sung by Homer—and again he killed causelessly and in cold blood, simply to see his victims fall and quiver.

And Belle Starr, the most famous woman-desperado of all the West—what sagas could be sung of her![11] Many the times she came into my aunt's millinery shop in the old Indian Territory, to purchase expensive and exclusive types of apparel fresh from the states. A handsome, quiet speaking, refined woman, my aunt said—she was of aristocratic blood, and natural refinement, for all she'd kill a man as quick as a rattler striking. Its a curious coincidence that two of the Southwest's most famous outlaws—Sam Bass and Belle Starr—were killed on their birthdays. Sometimes I feel as if the shotgun blast from the brush that mowed down Belle Starr, forecast the doom of the wild, mad, glorious, gory old days of the frontier. She was more than the wicked woman pious people call her—more than merely a feminine outlaw—she was the very symbol of a free, wild, fierce race. Will Rogers, in jest, spoke of erecting a monument to Belle Starr. Oklahoma could do worse. Whatever she was or was not, she symbolized a colorful and virile phase of American evolution.

When will a man rise up, bred from the soil, with the sun in his blood and the throb of the unfenced earth in his ear, to sing the saga of the West? Perhaps its too much to ask. Perhaps no man will ever be born with power to etch the pageant—no, that's not the word. Etch suggests stillness, something frozen and motionless; and the pageant of the West is furtherest from that. It is alive with movement; it burns, tingles, stings with motion and raw, quick life. It flows tempestuously on in swift and ever-changing color and flickering light. There are no mild eddies and interchange of soft light and dancing shadow. All is raw and bold and blazing, flooded by the fierce merciless flame of the western sun. It is a panorama that grips and repels with its blaze, that shakes and rends and maddens.

Just west of this place begins the real western half of the American continent. You will not see the real west until you cross the Callahan Devide. Where the high postoak ridges of the devide fall away into the high plains country to west and south, begins the West. Standing on the uplands I look westward and seem to see the whole vista of mountains, canyons, peaks, rivers, endless dusty plains, cactus-haunted deserts and high mesas stretching away from my very feet to the foaming shores of the Pacific. And I close my eyes and seem to glimpse a vast dim mighty caravan surging endlessly across those vast expanses—a restless river of changing glints of light and checkered colors, surging, eddying, brawling, swirling its spate into the waste-places, but sweeping onward, untiring and irresistible. What man can pick out the separate elements in such a flood? The individual mingles with the liquid masses and is lost—yet nowhere is the individual more strongly marked, more clear-cut; pioneers and buffalo hunters, miners and soldiers, sun-burnt women in home-spun, reckless dance-hall girls, gunfighters, gamblers, cowpunchers, outlaws—Spaniards, Saxons and Indians, mingled in one chaotic flood they roar blindly toward the sea.

I am proud that in all these patterns, men of my native state had a part. Nowhere in the West will you find a place where a Texan has not set his foot. Buffalo hunters, guides, officers, outlaws—they left their mark wherever men lived hard. In the old days of the cattle-kings, it was the custom, in range feuds, to send for Texan "warriors" as they were called—sometimes most of the men on each side were Texans, fighting for hire. They were loyal to the men who paid them. Men fighting side by side in one war, might be opposed to each other in the next. It was all a matter of chance. No feudal baron of Europe was served more faithfully and fiercely than the western cattle-kings were served by these wandering men-at-arms, who wore leather instead of steel, and were far deadlier with a six-shooter than the finest swordsman ever was with his blade. They were much the same breed—descendants of those medieval swordsmen. Texans took the first herds to Kansas, to New Mexico, to Canada. One man, right after the Civil War had ruined the New Orleans market, drove a herd of longhorns to New York without finding a market. He eventually sold them in Boston. Texans fought northern Indians as well as southern redskins. There were Texans with Custer—more's the pity.

I regret the fate of the brave unfortunate men with Custer, from whatever state they came, but as for that cold-blooded murderer, the only regret I have is that the dead lay over his corpse so thick that the Indians failed to find and scalp it. Long Hair, they called him, and his yellow locks fell to his shoulders. A few years hanging in the smoke of a filthy Sioux lodge would have tarnished that gleaming gold; would have more closely fitted the color of his soul.

The Indians didn't often have a chance to glut their vengeance to the full as at the Little Big Horn. But it was a splendid galaxy of war-chiefs that confronted the blue-coats—Gall, Crazy Horse, Rain-in-the-Face, others almost equally famous. I suppose Sitting Bull should have some credit, though like most politicians and priests, he was making "big medicine" in a canyon some miles away while the real fighting was in progress. Rain-in-the-Face is my favorite of that group. I have nothing against Tom Custer, whose career he ended so bloodily, but I admire guts in any man, and Rain had enough for a regiment. You know in the Sun Dance, when the raw-hides tore through Rain's flesh too quickly, Sitting Bull claimed that he had had no fair test of manhood and Rain bade Bull give him a test. The medicine man cut deep through the back muscles and passed the rawhide thongs through the slits, and they hanged him high. There he swung for two days, singing his war-chants and boasting of his bloody deeds—he boasted of murdering a couple of white men, a veterinary and a sutler, straggling from General Stanley's expedition, and thereby hangs a tale, and Tom Custer's doom was written in blood. At last they bound buffalo skulls to his feet, and by terrific efforts, the young brave tore free, rending the flesh and tendons in such a way that for years he had depressions as large as a man's fists in his back. But his boasts had been overheard, and Little Hair—Tom Custer—arrested him and threw him in a guardhouse to await execution. White men imprisoned there helped him escape. He sent Tom Custer a bit of white buffalo hide, with a bloody heart drawn on it with the artistry of the Sioux. It was his way of saying he would eat the white man's heart when next he met him.

They met in the howling, blind, red frenzy of the Little Big Horn. Tom Custer was a brave man; none braver on all the frontier. But when he saw his enemy riding at him through the drift of the storm, naked, bloody, painted like a fiend, lashed to his naked steed, he must have frozen with the realization of his unescapable doom. Unaccustomed fear shook his iron hand, and his shots went wide—the painted rider raced in, a naked knife glittered in the dust, blood spurted—and out of the melee rode Rain-in-the-Face, holding a quivering dripping heart on high—blood trickling from the corner of his mouth—blood that was not his own.

Like Samkin Aylward,[12] I warm to a man with the bitter drop in him. And whatever else they were or were not, the Indians were'nt fools enough to forgive a wrong, or what they considered a wrong. I've often thought of fictionizing the incident just mentioned, transferring it to another race and age—having Bran Mak Morn eat the heart of a Roman governor, or Conan the Cimmerian that of a Hyborian king. I wonder how much barbarity the readers will stand for. One problem in writing bloody literature is to present it in such a manner as to avoid a suggestion of cheap blood-and-thunder melodrama—which is what some people will always call action, regardless of how realistic and true it is. So many people never have any action in their own placid lives, and therefore can't believe it exists anywhere or in any age. Another problem is how far you can go without shocking the readers into distaste for your stuff—and therefore cutting down sales. I've always held myself down in writing action-stories; I never let my stories be as bloody and brutal as the ages and incidents I was trying to depict actually were. I think sometimes I'll let myself go—possibly in a yarn of the middle ages—and see if I can sell the thing. I don't know much slaughter and butchery the readers will endure. Their capacity for grisly details seems unlimited, when the cruelty is the torturing of some naked girl, such as Quinn's stories abound in—no reflection intended on Quinn; he knows what they want and gives it to them. The torture of a naked writhing wretch, utterly helpless—and especially when of the feminine sex amid voluptuous surroundings—seems to excite keen pleasure in some people who have a distaste for whole-sale butchery in the heat and fury of a battle-field. Well—to me the former seems much more abominable than the cutting down of armed men—even the slaughter of prisoners in the madness of fighting-lust. I can read of the Little Big Horn, of Little Turtle's slaughter of Saint Clair's army, of the slaughter at Nicopolis and at Mohacz and the Horns of Hattin, unmoved except by feelings of admiration for the courage shown; but I have never been able to read of the burning of Joan of Arc without the most intense feeling of horror and rage; the same is true of the execution of William Wallace, and of Robert Emmett; thought of them rouses in me another sensation—a savage satisfaction at the memories of King's Mountain and New Orleans, with the British soldiers falling like ripe grain before the American rifles—yet I deplore the Scottish troops that fell there. I have seen persons who were constituted right opposite from me; they found accounts of battles and whole-sale massacre either repugnant or without interest, yet avidly devoured articles and stories dealing with the persecution of the helpless. I've never been able to read the full history of the Spanish Inquisition; its too horrible. But I find highly enjoyable the chronicles of Montbars the Exterminator, who went mad from reading and brooding over that same Inquisition and started out to avenge all the French who perished thereby.

Another thing—I have no patience with writers, historical or fictional, who glorify Oriental monarchs, comparing them with western rulers, to the discredit of the latter; who decry the outrages committed by the westerners on the Orientals, and then gloss over the atrocities of the latter, holding up some western outrage as an excuse. Westerners have suffered a hell of a lot more outrages at the hands of the Orientals than vice versa. I am utterly unmoved when I read of massacres of Asiatics—especially Muhammadans—by Christians. They started it, blast their hides—back in the days of Peter the Hermit, when the Seljuks took Palestine and started maltreating pilgrims to Jerusalem. And before that, in the days of Muhammad, and of the Caliphs—and of the Moors in Spain. Not a blow struck against Islam but we owed it to them. Even Stanley Lane-Pool deplores the action of Milosh Kabilovitch, who struck down Murad in the hour of victory at Kossovo—he looks on it as a traitorous murder, apparently. Bah! Who ever heard of such infernal drivel. Which was worse—Milosh, who approached the Turk smiling, and suddenly drove a dagger in his guts, or Murad, who had just butchered a nation, and dragged thousands of innocent men, women and children into hellish slavery? I have intense admiration for Milosh—and for Ehud the Benjamite who stabbed Eglon the Moabitish tyrant—and for William Tell, whether real or legendary.

Speaking of tyrannies naturally reminds me of this country. I reckon the government will be giving medals of heroism to the bold soldiers who, armed only with sabres, rifles, machine guns, tear gas and armored tanks, routed the veterans with their awful sticks and horrible bricks.[13] This business ought to cause a big boom in enlistment for the next war. I remember a song they used to sing during the war, "When you come back—and you will come back!—there's a whole world waiting for you!" Yeah—with brass knucks and butcher knives.

Well, we've been having some elections in Texas, and on the first pass we dealt the Wall Street clan a body blow. I hear the big babies up that way sent down numbers of tickets already filled out for the boys to vote; they wanted to be sure their men went in. Well, the state of Texas is damned near sold out to the big interests, but not quite. Take Mr. Insull—the mister is meant sarcastically.[14] The city of Cross Plains can't even dam up Bee Branch, because it runs into Turkey Creek, which in turn runs into Pecan Bayou, which is a tributary of the Colorado River—because Mr. Beloved Insull owns the Colorado and all tributaries. As a result, the citizens of the town have to use water out of wells, that would ruin the system of a brass monkey. Brown County had one hell of a time kicking Insull and his cohorts off the Pecan Bayou so they could build their dam, but they did it, and thereby established a precedent that may help the next strugglers. I see they retired the poor fellow—his company, I mean—on a meagre pension of $17,000 yearly. I pity him in his abject poverty.

Anyway, the big interests rocked in the election. Allred, candidate for attorney general, as opposed to a man who was avowedly in favor of Wall Street, was not even allowed to speak over the radio, or to get his speeches published in the big papers, I understand. He had to go over in Louisiana, and talk from Old Man Henderson's station in Shrevesport—and we elected him about four to one. You may have heard some echo of Henderson's long battle with chain-store interests—a rather eccentric old fellow, perhaps, but a fighter from heel to bald spot. And we're going to elect Mrs. Ferguson governor again, or I miss my guess. Of course, Jim will be the real governor; he'd run himself, only he can't, because he's been impeached. The last election seemed to show that the Fergusons were very unpopular in Texas; but its not Sterling against Ferguson; the issue is deeper. Its the common people, mainly the country people, against the corporations and the richer classes. We've won the first toss. And I believe we're going to win the rest. The governors are always men from the East or South. We Western Texans can't elect a governor—yet. But you wait a few years, till the West is completely settled up. Sterling is strong in the Southeast, but he lost the vote of the common People in East Texas proper, by imposing military rule in the oil fields. And I believe that there's enough people in Northwest and East Texas to put a new governor in the capitol. I'm enclosing a copy of an oil field—East Texas—paper, as an example of Southwestern journalism. You won't find such virility in the big Texas papers. You have to go to the hinterlands, where the press isn't controlled by big business.

By the way, as an evidence of our democracy, it looks like this district is going to elect a full-blooded Syrian to the legislature. He runs a small dry-goods store in this town—a very short dumpy sort of fellow, brachycephalic, swarthy, curly-haired—an Elamitish type if I don't miss my guess. He and his family are the only Orientals in this town, the Jews having pulled their freight when times got hard. A funny thing in connection with this fellow—he was born near Lebanon, in Syria, but has been in this country so long he was a stranger when his brother and he revisited the old country a few years ago. In Damascus they mistook a Moslem washing-place outside a mosque—a holy place where the Muhammadans did their ritualistic ablutions—for a public toilet, and were mobbed by a gang of maddened Islamites, who chased them for blocks, and were only pacified by money, and the assurance of the culprits' native kinsmen that the offenders were only American barbarians whose ignorance was too abysmal to be resented.

I'm glad to hear that the southern climate helped your health. I agree with you in regard to cold weather. I despise it utterly, though it doesn't have such dangerous effects on me as you described—however, I was never in a really cold climate, and don't know what it might do to me. Its never been much more than sixteen below zero in this part of the country. I was really shocked to read how the cold hurts you, and would certainly advise a change to a warmer climate—though I can understand your reluctance to sever old ties.

Long's poem in the current Weird Tales is superb. I also like the story by Howard Wandrei—Donald's brother, perhaps?[15] If so, please extend him my congratulations and welcome to the fraternity of fantastic fictionists.

But its time, long time, that I brought this rambling to a close. What an ungodly length of letter to impose on anyone! I fear I create the impression of loose-mouthed garrulity—if that's the way its spelled. Such isnt the case. I have a reputation of taciturnity among a people not noted for volubility. I was raised in the postoak hills, and I know how to keep my mouth shut. I narrate and discuss matters with you, by letter, that I would'nt mention to my most intimate Texan friends. I trust your discretion, and anyway, you have no connection with the state or the people of which I might speak, and so are impartial and unprejudiced. I don't have to tell you that a lot of the things of which I speak are in strict confidence.

With best wishes, and hoping that the editors will see the light and soon give more of your work to the public,[16]

Cordially,
R.E.H.

P.S. Just a humorous note to taper off on; some weeks ago the guardians of the law called on a friend of mine and told him the jig was up. Seeing they had him cold, he cheerfully surrendered, and asked to be allowed to get his cap in the next room. They agreed—apparently forgetting that rooms have windows as well as doors. He must have had a devil of a time finding his cap, because the laws havent seen him since then.

Another shooting scrape in town before last. No casualties; just a minor wound inflicted on one of the men. Rotten shooting.

I notice that a New York reader of Weird Tales—in the current Eyrie—asks for reprinting of the "Necronomicon" and "Nameless Cults"![17]

Notes

1. I.e., Ernst Haeckel (1834–1919), German biologist, zoologist, and anthropologist, author of *The Riddle of the Universe* (1899; English translation 1900).

2. *John Barleycorn* (1913) is an autobiographical novel about alcohol.

3. REH discusses Tamerlane (1336–1405), Turkic conqueror of Islamic faith, in "Lord of Samarcand."

4. Ruy Gonzalez de Clavijo (d. 1412), *Embassy to Tamerlane, 1403–1406,* trans. Guy le Strange (London: Routledge, 1928; New York: Harper & Brothers, 1928), a translation of *Historia del gran Tamorlan* (1582). Gonzalez, an envoy in the Spanish embassy sent by Henry III of Castile, was the first Spanish traveler to reach the Middle East and write about it.

5. Bayard Taylor (1825–1878), American journalist, poet, and novelist. The book of travels is *Views A-Foot* (1846); see esp. ch. 23.

6. Stanley Lane-Pool (1854–1931), *The Story of Turkey* (New York: G. P. Putnam's Sons, 1888), p. 228.

7. John William Poe (1845–1925) became a lawman in Texas in 1878; he later went to New Mexico, where he joined Pat Garrett in tracking down Billy the Kid (he was present when Garrett killed Billy). Poe became sheriff of Lincoln County, New Mexico, in 1882, and later became a prominent rancher, businessman, and public official. Patrick Floyd Garrett (1850–1908) was a cowboy, buffalo hunter, gambler, and saloonkeeper before being elected sheriff of Lincoln County in 1880. He set out to capture Billy the Kid and was successful, but the Kid later escaped. Garrett went after him again and, upon locating him at the Maxwell Ranch, shot him on 14 July 1881.

8. Benjamin "Shotgun Ben" Thompson (1843–1884) and King Fisher (1854–1884) were noted Texas gunfighters.

9. William Clarke Quantrill (1837–1865), a Confederate guerrilla leader during the American Civil War. After leading a Confederate bushwhacker gang along the Missouri-Kansas border in the early 1860s, which included an infamous raid on Lawrence, Kansas, in 1863, he ended up in Kentucky, where he was killed in a Union ambush in 1865, aged 27.

10. Hendry (or Henry) Newton Brown (1857–1884) had participated in the Lincoln County War as a gunman for John Chisum's faction, later joining Billy the Kid and others in a cattle-rustling operation. When the others returned to New Mexico, he stayed in Texas. He worked for a short time as a cowboy in Texas and Oklahoma before drifting to Caldwell, Kansas, where he became city marshal in 1882. On 30 April 1884 he, along with his deputy and two other accomplices, was captured after robbing a bank at Medicine Lodge, Kansas. Brown was killed while trying to escape a lynch mob. There was speculation that he had been responsible for other unsolved robberies while serving as marshal.

11. Myra Maybelle Shirley Reed Starr (1848–1889), better known as Belle Starr, a famous American female outlaw. Richard K. Fox made her name famous with his novel *Bella Starr, the Bandit Queen, or the Female Jesse James* (1889).

12. Samkin Aylward is a principal character in Sir Arthur Conan Doyle's historical novel *The White Company* (1891).

13. A reference to the so-called Bonus Army, a group of World War I veterans who marched across the country to Washington DC, in May 1932 to demand the early distribution of a bonus that was not scheduled for payment until 1945. They hung about in makeshift tent cities for months; eventually their numbers swelled to about 20,000. On 28 July the police provoked a confrontation with the veterans, and in the ensuing riots two veterans were killed. President Hoover ordered the Army, under the command of General Douglas MacArthur, to remove the Bonus Army veterans from Washington. Troops entered the tent cities and used fixed bayonets and gas to evict the marchers and their families, then burned the makeshift housing.

14. Samuel Insull (1859–1938), capitalist and utility magnate who pioneered the concept of utility holding companies and offering publicly traded securities, and his brother Martin were indicted in October 1932 for embezzlement and larceny in connection with a scheme to shore up securities controlled by Martin. Insull's utility empire had been forced into receivership in April 1932, though the companies were fundamentally sound, because New York banks refused to renew notes due. The receivership became a hot political issue in that year's presidential campaign. Insull had gone to Paris; when he learned he was to be indicted, he feared he could not get a fair trial in the prevailing political climate and fled to Greece, which had no extradition treaty with the U.S. Seized from a Greek vessel and returned to the U.S. in 1934, he was acquitted on all counts, as was his brother.

15. FBL, "When Chaugnar Wakes" (*WT,* September 1932); Howard Wandrei, "Over Time's Threshold."

16. Following the rejection of *At the Mountains of Madness* in 1931, HPL submitted virtually none of his work—even new pieces—to the pulp magazines.

17. André Galet of New York City wrote to "The Eyrie": "If you are really sincere in your desire to please us (the readers) and if it is humanly possible, why not publish in your reprint department Von Junzt's *Nameless Cults,* or the *Necronomicon* by Abdul Alhazred? Yours for more stories like *Kings of the Night, The Outsider,* and *The Picture.*" *WT* 20, No. 2 (August 1932): 271.

[61]

Providence, R.I.
August 16, 1932

Dear R E H:—

I cannot even begin to compete with your highly interesting and generously proportioned letter of the 9th, but I can at least attest the sincere appreciation with which I digested that meaty document. I am grateful for the expressions of sympathy regarding my recent bereavement—an event which of course one has to recognise as inevitable, and typical of the plight of mankind amidst an indifferent universe.

It is curious how our natural fields of interest and familiarity in ancient history diverge—and yet perhaps not so strange after all, since each simply seizes on that phase of antiquity which most resembles the life and spirit of his own early environment. To me Greece and Rome are prime realities because they had the same general problems and attitudes which the settled nations of modernity have. They had measurably conquered the salient natural phenomena around them, and had won sufficient material security to expand other parts of their mental and emotional endowment that those directly connected with self-defence and ego-assertion. Important brain areas—such as those connected with pure intellectual curiosity and with the finer nuances of rhythm and coördination—which had been necessarily underdeveloped in the peril-beset barbarian, began to expand and enrich life among the people who had reached a stage of relatively stable adjustment to nature and to the problem of group-defence. Where the barbarian had only a few simple motives and pleasures, and used only a small fraction of his heritage as a highly evolved primate, the civilised man had the infinitely vaster variety of stimuli and rewards which accrued from a more all-around development of his capacities. What he lost in the process was more than balanced by what he gained—so that not until his later decadence did he need to mourn any of the simple ruggednesses he had left behind. It seems to me that a vigorous, intellectual, and orderly civilisation *at its zenith* (not the uncertain, decaying world of today) is about the best system under which a man can live. I can't see why the half-life of barbarism is preferable to the full, mentally active, and beauty-filled life typical of the age of Pericles in Greece or (to a lesser extent) the age of the Antonines in Rome or the 1890's and 1900's in pre-war England and France. The exaltation of the spirit of physical struggle to a primary and supreme value is obviously a purely artificial and temporary attitude, determined by the historic accidents of one stage only in the evolution of the social group. When this quality is regarded more intelligently—esteemed, that is, in its proper proportion beside other qualities (reason, taste, cultivation, talent, etc.) of equal importance—we cannot help feeling that the race has ascended in the scale of humanity—become better developed because more of the capacities and functions are recognised and put in use. There is no reason to lament anything until the esteem for physical prowess declines radically and disproportionately, (as in broken and beaten nations and races) so that the freedom, dignity, and integrity of the group are menaced. This latter condition, of course, is outright decadence—and when it finally arrives (as it probably must toward the end of any social group's career) we usually look back wistfully to a primal barbarian age when the lost quality was in its fullest flower. Yet in reality we do not need to wish for anything so primitive and exaggerated. What we had better wish for is that sound middle period of highest development when the finer functions of the brain and emotions are brought into play without occasioning any drop in the standard of defensive physical stamina. At least, such are my views. Accordingly I can't feel any great kinship with barbaric tribes, even when they happen to be my blood ancestors. As I told you once, my sense of *personal identification* leaves the English race when I go back to the period of early Saxon England—skipping over to Rome and causing me to view all antiquity through instinctively Roman eyes except at rare, elusive moments when the strange poetry of the frost-blighted North and its wild, yellow-bearded gods gets a transient hold on me. But it is always through a mist of dreamlike *strangeness* that I think of the frosty, barbaric North. I could not really imagine myself a skin-clad barbarian, or pretend to understand the thoughts and feelings of one; whereas I do feel perfectly at home among the people and events of orderly Roman history. Be it blood-treason or not, I can't view any clash of the Roman legions with the Germanic hordes except from the Roman side. As between Caesar and Ariovistus, I am at all times a follower of Caesar—by deep instinct, not choice. And I always think of the affair of the Saltus Teutobergiensis with the exultation of a German. My blood is that of victorious Arminius—but my deep emotional reaction is that of horror and sorrow at the fate of the daring P. Quinctilius Varus. I feel that Arminius and I would have had little or nothing to discuss or understand in common, whereas Varus and I would have the whole tradition of civilisation—the whole cosmic perspective of Hellenic and Hellenistic thought, and the whole Roman attitude toward the ordering of men and institutions for the common good—to share and experience as a bond of kinship. I can't envisage the background that produced Arminius, whereas that of Varus is well-known and homelike to me—because it is that which has, in basic psychological essentials, survived the Dark Seas to become the guiding force of civilised modernity. All told, I think that—for the average person—blood is thicker than water *only up to a certain point.* At all times, the force of *cultural environment*—i.e., of mental standards, traditional folkways, habitual attitudes, forms of art and social organisation, etc.—is a potent competitor of biological instinct; so that when the two are opposed, it is hard to say which will win the tug-of-war. When no *radical* race difference is involved—as, for instance, when two approximately Aryan strains are concerned, I think that cultural heritage is often more powerful than blood. If, in such a case, a certain group has adopted the cultural heritage of another group, the tendency of its members in thinking backward behind the period of the cultural adoption will be to identify themselves with the alien group whence their culture came, rather than with their own physical ancestors whose original culture was so different and is now so incomprehensible. That is, unless special factors have caused a continuous tradition of resistance to exist from the very time of the cultural metamorphosis. Thus the clean-shaven, short-haired, toga-clad Gallo-Romans who spoke Latin and sat in the Roman Senate a generation after Caesar had conquered their fathers actually thought and felt as Romans. They were regularly enrolled into Roman gentes, receiving such Roman names as C. Valerius, M. Fulvius, T. Annius, etc. etc.—and looked back at history from the Roman angle; seeming to share the victories of Caesar rather than the defeat of Vercingetorix. Thus, too, with the Celtiberians whom Scipio had subdued at a still earlier period. By the time of Augustus they were as Roman as the Julii and the Claudii—and by the time of Nero they were the most artistic and intellectual element of the Empire, celebrating the heritage of Rome as if it had always been their own. They gave the empire such names as L. Annaeus Seneca, M. Annaeus Lucanus, M. Fabius Quinctilianus, and M. Valerius Martialis. Thus, too, with others—in the time of Marcus Aurelius (himself of blond Gallic ancestry) the intellectual life of Rome was in the hands of Roman-thinking North-Africans of Semitic (Carthaginian) blood, while the Gallo-Romans (cf. Ausonius, Rutilius Namatianus, etc.) held the centre of the cultural stage at the last. There is reason to think that if the Empire had survived, the centre of power and civilisation would have shifted to Gaul and the Celtic race, though retaining its Roman character and looking back to Scipio, Horatius, etc. as its folk-heroes instead of to the heroes of early Gaul. Indeed—how could a Gallo-Roman of A.D. 450 understand the half-fabulous Haedui, Allobroges, etc. etc., whose very language and way of life were forgotten except when recalled through Roman writings? In blood these men were Gauls, but mentally—despite such non-Italian impulses as their northern biological makeup may have given them—they were Romans. It is significant that Gaul remained officially a Roman province slightly *longer than Italy itself.* Odoacer banished the shadow-emperor Romulus Augustulus and made Italy a Gothic kingdom (with the fiction of allegiance to the "Roman" emperor at Constantinopolis) in 476, but not until a decade later—in 486—did the Roman proconsul of Gaul, Syagrius, surrender to the youthful Frank Clovis.

And so it goes. But despite my inability to feel *personally identified* with barbarians, I nevertheless take an intense *objective* interest in them; being fascinated by the drama and pageantry of the heroic age as Virgil and his contemporaries were. I *admire* even when I do not *understand,* and of course I have a strong feeling of partisanship for barbarians whenever they are contrasted with *decadent* groups (Syrians, Alexandrians, etc.) as distinguished from civilisations at their height. I can fail to *comprehend,* but I can never *despise* him as I do a member of a broken, cowed, wily, and treacherous civilisation. In the hypothetical case of a Northern captive brought before a Lydian king or Syrian tetrarch, my sympathies would be wholly with the captive.

I have indeed been fascinated by many aspects of the Byzantine civilisation, especially since it was a legal prolongation (though not a cultural heir) of Rome's dominion. The appearance of its special characteristics was very gradual. When the West fell, and for some time afterward, Latin was the *legal* language; whilst the art tradition was a debased offshoot of Roman rather than Greek art. Justinianus was Latin-speaking, and in his time architecture was still largely Roman. His generals reconquered North Africa (a Latin-speaking province) and part of Italy from the Teutonic conquerors, so that at the close of the 6th century there were still Romans under a Roman Imperium. Heraclius, when he subdued Persia, was generally regarded as a Roman in private life. During his lifetime the Saracens took away most of the Latin-speaking portions of the Empire, so that from A.D. 700 onward we may consider the civilisation a purely Greek one. It was intellectually sterile, but not wholly unproductive artistically. Byzantine architecture coloured the architectural tradition of many parts of Italy—especially Venice—and Byzantine art in general lies at the base of all Russian art. Russia's influence passed certain Byzantine elements (especially the bulbous dome of churches) on to Scandinavia—so that in America today there are Swedish Lutheran churches (Providence has a sumptuous new specimen)[1] in whose outlines the influence of the old Greek Empire still lives!

As for violence in modern America—no, I didn't think the larger cities of Texas were stamping-grounds of the feudist and the bad man. One of my best friends taught in the university at Houston for a year, and never spoke of anything violently un-eastern except the cockroaches around his kitchen and bathroom water pipes! I had in mind, in all cases, the respective regions as a whole. The contrast is really between the strife-torn plains of the west and the quiet rural valleys of the east where people till the soil from generation to generation, separated by the same ancient stone walls and having no occasions for encroachment or violence. What really causes violence to subside is *tradition and continuity*. Old, settled races accept conditions as bequeathed from father to son, and have so many psychological influences tending toward the preservation of certain boundaries and non-encroaching lines of action that clashes are relatively infrequent. Then, too, in regions where European traditions are solidly carried over without a break there is always a recourse to law before any other remedy for unsatisfying conditions is tried. This system works, because in a thickly populated district the enforcement of any law having popular endorsement is relatively easy.

It is odd that the urban east-Texans are so ignorant of the primitive life at their very doorstep—but such is the way of the world. What is near is always overlooked—and they probably read about South America or China when they feel like imbibing the lore of violence and unrestraint. For that matter—what I don't know about Maine lumber-camps (as near to Providence as West Texas is to East Texas) would fill many compendious volumes. But certainly, these myopic fellows ought not to adopt a pose of superiority and scepticism when given evidence of the Homeric life around them. Such an attitude is the very reverse of intelligent and civilised, and merely confirms them in their state of ignorance. I have no use for the smug cockney type of fellow who knows nothing of the geographic and historic background of his general region. Such a person is imperfectly adjusted to the social pattern—and is no more a real inhabitant of his region than a foreign immigrant is.

As for Outside encroachments—and the subject of supernaturalism, immortality, etc. in general—I am, in theory, not so far from your own position. Actually, of course, we know absolutely nothing of the cosmos beyond the small fragment reachable by our five senses; hence dogmatism in any one direction is as illogical as dogmatism in any other. However, I am not as reluctant as yourself to piece out matters with a few reflections based on *probabilities*. The absence of *positive* knowledge does not stop certain views of things from being, according to present indications, *a damn sight likelier* than certain other views. And when anthropology teaches us that certain traditions of theology had a definite origin in some special condition leading to delusion, we are completely justified in maintaining that these traditions—with their manifestly false origin—*have not one chance in a million* of being the true explanations of the things they profess to explain. It would be too much of a coincidence if our ignorant and blundering forefathers should have *happened* to hit, without any real data and logical method at their disposal, upon infinitely profound truths in complex matters which even today are unreachable. When we know that the reason people believe in a thing is false, we have a right to guess that the belief itself is exceedingly flimsy. Today all the traditional assumptions regarding "god", "spirit", "immortality", etc. etc. are pretty clearly traced to delusive conditions, fears, and wishes of primitive life. *If such things as gods, immortality, etc. did exist, they could never have been really known by the people who made the myths.* The myths, conclusively, are false—being natural products of known forms of illusion. And it would be damned improbable if there were any real phenomena existing unknown in space and happening to correspond to these error-born myths! Looking at it another way—simply forget that the old myths do exist, since of course in sizing up an intrinsic situation we must judge it on its own merits and refuse to take the word of any biassed persons. Glance over the universe today, *in the light of the knowledge of today,* and see if anything in it or pertaining to it suggests such things as a central consciousness, purpose, ghost-world, or possibility of "life" when life's vehicle is destroyed. No person, thus facing the facts directly and keeping free from the mythical lore of the past, could possibly read into the cosmos the extravagant, irrelevant, clumsy, improbable, and unnecessary things which traditional theologians believe. There is no evidence whatsoever for the existence of the supernatural—*and where no positive evidence exists,* it is mere pedantry to continue to take an extravagant and gratuitous improbability seriously *merely for lack of definite negative evidence.* Theoretically, the improbability *may* be *possible*—but the chances are so overwhelmingly infinitesimal that they can well rank as negligible. Practically speaking, there is no earthly reason for believing in a deity, immortality, etc. In the absence of any official evidence, it is silly to give the *least* probable explanation an equal footing with explanations which are *really* probable. What little we know of physics and biology leads us to regard life as a form of energy—a mode of motion—in a material physiological medium. When the material medium has ceased to exist, there is no sense in assuming that the form of motion or energy determined by its parts can continue to exist. Thus according to everything which we do know, "immortality" is a wild improbability; and I am not so naïve—or so pedantic—as to accept *improbabilities* on equal terms with *probabilities*. What we learn from the study of small sections of force and matter indicates that phenomena are caused by the mutual interaction of forces following fixed patterns inherent in the cosmic order. This holds good for all the phenomena we know—on every conceivable scale. Lacking any contrary evidence, we may *reasonably guess* that this mutual interaction holds good for phenomena on *any* scale—even the largest—so that the entire cosmos may be provisionally considered as a huge field of force without beginning or ending, whose automatic and kaleidoscopic rearrangements of parts constitute the physical and material phenomena of which we can glimpse a fraction. Nobody tries to elevate this *reasonable guess* into a positive dogma, but one is certainly justified in saying that it is *probably* a lot nearer the truth than are the wild myths which were born of primitive ignorance *and which insist on being judged arbitrarily without consultation of the real natural evidence around us.* I certainly can't see any sensible position to assume aside from that of *complete scepticism tempered by a leaning toward that which existing evidence makes most probable.* All I say is that I think it is *damned unlikely* that anything like a central cosmic will, a spirit world, or an eternal survival of personality exist. They are the most preposterous and unjustified of all the guesses which can be made about the universe, and I am not enough of a hair-splitter to pretend that I don't regard them as arrant and negligible moonshine. In theory I am an *agnostic,* but pending the appearance of radical evidence I must be classed, practically and provisionally, as an *atheist.* The chances of theism's truth being to my mind so microscopically small, I would be a pedant and a hypocrite to call myself anything else. As for *arguments*—I can't afford to detest them, since they are all that ever bring out the truth about anything. We know nothing except through logical analysis, and if we reject that sole connexion with reality we might as well stop trying to be adults and retreat into the capricious dream-world of infantility. There is a craving for truth inherent in the human personality; and when childish mythmaking is outgrown, this instinct can be satisfied only through logical investigation. The greater the civilisation, the greater the demand for *real facts*—hence the early philosophic development of the Greeks, a superior race, contrasted with the irrational and inquiry-shunning religious orthodoxy of the less emotionally evolved Semitic nations. The Greek speculative mind is probably the most perfect product of this part of the space-time continuum—the most delicately and highly organised form which matter and energy have ever assumed in the history of the solar system and probably of the galactic system as a whole. The Greeks were certainly our superiors—to the extent, perhaps, that we are the superiors of the duller brachycephalic races. They showed an eager alertness in many fields of cerebral experience from which we of today either retire in defeat or shrink in indolence, timidity, or confusion.

As for liquor, I read with extreme interest your exposition of some of its aspects and effects, which confirms my contention that, in general, it is for oblivion rather than for mere heightened sensation that the Nordic (as distinguished from the Latin) drinks. I can sympathise with the argument of those who would tend to grant the hard-pressed classes the surcease of drink as a compensation for their burdens and helplessness; yet after all I can't believe that this is as great a favour to the oppressed as it seems on the surface. The more drink-sodden they get, the worse their biological stock becomes, and the less chance they have of getting out of their rut either by individual success or by concerted political action toward a more equitable social order. If some rich industrialists would like to keep the masses sober in order to make them good workmen, there are others who would like to keep them poisoned with alcohol to prevent them from thinking, organising, and exerting political pressure. It seems to me that at this late stage of social evolution, when social and economic factors are better understood than formerly, it would be wiser to study means for the reduction of general misery through the controlled allocation of labouring opportunities, the granting of old-age pensions and unemployment insurance, and the gradual undermining of the excess-profit motive in favour of a supply-and-coördination motive, instead of condoning the woes of the helpless and giving them poison to make them forget about it. However—time will tell. I greatly doubt, after all, whether the needed social changes will be brought about through the real intelligence and conscious planning of the lower orders. Perhaps it's just as well to let them have their poison for the time being, if it does them any good. Actually, I fancy that the part played by the masses in social reorganisation will be largely one of *intimidation.* They can't be expected to stand a mechanised civilisation which gives them less and less chance for food, shelter, and endurable comfort. After a certain stage, they will undoubtedly begin to feel that they aren't getting enough out of the existing order to warrant their upholding it—and from their point of view they will be right. Then the signs of uprising will appear, and even the entrenched industrialists will recognise that something will have to be done. Being men of sense at bottom despite their present confused myopia, they will probably see the need of some new division of the fruits of industry, and will at last call in the perfectly disinterested sociological planners—the men of broad culture and historic perspective whom they have previously despised as mere academic theorists—who have some chance of devising workable middle courses. Rather than let an infuriated mob set up a communist state or drag society into complete anarchical chaos, the industrialists will probably consent to the enforcement of a fascistic regime under which all citizens will be ensured a tolerable minimum of subsistence in exchange for orderly conduct and a willingness to labour when labouring opportunities exist. They will accept their overwhelmingly reduced profits as an alternative preferable to complete collapse and business-social annihilation. Such, at least, is a reasonable speculation—though it would be hard to guess at the probable time-period involved. And of course some unforeseen factor may make it all wrong anyway. But on the whole, I think the labourer's best friend is the man who tries to lighten his load a trifle, rather than the one who strives to feed him a poison which pushes him deeper in the gutter and makes each generation of his stock more and more diseased and mentally inferior. Under the latter policy, a nation (barring revolutionary upsets) would be likely to split into two races—an evolved upper type ruling over a debased horde of brainless semi-automata—as in H. G. Wells's story of "The Time Machine".[2]

It is certainly unfortunate that your boyhood included a period as exacting and oppressive as the soda-fountain interval—yet perhaps it formed a test of stamina which has strengthened your character in the long run. Certainly, you have survived it brilliantly enough; with unweakened imagination, and uncurbed creative zest. Still—one would wish that the discipline had been less exacting—achieving the same result in a way less painful while it lasted.

Yes—the social background of liquor is certainly responsible for a large part of its consumption. It takes tact and resistance to preserve a teetotalling policy in the face of existing conventions; though if one's dislike of the drinking tradition be sufficiently strong, one can usually find a way to keep dry without committing too many gaucheries. One may be regarded as a bit eccentric by many, and disliked as a prig by a few—but what's that to a man of independent convictions and a firmly fixed aesthetic attitude in the matter? I am of the third generation of non-drinkers on both sides, though there is plenty of liquor-consumption to be noted in my remoter heredity and in certain collateral branches. A country-squire sportiness which included drink among other elements probably caused my great-great-grandfather in the male line to lose everything he had in England, including a landed patrimony held since before Queen Elizabeth's reign, and end in obscurity while his sons and grandsons scattered to America and the colonies—and since that time (everything was sold in 1823, and my great-grandfather and grandfather settled in New York State in 1827) at least one line of his descendants has had no favourable opinion of the cup that cheers. On my mother's side the New England temperance tradition made a deep impression, so that my maternal grandfather[3] never took liquor except for the light wines of the European continent when he travelled there. Even those he took sparingly—and for the very un-convivial reason that he couldn't find any water fit to drink. His son—my late uncle, who died in 1918[4]—was less abstemious, and was far from benefited by his drinking habits—though he never let the latter lead him to swinishness. My mother used to hold him up to me as a sort of horrible example to avoid—which, coupled with my father's tradition of teetotalism, about turned the scales so far as my emotional attitude was concerned. How much this early bias had to do with my aesthetic distaste for the phenomenon of drunkenness I don't know—but my distaste is genuine and individual enough now, at any rate. In addition, I have a physical loathing for the smell of alcoholic beverages of all kinds. From beer to claret, and port to whiskey, a whiff of any one of them is almost an emetic to me.

It is still a mystery why the Celt, without undergoing any physical departure from the full Nordic type represented by the Teuton, developed a reaction from the gnawing, guzzling habits of the original stock—along with a modification of language and various folkways. Probably there was some obscure prehistoric contact with some non-Aryan civilisation, which did not develop into a blood amalgamation.

The Tartars certainly were an odd folk. I don't think, though, that one needs to be surprised at the way they throve; for *cheese* (a favourite comestible of my own, despite my entirely non-Mongol heritage!) is an extremely nutritious article, containing various dietetic elements in ample and well-balanced form. As for Moslem drunkenness—instances were numerous and occasionally notable. The sanguinary A. Hakam, Emir of Cordova around 800 A.D., was a notorious drinker—his habits provoking his orthodox Moslem ministers to the point of disaffection and disloyalty.

I am fearsomely ignorant of the history of Eastern Europe, and could let Bayard Taylor get away with all sorts of blunders without being able to correct him. Somehow I can't seem to get interested in anything except the direct line of culture—Greece–Rome–Western Europe–England—extending behind our own civilisation, together with certain picturesque cultures which immediately impinge on it. I'd hate to admit how little I know about the Slavonic nations, the Tartars, and even of Germany. None of my books give any clue to the date of the Danube canal in Vienna, but if I turn up anything at the library I'll let you know. Poland never did give me a very big kick. Even now, after all its period of subjugation, it is displaying a high-handed arrogance (as, for instance, against the helplessly isolated city of Dantzig) which does not invite any especial sympathy.[5] The Balkans certainly are a hopeless mess, with wide racial variations. Greece has some decadent Hellenic blood, but a lot of Slav is mixed in. The Roumanians have a genuine touch of the Latin, but the Bulgarians are largely Turanian. Serbia and its added parts is about as Slavic as any part of the area. No—I couldn't have said that *large* numbers of Balkan Slavs are invading New England. Aside from the Poles, our principal Slav (or near-Slav) invaders are the *Lithuanians,* who tend to become urban and congregate in crowded places like the Boston slums. Providence has relatively few of these latter, although Poles are thick in the western manufacturing section of the town. Czecho-Slovaks are indisputably the best of the Slav immigrants, but they prefer the Middle West to New England.

The mayor of Chicago is one. Providence—and also Connecticut—has had a number of Russians since the bolshevik upheaval, but these are generally orderly and well-behaved. They congregate in the north end of Providence—next to the older-settled Russian Jews, whose occasional knowledge of Russian made them convenient neighbours—and have a Greek church of their own. But Providence's foreign element, on the whole, is overwhelmingly *Latin*—Italian, (the most intelligent and assertive) French-Canadian, and Portugese. These three groups, taken together, form an enormous bulk; and make the "new" Providence as distinctly a Latin city as the "new" New York is a Jewish city. We also have a large group of Armenians, but not so many Syrians as other American cities have.

Such are the elements flung into juxtaposition with the old stock—and how little the divergent blends can ever have in common unless all traditional streams fade out into a pallid, backgroundless, neo-American utilitarian civilisation! I can understand how you felt when viewing the Slovene organiser. What a complete divergence and irrelevance betwixt his stream of ancestral memories and our own! The future is hard to predict. Present closing of immigration will be a help, but the higher birth-rate of the foreigners—if it is kept up—is against us. Still—there is undoubtedly a Nordic majority in the country, counting not only the old stock but the German and Scandinavians of the middle west. Incidentally—the labours of the Slovene Communist among the Mexicans ought to form good comedy material!

Glad the picnic didn't involve any heavy casualties. Possibly it was wise to omit the carnival features in view of the prevailing attitude. That feud itself certainly mirrors the inconsistency of human nature. The rustics welcome the presence of the carnival enough to patronise it, yet feel a bitterness toward it because of the natural result of that voluntarily granted patronage! Your own experience was surely harrowing enough—and I wish you could have identified the florid and semi-homicidal stranger while there was still a chance for reprisal! In general, the sport-witnessing public tends to be coarse and brutal, like the passive spectators at the gladiatorial games of old. They certainly welcome the low-grade thrill which comes when serious misfortune befalls the performers.

As for the "third degree" applied by police officers to prisoners—it has indeed come in for a vast amount of debating nowadays. Probably your position is right, for it certainly means peril to leave so much punitive latitude to minor officials with so little power of discrimination; and yet I can see the other side of the matter also, for perhaps nothing less drastic than rough handling would ever serve to extract the truth from hardened and organised criminals. It is understood, of course, that such methods are reserved for known members of the toughest criminal class. The drawback is that one can't exactly classify many prisoners—and also that it is hard to determine just how far to go in any specific case. To leave so much to the judgment of relatively untrained men is undeniably dangerous—hence I fancy that it is better to err on the side of leniency than on the side of severity. However, I think you take a somewhat impracticable—and essentially *romantic* rather than realistic—position when you call for 'fair play' between the forces of order and those who have knowingly put themselves outside the pale by violating the social agreements on which civil action is based. When a man deliberately sets himself against society, he cannot expect from society the chivalric treatment demanded in dealings between honourable equals. He has violated the agreement which every citizen has to make with society to secure the benefits of civilised life, and is no longer an honourable equal. By breaking his side of the rules of the game, he has forfeited the right to expect that those rules can be invoked in his favour. From then on, it is not the duty of the forces of order to be 'fair' with him in a sporting sense. It is their duty primarily to get hold of him and put a stop to his anti-social activities, and all else is secondary. However—one naturally expects that they will keep within the bounds of good taste in their procedure, and that they ill not inflict upon the prisoner any suffering not absolutely essential to his capture and imprisonment. I may add, of course, that this holds good principally for those older regions where the lines between the legal and the illegal are well-defined. It may well be that in pioneer sections, where legal processes are still necessarily uncertain, a more informal relation betwixt pursuer and pursued is advisable.

You would find that the ideology of the frontier could not work in a thickly settled community where everything depends upon the preservation of order. Standards differ with conditions. For example, you speak of it as 'more manly' to send *one man* to capture a disorder-breeding bully than to send a good-sized quota of men certain to apprehend him quietly. Now that opinion is based solely on the romantic conception of a game between equally honest individuals . . . . the old rule of even odds, and taking a fellow of one's size. Actually, the situation is very different. The bully has outlawed himself by breaking the rules on which the communal life is based, and he knew that fact before he started in. He has had—and discarded—his chance for social tolerance. At this stage he is simply a social liability to be gotten out of the way in the quickest and most effective manner. To send merely *one man* against him would be *flagrantly unfair to the community,* since this is not a childish game but an emergency in which the good order of the community is imperilled. The community has no obligations toward one who is arrayed against it (except in warfare, where the opponent does not owe allegiance to the community and is subject to another set of rules), and the forces of order are derelict in their duty to society if they do not adopt the *most certain* way to put the offender out of business. By sending only one man they would diminish their chances of capturing the outlaw and thereby increase the community's peril from him. It is their duty to get him in any way that is quickest and most nearly certain. The more men, the more effective—and the more fair to those orderly members of society who suffer from the anti-social acts of the bully. In a heavily populated community, *civic order is the first and paramount consideration.* Everything else is secondary to this, because a single infraction would breed others—leading to chaos. It *must* be a 'light thing' to arrest a man, because hesitation might enable him to perpetrate infinite harm. A mistaken arrest can never do as much harm as a mistaken abstinence from arrest may frequently do. When in doubt, one must choose the course which favours communal safety. Resistance to arrest must be rigorously suppressed, because such a custom strikes at the whole base of civic order. The more civilised the country, the more public opinion tends to be on the side of the police rather than on the side of the criminal. In Great Britain, Canada, and most of the colonies general sympathy is almost always with the police; this was the case with the American seaboard states to a great extent until foreign immigration upset the social balance. Indeed, it is still so among the more thoughtful part of the native population. However, America has never equalled Great Britain and the loyal colonies to this extent, since a certain antinomianism was inherited from the separatist and individualist tendencies of the first colonists. Still, with all allowance made, the native Americans of the East—and of urbanised regions generally—are far more solicitous for law and order than are either the foreigners or the Americans of pioneer regions. Reverting to the hypothetical case of the bully in Boston—it may 'not be particularly courageous' for half a dozen men to overpower an unruly specimen; but who expects the grim business of law-preservation to be a stage for the showing-off of personal merits? In this situation the paramount duty is to remove a certain obstacle to social functioning, and the proper thing is to do it. 'Courage' is a *perfectly irrelevant* thing in this matter. Any one of the six policemen who pile on a 'tough egg' to quiet him may be a man of the highest courage when confronted by a situation where courage is called for. This is simply an emergency of a different sort. There are cases enough where policemen *have* single-handedly captured violent criminals *when no aid was available.* They had a choice of letting the criminal go or facing the peril, but they did not hesitate. Yet if aid *had* been available, they would have been blameworthy indeed if they had not taken advantage of it; since their chances of doing their duty and freeing society of its enemy are lessened if they fail to use all means in their power. Remember that police are hired to produce certain results and perform certain defensive functions—not to make a parade of their personal chivalry and bravery. They must indeed be brave—for there are times when bravery *is* needed—but they must not try to test out that bravery when it is not necessary and when it might be the means of prolonging a social peril otherwise instantly conquerable. The state and civic order come first. When they are suitably safeguarded—but only then—it is time for the frills.

As to whether one of the old-time western desperadoes could have long escaped the police network of a modern city—imagination is free to draw its own conclusions. Conceivably, one determined man bred amidst border perils which call forth special aptitudes and methods could escape from six policemen unprepared for anything unusual. But when one reflects on the instant telephoning and telegraphing certain to follow; the descriptions circulated among city and state police; the *number* of pursuers involved; and the fact that shooting on sight would be the policy with a criminal of such proved desperateness—one hesitates to bet too heavily on a long career for the outlaw. The really determinant element in all matters of this sort is *thickness of population.* In relation to the importance and maintenance of order, the densely settled region and the open or sparsely settled region have very little in common. The different conditions breed different methods and facilities, and different emotional attitudes. In a settled district, complete and unbroken public order is the only possible norm, and popular emotion accepts it as such. It is a basic thing, taken for granted, and nothing is permitted to challenge it or interfere with its maintenance. When any individual or group stands out against it, the only thought or wish for the time being is to subdue or eliminate that individual or group. The idea of tolerating or condoning any less rigid standard of order is simply inconceivable to the popular mind. Even when a corrupt political machine condones crime, there is always a popular clamour and partial correction the moment such crime assumes the form of public disorder. Hence the tardy action against the Chicago gangsters, whose violence at last became public and general. The policy of a community in matters like these is based upon very deep and usually hereditary emotional considerations, hinging upon the popular conception of what is normal.

Your accounts of John Wesley Harden, Quantrell, Belle Starr, etc., are intensely interesting and in many cases illuminating; for in the east these are largely dim figures about whom little in detail is known. I agree that it is time someone arose to preserve in vital literature the deeds and traditions of the old southwest as it really was—and believe no one could fulfil that function better than yourself. You have assimilated a tremendous amount of historic data, and have a rare type of vigorous felicity in presenting it. What is more important still, you are phenomenally sensitive and responsive to the whole psychological background and sweep of pageantry. You feel the epic drama keenly and understandingly, and can throw a vivid, intelligent sympathy into your presentations. A pile of your letters is a choice slice of literature—and one can imagine what you could do if you really sat down to mirror inclusively and systematically the heroic march of events across the soil of your native region. I certainly hope you will attempt such a *magnum opus* some day, and believe it would have great chances of success.

You are right in estimating the difficulty of dealing with sanguinary themes without verging on the borderline of that which disgusts. There is no rigid set of rules governing such matters, for the net impression of any incident depends to a tremendous extent on surrounding circumstances involving both the incident itself and the manner of its narration. In the absence of rigid rules one has to depend mostly upon one's innate sense of appropriateness—taking into account the type of production one is composing. History and science can be franker than fiction—and indeed must be absolutely frank if they are to be of any value. The historical novel has some of the characteristics of history, and certainly should not tone things down so far as to give a false picture of the period covered. In general, I think that sensitive people are disgusted more quickly with repulsive details on a *small* scale than with equally sanguinary matters on a broad or epic scale. The mowing down of an army arouses a sense of disgust less quickly than does the vivisection of a single individual. In wholesale slaughter the problem is not so much how to avoid disgust, as how to avoid an appearance of disproportion and improbability. Criticisms of large-scale battle scenes are usually based not on the score of grisliness, but on that of *monotony*. That is, critics believe that where repetitions of descriptions of slaughter have a tendency to lose force through their frequency; and that a battle may often be more vividly conveyed by the glancing citation of typical incidents plus a general statement of its outcome. This may or may not be good criticism. Really, one has to make an independent judgment in each individual case. What is more universal is the truth that sanguinary passages become weak and almost *comical* when it is apparent that they have been dragged in by the heels—that the author has deliberately twisted his story to provide an excuse for introducing them. Such an arrangement violates one's sense of probability and proportion. Bloodshed—like everything else—should be depicted in fiction *only in that proportion in which it occurs in real life*. When an author is depicting an age and scene where bloodshed played an inconceivably greater part in life than it does in any well-known age and scene, his problem is indeed great—as you justly point out. The solution probably lies in preliminary explanation. Somewhere, earlier in the narrative, the reader must be specifically informed of the difference of conditions between the depicted scene and his own; and thus prepared for events which might seem out of proportion according to his ordinary bases of judgment. As for the scenes of *individual* torture such as appear in the work of Quinn, Capt. Meek,[6] and other pulp idols—I think most of them are in rather doubtful taste. While literature must reserve the right to portray *anything in its proper proportion*, it is certainly a fact that these descriptions are *out of all proportion* to the real significance in life of the various harrowing details involved. It is only too obvious that they have been devised to titillate the morbid emotions of a very low-grade class of reader—for the reaction of sensitive and intelligent people is usually something extending from mere boredom to violent repulsion. These torture-incidents are wholly without imaginative appeal or dramatic bearing, and cannot have any conceivable purpose except to cater to the diseased taste of a certain type of semi-illiterate scum. Too bad Wright is so much of a commercialist as to encourage them.

About glorifying Oriental monarchs and nations at the expense of our own—that is undoubtedly a sheer reaction against the undiscriminating chauvinism of that earlier school of writers who represented their own civilisation as always right, and every enemy as always wrong. Actually, we see history to be an impersonal turmoil of confused, groping motives and forces, with "right" and "wrong" as purely relative matters. In the specific matter of the crusades and similar East-West encounters, it is difficult to sympathise with the East because of the reasons you mention. The very beginning of the Moslem-Christian feud was a wholly aggressive sweep of Moslems over territory to which they had no right, hence we have no need to pity them in later passages-at-arms—even if we accept the theory of the economic determinists that the crusades were precipitated by a Western desire to reopen closed routes of trade.

Regarding the 'bonus army' and its dispersal—most persons in the east, especially those who saw the gathering at first-hand in Washington, seem to think that no other course could well have been pursued. The assemblage had no legitimate purpose—for legislation is not a thing to be influenced by gestures and threats except in the most extreme periods of readjustment—and there were many signs that its mood was becoming dangerous to the peace of Washington and its citizens. Every effort was made to avert the loss of life, and in the meantime all sorts of favours and offers of free transportation had been made to the city's uninvited guests. The idea of marching on a capital with the idea of influencing legislation is at best a crazy one and at worst a dangerously revolutionary one. No end other than the present one could have been expected. Still, one must sympathise with the 'marchers' themselves, for they were in most cases genuinely needy persons, largely ignorant and easily swayed. Chief blame rests with the demagogues who encouraged their manifestly futile and potentially dangerous flourish. But the important point is that no one wished them any evil at any stage of the proceedings. Pressure was used only when they became a probable menace.

The question of the bonus itself is much deeper, and subject to any amount of controversy. No actual *debt* is involved in a legal sense, and in the case of 'veterans' who did not see service in France it is problematical whether the gift ought ever to have been promised. On the other hand, so much was asked of those who actually did see service, that some special preference or compensation in their case is clearly a very graceful thing. The problem is whether this especial form of favour at this especial time is an advisable thing. If any order of precedence has to be adopted in relieving the needy, genuine veterans ought certainly to come first—but this arbitrary granting of certain sums to veterans *only,* and to veterans who are solvent as well as to those who are in need, is open to objection on many scores. Many persons of my acquaintance who are both war veterans and hard pressed financially are unqualifiedly against the measure—as, I believe, is the American Legion as a body. It is bewilderingly hard for any layman to have any really intelligent opinion on the subject. I find myself sometimes on one side and sometimes on the other. It might be that the enactment of such a measure under popular pressure would prove a valuable entering wedge in the future's necessary task of breaking down conservative resistance to federal aid programmes in general. On the other hand, it might prove the signal for other and more irrational clamours for special privileges on the part of various groups and interests. There would, perhaps, be campaigns of intimidation in favour of a 'farmer's bonus' or a 'boilermakers' bonus'. It might also set a precedent for the custom of mob assemblage and the physical threatening of legislators. Only later historians can render a truly impartial verdict.

Meanwhile any legislation which can loosen the myopic and self-complacent supremacy of the larger industries is to be encouraged. It would probably be impossible and impracticable to try to dissolve these industries into smaller ones, for the whole trend of effective operation is toward unification; but it is indeed practicable and advisable to combat as far as possible their irresponsible abuse of power and their control of governmental processes. I trust that your ticket may win in Texas—the Elamite and all! Incidentally—many thanks for the copies of the *Gladewater Journal,* which I read with the keenest interest. I really had no idea that such specimens of untrammelled personal journalism still existed—for none of it remains in the east, even in the most remote county districts. Independence of this kind is refreshing to contemplate, even though it now and then defends some view which riper scholarship would find somewhat naive and impracticable.

As for the *cold*—if 16 *below* isn't really bad, I'm sure I don't know what is! I couldn't be alive at anything approaching that figure—for indeed, 16 *above* is below my limit of safety. Providence never gets down near zero except for two or three times each winter, and has never been lower than 6 below. A below-zero temperature is recorded perhaps once or twice in every five years. Boston is colder than Providence, while the *interior* parts of the northern states—deprived of the equalising influence of the sea—are much worse. I couldn't possibly live in *inland* New England. Of all the climates I've experienced, Florida suits me best—though I've no complaint to make against New Orleans. I'm told that in winter New Orleans sometimes has cold snaps which Florida does not get so often.

Yes—Howard Wandrei is Donald's younger brother, and a very bright kid from all I hear. Donald is now in New York, and will probably come to visit me in Providence next month. He has resigned his post in the university and will try to keep afloat for a time through writing alone.

A couple of weeks ago I felt complimented when a Los Angeles composer—Harold Farnese, Asst. Director of the Inst. of Mus. Art and graduate of the Paris Conservatory (winner of the latter's 1911 prize for composition)—wrote for permission to set two of my "Fungi from Yuggoth"—"Mirage" and "The Elder Pharos"—to music.[7] Naturally, I told him to go ahead—and I shall be curious to see what sort of strains my bizarre images will inspire in him. Another rather pleasing incident was the appearance in the July *American Author* of an article on fiction-writing in which the work of Clark Ashton Smith, Edmond Hamilton, and myself is favourably cited and quoted in connexion with certain problems of narration.[8]

I've made several trips to ancient Newport since writing you last. On the 31st I expect to get north of Boston to see the total eclipse, and immediately afterward I hope to take a cheap rail excursion to Montreal and Quebec. I've never seen Montreal, and would like to do so once, even though I know it will not prove as fascinating as ancient Quebec. Montreal dates back to 1647, but is the metropolis of Canada and has become vastly modernised.

With every good wish—

Yrs most cordially and sincerely,

HPL

Notes

1. HPL refers to the Gloria Dei Evangelical Lutheran Church (1925–28) at 15 Hayes Street in Providence, built for a largely Scandinavian congregation by Martin Hedmark, a Swedish emigré.

2. H. G. Wells, *The Time Machine* (1895). HPL initially read the novel in November 1924, noting somewhat tersely that it was "pretty good" (HPL to Lillian D. Clark, n.d. [c. 24 November 1924]; ms., JHL). He characterized the novel as "better than most of Wells' fantasy—yet [it] has the same scientific coldness & social satire" (HPL to AWD, 16 March 1927; *Essential Solitude,* 1.76).

3. Whipple Van Buren Phillips (1833–1904).

4. Edwin E. Phillips (1864–1918), Whipple's only son.

5. The city of Danzig had been under the control of Prussia until 1919 and had a largely German population. After World War I, the Allies established the nation of Poland but decreed that Danzig was a "free city" under the protection of the League of Nations. In the summer of 1932 the Nazis in Danzig were voicing their determination to reunite the city with Germany; but on 14 June, Józef Pilsudski, Poland's minister of defense, deliberately provoked the Danzig Senate by allowing a Polish warship to escort three British destroyers into the port of Danzig. The Senate complained to the League of Nations, but no action was taken.

6. Sterner St. Paul Meek (1894–1972), a military chemist and early science fiction author, who published much of his work as Capt. S. P. Meek.

7. Harold S. Farnese (1885–1945) set the two sonnets from *Fungi from Yuggoth* (*WT,* February–March 1931) to music by September, but HPL neither heard nor saw the finished work. See *SLL* 4.159 [facing], for a page from Farnese's "The Elder Pharos."

8. J. Randle Luten, "What Makes an Author Click?," *American Author* 4, No. 4 (July 1932): 11–13, cited HPL, CAS, and Edmond Hamilton as models of narrative technique. See *SLL* 4.54.

[62] [ANS][1]

[Postmarked Providence, R.I.,
21 August 1932]

Just recd. your note. Here's another Newport view. Just got back from there, having blown myself to this trip to celebrate my 42nd birthday. Cliffs & rocks of this sort are found at various points all the way up the New England coast. ¶ I read of the recent Texas storm, but concluded that it did not affect your region much. But I thought of what you once said about the perilous geography of East Texas. ¶ I was greatly interested in the cutting—& hope that West Texas will soon have population enough to exert the influence it ought. ¶ As to the Farnese music to my "Fungi"—I think the tunes ought to beat the verses, for F. is really a composer of some note. ¶ Wandrei called on both Wright & Bates in person last week, though I don't know how much that will help him place his MSS.

Best wishes—H P L

Notes

1. Front: Surf and Rocks Along Cliff Walk. Newport, R.I.

[63] [non-extant postcard by HPL]

[Postmarked Newburyport, Mass.?
c. 1 September 1932]

[64] [ANS][1]

[Postmarked Providence, R.I.,
14 September 1932]

Greetings from a conclave of spectre-chasers! We are reading with appreciation some unpublished tales of yours just sent on by Dwyer. I've told Wandrei of your appreciation of his "The Little Gods Wait." Returned from Quebec via Boston, & made a side-trip to ancient Marblehead (the "Kingsport" of my tales) Best wishes—H P L

Ξαριξετε ή Αραβε

Δοναλδ Ϝανδραιι[2]

Thus am I left by your tales wordless!

Wandrei

Notes

1. Front: University Hall and Manning Hall. Brown University.

2. Wandrei was engaged in his second visit to Providence to see HPL (from 13 to 20 September 1932).

[65] [TLS]

[received 22 September 1932]

Dear Mr. Lovecraft:

I read, as always, your comments on the Greco-Roman world with intense interest. I agree with you that cultural environment and heredity is generally stronger than blood heritage. The matter of Romanized Gauls is a case in point. And in America today, many immigrants become so completely Americanized by the second or third generation that they seem to merge with the native population and to become as much a part of their adopted country and race as if their ancestors had come over on the Mayflower. There are plenty of exceptions to this latter case, of course, but they have no bearing on the original theory.

For myself, if I should be suddenly confronted with the prospect of being transported back through the centuries into a former age, with the option of living where I wished, I would naturally select the most civilized country possible. That would be necessary, for I have always led a peaceful, sheltered life, and would be unable to cope with conditions of barbarism. Thus, for my own safety, I would select Egypt rather than Syria, to which otherwise my instincts would lead me; I would choose Greece rather than Spain or Thrace; Rome rather than Gaul, Britain or Germany. As a matter of personal necessity I would seek to adapt myself to the most protected and civilized society possible, would conform to their laws and codes of conduct, and if necessary, fight with them against the ruder races of my own blood.

On the other hand, if I were to be reborn in some earlier age and grow up knowing no other life or environment than that, I would choose to be born in a hut among the hills of western Ireland, the forests of Germany or the steppes of Southern Russia; to grow up hard and lean and wolfish, worshipping barbarian gods and living the hard barren life of a barbarian—which is, to the barbarian who has never tasted anything else—neither hard nor barren. I never talked with an old pioneer of the true type, who, even admitting hardships that seem intolerable to modern people, and would kill folk of softer mold—I never talked with one, I say, who did not at last admit that to him that life was fuller, more vital and more full of real content than this newer phase. Of course such a man has usually been unable to adjust himself to changing conditions. To a man of intellectual accomplishments the life of a frontiersman would be intolerable; but to a man who has never known anything else, such a life would be full of vital interest.

I can not, however, agree with you that the spirit of physical contest is artificial. I may possibly have misunderstood your meaning in this case, since it is pretty easy to get out of my depth. Personally, I would never consider glorifying physical achievement above other things—a research worker in a laboratory, for instance, is of infinitely more value than the greatest athlete that ever lived. Yet I can not but think that a zest for, or at least an interest in physical struggles, ties to the very ribs of humanity. It is manifestly impossible for all men to derive pleasure from intellectual pursuits alone. The average man lacks the ability and the advantages, or perhaps I should say the opportunity. So he turns in many cases to the field of sport, for relaxation and exhilaration, and I can not but believe that if there is any artificiality in the matter, it leans toward the side of the purely intellectual pursuit. Yet I am not prepared to say that any pursuit of mankind is artificial. True, there is probably nothing about the football field, the prize-ring, the race-track or the baseball diamond that tends toward the advancement of art, science or literature. But surely we are not so bound to the treadwheel of progress that we must engage in only those pursuits which definitely make for the advancement of society. After a hard day's work I feel far more like seeing a prize-fight or a leg-show than I feel like delving into questions of science and philosophy. Understand, I am not upholding this feeling. I am only saying that the average man, like me, simply lacks the brains to find his pleasure and thrills in purely intellectual followings.

Looking back over a none-too-lengthy and prosaic life, I can easily pick out what seemed—and still seems—the peak of my life to date; that is, the point at which I derived the highest thrills—a word which my limited vocabulary causes me to overwork. I do not altogether lack appreciation for artistic endeavors. I am capable of becoming drunken on written words—the power, sweep and splendor of certain prose writers; often I have felt a wave of coldness sweep over me, with a physical accompaniment of "goose-flesh" at the pure beauty of great poetry. It is not hard for certain singers and musicians to bring tears to my eyes, or a white blaze of glory to my brain. All this, I realize, shows that the appeal is more to my emotions than to my intelligence, and possibly I am without genuine intellectual appreciation. Yet, mental or emotional, it is possible for me to keenly enjoy the triumphs and attempts of art.

Yet when I look for the peak of my exultation, I find it on a sweltering, breathless midnight when I fought a black-headed tiger of an Oklahoma drifter in an abandoned ice-vault, in a stifling atmosphere laden with tobacco smoke and the reek of sweat and rot-gut whiskey—and blood; with a gang of cursing, blaspheming oil-field roughnecks for an audience. Even now the memory of that battle stirs the sluggish blood in my fat-laden tissues. There was nothing about it calculated to advance art, science or anything else. It was a bloody, merciless, brutal brawl. We fought for fully an hour—until neither of us could fight any longer, and we reeled against each other, gasping incoherent curses through battered lips. No, there was nothing stimulating to the mental life of man about it. There was not even an excuse for it. We were fighting, not because there was any quarrel between us, but simply to see who was the best man. Yet I repeat that I get more real pleasure out of remembering that battle than I could possibly get out of contemplating the greatest work of art ever accomplished, or seeing the greatest drama ever enacted, or hearing the greatest song ever sung. I repeat, I do not seek to justify my particular make-up. But there it is. I love to watch a well-matched prize-fight, a well-fought football game. I have beat my way hundreds of miles to see both, and have endured cold, hunger and a certain amount of hardship, and I can not believe that my enjoyment of such spectacles is artificial. Animalistic it may be; unworthy it possibly is; bound to the tie-ribs of reality it must be.

I noted with interest your comments regarding the supernatural etc., and am not equipped to dispute any point of your theories. I never gave a name to my views—or lack of views—but I guess an Agnostic is what I am, if that means scepticism regarding all human gropings. Perhaps the main reason that I dislike to take a firm stand in any direction, is because of the respect I have for my father's intelligence. He is not by any means convinced that there is nothing in the matters mentioned. He is far better educated than I, and has more natural sense than I'll ever have. Scientist? He is a practical scientist if ever lived one. For more than thirty years he has been applying science in his daily life. There is no better physician in the state of Texas, though there are many who have made more of a financial success. The reason he is not a rich man is because he's been more interested in humanity than in dollars. The charity work he's done would run up into the hundred thousands, and the bills people have beat him out of would about equal that figure. He always sacrificed the business side of his profession to the scientific side. When other men were balancing their ledgers, figuring their per centages and suing for their bills, he was studying the latest methods, attending clinics and buying the latest books on medicine. He is a rare combination of a scholar and a worker. All that the finest medical schools of the South and Southwest could give him, he got, working his way through, frequently doing mental and physical work that would have been beyond the power of a weaker man. Even now, at the age of sixty-one, he does not only an office practice, but a country practice as well, that embraces parts of four counties, and has more strength, endurance and enthusiasm than I have. Hundreds of men are walking the world today who owe their lives to him, and many of these men were paupers, who were never able to pay him a cent. Nor did he ask it. Frequently he not only saved their lives, but fed their families as well. That's why he's not rich today. In the thousands of women he has delivered, he never lost one woman in childbirth. He was the first to introduce snake-antitoxin into this part of the country, and he never lost a snake-bite case, to the best of my knowledge. Publishers of the most up-to-date medical books have frequently written him, asking him to contribute reports on diagnosis and treatment for publications. All this is to simply show that he is no ignorant bumpkin, but a scientific man in the truest sense of the word—science applied, and not simply theorized on. There is scarcely any branch of medical science that he has not studied; any legitimate branch, I mean. Nor medicine alone, but theology, history and economics.

I have set in colleges and listened to dried up professors mouthing their supercilious viewpoints on life and death, and I could scarcely restrain my mirth, when I compared them with my father, who, while they were sitting at ease in some dusty nook, analyzing the universe from a detached and superior point of view, he was grappling with the raw, elemental vitals of existence in the city slums or the backwoods hills. In his early days much of his practice was in primitive communities, far removed from any of the inventions and conveniences of civilization. He went into miserable shacks and huts, and without weapons save his own will and intelligence and a few simple medicines of the time, grappled the destroyer and repeatedly overthrew him. Science? My father knows science; it is not an empty word or a theory with him; it has been a spear with which he has ten thousand times hurled back death from the quivering body of a helpless victim.

And if he, who has plunged his hands deep into the very guts of Life and Death, and seen things that an average man seldom even dreams, if he is not ready to deny the existence of a future state, then I for one do not care to deny it. These college professors I mentioned thought they knew things because they had read the books. He has read the books, and more than that, he has known Life in its reddest, rawest, most elemental phases. Honest men, thieves; white men, negroes, Mexicans, to all he has given, and gives, the same earnest attention. It has mattered little to him whether the man or woman under his care were a saint or a criminal, a rich man or a beggar. Many and many a time he have kept watch over the sick-bed of some poor pauper, himself neither eating or sleeping, oblivious to all else except the battle he was waging with the destroyer. And people have stood awed, seeing the intensity of that awful struggle, in which he literally held death at bay by the sheer power of his intellect and will, throughout the night, to stagger forth in the dawn, victorious.

Through the slums of eastern cities, in the outlaw-infested wilds of the old Indian Territory, in the silence and desolation of the Great Plains in the days before the law was brought there, in the sordid barreness of the squatters' hills, in the roar and madness of oil booms, he has moved unchangingly on his way, single-handed battling disease, madness, insanity, death.

And when I compare him with professors, and with mere scholars, I am merely amused. I respect their zeal for knowledge, but I can not attach too much importance to any man's theories, unless he has backed them up with actual work and toil and matched them against the elementals of Life, as my father has.

I'm enclosing a clipping, telling of the planned destruction of the old French Market in New Orleans.[1] That's an old landmark that seems to me should be preserved. It smelled like hell—what with the fish, lobster, wops etc., but it had a real air of olden times that wasn't altogether the scent. But you doubtless visited it. Many a plantain have I purchased there—and cooked in the manner of banana fritters; I know of no better dish. Did you get any genuine Creole gumbo while there? Cooked as only the bona-fide French of New Orleans can cook it, with rice, thyme, bay-leaf, minced ham, white chicken meat, crab and shrimp, it's a food for the gods. Nor have I ever tasted a drink half as good an old French-German woman on Canal Street used to mix—but those were the days of good whiskey. I supposed you visited Pontchartrain, the duelling oaks, and the ruins of the old Spanish fort. You should have—or maybe you did—take a boat up the river a few miles, in order to get a look at the old plantation houses which rose near the banks—at least they did in my time. Did you ever hear the old song, "The Lakes of the Pontchartrain"?

"Twas on one bright March morning, I bid old New Orleans adieu,
And on my way to Jackson, where I was forced to go,
'Twas there my Georgia money no credit did me gain,
And it filled my heart with sadness on the lakes of the Pontchartrain.

Through swamps and alligators, I wound my weary way,
O'er railroad ties and crossings, my weary feet did stray,
Till the shadows of the evening, some higher ground did gain,
Twas there that I met this Creole, on the lakes of the Pontchartrain.

"Good evening, fair young maiden, my money to me is no good;
"It if wasn't for the alligators, I'd sleep out in the wood."
"Oh, welcome, welcome, stranger, for though our house be plain,
"We never turn away a traveller from the lakes of the Pontchartrain."

And so on for several more verses. I can't get interested in these new song-hits, but I know a lot of old ones by heart, that have been passed down through the generations, from the hills of Scotland and Ireland, across the Piedmont and the Cumberlands, over the Mississippi and through the pine-lands, and onto the great plains, changing form as they went.

You are undoubtedly right in saying that it would be better to aleviate the miseries of the working classes, than to give them liquor. But who's going to do that? The workmen themselves are scarcely capable of working out their own solutions; and to all other classes we—and when I say "we" I mean the laboring masses, of which I am a member—we, I say, are less than the dogs that eat their crumbs. How can we develop intelligence and co-ordination when life is such a struggle for existence as to crowd all other considerations out? What are the philosophers and economists to a man whose days consist in back-breaking, brain-numbing toil from the time he rises until he falls dazedly into his bed that night? I agree with you that the only way the masses will ever get any favors is by force. But I doubt much if, in such event, the rulers will call in the socialogists; they're more likely to call in the gunmen and sluggers, and put down revolt by massacre and whole-sale slaughter.

As for liquor as a whole—I have no use, and never had any use, for any man or set that expected a person to make a swill-barrel of his belly in order to be sociable. I certainly think no less of a man because he refuses a drink. In fact, I was a rather rabid teetotaller at one time of my life, and wouldn't have taken a drink if the president had brought it on a golden platter. Even in my hardest drinking days, I've refrained from taking a drink, because I happened to be with a non-drinking man. I have a right to drink; the other man has a right not to drink. That's my attitude. I never regarded a man as priggish or eccentric because he doesnt drink, and I have no patience for anyone so narrow as to look on a non-drinker in that light.

As for law and law enforcement—I had no intention of casting slurs on the courage of Eastern law-officers. I don't think that at any time during our correspondence, I've cast any reflections on the courage of the people of the East, or any people, as far as that goes. I do say that it doesn't take the guts to be a law-officer anywhere today, that it used to take. As you yourself point out, the many inventions of civilization make it hard for the criminal to escape punishment; it naturally follows that the job of the cop is easier. I hardly think that such men as John Poe, Pat Garrett and Jack Hayes[2] looked on the apprehending of criminals as "a stage for the showing off of their personal merits." When one of these men went out after a desperado single-handed it was not because of an inflated ego, but a cool confidence in his ability to do the job alone. When Jack Hayes went into a thicket and killed ELEVEN Comanche Indians in hand-to-hand combat, he did not do this because he wanted to show-off. It was his job and he did it. He was confident of his ability, and he did not need a mob of men to help him. He was the greatest law-officer the west has ever seen, and he killed more men than the average cop ever arrests. The same thing can apply to Wild Bill Hickok. He was up against conditions that would freeze the guts of the average chief of police, wherever he lived. The west swarmed with desperadoes of the most terrible type—bandits from the gold-fields, renegades from all states, half-breeds, gunfighters and gamblers and wild cowboys from Texas, bringing the trail herds up the Chisholm. He went it practically alone. I have no love for Wild Bill Hickok—he killed too many Texans. But he was a power in the west. And he never had a mob at his beck and call. In fact, it was the other way around. He was repeatedly faced by organized crime of the most desperate sort. If he had been a mere swaggering swashbuckler, with a desire to strut and show-off, he wouldn't have lasted a week. As it was, he lived long enough to clean up every place he went, and had some eighty-odd slayings to his credit when Jack McCall shot him in the back of the head;[3] at the behest, by the way, of certain organizations not openly connected with the criminal element. It may have been an inflated ego that led men like him, and like John Poe, and Jack Hayes, into wild countries, to clean it up and make it habitable, single-handed, yet at least they succeeded. And I can assure you that it was no "childish game" in which they took part—unless murder, butchery and sudden death are childish. In one town in Kansas the outlaws took out the sheriff and chopped off his head with an axe. The governor sent Wild Bill Hickok there; he went alone, killed the ring-leaders of the gang, and ran the rest out of the country. He made the town fit for a man to live in, and he did it alone. In my own time one Ranger has cowed a ravening mob; and until very recently it was never the custom to send more than one Ranger to quell an ordinary disturbance.

Romantic or not, I find much to admire in the old type of officer, who, instead of having everything on his side as does the modern cop, worked against every disadvantage and yet cleaned up his country. His resources were comparatively few. His deputies were few, if any; the countryside was frequently hostile, or at least remained silently neutral. The outlaws had friends, secret hide-outs, frequently political pull. In the last analysis, law enforcement depended largely on the individual wearing the badge. I've seen that work out myself, to an extent, in boom towns. When Pat Garrett went after Billy the Kid, he had a posse, its true. But he asked no man to do his shooting. With his own hand he killed Tom O'Phalliard, Charlie Bowdre[4] and Billy himself, breaking up, practically single-handed, the most desperate band of outlaws that ever haunted the hills of the Southwest.

When Jack Hayes went from Texas to California in '49—the fact that he had to work his way, shows how rich the pickings were for a Texas law in those days—and the governor appointed him sheriff of San Francisco, he had not only the regular criminal element to deal with, but the organized Vigilantes as well. Within a year or so, he'd cleaned the town as its never been cleaned since. And he did it practically alone. I hardly think you'd have found a more practical and less romantic man than Jack Hayes. If he was aware of his manhood, it was scarcely to his discredit, since no man ever saw him strut or heard him boast about his deeds. Indeed, no one will ever know how many Mexicans, Indians and desperadoes Hayes killed, because he never would talk of his exploits. He was quiet, soft-spoken, modest, and I repeat, the best law officer that ever wore leather west of the Mississippi.

In regards law-breakers—I am the first to admit that frequently the confirmed law-breaker is a rat, who ought to be put out of the way. Yet I can not hold that any man who breaks a law puts himself beyond the pale of human consideration and is to be held as a rabid wolf. Frequently the breaking of a law is not wanton and vicious, but merely a mistake or the result of a momentary blind passion. I do not call for mushy sentimentality in dealing with offenders—but I do call for a little common sense, which quality seems lacking in a good many enforcers of the law. Even in the case of regular law-breakers, the individual is not always a cross between a maddog and a vandal. I've seen plenty of men who were driven to crime. Society stood smugly by and let them welter, but the instant they turned in desperation to some course not exactly ethical, there was a great howling and yelling about the individual's debt to society. Apparently society has no obligations to fulfil toward the individual. I hate a habitual criminal as much as any man. But I don't class as a criminal a man who commits a crime in a moment of passion—or one who steals to keep from starving. I've rubbed shoulders with many kinds of men in my life, and there was a good deal of the devil in most of them, and a little of the saint in some. When I was working in that drug-store I mentioned, I used to run accounts of my own with certain young fellows the management wouldn't credit. In other words, I sold them the stuff on my own responsibility, and if they failed to pay me, I made it good to the management out of my own pocket. I dealt with bootleggers, booze-runners, gamblers, and hijack men, and I never lost a damned cent. Even a fellow who scattered a trail of cold checks across the country and skipped, leaving his room-mate to hold the bag, paid me what he owed the night before he took it on the lam. I don't particularly hold this up as a sign of nobility in a passle of rats and wolves. These youths of course were not hardened criminals, at least I wouldn't call them so. Though some of them undoubtedly developed into such characters. Let me repeat that I do not seek to glorify crime. I merely object to a system that allows the gangster rat to go unpunished, while an ordinary citizen who has the misfortune to slip, is practically sure of being crucified for an example. I know the grilling methods of the police, for instance, are supposed to be applied only to the worst thugs. But I am hardly innocent enough to be fooled by that. If I didn't know of a few cases, I have other sources of information to fall back on. Eastern sources too, by the way. Not many years ago I heard a Chicago literary critic remark over the air that the police generally reserved most of their strong-arm methods for unattached offenders who had no gang-connections or political pull.

I'm afraid I wouldn't fit into the scheme of more civilized sections, or even in the scheme of this section, which is being civilized as fast as people from other states can do it to their own advantage. I've always been a quiet, law-abiding citizen, to the best of my ability. Yet I, in common with most of my acquaintances, have occasionally broken laws. Just now the brother of one of my best friends is hiding out somewhere—I don't know where. But if he were to come to me, I understand my duty as a citizen would demand that I instantly hand him over to the police. Well, I have few friends in this world, but if any one of them were to come to me, hunted by the law, I'd hold myself lower than a dog if I didn't do all in my power to aid him. If that's romantic and idealistic, I'm sorry, but I can't help it.

I was nearly fourteen years old before I lived—for any length of time—in a community which supported a law officer. Generally the nearest officer was the sheriff of the county, whose office was in the county seat. Sometimes there was a sort of constable, whose duties were so light as to be practically non-existent. The communities in which I lived were unsophisticated and primitive, made up largely of people with quick tempers and violent passions. Yet life was not a holocaust of murder and rape. Mainly we settled our problems among ourselves. Civil suits and litigations were comparatively few. If some swaggering bully began to impose himself too much on the community, somebody killed him. After a killing there was always some kind of a legal investigation. But fights that did not end fatally were seldom dragged into courts. I still think that if two gentlemen want to go out where no innocent bystander will be injured, and fight it out between them, its nobody's business but theirs. We were a taciturn, clannish people, not inclined to talk to strangers. A whole county could keep a secret and keep it well. Nor did a sheriff or officer dare resort to strong-arm methods to get information. You will understand that I am not suggesting these conditions to be applied to more thickly settled parts. I don't pretend to know anything about life in the East, for instance, and nothing I say here is to be taken as a sectional criticism. But as I remember it, Texas was a safer and more pleasant state to live in before the influx of people from other states forced a lot of protective legislature down our throats. If there was more honest fist-fighting, there was less theft, murder and underhanded knavery; more open hospitality and trust. Now men are becoming so cowed by law that they are becoming miserly, furtive and afraid to resent an open insult. I agree with a noted lawyer, now a candidate for the legislature, and a man whose intelligence I respect. He maintains that too many laws are being passed, and forecasts the time when the people will be made literal serfs, simply by the passing of myriad laws. These laws the rich can evade, but the poor can not. Frankly, that's one of my kicks; instead of being allowed to develop gradually along our own lines, and work out our own laws and culture, the state has been flooded with capitalism from other sections of the country, by people who wanted laws enacted for their own benefit, by which they could exploit the state, and be protected from reprisal while doing so. I resent the forcing of alien culture and habits on my native state, even if that culture is superior. Its superiority in a general sense doesn't mean that its the best thing that could happen to us. Yesterday Texas was a frontier; today its a grab-bag for big business—business which takes far more money out of the state than it ever puts in. The transition is painful to a person of old traditions.

There is a vast difference between the old stock native Texan and people from more civilized sections. Though now it is the style in many parts of the state to ape Eastern ways and despise the mannerisms of their fathers. Eastern ways are good for the East, where they naturally developed. I am not so sure than an imitation of those ways is so good. But the old Texan: a great number of the people who have flooded this state in quest of climate, health or money, do not understand us, and make no effort to, being fortified with a feeling of their own superiority. Many evidently expect to be shot at the minute they get off the train or the boat, and finding us not particularly sanguinary, immediately swing to the other side, and despise us for lack of spirit. They seem to mistake our natural courtesy for servility. Our code of politeness does no doubt seem exaggerated to a stranger from parts where life moves at a quicker tempo. Our habit of complimenting our friends, and deprecating ourselves, is merely part of our code of courtesy; the compliments are sincere, but when we deprecate ourselves, it does not mean that we lack self-esteem. Under our politeness generally lurks a keen vanity, and a sometimes dangerous pride. Beneath the veneer of our courtesy we are generally hot tempered and unforgiving. We remember our friends long, but we remember our enemies longer. Of course you know that these remarks can not apply to all Texans, now that the state is become thickly settled and complex. But it does apply to the people of the old original stock. Another thing, more cultured people are prone to sneer at a certain melodramatic tendency in people of the old stock. It is there; I would be the last to deny it. It crops out continually in my writing, occasionally in my speech, though never in my actions.

I have heard and read this tendency pointed out as an evidence that the old Southwesterner was more bluff than anything else. A greater mistake was never made, and can be classed with the fallacy that a bully is always a coward, and that a braggart never makes good his threats. Such men as Bat Masterson, Bob Ollinger, Henry Plummer, and Ben Thompson[5] were extremely melodramatic, but were no less deadly for that reason. Ben Thompson in particular—his whole life was a stage whereon he swaggered and posed; he lived pure melodrama to the day he was riddled in the old Jack Harris Theatre in San Antonio, and he shamelessly played up to the gallery gods. And he strewed his stage with thirty-odd dead men, as an earnest of his actorship. King Fisher, too, who died beside him on that red day when the curtain finally rang down on the red drama. By God, how appropriate it was that these deadly actors made their final bow in a theatre, of all places! King Fisher's melodrama ran more to his attire than his actions. His boots were of the finest calfskin, with fancy red stitching; his hat was a Mexican sombrero ornamented with gold braid; for a vest he wore a gold braided Mexican jacket; a red silk sash girdled his supple waist, and from richly hand-worked leather jutted the ivory butts of the finest pistols Colt could supply by special order. His chaps were made of the striped pelt of a royal Bengal tiger, commandeered from a wandering circus. I have heard that at one time a hundred and fifty men followed him. Yet King Fisher was not merely a taker of human life. If he had been, he would have killed Horace Greeley[6] that day in San Antonio, when Horace took him to task for his murders. Instead of resenting the impertinence, the King simply smiled and assured Horace that he had murdered no one recently. Horace then accused King of having ridden into Eagle Pass with sixteen human ears strung on his bridle reins—which was true. Still King Fisher showed no resentment at this uninvited criticism of his actions, merely smiling again and remarking that they were Mexican ears, and did not count. If Horace had ventured thus to reprove Hendry Brown or Bob Ollinger, I wouldn't have cared to vouch for his safety.

But to return to the present day: the native Texan is looked on as lawless. But if he is prone to reserve calling in the law as a last resort rather than a first, it is only necessary to remember that the time is not far back when men considered it their own personal business to protect themselves. When the uncle for whom I was named—a prominent banker on the coast—was mixed up in the "round bale war", he hired a private detective to guard his house and protect his family when he himself had to be absent, but he asked no man to protect him. He wore his protection slung on his own right hip. Anyway, when one of his associates was shot down in the streets, the gang that did it ran the sheriff clean out of town. Even when my uncle learned of a plot to murder him as he got aboard the Galveston train, he didn't ask for a police escort. He didn't even ask his friends to help him, but they were there in force, and the would-be killers backed down. I'm not telling this to show how brave my uncle was; I don't claim he was braver than anybody else. As far as that goes, he wasn't afraid of anything between the devil and the moon. But it just shows that in those days men considered protecting themselves their own personal job, unless the odds against them were too overwhelming.

As for the modern police system, I must confess that my admiration for it is not high. I hear much of its efficiency—and at the same time, in newspaper editorials, from the mouths of lecturers, speakers, reformers, and the pens of political and social writers, I hear that the nation is staggering with corruption and vice. Not many months ago a woman in an East Texas city said to me—and she held a responsible position and was in a position to know—she said, "The police don't exert themselves unless somebody pays them; promise one a hundred dollars and he'll work his legs off." Is that the sort of condition that prevails in cities? Is legal protection to be the privilege only of those willing and able to pay for it, while a man is denied the right to protect himself? For the carrying of weapons and the personal avenging of a wrong is forbidden by law. Another thing—a slight one. Once a friend of mine was walking down the street of a boom town, slightly jagged. Somebody smelled his breath, and he was thrown into jail where he spent the night, being released only on the payment of a fine. He was making no disturbance at all. Of course, the laws could not know that he would make none. Let us admit then, that they were right in casting him into jail. But—not long later I was in a drugstore where the son of a big oil magnate from the North was wild drunk and raising hell generally. Not a law ever showed up until he left. He was allowed to do just as he damned please. And if somebody had shot him, heaven and hell would have been moved to have sent the killer to the chair. Is there here a double standard of conduct? Are the obligations of the laboring man to society different from those of the rich and powerful? If our laws are so blindly just, why do the wealthy seldom ever suffer by their enforcement? There was a great tumult about Albert Fall serving his light sentnce;[7] yet for half of what he did, other men have spent a life-time behind the bars. No, I don't believe a really wealthy man can be touched by the law, usually, East or West. On the other hand I've known plenty of cases where ignorance was taken advantage of. Men were arrested without legal right, and bullied into paying fines that could never have been collected, had the victims known anything about law. Just like the Vice-squad racket, for instance. I followed that business pretty closely in the papers and magazines. I've known it worked on a smaller scale elsewhere. Where ignorant people, men and women, knowing nothing of legal procedure, were made to believe that they had committed some offense and simply shaken down.

As for the rest, we have the Vice-squad scandal in New York; the present investigation in that city, and the kicking of various officials out of office.[8] And there is the Lindbergh case. No feather in the police cap there, unless the hounding of an innocent girl to suicide is to be considered as such.[9] And there is Capone, whom they had to send up on a federal charge. Nor do I ever pick up a paper that I don't read about gangster activities, extortions, city scandals, dope rings, etc. The utter failure to enforce prohibition is likewise a case in point. No, I can't believe that the police machine works universally with anything like a smooth tread. These remarks need not be taken to mean that I am an anarchist, a criminal-sympathizer, or a rabid cop-hater. But I do believe that the system as a whole is too corrupt. I have respect and admiration for any fearless, honest officer of the law.

I'm enclosing a clipping which is probably a lot of bologna. If the outlaw had been Floyd, he'd more likely have killed the officer instead of throwing him out naked. A friend of mine recently returned from Oklahoma, where he'd gone to try his luck in the harvest fields, and he was quite enthusiastic about Floyd. From what he said public sympathy must be a good deal with the outlaw. I also hear that Floyd has been feeding a good many destitute people. They can hardly be expected to inform against him to the representatives of a society which lets them starve.

I note the mid-western farmers are raring up.[10] I've always said that if an agricultural revolution started, it would start there. I don't have the slightest idea that their blockade will do any good, but you can't blame people for trying to help their conditions. Legislate—legislate—but what good does that do when the people are betrayed by everybody they put in office? However, the farmer is just out of luck; he's not organized well enough to intimidate anybody, and it will probably end by their being mowed down with machine guns and ridden down by cavalry. Also a little hell busting in the Illinois mining district.[11] I suppose they'll have the troops out there, too. I'm surprized I haven't heard the term "Red" applied to the midwestern farmers. Now days if a man's hungry, he's a Red; if he wants a job, he's a Red; if he asserts his right to live, he's a Red; and should be clubbed on the head and dragged out as an enemy to organized society.

You're right about the muddle of history. Its a regular blind surging maelstrom as far as I can see. Lamb, writing on the crusades, seems to discount the theory of trade-routes, at least in connection with the First Crusade. As near as I can learn, he maintains that movement was begun by Urban[12] for his own particular purposes—he wanted to start a popular movement to counter-balance the power of his popish rival—and was carried out by the people, mainly through actual religious zeal, though this of course was modified, in the case of various nobles, by a desire to loot and carve out new kingdoms.

Glad you found the Gladewater paper interesting. Its one of the few organs of the people against the crushing tread of the big interests. The editor packs plenty of power, too; immediately after he accused the state government of sending Rangers to the East Texas fields to co-erce the voting, the order was countermanded. It had been announced that thirty-five Rangers were to be sent there to clean out "certain gangsters from the North." The editor of the Journal point-blank accused certain high officials of sending these Rangers to East Texas to bulldoze the voters in the coming election, and he added a warning which might easily have been read as a threat. Anyway, the thirty-five Rangers who were already on their way to the fields, were recalled, "lest their presence be misunderstood" it was officially announced.

I was surprized to learn that Providence weather is no colder than it is. Yet I might have known it, considering its position on the coast. Winters in this part of the state, when rainy, are generally mild, though drab and gloomy because of the continuous cloudy weather. Dry winters, especially those following drouths, are likely to be cold as the devil. I've seen people come here from northern and eastern states, and nearly freeze in the winter. That's because this cold is different from the still even cold which I understand prevails in those regions. Fairly warm days are followed by freezes, and its difficult to accustom oneself to the sudden changes. Then there is the wind; that's what gets many people from other states. These howling, raging blizzards, falling directly off the Rocky Mountains by way of the Staked Plains, are enough to freeze a brass monkey. You can't wear enough clothing so the wind don't blow the coldness right through you. Though, as I believe I told you about the sand-storms, there doesn't seem to be as many and as vicious blizzards as there used to be. There are lots of different climates in Texas anyhow, ranging as the altitude does, from sea-level to plains of four thousand feet and mountains a mile high. Last February I sat on a porch in the lower Rio Grande Valley, in my shirt-sleeves, being pleasantly cooled by a norther that was rattling the fronds of the palm-trees, and hugged myself in unholy glee to think that my friends up on the Callahans were being frost-bitten by that same norther. But I can't stand the low altitudes of that south country. This section isn't as cold as it is up on the plains, but its cold compared to other parts of the state. As I've probably said before, this town is on the highest point of the Callahan Devide, which is a watershed draining into the Brazos on the north and the Colorado on the south. The land dips somewhat to the north before beginning to climb toward the Caprock, and there are no ridges to break the swoop of the northers which whistle off the great plains. Therefore its much colder here than it is in even Brownwood, for instance, which lies only forty miles from here, but on the southern slope of the devide. In fact, this devide seems to act as a wind-break for most all Central West and Central Texas.

I sure agree with you about the relative merits of cold and heat. I detest winter. I despise to wear overcoats and scarves and all that sort of junk. I draw the line at heavy underwear. I wear the same light silk stuff in the winter that I do in the summer. But regardless of what I wear or don't wear, my feet and ears nearly freeze off. I remember one time when I was a kid, I was out skating—or rather sliding, for I had no skates—on a frozen pond. I must have been a bigger sap then than I am now, even. Because the ice buckled and cracked under my weight, and I couldn't swim a stroke and was out there by myself. But luck was with me that time, because the ice didn't break until I was near shore and the water was only knee-deep. But Judas, was it cold! As I'd been forbidden the pond, I said nothing about it, didn't have a chance to change my shoes and socks, or even empty the water out, and so splashed off to school in the teeth of a howling blizzard. I had only about a quarter of a mile to walk, but before I'd covered half the distance my stockings were stiff as boards, and the water didn't splash in my shoes, because it was solid ice. When I got to school, the teacher, who was enveloped in a fur coat, wouldn't let us go to the stove to warm, because we generally got into a fight if we did. I sat there until noon, at the back of the room where the heat couldn't reach, and I want to say that it was about as lousy a morning as I ever spent, viewed from a purely physical standpoint. Its a wonder my feet hadn't been frost-bitten.

While you were in the South on your recent visit, did you hear any legends of the Cave-in-the-Rock gang? That's a bit of scenery I've always wanted to visit. A friend of mine saw it a year or so ago, and said its really impressive.[13] It certainly harbored a desperate horde. Foremost of these were the Harps, who to my mind were the most terrible outlaws that ever cursed this Continent, not even excluding Boone Helm,[14] from whom Zane Grey apparently drew his hellish "Gulden" of "The Border Legion",[15] and who on one occasion, finding himself snowed in with a companion in the mountains of British Columbia, and out of food, murdered the companion, partly devoured his body, and took up his journey again, carrying a leg along for supplies on the way; who, when strung up along with the rest of the Plummer gang by the Vigilantes,[16] standing on a wagon with a rope around his neck, asked if he was expected to jump off, or be pushed off. On being told that he could do as he liked, he replied, "Every man to his own principles! Three cheers for Jeff Davis and the Confederacy! Hurrah for hell! Let her rip!"—and jumped off.

But I was speaking of the Harps, whose devilish blood-lust can be traced partly to an evident insanity, partly to resentment instilled by persecution as Tories in their early life. They eventually foreswore even the garments of civilization, wearing the garb of Indians, and going single-file through the woods. I hear that it was a most horrifying experience to meet them, trailing silently through the forest, their women and children treading noiselessly behind them, and all stamped with the mark of their bestial ferocity. A white man reverted to savagery is a more terrible thing than a true savage, as witness the Girtys.[17] Few there were who survived a meeting with the Harps in a lonely forest. They were too primitive and savage for the gang at Cave-in-the-Rock, who drove them forth in horror. Judas, the blood that was spilt along the Wilderness Road and the Natchez Trace!

Big Harp met his end at the muzzle of a rifle he had loaded himself, and a man whose entire family the Harps had butchered, cut around the outlaw's neck with a butcher knife and twisted his head off, breaking the spinal bones by sheer strength. They carried the head in a sack of roasting ears for a long way—and ate the corn, too, for supper, all but one young man who objected to the blood on the shucks and was jeered at—and finally stuck it up in a tree which was for years known as Harp's Head; until an old woman took down the skull and ground it up for one of the ingredients of a magic potion that she hoped would restore intelligence to her idiot son.

Fate played an ironic jest on Little Harp, the other brother. Two desperate-looking men volunteered to go up the river to the hide-out of Sam Mason, the river-bandit,[18] and try to collect the big reward that was on his head. They brought back Sam's head rolled up in a big ball of clay, and while the judge was about to pay them off, a bystander pointed at one of the men and shouted that the fellow was Little Harp, who'd disappeared after the killing of his brother. So they stuck Little Harp's head up beside Sam Mason's.

There have been, however, few more desperate rogues than those living in old New York, from all I can hear. In the days of the Hudson Dusters, the

Dead Rabbits and other gangs. Bill Poole, the leader of the "native Americans" must have possessed incredible vitality, to have lived fourteen days—I believe that was the right number, wasn't it?—with a bullet under his heart. "Good bye, boys; I die a true American!" That speech of his bade fair to become an American classic. He should have had more sense than to have gone into that Irish dive. Because a mick lets you kick him is no sign he wont shoot you in the back. Not that there were many of that gang who would take kickings from anybody, even Bill Poole. I'd have given five dollars to have seen the fight John Morrissey had with Poole. New York about that time—about 1850—must have been a most virile and interesting place. I'd have liked to have seen the fight Tom Hyer, Poole's friend, had with Yankee Sullivan for the heavyweight title. Heavyweights! Sullivan weighed about 155 pounds. What with Hyer falling on him after he was felled, and slugging him with his knees and elbows, its a wonder to me that Yankee survived. Sullivan was a tough nut, though. They say he gave Morissey a terrible beating, until John's ruggedness wore him down. There's a legend that Sullivan, after leaving New York, joined Walker's filibusters and perished nobly in Nicaragua.[19] That's balogna. He went to California and was hanged by the San Francisco Vigilantes.[20] But neither Sullivan nor Morrissey nor yet Tom Hyer was the toughest product of that time, to my humble mind. That honor—or whatever—ought to go to Chris Lilly who flourished in the early '40's. After killing his sweetheart, Rose Seven, one of the belles of Five Points, with a blow of his naked fist, he became enraged because one of her former suitors, Tom McCoy, the middleweight champion, insisted on shedding tears—probably more inspired by licker than grief—and making a scene. Chris must have been jealous of McCoy, even though the girl was dead. Anyway, they fought it out with the raw 'uns, on a place between Yonkers and Hasting, and after 120 rounds of terrible battling, they carried McCoy out of the ring dead. Lilly fled to New Orleans, where he quickly established himself as the bully of the quarters, and got matched with an English fighter. The Briton's manager had learned that Chris was a fugitive from justice, and told him if he didn't throw the fight, he, the manager, would squeal to the bulls. Chris tried to dog it; he did his damndest to lay down; but he was such a fighting brute, he couldn't do it. He finally went mad with rage and fighting lust, and rushing in on the Englishman, literally beat his life out with his naked fists. The dead boxer's manager made good his threat, and Lilly was arrested and taken back to the gallows that awaited him in New York.

But here I am spieling away about things that happened in your part of the country, forgetting that you naturally know more about them than I do. Anyway, I imagine life in New York was pretty interesting in the '40's, '50's, '60's, and '70's.

Well, the election is over. No fights anywhere. That alone shows how utterly cowed the people are. Sterling was elected by a narrow margin.[21] I'm disappointed but after all, not too surprized. There was too much money behind him for him to be defeated. Not that I'm a rabid Ferguson man. I looked on it merely as a choice of two evils. I was for Tom Hunter of Wichita Falls, but we can't elect a West Texas man, and he was defeated in the primaries. The Fergusons are from Central East Texas, Sterling from Southeast Texas. But I agreed with Jim about the forty million dollars resulting from the gasoline tax. Sterling and his mob intend to put it all on the highways, and, I hear, build some kind of an elaborate state building. Jim wanted to put a third on the highways, utilize another third for general purposes, and use the other third to pay the poor damn teachers of the state, hundreds of whom haven't received a cursed cent in months and months. I like good highways as well as the next scut, but I'd a sight rather see the teachers get their money than to see a lot of expensive highways built. But this state was always exploited. For instance: gas produced almost in our backyards costs us $.75 a thousand, while that same gas is piped through a gigantic pipe-line to Chicago, there to be sold to the citizens at $.19 a thousand. The great majority of the money-making concerns of the state are owned by corporations and individuals in New York or Chicago, who contribute little enough to the state, except the wages they pay, and many of their employes are imported from elsewhere. The Texas people have been as ruthlessly exploited as if they were painted savages. And what grates me, is, they've put up with it.

However, if revolution ever rises in America, the Southwest is the very last place where it will blaze up. The people of this section, especially the country people, are so enured to suffering and hardship that it would take a veritable cataclysm to cause them to rise. Their capacity for enduring hardship is incredible—more, it is appalling, because it only shows what their lives have been for generations. Right now, the midwestern farms are raising hell about conditions that are, apparently, quite new to them. From what I hear, read and am told by people from that section, those folks are not used to starving. They are land-owners in what must be the greatest farming country in the world, and they are used to plenty and a bit of prosperity. Sheer suffering is new to them, and they resent it. The depression, augmented by the recent drouth, has caused them to rise in wrath. But down here the depression merely emphasized a condition that has always existed in the western Southern states. We have not, it is true, experienced a disastrous drouth since the beginning of the depression. If we had, and had our only available food supply—what we raise ourselves—swept away, things might have been different. But the point I wish to bring out is, the average farmer in the Southwest has never been prosperous, nor his father, grandfather, or greatgrandfather, unless some of the latter happened to be slave-owners. Life has always been a bitter grind of poverty; and short of massacre and whole-sale rape by the ruling classes, I do not believe any semblance of a revolution could be stirred up down here. However, there is one point to be remembered: if such a rising should occur, I am afraid it would be far more desperate and bloody than the affair in the mid-west has been so far. I understand that in the more civilized sections, firearms have been practically taken out of the hands of the people in one way or another. There are few homes in the rural parts of the Southwest were there is not some kind of a gun—shotgun, rifle or pistol. I sincerely hope that no class-clash will ever come; for if it does, it will not be an affair of fists and sticks. To the best of my knowledge, the only fatality resulting from the midwestern disturbance was when an officer was demonstrating an automatic shotgun to a deputy and accidently blew his guts out. Damned clever, these cops.

I notice where a mug named Oliver Herford has decided Shakespeare was Lord Oxford.[22] It must have been a momentus decision, affecting the destiny of the world for Olivero got his map in the magazines. Personally, I never cared whether the Shakespearian plays were written by Shakespeare of Stratford-on-Avon, or Lord Oxford-on-Thames or Lord Bitchbelly of Hog-wallow-on-the-Tripe. Its a cinch somebody wrote 'em, because I've read 'em myself, unless I was suffering from an optical delusion, and if so, I enjoyed the delusion. Although there's only one character of Shakespeare that I have any real attachment to, and that's Sir John Falstaff. I have a sincere affection for that old bastard.

I also notice where an egg named Barlow says he's given the Soviets a weapon that will make disarmament necessary, because with it war would be too terrible to concieve.[23] He seems to think our dear bewhiskered cousins will use it idealistically. He has more faith in the Slavonic soul than I have. I can see them advancing the cause of humanity by anchoring a thousand miles off our coasts and dropping gas-bombs and projectiles down our collars. Yet I am unable to work up any particular emotion. To my mind the human race is merely a parasitic freak of two-legged fungi that polutes the universe, which would be better off—and much cleaner—without it. I have a strong prejudice in favor of life, but from a philosophic standpoint, honestly believe the universe would be better off without human varmints of any kind. Understand, I do not look forward with any enthusiasm toward being eliminated by a moujik with vodka-scented whiskers. But it looks like a choice of being shot by a Jap, sprinkled with insect-powder by a Slav, or starved by one's own benevolent capitalists. The time may come when the government will howl for the people to protect it. Meanwhile, it makes no attempt to protect its people. One thing I like about the British government—it looks after its subjects, wherever they are, so I hear. Not so with America. I've known of too many men who were coolly allowed to rot in Mexican, Central or South American prisons. This is no wild-haired suppositions. I've known several of these men personally and heard it from their own lips. One man was rescued by a British consul; one, a Catholic, by a priest. The rest rotted until their friends had paid out exhorbitant sums of money for their release. Those Latin-American prisons are pure hell. Did you ever see a picture of a Mexican hoosegow? We call them bull-pens, in Texas. Its generally just a roofless enclosure, a square, squat building, with high white-washed stone or adobe walls. No roof. The prisoners are not protected in any way from the blaze of the sun throughout most of the day. They are given no bedding, benches, or tables to eat on. They are herded together in these pens, guarded continuously by brutal soldiers, armed to the teeth and frequently bare-footed—the most ignorant and savage type of human being on this continent. The prisoners are given the sorriest kind of food imaginable, which they have to cook themselves. Rain, cold, heat, they have no protection against the elements. Many go mad and knock out their brains against the walls, or are shot in frenzied efforts to escape. I never passed one of those hell-holes that my flesh didn't crawl. I never heard of anyone escaping from one, except one desperate cowpuncher who fought his way out by sheer ferocity, killing four armed guards with a rock and his naked hands, and swimming the river by night, to regain the Texas side, badly wounded and half-dead from his suffering and exertions. No, the government doesn't exert itself to protect its citizens' lives, but you let a revolution or something threaten the profits or property of the big business concerns. Then you'll see the marines moving out, bayonets fixed. Sandino—bah! A real patriot, to my mind.[24]

When I wrote the above about the election, I made a mistake. Sterling had a lead and I thought all the returns were in. Later returns gave the Fergusons nearly four thousand lead. These returns are being questioned, and the Sterling gang is yelling about illegal voting, and the like, and demanding an investigation.[25] Feeling is running pretty high in Texas, as shown by the fact that people have quit discussing the election on the street. When people are loath to talk about something, its a sign they feel pretty strongly on the subject. Twenty years ago, guns might have been barking already. Now the people are mostly keeping their mouths shut and waiting. It is an instinctive way of avoiding trouble as long as possible. While I'm on the subject—aside from the election returns—I have found that the more highly civilized people are, the readier they generally are for dissentions and disputes. Why not? Rows among the civilized, however hot, seldom end in bloodshed. That's not the case among more primitive people; I think that's why such people avoid arguments instinctively, as much as possible, and are close-mouthed on almost every subject.

I hope Wandrei makes a go of it, but its a damned bad time to resign a job and try to depend on literary work alone. I wish I had a good solid job, myself, even if it didn't pay much. As I said, I'm glad to hear that the Californian is going to put your poems to music, and I'm eager for the result. If the music is anything like as good as the poetry, it will superb. Glad to hear that your work got its proper mention in the "American Author"; I didn't see the article mentioned, the magazine not being on any of the stands I frequent, but I'm glad the writer referred to you. It ought to boost you with the editors.

The eclipse was a flop here; only half-part, anyhow, and cloudy that day. I hope you had better luck, though they said over the radio that it was cloudy in New England, too.

I've recieved your card, since writing the above. Glad you had good weather for the eclipse. I imagine it was an impressive spectacle. Thanks very much for the generous amount of cards and folders. I have gotten the most intense enjoyment out of scanning them—sort of a glimpse out of another world, as it were. I added them to my permanent files, which, thanks to your generosity, present a fine pictorial panorama (if that's the phrase I mean) of the Eastern sea-board. I was especially interested in the views of Quebec, and could almost visualize old Wolfe and his red-coated boys swarming up the cow-trails and hacking into the Frogs on the Plains of Abraham.[26] I'll bet there's good licker in Quebec.

Have you noticed the most recent spat in Tokyo, where the little brown brother is frothing because the Bank of New York has been taking pictures?[27] They think—or pretend to think—that these pictures will be used by the American military department, to aid in future bombardments. They flatter us; we haven't got that much sense. It gives me a big laugh to hear the government asking for a recantation, apology or what-not. The Japs aren't going to apologize for anything—much less to us. Anyway, the big official on whom the responsibility rests, doesn't dare do anything that might reflect on the military regime of the empire; he'd be bumped off, just like other Japanese officials have been scuppered lately. The samurai is lifting his crest after his enforced submission to the West. Its the last flare of the old-time imperialist, to my mind. And in Germany the steel helmets are goose-stepping. The nations are heaping up the coals and stirring the fire; the pot's simmering and when it explodes the whole world is going rock. Well, let it burst any time it wants to; I'd as soon be bayonetted or shot as to starve or grind out a meagre existence under present conditions.

To give you a slight idea of what the farmer is up against, and people depending on his prosperity. Day before yesterday my father and I took some wheat to mill, that he'd gotten on a bill. We drove twenty-one miles, only to have the miller refuse to handle it. It showed signs of smut; the continued floods we've had for months have ruined most of the grain in this country. We brought it back and eventually sold it at twenty-five cents a bushel for chicken feed. My father allowed the farmer thirty-four cents a bushel for it, so you see how much we made on it. But the fellow had nothing else with which to pay his bill. At this rate we'll become wealthy fast! My father was irritated, at the mill, by the sight of big powerful-looking farmers staggering around, two men to the load, under grain sacks no heavier than those I handled with ease by myself—and God know's I'm not a particularly strong man. No doubt about it—the breed is getting soft and flabby. In fifty years I reckon we'll be too soft for anything.

Again, many thanks for the pictures, and with the best of good wishes,
Cordially,
R.E.H.

P.S. Glad you found the unpublished mss. of interest;[28] I doubt if they'll ever find a publisher, since Wright rejected them, and I know of no other market for that kind of yarn; hope Wandrei has success in his literary venture.
R.E.H.

Notes

1. Cf. *SLL* 4.85 (13 October 1932): "The prime objective of trip #1 was New Orleans, which I wished to see before the destruction of the French Market." HPL's trip to New Orleans was in June 1932.

2. John Coffee (Jack) Hays (1817–1883) came to Texas in 1837 as a surveyor. He served as Captain of a Ranger company from 1840, gaining fame for his fights with Indians and border bandits. He commanded a Texas mounted regiment in the Mexican War. When the war ended, he led a party to the California Gold Rush. He served as sheriff of San Francisco for four years, after which he was appointed surveyor-general of the state. He bought a large Spanish land grant and laid out and promoted the present city of Oakland, becoming wealthy and prominent in Democratic politics.

3. John ("Broken Nose Jack") McCall (1851?–1877), buffalo hunter, laborer, and freighter, fatally shot Hickok from behind on 2 August 1876. At his trial, McCall testified he had lost $110 to Hickok at cards the day before the shooting; he also claimed that Hickok had killed his brother in Kansas (this was untrue). He was acquitted by the Deadwood jury. In Cheyenne some time later, a deputy U.S. marshal overheard him boasting about lying to the jury, and he was arrested, tried in federal court, and hanged in 1877.

4. Tom O'Phalliard (or O'Folliard) (1858–1880) and Charlie Bowdre (1859–1880) were cohorts of Billy the Kid.

5. William B. Masterson (1853–1921), legendary western gunfighter. For Robert A. Olinger, see letter 23, n. 1. Henry Plummer (1837–1864), a gambler, masterminded gangs of thieves around Lewiston, Idaho, and Bannack and Virginia City, Montana. At the latter two towns he even contrived to become city marshal, the better to cover his outlaw activities. Vigilantes put an end to his career by hanging him and over twenty of his men c. January 1864. Plummer's gang was probably the inspiration for REH's "Vultures of Wahpeton." For Thompson, see letter 60, n. 8.

6. Horace Greeley (1811–1872), New York newspaperman and politician, famed for the quote widely attributed to him, "Go West, young man, and grow up with the country."

7. Albert Bacon Fall (1861–1944) was Warren G. Harding's Secretary of the Interior (1921–23) and the man most responsible for the Teapot Dome scandal. Convicted in 1929 for his part in the affair (the first U.S. cabinet officer convicted of official wrong-

doing), he was sentenced to one year and one day in prison. He began serving his sentence 11 July 1931 and was released 10 May 1932, his health permanently ruined.

8. Ongoing investigations into official corruption in New York City had revealed that many vice officers were extorting money from prostitutes, bootleggers, and others, and were arresting and giving false testimony against those who refused to pay them. A new police commissioner made significant changes in vice-squad operations beginning in 1931, but cases continued to make headlines throughout 1932. Other investigations resulted in the removal of judges and finally in the resignation of Mayor Jimmy Walker.

9. Aviator Charles Lindbergh's young son was kidnapped from the family's home 1 March 1932. The police chased down many fruitless leads, and Lindbergh paid $50,000 in ransom to one mysterious figure who seemed to know facts that had not been publicized, but his son was not returned as promised. The child's body was found on 12 May 1932 four miles from the Lindbergh home. Violet Sharpe, an English maid in the home of Anne Morrow Lindbergh's parents, had been out with friends the evening of the kidnapping. She was so harassed by the police that she committed suicide on 10 June 1932. Bruno Richard Hauptmann was finally arrested for the crime in 1934.

10. The National Farmers Holiday Association, seeking to bring prices for farm produce in line with production costs, called for a general selling holiday (i.e., a moratorium on sales by farmers) to begin at midnight on 20 September 1932. Farmers supporting the holiday picketed roads seeking to prevent others from getting produce to markets. Public officials in Sioux City, Iowa, asked Governor Turner to send National Guard troops to clear the pickets. The strike quickly spread to other Midwestern and some Southern states.

11. Illinois coal mines had been shut down by strikes since 1 March, with 49,000 miners out of work. By September, "war" had begun between miners wanting to return to work for the $5.00 per day wage being offered by mine owners, and those who wanted to hold out for the $6 per day wage prevailing before the strike. The "war" reached such violent extremes—including street fighting and bombings—that Governor Emmerson sent two troops of National Guardsmen to Taylorville on 19 September. On 26 September a bloody melee in Springfield left one policeman dead and twenty persons injured.

12. Pope Urban II (1042?–1099) issued the call for the First Crusade in 1095. See Harold Lamb (1892–1962), *The Crusades: Iron Men and Saints* (New York: Doubleday, Doran, 1930), pp. 326–29.

13. Cave-in-Rock, a natural feature about which a town grew up in southern Illinois, near the mouth of the Ohio River, was headquarters for some of the most desperate outlaws along the river c. 1790–1830. Tevis Clyde Smith, Jr., his grandfather J. E. Smith, and perhaps other members of his family traveled to Western Kentucky, the elder Smith's homeland, in 1931.

14. Boone Helm (1828–1864), born in Kentucky, developed a reputation as a thief and murderer in the California gold fields; later fled to Oregon, where he became a mountain man and on one occasion claimed to have eaten part of the corpse of a companion who had committed suicide; was finally hanged with other members of Henry Plummer's gang.

15. Zane Grey (1872–1938), *The Border Legion* (1916).

16. See n. 6 above.

17. Simon Girty (1741–1818?) was captured and held by Seneca Indians, along with his brother, for several years. During the early part of the Revolutionary War he served the British as a soldier, spy, and Indian interpreter in Pennsylvania. In 1778 he turned renegade and led Indian raids against white settlements. He continued to stir up Indians against the settlements as far as Detroit and Kentucky throughout the 1780s. During the War of 1812 he again sided with the British. He is thought to have gone to Canada after the war and to have died there in 1818.

18. Sam Mason (d. 1804) is the earliest bandit associated with Cave-in-Rock, c. 1797. He later removed to the Natchez Trace, where he continued to lead a gang of thieves. He met his end in 1804, but there is some doubt whether the bounty-hunter who killed him was indeed "Little" Harpe.

19. A reference to a group of irregular military adventurers led by William Walker (1824–1860), who seized control of Nicaragua in 1855.

20. The Hudson Dusters and Dead Rabbits were New York gangs. Bill Poole (d. 1859) was a leader of the Bowery Boys, later led his own gang, and was a political ally of the Know-Nothing Party, rivals of the Democratic machine at Tammany Hall. He was shot in a Manhattan saloon by three Tammany toughs. He did indeed linger 14 days, and his dying words, quoted here, inspired several melodramas. Boxing and politics went hand-in-hand in mid-19th-century New York, with "Native Americans" often pitted against the Irish immigrants of Tammany Hall. Tom Hyer (1819–1864), a friend of Poole, defeated "Yankee" Sullivan (born James Ambrose in Ireland) for the first heavyweight championship of America in 1849. Hyer then retired from boxing. John Morrissey (1831–1878), born in Ireland, was brought to America in 1834. He became a power in Irish-American affairs and a top man at Tammany Hall. He defeated Sullivan in 1853 for the title vacated by Hyer. Disgusted at losing to his Tammany rival, Sullivan went to California, where he ran afoul of San Francisco's Vigilance Committee and was found dead in his jail cell. Morrissey, after retiring from the ring, was twice elected to Congress, then won election to the New York State Senate. Ill health prevented his serving in the latter. All the above are mentioned in Herbert Asbury's *Gangs of New York* (1927), which REH may have read. It is also possible that REH got some of this information from *Ring Magazine* or the *Police Gazette.*

21. REH refers to the second Democratic primary, a run-off between Ross S. Sterling (1875–1949), of Houston, and Miriam Amanda ("Ma") Ferguson (1875–1961), of Bell County. In Texas politics at the time, winning the Democratic primary was tantamount to being elected to office; the general election against token Republican opposition was little more than a formality. Mrs. Ferguson was the wife of James E. Ferguson (1871–1944), governor from 1915 to 1917. Impeached early in his second term, Ferguson could not again run for governor; Mrs. Ferguson was elected in 1924, making it clear that her husband would be making decisions. Defeated in 1926 and again in 1930 (she did not run in 1928), she ran against incumbent Sterling in 1932. See further n. 24.

22. REH refers to Edward de Vere, Earl of Oxford (1550–1604), thought by some (including Mark Twain) to have written Shakespeare's plays.

23. The *New York Times* (13 August 1932) reported that American engineer and inventor Lester P. Barlow of Stamford, Connecticut, told German newsmen that he had revealed to the Soviet government plans he had developed showing the possibility of destroying large cities from the air. He had originally brought these plans to the atten-

tion of U.S. government officials and members of Congress in April of that year, and was in Berlin to seek meetings with German officials. His purpose in revealing the plans was to impress upon these governments the necessity of total disarmament.

24. Augusto Cesar Sandino (1893–1934), Nicaraguan guerrilla leader, waged warfare against U.S. Marines (1927–32) in an attempt to end U.S. intervention in Nicaraguan affairs. When the Marines withdrew, Sandino agreed to amnesty terms.

25. "Ma" Ferguson defeated Ross S. Sterling, 477,644 votes to 473,846, in the Democratic primary run-off. She went on to defeat the Republican candidate for Governor, Orville Bullington, by more than 200,000 votes in the general election.

26. Major General James Wolfe (1727–1759) commanded the British Army expedition against Quebec; in 1759 he led his army up the heights to the Plains of Abraham outside the city, where he defeated the French under Marquis Louis Joseph de Montcalm de Saint-Veran (1712–1759), completing the British conquest of Canada. Both commanders were mortally wounded in the battle.

27. In early September 1932, Japanese newspapers accused the National City Bank of New York of espionage when the bank had pictures taken of a number of Tokyo businesses. The bank claimed the pictures were "to be used as promotion matter illustrating business and industrial development in the Far East."

28. Probably "The God in the Bowl" and "The Frost-Giant's Daughter."

[66] [ANS][1]

[Postmarked Providence, R.I.,
22 September 1932]

Many thanks for the interesting issue of the always-vigorous Gladewater Journal! The editor is surely up to his usual form. Was pleased to read in the press some time ago of the triumph of your candidate—"Ma" Sterling. Wandrei returned to N Y last Tuesday—I was sorry he had to leave so soon, especially since his visit was hampered by rainy weather & a bad case of sunburn on his part. He will, however, be in the east until January; & may get to Providence again—although at a time when I can't do much outdoor sightseeing. ¶ Derleth has just won a three-star citation in O'Brien's Best Short Stories of 1932—& a 2-star mention for another story.[2] The kid is coming along! ¶ The man who set my Fungi from Yuggoth to music (Harold Farnese of Los Angeles) wants me to collaborate with him on a fantastic music-drama, but I don't think I'm qualified for that type of composition.[3] ¶ Clark Ashton Smith has just written a fascinatingly clever conclusion to Beckford's unfinished 3rd Episode of Vathek—he'll probably try it on Wright.[4]

Best wishes—

H P L

Notes

1. Front: University Hall and Manning Hall. Brown University.

2. HPL alludes to Edward J. O'Brien (1890–1941), *The Best Short Stories of 1932 and the Yearbook of the American Short Story* (New York: Dodd, Mead, 1932). AWD's "Old Ladies" (*Midland*, January–February 1932) received a 2-star ranking, and "Nella" (*Pagany*, Winter 1932) a 1-star ranking.

3. Farnese proposed to collaborate with HPL on a musical drama in one act set on Yuggoth to have been called *Fen River*. HPL declined.

4. Wright rejected the story. RHB published William Beckford's "The Story of the Princess Zulkais and the Prince Kalilah" in *Leaves* No. 1 (Summer 1937): 1–16, followed by CAS's "The Third Episode of Vathek" as "Conclusion to Wm. Beckford's Story of Princess Zulkais & Prince Kalilah," pp. 17–24.

[67]

10 Barnes St.,
Providence, R.I.,
Octr. 3, 1932

Dear R. E. H.:—

Your highly interesting letter duly arrived, and I have absorbed its contents with the usual blend of pleasure and appreciation. Also your note of 24th ult. Glad you found the various views, etc. of interest. Under separate cover I am sending quite a little bundle of views of sundry antiquities—Portland, New York, Philadelphia, Richmond, etc.—which I found to be duplicates upon recently going over my files. I don't think many of these repeat views I've sent before—and I fancy you'll find them at least worth looking over.

As to the relative merits of barbarous and civilised life—judged abstractly and intrinsically—I still think that the odds *may* be in favour of civilisation for those who utilise its advantages to the full. Naturally persons who have changed from a free-and-easy pioneer life to a more urbanised form feel a lack of something accustomed—but there is always a tendency to exalt the conditions of one's youth, whatever they may have been. Moreover, it is likely that in most cases the persons making the transition have not been able to utilise the advantages of civilised life to the full. The transition is apt to come a trifle too late in the history of the individual to permit him to extract the most good from the intellectual and aesthetic advantages of civilisation. Therefore, the thing he weighs unfavourably against his old pioneer existence is by no means civilisation at its best. Both barbarism and civilisation have their advantages, and it is probable that some individuals naturally prefer one type to the other. Yet I think that certain types of civilisation add much more to life, than they subtract from it. It is probable that the idyllic picture of barbaric life contained in literature and some kinds of history is an over-flattering one, and that if we were to know the actual facts we would find many important and hardly-suspected flaws. On the other hand, I will agree that when a civilisation has passed its peak and become decadent, its members very often sink into an ennui which makes them less happy than they would be under barbarism. Some of its members, at least. The whole question is a complex and baffling one, and perhaps no conclusive answer is possible.

About games—I'm sure I didn't single out *physical* contests as especially artificial. What I did point out was simply that all *arranged* competitions—mental, fortuitous, or physical—which operate under *arbitrarily devised* conditions and rules, are essentially *artificial as compared with the natural battles of force which they mimic and symbolise.* Thus chess—an intellectual exercise under arranged conditions—is palpably artificial as compared with the use of intellect in grappling with the actually unknown. The intellectuality which wins a difficult chess game is obviously put to a more trivial and artificial end than that which tries to measure the universe or ascertain the structure of matter. And thus with a physical game like football. The enterprise and prowess displayed in downing an opponent are genuine enough; but their employment in this capacity—where the contest is deliberately arranged and arbitrarily conditioned—is undeniably more *artificial* than would be their employment in defeating an actual invading army which threatened the life and liberty of the group. The crux of the whole matter lies in the *arranged and arbitrary nature* of games. There is a basic difference between the tense drama of meeting and overcoming an *inevitable* problem or obstacle in real life, and the secondary or symbolic drama of meeting and overcoming a problem or obstacle *which has merely been artificially set up.* The chess-player has no breathless sense of uncovering unknown secrets of the cosmos, as the real research scientist has; while the football-player lacks the intense exaltation of knowing that his efforts are necessary to save his country from disaster. Accordingly, I feel quite justified in believing that games and sports ought not be ranked among the major phenomena of life. However—let it not be thought that I am denying them any place whatever in the scheme of things. They have, undoubtedly, the poetic value of symbolism. Chess, by bringing into play the same human forces which are used in conquering the unknown and planning life, is a sort of ceremony in celebration of these forces—an exaltation of the forces as intrinsic things in themselves, all apart from the question of object. And football, by involving the same forces as those which resist enemies and preserve civilisations, may be regarded as a ritual exalting such forces independently of their object. All this is psychologically sound and aesthetically legitimate provided we do not try to invest these mimicries and symbolisations with the full dignity and importance of the *natural* struggles which they symbolise. My own complete personal indifference to games of every sort is merely an individual characteristic, and in no way represents my general views regarding the field in question. This, I trust, clears up the doubtful point. As you see, I don't consider physical games any more artificial than mental ones; but I consider *all* games more artificial than inevitable struggles in real life where the occurrence and conditions are not prearranged.

Your description of the fight with the Oklahoman is surely vivid. Regarding your enjoyment of the event—I think individuals differ widely in their attitude toward *intrinsic processes* as distinguished from *ultimate objects.* A fight *for its own sake* would mean nothing to me, either at the time or in retrospect, but on the other hand I would take the greatest satisfaction in having defended myself from aggression, or in having wiped out an insult, by means of combat. Likewise in the mental field. A friend of mine[1] is tremendously fond of chess, cryptograms, difficult puzzles and anything which sets the cells of his mind working intensely and involvedly—irrespective of purpose or object. Now all that leaves me absolutely cold. I can't get the slightest fun out of the exercise of my mind (or body either) merely for the sake of the exercise. But on the other hand, I take keen delight in using my mind to study out some problem in science, philosophy, or history which really puzzles me. Emphatically, I belong to a definite type of personality in which there is a lack of interest in *intrinsic processes.* The things which interest me are not details, but *broad vistas* of dramatic pageantry in which cosmic laws and the linkage of cause and effect are displayed on a large scale. I love the sweep of history and the excitement of age-long struggles of cultural forces—yet care little for the details of a single diplomatic problem or the particulars of a street-corner fist-fight. I would make a very poor scientific research worker, since in accurate research everything hinges on a tremendous absorption in significant details.

Your description of your father and his work is magnificently interesting, and I can well imagine what an indispensable force in the community he is. Medical practice in a thinly settled section involves responsibilities unheard-of elsewhere; so that the practitioner must have not only a phenomenally wide range of medical attainments, (to compensate for the lack of available specialists to call in) but a quality and force of character of the sort usually associated with leaders. Doctors of that kind seem to be harder and harder to find—for those bred under easy urban conditions are increasingly reluctant to assume the burdens of rural or pioneer practice, and increasingly prone to fall into the commercialistic attitude inculcated by the cruder spirit of the times. Your father's exaltation of his work itself above the possible financial results is something which cannot be sufficiently admired and praised—the true attitude of the scholar and gentleman as distinguished from the petty tradesmanship of the modern majority. I am glad that, even in the face of inadequate material rewards, he has a son so thoroughly and intelligently appreciative of his qualities and efforts!

As for the question of the supernatural—one ought really to think as independently as possible, and above all things to avoid being influenced by any one person—or even any few other persons. It is of course a well-known fact that all sorts of individuals, including those of the highest mental quality, hold all sorts of beliefs—so that one may find persons of the greatest eminence on *both* sides of every question. In such a case of opposite opinion *someone* must obviously be wrong—and only a wide amount of impersonal correlation can enable anybody to make a guess as to which the wrong one is. The reason for this is that most persons possess an emotional bias resulting from the teachings (right or erroneous) of early childhood, which unconsciously influences their intellectual decisions in all matters where there is any latitude whatever. The only persons who are apt to escape this bias are those with a special interest in the intrinsic truth or untruth of the questions involved—an interest stronger than the sense of conformity which would ordinarily cause the externally-imposed influence to operate. Thus we cannot justly defend a given intellectual position merely because certain men of high calibre happen to hold it. If we look about more widely, we shall see that other persons of high calibre hold an exactly opposite position. All we can do in such a case is to study the evidence itself, analyse what a vast number of different students say about it, and see whether any of the opinions (on either side) seem to be influenced by hereditary or environmental predispositions antagonistic to a perfectly impartial appraisal. In dealing with this latter point it is useful to study the trend of group opinion over a long period of time. In the case of a gradually declining belief which older men tend to cling to and younger men tend to drop, there is great reason to suspect that the belief is unsound—that those who cling to it do so because of early emotional bias, and that perfectly impartial minds approaching the problems freshly and unprejudicedly would never even think of assuming the improbable things which old tradition (formed in primitive ages, when information was lacking) takes for granted. Incidentally—I think you are a bit hasty and thoughtless in making a blanket attack upon the position of those whom you contemptuously group as "professors and *mere* scholars". It is a popular thing to attack those who have devoted their lives to truth, but I really can't see the force and validity of such attacks. I fancy that those who make them are apt to confuse serious scholars with a certain semi-charlatanic element who publicise inconclusive findings with the feigned authority of scholars—but really, one ought not to blame genuine truth-seekers for the faults of their imitators. What, after all, *is* the knowledge that a serious research worker has? Is it different in essence from knowledge acquired with a less direct regard for abstract truth as an object? There is something a trifle naive in the traditional popular contempt for "book l'arnin'", for what do books contain if not *the recorded results of direct observation?* True, in all technological matters where *process-skill* and concrete application count equally with intrinsic information, the mastery of books must be supplemented by first-hand applications of the principles learned. But who denies that? The despised professors themselves are the first to insist on thorough, practical laboratory work, and to point out that no one is the real master of a technique, until he has served a thorough apprenticeship under the varying outer-world conditions which he will habitually have to meet. Your idea of a professor or scholar is a purely conventional one—unfortunately fostered by literature and bolstered up by the spectacle of inferior members of the class, but far from representing the facts concerning the highest type of truth-seeker. They err—being human—but no more than anyone else; and over against this human fallibility we must remember the advantage they have in being trained in the special art of weighing evidence, eliminating inessentials, and thinking things through according to unswayed logic. They realise the value of practice in practical arts, and very seldom question the methods of "practical men" except when some unusual circumstance—like a new discovery or sudden change of basic conditions—makes it logical and necessary to do so. There are times, of course, when shifting conditions invalidate certain traditional rule-of-thumb methods and blindly popular values. In such cases, the informed scholar must necessarily differ from the nose-to-grindstone worker who has never analysed the conditions and bases of his (no doubt effectively performed) work—but even here he will soon be agreed with by the less thoughtless and habit-moved wing of the "practical workers". It is the popular custom to magnify the mistakes and bad guesses of the professorial element, and to cover up and excuse those of the "practical" element. Thus everybody takes a whack at poor old Woodrow Wilson and his international theories, while only a few see the absurdity of the "solid practical people" in blindly accepting pre-1929 prosperity as a fixed economic state. But more than this—there is a field of purely abstract knowledge, which does not involve matters of policy, technique, and administration, in which *no one but the avowed scholar* has any reason to claim authority . . . . . a field of sheer "is-or-isn'tness" concerning which no practical pursuit qualifies one to act as judge. If a "practical man" does have an intelligent opinion in any part of this field, it is not because of his practical experience in his own work, but simply because of his abstract natural mentality—which would be the same even if he were not engaged in practical work. All that specially qualifies one for speculation in this field is the thorough mastery of the sciences concerned, plus a general training of the intellect in matters of evidence-judging—the usual equipment of the best type of professional scholar. Some of the subjects coming within this field of the impersonally and non-technically abstract are intra-atomic chemistry and physics, non-Euclidean mathematics, astronomy, pure biology, (apart from human physiology) history, anthropology, palaeontology, philosophy, etc. etc. You can easily see the difference between this type of knowledge and the technological type—medicine, engineering, military science, economics, government, etc.—in which practical experience is just as necessary as pure study. Now the subject of the supernatural clearly belongs to the abstract and impersonal field as distinguished from the technological. Nothing in *practical experience* especially qualifies anybody to pass on the validity of transmitted folklore as scaled against the evidence of the external world. It is a matter for the pure scientist and absolutely no one else. On the one hand we must have some idea of what is known of life and the universe—biology, chemistry, physics, astronomy, etc.—and on the other hand we must have some idea of the forces behind the formation of the conventional beliefs of primitive times, which our ancestors blindly and uncritically force upon us without regard for reason . . . . an idea obtainable only through such studies as psychology, anthropology, history, and so on. No one but the scientist can give us such ideas—and what is more, no *one* scientist can handle more than a small fraction of the whole matter. For instance, the kind of researcher who studies the dimensions of the universe is of another kind from the one who studies the structure of the atom, while both are unlike the one who investigates the origin of concepts in the primitive human mind. Obviously, it takes a whole staff of unbiased experts to dig up the necessary data, and even then each one of the experts is too one-sided to have any special authority on the conclusions derivable from the piecing-together of all the evidence. To accomplish this piecing-together we need scholars of another type—those especially trained in the analysis of evidence *as evidence* and the use of reason in eliminating falsehood and arriving at the truth—or approximations of the truth. This type corresponds to what we traditionally call the *philosophers,* and includes today such men as George Santayana, Oswald Spengler, John Dewey, Bertrand Russell, Joseph Wood Krutch, and (although he originally started out as a biologist) J. B. S. Haldane. I do not know of any eminent living member of this type of thinker or philosopher who believes in the supernatural. As a rank layman, I have no right to a dogmatic or first-hand opinion on any special subject; but when I view the evidence in the matter of the supernatural (or such of it as a layman can grasp) and analyse the conclusions which different thinkers of eminence draw regarding it, I cannot help drawing the mere common-sense conclusion that traditional beliefs are false and meaningless, and that the real testimony of the external world does nothing whatever to confirm such wild and gratuitous myths as those of immortality, cosmic purpose, and so on. There is no more reason to believe in that stuff than there is to believe in witches—which the most learned and intelligent people once did, when there was less realistic evidence at their disposal to discipline fantastic flights of emotion and imagination.

Octr. 5

Regarding social and political matters—I certainly realise the virtual impossibility of securing equitable legislation, yet would hesitate to say whether some closer approximation than the present could not be secured. While any nominally accepted social pattern will undoubtedly be administered in a corrupt way, it is nevertheless true that some patterns allow much more latitude for one-sidedness than do others. Certain deep-seated changes in a racial or national ideology are likely to reduce extreme manifestations in certain directions. For instance—despite all graft and corruption, the civic authorities of the U.S. no longer allow the slum population to starve and wallow in filth as they did a century ago and before. No matter how dishonest a city administration is, it insists on certain rudimentary sanitary regulations formerly neglected, and also provides food in some way or other for the destitute. The reasons for the change are many, and in most aspects not especially altruistic. It is recognised that unsanitary slums breed disease which spreads outside their bounds, and also that starving masses menace social security. Also, there is an aesthetic dislike of widespread suffering—a thing so contrary to the spirit of harmony which lies at the basis of all beauty—which moulds the policy of the more cultivated wielders of power. But whatever the cause, it remains a fact that a new instinctive standard has arisen, which substantially changes the actual conditions in the province involved. No matter how much below the new standard a corrupt administration may fall, the results are always better than they were before the standard was adopted. And so with the problem of the distribution of wealth. No one expects the reigning commercial interests to relinquish any more than they have to, but it is probable that changes will come when they see that the existing impasse is no longer profitable to them. They cannot continue to reap vast profits when fewer and fewer people have any money to spend—and there is no likelihood of any great increase in purchasing power when intensive mechanisation is throwing more and more people out of employment. Moreover, the danger of social revolution increases as popular suffering increases. The explosion came in France, and a still worse one in Russia—and no nation can safely consider itself immune. All this points to the slow and reluctant growth of a new standard of wealth-distribution—based on selfish expediency, of course, yet none the less beneficial to those suffering under the present standard. It will hold that the existence of large pauper classes—permanently unemployed and unemployable—is dangerous to national equilibrium, and will therefore list among the national necessities some plan of artificially spreading out remunerative employment and compensating those who cannot secure it. At the same time the threat of popular revolution will probably create a minimum wage provision ensuring some degree of basic comfort to the formerly hard-pressed unskilled labourer. An illustration of how such concessions will be extorted is afforded by the incident of the present soldiers' bonus agitation. Here we have a special group seeking a privileged position in the matter of relief, and indulging in large-scale intimidation both physical and political. Though nearly all economists consider the measure unsound, it is likely to be passed in the end—especially in view of the action of the American Legion at its recent convention. (Incidentally, the chief Providence post has been considering withdrawal from the Legion because of the new attitude which reverses last year's policy and violates the non-political clause in the order's constitution.) This incident is probably a very fair sample of the way in which pressure will be exerted to bend the holders of the national wealth into larger and larger handouts. Though at present bitterly opposed by conservatives, this legalised holdup principle is probably a valuable safety-valve for an economically top-heavy nation. Without the relief afforded by legalised holdups, we might eventually suffer the non-legalised holdups exemplified by the French and Russian revolutions. Similar blocs and intimidative societies, composed of labourers and other economic sufferers, will be likely to force the visible government into necessary measures like artificially regulated employment conditions (shorter hours, fewer working days, minimum wage schedules, more persons employed), unemployment insurance, old-age pensions, and the like. The industries behind the government will yield, because they will be afraid of total economic and social collapse if they don't. Their motive in handing out will be the same as that of their earlier grabbing in—simple desire for survival under the best obtainable conditions. It is a case of dog eat dog, like everything else in life. Every man grabs all he can, and the strongest combination wins. Equitable distribution implies merely a more even balance of strength between opposing combinations. To compensate for the need of reducing profits, the major industries will probably combine and coördinate even more extensively than at present, in order to avoid the waste of duplicate manufacture and unusable surpluses. Something roughly resembling the Soviets' "planned economy" will probably be adopted by the industries of the most capitalistic nations. Agriculture will probably become a corporation matter—with land owned on a large scale by vast organisations, and formed by employees enjoying the advantages of minimum wage laws, unemployment insurance, regulated leisure, and the like. Now of course all these alleviative measures will be administered corruptly. As of old, officials will get rich on graft, and individual cases of hardship will appear. But it would be foolish to claim that the lot of the majority could be as bad as before, when so many liberal and non-misinterpretable safeguards for the distribution of wealth will exist. The change in the legalised norm will provide a change in the foundation on which corruption preys; and what is left after corruption has had its fling will be much more favourable to the masses than the corresponding residue today. This will, of course, be accompanied by a general shift in the popular instinctive ideology (as in the already-accomplished matter of slum sanitation and municipal relief); so that it will no longer be thought possible to allow industries to depress living conditions below a certain level. Such changes in basic, taken-for-granted assumptions are slow in coming, but when they do arrive they have vast potency. For example—what state would think today of tolerating the cruel and barbarous punishments of two centuries and more ago—ear-cropping, branding, drawing and quartering, breaking on the wheel, burning at the stake, etc. etc.? This shift implies a readjustment of public psychology (though not, of course, a change in human instinct itself) which creates an entirely new set of unconscious inhibitions and spontaneous impulses. Similar—or rather, homologous—readjustments of public psychology appear to be taking place regarding economic relationships, and the outcome will probably be a general state of mind in which it will not occur to anybody to try to deprive large sections of the community of the legally ensured security which seems artificial to us, but which will seem only a natural and inevitable attribute of organised society to the generations ahead. Russia is an excellent example of an altered instinctive ideology—though its alterations extend too far, and were secured at too tragically high a cost, to recommend them to the western world. All this explains why I doubt the truth of dogmatic pessimism just as much as I doubt that of dogmatic optimism. What I have outlined, of course, is only a probable—or perhaps I should say no more than *possible*—turn of events; but it has so many foundations in reason, and is predicted by so many observers of apparent good sense, that I feel it is not likely to be ruled out summarily as a conceivable future. Actually, the turn which history may take cannot be forecast with certainty. Obscure and hardly-realised factors may have the power to sway events into one or another of many widely separated channels. One never can tell. As for your belief that the dominant interest will call in gunmen and sluggers instead of sociologists when mass pressure grows too powerful for comfort—I would say that while they may do so, tentatively, *at first,* they will not find it expedient to carry such a policy through to its logical end. The reason for this is, first, that they could not trust their gunmen and sluggers. The masses might outbid them and hire the thugs themselves on the promise of greater booty in the event of victory. Also, the thugs might dicker with both parties and seize power themselves as a new oligarchy—to the disadvantage alike of the older oligarchs and of the dispossessed. But secondly—and more importantly—it is probable that the farthest-seeing industrialists realise the lack of profit in a forcibly established equilibrium with starving and unemployable masses at the bottom. Popular purchasing power can never increase as long as money is highly restricted, and unless the unemployable are placated by a sizeable "dole", (which in itself would mean a vast drain on profits) they will always constitute a sullen and discontented nucleus that must be kept down through the application of costly and burdensome pressure. I think the industries will call in the sociologist because they will at last believe that his prescription will ensure them a greater residue of profit—through the elimination of threats to the general equilibrium—than could any alternative course. In all this struggling it is evident that both sides are basically just alike—i.e., composed of the same individual units . . . human beings motivated by the inextinguishable each-for-himself urge. One may logically take sides only so far as one of the many alternative systems promises a better equilibrium—with a more harmonious minimisation of general suffering, and a better opportunity for the development of man's highest potentialities—intellect and the arts—than the others seem able to promise.

I agree with you that the southwest—and most other dominantly agricultural regions—would be the last part of the country to join any radical social revolt. The acutest outbreak would come from a dispossessed and unemployed industrial element—largely foreign, and led by foreign agitators or others permeated with foreign theories. Also, I think that if any revolt of native Americans were to occur, it would have less radical objects than would a revolt of foreign labourers. Meanwhile I trust that the efforts of Texas to tone down the dominance of oil corporations may have some success. Until some major readjustment can be reached, there is nothing to do but to try to curb the power of the arrogant industries whenever some especially flagrant excess crops out. Once in a while there will be ways to limit their encroachments in one direction or another.

Regarding international matters—one may justly be sceptical about some of the titanic death-dealing inventions reported from time to time, yet none the less it seems clear that the next large-scale general war will be a far more destructive affair than any hitherto experienced. It may conceivably precipitate a chaos leading to the end of western civilisation—a denouement which different people anticipate with different emotions. Obviously, it would pay to cultivate a habit of international arbitration calculated to reduce the number of open conflicts—though it is folly to expect debate to deter nations from war when really deep issues are involved, and chances for success exist. As for the human race—one may not justly regard it as either an advantage or a detriment to the universe. It simply exists as an inevitable and very temporary natural phenomenon, and the whole fabric is neither better nor worse for the fact of its existing. Indeed, the whole fabric knows nothing whatever about it. Life is a somewhat uncommon cosmic phenomenon resulting when carbon, hydrogen, and nitrogen atoms become combined or ionised in a certain way during the cooling of a planetary body's crust, and the subsequent course taken by it depends wholly on the accidental conditions of the planet's history. Probably nothing even remotely like the human race has ever existed before, exists now, or will ever exist again. It would mean too vast a coincidence to have the exact conditions of its evolution repeated anywhere else. No one outside this microscopic earth knows or will ever know that the human race exists. When the breed is extinct, there will be none (unless some other terrestrial species arises to consciousness) to recall that it ever existed. And when this planet is finally frozen to lifelessness by the fading of the sun, there will certainly be not a conceivable grain of evidence left to tell anybody (assuming the existence of other organisms somewhere amidst the scattered galaxies) that any life has ever existed on it. It is all the same to the universe whether man exists or not—hence it flatters the importance of a perfectly negligible type of temporary material organisation to claim that its absence would be preferable to its presence. In truth, man's existence doesn't matter a damn to anything or anybody save himself. From his own standpoint, it might be more merciful for him if he didn't exist.

As for international matters—the American government certainly is lax in protecting citizens abroad. I had not seen any detailed description of a Mexican 'bull-pen' before, though I always understand that Latin-American prisons were crude and brutally conducted. Your account is certainly vivid. Concerning Nicaragua—I suppose the U.S. wants to keep hold of it in order to prevent any other powerful nation from constructing a canal through it. That is not an especially flagrant national policy—as judged by the realities of history—provided the Nicaraguans are not oppressed. I'd have to know more about the matter before taking sides in the Sandino rebellion. Japan is certainly getting itself into an hysteria of nervous apprehension, as attested by the fear of American photographers. Just what the future will be in regard to Japan is still a puzzle. I think it is only fair to let Japan control Manchuria if its out-reaching is stopped there. From all I can see, Manchuria is necessary to Japan. But of course, steps must be taken to prevent the Japanese from going further—controlling China as a whole, and obtaining the hegemony of the Pacific. Sooner or later, there will probably have to be a war between Japan and the U.S.—and perhaps other western powers. The position of Soviet Russia in such a war remains to be seen.

Concerning the subject of law and order—let me hasten to correct what seems to be a misapprehension on your part. From your present letter I gather that you thought my previous letter referred to the pioneer western sheriffs as regarding their work 'as a stage for the showing-off of their personal merits'. Now in reality this was very far indeed from what I said—since no one admires the bravery of pioneer officers, working against odds, more than I. What I did say was that a *modern city policeman* would be using his work as a stage for the exhibition of his merits if, *having plenty of aid and organisation at his disposal,* he imperilled the public peace by neglecting to avail himself of that aid and organisation in order to *imitate* the lone-handed bravery of the early westerner who *did not* have aid and organisation at his disposal. He would be staging a piece of reprehensible bravado because he would be refusing to give the public the maximum protection which it is capable of being given. It was not so with the old western sheriff. He *did* give the public as much protection as he could; and his lone-handed bravery was not a matter of showing off, but merely a necessity caused by the fact that no better means of protecting the public was at his disposal. Bravery under those circumstances is not bravado, but is instead a highly admirable exercise of character. In modern cities, however, all is different. There is no need in such places of using the one-man methods of the frontier—in fact, such methods would get nowhere amidst the problems of a thickly settled district. The most effective way of preserving the peace in cities lies in competent organisation and a numerous police personnel trained in intelligent team-work. To be sure, not so much courage and initiative are demanded of each man as under the pioneer one-man system—but *what of it?* The business of a policeman is to catch crooks, not to display bravery. When the work calls for bravery, we admire the sight of it; but we do not want our policemen to impair our security by deliberately repudiating their advantages in order to bring their personal bravery more constantly into play. The western sheriff, I'm sure, wouldn't have done that. He was constantly a figure of one-man heroism *because he had to be*—not because he passed up possible advantages in order to draw more heavily on his bravery. If he had deliberately forfeited advantages, he would have been disloyal to the citizens who chose him to protect them. Officers are appointed to keep down crime and disorder—not to exploit their personality. All of which is not incompatible with the fact that only brave men can be good officers, and that the one-man pioneer officer naturally had to use more courage and initiative than the average member of a modern police force.

This—not what you thought—is what I was driving at. I was replying to your opinion (with which I still diametrically disagree) that it would be more manly for a police force to send *one man* to deal with an exceptionally disorderly saloon bully than to send six men and have the matter neatly cleaned up in an adult way. I still say that it would be a bit of childish romanticism to send one man—who could probably do nothing to bring the disorder to a rapid end—instead of six, who would have the offender quietly in a patrol-wagon in five minutes, thus allowing the peaceful affairs of the neighbourhood to continue their course. The sending of only one man could not be other than a feebly theatrical gesture, based on a total misconception of the elements involved and regarding the prosaic job of wiping out a nuisance as chivalric tournament or game in which the quixotic spirit of equally matched combatants had a place. This sort of situation is not a romantic fight, in which the forces must be evenly matched. It is not, properly speaking, a fight at all; since the object of the police is not to *injure* the bully but merely to remove him as unhurt as possible to a proper place of confinement. The one duty of the police is to get rid of the nuisance as quickly and cleanly as possible, and if they neglect any aid to doing so they are derelict in their obligations toward the public. To send one man instead of six, when six are available, would be a public offence well meriting demotion and prosecution for the sergeant or lieutenant responsible for the order. I honestly do not see how it is possible to hold any other view—nor do I see what relation this hypothetical case has to the one-man tactics of the old-time western sheriff who did not have any auxiliaries at his disposal. What I called "childish" was *not* the intrepid warfare of pioneer lone-handers against the desperadoes of their age and place. I simply said that it was childish to *neglect to use force actually at one's disposal.* It would be childish, for instance, for a bunch of four policemen to see a drunken brute terrorising a neighbourhood with a revolver, and yet to allow only *one* of their number to try to stop him—on the romantic ground of "fair play". Before *one* man could handle him, the brute might shoot a dozen people; whereas if all four pitched in, they could disarm him before his weapon could injure more than one or two. I would call the limitation of the punitive force to one man not only childish but criminal. For remember the basic truth—*policemen are appointed to safeguard the community, not to play games of chivalry.*

As for lawbreakers—when I said that they deserve no consideration I did not mean that they are to be treated with mediaeval rigour. I meant, merely, that they are not to be considered as equals of the law's proper officers in the matter of pursuit and combat. This pursuit and combat cannot be regarded as a romantic game in which the officer must obey a set of chivalric rules and forfeit advantages through sentiment. The criminal has knowingly and voluntarily put himself outside the pale of ornamental sporting regulations—and indeed, he himself wouldn't observe any of those regulations toward the officer! The only obligation resting on the officer is to get the criminal and eradicate the nuisance caused by the criminal in as short order as possible—using every advantage at his disposal. If this involves the capture of one man by six, well and good. It's no time for boyish punctilios. The officer who doesn't use every advantage at his disposal for the protection of the public is himself a criminal. But remember, I'm talking only of *capturing* the offender and suppressing the nuisance he creates—not of dealing with him later. Truly enough, criminals differ in degree of reprehensibility; and a wise judge will certainly temper his sentences with mercy and common-sense when such are called for. But this has nothing to do with the policeman. His job is to suppress all disturbances of the peace in any way he can for the benefit of society, and when he sees a person acting in an anti-social way he must get that person into custody in order to eliminate the trouble. If, later on, the judge finds that the person does not merit further punishment, well and good. But at the outset, it is the policeman's duty to suppress disorder without asking questions. Now and then innocent people will undoubtedly be arrested, but what system is ever free from mistakes? These accidental victims themselves would not wish the police to be any more lax, since on another occasion the question of arrest might involve criminals who were doing them harm. When in doubt, the wise policeman always arrests. A wrongly arrested innocent man can always be released—but a wrongly non-arrested criminal is not so readily captured after he has once made his escape. As to those who are "driven to crime"—that is for the judge, not the policeman, to deal with. The policeman's job is *to stop crime*—by whomever committed, and for whatever reason. If, in the end, the court finds palliating circumstances, it may very well give certain individual offenders a second chance. It is not often, though, that a man is really 'driven to crime'. Much of that legend is sentimental propaganda launched by those romantic souls (more common in the U.S. than in Canada or Great-Britain) who instinctively sympathise with lawbreakers rather than the law. Actually, there are dozens of charitable agencies which can relieve the plight of the man who goes under in the social struggle. Still—let it not be denied that in a few cases the commission of technical crime may have been part of a necessary struggle for survival. In such rare instances it is for the judge of the court—and for no one else—to grant special leniency. It is of course understood that all my remarks have been applied to what may be called *substantial* crimes—crimes involving violence, real theft, and other serious encroachments on the good order of society. The question of petty law-breaking—motor overspeeding, playing cards on Sunday, fishing out of season, etc.—is something entirely separate and distinct. Here, of course, the policeman ought to use his own individual tact and avoid making arrests when he knows that no adverse social consequences will result from their omission. Another thing—in cases involving disturbances and other semi-substantial offences, the officer may sometimes have good justification for not making an actual arrest *after he has put a stop to the anti-social condition involved.* The point is, that the *anti-social manifestation must be stopped.* That is primary. Whether, in petty cases, to place the responsible person or persons in technical custody, is a secondary matter to be decided on its own merits. As to whether society has obligations to fulfil toward the individual—I would say that it has, but only so far as the original social contract involved in its formation is concerned. The individual must conform to the rules which his ancestors voluntarily—by consent if not actively—formulated, and certainly cannot expect society to protect him against the consequences of breaking those rules. Still more—I don't think an individual can expect society to protect him in rule-breaking even if the rules happen to have been imposed involuntarily on his group from outsisde. He may be intellectually justified in thinking the rules unjust, but he cannot expect society—so long as it upholds the rules—to fight against itself by condoning their violation. If he feels justified in starting a revolution against authority, well and good. But he must not, in such a case, expect the society which he has made his adversary to yield him aid and comfort! By the way—don't confuse what I say about the duty of police officers with the theoretical duty of the private citizen to help in the apprehension of criminals. This latter theoretical duty is very shadowy, and certainly cannot be compared with the policeman's professional duty. The private citizen is not specially appointed and paid to catch criminals, nor has he taken any oath of honour to engage in such pursuit. Ordinarily, a man of good breeding does not allow any civic theory to make a spy and tattle-tale of him. He minds his own business, and does not think it necessary to telephone the police station even if he happens to have heard of the whereabouts of some fugitive—provided, of course, the fugitive is not a real social menace, or wanted for some especially atrocious crime. Most citizen coöperation has to do with the thwarting of crimes actually in process of commission—as when one rushes to the aid of a man whom one sees attacked by footpads.

Moreover, it is tacitly understood that the private citizen's personal honour has precedence over any theoretical duty in the matter of shielding relatives or friends from arrest. When one takes a stand for law and order, it must not be thought that a fanatical suspension of all the canons of proportion and all the laws of common sense and ordinary consideration is recommended!

As for the laws themselves—it is certain that their *number* is too great, as so many have said; but that does not mean that the strict enforcement of certain basic and necessary laws is not a desirable policy. I know nothing of frontier conditions, but I can assert with confidence that in a populous and long-settled region the effect of an orderly restraint of violence is *not* (as you say it is in the west) to promote murder, furtiveness, and underhanded knavery. On the other hand, much more crime would undoubtedly exist if no restraint were there—for our foreigners are shifty, mercurial, and quarrelsome. As I have said, our native population is naturally so law-abiding that it has virtually no friction with the authorities. I have never had any law clash with me, and don't know anybody else who has felt police pressure except for motor overspeeding or tardy shovelling of snow from some sidewalk. I have never seen any act of adult human violence committed, and don't know anybody else around here who has, except in war. People—that is, native Americans—know the functions and privileges of the citizen, and never think of overstepping those bounds under any ordinary conditions. They refrain from encroaching on others in exchange for the absence of encroachment on them. A substantial crime committed by a native American hereabouts gets front-page headlines, while the same thing committed by an Italian would be buried in the middle of the paper. Of course it is illegal to carry firearms in all eastern states—otherwise the thugs would have it all their own way. Ability of the police to arrest revolver-toters (occasionally they examine suspicious characters in the haunts of such) has prevented more than one holdup, murder, or burglary. What helps a lot in the east is the sort of simple good sense which results from the long adjustment—over many generations—of the people to one another and to the communal way of life. Well-bred men virtually never fight, because the social code frowns on the sort of language and conduct which precipitate fights among less restrained people. It is plebeian and ill-bred to give offence, and no one wishes to be caught doing it. Arguments never involve violence; because reflective people understand that the opinions of individuals naturally differ, and that—in consequence—it is no affront to a man not to believe the same things that he believes. As a result, we are as eager for debate as the Greeks of classic times—our object being simply the truth. The idea of violence attending a simple difference of opinion would be ridiculous hereabouts. This general mood extends even into politics—although the best men tend not to mix in politics more than they have to. Even when campaigners make wild charges in speeches there is never anything personal in it—and two candidates who have been calling each other 'grafter' and 'tool of the interests' will dine together the same night in perfect personal amity. Real quarrels and feuds—based on actual insults or injuries—result in silence and estrangement rather than violence. It seems tacitly understood that a non-physical wrong (aside from a crude verbal insult, so seldom given) is not to be resented in a physical way, although a physical wrong (rare as it is) is. Whether the duel—which became obsolete here around the 1830's—was a wholesome safety-valve for festering feelings is a matter for debate. All these conditions hold good for the whole Atlantic seaboard and such inland regions as are strongly connected with it. In Canada and Great Britain they are even more emphatic. The average non-slum person lives and dies without ever having seen any display of physical violence among adults. At the same time, however, there is never any inclination among intelligent people to criticise the different conditions of the frontier. It is understood that folk-attitudes are the result of antecedent and surrounding conditions, and the pioneer's struggle with nature, Indians, and solitude amply explains his ready recourse to the physical. It is a repetition of what occurred when all the Aryan race were correspondingly environed in the infancy of the old world. Nowhere is the drama of the frontier more poignantly appreciated than in the peaceful east—and we realise, too, that we have lost a certain amount of ancestral resourcefulness which those under more primitive conditions have retained or revived. I can sympathise with you in your opposition to urban methods introduced before the region is urbanised enough to need them. Certainly, the laws of any section ought to be drawn up with the profoundest regard for that section's local conditions and historic background. I greatly enjoyed your analysis of the traditional Texas character, and hope that you will eventually try to expound and mirror it in literature. Your knowledge of the region, its traditions, and its historic characters is a phenomenally wide, intelligent, analytical, and sympathetic one—an admirable background for the creation of convincing fictional figures and events centreing therein.

Regarding police corruption—it is important for the observer to realise (1) that its effects on the general outward order of a city as encountered by the average respectable citizen are vastly less considerable than one would think from the speeches of reformers, and (2) that although simple graft is virtually universal, the famous close alliances betwixt gangs and police occur only in very large cities with extensive foreign (usually Italian) populations. To imagine that the great bulk of ordinary crimes are not genuinely dealt with by the police, or that absolute peace and safety do not exist for the ordinary respectable citizen in the non-slum districts of any normal eastern city, is to be as naive as the easterner who expects to be shot at the moment he enters the west. Reformers naturally dwell on the seamy side of things—but anyone with common sense knows that arrests and convictions are constantly taking place for genuine crimes committed against persons of every kind, rich or poor. It is of course probable in the long run that wealthy persons fare better in the courts (either when arrested or when acting as complainants) than persons without money or influence—since they are able to command better legal advice. But the *extent* of this very natural and inevitable tendency is ridiculously exaggerated by propagandists. I have seldom noticed that any wealthy person guilty of a crime like murder escapes arrest and conviction any more readily than a person without means. If some get off through sentimental technicalities, the same thing is also true of many non-wealthy persons. The cases most often cited—like that of Secretary Fall, Sinclair, Charles W. Morse,[2] etc.—are those of men guilty only of business crimes; where the line between actual crime and socially tolerated sharp practice is very ill-defined. If they get off relatively lightly, the same can often be said of poor men as well—for there are hundreds of cases of humble defaulters, sharp dealers, and other commercial violators admitted to early parole or probation. The radical propagandist likes to play up individual instances where injustice has been conspicuous, but the general picture he presents is one of fundamental erroneousness. To imagine that the police do not, as a rule, exert themselves to work on crimes unless the victim happens to be wealthy, is to entertain a wholly false picture. No doubt in certain cities a tip is a good incentive toward extra work—but against that side of the picture we can array the ordinary record of any week's police activity, with scores of arrests and convictions for crimes against non-wealthy persons. Reformers and propagandists single out flagrant instances and harp upon them—they do not think or talk temperately. For instance—it would be futile to try to generalise from the case of the oil magnate's son which you cite. You say that he was allowed to disturb the peace in a boom town, although humbler men were arrested for far less cause. Well, I can say with certainty that no such thing could happen in New England, where we have a respect for law and order for its own sake, apart from personalities. When Brown University students get riotous down town in Providence, the police deal with them exactly as they would with any gang of peace-disturbers—without paying attention to whose sons they are. Arrests are made, nightsticks are used, and full-sized fines are paid in court afterward. Sometimes sentimentalists protest against this firm treatment of "high-spirited boys"—but I never heard of a policeman being 'broken' through plutocratic pressure for doing his duty in this way. Also—any man caught driving a motor-car under the influence of liquor is arrested and fined, and loses his motor licence. It makes no difference who he is—and some extremely wealthy and influential citizens are at this moment without a motor licence for this reason.

There is really no excuse for irresponsible theorising in matters like this, where so much first-hand evidence is available. The proof of police efficiency—with all due allowances for corruption—is in the daily life of the citizen; and here we know absolutely that virtually 98% of our respectable and law-abiding population are thoroughly protected from disorder, free from the menace of false arrest, and sure of reasonable attention when the victims of crime. Accost at random, on the street of any normal eastern city, 25 average citizens of the quiet type which may be classified as essentially decent and law-abiding. Ask each one whether he has ever been persecuted by the police, or whether he has ever had any reason to complain of their protection of him. The chances are that 23 out of the 25 would be astonished by the question. They would say that they had certainly never run afoul of the law except in speeding or other technical and trivial matters, and that they had no reason to think the police lax in attending to any complaints of theirs. If I were among those questioned I could say just that. I have had stolen property returned by the police—and I recall a case where a friend of mine (son of an important political figure, hence theoretically in the unduly favoured class) *failed* to get back stolen property of his. In both of these cases it is obvious that the police were performing their simple, unbribed routine duty . . . happening to succeed in one case, but not happening to do so in the other. When you realise that the average respectable man in an eastern city has never seen any substantial display of physical violence among adults, and has never had any unpleasant dealings with the law and its officers, you can get a common-sense idea of the general working out of the Anglo-Saxon law and order ideal. This will be a far truer picture than the speeches of reformers, or the whisperings of those who have witnessed exceptional incidents, can furnish. There is no question at all about the soundness of the ideal, because *it works.* Its benefits are so overwhelmingly greater than its lapses and misapplications, that it would be folly to challenge its soundness. It is the logical evolutionary product of society—the natural state of things when a people become numerous and settled. In a heavily populated district it is impossible and absurd to consider the individual's physical protection "his own business". A complex society cannot waste the energy of its members in individual defences against physical perils which the social fabric as a whole can much more effectively reduce to a minimum. The energy of the people must be saved for actually significant activities—things of the intellect—many of which could not exist at all under conditions of constant physical peril. Internal lawlessness is just as much an enemy of settled society as the Indians, the French, and the rigours of nature against which the orderly population of the east had to cope. As a result of conquering all these things, we are free to develop the human personality in a fuller, broader way than is possible under the conditions of constant turbulence. Naturally there is a loss of certain resourceful qualities peculiar to primitive man, but the gain more than balances it. Later, of course, decadence ensues, and the megalopolitan type loses more than it gains; but it would hardly be accurate to say that any American city except New York has definitely reached this overripe stage.

But I am far from opposing the work of the reformers whose reports I have mentioned as one-sided and overcoloured. That corruption would be greater but for the zeal of these men in singling out exceptional conditions, is an undoubted fact. It is in cities of the largest class—of a million or more population—that police corruption usually extends so far as to become a serious problem—though even there no respectable person is often in danger unless he is engaged in certain trades affected by racketeering. However, this racketeering menace is enough to warrant drastic civic action, and such action has not been absent during the past year. In Chicago the basic sense of law and order—paralysed for a while—has reasserted itself in the formation of a citizens' committee which furnishes a special protection temporarily denied by the corrupt police. In time, there is no question but that the gang matter will be straightened out. New York, too, is making an honest effort to shake off the worst features of its corrupt machine. And remember that even in Chicago or New York no respectable citizen has ever been in peril unless he has happened to be in one of the trades on which the racketeers prey. For 90% of the decent people, both of these corrupt cities have always been perfectly safe. Even the widely advertised vice squad racket has its other side. Raids were seldom made except in actually shady localities, and the number of innocent victims shrinks somewhat when we confine the term to persons *always* innocent of the charges preferred. It's a safe bet that *very few* persons actually leading continuously respectable lives, and keeping clear of neighbourhoods they knew to be shady, were ever involved in vice-squad trouble. Nevertheless, the extirpation of the racket was certainly a thing to be desired.

Altogether, we may say that the existing general system of police protection—despite its rotten spots—not only accomplishes more good than harm, but is an absolute necessity for the older and more urbanised parts of the country. What critic has anything better to offer? The primary problem is the suppression of general disorder so that a large population can perform its functions without getting all tangled up in itself—and it can be said that the existing system *does accomplish that end* as well as could any system at our disposal. There is plenty of room for improvement, but no friend of the country could logically wish the overturn of the basic design, with its ideal of rational law and order.

As for the lawless gangs of *old* New York—very differently organised and motivated from the economically-inspired gangs of today—they surely present some extremely dramatic situations. It must be remembered, however, that they were as definitely confined to an underworld as are their unworthy successors; and that no respectable New Yorker of the 1850's ever heard of them except through minor items in the press. Their battles all took place in slum areas given over to indescribable crime and squalor—areas into which no ordinary citizen ever set foot. In those days city slums were filthy and monstrous to a degree incredible in this generation. Nothing on this continent today is comparable in horror, disease, and general vileness to the Five Points or Cherry Street of the middle 19th century. Such districts were virtually fabulous and forbidden ground to the respectable people of their time—and even to this day not more than one New Yorker in a hundred has ever visited their relatively tame successors. Slumming was confined to a small and venturesome element of young bloods—for at that period no obviously respectable person was safe from assassination in the hell-roaring region east of the City Hall. You could probably have visited in New York for months in 1850 without coming across anybody—business-man, professor, clerk, mechanic, or any other normal type—who had ever been in contact with gangdom and its territory. Incidentally, it is only in the last few years that people outside New York have taken their present interest in the old gangs. This phase of local history was exceedingly obscure until modern gangdom revived the subject with the Rosenthal murder of 1912.[3]

In their general attitude toward the problem of law enforcement, people probably fall into several distinct types, as determined by historic tradition, personal environment, and individual temperament. I can easily imagine that one used to pioneer problems and methods would not have the ready sympathy with the eastern standard that an easterner would; yet the different needs of a settled and an unsettled country ought to be apparent, upon reflection, to any unbiassed observer. Another thing which inclines you toward the anti-legal position is your keen sense of the drama of physical struggle. You are inclined to admire the element of combat so much for its own sake—or for the sake of the primal drama it symbolises—that a social order which has to tone down the element tends to strike you as flat and pallid. This is a very natural reaction—yet after all, you will have to concede that all evolution involves the necessary sacrifice of picturesque things. The real value—as distinguished from the romantic or decorative value—of constant physical combat is confined to a relatively early stage of social development. When it is a necessary survival-measure, or a necessary mode of maintaining position and securing progress, bodily combat is indeed an important feature of life; but later on life naturally takes forms which largely relegate it to a symbolic, ornamental, or recreational position. The determinant survival-element at such later stages is mental acuteness, will, or coördinating power. Now it is the habit of those devoted to the old way of life to hate and sneer at the new—to look down on the "suave, tricky" modern, and exalt the memory of the bold, manly ancient who accomplished his will through force instead of calculation. This is because a fixed set of values has been accepted—but one might naturally inquire whether the set in question is the only possible one, or whether the new natural order may not have given birth to a new set, based on intelligence, and just as valid for the modern age as the old set was for the departed age. In other words, why mourn and exalt a thing which belonged to another order of existence, when another thing may be far better for the present order? By what standard is one age and its methods entitled to preference over another age and its methods? Why take for granted that fists are better than brains? In this matter I try to be as balanced and impartial as possible. I certainly regard the intellect and aesthetic sense as the highest development of human personality, and believe that the goal of civilisation must necessarily be a state in which they can have the maximum opportunity for unhampered operation. At the same time I am not blind to the need of preserving a certain amount of the old physical stamina as a supplement to the newer qualities. Several fundamentals of graceful existence—independence, personal inviolateness, and so on—involve emotional attitudes of ego-defence which once depended wholly on the physical, and still do to a limited extent; while group-survival depends on a willingness to resort to the physical when other means will not assure the group a favoured position among other groups. Any individual or group which wholly loses its physical stamina in connexion with the will to be free from encroachment is at a serious disadvantage and may be considered as definitely decadent; hence there is undoubtedly a strong validity in the Aryan standard which makes sturdy inviolateness (backed up when necessary by physical force) a criterion of merit. Races marked by an absence of this stamina and insistence on inviolateness are destined for decay and subordination. In recognising this condition, I am quite on your side—as against utter despisers of physical stamina and combat like Frank B. Long and others of the younger generation. I realise that a reserve of combative force, and a willingness to bring it out on occasion, is at the base of individual and national integrity—and that consequently the significance of primitive combat as a symbol is still valid and potent, even in regions where such combat is no longer a daily ingredient of life. Indeed, I have a hearty appreciation of the drama of old struggles, and understand their connexion with the general march of history. Where I differ from you is that I do not advocate giving this physical foundation too extreme and undivided a worship. Necessary though it is for the maintenance of a healthy state, it does not include all that it is the business of a state to achieve. Richer, broader sides of the human spirit develop when the sheer struggle for survival lessens, and the struggle itself must not be allowed to eclipse these valuable fruits. These new things are just as valuable as the old, and a blind worship of the old at the expense of the new is more or less pointless. As the race develops, those aspects of it which place it most in touch with the universe become naturally its paramount objects, and the growth of intelligence provides a new instrument for use in the business of survival. The physical becomes less an end in itself than one of several means to an end, and the focus of human interest shifts from physical struggle to the struggle of the will and intellect—so that in the solid literature of the 19th and 20th centuries the problems and conflicts are dominantly psychological rather than physical. A man's mental and emotional life comes to be of deeper significance than his physical life, and is so recognised by the sensitive artist. Now all this is natural—an inevitable product of social evolution—and there is no point in regretting it or continuing to regard the physical as inherently nobler than the psychological. Both have their function, and each separate region must base its use of the two elements upon its own peculiar conditions and place in the cycle of social evolution. It does not become the settled urbanite to despise the mainly physical life of the frontier, or the frontiersman to despise the orderly and mainly calculative life of the settled cities. One regional type is just as natural as the other—and the only mistake is in trying to apply the standards of the one to the other. Thus I realise fully that the frontier demands a set of conditions wholly distinct from those of an urbanised (or any sort of settled and governable) region. The inability of the law to cover vast desolate areas and ensure redress for injuries makes it imperative for the individual to have a certain amount of freedom in matters of defence and reprisal. I would be the last to advocate the denial of weapons, for instance, to those who require them in order to survive and defend their property—the last, too, to belittle the worship of physical prowess surviving in a region where such prowess is still a paramount factor in social adjustment. What I do object to, however, is the unwarranted assumption on the part of some that the frontier-physical way of life is intrinsically preferable to the civilised-settled way, and that the settled region is reprehensible in its insistence on the degree of law and order demanded by its own conditions. I have no use for large cities, but I do have a high regard for *civilisation itself* as exemplified by the small town and long-settled countryside. I believe that the security of such places gives the human spirit a fuller opportunity for extensive and symmetrical development—in a majority of cases—that it could obtain under any other set of conditions, hence I uphold most firmly the standard of law and order upon which this security is based. I do not think that any sentimental regard for primitive backgrounds, or for the coddling of the individual at the expense of society, ought to be allowed to interfere with the best possible maintenance of that state of public peace which gives every man the maximum opportunity to develop his highest faculties. Law and order—the ideal of an unbroken public peace—is of course just as compatible with a liberalised social order as with a despotic one. There is nothing about the probable future system of redistributed wealth and ameliorated working classes to cause any lowering of the existing standard. Rather will there be an increased sentiment for a better and more equitable enforcement of that standard. Even in Soviet Russia the standard of law and order is absolutely inflexible . . . . just as it was in Imperial Rome. It is a necessity of every coherent and enduring civilisation.

Octr. 7

No—I didn't see the Cave in the Rock or hear any legends of its desperate frequenters. I did, however, visit the so-called Devil's Punch-Bowl north of Natchez,[4] which is said to have been a haunt of all sorts of sinister characters, piratical and otherwise, including your old friend Murrell. It is a weird place—a great hollow in the earth not far from the river bluff. What could have caused it is still a mystery—one fantastic theory attributing it to a bygone meteorite. There are the usual legends of buried treasure connected with it, and it has been dug over many times in the past. Its size—now several acres—increases as time passes, owing to the gradual caving-in of the banks. It is thickly grown with underbrush and trees, and is wholly uninhabited. Not many of the younger generation in Natchez know about it, and only one guide-book gives any workable idea of how to get to it. It is unmarked, and one can reach it only by traversing one of the small negro farms perched on the high ground between its brink and the sunken line of the Natchez Trace. I think I mentioned—and probably you know of old—that all the old roads around Natchez are deeply sunken below the surface of the surrounding terrain, on account of the highly friable nature of the yellow alluvial clay. They are like cañons running between high perpendicular walls—and are usually shaded by the huge live-oaks that grow on the brink of those walls. What you write of the *Harps* is indeed dramatic and sinister in the highest degree—vaguely suggesting the hideous clan of Sawney Bean in old Scotland.[5] The ending of both was surely ironic enough—and their whole history deserves incorporation in literature. One thing you ought to do sometime—in addition to writing on the traditions of Texas—is to prepare a history of the border ruffians of all sections in such a way as to make each one stand out clearly—geographically and chronologically. We hear fleetingly of these characters, yet always tend to get them mixed up as to time and place. A systematic book about them would help to fix their respective positions in the historic stream, and coördinate them as a definite chapter of history. I don't know of anyone better fitted than yourself, as regards both erudition and zest for the subject, to perform this task. Your historical side is far too valuable not to be expressed in permanent published form. Thanks, by the way, for the cuttings. Pretty Boy Floyd seems likely to grow into a legend of the true border type, though perhaps he is not quite as wild a character as his remote predecessors. It will be dramatically interesting to see how this case turns out.

Alas, yes—I knew that the old French Market was doomed. It has been threatened for years, and one of the reasons I made my New Orleans trip this last spring was that I wanted to be sure to see it before it went. Opinions still seem to differ as to just *how much* will be torn down. Many in New Orleans last June thought that the renovated section nearest Jackson Square might be preserved as a sample of what the whole was. I explored the whole thing, though with my handkerchief pressed to my nose, and took coffee more than once at the renovated section. Assuredly the place needs an exhaustive cleaning-out and fumigation, but it seems to me that the general frames of the existing buildings could be made sanitary. I don't see why destruction is necessary. Unfortunately New Orleans seems to have a little too much of the "civic progress" idea. In a way, the inhabitants appreciate the priceless heritage of antiquity which they have; for much of the Vieux Carré has been carefully restored, while the mourning for the burned-down Opera House is obviously sincere. On the other hand, there is a streak of callousness somewhere—as witness the utilitarian destruction of the old St. Louis Hotel (torn down because nobody would pay for the rat-proofing of its cellar) in 1916, and the razing of a whole block of ancient houses for the new court-house. Price thinks that a great part of the old quarter is doomed—and certainly, modern business is eating into it dangerously from the Canal St. side. Royal St. is predominantly modern (though a few old edifices have been saved) as far in as Bienville. As for Creole cooking—I didn't sample much of it because my cash was so low that I had to eat at cheap lunch rooms where things are more or less standardised. There was, though, a certain local tinge to some of the dishes. One curious local phenomenon is what is called a "poor boy" sandwich—a long roll filled with pork or beef and very highly seasoned. I like these—except that the plethora of crust was a bit hard on my gums. Creole cooking as a whole might have been somewhat wasted on me, because of my lifelong detestation of all *sea food,* which is a New Orleans specialty. I can't bear any kind of fish, shell-fish, or anything of the sort—it acts on me like an instant emetic—hence many of the most celebrated Creole dishes would have been off my list. Yes—I saw the dwelling oaks in City Park, and visited Lake Pontchartrain, and the old brick fort (or what's left of it) near the mouth of Bayou St. John. I did not, however, take the river trip, because most of the plantations on the banks were washed away in the floods of 1927. Such plantations as I saw were a little farther from the river—some on the road from Baton Rouge, and one fine old plantation-house (Three Oaks) in St. Bernard Parish between Jackson Barracks and Chalmette battlefield on the present grounds of the Am. Sugar Refinery. I liked New Orleans tremendously, and hope I can get there again some time. There are streets in the Vieux Carré which take one back 100 to 150 years, and endless examples of distinctive and fascinating architecture. The many patios are an endless delight—no two alike, and a very liberal number open to the public. I crossed over to Algiers on the ferry, but did not find that side of the river very interesting. The climate suited me precisely—never too hot, and too cold only one day. No—I never heard that ballad "The Lakes of the Pontchartrain". It is certainly typical of the genuine folk ballad, and I hope its text and tune have been preserved by those who collect such things. You are to be envied your knowledge of these old songs, since they appear to be fast disappearing from public knowledge. Some time you ought to consult collections of ballad lore, and see if any songs you know are left out. If so, you ought to bring the missing specimens to the attention of folklorists. Mobile is another fine old city, though not quite so distinctive as New Orleans. Vicksburg, too, is delightfully attractive. But my real favourite of all the towns of that region—a place where I'd really like to live—is old *Natchez.* That town takes its place beside

Charleston, Marblehead, Newburyport, Portsmouth, and Quebec as one of my supreme favourites. I think I described it to you in my letter from New Orleans. To this day it preserves the leisurely and beautiful air of the 1820 period—and the scenery is incomparably exquisite. It has the air of *unmixed* antiquity which busy New Orleans lacks, while the landscape is a thousand times finer than that of Louisiana. On the whole, I think Natchez is the high spot of my southern trip. It also marks the farthest west I have so far been.

The cooling days—which are now making outdoor reading and writing impossible—give your remarks on climate a twofold and melancholy interest! When I visit Texas, it certainly won't be in winter! Like you, I hate overcoats and such paraphernalia—and despite my sensitiveness to cold I wear them as little as possible. I never wear heavy underwear, either—for it isn't needed in a well-heated house, and warm outer clothes will do just as well for outdoors. Cold gets at me in several different ways—enough to puzzle a doctor. First of all—and before I feel any real discomfort—my muscles stiffen up and become clumsy so that I can't write. I can't write decently under 73° or 74°. From there on down to freezing the effect of a falling temperature is simply increasing discomfort and sluggishness; but after that it begins to be painful to breathe. I can't go out at all under +20°, since the effects are varied and disastrous. First my lungs and throat get sore, and then I become sick at the stomach and lose anything I've eaten. My heart also pounds and palpitates. At about 17° or 16° my muscular and nervous coördination gets all shot to hell, and I have to flounder and stagger like a drunken man. When I try to walk ahead, I feel as if I were trying to swim through some viscous, hampering medium of resistance. Finally, at 15° or 14°, I begin to lose consciousness. Once in Jan. 1928 I passed out entirely, so that the fellow who was with me had to drag me into a warm place to thaw out. Nor is the effect of such an exposure merely temporary. I remain as sick as a dog for hours afterward, and for days I have pain in breathing. If I get many such exposures in succession, the effects last all through the winter. One of those effects is a monstrous swelling of feet and ankles which prevents my wearing shoes. This is probably caused by some interference with the heart action—and it keeps up until the next late spring. I haven't had this trouble since 1930—for during the last 2 winters I have carefully stayed in on all very cold days. Obviously, winter is no time for me—and I may yet have to move down to Florida. My advantage comes in summer, for I literally don't know what it is to be too hot. The hotter it gets, the more energy I seem to have—mental and physical alike. I perspire freely, but am comfortable for all that I can relish temperatures of 97° and 98°, and never want it cooler than 80°. Of course, I don't know how I'd be in those inland regions where the summer temperature gets up around 120°—but judging from the available evidence I could stand it better than most. I believe I'd like the tropics or subtropics—and certainly mean to travel in the West Indies some time.

Coming down to my recent trip—as my postcard indicated, the eclipse was a decided success for me, though many places in the totality zone were clouded. A friend of mine—W. Paul Cook—and I picked ancient Newburyport (of which I've probably sent you views) as a post of observation, and although there were clouds in the sky, the sun and moon were entirely clear of them at the climactic moment of totality. We reached Newburyport long before the eclipse started, and chose a hilltop meadow with a wide view—near the northern part of the town—as our observatory. Naturally the clouds made us apprehensive, but the sun came out every little while and gave us long glimpses of all stages of the phenomenon. The landscape did not change in tone until the solar crescent was rather small, and then a kind of sunset vividness became apparent. When the crescent waned to extreme thinness, the scene grew strange and spectral—an almost deathlike quality inhering in the sickly yellowish light. Just about that time the sun went under a cloud, and Cook and I commenced cursing in seven different languages! At last, though, the thin thread of the pre-totality glitter emerged into a large patch of absolutely clear sky. The outspread valleys faded into unnatural light—Jupiter came out in the deep-violet heavens—ghoulish shadow-bands raced along the winding white roads—the last beaded strip of glitter vanished—and the pale corona flickered into aureolar radiance around the black disc of the obscuring moon. We were seeing the real show! The earth was darkened more deeply than in the eclipse of Jan. 24, 1925, (which I saw—though half-frozen—from Yonkers, N.Y.) though the corona was not so bright. We absorbed the whole spectacle with the utmost impressedness and appreciation. Finally the beaded crescent reëmerged, the valleys glowed again in faint, eerie light, and the various partial phases were repeated in reverse order. The marvel was over, and accustomed things resumed their wonted sway. I may never see another—but it is not everyone who has, like me, witnessed two total solar eclipses.

The Montreal-Quebec trip—which I took alone—was also a decided success. Montreal is more Anglo-Saxon than Quebec, and does not seem at all foreign except in the French section east of St. Lawrence Boulevard. Actually, there are about twice as many French as English in the population, (600,000 Fr., 300,000 Eng.) besides some 150,000 foreigners of all sorts—Jews, Italians, Greeks, etc. It is certainly a cosmopolitan metropolis. One district—Westmount—is a separate and wholly Anglo-Saxon municipality. All official signs are bi-lingual—

NO PARKING	ARRETE DE TRAMWAYS	RAILWAY CROSSING
—	—	—
NE STATIONNEZ PAS	CAR STOP	TRAVERSE DU CHEMIN DE FER

etc. etc.—and the street signs vary in language. In the English section the main street is placarded as ST. CATHERINE ST., but across the Boulevard in the French quarter it reads RUE STE. CATHERINE. The whole province of Quebec is officially bi-lingual, the French there being more tenacious of their language and customs than in Louisiana. Montreal shows no signs of becoming wholly Anglicised like New Orleans—although 50 or 75 years ago, N. O. was much like Montreal, with Canal St. playing the part of St. Lawrence Blvd. Montreal is a highly attractive city, well set off by the towering slope of Mt. Royal, which rises in its midst and from which it was named. The ancient part—containing the old cathedral (1824), the seamen's chapel of Notre-Dame de Bonsecoeurs (1771), the Chateau de Ramezay or old Governor's house (1705), the ancient Bonsecoeurs Market (a domed building, formerly the City Hall, and still unthreatened by destruction), the centuried Sulpician Seminary, etc.—is that closest to the southern waterfront. Here one may find some very old French houses of stone or brick-and-stucco, though all are in a decrepit condition. You could trace a vague architectural likeness to some types of New Orleans houses though they lack the subtropical and Spanish ingredients. No patios or balconies. The newer French houses are not like the later Creole houses of N. O., but follow a peculiarly Canadian plan—with outside staircases in the double and triple houses, to save room inside. English houses are not, as a rule, as tasteful as the newer houses in the U.S.—or at least in New England. The Canadians have not reverted to classic Georgian designs as New Englanders have. All told, however, the general effect of Montreal is much like that of any large, high-grade American city—except for the profusion of horse-drawn vehicles. I explored it thoroughly, and also visited the well-known Lachine Rapids. Here once dwelt the celebrated La Salle—who met his end in your own Texas. After doing Montreal I was glad to get back to the more unbroken antiquity of Quebec City—for that is a thing utterly unique among the cities of this continent . . . . an absolutely perfect bit of old provincial France. As in 1930 I revelled in its historic atmosphere—the precipitous cliff, the frowning citadel, the red roofs and silver belfries, the climbing lanes and winding alleys, the ancient doorways and facades, the city walls and gates, the unexpected vistas and dizzy flights of steps—and I also took a 'bus and ferry excursion around the neighbouring Isle d'Orleans, where the old French countryside remains in a primitive, unspoiled state—just as when Wolfe landed in 1759. Memories of Wolfe are many, and on the adjacent mainland his headquarters (a curve-roofed farmhouse) still stands. (Incidentally, the route of Wolfe up the Heights of Abraham behind Quebec is still visible—though made easy for the visitor. Atop the cliff a wide expanse is preserved as Battlefields Park, though the actual scene of the Wolfe-Montcalm clash is built over. Wolfe's front line roughly coincides with the modern Rue de Salaberry.) On the island there are endless brick farmhouses with curved eaves, wind and watermills, wayside shrines, and quaint white villages clustering around ancient silver-steepled parish churches.

Nothing but French is spoken, and the rustic population live where their ancestors have lived for 200 years and more. They seldom visit even nearby Quebec—though there is a motor-coach line which meets the ferry and makes a circuit of the island twice each day. I explored several of the churches—some of which are magnificently adorned for rustic fanes. The parish church of St. Jean surprises the visitor by possessing an obviously English Georgian steeple, so that at a distance it looks like one of our New England churches. This is probably due to the influence of British government engineers who supervised its rebuilding after a wind destroyed the original in 1775. It is, however, painted a glistening silver like the steeples of all French churches.

Well—I hated to go home, and when passing through Boston eased the transition by making a side-trip to ancient Marblehead (the Kingsport of my tales). I have probably described this ancient seaport to you before, and sent you views of it.

As for the authorship of the Shakespearian plays and poems—I can't take very seriously the various attempts to attribute them to persons other than W. S. of Stratford and London. All the evidence given in such claims seems to me very thin and forced, while a great deal of evidence on the other side exists. Many seem to think that no one with Shakespeare's limited education and commonplace background could have written the existing works—yet on the other hand I don't believe that they could have been written by anyone *without* a limited education and commonplace background. The historical and other errors in the plays are numerous and often absurd—and cannot be explained away as common attributes of the Elizabethan age. Not one of the men—Bacon, Oxford, etc.—to whom people have tried to credit the plays could have made such mistakes. Ben Jonson's "Sejanus" and "Catiline" shew the exactness of the scholarship prevailing among the really educated men of Shakespeare's time. There is also in Shakespeare a sort of fawning affection for royalty and nobility which eloquently bespeaks the emulous plebeian rather than the actual nobleman. To me, the plays and poems seem just about what would naturally be written by a man of prodigious natural genius in the position of William Shakespeare of Stratford. Some are obviously collaborated, but a certain thread of unity runs through them all. I don't for a moment believe that anyone but W. S. is primarily responsible for them.

Did I give you Wandrei's *new* temporary address in new York? It is *84 Horatio St., Apt. 4B, New York, N.Y.* That is the northern part of the Greenwich Village section, not far from the Hudson River waterfront. A good many colonial houses still remain in that locality—as you may see from one of the postcard sets I sent the other day. He'll be very glad to hear from you at any time that you decide to write. I imagine that after a year of free-lancing he'll be glad enough to go back to the U. of Minn.—where I believe he is virtually sure of getting an instructorship again. He had an idea of spending the coming winter in Southern California (incidentally passing through Auburn en route to see Clark Ashton Smith in person for the first time), but does not now think he can swing it financially. I hope he can get to Providence again before returning to St. Paul.

As for the Farnese music-drama proposition—I know the difference between different kinds of technique too well to fancy I could write successfully in that medium. Dramatic construction is virtually an alien art to those experienced only in narrative technique, and a first attempt in that new line would be a pretty sorry piece of work. Of all those I know, I think only Clark Ashton Smith could handle a job of that kind. Still—I'm letting Farnese unfold his ideas more fully. I find that he is a native of *Monaco,* educated in Paris. Which reminds me that for the last couple of years, the famous scientifically-equipped yacht of the late Prince of Monaco (a noted oceanographer)—*L'Hirondelle*—has lain at anchor awaiting a purchaser in Providence harbour. I had known of *L'Hirondelle* virtually all my life—and it seemed curious to have it tie up less than a mile away from my doorstep for a long stay. It is still here, but an auction sale may soon remove it. Last winter it had as a neighbour the ancient convict ship *Success*—oldest ship afloat, and now a museum—which berthed here for about 6 months. Quite a bit of colour for the old waterfront!

Smith's conclusion to the "Vathek" episode is splendid, and I ardently hope Wright will take it—although I fear he won't. He has just rejected a fine prose-poem of his—"The Maze of Maal Dweb".[6] My opinion of Smith's style is exactly like your own. I don't care for humour as an ingredient of the weird tale—in fact, I think it is a definitely diluting element. That is my chief objection to Long's work—he so often likes to snicker at nothing in particular.

Derleth's 3-star citation was for "Old Ladies" in *The Midland;* the two-star for "Nella" (I don't know where it appeared). Neither one is a weird item. Derleth's weird stuff is not his most serious work, and I doubt if it will ever count very heavily with him. As a serious artist, he tends to create delicate reminiscent studies in the vein of Marcel Proust. Actually, he has the makings of a very solid literary figure in him. He will go far—as far, perhaps, as anyone now writing for W.T.

Well—I hope that you are not bored *quite* to death by this endless and rambling scrawl! I'm looking forward to the chance of reading your new material in W.T.—haven't had time to glance at the magazine for 2 months!

With every good wish—

Yrs most cordially and sincerely—

HPL

Notes

1. I.e., James Ferdinand Morton, Jr.

2. Harry F. Sinclair (1876–1956), an oil industrialist, was caught up in the Teapot Dome scandal through his association with Albert B. Fall. He was eventually tried for

fraud and corruption, found guilty, and was fined and served a six-month prison sentence. Charles W. Morse (1856–1933) was a speculator whose failed attempt to corner the copper market was one of the precipitating events of the Panic of 1907. He was convicted the following year of making false entries in books of one of the banks he owned, and misapplying funds, for which he spent two years in prison.

3. On 16 July 1912, Herman Rosenthal, the Jewish owner of a gambling house in New York City, was shot and killed by four Jewish gunmen outside the Hotel Metropole. Suspicion quickly fell on Lieut. Charles Becker of the N.Y.P.D.: some months earlier, Rosenthal had publicly stated that Becker had doublecrossed him in regard to supplying police protection for his gambling activities. After a long and sensational trial, Becker was found guilty; a second trial produced the same result, and he was executed on 31 July 1915. (The four gunmen had been tried and convicted earlier and were executed on 13 April 1914.) Some historians believe the case against Becker was insufficient. The affair revealed the existence of a Jewish mob and the workings of other criminal gangs in New York.

4. HPL refers to an immense semicircular depression in a bluff above the Mississippi River just north of Natchez, Mississippi.

5. Sawney Bean was a mid-15th-century Scottish highwayman, mass murderer, and cannibal. He and his large family preyed upon travelers along the desolate Galloway seacoast for more than 25 years. The Beans' murder victims are thought to number over 1,000. A force of 400 men with bloodhounds finally tracked down and, after a pitched battle, captured the family in their cave, in which were found numerous mutilated cadavers. Showing no remorse nor repentance for their crimes, the Beans were burned at the stake.

6. CAS, "The Maze of Maal Dweb" (*WT,* October 1938). CAS self-published the story in *The Double Shadow* (1933) under the title "The Maze of the Enchanter."

[68] [ANS][1]

[Postmarked Providence, R.I.,
15 October 1932]

Thanks prodigiously for the splendid set of lethal reminders—which will go under glass in my cabinet of curiosities. It will form a splendid companion piece to the mottled & sinuous glider which Whitehead captured & bottled for me in Florida in 1931. ¶ Your prose-poem accompanying the set is one of the most vivid things I have read lately, & I wish it could be published somewhere. It has a magnificently weird, haunting cadence & imagery, & seems to call up a potent atmosphere of power, death, & silence. ¶ I wouldn't have enjoyed meeting the original wearer of the adornment in his native freedom![2] ¶ Probably you've heard the dismal news that *Strange Tales* is being discontinued. I'm tremendously sorry for those who, like you, had secured an entree to its pages. ¶ I see that Price is back in New Orleans—1416 Josephine St., in the American section near Jackson Ave. He's sold quite a bit lately. ¶ Best wishes, & renewed thanks for the vastly appreciated addition to my museum shelf.

Most gratefully—
H P L

Notes

1. Front: Windings of the Trail and River, Mohawk Trail, Mass.
2. REH had sent HPL a set of rattlesnake rattles along with a short prose poem about the snake, published as "With a Set of Rattlesnake Rattles" (see Appendix).

[69] [TLS]

[c. October 1932]

Dear Mr. Lovecraft:

I hope you decide to collaborate on the proposed musical drama. Don't tell me you're not qualified for that sort of thing. You're capable of any sort of literary expression, to my humble mind. You'd instill new vigor and fresh imagination in the dramatic world, which, from what I hear, is badly in need of some such stimulus. If the Californian did his part half as well as I know you'd do your's, the success of the venture would be assured. This is no mere polite maundering on my part, but my honest opinion.

Sorry Wandrei's visit was handicapped by rain and sun-burn. Rainy weather is always depressing—to me at least; and while never having experienced sun-burn, having the hide of a bull, I imagine it's a pretty uncomfortable handicap. I hope he'll get to return to Providence before leaving the East. I've been laying off to write him for some time, but somehow haven't got around it.

Good for Derleth! Which of his stories got the citations? I've known for years that he was of "the right girt", as John A. Murrell used to say. He's deserved much more notice from Weird Tales readers than he's gotten—doubtless because of the shortness of his stories; the readers seem to like 'em long, generally. More power to him; I wish him all the luck in the world.

And I hope Clark Ashton sells his "Vathek" episode. His style is unique—to me at least—with just a tinge somehow reminiscent of Petronius. I don't mean that he tries to copy the classics, or anything like that; but his work has a subtle mirth that I can only describe as classic. I've gotten some real belly laughs out of his subtly turned hints and allusions. This, to my mind, keeps some of his tales from being weirdly perfect—humor however subtle not fitting in with true horror—but gives them a piquant zest all their own. That he is capable of writing straight horror-stuff is evident by such tales as "The Return of the Sorcerer" in Strange Tales, which was, as I wrote the editor, one of the most intolerably hideous stories I ever read—in other words, a sheer masterpiece.[1] As I have said before, I rate Smith second only to yourself in the art.

Thanks for the congratulations regarding the election. It remains now to see whether Jim will double-cross us when he gets in office, like so many other candidates have done. Anyway, he'll never get in, if the Sterling mob can keep him out. They took the fight to the state convention; the convention affirmed Mrs. Ferguson's nomination, and now they've dragged it into court. It looks like a deliberate plot to take the voting power away from the people. It's rumored that the idea is to keep the matter in court until after the election, so as to jockey the Republican candidate into office, by the simple process of having no other name on the ticket. The common people nominated Mrs. Ferguson; the big interests are fighting teeth and nail to keep her out of the chair. Some claim if Jim gets in, he'll sell us out t the railroads; better railroads than Wall Street owned oil companies. I don't know. It looks like the courts, the laws, the government, all wealth and authority and power are combined to crush the last vestige of freedom out of the common people. Men that rise to lead the people sell them out and betray them. Where can a man turn? I wish I had vision, or a fanatical faith in something or somebody that creates an illusion of vision. All roads look blind to me. I see nothing but ruin, chaos, and a rising tide of slavery.

But I am prone to harp on these things; please excuse me. I know I must grow boresome.

With best wishes,

Cordially,

REH.

Notes

1. CAS, "The Return of the Sorcerer" (*Strange Tales,* September 1931).

[70] [TLS]

[received 2 November 1932]

Dear Mr. Lovecraft:

I want to begin this letter by an apology. I am afraid my last letter may have appeared rather churlish in spots, though rudeness was not my intention. The fact is, I wrote while in the grip of one of the black moods which occasionally—though fortunately rarely—descend on me. With one of these moods riding me, I can see neither good nor hope in anything, and my main sensation is a blind, brooding rage directed at anything that may cross my path—a perfectly impersonal feeling, of course. At such times I am neither a fit companion nor a gentlemanly correspondent. I avoid personal contacts as much as possible, in order to avoid giving offense by my manner, and I should never, at such times, venture to write a letter to anyone. I am likely to offend where I do not intend, for the passionate pessimism in my mind is prone to make my manner, verbal or in writing, brusque and surly. These moods are hereditary, coming down the line of my purely Irish branch—the black-haired, grey-eyed branch, of which, as far back as family history goes, both men and women have been subject to black fits of savage brooding, which has been, in some cases, coupled with outbursts of really dangerous fury, when crossed or thwarted. My great-grandfather, whom I seem to resemble in many ways, lost his life in that manner, being the victim of an attack of appoplexy brought on by his uncontrollable rage. All this delicate and intimate data I would not be shouting from the house-tops, nor would I mention it here except for the fact that I feel you are due an explanation of possible surliness on my part. In cases where we disagree, your arguments are so well-balanced and show so much gentlemanly consideration and restraint, I would not wish to seem churlish, though my last letter may have created that impression. I will admit that when a better educated man than myself takes advantage of his superior culture and experience to cut and slash my self-esteem to shreds, and hold me up to ridicule and contempt, I feel a primitive urge to do him bodily violence. But you have never done this on any of the points on which we disagree, though I know many of my arguments must have seemed crude, naive and biased in the extreme. It is a new experience to me to encounter such consideration in one of superior accomplishments, and I appreciate it. So if I have at any time offended you with my clumsiness or surliness, please be assured that it was entirely unintentional. As a proof of my sincerity, I may mention that this is only the third time in my life that I ever apologized to anybody for anything.

As for my aborted views on conditions in general—I see that I have so tangled up my remarks and theories that misunderstanding was bound to result. It isn't your fault; it's my own lack of vocabulary and clumsiness of expression. When I get out of my depth—which is easy—the Devil himself couldn't get what I'm trying to say. So I won't try to untangle myself, except to say the following: that I really do not hold the scholarly class in wholesale contempt. On the contrary I have a high regard for it. When I spoke of certain professors as dusty fossils, I did not mean the profession as a whole, but I had in mind certain individuals I have known who really would come under such a classification. It's just another example of my vagueness of expression. Maybe I have in my system an unconscious bitterness and resentment at times, resulting perhaps from a realization of my own sketchy education and lack of real culture. Nor do I have any contempt for the East or the people of the East. I realize, as you say, that conditions vary according to environment, traditional mode of life, etc., and I would be the last to assume that the people of one part of the country are superior to those of any other part. Nor do I glorify the physical to the expense of the mental or intellectual. I am so constituted that physical things appeal to me more than mental, but simply because I would rather watch a football game than to see a scientist work out a really important problem in economics or mathematics, or the like, does not mean that I have any hero-worship for the first, or contempt for the latter. I would rather see men match physical strength than to match their wits in any sort of a contest; that does not mean that I place physical ability above mental ability. It means, doubtless, that I am more of the physical man than the mental. And I'm afraid I'll remain that way to the end, rightly or wrongly. And for that reason alone, I should never impose my gropings on abstract things on anybody. When the argument gets away from something I can see and feel and handle, I'm out of my depths. I say all this not in self-abasement or undue humility, but simply because I always try to be as honest as possible with my friends and with myself. I must be myself, whatever my faults. I might pose, and pretend an intellectuality and an interest in the higher things, but I wouldn't fool anybody, and I wouldn't try it if I could. When I say that I'd rather watch a football game, a prize-fight, a horserace or a really able dancing girl, than to delve into the mysteries of the universe, however magnificent and awesome, I'm simply being honest. I'm not trying to uphold my preferences. Each man to his own path; I have no sneer for scientist, poet, scholar, horse-trader or pugilist.

I, myself, was intended by Nature to be an athlete. If events had flowed smoothly and evenly from the time I first entered school, I would at this instant be engaged in some sort of professional athletics, rather than struggling with a profession for which I am not fitted. The chain of circumstances which altered the course of my life is too lengthy and involved to impose upon you. But I will say that I extremely regret those circumstances, and had rather have been a successful professional athlete than the very minor writer I have become—in honesty I will go further and say that I had rather have been a successful professional athlete than to be a great writer. This is not to be taken as a slur on the writing profession. You said once, in one of your letters that the main object in life was to get as much happiness out of it as possible—I trust I do not misquote you. The fact is that I believe I would have gotten more content out of an athletic career than I have out of this bitter grind, which I took up simply because it seemed to offer more freedom than anything else in the way of a job. Let me repeat that when I voice a preference for anything I am not depreciating its opposite. I merely speak my own choice in the matter. A thing may be good or bad for the race as a whole; it may be magnificent or foolish. I have only my own sensations to go on. If anything gives me pleasure, while harming no one else, then it is my instinct to lean toward it, however trivial. If anything bores or confuses or pains me, it is my instinct to avoid it, however splendid. I have endured confusion, boredom, and even pain in consideration of others; but I can not say that I enjoyed it.

I lack your broad and sweeping viewpoint; I sincerely admire it, but I could not copy it to my own advantage, any more than I could wear with comfort the coat of a man bigger than myself.

And another thing, before I forget it—my deep admiration for physical prowess and my continual harping about deeds of blood, may sound like I was trying to make an impression of boldness and fearlessness on my part.

Please believe that I am not seeking to make any such impression. I'm a man cautious to the point of absolute timidity. The only way a man can get a fight out of me, is simply to get me in a corner where I have to fight. In that case, of course, I'm prone to give him all I have, including teeth and hob-nails, just as anybody will when cornered. It's just another incongruity of nature that a man as peace-loving as I am should be so violently interested in deeds of gore, and be unable to realistically write about anything else. When my fictional characters can't slash and slug and litter the pages with one another's carcasses, I'm an utter flop as a tale-spinner.

Your remarks concerning your trips interested me as usual. I'll bet that "Devil's Punch-Bowl" was a fascinating place. I'm not surprized that the young bloods of Natchez knew little about it. It's appalling the way the younger generations of Americans are losing hold of the traditions and folklore of their country. For instance, a year [or] so ago a man of fair education, raised in this state since infancy, asked me if I knew anything about a fellow named Bigfoot Wallace! Ye gods! Even I can remember when Bigfoot's exploits were subjects for innumerable tales of the old-timers.[1]

I appreciate your remarks pertaining to my incorporating the border villians in print. It's a matter I've been thinking about for a long time, and intend to try, if times ever get better so I can afford to do some work on my own, instead of pounding out fiction all the time. There are numbers of good books on the subject, but each book generally deals with only one time or one place. I'd like to start at the Atlantic sea-board with the early colonists and work gradually westward, carrying the work not later than the early 1900's. The latter phase of gang-life does not fascinate me. Concerning the Harps, I seem to have a vague idea that they were from Virginia where they were Tories during the Revolution. They seem to have been slightly negroid in blood-strain. About the only crime they didn't share with Sawney Bean was that of cannibalism—and there's no actual proof that they didn't. Big Harp, while confined in prison from which he later escaped—he developed a religious mania there and posed as a wandering preacher up to the day of his death—confessed that the only deed he regretted was the murder of his youngest child, whose brains he dashed out against a tree, throwing the body into the bushes to rot. He and Little Harp used to come into a lonely settler's cabin and ask news of those damnable outlaws, the Harps. If the people recognized them, their doom was sealed—the doom of the people, I mean. If not, Big Harp called pious blessings on the heads of the humble settlers, and invoked the wrath of the Lord to protect them from the hellish Harps. Then the outlaws would ride away, to commit some other depredation. The last time they pulled this stunt, Big Harp got so worked up in his role of protector that he loaded the settler's rifle from his own pouch, the man being out of powder, as protection against the Harps. A few hours later that man joined the posse pursuing the outlaws, and Big Harp got his own bullet in his spine.

Too bad New Orleans is going so modern. I'm glad I saw it before the vandalism had gotten completely under way. I was interested in your remarks concerning French food. I've encountered the "poor boy sandwich" phenomenon in Galveston and similiar places. I think if I were in the restaurant business I'd exploit a "pauper's sandwich" which is going to be a necessity if things get any lousier. Too bad sea-food disagrees with you. Now with me, as with many inland dwellers, it constitutes a rare delicacy. And the word "rare" is quite descriptive. Oysters are about the only sort of sea-food which finds its way this far up-country.

When I get in a sea-port town, I revel in oysters, shrimps, crabs, sea-fish, and the like, to my heart's content. I find one thing about such food; it doesn't seem to stay with you and give you any real strength. I eat it in enormous quantities, and then in a few hours I'm ravenously hungry again. Maybe its because, like most people in this country, I'm a beef-eater. Indeed, only beef in some form or other seems to be the only food that gives me the necessary nutriment.

But I'm not narrow in my tastes. I'm a big eater and I get a real kick out of gorging. Any kind of meat—fish, fowl, beef, turtle, pork; practically any kind of fruit; I'm not much of a vegetarian. Milk—I see people coaxing children to drink milk, and I can't understand their dislike for it. I always drank it in huge quantities, and believe its one reason I was always so healthy. Cheese—give me limburger cheese, German sausage and beer and I'm content—yes, and a bit of what they call "smear-cake"—a rather unsavory name, for what we call cottage- or cream-cheese. Mexican dishes I enjoy, but they don't agree with me much. However I generally wrestle with them every time I go to the Border. Tamales, enchilados, tacos, chili con carne to a lesser extent, barbecued goat-meat, tortillas, Spanish-cooked rice, frijoles—they play the devil with a white man's digestion, but they have a tang you seldom find in Anglo-Saxon cookery. You know a coyote nor a buzzard never will touch a Mexican's carcass—they can't stand the pepper he ate in life-time. The last time I was on the Border I discovered one Pablo Ranes whose dishes smoked with the concentrated essence of hell-fire. I returned to his abode of digestional-damnation until my once powerful constitution was but a shell of itself. I aided Pablo's atrocities with some wine bottled in Spain that kicked like an army mule, and eventually came to the conclusion that the Border is a place only for men with cast-iron consciences and copper bellies.

That old ballad I quoted from, "The Lakes of the Pontchartrain", must have been fairly popular at one time, though just when I couldn't say. I used to correspond with one R. W. Gordon who was collecting old songs for an anthology—though I never got the chance of examining the completed work. The best thing of its kind I ever saw was an anthology compiled by Carl Sandburg,[2] in which I found numbers of old songs I knew by heart but had never seen in print. Its cheering to find men collecting these old ballads, which seem to be forgotten by practically all people. Folks don't sing like they used to. The '49'ers crossed the Plains to the tune of:

"I come from Alabama
With my banjo on my knee,
I'm goin' to Louisiana,
My true love for to see.

It rained all night the day I left,
The weather it was dry,
The sun so hot I froze to death—
Susanna, don't you cry!

Oh, Susanna,
Don't you cry for me!
I'm goin' to Californy
With my banjo on my knee!"

During the Civil War, one side sang,

"John Brown's body lies a-moldin' in the grave,
John Brown's body lies a-moldin' in the grave,
John Brown's body lies a-moldin' in the grave,
But his soul goes marchin' on!"

And the other side sang, among others,

"We'll hang Abe Lincoln to a sour-apple tree,
We'll hang Abe Lincoln to a sour-apple tree,
We'll hang Abe Lincoln to a sour-apple tree,
As we go marchin' on!"

Then there was another which went something like this:

"Old Johnny McGruder, he went on a spree,
He captured a gunboat and started to sea,
He hauled down the colors, both red, white and green!
Hurrah, hurrah, for the bonny Blue Flag!"

And,

"Up with the bars, and down with the stars!
We'll rally 'round the flag, boys,
Rally once again!
Shouting the battle-cry of freedom!"

The boys hazing the herds up the old Chisholm used to chant,

"Ki yi, ki yi -yoh! Get along, little dogies!
Its yore misfortune and none of my own!
Ki yi, ki yi -yoh! Get along, little dogies!
You know Wyoming will be yore new home!"

Not all the songs came by the southern route; here's a verse from one you've probably heard in the rural districts of your country,

"Tom Quick he lived in the Sullivan hills,
By the Delaware's rolling tide;
'Midst the whispering trees and the rippling rills,
Away from the world and all of its thrills,
He hunted far and wide."

And this one used to be very popular, which began, or at least contained the lines, possibly as a refrain,

"Blue-eyed bonny, bonny Eloise,
The pride of the Mohawk Vale."

Which I reckon refers to the Mohawk Valley in—New York state, isn't it? And I'm sure you're familiar with the old New England ballad relating the fate of "Deacon Jones's oldest son" who "just had turned his twenty-one." Who was nipped in the heel by a "venomous rep-tile", and the ballad of which concluded with the warning,

"Come all, young men,
And warning take,
And never get bit
By a big black snake."

Referring back to your letter: I was intensely interested in your comments on the possible trend of future economic conditions. It may be that you are right. I'm not enough of an economist to dispute it, even if I had any desire to. However, I see no reason why the dominant interests would be unable to coerce the masses by force. They have the navy on their side and the regular army; they have every flat-foot cop and detective in the country; they have money, power—the ability to fill their ranks with professional fighters, just as the companies employ strike breakers and private detectives to shoot down strikers. The masses have only their empty hands and empty bellies. As for lack of profit—what's to prevent them from actually enslaving the people? A remark no doubt wild and visionary—yet if the Russian people aren't slaves, I don't know the meaning of the word. What's to prevent the dominant classes in this country from carrying out a similiar idea under slightly different conditions? Slavery is far from being extinct in this country today—though of course its present form has nothing to do with whole-sale enslavement, or with what I just mentioned.

But if peonage, where a man gets a Mexican, negro, or even a white man, in debt to him, and keeps him toiling for years to pay out that debt, isn't slavery, then I don't know what it is. There's been something of a scandal concerning such practises along the Mississippi River recently. Another meddling reformer, I suppose. Nevertheless such things do exist, and are no credit to our boasted civilization.

That word reminds me of our discussion concerning what I said about my preference for a theoretical former existence. I didn't say that barbarism was superior to civilization. For the world as a whole, civilization even in decaying form, is undoubtedly better for people as a whole. I have no idylic view of barbarism—as near as I can learn it's a grim, bloody, ferocious and loveless condition. I have no patience with the depiction of the barbarian of any race as a stately, god-like child of Nature, endowed with strange wisdom and speaking in measured and sonorous phrases. Bah! My conception of a barbarian is very different. He had neither stability nor undue dignity. He was ferocious, vengeful, brutal and frequently squalid. He was haunted by dim and shadowy fears; he committed horrible crimes for strange monstrous reasons. As a race he hardly ever exhibited the steadfast courage often shown by civilized men. He was childish and terrible in his wrath, bloody and treacherous. As an individual he lived under the shadow of the war-chief and the shaman, each of whom might bring him to a bloody end because of a whim, a dream, a leaf floating on the wind. His religion was generally one of dooms and shadows, his gods were awful and abominable. They bade him mutilate himself or slaughter his children, and he obeyed because of fears too primordial for any civilized man to comprehend. His life was often a bondage of tabus, sharp sword-edges, between which he walked shuddering. He had no mental freedom, as civilized man understands it, and very little personal freedom, being bound to his clan, his tribe, his chief. Dreams and shadows haunted and maddened him. Simplicity of the primitive? To my mind the barbarian's problems were as complex in their way as modern man's—possibly more so. He moved through life motivated mainly by whims, his or another's. In war he was unstable; the blowing of a leaf might send him plunging in an hysteria of blood-lust against terrific odds, or cause him to flee in blind panic when another stroke could have won the battle. But he was lithe and strong as a panther, and the full joy of strenuous physical exertion was his. The day and the night were his book, wherein he read of all things that run or walk or crawl or fly. Trees and grass and moss-covered rocks and birds and beasts and clouds were alive to him, and pertook of his kinship. The wind blew his hair and he looked with naked eyes into the sun. Often he starved, but when he feasted, it was with a mighty gusto, and the juices of food and strong drink were stinging wine to his palate. Oh, I know I can't make myself clear; I've never seen anyone who had any sympathy whatever with my point of view, nor do I want any. I'm not ashamed of it. I would not choose to plunge into such a life now; it would be the sheerest of hells to me, unfitted as I am for such an existence. But I do say that if I had the choice of another existence, to be born into it and raised in it, knowing no other, I'd choose such an existence as I've just sought to depict. There's no question of the relative merits of barbarism and civilization here involved. It's just my own personal opinion and choice.

I reckon The Five Points district in old New York was pretty squalid from all I hear about it, yet I find it interesting—reading about it, I mean of course. Pugilism and the underworld were pretty closely linked in those days; thus we find the early champions, Hyer, Yankee Sullivan, and Morrissey, hobnobbing with thugs and gangsters that a present-day boxing champion wouldn't be seen with. Morrissey, at least, rose above his environments. At least, I suppose it was a rise; he became a member of the New York legislature. Billy the Kid was born in the New York slums; I wouldn't be surprized if it was in Five Points that he first saw light. Quite a number of Western outlaws originally came from the East. Quantrill, for instance, was born in Ohio, of New England stock. John Brown was from Connecticut.[3] Henry Plummer, called by a noted historical writer, "the most consumate villian", who, under the guise of his sheriffship, managed one of the most blood-thirsty gangs of robbers and murderers the West has ever seen, was a native of Boston. And of course the Girtys and the Butlers were New Yorkers.[4] Speaking of the latter, Cherry Valley in New York state has always had a fascination for me because of the massacre committed there by Walter Butler and Joseph Brant[5]—though I believe it is maintained that Brant was not there, and that the slaying was done mainly by Senecas instead of Mohawks. Walter Butler must have been a genial soul—one which I'd have enjoyed seeing kicking in a noose. He was an Irishman, wasn't he? One of the Le Boteliers of Ormond originally, I doubt not. I always took sides against them in their feud with the FitzGeralds. I'll bet the Eastern states are teeming with spots of fascinating historical interest, similiar to that just mentioned. I never was much in reading Indian yarns, but stories about the Long House always interested me.

The Eastern Indians were quite apparently of a much higher type than those of the West. For one thing, they tended toward the dolichocephalic type, whereas the typical Western Indian was brachycephalic. This has not been perfectly explained; at least if it has, I haven't encountered the explanation. Some authorities seem to think—what I had decided myself before encountering the theory in print—that there was a prehistoric connection between the primitive Mongolian type and a Caucasian race, from which hybrid breed the Indian sprang. It can not be denied that the red Indian seems much less repugnant and alien to the white man than the negro, Malay, Mongol or Chinaman. Indeed, I see no reason why the race should not be admitted on an equal footing, determined by education and advancement rather than color. I have no Indian blood in me, but I certainly would not be ashamed of it if I did. I have a number of cousins who are of mixed blood, boasting both Cherokee and Chickasaw strains, and this mixture does not result in any inferiority on their part.[6] The greatest athlete this continent has ever seen was a Sac and Fox Indian.[7]

But returning to the inferiority of the Western Indians: I am not aware whether this was due to their nomadic life, or whether the life was due to their inability to develop a settled mode of living and agriculture. At any rate, it was not until the advent of the white man that the Western tribes amounted to much. The introducing of the horse into the country was what made them powerful. In some cases alliance with the whites increased their power. This was especially true of the Pawnees, who had been harried and slaughtered for generations by the Sioux. They were shrewd enough to throw in their lot with the settlers, and whole companies of regular cavalry formed of Pawnee braves were used in the Sioux wars. Their uniform presented a rather peculiar aspect, since they always cut the seat out of the breeches. When they started across the prairie on a charge, they started shedding their clothes, and before the concussion came, were riding in their loins-cloths, yelling and shooting like madmen.

They were good fighters, especially against hereditary foes, but they were hard to control during the battle and afterward. They wanted to deal with prisoners in the old tribal way. I know of at least one instance where Pawnee privates took a Sioux prisoner away from their white officer and burned him alive. Well, the Sioux were no babies in atrocities themselves. One of their favorite jests was to cut off a victim's head and thrust it into his disembowelled belly.

The Pawnees used to wander down into Texas, where they continually clashed with the Comanches, who were probably the most ferocious fighters this continent has seen. Some noted western explorer, whose identity I've forgotten, once met a band of Pawnees journeying southward, to steal horses from the Comanches, they told him. Later he encountered them again, returning to their homes on foot. They had not only failed to steal the horses of the Comanches, but these wily barbarians had stolen all their own mounts. The Comanches raised hell with the Spaniards and later the Mexicans—into which, by the way, the bulk of the Comanche tribes was eventually absorbed. The Mexican mode of dealing with these tribes was a mixture of cringing and treachery. One time a band of Pawnees was encamped on the outskirts of San Antonio, and one of the women was seized by a big Comanche who tried to carry her off. A Pawnee brave brained him with a hatchet. The Comanches attacked the Pawnees, who were outnumbered and withdrew. Mexican soldiers joined the Comanches, and they hurried to cut off the retreating Pawnees and ambush them. The Pawnees discovered the ambush, made a flanking attack, and practically wiped out the whole combined force.

The Comanches were the prime horse-thieves of the West. They measured their wealth by the number of horses they owned. It was a dishonor for a brave to lose his horse. Sometimes a number of young warriors would find themselves without steeds, owing to losses in war or otherwise, and would "smoke horses" with more fortunate braves. The horseless ones sat down in a circle about a fire, naked to the waist, smoking their pipes. The braves from which they wished to borrow, would mount and race around the circle at full speed. Each time a brave passed the warrior who wished to borrow his mount, he would strike the sitting man across his naked back with a rawhide whip, with all his power. These whips cut like a knife, and the first stroke would start the blood spurting. This process would continue until the victim's back was raw beef. It was his part to continue placidly smoking and recieve the blows without wincing. At the end of the affair, the mounted warrior would lead his horse to the other and say, "You ride my horse, but you carry the scars of my whip."

I'm glad you saw the duelling-oaks of New Orleans before somebody cuts them down to build a hot-dog stand. A distant relative of mine exchanged shots with a brother of the governor of Louisana there, many years ago. He was evidently too drunk to see the sights of his "navy" because he didn't score a hit, and carried five or six slugs in his flesh off the field of honor. The argument came up over a fight between a couple of newsboys, and was quite trivial to get shot about. But the victim had been with Walker in Nicaragua, and the men who survived that campaign had their lives nailed to their spines. You'd think I was a liar if I narrated the wounds he survived, to die at last of old age. He was one of the few filibusters who escaped when the rest were victimized—mainly owing to old Cornelius Vanderbilt, damn his filthy soul.[8]

The duel was never too popular in Texas—not nearly so much as in the older Southern states. Life was too uncertain here. When everyday existence is a continual battle, men are not likely to devise and uphold elaborate systems of getting themselves formally shot.

There have been duels, of course, but most of the shooting-scrapes of early Texas were informal affairs. Enemies met unexpectedly in saloons or on the streets, and each man went for his gun. The one to unleather his six-shooter first generally survived, unless he missed. Often enough "the Texas drop" was employed, which simply consisted in catching your victim off-guard, or drilling him through a window or from behind a brush fence. When men have to fight all the time for their lives, they are very likely to take all the advantages they can.

The most famous duel in Texas was that between Felix Houston and Albert Sidney Johnston, in which the latter was wounded in the hip. Houston was a soldier of fortune, who resented the other being promoted over his head.[9] Another was that between George Scarborough and John Selman in El Paso, in 1895, I believe it was. They went into an alley behind a saloon, stepped off their paces, turned—Selman reached for his gun and found only an empty scabbard. Somebody had slipped out his six-shooter without his knowledge. Scarborough shot him down before he had time to see that Selman was unarmed.[10]

John Selman was the man who killed the famous John Wesley Harden. After Harden [was] released from the penitentiary, he came to El Paso, and according to some, began to practise law. Outside of holding up a gambling house, he was apparently living a law-abiding life, though some connected him with the murder of one McRose, who was mowed down by a charge of buckshot one night near the international bridge. Harden fell afoul of the Selmans in this manner: his sweetheart knocked a dance-hall woman in the head with a pistol, and young John Selman, who was an officer of the law, arrested her and threw her in jail. Naturally this infuriated Harden beyond measure, and he swore to massacre everybody wearing the name of Selman. According to accounts, young John decided the climate was too torrid for him. Anyway, he left town in a hurry and didn't come back until after the fireworks were over. Which were not long delayed. That very night, as John Wesley Harden stood at the bar, shaking dice for the drinks, old John Selman entered the saloon quietly and shot him in the back of the head. Albert B. Fall of Teapot Dome fame, then a rising attorney, defended Selman and naturally he was acquitted. He would have been anyway; everybody felt safer with Harden out of the way. Selman was killed soon afterward by George Scarborough in the manner above related, and Scarborough himself was killed not long later by Kid Curry and his gang in Arizona.[11] Mannen Clements, Harden's nephew,[12] swore to kill Fall for insulting his relative's memory during the trial, and on at least two occasions he attempted it, but without success, owing to circumstances. He himself was at last killed in a barroom in a most mysterious fashion, and it has been hinted that Fall knew more about the matter than he ever admitted. Incidentally, Fall defended Brazel who killed Pat Garrett, the killer of Billy the Kid, and won an acquittal.[13]

But I was talking about duels. The only one that ever took place in this locality, so far as I know, was at a dance a good many years ago, between two cowpunchers, members of feuding families. Mutual friends stood by with guns drawn, to see fair play, while the boys stepped off their paces, turned and fired simultaneously. Both fell, one dead, one dying; their bodies were placed in a spare room and the dance went on. Dances in those days were too rare entertainment to be spoiled by murder.

Ben Thompson, a famous old-time Texas gunman, once fought a duel in New Orleans with one Emil de Tour, along in 1858 or 1859, I think it was. The Frenchman insulted a young lady on Canal Street, and Thompson, though a stranger to both, resented it to the point of knocking de Tour down and stamping him into unconsciousness. When the bould Frog recovered, he challenged Thompson, and the young Texan—he couldn't have been more than eighteen or nineteen—accepted with alacrity. The details of the chroniclers are veiled in doubt. They merely say that they fought in a dark room with knives and Thompson killed his man. But I got the facts from an old-timer who knew Thompson and had heard the tale from his own lips. Thompson was to give the word to begin. Standing in utter darkness, where neither could see the other, he gave the word and at the same instant stepped quickly and noiselessly aside. As he knew would happen, de Tour sprang like a tiger at the sound of his voice, and Thompson, thrusting by the sound of the rushing body, sank his knife to the hilt in the Frenchman's heart. The dark room and the knives were Thompson's idea. He had no patience with the formal code of the duello.[14]

French duelling suffered when the Americans swarmed into New Orleans. The French form had become, to a large extent, a sort of polite exercise, where honor was satisfied by a scratch or a drop of blood. While it is a fact that many bloody battles were fought under the Oaks and elsewhere by Frenchmen—sometimes with sabers in which case a fatality was inevitable—yet in later days milder conditions dominated. The Americans changed this. They were practical—blood-thirsty, if you will. They introduced butcher knives, rifles, navy pistols, and shotguns—the latter often at half-a-dozen paces with an open grave between the combatants. The gory results shocked the French into disapproval of duelling. Not that this is any depreciation of French courage. It is quite true that as a nation and as individuals they have always shown a fine brand of courage, however shifty their politics might have been. The reason the English under the Black Prince and such leaders defeated them so often and against such odds, was due entirely to the longbow in the hands of the English yeoman, the most terrible weapon concieved by man, up to the invention of gunpowder. Man to man, the French knights were the equal of the English. But having made pitiful serfs out of their common people, they had no sturdy reserve force to fall back on, and could not put an army of hardy foot soldiers in the field, as the English did. In the last analysis, it is the common people who win wars, even if directed by their aristocrats. A point the upper classes of America might well remember.

I admire many points of the French character, but I can not include their literature. This is no criticism, only my own personal viewpoint. I certainly don't consider myself a critic, but I know what I like and what I don't like. And I don't like French literature. If I were able to read it in the untranslated original, I might like it better, but I doubt it. There's a polished hardness about the literature of the Latins that I don't relish. Even when it lacks this polish, I don't care for it. To me, for instance, Rabelais is neither wise nor witty, though perhaps I shouldn't pass judgment on him, since his stuff nauseates me to such an extent I've never been able to read much of it. Balzac is better, but I never could get interested in him. Dumas has a virility lacking in other French writers—I attribute it to his negroid strain—but his historical fiction lacks, at least to me, the gripping vividness of Sir Walter Scott, for instance—a man whose works I highly value, regardless of what modern critics think. I don't go by what critics think, but by my own likes and dislikes. Gautier bores me immeasurably. I like Villon's poems, and Verlaine's and Baudelaire's, but don't think any of them can equal the greatest English poets. D'Maupasant has power—undoubted power. Too much power for me to read extensively. Talk about Nordic gloom—his tales of French peasant life are enough to make a man want to cut his own throat. After reading some of his more realistic yarns, I've been unable to see any good in anything, except thankfulness for the fact that I wasn't a Frenchman.

I'm narrow in my literary likings. About the only poets and writers I can stand regularly are the British and American ones. I find the old Scandinavian sagas fascinating, but I can't work up any interest in modern Scandinavian writers. They seem further removed from the pristine Viking type than the English writers. Russians seem men wandering in mazes, never getting anywhere. Gorky seems to ramble interminably, without doing anything. Some Slavonic tales are gripping by their sheer somberness, but taken as a whole their literature fails to arouse my enthusiasm. That phrase—taken as a whole—is misleading, seeming to indicate that I was deeply familiar with that literature. I'm not, of course. What I meant was that part of the literature which I have read.

I wouldn't take anything, though, for my early readings of Scott, Dickens and other English writers. I doubt if I could read Dickens now—with the exception of "Pickwick Papers" which is my favorite of all his books. He gets on my nerves, not so much by his tedium as by the spineless cringing crawling characters he portrays. I don't doubt he was drawing them true to life, but that realization makes the matter more damnable. Nicholas Nickleby was about the only one of his characters who had any guts at all. Why good gad, his characters submitted to indignities and insults and outrages that made me grind my teeth merely to read about. And I'm a peaceable man. The same can be said about "The Vicar of Wakefield", one of the most abominable books ever penned. I've never had any respect for Goldsmith since reading it. The old cuss in the book had one daughter seduced, if I'm not mistaken, and the other abducted by the same egg. So he stood around mouthing pious platitudes—the old jackass. And when his son wanted to fight the abductor a duel, a squall of disapproval was raised to the shamed skies. I read this abomination as a part of my high-school work, and in writing my report, I let myself go the only time I ever did in school, and gave my own honest opinion in my own honest words, allowing myself the freedom of frothing at the mouth. I expected to flunk the course, so many teachers being slaves of the established, but that particular teacher was a black-headed Irish woman who evidently entertained similiar ideas on the subject to mine, and she gave me a good grade instead of the tongue-lashing I expected. Somewhere I read an essay on that book, and the writer spoke of the Vicar as the highest type of human imaginable, praising his meekness and humility and long-suffering and Christian spirit. Bah! A whole flock of bahs. In some cases humility is out of place. To my mind he was a lousy old worm, ten times lower-down than the libertine that misused his daughters.

I was talking about duels awhile ago, and I said the custom was never much in fashion in Texas, which is true. But there was a form of duelling extant here, which was a little too tough for even most of the early settlers of the West. It was employed by the Comanches; the contestants had their left hands tied together, and fought with knives in their rights until both were carved to pieces. This never found much favor with white men; it was too bloody and definite. One of the most desperate men in the state refused to fight that way, when challenged by my father, when he, my father that is, was a young man. The other fellow had had the best of a fist-fight, but a fist-fight didn't settle matters in Texas—not in those days. With guns and fists this fellow was a real scrapper, but steel was something different. Though urged by my father, he refused to fight Indian-style; and when my father, enraged, laid the edge of his knife to the fellow's throat and damned him for every scoundrel under the sun, he said nothing, nor did he reach for his gun, standing white and shaking. He didn't like the feel of the edge; not many men do.

You'll have to excuse me if I seem to ramble about in this letter and my style seems jerky. I'm restless as hell and can't seem to concentrate long on any one thing. I wish to God I could go to the Dallas Fair today—not that I give a damn about Dallas or the fair either, but Texas University plays Oklahoma University there, and I'd like to see the game. There's a big French-Indian fullback on the Texas team that charges like a wounded bull, and—but I won't bore you with athletic details. But the hell of living so far away from any center of population is that one seldom gets to see any first-class sports.

More hell popping in Illinois; employers, officials and scabs shaking in their boots and squawking for more National guardsmen. The Insulls scooting hither and yon, possibly with their suitcases full of embezzled dough. I don't give a damn whether they catch them or not. I've always detested old Insull, but when he was on top of the heap people licked his boots and kowtowed to him, and he was allowed to get away with anything. They didn't yell cop till he hit the toboggan. It's just like the bootleggers. As long as they can pay off, they stay out of the jug. It's when laws and lawyers have them busted that they get the hoosegow. That's no idle speculation. I've known some of them personally. Not that it makes a curse to me. The only reason I have it in for the bootleggers is because of the awful muck they hand out as liquor. If I had a case of good beer on hand, I wouldn't be nervous and restless like I am. I'm in favor of the open saloon; and legalized prize-fights and horse-races, licensed gambling halls and licensed bawdy-houses. I wish I was in Mexico right now.

A bit of Hades in Belfast. Excuse me while I take time out for a few hyena-laughs. England's dear little Ulster pets are raring up. Evidently all the rioters in Ireland are not confined to the South. I can think of no more amusing sight than an Orangeman and a Black-and-Tan knocking the socks off each other.[15] What with Belfast and India, the empire-builders must be having a sweet time. I notice they didn't quite have the guts to let Gandhi starve himself into the Great Beyond.[16] Whatamanwhataman. Not that I have any contempt for Gandhi. I honestly have a sincere admiration for him. He may be a visionary, but he is evidently sincere. I don't know if he's right or wrong, but I admire him just the same.

Your case in regard to cold weather is indeed puzzling. I never heard of anything like it. I sympathize with you, for it must be considerable of a handicap. I certainly hope you never have any permanent bad effects from it. As for myself, my only physical weakness, so far as I know—outside of flat feet!—is a bad heart. I inherited a weakness of that organ, and about the age of eighteen suffered from what is commonly known as an "athletic heart", or dilation. After recovery, there was still a weakness that I occasionally notice now. Strenuous exertion, long sustained, or violent excitement is likely to knock me out. The last thing of the sort was several years ago, when Dempsey knocked out Jack Sharkey in his come-back.[17] For days before the fight I was in a state of nervous tension, and during the battle, to the broadcast of which I listened in a theater, my heart went back on me. Or rather, it went back on me at the conclusion of the fight, when Dempsey finished Sharkey with a terrible smash to the jaw that came clearly over the air like the sound of a woodsman's axe cleaving a tree-trunk. I sprang up with an involuntary yell—unnoticed because the whole theater was in uproarious pandemonium—and toppled back into my seat, half-conscious. But the attack lasted only a few seconds; in fact I rose and followed my companion out so quickly that he thought I had merely been delayed by the crowd. But I was in a daze, and hardly knew what I was doing. I don't remember hearing the announcement of the winner—but I knew; I knew only one man in the world could strike a blow like that which had resounded over the air.

By the way, I suppose your remarks about an individual having no right to expect "aid and comfort" from society in resenting rules forced on his group from without, you are referring to what I said about laws and legislations forced on Texas by outside interests. Let me assure you that I never expected favors from any force, group or individual I ever opposed. I never saw any mercy shown in any sort of a battle, and I never expect to. Nor do I ask it. If I'm fighting a man, I fully expect him to do everything in his power to win, by fair means or foul. I expect him to gouge, bite, and kick, and if he's strong enough to fell me, I see no reason why he shouldn't stamp out my brains. I've never been shown any mercy, and I'm not overstocked with it myself. The fact that I resent this over-legislation, this exploitation of my native state, doesn't mean I expect pampering from those it is my instinct to oppose. But I do resent it, even if I can't do anything about it. Just because a man is strong enough to stamp my teeth down my throat without retaliation on my part, doesn't mean I've got to thank him for it. As for laws, we've got more laws in Texas than we ever had before, and infinitely more crime. The increase in crime can not be traced merely to the increase in population. We have four death penalties in Texas—or I should say laws providing for the death penalty for four offenses—murder, rape, kidnapping and robbery with firearms. Yet each year sees a mounting number of murders. Kidnapping is comparatively rare. I'm sorry to say there's some rape. Robbery with firearms seems somewhat on the wane—not so much because of the death penalty provided, which is seldom invoked, but because of the destruction of a few noted outlaw gangs, which were doing most of the robberies. But the list of killings is rather appalling. I can prove this by statistics, if necessary. I used to work in a law office myself, incidentally.

While I am on this matter, let me say that I am sincerely glad that the police system in the East is as good as you say it is. After all, it is corruption and not the system itself that I object to. I am always glad to recieve evidence of honesty and integrity in any and all walks of life. I am quite ready to accept your word for it, without putting the matter to the proof. But—the perfection of the Eastern police system does not mean that the system in all parts of the country is perfect.

When I mentioned the case of my friend being arrested for having liquor on his breath, while the oil magnate's son was allowed to go unmolested, I was not generalizing from that single case. It was only one of many I could quote. In order that you may realize that I am not indulging in irresponsible theorizing, in regard to my own state, I am going to quote a few cases taken at random. Understand, I am talking about Texas, not the East, North, or South. I am enclosing a few clippings from newspapers which dare to tell the truth about things. Let me say one of my kicks at law-enforcement is the difficulty to convict an officer of the law for any thing he may do. Let me quote a case in point. In a certain town where I happened to be staying, an officer had trouble with a certain private citizen. There was no question of law enforcement. It was a private matter, involving family affairs. According to general opinion, the citizen was in the right of it. The officer came up to him suddenly on the street one day and shot him down without a word. I did not see the affair, but my room-mate did, and he said it was cold-blooded murder; he said the officer approached his victim without a word and suddenly drew and dropped him without warning. The murdered man was unarmed; he made no threatening move of any kind. The officer later said the man had threatened his life; I don't believe that. I was well acquainted with the murdered man and a more harmless, inoffensive mortal never lived.

If you were as familiar with the working of Texas law as I am, you wouldn't even ask if the officer was acquitted. Of course he came clear. My best friend attended the trial, and he told me it was a farce. No real attempt was made to prosecute the killer. Why? Hell, nobody doubted why. Because the fellow was an officer of the law. "You can't stick a law." An old saying in these parts and a true one. From what you say, this could not have happened in the East. But it DID happen in Texas. This is no idle romance. If necessary, I can supply names, data and records; but only in return for assurance of treating the matter confidentially. I have no desire to risk my own life digging up things out of the recent past.

Doubtless you read, a few years ago, of the killing of a couple of young Mexicans of highly-connected families, by an Oklahoma officer. He said one of the boys tried to draw a gun. Well, why shouldn't he, accosted suddenly in the night by a stranger, in a locality always more or less haunted by hijackers and bandits? He might have drawn the gun, or he might not. At any rate, he had no way of knowing he was being accosted by an officer. Why did these officers interfere with these boys? At the trial they gave as their reason that the car was carrying a Kansas license! As Will Rogers remarked, when did it become an offense to drive through Oklahoma with a Kansas license? (Naturally the officer was acquitted.)

In Texas there was—and is, so far as I know—a big reward offered for bank-robbers—dead, only. Shortly after these rewards notices were posted, several Mexicans were killed in a West Texas town, by officers who said they were trying to rob the bank. Investigations proved that these officers had hired the Mexicans to come to town, and to enter the bank; then they shot them down in front of the bank in cold blood, to collect the reward money. I never heard just what was done to these officers, but I'm pretty sure they were'nt treated too harshly. And there was a law in a larger Eastern Texas town who hired a negro instead of Mexicans, to rob a bank, in the course of which a bank-clerk was badly wounded. The officer killed the negro and claimed the reward. He got off with a penitentiary sentence.

If people seem bitter against the enforcers of the law, it is but necessary to remember that perhaps they have some slight reason. When I resent such things as I've mentioned, I don't consider myself a criminal. It isn't law-enforcement I resent, but the vandals that parade under the cloak of law. Condoning everything a man does, simply because he happens to wear brass buttons, is something I have no patience with. I won't bore you further, but will merely refer you to the clippings, which you can be assured are not the results of newspaper sensationalism. There are many fine men in Texas in ranks of the law; without them chaos and anarchy would result. But surely it is not fanaticism or outlawry to wish to eliminate the worst spots of corruption and injustice. I'll say one thing more: I hope those Florida guards that murdered the lad from New Jersey in that prison-camp, get the works, just as I'm sure they won't. There are conditions existing in Southern prison-camps that no amount of sophistry can justify. I've seen men whose backs bore the scars of the lash inflicted, not because they would not work, but because they were physically unable to do the work laid out for them—that remark just incidentally.

There was one man prison could not break. I make bold to say no prison-system in the United States, or anywhere else could have broken him, for in those days Texas prisons were hell on earth. John Wesley Harden. He was a bloodthirst killer, a murderer—what you will. Yet I respect him more than I respect some of the men that hunted him. He did his own killing. For only one of these killings was he tried—that of Deputy Sheriff Webb. I have little sympathy for Webb. He met Harden in a social way, and sought to take advantage of him, for the sake of the reward. The sheriff of another county than Webb's, a friend of Harden, introduced the men in a saloon. Webb went for his gun and dropped with Harden's bullet through him.[18]

John later went to Florida, where he was trailed by some Rangers. His capture was effected by a Florida sheriff, who caught his arms from behind when he sought to draw his guns. He suffered a crippling kick from the outlaw, and, I've heard, was gypped out of his share of the reward. During the melee, which took place on a train, a young boy got scared and started to duck out of the way, whereupon one of the officers shot him down. The boy was in no way connected with Harden.[19]

John Wesley Harden drew twenty-five years in the penitentiary. But he refused to work. He wasn't lazy. He'd done harder work rustling cattle and hazing them up the trails than any of the prison guards had ever dreamed of. But he was unconquerable. They could rob him of his liberty. They couldn't make a slave of him. And they didn't. It was because of no softness or sentimentality they failed. All that they could do, they did. They beat him in a manner that would have killed a lesser man. They hanged him by his thumbs. They starved him. They threw him into a dark cell to rot on moldy bread and stale water. A softer man would have died or given in. Not John Wesley Harden. He was steel springs and whale-bone. They couldn't kill him, short of shooting him or cutting his throat. And probably they hesitated about that because of the numerous relatives he had outside the bars. Some people resent the murder of their kin, even by the laws.

John Wesley Harden licked them. He was one man civilization never tamed. Finally they put him in a vat, where he had to pump water or drown. He didn't touch the pump. The water rose over his head and the prison officials lost their nerve. They emptied the vat, dragged Harden out, half-drowned, but unconquerable, and threw him into a cell. After a year, he finally agreed—not by coercion, but of his own accord—to accept a position in the prison shoe-shop, where he was allowed time to study law on the side. All the vaunted power of civilization could not shake him. In him the individual was never subjected to the advantage of the mass. Nor was it civilization which finally cut him down; he met his death as I have narrated, at the hands of John Selman, a character as wild and untamed as Harden himself.

I sure envy you your magnificent sight of the eclipse, and was absolutely enthralled by your vivid and colorful description of it. I hope you'll include that description in a story of some sort some time. You're very fortunate in having seen two total eclipses. I've never seen one, and it's a thousand to one shot I never will.

I was fascinated, too, by your descriptions of your Canadian invasion, and my mouth fairly watered as I thought of the grand liquors within your reach—unheeded by you, alas! But what I would have done to them! Quebec must indeed be a glamorous place of quaint and picturesque architecture and traditions. Aside from the liquor, your descriptions of the city really instilled in me a vast desire to see it some day, though it is a wish with scant chance of fulfillment.

I don't doubt that you're right about Shakespeare. I never paid much attention to the anti-Shakespeare theory myself.

Thanks for Wandrei's address. I'm so swamped with work that I hesitate to begin any new correspondence, but I do intend to write him some day, as he is an author whose work I sincerely admire.

And let me thank you for the pamphlet of poetic criticism which you sent me.[20] I have studied it with an appreciation I do not accord every critic. I am again impressed, as so many times before, by the extent of your artistic education. I am also impressed by the realization that I haven't a chance to ever become a poet. As you so ably put it, "—speaking in images, comparisons, suggestions, and implications rather than in coldly explanatory statements or logical expositions." I can't achieve this imagery. I have to say what I mean in bald narrative style, which is as far from real poetry as an ant-lion is from a lion.

Say, by the way, your comments about individuals having no right to expect favor from the opposition (which is quite true) could be well applied to the defeated party in Texas just now; the anti-Fergusonians. For the first time in more years than I like to remember, the old Texans have won an election. We won it fair. Not a shot was fired, not a voter slugged. And you ought to hear the mob howl! After all who represents society? Is it the millions of people, who, if they are poor and not individually important, still compose the great bulk of the population?—or is it the handful of special privileged business men, absentee owners, and politicians who have grabbed the reins of the state? Primitive backgrounds possibly should not, as you remark, be allowed to hinder the march of progress. But what if that progress is used as a camoflage for wholesale exploitation? The people expressed their will in the election; yet now the opposition howls that society is being defied, civilization threatened, and chaos imminent. I repeat—*which group represents society?*—the great common majority, or the wealthy and powerful minority?

Jim Ferguson's wife was nominated in the teeth of such obstacles as have seldom confronted any candidate. She was opposed by big business; wealth, power; by the bulk of the so-called intellectual class; by thousands of white-collar workers who might have found themselves without a job had they ventured to vote against their bosses; as well as by thousands of honest people, who sincerely considered it to their best interests to vote for the exploiters. Add to that, the fact that most of the Republicans in Texas seem to have cast their votes for Ross Sterling. It was the common people who nominated Jim Ferguson's wife—the common folks, the poor people, the ignorant, the down-trodden, the oppressed—the scum of the earth, as it is the fashion to designate them. Jim Ferguson, with his ragged followers, whipped Sterling to a standstill: in the primaries; in the run-off; at the State Convention; in the courts. Now from the Sterling mob goes up an awful yell, and scores of them are preparing to bolt the party and vote for the Republican candidate; including a number of college professors who formed an organization to promote "good government" and primly set to work to defeat Jim and his uncultured tatterdemalions. They would hand their state over to a tribe of Vandals, if the Vandals wore good clothes and had a civilized air, rather than to side with their own race which is considered backward and out of style. The losers don't like the taste of defeat; they're not used to it. This is the first licking the exploiters of Texas have got since Jim Hogg ran the Standard Oil Company out of the State back in the '90's.[21]

Our candidate for attorney-general had to go into Louisiana in order to broadcast his speeches; and we elected him by a terrific majority. And now he's sinking the gaffs in the looters.[22] I don't give a damn about the Fergusons. But I do give a damn about the people, the common, the low-down, the ignorant people whom the great call the scum of the earth. This has been their victory. They came down from the hills, out of the forks of the creeks, from the mesquite flats, the post-oak ridges, the river-bottoms, the tenement-destricts, the oil-field shacks: with their hickory breeches sagging their suspenders, their shoe-soles worn through, their shoulders slumping and their calloused hands hanging from years of bitter toil. Their victory won't help them much materially, perhaps; it matters little to the poor who is in power. But I rejoice in that victory. It is the last stand of the old Texan race. They'll never win another triumph. They are fading into oblivion, following the red-men. And I am ready to go with them; for with all its faults, follies and cruelties, it's my breed and my race, and I am alien to all others.

"Not of the princes and prelates, with periwigged charioteers,
Riding triumphantly laurelled to lap the fat of the years,
Rather the scorned, the rejected, the men hemmed in with the spears.

"Not the ruler for me, but the ranker, the tramp of the road;
The slave with the sack on his shoulder, pricked on by the goad;
The man with too weary a burden, too heavy a load.

"Let others sing of the wine and the wealth and the mirth,
The portly presence of potentates godly in girth—
Mine be the dirt and the dross, the dust and the scum of the earth.

"Theirs be the music, the color, the glory, the gold;
Mine be a handful of ashes, a mouthful of mold.
Of the maimed, of the halt and the blind in the rain and the cold—
Of these shall my songs be fashioned, my tales be told."[23]

I hardly know how to thank you for the bundle of cards you recently sent. I have gone over them again and again, with the utmost appreciation, and they go into my most valued files. Any one can get a good idea of Eastern, Southern and Canadian architecture and scenery, just by studying them. The systematic way in which they are arranged is a great aid in this study, and altogether, it is about the most valuable addition to my collection that I have recieved in some time. Again, many thanks!

I recently recieved your postcard. Glad you liked the rattles. And thank you for the kind things you said about my maunderings concerning them; there was no conscious literary effort; I was just sort of rambling along. But I'm glad my random comments proved of some interest.

Yes, a bulletin from the AFG announced the crumpling of Strange Tales,[24] and on its heels came back a yarn the magazine had bought but hadn't paid for. I wasn't surprized. Strange Tales was too narrow in policy to have lasted long, though in good times the magazine would have stood up longer than it did. By the way, before I forget it: Belknap Long, who wrote the introduction to Danziger's "Portrait of Ambrose Bierce"—is Frank Belknap Long Jr.'s father? [25]

I'm enclosing a clipping telling of the end of one, who, in his own way, was as deadly as the creature whose remains I sent you recently.[26] He was raised in the house which stands right across the street from where I now sit. There were four of the boys—all bad, in the Western sense of the word. I remember well the first time I ever saw any of them. I was a kid in my early 'teens. I rode into town one cold, grey winter evening. The grey clouds merged in the mist which seemed to change the air to damp smoke. As I went up the street on foot, a lean, hard-looking youth stared at me aggressively, and made some sneering remark about my "wild" appearance. To which I responded with an oath, in the accustomed repartee of the times, "I'm wild and wooly and full of fleas, and I never been curried below the knees!" His comment had been occasioned by my slouch hat and spurs, which were even then a rather rare sight in an oil-boom town. Later I encountered this same fellow, just as I was climbing on my mustang, and we had another slight clash of words as I rode off. I didn't know him, and it didn't occur to me that he was trying to start a fight. When I later learned who he was, I realized I'd been lucky. I wouldn't have had a chance; he was too handy with both knife and pistol. But he was a younger brother of the man described in the enclosed clipping, and probably the worst of the bunch. At present he's doing time in a Texas penitentiary. I haven't seen any of them for years, except the oldest brother, who visited the old home-town last spring, just a few months before he was killed in Mississippi during a bank hold-up. They said he'd recently finished a stretch in Leavenworth, but he looked well-groomed and sleek as a prosperous travelling salesman. This last killing leaves only the younger boys; the fellow I mentioned, and a still younger one, a kid of eighteen or nineteen, who's doing a life-stretch in Oklahoma for a kidnapping job. Those boys were just born out of their time. They were crude, and this system can tolerate anything rather than crudeness. If they'd worn dress-suits, spoken good English, and robbed the helpless and ignorant by approved legal means, they might have been lions of society, like most successful thieves of that type.

By the way, you mentioned that my "Children of the Night" got a mention in the O. Henry Memorial prize annual.[27] What is this annual, and is it possible for me to get a copy of it? The reason I ask, is I gather its something of a boost to get mentioned in it, and it's just possible that I might be able to boost myself with an editor sometime. Any information you can give me about this business will be greatly appreciated.

But I won't impose on you any longer. I've already maundered along beyond all patience. Thanking you again for the poetry pamphlet and the generous bundle of scenic cards, I am,

Cordially,
REH

P.S. Have you read my "Cairn on the Headland" in the latest Strange Tales? If not, I'll be glad to lend you my copy. It was the artist's idea, not mine, to deck Odin in a solid steel cuirass![28]
R.E.H.

Notes

1. See letter 38, n. 2.

2. Carl Sandburg (1878–1967), ed., *The American Songbag* (1927).

3. John Brown (1800–1859), abolitionist whose abortive raid on the Federal arsenal at Harper's Ferry, Virginia (now West Virginia), gave opponents of slavery a martyr to their cause.

4. For the Girtys, see letter 65, n. 20. John Butler (1728–1796) helped recruit and commanded Indian forces in the British drive down the Mohawk Valley of New York during the American Revolution. As the leader of Butler's Rangers, he was active in the British cause throughout the conflict. His son, Walter (d. 1781), led an attack by Tories and Indians at Cherry Valley, New York, in 1778, and was active in stirring up Indians against rebellious New York settlers until his death following a Mohawk Valley raid in 1781.

5. Joseph Brant (1742–1807), son of the Mohawk chief Thayendanegea, fought with the British during the French and Indian wars and the American Revolution. As secretary to the British Superintendent for Indian Affairs, he was instrumental in bringing the Iroquois nations into the Revolutionary conflict on the side of the British. Brant and the Butlers (particularly Walter) play a large part in a series of novels by Robert W. Chambers set in frontier New York during the Revolution. Of these, *The Maid-at-Arms* (1902), *The Little Red Foot* (1921), and *America; or, The Sacrifice* (1924) were in REH's library. Walter Butler probably inspired the character "Lord Valerian" in REH's "Wolves Beyond the Border."

6. Dr. Isaac Howard's sister, Willie, married William Oscar McClung, whose mother, according to according to the McClungs' daughter, was a Choctaw.

7. James Francis "Jim" Thorpe (1888–1953), who won the pentathlon and decathlon in the 1912 Olympic Games (later disqualified when he admitted having played semi-professional baseball in the summer of 1911) and played professional football and baseball. He was indeed part Sac and Fox Indian, and as a child was given the tribal name Bright Path.

8. Cornelius Vanderbilt (1794–1877), American capitalist and transportation magnate, was instrumental in bringing about Walker's downfall in Nicaragua, after Walker had seized Vanderbilt properties in that country and turned them over to business rivals.

9. Felix Huston (1800–1857) was a lawyer in Mississippi when the Texas Revolution began. He spent a large sum of his own money raising a force that he equipped and brought to Texas, too late to join in the fighting. Late in 1836 he was nominated to take command of the Texas army, but his extremely aggressive attitude toward Mexico led to his being relieved of the command. Albert Sidney Johnston (1803–1862) was sent to take over, but Huston challenged him to a duel and seriously wounded him. Huston later served with distinction against the Indians. Johnston went on to distinguished service in the Mexican War, with the U.S. Army in various posts in the West, and as a Confederate general in the Civil War. He was killed during the battle of Shiloh.

10. George Scarborough (1859–1900), cowboy and lawman, was serving as deputy U.S. marshal in El Paso when he killed John Selman (1839–1896) in a dispute. He was acquitted of murder.

11. Scarborough died on 6 April 1900 of wounds received while with a posse chasing Harvey ("Kid Curry") Logan (1865–1904) and a gang of cattle rustlers in New Mexico.

12. Emmanuel Clements, Jr. (1869–1908), cowboy and law officer, was generally known as "Mannie," while his father, Emmanuel Sr. (d. 1877), was called "Mannen."

13. Garrett was killed on his New Mexico ranch on 29 February 1908, under circumstances still debated by historians. He was in the company of Wayne Brazel, who owned a neighboring ranch, and Carl Adamson, who had supposedly topped Brazel's offer for the ranch. Accounts of the murder are conflicting: although Brazel con-

fessed and Adamson corroborated, there were many contradictions in their stories, and physical evidence at the scene cast further doubt. Some believe Brazel was the murderer; others believe Adamson guilty; still others believe evidence points to Adamson's cousin, Jim ("Killer") Miller, a notorious murderer-for-hire. The only certainty is that there was a conspiracy to murder Garrett.

14. This account of Thompson's duel with de Tour can be found in W. M. (Major Buck) Walton, *The Life and Adventures of Ben Thompson* (1884).

15. Unemployment riots broke out in Belfast on 11 October 1932; British troops arrived the following day. Sporadic violence continued, and when the Prince of Wales arrived on 16 November to dedicate the new Northern Ireland Parliament building, he was guarded by 20,000 British troops. Ulster Protestants ("Orangemen") boycotted his appearance. "Black and Tans" were ex-servicemen recruited into the Royal Irish Constabulary during the Anglo-Irish war of 1919–21.

16. Mohandas K. (Mahatma) Gandhi (1869–1948), Indian nationalist leader, began a fast in his jail cell on 21 September 1932 to protest an electoral change he believed would perpetuate unfair treatment of "untouchables" under the caste system. On 27 September a compromise plan agreed to by representatives of caste Hindus and untouchables was approved by the British colonial government, and Gandhi ended his fast, which had made headlines around the world. He renewed the fast when Hindu legislators attempted to weaken the agreement and preserve the caste system.

17. Jack Dempsey defeated Jack Sharkey in seven rounds on 21 July 1927, in a match to see who would challenge Gene Tunney for the heavyweight title he had won from Dempsey in 1926.

18. Hardin killed Sheriff Charles Webb of Comanche County on 26 May 1874 in Comanche, Texas. Most accounts make no mention of treachery on Webb's part, just an honest attempt to capture the outlaw. REH's version no doubt comes from Hardin's self-serving autobiography, *The Life of John Wesley Hardin* (1896; rpt Norman: University of Oklahoma Press, 1961).

19. Hardin was captured on 23 August 1877 on a train in Pensacola, Florida, by Texas Ranger John Armstrong. Reliable accounts make no mention of his being pinned from behind; rather, his gun seems to have caught on his suspenders, and Armstrong knocked him senseless with the barrel of his Colt "Peacemaker." The "young boy" who was killed took a shot at Armstrong, who fired back. The young man climbed out a window and ran a few steps before collapsing.

20. *Further Criticism of Poetry* (Louisville, KY: George G. Fetter, 1932). HPL's title was "Notes on Verse Technique." See letter 34, n. 4.

21. James Stephen Hogg (1851–1906), governor of Texas (1891–95).

22. James V. Allred (1899–1959) was elected Texas attorney general in 1930 and again in 1932. He won popular approval with a continuing campaign against monopolies and big businesses and against the efforts of large corporations to influence state taxation and fiscal policies. He was elected governor in 1934 and 1936.

23. John Masefield (1878–1967), "A Consecration" (1902), stanzas 1, 4, 6, and 7.

24. I.e., the American Fiction Guild, a writers' organization, to which REH had belonged since at least the spring of 1932. See letter 54.

25. Belknap Long is HPL's friend Frank Belknap Long, Jr. He revised and wrote the preface to Adolphe de Castro's *Portrait of Ambrose Bierce* (New York: Century Co., 1929; REHB 56) after HPL refused to do so because de Castro would not pay him in advance.

26. See letter 73, n. 4.

27. In the *O. Henry Memorial Award: Prize Stories of 1931,* ed. Blanche Colton Williams (Garden City, NY: Doubleday, Doran, 1931), p. 359, REH's "The Children of the Night" was listed in a group of "Stories ranking second" for that year.

28. The illustration for "The Cairn on the Headland" was by Amos Sewell.

[71] [TLS]

[c. November 1932]

Dear Mr. Lovecraft:

Here's a clipping that might be of some interest, not because of its athletic significance, but because it bears out some former remarks of mine concerning the various types of Southwesterners. The difference between the typical North Texan and the typical South Texan is becoming so marked that even the newspapers are noting it, as shown in the enclosed clipping.

T.C.U., represented by the blond warriors, is in Fort Worth, where I've seen more pure blonds than anywhere else in the state—or any other state I've ever been in. Out of nineteen people met on one block, I've counted sixteen of that complection. The further south you go, the more brunets you see. This is mainly because of the great numbers of Mexicans, Bohemians, Bavarians, and Poles settled there. Again, that section of the country has been settled longer than north and west Texas, and the people have had more opportunity to mix with people of Slavonic and Spanish strains. North west Texas was settled mainly, not by people from south and east Texas, but by people from such states as Alabama, Georgia, Tennessee, Arkansas, and Mississippi, of pure Celtic or Anglo-Saxon blood. These have not mixed so easily with Indian and Spanish strains. Yet, it is a curious fact that there are more brunets among the unmixed Anglo-Saxons of south Texas than there are among those of the north and west.

In this part of the country, that is, among the Callahan hills, there are comparatively few pure blonds, yet they outnumber the pure brunets; the characteristic type is of blue or grey eyes, with medium to dark brown hair, and a medium complection.

In the lower Rio Grande valley, among the irrigated districts, blonds predominate, because of the great numbers of Germans and Scandinavians from the Middle West. They are easily distinguishable from the native stock. Put a blond Scandinavian beside an equally blond native Texan, and it's easy to tell them apart. It's not so easy to distinguish brunet aliens from brunet natives. Why this should be, I can't pretend to say.

Incidentally, the blond T.C.U. team has the advantage in weight, height and strength, and is perhaps the most powerful defensive line in the nation, while the brunet Texas University team has the edge on speed and spirit, and shines most brightly on the offense.[1]

So much for Southwestern racial contrasts—or what ever they are.

Cordially,

R E H

Notes

1. Texas Christian University played Texas University on November 11, 1932. T.C.U. won, 14–0.

[72] [ANS][1]

[Postmarked Providence, R.I.,
13 November 1932]

Thanks exceedingly for the very interesting cutting & comment regarding North & South Texas types. The difference certainly does appear to be phenomenally striking—& not altogether due to foreign blood, since the list of South Texan brunet athletes contains a good sprinkling of old American names—Stafford, Hilliard, Fagan, DuBose, Birdwell, Blanton. The prevalence of pure blond types in Ft. Worth—which you mentioned once before—is very striking. Scandinavian types sometimes have a distinguishing physiognomy—due mostly, I fancy, to modifications caused by diet & climate, but in part to the tincture of Lapp-Finn Turanian blood which some of the peasantry possess. ¶ I have often thought that, on the whole, blond types are more frequent in the South—Virginia, Carolinas, Georgia—than among the old stock in the North, but I may be wrong. Of course, one can never judge from the crowds on the streets, for in the North these are likely to be 3/4 foreign—or even 9/10 foreign in New York City. ¶ It's getting devilish cold up here! Hope winter isn't quite so near in your part of Texas. Best wishes—
H P L

Notes

1. Front: Unknown.

[73]

10 Barnes St.,
Providence, R.I.,
Nov. 7, 1932

Dear R. E. H.:—

Your intensely interesting letter duly arrived, and I have digested it with the usual pleasure and appreciation. Let me say at the outset that there was no need of regretting anything in your former letter, since I never take offence at any genuine effort to wrest the truth or deduce a rational set of values from the confused phenomena of the external world. It never occurs to me to look for personal factors in the age-long battle for truth. I assume that all hands are really trying to achieve the same main object—the discovery of sound facts and the rejection of fallacies—and it strikes me as only a minor matter that different strivers may happen to see a different perspective now and then. And in matters of mere preference, as distinguished from those involving the question of truth versus fallacy, I do not see any ground whatever for acrimonious feeling. Knowing the capriciousness and complexity of the various biological and psychological factors determining likes, dislikes, interests, indifferences, and so on, one can only be astonished that any two persons have even approximately similar tastes. To resent another's different likes and interests is the summit of illogical absurdity. It is very easy to distinguish a sincere, impersonal difference of opinion and tastes from the arbitrary, ill-motivated, and irrational belittlement which springs from a hostile desire to push another down and which constitutes real offensiveness. I have no tolerance for such real offensiveness—but I greatly enjoy debating questions of truth and value with persons as sincere and devoid of malice as I am. Such debate is really a highly valuable—almost indispensable—ingredient of life; because it enables us to test our own opinions and amend them if we find them in any way erroneous or unjustified. One who never debates lacks a valuable chart or compass in the voyage for truth—for he is likely to cherish many false opinions along with sound ones for want of an opportunity to see each opinion viewed from every possible angle. I have modified many opinions of mine in the course of debate, and have been intensely grateful for the chance of so doing.

As for the question of the physical versus the speculative and the aesthetic—I can see your point of view completely, and do not believe that any real controversy is involved. One's interests in such fields are largely guided by one's general conception of the cosmos as determined by temperament—and in both cases the underlying process is an emotional reaching-out after whatever gives one's ego the greatest sensation of stability, important existence, meaning, and potential expansion. Whether that sensation is to be secured best through physical or non-physical channels, is in each individual determined by dozens of separate causes—hereditary, environmental, and accidental. Preferences between channels are really irrelevant. In my own case, physical matters seem relatively (but not absolutely) uninteresting and unimportant because it is my instinctive and unalterable habit to take the cosmos as a primary unit of perception, calculation, and evaluation. The cosmos is everything—the individual nothing. All that—in my instinctive feelings—forms any rational measure of the individual is his degree of ability (infinitesimally fragmentary in even the greatest of philosophers and scientists) to comprehend the knowable fraction of the cosmos and correlate himself with it. That is what being a human being is—to possess consciousness and comprehension. As Descartes put it, "Cogito, ergo sum". In a primary sense—other things being equal—one man can be greater than another only through having a greater comprehension of the universal flux of worlds and aeons, and a greater recognition of his place in it. We live, in a human sense, only so far as we understand. Consciousness is life—uncomprehending physical functioning is a mere vegetative or quasi-inorganic existence shared with bacteria and does nothing to determine or promote our status as human beings—i.e., as conscious graspers of some fragment of universal reality. To be strong, or to exceed another in strength, is devoid of any *large* significance which I can recognise, try though I may. Any bull or elephant is stronger than any man, and any locomotive, motor-truck, thunderstorm, or earthquake is stronger than any bull or elephant. A man is greater than a bull, elephant, locomotive, motor-truck, thunderstorm, or earthquake only because he has more consciousness than any of these other transient foci of energy. A relatively feeble man with strong consciousness can drive and harness physically strong men, bulls, elephants, locomotives, and motor-trucks, and can even do something toward predicting thunderstorms and earthquakes and avoiding their worst consequences. Humanity means mind—but the physical is shared by all the less highly organised forces of the cosmos. With these underlying assumptions, it would be hard for me to attach any primary importance to the physical. I do, however, recognise its secondary importance in making consciousness effective and in safeguarding the fruits of consciousness; hence (as I said before) never share the views of those idealists or pacificists who actually despise it. Indeed, I have just as much of a controversy with them as with these opposite extremists who primarily enthrone the physical. As a matter of fact, the natural principles of aesthetics demand a certain amount of harmony in any organism; and such is the origin and construction of the human animal that it would be disharmonic and ill-proportioned if lacking in a certain amount of physical development and physical assertiveness. Decidedly, I have nothing in common with the fanatical anti-physicalism of such extreme ascetics as the genuine Christians or the "Yogis" and other mystics of the East. On the contrary, I thoroughly endorse the Horatian precept of "mens sana in corpore sano",[1] and am keenly sensitive to the vivid drama of physical force—acting in its proper proportion—in the stream of history. I feel to the full the glory of Thermopylae and of Zama, and have a corresponding dislike of the shifty and obsequious mental activity which—like that of the Hellenistic Greeks and the Jews—is not backed up by enough physical stamina to ensure its own honesty and independence. In other words, I take what appears to me to be a rational middle ground, trying to avoid overemphases in either direction. Or to express it more specifically, I do not care for the physical for its own sake, but respect it highly when it is used in the defence of ideas and civilisations, and appreciate both its dramatic value in history and its aesthetic necessity in the balanced, well-rounded human personality.

By the way, though—I must disagree with you when you speak of writing as a profession for which you are not fitted. With your intense sensitiveness to the colour of the past, the pageantry of time and change, the atmosphere of places, and the tense drama of interacting civilisations, nations, and individuals—and with your spontaneous, zestful use of fluent, graphic language and vividly significant imagery—I would be tempted to say that you are a natural-born author if there ever was one! Anybody who responds to life as you do—finding everything around you a basis of expanding circles of associative reflection and emotion which apparently clamour for expression—is by that very circumstance essentially of the stuff of authors. Indeed, I'd call that responsiveness the real test of a genuine artist as opposed to a mere fluent technician. Of all the writers with whom I've been in contact, I don't know of one who really has more to say, or who says anything with a more convincing gusto, than yourself. Even though you may specialise in deeds of prowess, your range of expression is by no means confined to such matters. For one thing, you have a tremendous power to evoke the atmosphere of awesomely and immeasurably remote ages as hinted by worn-down monoliths and cyclopean ruins. Again, you can make a locality live through your instinctive choice of descriptive elements taken from the landscape, climate, and denizens. And your sense of history as a dynamic drama is something notable and full of tremendous possibilities. I certainly hope you can get a chance to try, sooner or later, that book of eminent outlaws which may place its subjects in true chronological perspective; and I also hope you can eventually get at some kind of history of the Texan or Southwestern life-stream which you know so minutely, subjectively, and sympathetically. The damnable thing is that you have to limit yourself by catering to the artificial, conventional, and oversimplified needs of the wretched pulp magazines. You are lucky to be able to suit them at all—but it's none the less a shame that you have to use your time and energy on this kind of thing instead of the boldly independent fiction and powerful historic material which you would produce if absolutely untrammelled. Yes—I read "The Cairn on the Headland", and thought it splendidly powerful. The atmosphere of brooding menace is magnificent, and all the accessories—such as the ancient crucifix from the tomb—are vividly adequate. Too bad the "artist" didn't follow the text closely enough to give the liberated god the awesome and terrible form suggested—but all of these fellows (except good old Rankin) lack imagination. By the way—I think you take a bit of liberty with tradition in making Odin such an emphatically *evil* deity. As the god of my forefathers before 600 A.D. he has always been a favourite of mine—indeed, I have always thought it unfortunate that men fell away from him and adopted the hypocritical Asiatic slave-cult of Christus which political accident had foisted on the Mediterranean world, and which is radically and basically unsuited to a vigorous Aryan people.

Another recent thing which impressed me as tremendously fine—potently frightful in its echoes from black gulfs and unsuspected secrets of the planet's elder aeons—is "Worms of the Earth".* The subtle way in which you *suggest* the abysmal horror of those retrograded *things* is truly inimitable. About the O. Henry Memorial Prize Annual—it is a publication which lists and classifies the year's short stories in much the same manner as Edward J. O'Brien's "Best Short Story" annuals, though on a basis less purely aesthetic and more related to the conventional standards of the professional magazine press. It is issued by a sort of "foundation"—endowed with money for the purpose—and the story selected as absolutely the best receives a cash prize. That—and certain others—are reprinted as an anthology, and the balance of the year's published stories are listed in grades corresponding to O'Brien's single, double, and triple starred classes. Because of the somewhat different principles of selection, it is only occasionally that an "O. Henry" classification corresponds precisely with an O'Brien classification. Because of its primarily conventional standards, this annual has never interested me as much as O'Brien's; and it is only through a correspondent that I recently learned of the verdicts in its last two numbers. In fact, I hadn't learned about the *1932* verdicts when I wrote you. In the 1931 book, as I said, your "Children of the Night" received a class II rating, along with Long's "Black Druid"†—these being the only products of our group to rate above class III. In the latter group are Francis Flagg's "The Picture", Long's "Visitor from Egypt", Smith's "Rendezvous in Averoigne", and Whitehead's "Passing of a God". Both the Smith and Whitehead items ought to have had a decidedly higher rating. There seems to be a fourth class, tho' (I haven't seen one of the annuals in years, hence am hazy as to the exact system)—in which Flagg's "Jelly Fish" and Smith's "Phantom of the Fire" are listed. In the current 1932 annual, I am told, my "Strange High House in the Mist" makes class I. Class II includes Whitehead's "Black Beast" and "Cassius", and my "In the Vault". In class III are Long's "Horror in the Hold" and Whitehead's "Black Terror" and "Mrs. Lorriquer". My correspondent (who copied from memory) also says that Smith's "Gorgon" and "Testament of Athammaus" are listed in some minor class, though he can't recall which.[2] None of our group except Derleth make the O'Brien annual this year—and even his cited items are not of the weird order. It will be as a delicate realist that Derleth will seriously develop. As for poetry—and the brochure I sent—you certainly err in saying 'that you haven't a chance to become a poet' . . . . except in the sense that you can't *become* what you *already are!* Why, great Scott, if ever anyone was a

*In that tale, why do you spell *Eboracum* as *Ebbracum?*

†Long Jr. himself—not his father, who is a dentist—wrote the preface to old de Castro's Bierce book, and also revised the text. I passed up the job because de Castro wouldn't meet my price. At that period Long had a temporary affectation of leaving off his first name.

natural poet, you are the one! How can you say that your style is a bold, narrative one when as a matter of fact it is *spontaneously full* of just the sort of images, comparisons, suggestions, and implications which make real poetry? Of course a given piece of poetry has to have a sort of framework or skeleton of plain statement—description, narration, or definition, as the case may be—upon which the figurative images or symbols are draped. We complain only when the images and symbols are wanting or too few, or when the *main effect* is aimed at with other than an image or symbol. Far from being barren and prosaic, your style both in prose and verse is one of the most poetic I know. One could pick powerful and apt images by the dozen from any one of your best stories or poems. Take your rattlesnake prose-poem, for instance—"let him dare to walk *where the rank grass quivers without a wind*" . . . . etc. If that isn't *poetic implication* of the first order, then I'll resign from the N.A.P.A. Bureau of Critics! Poetry is really a tremendously strong point of yours, and something which deserves a large share of your attention. You'll recall my saying this before—and remarking what a fine natural ear for metre you have. It truly astonished me when you mentioned some time ago that you had not studied the various metrical forms. (N. B. I suppose you know that your "Black Stone" is in the new "Not at Night" anthology.)

By the way—I must express again my thanks for that splendid set of rattles. I appreciated them anew when I compared them the other day with a set my grandfather had—now in the possession of my surviving aunt. This set is much smaller than the one you sent, and has only six rattles instead of seven. I am certainly vastly indebted to you for this extremely welcome addition to my collection.

About New Orleans—it isn't spoiled yet by any means! I'm not sure but that most of the changes I mentioned were all accomplished at the time of your visit. Aside from a slight eating of modernity into the Canal St. side of the quarter, the real devastation embraces not much more than a single block—that bounded by Royal, St. Louis, Chartres, and Conti Sts., where the relatively new Court House is—and I believe that devastation was effected some 20 years ago. The old St. Louis Hotel was torn down in 1917, and the French Opera House burned in 1919—and since then no radical destruction has occurred. The loss of the old French Market, though extremely unfortunate, will scarcely impair the general aspect of the ancient quarters as a whole; and to offset the destruction there is a steady wave of reclamation and restoration guaranteed to preserve many of the more important reliques. The Italians, for instance, have been cleared out of Gen. Beauregard's house—which is now a museum open to visitors—and I think I told you that the city has installed small, old-fashioned lamp-posts (though containing powerful electric lights) throughout the Vieux Carré. Of course, one cannot predict the future. As I said, Price is a pessimist about the survival of the old houses and atmosphere; but the change may not be as rapid or as complete as he fears. By the way, he has doubtless written you of his return to New Orleans—where he now dwells at 1416 Josephine St., in the old American section far south of the quarter. And so the "poor boy" sandwich has spread westward to Galveston! Curious that it should go west and not north or east—for it is absolutely unknown in Natchez or Mobile. As for sea-food—it is simply *intensely repulsive* to me. If I could get it down without tasting it, I don't imagine it would disagree especially with my stomach—but the taste or smell of it revolts me to the point of nausea and (if too intense or prolonged) actual regurgitation. I know that this aversion is not widely shared, and likewise realise how avidly most inland dwellers take to fish. Visitors to Providence from the west always ask to be taken to shore dining places where clambakes are featured, or restaurants featuring oysters, lobsters, swordfish, or other alleged delicacies of the sea—indeed Rhode Island is almost as famous as Louisiana for sea-food. But that doesn't mean anything to my palate. From earliest infancy every sort of fish, mollusc, or crustacean has been like an emetic to me. My room at 10 Barnes is a former dining room, so that my dressing-alcove (a former pantry with running water) connects with the kitchen by means of a dish-passing aperture now closed but permeable by strong cooking odours. Whenever fish is cooked, I am in misery—and I sometimes get a headache in winter when I can't keep the smell thoroughly aired out. But thank Odin it doesn't happen very often! Aside from sea-food, my principal dietary aversions are tripe, liver, sauerkraut, spinach, any *underdone* meat, any dessert with caraway seed, custards, and (as I've said before) alcoholic liquor or anything with its flavour. At the other end of the scale, my three favourite dietary articles are *cheese,* (preferably of the common hard variety, medium strength. I hate Roquefort, dislike cottage cheese, just tolerate Camembert and Brie, and am neutral about Limburger—which latter I've tasted only once, at Whitehead's a year ago last spring) *chocolate,* (in nearly any form—cake, frosting, sweet milk chocolate, etc.) and *ice cream* (preferably vanilla or coffee—the latter being a popular New England flavour, though largely unknown elsewhere). Quite a triad! I like meat courses very highly seasoned—the Latin idea—and desserts very sweet. Don't care for tea (but take it with lemon if at all) but like coffee—taking both very sweet (about 5 lumps to an average cup). Coffee with little milk—but always some. Don't like milk to drink. Of meats, I fancy I rather prefer beef for all around consumption, but like most others pretty well. Fond of sausage—especially the old fashioned baked or fried sort. Like fowl—but white meat only. Can't bear dark meat. My really favourite meal is the regular old New England turkey dinner, with highly seasoned dressing, cranberry sauce, onions, etc., and mince pie for dessert. Pie is my favourite dessert, and blueberry (for summer) and mince (for winter) are my preferred kinds—with apple as a good all-year-round third. Like to take vanilla ice cream with apple and blueberry pie. Fond of most fruit, anyway—peaches, pears, strawberries, apricots, bananas. Like Italian cooking very much—

especially spaghetti with meat-and-tomato sauce, utterly engulfed in a snowbank of grated Parmesan cheese. Spanish cooking pretty fair, but not up to Italian. Like tamales and chili con carne. Am fond of stuffed green peppers with tomato sauce . . . . in general, I doubt if the buzzards will stage much of a fight over my mortal remains when I explore the west and get dropped by some rampageous two-gun desperado! I'm not, however, a heavy eater—take only 2 meals per day, since my digestion raises hell if I try to eat oftener than once in 7 hours. In winter, when it's too cold for me to go out much, I subsist largely on canned stuff. I always get my own breakfasts, anyway—doughnuts and cheese. I have financial economy in eating worked out to a fine art, and know the self-service lunch rooms where I can get the best bargains. I never spend more than $3.00 per week on food, and often not even nearly that. In New Orleans I patronised Thompson's (in St. Charles St. near Canal), the Gluck chain, and a cheap place next to Lafayette Park called the "Chocktaw", which changed its name to the "Palm" during my sojourn. All these lay between the Vieux Carré and my hotel, (where I got an inside room and bath for a dollar a day) which was in St. Charles about half way out to Lee Circle and the public library. Ah, me—I wish I were back in New Orleans (or better still, Florida) for the winter!

Quebec is certainly great in its season—absolutely the most picturesque and beautiful city on this continent, unless Mexico has some marvellous hill town which I've never heard about. I can't say that the frequent "Vins, bieres, et liqueurs" signs offered any kind of temptation—for in a living wonderland like old Quebec one doesn't want to be drugged and drowsed in any artificially distorted half-perceptions. One wants to have the full benefit of one's personality and perceptions to enjoy and absorb the actual glamour of the very real scenes and vistas which extend on every hand. Boy, what a place! The 18th century—the 17th century—even the middle ages seem to hover around. Did I say that I saw a genuine barefoot friar with brown robes, sandals, and tonsured head? The place is simply an incarnation of history—what New Orleans must have been around 1800, plus a wildly beautiful landscape setting unknown to Louisiana.

I was greatly interested in the old ballads you cited. "Oh, Susanna" was widely sung in New England—probably with a slightly varied wording. I never heard "Tom Quick" or "Bonny Eloise", but believe I came across something like "Deacon Jones" in Wilbraham, Mass. (the "Dunwich" country) in 1928. This ballad was locally adapted to make Wilbraham Mountain (pronounced, of course, "Wilbrum Mountain") the scene of the fatal encounter. For some reason or other, New England and certain other northern regions seem to be almost as badly snake-infested as the tropics. The thick settlement of the countryside drove them out to some extent, but they are reported on the increase now that the urban drift is leaving large rural areas comparatively deserted again.

As for economics—of course all predictions are largely guesses. However—when you reflect on the France of 1792 and the Russia of 1917 you can see that the power of a dominant group to preserve its supremacy by force is not always to be relied on. In the United States I think that mass pressure in certain directions is likely to cause ultimate governmental changes because the dominant industrial group will find suppression too costly. Also, the loss of purchasing power by the majority (almost inevitable in a machine age under a laissez faire policy) will vastly cut down profits even in non-depression times. In the end, I doubt if the ruling industries will find their supremacy worth maintaining. It simply won't pay—reckoning in the lessened profits, the enormous outlay for forcible mass-suppression, and the constant psychological tension afforded by the possibility of revolution. Remember that a mercenary army protecting a small group is always likely to seize power itself, for its own benefit, (as in the case of Rome's praetorian guards) or to go over to the other side in the hope of increased personal rewards (as in the case of the Russian army just 15 years ago today). It looks to me as if common sense would prompt the ruling industries to loosen up a trifle sooner or later—contenting themselves with less immediate profit-grasping in exchange for the greater security, stability, and long-range advantages offered by a more public-spirited policy. I don't imagine that anyone will be perfectly suited, but I think the tension and hardship will be rather less than at present. As for peonage or actual slavery—that is hardly a practical possibility except with inferior or badly-cowed race-stocks. The whole psychological equilibrium which made it possible in mediaeval and ancient times has been permanently destroyed. But it really wouldn't be so bad to enslave niggers, Mexicans, and certain types of biologically backward foreign peasants. I'm no abolitionist—in fact, I'd probably have been almost ostracised in New England in the hectic days of Charles Sumner, Wendell Phillips, and Bostonese pharasaism in general. Of course, slavery ought to be regulated by stringent laws as to the treatment of slaves—laws backed up by frequent governmental inspections, and sustained by a carefully directed public sentiment as to humane conditions. In the 18th century, when we had negro slaves in Rhode Island, there was never any discontent or talk of ill-treatment. On the large estates of King's County (estates duplicating the plantations of the South, and quite unique for the North) the blacks were in general simply contented—having their own festivities, and indulging in a kind of annual Saturnalia in which large numbers met and elected one of their number "King of Africa" for the ensuing year. One of my ancestors—Robert Hazard[3]—left 133 slaves in his will. What caused slavery to decline in the north was the complex economic readjustment which rendered large-scale agriculture and stock-raising no longer as profitable as maritime commerce. When it no longer paid to keep niggers, our pious forbears began to have moral and religious scruples about the matter—so that around 1800 Rhode Island passed a law limiting slavery to blacks over 21, and declaring all others, and all subsequently born, free. Later this was amended to free the adult negroes—though most stayed right on with their masters as nominally paid servants. In the next generation, when slavery was defunct in the north but seen to be still a source of profit in the south, it occurred to northern politicians to become very Quixotic and devoted to the ideal of freedom—hence the impassioned frock-coated moralists of the abolitionist school, calling upon heaven to end the unrighteous curse of human bondage. But on the whole I don't think slavery would form a practical policy for the future. Psychological conditions have changed. I don't think inferior races, or persons of very inferior education or capacity in any race, ought to have the political franchise; but I think it is the best public policy to give them as much freedom as is consistent with the maintenance of the civilisation on an unimpaired level. This leads one to your question as to *what actually represents society, civilisation, or the state as a unit to be upheld and defended* . . . . . a question which has often excited long and careful speculation on my part, and to which *I do not think it is possible to give any one simple answer.*

In trying to determine what *society* or *civilisation,* as a defence-worthy unit, really *is,* we can best begin by attempting to see what it very obviously *isn't.* Then, by elimination, we may be able to narrow down our idea a bit. Looking at the matter broadly, objectively, and unsentimentally—without regard for any traditional ideal or condition to which blind lip-service or passive, mechanical compliance has been given—I think we can safely strike out two types of extremism, one at either end. First, it is clearly disproportionate and inharmonic to sacrifice all the interests of the majority to any small group exclusively determined by some purely arbitrary principle such as the accident of personal lineage or the chance possession of material resources. But secondly—and on the other hand—it is equally disproportionate and inharmonic to sacrifice the fuller life of the mind and emotions which part of the group is able to achieve through personal development, to the capricious wishes of the undeveloped and sometimes undevelopable numerical majority. To reduce the matter to underlying principles: (a) On the one hand, it is undesirable to inflict pain and hardship, which could otherwise be avoided, upon the bulk of the people for the sake of propping up to disproportionate heights any arbitrary fraction of the people; or even to impose avoidable minor discomforts or restrictions on the majority for the sake of any minority-elevation *which is not justified by an actual intellectual and aesthetic superiority on the part of the chosen minority*—a superiority constituting the attainment of a cultural level which *none* of the whole group could attain through any arrangement other than a slightly unequal distribution of privilege. That is, unequal privilege is justified only when it enables a higher degree of human development (in which the individually superior members of the less privileged majority can gradually share until they become incorporated in an increasing privileged minority) to arise within the group, than could have arisen without it. (b) Looking from the other angle, we may consider it clearly undesirable to load power and needless favours (favours, that is, beyond the assurance of a decent living and the opportunity to rise) on the wholly undeveloped majority, when that loading would defeat the increased fulness of life to which a considerable and constantly growing number of individuals could attain if aided by a more intelligent and far-sighted apportionment of privilege. One may add that if this blind loading of power on the undeveloped is persisted in, it will probably result in their really getting less out of life than as if they had permitted a smaller group to develop, evolve more effective means of mastering environment and of extracting more satisfaction from the experience of living, and finally diffuse many of the advantages of these gains among the majority.

Behind this, of course, is a whole philosophy of life—and in deciding what a sound life-philosophy is, I believe I am about as sincerely objective, impersonal, and impartial as anyone well can be. I have no class sympathies—only a desire for truth and rational arrangement. In my opinion, the human being as born into the world with a blank consciousness is *only the raw material of a genuine human personality*. What determines the value and importance of a person, aside from his biological heritage, is the degree to which his physiological mechanism is developed into a conscious experiencer of the universe, and trained to make his relationship to the universe and to the group an harmonic one. In other words, we cannot with any good reason claim that a wholly undeveloped man is of as much value as a developed man. He may have the psychological capacity to become a developed and consequently valuable man, but until he is developed he has not the general value in the cosmic pattern which the developed man has. This, of course, is a generalistion, as all sociological principles necessarily have to be; and does not overlook the individual examples of high value among the undeveloped, due to mental superiority or to spontaneous presence of isolated qualities of harmonic excellence, and of low value among the developed, due to mental inferiority or to the presence of psychological twists antagonistic to harmonic adjustment. Generalisation is often cruel and often unduly flattering—but there is nothing else on which we can base a social policy. The more truly civilised we are, though, the more flexible and accomodative of the exceptional individual our social policy becomes. Well—the sum of the matter is, that we cannot, in view of what the cultural capacity of mankind has been shown to be, afford to base a civilisation on the low cultural standards of an undeveloped majority. Such a civilisation of mere working, eating, drinking, breeding, and vacantly loafing or childishly playing isn't worth maintaining. None of the members of it are really better off than as if they didn't exist at all, and those who are either exceptionally sensitive or exceptionally superior—or both—are infinitely worse off than as if they didn't exist. To be more specific, the process of being alive and conscious is too intrinsically painful—too predominantly painful, after all allowances for natural pleasure are made—to make it worth enduring by any man who has lost the primitive zests of savagery, unless he has a chance of enlarging his grasp on life by a mental and aesthetic development much greater than that of the undeveloped majority. No settled, civilised group has any reason to exist unless it can develop a decently high degree of intellectual and artistic cultivation. The more who can share in this cultivation the better, but we must not invidiously hinder its growth merely because the number of sharers has to be relatively small at first, and because it can perhaps never (Russian claims to the contrary notwithstanding) include every individual in the whole group. Even at the cost of a little limitation of privilege here and there, we must give the real natural capacities of the best of the group a chance to show what they can do toward dispelling the horror and the weariness of the undeveloped consciousness. But remember that this isn't blindly subscribing to any traditional aristocratic or plutocratic system. What is needed is simply a system which will enable at least some persons—as many as possible—to develop their potentialities to enough of an extent to make life worth living, and which will sustain an environment (economic, civic, educational, architectural, social) in which such developed personalities can function with a minimum of pain and disharmony. This doesn't mean restriction of privilege to the eldest sons of certain persons or to the possessors of so many millions of dollars, but merely the modelling of general institutions to facilitate the development of those capable of achieving it, and to make the prevailing conditions congenial to developed persons. If at times the circumstances of birth, or the chance possession of faculties and opportunities giving command of extra financial resources, may give one person a somewhat better prospect of development than another may have, we need not become fearful (as the Russian bolsheviks are) that this will necessarily lead to the reëstablishment of a narrow aristocracy or plutocracy. Only irrational envy could possibly find anything to resent in individual cases of special opportunity, so long as a sincere effort is maintained to keep the general road of advancement open, and to uphold a dominant standard of intrinsic personal development rather than one of birth or money. A man of sense is content to put up with occasional inevitable bendings and lapses of a dominant ideal, so long as the general reign of the ideal is not seriously threatened. Often a fanatical attempt to abolish the defects results in chaos amidst which the whole ideal is lost.

And so, as I have said, my ideal of a government fitted to the machine age is a fascistic one, with certain basic points so firmly embedded in its essential ideology that no laxity or latitude of administration could wholly nullify their operative force. Such points would include the government's control of industry in a manner designed to spread work and reward it adequately, and to eliminate the profit motive as much as possible in favour of the demand-supplying motive—a control probably amounting to ownership in the case of the largest industries—plus a system of pensions and benefits for the unemployed and unemployable. It would likewise include adequate public education both for industry and for the increased leisure of a mechanised era—an education not merely utilitarian, but liberal enough to develop the citizen's capacity for savouring life on a decently cultivated plane, so that his leisure will be that of a civilised person rather than that of a cinema-haunting, dance-hall frequenting, poolroom-loafing clod. No curb would be placed on private education, individual specialisation, or the establishment of higher and higher cultural standards on the part of persons and groups, in any case where such could be effected without upsetting the general economic equilibrium. There would be no place for the bolshevik's savage persecution of the liberal arts which he hates and calls "bourgeois", or for his callous discouragement of all the pure intellectual and aesthetic effort which aims not at the serving of material wants, but at the satisfaction of the profoundest innate and abstract elements of the human spirit. In the conduct of such a government I certainly think that a highly restricted franchise and office-holding eligibility would be absolutely essential—and I do not think it would be greatly resented if restriction followed logical and impartial lines for reasons well known to all. The idea that untrained persons can possibly understand the least thing about practical civil administration in an economically complex machine civilisation involving the most intricate engineering problems (a civilisation thrust on us by the blind historic flux, which we must accept whether we like it or not) is so grotesque and absurd that only blind custom based on a traditional and ineffable group stupidity can conceivably cause any sober adult to entertain it seriously in the disillusioned year of 1932. Democracy—as distinguished from universal opportunity and good treatment—is today a fallacy and impossibility so great that any serious attempt to apply it cannot be considered as other than a mockery and a jest. In primitive times the average man was more or less able to understand the nature if the governmental problems around him—understand, that is, what immediate measures would best effect his wishes in the long run, and what practical steps would, through a relatively simple chain of cause and effect, be able to ensure the successful adoption and maintenance of such measures. In the involved world of today no such comprehension is possible. Under the highly technicalised government which any large industrial nation must have, the citizen of only average information and intelligence can possess only the faintest idea of what the very simplest political principles mean, while he has not the remotest chance of grasping anything whatever about the more advanced and intricate problems of policy and administration. This applies, moreover, not only to the simple and uncultivated man, but to all economic and technical laymen, whether they be ploughmen or Sanscrit professors, street-sweepers or sculptors. For such uninformed persons to cast votes determining national measures, or even to fancy that they can guess what most of such measures are about, is a subject for uproarious cosmic laughter. And for such persons to be eligible for administrative office is something at which Tsathoggua and Yog-Sothoth must virtually split their sides in unrestrained and convulsive hilarity! Government "by popular vote" means merely the nomination of doubtfully qualified men by doubtfully authorised and seldom competent cliques of professional politicians representing hidden interests, followed by a sardonic farce of emotional persuasion in which the orators with the glibbest tongues and flashiest catch-words herd on their side a numerical majority of blindly impressionable dolts and gulls who have for the most part no idea of what the whole circus is about. The sacred common peepul indulge their sovereign democratic right to exercise the franchise in the control of their great commonwealth—and are saddled with a set of rulers whom they didn't really choose, and about whose real capacities and policies they know absolutely nothing . . . . and couldn't understand if they were told. And that goes for economically and administratively untrained poets, teachers, and artists as well as for garage helpers and plumbers' apprentices. A rational fascist government would have to change all that. Both office-holding and voting ought to be confined to such persons as can pass a really serious and practical examination in economics, history, sociology, business administration, and other subjects needed for the genuine comprehension of modern governmental problems. No one unable to pass such an examination—not the bluest-blooded boaster of sixteen heraldic quarterings, the richest millionaire manufacturer, or the profoundest mathematician or scientist, any more than the stupidest elevator-boy or furnace-cleaner—ought to have the least share in administering the affairs of the nation. But of course it would be the universally understood duty of the public (and free) educational system to give everyone (aside, perhaps, from the members of certain alien race-stocks whose heritage makes them unsuitable factors in the management of a nation of the given race-stock) an equal opportunity to qualify for the civic franchise. Nothing but a lack of inclination to specialise in this direction, or a mental capacity not above the average, would prevent any citizen from becoming a voter and potential office-holder. And so it goes. Of course, it would take an emergency—and probably an able leader such as the America of today cannot boast—to put such a programme of fascism into effect. That's the way Italy got the fascist government. There would, amusingly enough, be a tremendous amount of opposition from both ends of the present social scale—the enthroned plutocrats who would fight to save their increasingly dangerous money prerogatives, and the sentimental *amis du peuple* who would fight to save the illiterate masses a mockery of power which they don't know how to use and which never gets them anywhere anyhow. The fascist, obviously, must be prepared to be a decidedly unpopular character! All that could establish such a programme except by slow degrees is a series of governmental crises. If, for example, the bonus army were to overthrow the government and set up a government of its own with officials chosen from the ignorant mob, there would soon be a complete tangle and chaos, with such a breakdown of common utilities and necessities that some strong influence would have to intervene. A strong organisation of fascists, led by university economists and students of history and with official administrative posts filled with members of the old executive class (duly chastened by the proletarian menace and willing enough to work for any competent and responsible government, plutocratic or not), would then have a very good chance to sweep into power—backed by the militant and enthusiastic youths of the intelligent middle class. It would, of course, have to be more or less military in character, relying on force and stamina for a decade or more to keep both plutocrats and proletarians from ruining things. But once the ideology was established, its possibilities for effective and harmonious civil functioning would be enormous.

Nov. 8

As for the present situation in Texas—even if, as some suggest, the Ferguson following is not of the type to give the most stable sort of government, it is probably better to try them than to allow outside corporations to dominate the state against the interests of the native agriculturists. When ideal weapons are lacking, one must use whatever one has—and if a lesser evil can dispose of a greater one, there is every reason to be thankful. The first job of the Texan is clearly to crush outside plutocratic control. Then will come a time to look inward and see what can be done toward orderly and effective government. Tomorrow I shall be able to learn from the paper whether "Ma" triumphed over the Republican candidate.

Regarding the behaviour of police in Texas—I must confess myself completely dumbfounded and bewildered by the array of data you bring up! No wonder our lifelong and instinctive reactions to law-enforcement have been antipodally different—for truly, I never dreamed of the existence of such conditions as your reports indicate! It sounds like a piece of sensational and extravagant fiction in this day and age—and if it weren't that you bring up cases observed at first-hand to supplement the printed accounts, I'd say it was all a hoax on the part of the Gladewater editor. Indeed, I really did think so for a moment—for I read the cuttings before beginning your letter. From the text I assumed that the editor was merely following out a chronic "agin' the gov'munt" policy and exaggerating certain incidents into imaginary cases of persecution through suppression of vital provocative factors on the part of the alleged "victims"—a common practice, of course, among sensational and malcontent journalists such as those who wrote for the communist press. I would, I thought, be able to convince you that your impression of police persecution was an erroneous one fostered by continual and irresponsible newspaper propaganda—when lo! in your letter I found first-hand corroboration of all the apparent extravagances of the reporter and editor! All I can say is—I'll be damned! I never heard of such a thing before—do you mean to say that this is an habitual condition in Western Texas? It must be a kind of degenerate survival of the original pioneer disregard for law and order—for of course in a region where the ideology is antagonistic to regulation of conduct, it follows that the nominal forces of regulation will themselves be only loosely regulated despite their avowed purpose. The *instinct* for orderly conduct and mutual non-encroachment which is taken for granted in a long-settled community, and which applies to police as well as native citizenry at large, is probably absent. This of course brings up a curious point in comparative moods and deeply-seated attitudes on the part of residents of East and West. In regions of a settled tradition—England, Canada, the American Atlantic seaboard, etc.—the inviolability of the individual from physical attack is a principle of infinite strength and depth. The idea that each person has his legitimate place, and that he must never be molested or interfered with as long as he does not molest or interfere with others is ground into everyone from the cradle, and forms a spontaneous psychological background which persists and colours the whole tone of life. The raising of a hand or weapon to injure another—or intrusion of any sort upon a person who is quietly minding his own business—is a process so universally condemned and associated with the lowest types of the community that it cannot be indulged in lightly. Subconscious inhibitions operate against it—for it is impossible to form a conception of the native American as a casual assailant and interferer. The image of ready violence and lax disregard of traditional inhibitions is inextricably associated with such foreigners as Italians and Poles. It is not that the more insensitive people have any real *conscious* scruples against violence and lawlessness—it is simply that it seldom occurs to them to be violent or lawless. They haven't enough imagination to picture native Americans (except in cowboy moving pictures) being freely and casually violent and lawless. That is why tales of pioneer regions fascinate them so—as bits of glamourous and half-incredible historical mythology. Well, the application of all this to police problems would seem to be simply this—that police officers themselves are unconsciously held to certain approximate patterns of basically orderly and lawful conduct, even when corrupt in many ways. That is, they might accept graft from gambling and other joints, and might deal sharply with gangsters and other recognised members of the underworld; but it would take a hard psychological wrench to make it even occur to them to interfere with actually honest, law-abiding citizens quietly going about their own business. On the other hand—although I freely confess that it never definitely and vividly occurred to me before—I suppose that in a region where traditions of law and order have not had time to develop, the police feel the same freedom to do just about as they please as the rest of the citizenry do. Being without the settled instinct against violence and interference, they doubtless give caprice and malice free rein except when restrained by the prospect of tangible rewards—or the fear of punishment. It's a curious psychological problem—this difference between regional ideologies. We see it in comparing South and North America—the one, with its Latin heritage, takes naturally to revolutions and government by violence; the other, dowered with Anglo-Saxon feeling, does not. And so with West and East. It is impossible to explain the one in terms of the other. In this part of the country all complaints against the police regarding violence or interference come from radical and criminals. Radicals complain that their meetings are broken up, or that officers handle them roughly in strike riots—but of course one realises how little all this means. Criminals complain of occasional "third-degree" questionings, and undoubtedly some excesses do occur at more or less rare intervals—but this concerns only the known and hardened offender. In all my life, I never heard any such complaints against the police here (and I've talked with anti-government radicals, at that!) as those which appear to be so well justified in Texas. I am especially astonished at what seems to be a chronic feud between the Southwestern police and the poor and homeless, because in the East the exact reverse is true. Dozens of destitute persons are fed and lodged every night at police stations, while unfortunate drifters of every sort are allowed to roam unmolested as long as they behave themselves. During the depression even beggars are winked at—and once last summer (this is a good incident to remember as a symbol) I personally saw a down-and-outer beg successfully *from a policeman.* The officer dived down in his blue trouser pocket just like any well-intentioned citizen, and slipped the beggar a coin with a good-natured grin and some remark which I could not catch. All this may sound odd to you—but if it weren't a real and permanent condition I'd know it by this time. As you see, I knew so little of any other condition that I was all at sea regarding your attitude. And all reliable accounts indicate that police conditions are even better—in that there is less graft—in Great Britain and Canada. I'm not trying to paint an exaggerated picture, or to deny that graft-pull, uneven enforcement of petty laws affecting the criminal class, occasional over-zeal in dealing with stubborn crooks and radicals, etc., etc., can be found. These things, in varying quantity, always tend to crop out (though less so in England and Canada than here) in regulatory organisations, but are subject to constant repression. What I'm driving at is simply that there are no outrages or interferences with law-abiding persons, rich or poor, and that no breach of the peace is ever tolerated, be its source influential or humble. This condition is not hard to prove. Absence of complaints except from criminals and radicals is itself a significant thing, and one may further note that *the policeman is essentially a well-liked and popular figure* here, in England, and in Canada; not only among prosperous persons, but even in the slums where the most helpless and unfortunate elements dwell. Individual officers may be brusque and unpopular, but the general principle is unmistakable. Cases of police discipline for lax or hasty conduct are frequent—shewing how taken-for-granted an equitable programme is. Only the other day a motorcycle sergeant in

Providence was reduced two pay grades for the injudicious arrest of a motorist with whom he exchanged harsh words at a crossing—and it is significant to note that the arrested driver was a man so poor that he would not have been able to pay his fine if convicted. If you study the matter carefully, you will see that it isn't as remarkable as it seems. The human mind is a plastic and impressionable thing, and its responsiveness to heavily inculcated and freely accepted tradition is prodigious. Strange as it seems in view of the instability of most phases of human character, there are certain sets of understood inhibitions which various groups do accept and follow with remarkable fidelity and a complete sense of easy naturalness. Take the whole law-abiding attitude of settled countries, for one thing. Likewise, note the instinctive truthfulness and cognate qualities which West Point hammers into an army officer. Price could tell you about that—he's been through it. The instinctive incorruptibility of the London police force is another widely famous and perfectly authenticated thing. So, in the face of all this, the comparatively honest and completely non-interfering character of East-American police forces is not to be wondered at. It is a natural product of recognisable historic factors. The most notable exceptions are in the rural districts of those parts of the far South where the settled influence of the old tidewater civilisation did not extend. Florida in particular has its prison-gang troubles, although even there there is no molesting of law-abiding citizens. The prisoners who suffer are always genuine criminals properly sentenced—though of course that does not excuse inhumane treatment. I am glad that in the recently reported case the offender was suitably punished. But don't fancy that Florida, Alabama, and Mississippi represent the old colonial East of settled habits. They don't, for they are all semi-pioneering regions settled by second waves of migration from the oldest belt and sharing the relative instability of places where the social forms are altered to suit new conditions. You can often read of odd conditions in Florida or the inland South, but you wouldn't find them in Savannah or Charleston. Wherever the *European* spirit has had a chance to take root or develop unhampered by pioneering conditions, you will find a basic sense of civic regularity and personal non-encroachment utterly different from anything which a rough-and-ready environment can breed. It will spread later on to the pioneer regions—unless indeed decadence sets in first. That is one of the dangers of America's future—which reminds me of the recent bitter quip of a French sociologist, that America is the only country which as a whole has passed from barbarism to decadence without ever having been *civilised.*[4]

As outlined by you—and by the *Gladewater Journal*—the situation in Texas seems so extreme, and at the same time so deeply seated, that one is quite bewildered as to what to do about it. Some phases, as I said before, sound like the chapters from a novel (such as the policy of *agents provocateurs* in inciting Mexicans and negroes to rob a bank for the sake of shooting them and claiming the reward), and involve almost no precedent in American social and political experience. Of course it is perfectly clear that no such conditions ought for a moment to be condoned—indeed, the only question is *how* to put a stop to the phenomenon and to the causes behind it. First of all I think it ought to have serious publicity in order to bring wide public sentiment to the side of any attempt to abolish it. The *Gladewater Journal,* of course, is merely local in circulation, and does not reach those who ought to know of the conditions. Moreover, its style is (well-meaningly enough) so sensational and sentimental that an outside reader would suspect distorted propaganda in the absence of corroborative evidence. What is needed is a clear, factual report presenting the cases one after another without emotion and with enough verified detail to make corroboration easier for investigators. Such a report ought to go primarily into the hands of the most intelligent and cultivated Texans—persons with a certain amount of influence in determining the trend of state affairs. It is inconceivable that they could remain unmoved, or continue to support administrations tolerating such conditions, if *genuinely* convinced of the truth of these flagrant cases. That's the reformer's first business—to get the facts across in really scientific and effective fashion, and free from the atmosphere of sentimental propaganda. Do that, and I'll wager the really disinterested intellectual elements of Texas would gladly support a drastic programme of reform and police reorganisation. Nor should a certain amount of outside aid be scorned. The more the nation in general knows about the situation, the greater the psychological force behind reform. Great help in such cases is often afforded by certain nation-wide organisations like the American Civil Liberties Union. If the Ferguson government has won (I'll know tomorrow), and if it is really as interested in good government as it claims, there ought to be a splendid chance to start a shaking-up during the coming term. Really—with your intense feeling in the matter, it wouldn't be a bad idea for you to compile a brochure of flagrant cases for publicity purposes—that is, if you could arrange for its proper and effective distribution. If local conditions made it dangerous for you to appear as the author, you would not have to sign it—the contents would speak for itself. You could have the text re-written slightly to remove all identifying earmarks of style. However, I dare say the obstacles in the way of reform are tremendous. If no legal mechanism for improvement can be put in motion, it is possible that—considering the nature of the emergency and of the local conditions—some orderly but extra-legal secret organisation of force like the Vigilantes or the original Ku Klux Klan might be helpful in checking the unjustified encroachments of irresponsible officers. The Klan between 1866 and 1869 performed genuine miracles in freeing the South from the incredible saturnalia of misrule instituted by "carpet-baggers" and "scalawags"—a phenomenon which (though not typical because created by special transient conditions) possibly resembles the present Texas situation more closely than any other partial parallel. Reprisals against officers guilty of high-handed or inhumane procedure might prove a highly valuable corrective if constantly and adequately administered. It is strong medicine—but the case seems to require something strong! In the end, it is perhaps true that nothing but a gradual sociological evolution involving higher local standards of law, order, non-encroachment, and non-violence will ever make the regulating machinery as free from cruelty, unevenness, and high-handedness as the corresponding machinery of long-settled regions. That is a side of the matter for which no one is to blame—a matter of inevitable historic forces remediable only through time, thicker settlement, and the dying-out of frontier conceptions which accept frequent homicide, legal irregularity, and physical violence as matters of course. That state would now appear to be caught in the unpleasant gap betwixt pure frontierism—where the reign of violence is offset by a primitive sense of fairness which semi-settlement begins to undermine—and pure urbanism, where the loss of tribal chivalry is compensated for by the growth of a law-abiding and anti-violence ideal. Since movement backward in the time-stream is impossible, (notwithstanding the hopes of Gandhi and kindred mystics) all cultural forces ought to be bent toward a movement forward—toward higher standards of the sanctity of human life, the immunity of the individual from physical aggression, and the preservation at all times of a regularly administered civil order amidst which one-sided official action and ready violence either unofficial or official can have no tolerated place. Constant insistence on this ideal by writers and educators might have some slight effectiveness in hastening the historic evolution toward it. It would, by the way, be of considerable sociological value to compare conditions in Texas and its adjacent terrain with those of other regions in the corresponding stage of late pioneering—Arizona, Wyoming, etc. Of course, no two regions possess exactly the same problems; but approximate parallels often afford valuable suggestions. Anyway, I wish you luck in any crusade you may start—and hope meanwhile that the Fergusons may have their chance to do what they can.

Novr. 10

Well—I see "Ma" got in! Congratulations—and let's hope for some tangible progress in the liberation of Texas from industrial and financial carpetbaggers. Whether the nation at large will accomplish any real political evolution under the new administration remains to be seen. At least, the Democrats are less openly enslaved by the plutocratic fetish than the Republicans were. The trend of the age, as reflected in the sincere opinions of nearly all types of disinterested thinkers, is toward government oversight or control of large production enterprises, planned economy with minimisation of the profit motive, and automatic and mandatory relief of the unemployed and unemployable. This kind of thing is bound to come somehow, and it remains to be seen how far we get toward a transition in the next four years.

As for barbarism versus civilisation—you have given a magnificently graphic and comprehensive picture of barbarian life; indeed, I don't know when I've ever seen a more understanding and convincing summing-up of the oddly-motivated, shadow-haunted existence of our primitive forbears. You certainly seem to have no Rousseau-like illusions about the noble children of Nature in the happy Arcadia of the Golden Age! That you can still wish you had been born a barbarian in spite of your clear realisation of the life involved, is one more proof of the inexplicable diversity of human tastes. To me, the few possible advantages of barbarism seem infinitely overshadowed by the overwhelming mass of hopeless lacks and disadvantages—so that I feel sure I would never have found enough to live for in primitive times, except perhaps as a history-chanting bard or mystery-making shaman. And even these possibly tolerable situations would have formed only a pallid and unsatisfactory ghost of what a mature civilisation might give. The civilised man is sensitive to a million phases of pleasurable intellectual and aesthetic experience to which the barbarian is blind and callous. By acquiring civilisation he gains far more than he loses. No—I could never have been content in any ancient environment other than that of Greece or Rome. I can understand Graeco-Romans and feel as one of them—but barbarians (much as I enjoy reading of them as dramatic factors in history) are essentially alien to my sphere of comprehension. I admire many of their qualities, but cannot identify myself with them. However, I believe that many persons share your point of view either consciously or unconsciously.

Your various sidelights on the desperadoes of old—as well as on some of later times—proved as usual highly interesting. This vestigial persistence of an early phase of social organisation is a very fascinating thing from the point of view of panoramic history, and occasionally brings out unusual qualities of human character. The resistance of John Wesley Harden to prison conditions is certainly a most notable instance of determination and independence, and makes one regret that some of those "bad men" could not have had their energies steered into more fruitful channels. The stuff of great men was undoubtedly wasted, in many cases, in lives of meaningless slaughter and futile plunder gained only to be lost. I read the account of Cole Oglesby and his brothers with additional interest because of your close contacts with the family.[5] I'm certainly glad your arguments with the clan didn't progress any further than they did! It must give one an odd sensation to read of the dramatic deeds and end of a person whom one has long known at close range. As for the relative severity of society toward offenders of this type and toward offenders whose depredations are committed more smoothly under the cloak of law—while I deplore the tolerance of the latter, I can't say that I find the difference in treatment wholly unjustified. These desperadoes endanger human life as well as mere property, and are general public nuisances and obstructions in addition to the harm they cause their victims. Clearly, they require immediate elimination first—but of course I regret that the elimination process is not continued to include the subtler and more legalised criminal as well. Probably such an extension will occur in the next few years, for sentiment toward that end has been growing for over a generation. War against the racketeer—who occupies a middle ground betwixt the open highway man and the law-cloaked promoter or financier—may form the beginning of a slow drive to rid society of the type of operator who collects resources through smooth coercion and manipulation. Russia is trying valiantly to get rid of this latter type.

As for the duel—it gave me quite a kick to learn that the New Orleans man who fought the governor's brother after an argument over a newsboy scrap was a relative of yours! I read all about that duel in a book on New Orleans and its traditions published in 1886, and recall how trivial the causes of many of the affrays were. I also recall mention of your relative's Nicaraguan connexions—though details escape me, since I crammed so much New Orleans lore into my head during the brief fortnight of my sojourn. I spent most evenings at the public library, and also read through a very ample book (the one mentioning this duel) lent me by the genial proprietor of my hotel. The triviality of most duels' causes is a good testimony of the essential naiveté, childishness, and artificiality of the whole public mind all over the world until comparatively recent times. This triviality—which made the taking of human life a light matter joined to the most frivolous issues—was undoubtedly one of the chief causes of the bad repute into which duelling eventually came. I am still inclined to wonder whether the entire abolition of the institution and its principle is wholly advantageous. Disregarding the silly causes over which men often fought duels in the past—and still do in some Latin countries—there are some grave personal injuries in life—involving the dignity of the spirit and hardly atonable through the processes of law—which would seem externally and unalterably to demand some drastic expiation in an orderly and harmonious way among gentlemen of sensitive organisation and high cultivation. Slum denizens and foreigners maintain the folkways of the primitive, and lightly and indiscriminately punch or slash their feelings into equilibrium; but responsible men cannot do this in a settled and complex society. In the age of the duel they had a dignified and legitimate catharsis for such feelings of outrage as are too deep and powerful for expression in indirect and sublimated ways; but today such an avenue is lacking—so that strong feelings have to fester, and occasionally crop out in dreary, calculative revenges or in those relatively rare and always ungraceful crimes of violence which sometimes blaze out on the front pages of newspapers. It may, though, be remarked that with an advancing comprehension of life and its ultimately meaningless values, our sense of deep and inexpiable outrage—and our belief in the basic worth or essential meaning of revenge, reprisal, atonement, satisfaction, and the like—enormously diminishes. What a primitive man—or even a man of the 19th century—took as a grave affront or unpardonable injury, a sophisticated man of 1932 often takes as a joke, a trifle, an irrelevant incident, or a mere display of silliness and ignorance on the part of the alleged affronter or injurer. There is, however, among vigorous and non-decadent peoples a certain irreducible minimum of injury-forms which cannot be dismissed as trivial or meaningless. (This is so, because when a race loses the natural resistance expressed in the retention of such a minimum, it is no longer able to withstand encroaching influences and becomes a satellitic or parasitic race surviving only through slyness or sycophancy.) On account of this minimum, still valid for most Western European races, the total abolition of the duel is to my mind a not wholly unmitigated blessing. The only duel in my family of which I have any knowledge was fought in 1829, in upper New York State, by my father's maternal grandfather William Allgood (of the Allgoods of Nunwick and Brandon White House, near Hexham—an old Roman station not far south of Hadrian's Wall—in Northumberland)—who was born in England in 1792, graduated from Oxford, and came to the U.S. by way of Canada in 1817. The affray, as reported by family tradition, was the outgrowth of unpleasant remarks on national differences (memories of the War of 1812, in which the Americans vainly tried to conquer and annex Canada, were then fresh in Northern N.Y.) exchanged with a citizen of Rochester. Pistols were used, both participants were slightly grazed, and everybody appears to have been satisfied, since no more of the matter had been reported to posterity. It appears that my forbear was the challenger in this matter—though not without reasonable provocation. He died a peaceful natural death in 1840. I am aware of the comparatively harmless character of French duelling, and can imagine how the Creole blades of New Orleans must have felt when the more savage frontier Americans (all of whom, at first, they called "Kaintocks", from their memories of Kentucky flatboatmen) began to introduce more sanguinary methods. Knife duels in the dark are quite famous in frontier literature—Bierce's "Middle Toe of the Right Foot" being based on such a practice.[6] The Comanche duel certainly sounds like an ultimate refinement of sadism, and I don't wonder that it failed to win popularity among white men. I'm certainly glad that the bully you mention refused to accept your father's challenge to such an encounter! I've read of the Houston-Johnston duel. No doubt you've seen the fine equestrian statue of Gen. Johnston on a mound near the entrance of the Metairie Cemetery in New Orleans.

About the Indians—they certainly must have had wide racial differences in different parts of the New World. We shall probably never know the precise circumstances of the first peopling of the Americas, but it is pretty well agreed that there were no actually autochthonous inhabitants. Whatever men were here, came from Asia or Oceanica on the west or Europe-Africa on the east. Most of the early arrivals were clearly Asians of Mongol affiliations, but different types found today or deposited on Mayan monuments conclusively prove the existence of other strains. The nature of Mayan-Aztec art suggests to many a vague connexion with Indo-China and Burma—the culture of Angkor, etc.—and it is possible that some diffusion of blood across the Pacific in canoe migrations from island to island occurred in addition to the universally recognised migration of the bulk of the inhabitants across Bering Strait. It is also possible that a great archipelagic civilisation of the Polynesian race once existed in the Pacific and transmitted both blood and cultural elements to America. On the east coast, I feel certain that some elements from the old world must have lodged in very small quantity. The hawklike quasi-Semitic physiognomy of the eastern Indian has always suggested to my mind a possible admixture of Phoenician blood from Tyrian and Carthaginian galleys swept across the ocean by storms. Likewise, one can never tell how many northern sea-rovers may have been cast alive upon the shore of the unknown west. I don't know whether one could safely say the eastern Indian was superior in biological capacity to the western—for the Pueblo and kindred cultures of the southwest probably surpassed anything the east could boast, and of course the Mexican-Central American cultures were vastly above any other native growths on the continent—were, in fact, virtually true civilisations. More—the Indians of the far northwest—Haidas and Tlingits of British Columbia and southern Alaska—are of an exceedingly high type. Compared with these, the Indians of the east were relatively primitive, although the Iroquois and the Mobilian group of tribes of the far south showed signs of being about to develop settled cultures above those of their neighbours. The Iroquois and their near kin undoubtedly had a culture of far greater depth and stamina than that of the Algonquins, though there does not appear to have been any racial difference. The tribes of New England were purely Algonquin, although the Iroquois encroached on what are now western Massachusetts and Vermont. The Iroquois were always untamable, though some of the Algonquins could be reduced to slavery. Indian slaves, however, could never be broken as completely as negroes; and were always considered as somewhat dangerous to have. Most of those in New England were sold or traded in the West Indies early in the 18th century. If any Indians were or are culturally inferior to any others, I'd say they were the nomadic plains tribes—or else such northern Algonquins as the Ojibways, who have so little sense of the future and of practical preparations that they allow winter to find them houseless and defenceless against the cold—hibernating and half-starving in snow-banked wigwams until the next spring, when they once more emerge and soon forget that they must again undergo what they have been through. As reckoned among the race-stocks of the world, the Indian is certainly not inferior. Neither, for that matter, is the Mongolian race as a whole. It is simply our reaction against the alien and the unaccustomed—together with the circumstance that our immigrant specimens are generally of a low type—which causes us to look down on the Chinese and Japanese. Both of these races, as rationally judged by their history, literature, philosophy, and art, are among the superior biological forms of the planet—and no one who is acquainted with their better classes is ever able to retain that feeling of repulsion which the ordinary American, Australian, or New-Zealander usually feels. Amusingly enough, there is a reciprocal feeling of repulsion on the part of high-grade Chinese—it being the opinion of the typical cultivated mandarin that Aryans are inherently vulgar, loud-voiced, coarse-mannered, and ugly to boot, with their leprously white faces, disgusting hairiness, and grotesquely long noses! Japanese do not seem to share that feeling—being indeed closer to the white race as a result of some prehistoric admixture. Of course the Mongolian race has its degenerate offshoots just as the white race has—these including the stunted tribes of the Siberian steppes, and the Esquimaux of the arctic. The Indian, however, is as biologically fine as the best Chinese type—with perhaps some added qualities in the way of stamina. If Europeans had delayed their discovery of the New World for another thousand years, they would have found another great civilisation—a civilisation utterly unlike any other in existence. The world stream of culture has really been the loser through the premature cutting off of spontaneous and unhampered Indian evolution. Taking mankind as a whole, there are just two race-stocks whose biological variations in the direction of the primitive, and whose consistent lack of spontaneous intellectual and cultural growth unmistakably stamp them as inferior. These are the *australoid,* including Australian blackfellows, the extinct (as a pure stock) Tasmanians, some Melanesians, and the black tribes of Southern India; and the *negro,* including all offshoots of the thick-lipped, flat-nosed, kinky-haired, gorilla-like type whose historic habitat is central and western Africa. Of these the *australoid* (who even has the same heavy eye-brow-ridges of the extinct Neanderthaloid semi-humans) is unquestionably the lower, but both represent most unmistakably stocks which branched off from the main stem at a definitely pre-human stage, and which did not develop as far as the dominant stock which ultimately matured and divided into Mongols, various Caucasian races, and other subtle shadings and mixtures. During the past year the eminent ethnologist Sir Arthur Keith has revived some older theories regarding the origin of races—suggesting that many race-divisions took place at comparatively early evolutional stages, and that the similarities of some stocks are not due to a recent common origin, but to an approximately *parallel evolution* after a very early—even pre-human—cleavage. He now believes that many of the primitive skeletons like the Java, Pekin, Piltdown, etc. men may represent the ancestors of certain fully human races instead of representing (as hitherto supposed) merely stunted offshoots. But it is not yet time to pass dogmatically on points like this. We haven't discovered enough to be positive. Keith now suspects that the Java pithecanthropus may be a direct ancestor of the *australoid*—but is very properly unwilling to be positive about it.

Novr. 11

About Ulster—I'm afraid I am on the other side of the fence from you, because I can't see but what the sentiments of the majority of the inhabitants ought to be respected. It is merely academic and theoretical to complain that the ancestors of those inhabitants were high-handedly settled in the country 300 years ago at the expense of the proper natives. To unscramble all the injustices of history would be to plunge the world into meaningless chaos—am I to be kicked out of Rhode Island because my ancestors kicked the Narragansetts and Wampanoags out in the 17th century? Such reasoning is purely sentimental, and irrelevant to present realities. Whatever was done in the reign of James the First, the existing Protestant inhabitants of Ulster are not to blame for it. They were born—through no will or fault of theirs—where they now are; and no one can sanely dispute the fact that they are, more than any others could possibly be said to be, the legitimate inhabitants of the region at the present time. As such, their own wishes form the supreme criterion to be observed in determining their governmental allegiance. They very sensibly prefer to preserve the civilisation and institutions to which they are accustomed, and it would be a barbarous enormity of the worst sort to throw them forcibly into the clutches of the Free State—with its hostile national policy, and its disastrously Quixotic attempts to foist a romantically revived dead language on the people. They ought to be allowed to join it; but to allow the settled civilisation of Belfast and Londonderry to be dragged away from their inhabitants would be as great a crime as those earlier and reversed culture-substitutions which the Free-Staters so continually—and quite properly—condemn. If I were an Ulsterman I would fight tooth and nail to keep my native land within the purely English-speaking civilisation to which it now irretrievably belongs . . . . and indeed, the people of Ulster were actually on the point of doing just that—even against the edict of England itself—when the crash of the Great War deflected and patched up the 1914 crisis. If the Free-Staters can't be contented with a free hand in all the parts of Ireland which the members of their own culture-group actually inhabit, they certainly do not deserve a continuance of the sympathy which the general outside world has hitherto extended them so freely. Their claim to Scottish-Presbyterian Ulster is almost as absurd as the sentimental claim of the Zionist Jews to essentially Arab-Moslem Palestine. As for India and Gandhi—the Hindoo culture is about as sloppily decadent a mess as ever degenerated from an Aryan civilisation, and the political incapacity of the people is such as to produce complete chaos if British rule were ever withdrawn. The place is only a damned nuisance, for the bother of ruling it probably overbalances whatever commercial advantage its possession brings; but the trouble is that some other powerful nation—probably Soviet Russia—would gobble it up and use its strength in a potentially hostile way if it were ever cut adrift as some would like to see it. Same way with the Philippines—giving them "independence" merely means ultimate delivery to Japanese control. So my hope is that our race will hang on to these Asiatic pivots as long as it is practicable to do so—not because they are of any immediate good, but because their relinquishment means increased power for possible enemies. However—I certainly have a vast personal admiration for the stamina of old Gandhi. I can see how he must look at these things, and can sentimentally sympathise with his idyllic conceptions even while realising that he forms a potential peril to civilisation. If he can help to soften some of the cruel cleavages of the Hindoo caste system—as he is certainly trying valiantly enough to do—he will have amply justified his existence in spite of all the trouble he has caused in other fields.

As for literature—French and English—I don't quite concur with you on all points. While I believe that French *poetry* can never even begin to compete with English, and while I likewise feel very strongly that no Latin can ever equal a Nordic in matters of phantasy and mysticism, I think that in some matters the French actually excel us. In serious fiction, for example, Anglo-Saxon authors are too prone to be content with surface glamour and conventional views of life; while Frenchmen dive down and analyse and produce novels which seem, at their best, like actual fragments of reality. I could never feel any pervasive sense of reality in any important English novel, whereas Balzac seems to lift the curtain upon a vital and actual world. Gautier is sometimes tedious—but how could you find him so in "La Morte Amoreuse", "Avatar", and "One of Cleopatra's Nights"?[7] Flaubert is a genuine master who can never be excelled in certain directions—and I think that de Maupassant's gloom is only about the average amount which pervades human life. De Maupassant is probably the greatest short story writer of all time—he never truckled to the cheap clamour for artificial and insipid happy endings. Baudelaire, in his narrow special field, is a Titan. Zola presented life with tremendous vitality, Anatole France belongs with the classics as a mordant and sanifying ironist, while the keen intellect of Remy de Gourmont cleared away many a cobweb in its day. I could never get interested in Dumas, for he seems to me rather cheaply theatrical and melodramatic. I never get the illusion that his characters are alive, as I do with Balzac. Rabelais—despite his enormous repute as a classic—I must admit that I have never read. Some day, even though his work may have its repellent side, I must repair this defect in my education. The greatest writers of fiction were probably the Russians of the 19th century; but unfortunately they deal with a neurotic race and culture so unlike those of the Western World that we cannot grasp their full sweep except through objective study. Dostoievsky and Turgeniev are probably the greatest. Many exalt Tolstoy, but I find him too full of maudlin mawkishness to command sympathy. The writers of Scandinavia stand very high, and are among the greatest of all analysts of the human mind and motives. Ibsen—Strindberg—Lagerlof—Hamsun—and the late Georg Brandes was almost the greatest living critic of his day. Modern Scandinavians have become adult along with the rest of civilisation, hence realise that there is more significant drama in the hidden operation of the human spirit than in any phenomena of the external world. As for English literature—I think its prime glory is its *poetry*—Chaucer, Spenser, Shakespeare, Milton, Coleridge, Shelley, Keats, etc. Fielding, Sterne, and Smollett are probably the greatest novelists—though Thackeray and Meredith aren't bad. Scott has his points, but never seems very lifelike to me. Dickens I can't endure, for his characters are no more than parodies and abstractions. Galsworthy—who has just won the Nobel prize—is very solid, though I cannot help finding him often tedious. Joseph Conrad—a Pole by birth—is infinitely powerful. G. B. Shaw will be remembered—but in general I doubt if the present age will be looked back upon as great. I don't care for Kipling—his style becomes hopelessly dependent on artificial mannerisms. As for "The Vicar of Wakefield"—I concur with you in despising the sub-human spinelessness of Dr. Primrose, and have often reflected how such exaltations of flabby meekness form a *reductio ad absurdum* of the whole misfit Christian ideal and tradition. The trouble is not with Goldsmith—who drew a certain type of person quite faithfully (albeit, perhaps, with some exaggeration) from Nature—but with the inherent hypocrisy of mankind, which permits of the nominal worship of an ideal and way of life that any self-respecting Aryan would be ashamed to act upon. Granting the truth of Christianity—which was the custom in Goldsmith's day—there could be no other course than an acceptance in full of the craven humility of the Vicar as the highest possible type of human conduct. The whole thing is plainly outlined in the Bible—and if one accepts that one has to accept the ideals it teaches and demands. Of course, the way Christians commonly hedge around the matter is to say that such meekness is indeed the supremely perfect type of conduct, which all men should strive for, but that most human beings are too imperfect to live up to the ideal. Thus they pretend to exalt something they really despise, and pretend to despise a normal type of manly conduct which they really venerate. They preach other-cheek-turning—yet would ostracise a man who really tried to put it into practice. That's what comes when a virile race, moulded by the worship of warlike gods and governed by an ancient Teutonic code of honour based on personal inviolability and respect for unbroken strength and liberty, allows itself to be bamboozled into adopting an alien and unsuitable slave religion spawned in the decaying Orient to meet the emotional needs of a crushed nation of cringing and sycophantic Semites. I have no use for such duality and pretence, and believe that the Western World ought to repudiate the Christian delusion openly and honestly. Many individuals, indeed, are doing so—in fact, virtually no philosophic thinkers now call themselves Christians—but the stolid legions of the unthinking continue to wear the misfit label, as unconscious as their forbears of the grotesque hypocrisy and mendacity involved. I'm glad, by the way, that a fortunate chance allowed you to express your opinion of the spineless ideal in school without suffering for it.

About cold weather—yes, my extreme sensitiveness and set of physical symptoms certainly are puzzling and extraordinary. Some day I'll have to trek equatorward for good, I suppose, and settle in some place like St. Augustine. Sorry your heart is liable to capricious spells—and trust you are judicious in avoiding the sort of overexertion and excitement which invites trouble. The incident of the theatre seizure certainly proves your devotion to sports—which reminds me that it's really too bad you can't get to see more of the major athletic events which interest you so enthusiastically. Hope your favourite side won in the football game you mention.

Well, I certainly have covered a lot of paper! I trust you can pardon my verboseness and boresomeness, as well as my occasional expression of sincere opinions which differ from your own. As a matter of fact, all my favourite major correspondents are persons with whom I differ on some subject or another—usually many subjects—so that my long letters always tend to fall more or less into the debate class. Just now—or rather, after I get some less agreeable work done—I'm preparing to demolish the critical position of a chap who despises weird literature and exalts smart sophistication—and after that I shall tackle a fellow who retains a more or less sheepish belief in the occult. Hammering toward truth amidst a chaos of conflicting opinions is something which has always seemed to me especially fascinating.

The failure of *Strange Tales* is certainly most unfortunate. Clark Ashton Smith loses $500.00 by it—for he had stories accepted ahead amounting to that value—unless he can place the same material elsewhere. But I trust that good old *Weird*—and the *Magic Carpet*—will continue to carry on.[8] Best of luck to you in your writing!

With every good wish,

Yrs most cordially and sincerely,

H P L

P.S. Second magazine rights to my "Erich Zann"—in the Hammett anthology—have just been purchased by the London Evening Standard.

[P.P.S.] Late news—Derleth has just heard from O'Brien that his "Five Alone" will make the 1933 Best Short Stories.[9]

Notes

1. "A sound mind in a sound body." The quotation is not found in Horace but in Juvenal, *Satires* 10.356.

2. FBL, "The Black Druid" (*WT,* July 1931); Francis Flagg (pseud. of Henry George Weiss), "The Picture" (*WT,* February–March 1931); FBL, "A Visitor from Egypt" (*WT,*

September 1931); CAS, "A Rendezvous in Averoigne" (*WT,* April–May 1931); Henry S. Whitehead, "Passing of a God" (*WT,* January 1931); Flagg, "The Jelly-Fish" (*WT,* October 1931); CAS, "The Phantoms of the Fire" (*WT,* September 1931); HPL, "The Strange High House in the Mist" (*WT,* October 1932); Whitehead, "The Black Beast" (*Adventure,* 15 July 1932) and "Cassius" (*Strange Tales,* November 1932); HPL, "In the Vault" (*WT,* April 1932); FBL, "The Horror in the Hold" (*WT,* February 1932); Whitehead, "Black Terror" (*WT,* October 1932) and "Mrs. Lorriquer" (*WT,* April 1932). CAS's "The Venus of Azombeii" (*WT,* June–July 1932) and "The Gorgon" (*WT,* April 1932) were listed in "Stories ranking third"; "The Testament of Athammaus" (*WT,* October 1932) was not listed.

3. Robert Hazard (1635–1710) was HPL's great-great-great-great-great-grandfather. He had a house so large that he was once asked whether he rode from front to back door on horseback.

4. The remark—"America is the only nation in history which miraculously has gone directly from barbarism to degeneration without the usual interval of civilization"—has been attributed to Georges Clemenceau (1841–1929), French journalist and politician, and prime minister of France (1906–09, 1917–20).

5. HPL is commenting on a clipping sent by REH (see p. 453). REH, however, conflates two related families. Elbert (Cole) Oglesby was killed 18 October 1932 when he drew a gun on an Oklahoma City policeman seeking to question him about a stolen car; his death was undoubtedly the subject of the clipping. He had been indicted for murder in Abilene, Texas, in 1928 and spent time in the jail there, and was also a suspect in a bank robbery in Columbia, Mississippi, in January 1932. Weldon Oglesby, younger brother of Cole, was sentenced on 23 September 1930 to life in prison for a holdup in Tulsa. Ernest Oglesby, Cole's cousin (their fathers were brothers), was sentenced to two years in the Texas penitentiary in 1928 for a theft in Stephens County. He was in the penitentiary at Huntsville as of the U.S. Census enumeration on 24 April 1930, but a news article on 29 August of that year reports that he had engineered the escape of himself and three others from the Wilbarger County jail at Vernon, stating that he was "under sentences totalling 90 years assessed in various West Texas counties." He was convicted of killing an officer in Oklahoma in 1933 and executed in 1934 (see letter to HPL, 24 March 1934). The mother of Cole and Weldon was an older sister of the notorious "Newton boys," bank and train robbers, and the Oglesbys may have occasionally joined their cousins in criminal activities. Cole Oglesby and Joe Newton, for instance, were convicted in Eastland, Texas, of burglary and theft in 1930.

6. Ambrose Bierce, "The Middle Toe of the Right Foot," *Tales of Soldiers and Civilians* (1891); *LL* 91.

7. "La Morte amoureuse" (translated as "Clarimonde") and "One of Cleopatra's Nights" can be found in Lafcadio Hearn's translation of Gautier's *One of Cleopatra's Nights and Other Fantastic Romances* (1882; *LL* 346). "Avatar" can be found in *Tales Before Supper,* trans. Myndart Verelst [pseud. of Edgar Saltus] (1887; *LL* 347).

8. *WT* lasted until 1954, but *Magic Carpet* (*Oriental Stories* retitled in January 1933) ended with the January 1934 issue.

9. AWD's "Five Alone" was on the Roll of Honor in O'Brien's *The Best Short Stories of 1933* (1933).

[74] [nonextant postcard by REH]

[c. November–December 1932]

[75] [TLS]

[December 1932]

Dear Mr. Lovecraft:

Having read your latest letter with the greatest interest and appreciation, I'll try to answer it now, after having been delayed several times, owing to various circumstances.

I'm glad nothing I've said has proved offensive. Force of habit often makes me sound more aggressive and dogmatic in argument than I intend. This comes from having spent considerable time in rough-and-ready environments, where arguments are likely to be riddled with biting personalities, loud and arrogant assertions, and profanity. In such arguments it is impossible to win one's point by logic alone; in self-defense one is forced to adopt an aggressive attitude. This attitude is likely to become a habit, intruding into discussions where it is out of place. I've seen arguments decided, not on their actual merits, but simply because one contestant could yell louder than the others. Such disputes, also, are pretty liable to turn into fights. I'm sorry to say that it isn't among working men alone that I've encountered an irritating attitude in debate; I've discovered this attitude in several so-called intellectuals, who seemed more anxious to show up their opponents as fools, than to reach any logical conclusion. My method, in the teeth of such circumstances, has always been to avoid debate as much as possible, and when unavoidable, to be as tough as my opponents. This has brought about the unconscious mannerisms I deplored at the beginning of this paragraph. So if at times I seemed unduly agressive and vindictive, please believe that it is unconscious and due to the causes noted above.

Your attitude regarding the relative merits of the physical and mental seems very well balanced, to me. For myself, it is impossible for me to divorce man's mental life from his physical. After all, mind itself is a physical process, so far as we know, depending upon the workings of the material matter of the physical brain, fed in turn by glands, veins, and cellular matter, all of the earth earthly. "Safeguarding the fruits of consciousness"—I quote from your recent letter; that's a splendid phrase to my mind. And the fruits of consciousness are hardly more mental than physical, to my mind. Consciousness itself is a physical process, as far as I can see, depending, at least, on things physical. The finest intellect in the world is dependent on the slushy grey stuff of the brain, which in turn depends upon the physical skull that locks it in, the hands and feet that obey its instructions, and the mouth, teeth and intestines that feed it. That same splendid intellect can be destroyed in a twinkling by the impact of a club or stone against its bony case. And the club or stone can be wielded by an ignoramus, an idiot or an ape. If the physical is bounded, limited, guided or destroyed by the mental, the same can be said in the other way, though in some cases to a lesser extent.

As for relative strength—I can't to save my neck see why I should despise, neglect or ignore my body because a bull, elephant or electric dynamo is stronger than it. I realize that I could never equal the strength of a bull, yet my own comparatively puny thews have stood me in good stead time and again, against both men and animals. Yesterday, for instance, I helped shift a load of hay-bales from one barn to another, helped load a wagon with corn, and later did the bulk of unloading and storing fifteen hundred pounds of ground feed. All this work could have been done more easily and quickly with machinery, but I didn't have any. The fact that a gorilla could shoulder a heavy sack of grain and carry it to its proper place in the barn easier than I could, didn't alter my problem any—that of getting the stuff stored. When I escort a girl through the crush of a football crowd, the knowledge that a rhinoceros could charge through the throng and clear a way for her more effectively than I could, doesn't mean that I'm going to let her get squshed, as long as I have shoulders and elbows. Once I outran a mad bull in a short sprint to a rail fence. Now a jackrabbit could have reached the fence quicker than I, and a monkey could have climbed it a sight easier. But my own human muscles did the job well enough to haul me out of reach just as he reached for me. This may seem like a trivial example, but it was important to me. A foot and a half of bull's horn through the guts is no trifle to anybody. If a belligerent drunk announces that he is going to kick my head into the next county, I know very well that a trip-hammer could flatten him quicker than I, but that doesn't have much bearing on the case.

What I'm trying to show, is that every day, men on farms, ranches, and in oil-fields, mines, factories, small towns and country villages, are confronted with problems that require muscles as well as minds to solve. This is a matter that purely mental workers can easily lose sight of, and I think is partly the reason for the contempt with which the physical is looked upon by such persons as you mention holding to "fanatical anti-physicalism". I've known a few of these persons, mainly among the young intelligensia, or however it is spelled.

As for the importance of physical power—there is an element of vanity in the developing of a strong body, but no more than there is in the developing of a fine mind. The true athlete does not develope his muscles and co-ordination simply because of vanity, but because of pure love of the game. Strength is more or less relative, and like intellect, can not be defined by any definite limits, or measured by any accurate gauge. Of two strong men, each generally exceeds the other in some manner. One can lift more, the other can break a thicker stick, for instance. For example, my best friend and myself; (I trust this does not sound as if I were holding up myself for a strong man; I am not, particularly; I am just using this matter as an example.) My friend has a more powerful grip than I, but I can strike a much harder blow than he can; he can take a harder punch in the belly than I, but I can take more on the jaw than he. It could not be said that either of us was the other's definite superior in physical make-up. So if a man is motivated by personal vanity, in desiring to strut and swagger over other men, it is futile for him to waste his time in physical development. Regardless of how strong he becomes, he will always find men who will outclass him in one way or another. It is foolish for a man to be arrogant or conceited simply because he can lift more weight or break thicker sticks than the average man; it is foolish for him to develop himself simply because of the promptings of his vanity. But it is not foolish for him to wish to feel capable of standing on his feet and holding his own in any company. A man need not wish to feel superior to other men, but he should at least feel himself their equal. It is not particularly conceited on his part to wish to be able to always hold up his end of the game, regardless of what it may be; to do as much work as the next man; to be able to always do his part, without having to call for help; and to be able to help some weaker mortal, if it should be necessary; and to be able to stand up and take his own part against encroachment.

We live, after all, in a physical world. Few of us are fortunate enough to be able to move in a mainly mental sphere. This is especially true of this part of the country.

Humanity, as you say, means mind. But mind again rests on physical forces. In your example, the weak man who harnesses bulls, engines and stronger men, is still dependent on the physical. It is not his brain alone which harnesses these powers; he has the advantage of all the brains that have gone before him. And not alone of the brains, but of the millions and millions of grasping, groping, toiling human hands that, with their guiding brains, built slowly the edifice upon the summit of which he sits with his fingers on the reins of the lightnings. Without these hands he were helpless, no less than without the aid of the brains before him. Without the living hands that do his bidding he is helpless. He controls machines built by machines, but first these machines took shape under the clumsy, toiling fingers of flesh and veins and bone. Mind can not be divorced from the flesh. Our whole structure of progress rests, in the last analysis, on the hands of the unknown workers, from the engineers in the most modern factory back through the dim ages to the first ape-man squatting laboriously over the half-formed flint. Mind without Force is useless as Force without Mind; to me they seem inseparable. If the brain guides the hand, the hand carries out the instructions of the brain. Now a man born without hands or feet might become the greatest power of the modern world; yet he would be simply employing the hands and feet of others, and of all those gone before him.

And so I do not feel that I am wasting my time when I work at weights and punching bags to increase my wind and harden my muscles. I live among people who work with their hands. If the writing game continues to deflate, it's probable that I'll have to earn my living by some sort of hard labor, since I am not trained in any trade or profession. Last summer men died like flies in the grain fields of the Southwest and Midwest. They were men who were unused to such work; they were unfit. Their wind was bad, their muscles flabby. Confronted by the choice of working at back-breaking labor in the blazing sun, or starving, they chose the work, and died, simply because they were unfit physically. Many of those men were superior mentally to the farm-hands working imperturbably beside them. But no man knows, in this physical world, when he'll be called upon to demonstrate his right to survive, not by the craft and knowledge stored in his brain, but by the sinews and springy bones of his material body.

Therefore I feel that if it is possible, a man should try to give himself as much strength as is possible, as well as developing his mind to the utmost. The average modern man may never need such strength; but he might need it bad some time. As an example (one of many such I might cite), the friend of mine mentioned above, of the powerful grip. Last summer he was working on the high-way, and at the time was helping build a barb-wire fence. While holding a wire against a post with one hand, and driving a staple with the other, the taut strand snapped suddenly, between his hand and the post. You can imagine the result, if you have ever seen the ghastly havoc barbed-wire can wreak on flesh, animal or human. But my friend escaped unhurt, simply because he was strong enough to retain his grip on that broken wire and keep it from being ripped through his hand. The powerful recoil jerked him backward and almost off his feet, but he held on—a feat which no ordinary man would have been capable of. He didn't have time to let go cleanly, of course. Hold on was the only thing to do. If his grip had been just a little weaker, the barbs would have been jerked through his fingers, mangling his hand in a way not pleasant to think about. Again, the father of another friend, shooting an oil-well, having lowered the nitro-can, was horrified to see it shoot out of the shaft, having been expelled by a gas-pocket. There was but one thing to be done, and he did it. He grasped the "can" firmly in his arms in midair, and held on, cradling it with his body. That took quick thinking, but it also took unusual bodily strength. Had the "can" escaped his arms, struck against the timbers or fallen on the floor, the impact would have set it off and blown to bits the rig and everybody in it. It's a wonder it didn't anyway. But there was one of many cases where a keen mind tied to powerful muscles saved human lives.

I think it was Brisbane[1] who deriding sports and physical development, spoke of the uselessness of athletics, since anything a human being could do, could be outdone by an animal. He would not box since a mule could kick harder than a man could hit, nor run a footrace because a rabbit could outrun a man, nor wrestle because a python could crush any human wrestler. To be consistent he should not eat because a hog could eat more than he, or drink because a camel could drink more, nor sleep because a hibernating bear could outsleep him, nor indulge in sexual intercourse because a bull has more vigor in those lines; nor should he learn to swim because a whale can outswim him, nor dance because a whirlwind can outspin him, nor should he ever walk anywhere because a horse, a machine, or an electric wheel-chair can take him there much faster. But some of these things are necessary to life, he might say. Well, so are some of the things he denounces; necessary at least to some people. Such men as Brisbane have made their mark; they sit at the top and have the hands of thousands to do their bidding. They forget that there are millions of humans to whom life is still more of a physical struggle than anything else.

And he entirely ignores the sheer physical joy of muscular exertions, which is separate and apart from any mental enjoyment. A man may get a mental kick out of indulging in some form of athletics, but the fleshly thrill is there too, and stronger than the other. Vanity, and a feeling of self-expression aside, there is a real pleasure in feeling the rich red blood humming through your veins, the springy response of hard flexible muscles, yes, and the berserk exhilaration of good blows taken and dealt. For myself, some form of at least moderately strenuous exercise is absolutely necessary. Without it I become sluggish and bad-tempered; my health goes on the rocks, and affects my disposition and my literary (?) output. My mental ability is so tied up with my physical condition that I am unable to separate them. Unimportant to the world at large, yes; but extremely important to me, and it is I who pay my bills, and not the world—nor Mr. Brisbane, either.

I have known a few youngsters, of both sexes, whose scorn of the physical was biting beyond words. These persons considered themselves possessed of artistic appreciation. Yet what is more beautiful than a splendid human body in co-ordinated motion? The lithe finely poised figure of a dancer, the pantherish body of a boxer with the wedge-shaped torso, the long swelling muscles rippling under the smooth velvety skin, the easy glide of onset and retreat, the perfect balance and carriage, the suppleness of limb—where is a finer model for an artist or sculptor? How can people go into ecstasies over a cold lifeless lump of marble hammered and chipped into a semblance of humanity, and despise the warm, vibrant, pulsing original? What is art but a poor copy of reality at best? I suppose that these afore-mentioned "artists" who rave over the sculpturings of the Grecians, would have looked with contempt or indifference at the sinewy models whose god-like features the ancient masters copied. In admiring the skill with which the artist or the sculptor reproduces reality, I do not forget my admiration for the reality he mimics. Personally, while I enjoy looking at the statue of a wrestler, a gladiator or a discus-thrower, I much prefer to watch the actual model in action. This is not spoken in depreciation of the sculptor or the artist. I greatly admire the skill which lends a painting or an image the illusion of reality, and mimics the flesh in the last small detail of joint, muscle and finger-nail. But I say it is hard for me to understand these people who say they have artistic appreciation and a love of beauty, who see the beauty in a marble imitation of a physical god, and yet see no beauty at all in a living pulsing vibrant god of muscles, in fighting togs, bathing trunks, track shorts, or football harness.

Maybe it's the sweat, dust and strain of competition which repells them. But I have an idea that the athletes of ancient Greece sweated and bled, and strained, yes, and cursed like pirates, too, when they were stacking up their records. And there's considerable sweat and strain in hacking out a fine statue from marble, I should think.

As for me, I don't pretend to be an artist, or to love beauty particularly. I enjoy the beauty of a perfect figure, but primarily it's not beauty that interests me in athletics. It's the strife, the struggle; the impact of sweaty, straining, iron bodies; the creaking and snapping of mighty thews, the berserk onslaught and the ferocious defense. Anyway, beauty is relative, I think. On my favorite football team there is a fast flashy halfback, whose specialty is speed and elusiveness. He is beautifully built, from an artistic point of view. There is also a powerful fullback, a French-Indian, with broad massive shoulders and a slouching catlike gait. Now to some the most beautiful sight is to see the first mentioned lad go weaving down the field at blinding speed, avoiding tacklers with perfect control. But to me a more beautiful sight is to see the Indian fullback, with his bull-like strength, backing up the line and piling up blockers and ball-toter by sheer power and ferocity. It's not the artistic kind of beauty; but there is a beauty in the business of a job well done, of strength and fighting fury working in unison. Who can measure beauty with a set gauge? It's a word much overworked. Beauty to me is something that gives me pleasure to look upon, whether it is a sunset of blue and rifted gold; the sparkle of a diamond; the daintiness of a feminine countenance or the perfection of her figure; the lashing waves of a grey winter sea breaking along a frosty rock-strewn coast; the sleek rotundity of a thoroughbred pig; the tapering lines of a race-horse; a cluster of scarlet and russet autumn leaves; a thick luscious steak chicken-fried to a turn; a wedge of wild geese etched against a cold clear frosty sky and sounding their heart-tugging call as they race southward; a slender runner, with slender wire-hard limbs and a mop of yellow hair blowing in the wind; or a fullback built for fierce power and stamina, with broad thick shoulders, squat neck, low forehead, square jaw and massive limbs, in terrific action.

It is difficult for me to express the appreciation I feel for the kind things you said about my work. I know of no critic whose opinion I value so highly as yours, and for you to praise my efforts is indeed an honor. It renews my self-confidence, and inspires me to further efforts. However, if I possess any ability in the line of weird literature, I owe it mainly to a long and careful study of your technique. I have not tried to copy you; but I have studied your methods, just as I study the other masters of literature.

I'm glad you liked the yarns mentioned. The editor took liberties with "The Cairn on the Headland". In the original version, O'Brien was born in America. The editor changed this and made O'Brien a native of Ireland, but neglected to change the line: "We were countrymen in that we born in the same land." That would seem to make "Ortali" an Irishman, too, when I intended him for an American-born Italian. In making Odin a purely evil spirit, I did that partly for dramatic effect, and partly because I was writing from the viewpoint of the ancient Irish. They must have considered that god an utter devil, considering the murdering, looting and destroying habits of his worshippers. Their shrines and monasteries were burned and demolished, their priests slaughtered, their young men and young women butchered on the altars of the one-eyed deity, and over all towered Odin. Seeing his effigy looming through the smoke of destruction and the flame of slaughter, dabbled with blood, and bestriding mangled corpses, the victims must have seen in him only the ultimate essence of evil.

Concerning "Worms of the Earth"—I must have been unusually careless when I wrote that, considering the errors—such as "her" for "his", "him" for "himself", "loathsome" for "loathing", etc.. I'm at a loss to say why I spelled Eboracum as Ebbracum. I must investigate the matter. I know I saw it spelled that way, somewhere; it's not likely I would make such a mistake entirely of my own volition, though I do frequently make errors. Somehow, in my mind, I have a vague idea that it's connected some way with the Gaelic "Ebroch"—York.

I read with much interest your remarks on the prize annuals, O'Brien's, etc., and am glad to see that so many Weird Tale writers have got recognition. No, I didn't know my "Black Stone" had landed in the "Not At Night" anthology. I'm so far off the beaten track of literature,* that I get only vague hints of what goes on in the world of pen and ink.

Thank you very much for what you said about my verse. As I said above, I value your opinion most highly, and for you to speak of me as "a natural poet" gives me more real pleasure than I'd get out of having O'Brien name a yarn of mine as the best story of the year. That's no exaggeration. When you speak well of my work, I feel like maybe I have got something, after all. I wish I could give more time to verse, but the necessity of making a living crowds it out. Indeed, I've afraid I've lost the knack of rhyming. I've scarcely banged two lines together in years. The last verse I sold was stuff written years ago, and revamped; that is, pulled out of the unpublished archives and polished up a bit. Occasionally I go over rhymes I wrote a long time ago, and find I can iron out kinks that appeared impossible at the time of the original forging.

Glad you liked the rattles, and I'm sorry I couldn't get a bigger set. I'll try again next summer. If I could find a den of hibernating reptiles, and blast

*geographically.

them out—that reminds me of a comical thing that happened several years ago. Some fellows found such a den as above mentioned, and dynamited it. One of them stood too close to the cave when the charge went off. The air was full of stones, dust, and reptilian fragments, and the first thing he knew, there was a four-foot rattler around his neck! The explosion had blown it bodily into the air, and dropped it on the person mentioned, with very little damage to the snake. But it was blind and stunned, and the fellow dislodged it without damage to anything but his nervous system, which was jittery and jibbery for days afterward. I've seen thirty or forty big snakes hanging on a barbed-wire fence after the discovery of a hibernating den, and some lairs have been found containing a hundred or more. There aren't the snakes in this part of Texas there used to be, but they'll come back. Already the owls, hawks, and ravens are returning by the thousands. The country swarms with fat jackrabbits and cottontails, and these birds of prey live off them. And the like of rats and mice you never saw. I make no attempt to explain this invasion of rodents and hunting birds. But here they are!

It's too bad sea-food affects you so adversely, particularly since you live in sea-port town. I fear you would suffer on the Corpus Christi waterfront; what with the rotting fish and shrimp along the beach, the fishing boats full of finny things, and the shacks where bait is sold in large quantities, the odor has occasionally nauseated even me, and I am even less susceptible to such things than the average. A ship ought to be able to make that port in a thick fog with no port-lights showing, by simply following the smell! The smell along the wharfs of Galveston, Aransas and Rockport is none too sweet, but that of Corpus Christi surpasses them all put together.

I noted your likes and dislikes in the food line, with great interest, having a weakness in that direction. In fact, I'm something of a gourmand—I believe you spell it that way. I, too, am a cheese addict. My favorite is Swiss; I also like limburger, cottage, pimento—in fact, almost any kind. I know of few greater treats than a slice of Swiss cheese, between two good thick pieces of white bread, with a slice of minced ham, pimento loaf, or balogney, washed down with a bottle of foaming ice-cold beer. Like you, I detest spinach, and am not fond of underdone meat. I like mine well-cooked. I'm not enthusiastic over sauerkraut, and I never ate any tripe. But liver is a favorite dish of mine, especially when fried with onions. I like chocolate passibly well, though sweets in any form take the place more of an appetizer for more solid foods, with me. I go for ice-cream in a big way, though. Although after working in that drug-store I mentioned, it was months before I could regard the stuff without almost gagging. I often made a meal off it, when there was too much of a rush for me to take off time for lunch—or dinner, rather. The midday meal has always been dinner to me. My favorite is home-made cream; "sto'-bought" can never equal the other, when well made. I remember the peach-cream I used to eat at my grandmother's home, up in Missouri. She had a big orchard, including many fine trees of Elbertas, which, when allowed to ripe properly, are hard to beat. At night, when everything was still, I'd wake up occasionally and hear, in the quiet, the luscious squshy impact of the ripe peaches falling from the laden branches. These peaches, mushy-ripe, and cut up in rich creamy milk, made a frozen delicacy the like of which is not often equalled. The peaches in this part of the world are nothing extra.

I'm not a great eater of cakes or candy, pudding, custards, or pies. The latter more than the others. I like most kind of pies—chicken, pumpkin, mince—especially with pecans mixed in the meat—, apricot, peach, apple, etc.. As far as that goes, I like most all kinds of food, but of course have my preferences. For drinks, I like tea, that is, iced tea in warm weather, with crushed mint-leaves and lemon, not much sugar. I care little for hot drinks, even in the winter, though I don't object to cocoa occasionally. I've never drunk a cup of coffee in my life, so I don't know whether I'd like it or not. (Incidentally, I don't use tobacco in any form, either, and haven't since the age of fourteen.) I don't care for highly seasoned food, ordinarily, though I like Mexican dishes every now and then, as well as spaghetti, macaroni and vermicelli. I like most all fruit, but eat vegetables mainly out of a sense of duty, except corn, which I admire boiled on the cob. I can eat a ton of it that way. French fried potatoes are all right, and yams, fried in their juice or baked in their jackets go well with fresh pork spare-ribs and back-bone. Turnip-greens and boiled bacon are palatable occasionally, when served with properly made corn-bread. I believe the finest, richest fowl-meat extant is goose. But fried chicken is hard to beat. I care less for sausage than any part of the hawg, but I can sure put away ham—boiled, baked, or fried. I mentioned my preference for beef, I believe.

You struck a responsive chord in me when you mentioned turkey dinner. Thanksgiving! Baked turkey, with dressing made of biscuit and cornbread crumbs, sage, onions, eggs, celery salt and what not; hot biscuits and fresh butter yellow as gold; rich gravy; fruit cakes containing citron, candied pineapple and cherries, currents, raisins, dates, spices, pecans, almonds, walnuts; pea salad; pumpkin pie, apple pie, mince pie with pecans; rich creamy milk, chocolate, or tea—my Southern ancestors were quite correct in adopting the old New England holiday.

I hope you had as enjoyable Thanksgiving this year as I did. I don't know when I enjoyed a holiday more. Early that morning, the chores being done, my friend "Pink" Tyson and I drove to Brownwood, forty miles to the southeast, to see the football teams of Howard Payne College and Southwestern University battle it out for the championship of the Texas Conference. Arriving there we went to the leading hotel and looked over the Southwestern boys, and a bigger, more powerful team I havent seen in years. With them we listened awhile to the broadcast of the Colgate-Brown game, and I thought about you, and wondered if by any chance you were seeing the game. After dinner at the home of a friend we helped him unload a bunch of steers, in order to facilitate an early arrival at the game. They were the finest, fattest, big Hereford critters I've seen in a longest time; and one of them was the meanest and wildest I ever saw. The three of us fought him all over the hill (on foot), and after we got him in the corral, we couldn't get the ropes off. We had two ropes on him, or he'd have killed some of us. When he'd plunge at one of us, the other would haul him back, and so on. As it was both of us had some narrow shaves. We finally got one lasso off his horns, but to save our necks, we couldn't get the other off. We had him hauled against the corral fence, and every time we slacked the rope, he took every inch of it, and tried to murder us. At last I threw a doubled lariat around his huge neck and snubbed his head down against the fence, and held him there while the rope was cast off his horns. Then it was every man for himself! After that we picked up another friend and repairing to the stadium, witnessed one of the fiercest, closest and hardest-fought games I have ever seen, in which a comparatively light, but hard-fighting Howard Payne team triumphed for a fifth straight championship. After the game we returned uptown, got a table at a window through which we could watch the shirt-tail parade and the other antics of the celebrating collegians, and while we watched and gorged ourselves on roast turkey and oyster dressing and ice cream, we decided international championships, selected All-Americans, and agreed that Colgate would be the choice for the Rose Bowl game with the University of Southern California. After that Pink and I drove back through the forty miles of hill country, through one of those still, clear, crisp star-filled nights that you enjoy only during good football weather. Simple and unsophisticated enjoyment, yet somehow I got more kick out of the whole affair than I've gotten out of more expensive and less innocent pleasures. We didn't even take a drink of liquor.

I'll remember that game for one reason, if for no other. It was the last game of that big Indian fullback I've mentioned before. His playing has always fascinated me with its primitive ferocity, and I've followed his career ever since I saw him play for the first time four years ago. I'll never forget that first sight of him, as he seized the ball and came ripping along the line, his bare black mane bucking through the melee. Did you ever watch a cowpuncher breaking a wild horse on the other side of the corral fence? All you can see is the puncher's head bobbing up and down along the top of the fence, with the plunges of the horse. That was what I was reminded of as I saw that black head heaving among the helmets. Bucking is the only word to describe it. He was charging at blinding speed and at the same time driving with all the power of his iron legs. He struck the line like a thunderbolt, stretched a tackler out half-stunned with a devastating stiff-arm, ripped through the swarm and fell headlong, his knee broken by the incredible strain of his own efforts. The next year he was back, stronger than ever. As time went by, and his body adapted itself to the terrific punishment he took with each game, he lost a good deal of his speed. Nature demands compensation. In his case speed and a certain amount of skill was sacrificed for sheer power. He carried the ball less and less, but his blocking, line-backing and desperate plunges made him still the most valuable man on the team. And Thanksgiving of this year he played his last game—unless he should happen to go into professional football.

During the first quarter, his line plunges and the off-tackle thrusts of the quarterback placed the ball on the one-yard line, and the big fullback crashed over for a touchdown. The place-kick was blocked. Southwestern came back fighting mad and ripped the Howard Payne line again and again. Always the big fullback was in the midst of the battle, fighting with every ounce of his iron frame and ferocious spirit. Then toward the last of the game, something happened. I don't know what it was. I was watching the ball, when a yell went up, and we saw the big Indian down. His leg was hurt. They carried him off the field and laid him on the side-lines, where they began working over his injury. A big German lad was sent in in his place. He was good, but he was not Hoot Masur. Southwestern began an implacable drive. They marched irresistibly down the field, fighting for every inch. At last, on the sidelines, the injured player rose, with the aid of his companions. He began to limp up and down the lines, leaning heavily on a team-mate. Doggedly he plodded, half-dragging his injured member, his heavy jaw set stoically. Out on the field his team-mates, crippled by his loss, were being pushed slowly back toward their own goal. The fullback let go of his supporter, and walked alone, limping deeply, moving slowly. From time to time he worked at the injured leg, stooping, flexing, trying to bend his knee. Then he would resume his endless plodding. I forgot to watch the game in the fascination of watching that grim pathetic figure toiling along the sidelines—up and down—up and down. The sun was sinking, and the long shadow of the grandstands fell across the field. In that shadow the fullback plodded. Once, somewhere, I saw an old German print or wood-cutting, depicting a wood-cutter in a peaked hood carrying a bundle of sticks through the Black Forest. I was irresistibly reminded of this print. The peaked hood was there, even, the peaked hood of a grey sweater-like garment worn by football players when not in the game. There were the same massive shoulders, made abnormally broad by the bulge of the shoulder-pads beneath the sweater; the same slouching, forward bending pace. The shadows of the forest were to an extent repeated in the shadows of the grandstand. Only the bundle of sticks was missing, but the figure etched in the shadow stooped and toiled as if it bore the weight of a world on its shoulders. There was tragedy in the sight; he was eating his heart out because he was not back in the game, stopping those merciless onsets, giving freely of his thews and heart and blood, eating up punishment that would have snapped the bones of a lesser man. There was nothing of the story-book sob-stuff about the business. But to me, at least, there was a savage pathos in the sight of that grim, mighty figure plodding up and down the lines, striving vainly to work his bitterly injured leg back into shape, so he could re-enter the game. At last, when his captainless team was making its last stand, with its back to the wall, he sank down to the naked ground and covered his eyes with his hands. He would not watch the defeat of his mates. But that defeat did not come. Fighting like madmen, they broke up the attack just half a foot from the goal-line. The final score: Howard Payne 6, Southwestern 0. The fullback's touchdown in the first quarter was the only score. As the grandstands emptied and people rushed down onto the field to congratulate the winners, I saw him limping slowly through the throng, toward his team-mates.

Drama? You will see it on the football field, raw and real and naked, unaided by footlights, stage settings, or orchestras.

While I'm on the subject I'll continue the remarks I made about those teams clippings concerning which I sent—the West Texas blonds and the South Texas brunets. The strength and stamina of the Vikings proved too much even for the fiery fury of the black-haired Low-Country men, and after a desperate bruising battle they won, 14–0. I heard the broadcast of the game in a hotel in Abilene, with the Howard Payne team which was there to play Simmons University that night, and had an opportunity of observing the predominance of blonds among this other Western team. The game first mentioned was a clash of fire and ice, the blazing spirit of the Southrons bursting in vain against the cool, implacable power of the Westerners. The quarterback of the Texas team was laid out for the rest of the season, and Stafford, the great Texas University halfback, blocked out John Vaught of the opposing team with such ferocity that he tore two of his ribs loose from his breastbone. Yet Vaught played throughout the game, and through all succeeding games—which is why he is counted one of the best guards in the nation. But the full attainment of savagery was reached the next week, when the blond victors went to Houston to play the Rice team. Maddened by a former defeat, the defending team went into the game wrought to a pitch of frenzy. They were crying mad and out for blood. They went in slugging, battling with the desperation of wounded tigers. They tore into the TCU team as if they intended to sweep it off the earth. They broke Red Oliver's jaw, they dislocated Pruitt's knee, they fractured three of Boswell's ribs close to his spine and wrenched his vertabra, they nearly broke Spearman's back, they subjected the already crippled Vaught to a merciless hammering, though his incredible ruggedness kept him in the game. The great Rice backs, the Driscolls, MacCauley, and Wallace, ripped the famous TCU line again and again, driving over a touchdown by pure ferocity. Reeling and staggering under the punishment, the blond Highlanders held them to a single score, and finished that cruel, bruising battle winners again, to come on to a championship of the Southwest Conference which includes all the larger Texas colleges and Arkansas University.

But I must ask pardon for devoting so much space to a profession in which you have no particular interest. In my intense ardour for sports I am prone to forget that I may become boresome.

As always, I read your comments on political and economic possibilities with the greatest interest. You make even economics fascinating, which, as treated by any one but yourself, is to me the most wearisome of all sciences. I am not prepared to disagree or take issues with you on any point you advance. However, in the case of the oppression of people by a ruling class, or classes, it is quite true that the revolutions of Russia and France show that tyrannies *ultimately* fall; however each overthrow was preceded by many centuries of oppression, in which generation after generation groaned under the crushing heel, before the change came about. Change apparently being one of the laws of Nature, we can not expect despotisms to endure indefinitely any more than republics, democracies, of periods of chaotic anarchy. I do not expect a permanent state of slavery, but I do look for a period of more or less length, in which class and individual liberty will be practically unknown—oh, it won't be called slavery or serfdom. They'll have another name for it—Communism, or Fascism, or Nationalism, or some other -ism; but under the surface it will be the same old tyranny, modified, no doubt, to fit modern conditions. The victims probably won't realize they are slaves for a long time, until conditions get too utterly hellish. Then they'll doubtless rise, overthrow the existing rule, and institute another regime, in which the people will for a short space held the reins in chaos and confusion, then natural rulers will institute another mode of government—different in name and outward aspects, but fundamentally the same as the old, or capable of becoming modified to resemble the old type: and which will itself drift irresistibly toward eventual serfdom and ultimate dissolution. Of course all this is my own idea, and I don't pretend to be a student of economics or politics or socialogy, but it seems to me that the trend of all governments and forms of governments has been toward centralization, the creation of special privileged classes, and the abolition of individual rights and liberties. It seems to me that a race, passing from the bloody darkness of semi-barbarism, basks for a short period in the light of culture and freedom, which phase is followed by an era of vast commercial prosperity, during which, unnoticed by the brainless mob which is too busy rolling in material luxuries, their rights are subtly taken from them. The over-inflated prosperity passes, and the people awake to poverty and enslavement, in one form or another. Just now, the method seems to be the confiscation of property through exorbitant taxes, coupled, indirectly perhaps, with government competing with private business. When the government goes into big business openly, the independent, whether individual or corporation, will be crushed, because the government has such vaster resources at hand. You mentioned that military enforcement of class privilege is an unstable thing. You are absolutely right. I think that the military dictatorship is inevitable, following the overthrow of the commercial masters, either by the mob, or by the military itself.

I do not think that actual peonage is impractical, considering the vast resources of slaughter in the hands of the rulers. Suppose the people are far more highly enlightened than Russians or Mexicans. Psychological equilibrium may be altered, but one ruthless and able man could overbalance all the psychology in the world. One ruthless efficient fighter in an airplane loaded with gas and explosives could make raw beef out of a whole city full of unarmed people, and their brains would spatter, their flesh shred away and their bones splinter just as easily as those of uneducated peasants. I'm probably wrong, but I honest believe that a small group of men, guided by one brain such as Stalin's, or Mussolini's, could, with the aid of a comparatively small army, enslave a whole continent, regardless of the intellectual status of the people. Such event is a very remote possibility. A dictator would doubtless approach the matter in a more subtle way than by whole-sale slaughter. But classes opposing him would be ruthlessly destroyed, and the result would be the same—the old, old fundamental of kingship: one man or one small class of men ruling the rest under one or the other of the ten million high-sounding names used to dress the raw reality of slavery. Again, remember, however high the intellectual level of the American people may be, it would take only a generation of serfdom to reduce them to the mental level of an uneducated European peasant—three, at most.

Your impartial viewpoint is admirable. For myself, I must admit that I am motivated more often by emotion and sentiment than by cold logic. I have said before, I think, that my nature is emotional rather than intellectual. Possessing many powerful prejudices, it follows that many of my views must be narrow and biased; knowing this, I try to be just, but I know that my failure is frequent. I am unable to identify myself with any definite class or political movement. As for the classes, the arrogance of one, the smug complacency of the other, the stupidity of another, equally repells and antagonizes me. If it came to a show-down, I suppose it would be natural for me to throw in with the working classes, since I am a member of that class, but I am far from idealizing—or idolizing—it or its members. In the last analysis, I reckon, I have but a single conviction or ideal, or whateverthehell it might be called: individual liberty. It's the only thing that matters a damn. I'd rather be a naked savage, shivering, starving, freezing, hunted by wild beasts and enemies, but free to go and come, with the range of the earth to roam, than the fattest, richest, most bedecked slave in a golden palace with the crystal fountains, silken divans, and ivory-bosomed dancing girls of Haroun al Raschid. With that nameless black man I could say:

> "Freedom, freedom,
>
> Freedom over me!—

And before I'd be a slave,
I'd like down in my grave
And go up to my God and be free!"

That's why I yearn for the days of the early frontier, where men were more truly free than at any other time or place in the history of the world, since man first began to draw unto himself the self-forged chains of civilization. This is merely a personal feeling. I make no attempt to advocate a single ideal of personal liberty as the one goal of progress and culture. But by God, I demand freedom for myself. And if I can't have it, I'd rather be dead.

Your view of society and civilization seems to me very well balanced, and fair. And your ideal of a modern government, is really magnificent. I must strongly agree with you that no one should be allowed to vote until he has passed an examination fitting him for such privilege. This may seem paradoxical in the light of what I just said about personal freedom, but I mentioned that that was my own personal ideal. Individual liberty doesn't necessarily entail blind dabbling in governmental affairs. Occasionally I have refrained from voting, simply because I didn't feel that I understood the matters involved well enough to take sides, and I didn't feel any limitation of liberty thereby. I likewise—as do you—strongly advocate unlimited educational advantages, so that anyone could qualify himself for the franchise. Altogether your ideal government is a splendid one—but I fear that it would not long endure on the just and fair lines you lay out. I probably have a nerve in making that remark, considering my ignorance of things social and economic. And yet I feel there is one element which (aside from the inevitable abuses of power by men of unbalanced ego, inordinate ambitions, or other motives) would ruin the equillibrium. That is the terrific animal vitality of a certain class of people. Or should I say type, for they are found in all classes, from street-sweepers to millionaires. These men—and women—are possessed of extreme natural individualism, restlessness, turbulence, and physical vitality. They are, I suppose, of the type called extroverts. From their ranks come explorers, soldiers, athletes, wanderers, and outlaws.

They are so constituted that only strenuous physical action can satisfy them. Some, favored by birth or circumstances, become soldiers, explorers, empire-builders. For every one of that breed who becomes famous in the ways mentioned, there are ten or fifteen who become dare-devil aviators, prize-fighters, football players, regular soldiers or sailors, or wandering workmen. Then there is a goodly number who turn gangster, gunman, gambler, outlaw. (Not all men drift into crime by necessity or changeless destiny of environments. Some deliberately turn to such paths because of the turbulence and restlessness of their souls.) Such men are very, very seldom artistic, scholarly, or intellectual. Generally they care nothing whatever about the arts, sciences or esthetics. In a society founded on intellect, there is no place for them. And yet they constitute a vital element of civilization. It would be impossible to educate such men into a state wherein they would occupy their leisure by study and philosophical contemplation; every fibre in their mental and physical being opposes such a thing. To expect one of these mentally impatient and physically terrific beings to sit down and wade through a book on art, economics, philosophy, or history, would be not only futile, but sheerly cruel. There is a tingling and stinging of their blood and tissues which demands that they be up and expending their terrific energies on some strenuous task or amusement. These men are not all fools or dolts. They help to build the world. I have known many of them. But they demand continual hard work and hard play of some physical sort, and when denied that, in a legitimate way, they turn to other paths less innocent. They work hard, drink hard, love hard, hate hard, and play hard; but they do not think, in the intellectual sense. Yet the most highly developed of this type demand success, recognition, wealth. Under the conditions you describe, no doubt such success could be attained, to a more limited extent than at present. But consider the less developed of the type. There again we find unlimited physical energy, and little mental ability or ambition. When they work, they work hard; when they do not work, they turn to the dance hall, the speakeasy, the athletic field. I do not believe that it would be possible to educate this race into employing their leisure any other way. Mental and artistic pursuits are senseless and repugnant to them, because of their peculiar make-up, for which they are in no way responsible. Yet, what of increasing mechanical devices, the leisure of all increases. That is well enough for people who wish to improve their minds. But what of the millions and millions who have no such wish—or ability? With no hard work to fill their hours, they will weary of the endless round of animal pleasures and tinsel enjoyments. They will begin to feel the old restlessness and the stinging in the veins. In the tame, flat world of the future, there will be no legitimate way of working off that physical superabundance of animal vitality. They will grow moody and discontented. Crime will grow steadily, as the people's discontent evidences itself in contentions, bursts or passion, and deeds of violence. Crimes will grow into riots, riots into revolutions. To save civilization, society will bring down the crushing heel again. Again I return to the question of slavery, as the only salvation of the civilization that has been allowed to crawl up from the depths. Hard, continuous work, with livable conditions and part-time relaxation, will keep the people, if not contented, at least docile for a time (as long a time as we can expect any phase of evolution to endure). Expanding their energies in labor, they will have no time for systematic plotting and complaint. In their short leisure-hours, they will be too busy enjoying their old pleasures—made sweet to the taste by rarity—to rebell. But in a machine age, how is this work to be furnished? I can only venture a theory, an imaginative picture of an age in which vast projects will be carried out, dwarfing the pyramids and the wonders of ancient times, at first simply to keep the dangerous mobs employed, later also for the whims and fancies of an inevitably created aristocratic class, at once merely titannic, and degenerate. I seem to see a world like the dream of a crazed artist, reared by serfs and ruled by madmen with the intellects of gods.

All this is maundering, no doubt. I have no right to even conjecture, considering my lack of knowledge of the trend of world events. Anyway, the whole modern structure is more than likely to be swept away by a war or a series of wars. I care not. Individual liberty is a dream that is out-worn and will never be reborn. I have no other ideal.

Concerning police irregularities in Texas—you are quite right in saying that Texas is in the throes of change from a frontier existence to a civilized one.* Of course the good police outnumber the bad, else life would be intolerable, but there is abuse, as you discerned from the clippings and incidents I sent you. As a result, there is a pretty wide-spread resentment against such abuse, which is not confined to actual law-breakers. You remember the case I mentioned, wherein an officer shot down a private enemy on a public street and was acquitted. This same officer, later, maltreated another civilian almost fatally. It seems there was a poker game going on, in which the officer lost heavily. At last, doubtless fired by liquor as well as resentment, he attacked the civilian, who ran out of the house in an attempt to escape. The officer pursued him, caught him, gave him a frightful beating with his gun-barrel, and left him lying senseless in an empty lot, with his skull fractured. This was seen by witnesses. The officer resigned from the force, but I did not hear of it if he was punished further. A friend of his on the force, I heard—and quite believe—upon hearing another civilian criticise the action of the first officer, knocked the man down with his pistol-barrel, and likewise resigned. The two then established themselves in a detective agency. If resentment for officers in general results, it is lamentable, but scarcely to be wondered at. In that very town, not so terribly long ago, a powerfully built youth, maddenned by liquor and marihuana weed, nearly killed a policeman. In this case, my sympathies were wholly with the officer. As near as I could learn, he was trying to lead the boy out of a cafe, when the youth struck him down from behind with a chair, and then nearly stamped the life out him. But nearly every one I talked to of the case, expressed full sympathy with the boy, and hoped he'd be acquitted of the charge brought against him of attempted manslaughter. It wasn't that they condoned lawlessness or illegal violence; simply that abuses of law-enforcement caused resentment toward the enforcers. Incidentally, the offender was given a light suspended sentence—three years, I think.

*As for inhibitions of honesty, however, I'm not ready to agree that we are morally inferior to anybody else; thousands of people from more civilized sections have come here lately, and I haven't observed that their percentage of honesty is any greater than that of the natives.

Again, a friend and I were riding into the business part of a town with a couple of cops who had picked us up—not by way of arrest! They'd merely offered us a ride. It was rather late, and seeing a kid walking along the side-walk, they drew up to the curb and ordered him in a domineering manner to stop and answer their questions. If there was any real reason for this procedure, I failed to see it. The boy was rather poorly dressed, but he was proceeding on his way, apparently minding his own business—a kid in his early 'teens, I should say. The cops asked him who he was; and where he had been—he told them to some sort of a school-rally, I think. They asked him where he got the scratches on his face and hands, and when he said from falling while skating, they practically told him he was lying, accusing him of fighting in the alleys. They concluded by berating him for disrespect—he having become somewhat sullen under this badgering—and profanely ordered him off the streets, saying that there was a curfew law in the town; a straight lie, to the best of my knowledge. Now this may seem like a small thing. But a boy of that age is likely to be molded into any pattern by trivial things. He went his way, smarting, without doubt, at the wanton tongue-lashing he had got, and resenting it. A few such beratings, and he could hardly be blamed for looking on the police as persecutors instead of protectors. That viewpoint might well color his whole life's actions, and tip the balance from honesty to criminality.

I've never had but one brush with the police, but I must say that did not increase my respect for the system. I was about eighteen or nineteen, and with a couple of friends of about my own age, made a flying visit to Dallas. It was the first time any of us had driven by the traffic-lights, and the lad driving, not knowing the regulations, got confused, made a mistake and drove across a stop-light. We were stopped by the cop on the next beat, and the usual lambasting followed. The officer on whose beat we had comitted the offense was fair enough. I have no complaint to make about him. No one could have been more gentlemanly. But the cop who stopped us seemed to consider our blunder a personal insult. He lashed himself into a perfect rage. We had not sinned through intent, but from ignorance, though of course the officers had no way of knowing that. We were glad to be told the rules and regulations; we did not resent being halted and questioned; we would even have gone into court and paid a fine without undue protest. But we did resent being treated like gangsters and thugs. We explained the situation, and our willingness to conform with the law if it were explained to us, but the policeman who was so wrathy refused to be mollified. It was so damned unnecessary. If we had offered him any incivility, his resentment would be understandable. But none of us made any reply to his insults, not caring to be haled into court to pay a fine for "abusive language", "resisting arrest", "assault on an officer of the law", or some such charge. He loudly regretted that the offense had not occurred on his beat, so that he might run us in to spend our stay in Dallas in jail, urged the older officer to throw us in, intimated that we were fleeing from the committing of some dark crime, and concluded by accusing us of stealing the automobile in which we were riding. Well—the man doesn't walk the earth who can call me a thief on his own power without getting my knuckles in his mouth; it isn't particularly entertaining to be forced to swallow that insult because the individual who utters it is clothed in brass buttons. In the midst of his berating, a young negro started to absent-mindedly walk across a stop-light, and the policeman ceased his abuse of us to leap at the offender and snarl: "Get back there, you black bastard!" Then he wheeled back to us with a triumphant glare, as if to see how we were impressed. I must admit our only feeling was one of disgust. If it had not been for the other cop, who refused to arrest us or give us a ticket, that gentleman would have made it as unpleasant for us as possible. Understand me—that incident did not sour me against the police system as a whole, or make me a violent cop-hater. I supposed at the time that such varmints as that one, were so rare as to be almost unique in his case. My later conclusions were forced on me against my will. I could give other incidents, but there's no need of inflicting them on you. I need hardly to say that I wish all these remarks about the police and law-enforcement to be considered absolutely confidential. I hardly know how I got to spilling all this stuff; I never put any of it on paper before, and I wouldn't be doing it now, except that I feel I can trust your discretion. The fact that I could prove my assertions wouldn't do me much good, if I should make enemies.

I'm afraid a written statement of affairs wouldn't do much good, unless signed by some one in authority; even if I dared to publish such a paper. So much stuff is circulated in campaigns and the like—charges, refutations and counter-charges. The Fergusons may make some reforms. I don't know. If the Gladewater Journal doesn't have any effect, I'm afraid nothing I could write would, except to make dangerous enemies. The Journal has an enormous state-wide circulation, and in spite of its sentimental style (which is deliberate, in order to catch the attention of the common people who respond to the truth more quickly when presented in such fashion) is considerable of a political power.

But reform is difficult in this state, where lines are so loosely drawn. There is so much of a grab-bag, to-hell-with-everybody-but-me spirit. In the general grabbing, the weak are so often ruthlessly trampled, and common decencies lost sight of. For generations Texas has been the prey of certain particular breeds of vultures: magnates from other sections, who wish only to exploit and loot the state; and native promoters and politicians who are eager to sell the birthright of their people in return for personal graft. That is not to say by any means that the people who come to Texas are all commercial pirates, or that all the native promoters and politicians are grafters. But both breeds do exist in goodly number, and have, since the Civil War.

The state has always had such vast resources. So many men have come here with a single idea—that of getting rich as quickly as possible, and by any means, and then returning to their own section with their loot. Such men can have no sympathy with, or care for, the state or its people. But it would take too much space here to go into the social and historical factors behind this present tangle. I think I'll prepare such a treatise, however, and send it to you later on, in which I'll try to present the salient features in the development of Texas, and their connection with present-day conditions.

Concerning barbarians and civilization: it is quite true a civilized man, if suddenly thrown into a barbaric life, would find it intolerable. But one born to such conditions feels no lack of a fullness in life, any more than the Indians before the coming of white men, felt any lack of, or need for, whiskey; or any more than the Europeans felt the lack of tobacco, before they knew anything about it. Whiskey and tobacco are artificial stimulants, unnecessary, except when a taste has been deliberately developed; so are many other of the adjuncts of civilization. We can not get along without them now; but we would be better off if we had never discovered or developed them. As for being a shaman or minstrel among barbarians—those are the very last things I should wish to be, were my lot cast among the uncivilized. It is evident that a shaman, however fantastic and barbarous his thoughts and methods, represents the nearest approach to civilized man, in his tribe and age. Therefore, he is able to glimpse, in a dim way, some of the vistas that lie above (I say "above" for the sake of argument; I am by no means sure that "progress" is necessarily a step upward.) and to feel the lack of intellectual attainment—, oh, very, very dimly, without doubt. Yet he is stirred by gnawings and vague urges that never trouble the war-chief, the hunter, or the brave, who accepts the dreams of the shamans as truths not to be questioned or worried about. So the condition of the shaman is a faint reflection of what the condition of a civilized man cast among savages would be. This would seem to be borne out by the nature of the shaman. Whether white, black, yellow or red, the witch-finder, voodoo man, priest of Odin, or shaman, seems generally to have been a gloomy, brooding, shadow-haunted mortal, groping vaguely in the shadows. On the other hand the warrior, the ordinary tribesman, has often been a jovial cut-throat, in as far as the hard physical conditions of his life would allow him, swaggering imperturbably through blood and slaughter, gorging, guzzling, breeding, killing, and eventually dying in some ghastly fashion—never troubling his head about abstractions, and really living his life to its fullest extent—however shallow that might seem to a modern man, he found it full. No; I would not have cared to be a bard or shaman; if I had been a barbarian, I would have wanted to be a complete barbarian, well-developed, but developed wholly on barbaric lines; not a distorted dweller in a half world, part savage and part budding consciousness. Just as a man, dwelling in civilization, is happier when most fully civilized, so a barbarian is happier when fully barbaric.

Concerning duels, I hardly think we have any right to judge our ancestors by modern standards, or to condemn them harshly because so many of their duels seem to have risen from causes utterly trivial to us. We can not apply modern standards altogether to those earlier times, when men stood in somewhat different relations than at present, and were judged by different standards, determined by long trains of preceding events and customs, many of which have lost their meaning in modern times. We moderns, for instance, are so careful of our precious lives that we can not understand how a man could risk his, or take another's, over what seems to us a light matter. It could not be otherwise. We are not used to risking our lives through necessity, and we can not be expected to risk them recklessly. But the early Americans grew up in an atmosphere of peril, especially on the frontier. The very fact that a man was a frontiersman, was evidence that he was ready to risk his life lightly. He fought like a blood-mad mountain lion to preserve his life, but he would frequently walk carelessly into danger. When he was so ready to risk his own hide, it follows that he would scarcely be more careful of some other person's. He often valued his honor more highly than his life, and if he often seemed over-touchy in regard to his honor, it must be remembered that he alone was responsible for that honor and its upholding. From defending himself against enemies, it was natural that he was ready at all times to resent the slightest hint of insult or encroachment. If he had shown himself laggard in his own defense, there were plenty of individuals who would have soon made life unbearable for him. Major Henry, for instance, the gentleman of the New Orleans duel, once rode a mule across a plaza in Nicaragua, at a walk, through a hail of bullets. He rode across, and walked back, carrying a few bullets in his hide, the mule having been shot out from under him. His only reason for doing so was because of a wager of a dinner, with his brother officers. When a man takes such terrible risks simply because of a whim, it is not incongruous that he should readily shoot out any sort of an argument, whether important or not. This readiness to die or kill was simply a frontier characteristic, inexplicable to moderns, yet without which the settlement of America would never have been accomplished.

I feel, like you, that the total abolition of the duel was not altogether a move for the better. There are wrongs that ought to be settled individually and without recourse to law. As far as that goes, some wrongs are too great to be righted even by a duel. Some injuries deserve, not a fair fight for the perpetrator, but the death of a dog.

In regard to Indians, I believe—excepting the civilizations of Mexico—that the mental status of the Eastern Indian was somewhat higher than that of the Western, especially those of the great plains. I am speaking, of course, of the Indians found in what is now the United States. The Pueblos of course, had a culture of their own; but their pottery making, blanket weaving and house-building was not sufficient to stave off the invasions of the more barbarous Pimas and Apaches. The Sioux, Cheyennes, Utes, Comanches, Apaches, Pimas, Navajoes, Kiowas, Blackfeet, Arapahoes, Pawnees, Omahas, Konsas, Osages, were not, I think, quite the equals of the Iroquois, Natchez, Delawares, Seminoles, Chickasaws, Choctaws—and I can say with conviction that they were generally inferior to the Cherokees. Considering the so-called inferiority of any race, I realize the term is relative and varies with the varying viewpoint. I do not, for instance, consider myself particularly superior to a Chinaman, but I'd hate like hell to be changed into one, and I'd knife him if he tried to marry, say a sister of mine. The Indian might have developed a permanent civilization, if left alone long enough, but I must admit I have certain doubts on the subject.

It is natural that we should take opposite sides in the Ulster question. No, I wouldn't want you to be kicked out of Rhode Island because your ancestors gypped the Wampanoags out of the land; but a descendant of those Wampanoags might be pardoned for feeling differently. However, if you'll glance over my comments again, you'll find that I said nothing about booting the Orangemen off the land their ancestors stole from my people. They can stay there until they rot, as far as I'm concerned. And as far as incorporating Ulster into the Free State, personally, I wouldn't take it as a gift. I'm ready to admit they're right in their present squabble with the South Irish. But that's as far as I can go. It's too much to expect me to side against my own flesh and blood with their hereditary enemies. It really doesn't make any difference to me whether the South Irish are right or wrong, any more than I care whether a member of my immediate family is right or wrong in a dispute with an outsider. If the Irish are oppressing the Ulstermen, it's no more than can be expected. After three hundred years of oppression and abuse, are they to expect perfect fairness and justice from their former victims? Wrongs breed wrongs; when a man beats a muzzled bear, he needn't howl, if, when the bear breaks his muzzle, he sinks his fangs into him, whether he happens to be holding a club then or not.

Considering the Philippines—if we were allowed to fortify them, they would be a strength. As it is, they're a weakness. Instead of being a rifle aimed at the heart of Japan (as would be the case were they fortified and a goodly portion of our Pacific fleet stationed there), they tend to divide our forces, to scatter our lines, and to subject American citizens to danger, in case of war with Japan. I think it would be a point of strategy to abandon those islands entirely, and concentrate our forces about Hawaii. That Japan would gobble them is certain, but I scarcely think they would add much to her ultimate strength, increased as it is so enormously by her grabbing of Manchuria.

No doubt the French excel us in many phases of literature. The point is that personally I can't endure much of the stuff. After wading through a few chapters, my teeth get on edge and I am aware of an almost overpowering desire to spring from my chair and kick somebody violently in the pants. That is all but Voltaire. I get a big kick out of that lousy old bastard. English poetry is probably the highest form of English literature. But my favorite writers, both of prose and verse, are British and Americans. They are A. Conan Doyle, Jack London, Mark Twain, Sax Rohmer, Jeffery Farnol, Talbot Mundy, Harold Lamb, R. W. Chambers, Rider Haggard, Kipling, Sir Walter Scott, Lane-Poole, Jim Tully,[2] Ambrose Bierce, Arthur Machen, Edgar Allen Poe, and last, but no means least, yourself. Maybe the French excel the British in some ways, but where is the Frenchman who writes, or wrote, with the fire of Jack London, the mysticism of Ambrose Bierce, or the terrific power your own weird masterpieces possess?

For poetry, I like Robert W. Service, Kipling, John Masefield, James Elroy Flecker, Vansittart, Sidney Lanier, Edgar Allen Poe, the Benets—Stephen Vincent better than William Rose—, Walter de la Mare, Rupert Brooke, Siegfried Sassoon, Francis Ledwedge, Omar Khayyam, Joe Moncure March, Nathalia Crane, Henry Herbert Knibbs, Lord Dunsany, G. K. Chesterton, Bret Harte, Oscar Wilde, Longfellow, Tennyson, Swinburne, Viereck, Alfred Noyes, and, again, yourself.

I never read any of Conrad's work. I've never read any of G. B. Shaw's muck, either; he's probably a genius. He's also a poser, an egomaniac and a jackass. I see he's coming to America at last. Very condescending on his part. If I had my way, he'd be met on the wharf by a committee of welcome in top-hats and ivory-headed canes who would tender him the keys of the city, and pull all his whiskers out, hair by hair. Of all these foreigners, I prefer Kipling's works. He's made remarks about America that made me want to break his back, but I've got much solid enjoyment out of his prose and verse. He has guts at least, which so many modern writers utterly lack.

As for American writers, I think yourself and Jim Tully are the only ones whose work will endure; among the writers now living, I mean. Upton Sinclair may get by because of the pictures of economic and social life he draws. As for Drieser, Sinclair Lewis, Louis Bromfield, Ben Hecht, Sherwood Anderson, F. Scott Fitzgerald, George Jean Nathan, Floyd Dell, Mike Gold,—three ringing razzberries for the whole mob. They may be artists and I'm certainly no critic, but I know what I like and what I don't like, and to me they're all wet smacks. I don't know of anything I'd enjoy more than striking a match on a pile containing all Mencken's works, and if he was sitting on top of the heap at the time, it would be all right with me. I'd rather read Zane Grey the rest of my life.

As I said on my card, I am extremely sorry to hear of Whitehead's untimely demise. He was a writer of real ability, and, from all accounts, a brave and honest gentleman. Rest his soul wherever it lies.

Well, I've rambled even more than usual. I hope I haven't bored you too much with my maunderings. I'm enclosing a few rhymes I discovered among the archives and thought might interest you a little. You can return them at your convenience; no hurry. If I wasn't so lazy I'd make copies of them.

Some of the unevenness of the rhythm is intentional. By the way, could you give me the address of the "Not at Night" people?

And so, wishing you a very merry Christmas and a happy New Year, I remain,

Cordially,

R E H.

[Note by HPL at head of letter, presumably to Frank Belknap Long:] return this to Grandpa or incur the direst consequences!

Notes

1. Arthur Brisbane (1864–1936), American newspaper editor, chiefly for the Hearst papers.
2. Jim Tully (1886–1947), American reporter and writer about his life on the road and the American underclass.